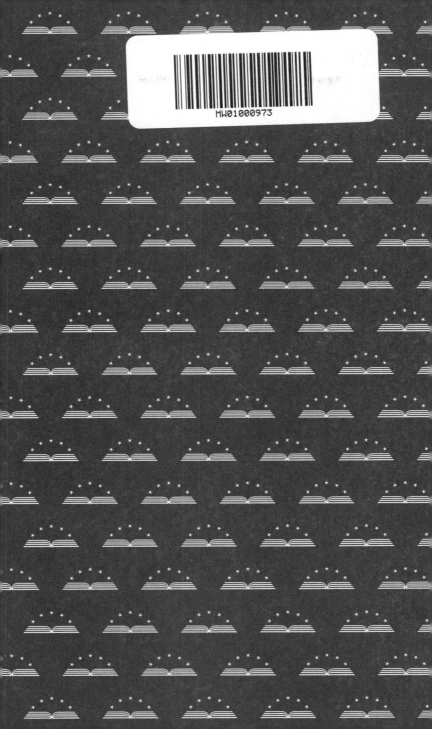

MW01000973

WALKER PERCY

WALKER PERCY

THE MOVIEGOER
& OTHER NOVELS
1961–1971

The Moviegoer

The Last Gentleman

Love in the Ruins

Related Writings

Paul Elie, *editor*

THE LIBRARY OF AMERICA

Published in the United States by Library of America.
Visit our website at www.loa.org.

This paper exceeds the requirements of
ANSI/NISO Z39.48–1992 (Permanence of Paper).

Distributed to the trade in the United States
by Penguin Random House Inc.
and in Canada by Penguin Random House Canada Ltd.

Library of Congress Control Number: 2023945374
ISBN 978-1-59853-775-8

First Printing
The Library of America—380

Manufactured in the United States of America

Contents

One

T HIS MORNING I got a note from my aunt asking me to come for lunch. I know what this means. Since I go there every Sunday for dinner and today is Wednesday, it can mean only one thing: she wants to have one of her serious talks. It will be extremely grave, either a piece of bad news about her stepdaughter Kate or else a serious talk about me, about the future and what I ought to do. It is enough to scare the wits out of anyone, yet I confess I do not find the prospect altogether unpleasant.

I remember when my older brother Scott died of pneumonia. I was eight years old. My aunt had charge of me and she took me for a walk behind the hospital. It was an interesting street. On one side were the power plant and blowers and incinerator of the hospital, all humming and blowing out a hot meaty smell. On the other side was a row of Negro houses. Children and old folks and dogs sat on the porches watching us. I noticed with pleasure that Aunt Emily seemed to have all the time in the world and was willing to talk about anything I wanted to talk about. Something extraordinary had happened all right. We walked slowly in step. "Jack," she said, squeezing me tight and smiling at the Negro shacks, "you and I have always been good buddies, haven't we?" "Yes ma'am." My heart gave a big pump and the back of my neck prickled like a dog's. "I've got bad news for you, son." She squeezed me tighter than ever. "Scotty is dead. Now it's all up to you. It's going to be difficult for you but I know you're going to act like a soldier." This was true. I could easily act like a soldier. Was that all I had to do?

It reminds me of a movie I saw last month out by Lake Pontchartrain. Linda and I went out to a theater in a new suburb. It was evident somebody had miscalculated, for the suburb had quit growing and here was the theater, a pink stucco cube, sitting out in a field all by itself. A strong wind whipped the waves against the seawall; even inside you could hear the racket. The movie was about a man who lost his memory in an accident and as a result lost everything: his family, his friends, his money. He

5

found himself a stranger in a strange city. Here he had to make a fresh start, find a new place to live, a new job, a new girl. It was supposed to be a tragedy, his losing all this, and he seemed to suffer a great deal. On the other hand, things were not so bad after all. In no time he found a very picturesque place to live, a houseboat on the river, and a very handsome girl, the local librarian.

After the movie Linda and I stood under the marquee and talked to the manager, or rather listened to him tell his troubles: the theater was almost empty, which was pleasant for me but not for him. It was a fine night and I felt very good. Overhead was the blackest sky I ever saw; a black wind pushed the lake toward us. The waves jumped over the seawall and spattered the street. The manager had to yell to be heard while from the sidewalk speaker directly over his head came the twittering conversation of the amnesiac and the librarian. It was the part where they are going through the newspaper files in search of some clue to his identity (he has a vague recollection of an accident). Linda stood by unhappily. She was unhappy for the same reason I was happy—because here we were at a neighborhood theater out in the sticks and without a car (I have a car but I prefer to ride buses and streetcars). Her idea of happiness is to drive downtown and have supper at the Blue Room of the Roosevelt Hotel. This I am obliged to do from time to time. It is worth it, however. On these occasions Linda becomes as exalted as I am now. Her eyes glow, her lips become moist, and when we dance she brushes her fine long legs against mine. She actually loves me at these times—and not as a reward for being taken to the Blue Room. She loves me because she feels exalted in this romantic place and not in a movie out in the sticks.

But all this is history. Linda and I have parted company. I have a new secretary, a girl named Sharon Kincaid.

For the past four years now I have been living uneventfully in Gentilly, a middle class suburb of New Orleans. Except for the banana plants in the patios and the curlicues of iron on the Walgreen drugstore one would never guess it was part of New Orleans. Most of the houses are either old-style California bungalows or new-style Daytona cottages. But this is what I like about it. I can't stand the old world atmosphere of the could contain such happiness. Yet in the case of Marcia and Linda the affair ended just when I thought our relationship was coming into its best phase. The air in the office would begin to grow thick with silent reproaches. It would become impossible to exchange a single word or glance that was not freighted with a thousand hidden meanings. Telephone conversations would take place at all hours of the night, conversations made up mostly of long silences during which I would rack my brain for something to say while on the other end you could hear little else but breathing and sighs. When these long telephone silences come, it is a sure sign that love is over. No, they were not conquests. For in the end my Lindas and I were so sick of each other that we were delighted to say good-by.

I am a stock and bond broker. It is true that my family was somewhat disappointed in my choice of a profession. Once I thought of going into law or medicine or even pure science. I even dreamed of doing something great. But there is much to be said for giving up such grand ambitions and living the most ordinary life imaginable, a life without the old longings; selling stocks and bonds and mutual funds; quitting work at five o'clock like everyone else; having a girl and perhaps one day settling down and raising a flock of Marcias and Sandras and Lindas of my own. Nor is the brokerage business as uninteresting as you might think. It is not a bad life at all.

We live, Mrs Schexnaydre and I, on Elysian Fields, the main thoroughfare of Faubourg Marigny. Though it was planned to be, like its namesake, the grandest boulevard of the city, something went amiss, and now it runs an undistinguished course from river to lake through shopping centers and blocks of duplexes and bungalows and raised cottages. But it is very spacious and airy and seems truly to stretch out like a field under the sky. Next door to Mrs Schexnaydre is a brand new school. It is my custom on summer evenings after work to take a shower, put on shirt and pants and stroll over to the deserted playground and there sit on the ocean wave, spread out the movie page of the *Times-Picayune* on one side, phone book on the other, and a city map in my lap. After I have made my choice, plotted a route—often to some remote neighborhood like Algiers or St Bernard—I stroll around the schoolyard in the last golden light of day and admire the building. Everything is so spick-and-span: the aluminum sashes fitted into the brick wall and gilded in the sunset, the pretty terrazzo floors and the desks molded like wings. Suspended by wires above the door is a schematic sort of bird, the Holy Ghost I suppose. It gives me a pleasant sense of the goodness of creation to think of the brick and the glass and the aluminum being extracted from common dirt—though no doubt it is less a religious sentiment than a financial one, since I own a few shares of Alcoa. How smooth and well-fitted and thrifty the aluminum feels!

But things have suddenly changed. My peaceful existence in Gentilly has been complicated. This morning, for the first time in years, there occurred to me the possibility of a search. I dreamed of the war, no, not quite dreamed but woke with the taste of it in my mouth, the queasy-quince taste of 1951 and the Orient. I remembered the first time the search occurred to me. I came to myself under a chindolea bush. Everything is upside-down for me, as I shall explain later. What are generally considered to be the best times are for me the worst times, and that worst of times was one of the best. My shoulder didn't hurt but it was pressed hard against the ground as if somebody sat on me. Six inches from my nose a dung beetle was scratching around under the leaves. As I watched, there awoke in me an immense curiosity. I was onto something. I vowed that if I ever got out of this fix, I would pursue the search. Naturally, as soon as I recovered and got home, I forgot all about it. But this morning when I got up, I dressed as usual and began as usual to put my belongings into my pockets: wallet, notebook (for writing down occasional thoughts), pencil, keys, handkerchief, pocket slide rule (for calculating percentage returns on principal). They looked both unfamiliar and at the same time full of clues. I stood in the center of the room and gazed at the little pile, sighting through a hole made by thumb and forefinger. What was unfamiliar about them was that I could see them. They might have belonged to someone else. A man can look at this little pile on his bureau for thirty years and never once see it. It is as invisible as his own hand. Once I saw it, however, the search became possible. I bathed, shaved, dressed carefully, and sat at my desk and poked through the little pile in search of a clue just as the detective on television pokes through the dead man's possessions, using his pencil as a poker.

The idea of a search comes to me again as I am on my way to my aunt's house, riding the Gentilly bus down Elysian Fields. The truth is I dislike cars. Whenever I drive a car, I have the feeling I have become invisible. People on the street cannot see you; they only watch your rear fender until it is out of their way. Elysian Fields is not the shortest route to my aunt's house. But I have my reasons for going through the Quarter. William Holden, I read in the paper this morning, is in New Orleans shooting a few scenes in the Place d'Armes. It would be interesting to catch a glimpse of him.

It is a gloomy March day. The swamps are still burning at Chef Menteur and the sky over Gentilly is the color of ashes. The bus is crowded with shoppers, nearly all women. The windows are steamed. I sit on the lengthwise seat in front. Women sit beside me and stand above me. On the long back seat are five Negresses so black that the whole rear of the bus seems darkened. Directly next to me, on the first cross seat, is a very fine-looking girl. She is a strapping girl but by no means too big, done up head to toe in cellophane, the hood pushed back to show a helmet of glossy black hair. She is magnificent with her split tooth and her Prince Val bangs split on her forehead. Gray eyes and wide black brows, a good arm and a fine swell of calf above her cellophane boot. One of those solitary Amazons one sees on Fifty-seventh Street in New York or in Neiman Marcus in Dallas. Our eyes meet. Am I mistaken or does the corner of her mouth tuck in ever so slightly and the petal of her lower lip curl out ever so richly? She is smiling—at me! My mind hits upon half a dozen schemes to circumvent the terrible moment of separation. No doubt she is a Texan. They are nearly always bad judges of men, these splendid Amazons. Most men are afraid of them and so they fall victim to the first little Mickey Rooney that comes along. In a better world I should be able to speak to her: come, darling, you can see that I love you. If you are planning to meet some little Mickey, think better of it. What a tragedy it is that I do not know her, will probably never see her again. What good times we could have! This very afternoon we could go spinning along the Gulf Coast. What consideration and tenderness I could show her! If it were a movie, I would have only to wait. The bus would get lost or the city would be bombed and she and I would tend the wounded. As it is, I may as well stop thinking about her.

Then it is that the idea of the search occurs to me. I become absorbed and for a minute or so forget about the girl.

What is the nature of the search? you ask.

Really it is very simple, at least for a fellow like me; so simple that it is easily overlooked.

The search is what anyone would undertake if he were not sunk in the everydayness of his own life. This morning, for example, I felt as if I had come to myself on a strange island. And what does such a castaway do? Why, he pokes around the neighborhood and he doesn't miss a trick.

To become aware of the possibility of the search is to be onto something. Not to be onto something is to be in despair.

The movies are onto the search, but they screw it up. The search always ends in despair. They like to show a fellow coming to himself in a strange place—but what does he do? He takes up with the local librarian, sets about proving to the local children what a nice fellow he is, and settles down with a vengeance. In two weeks time he is so sunk in everydayness that he might just as well be dead.

What do you seek—God? you ask with a smile.

I hesitate to answer, since all other Americans have settled the matter for themselves and to give such an answer would amount to setting myself a goal which everyone else has reached—and therefore raising a question in which no one has the slightest interest. Who wants to be dead last among one hundred and eighty million Americans? For, as everyone knows, the polls report that 98% of Americans believe in God and the remaining 2% are atheists and agnostics—which leaves not a single percentage point for a seeker. For myself, I enjoy answering polls as much as anyone and take pleasure in giving intelligent replies to all questions.

Truthfully, it is the fear of exposing my own ignorance which constrains me from mentioning the object of my search. For, to begin with, I cannot even answer this, the simplest and most basic of all questions: Am I, in my search, a hundred miles ahead of my fellow Americans or a hundred miles behind them? That is to say: Have 98% of Americans already found is their peculiar reality which astounds me. The Yankee boy is well aware of it, even though he pretends to ignore Holden. Clearly he would like nothing better than to take Holden over to his fraternity house in the most casual way. "Bill, I want you to meet Phil. Phil, Bill Holden," he would say and go sauntering off in the best seafaring style.

It is lunch hour on Canal Street. A parade is passing, but no one pays much attention. It is still a week before Mardi Gras and this is a new parade, a women's krewe from Gentilly. A krewe is a group of people who get together at carnival time and put on a parade and a ball. Anyone can form a krewe. Of course there are the famous old krewes like Comus and Rex and Twelfth Night, but there are also dozens of others. The other day a group of Syrians from Algiers formed a krewe named Isis. This krewe today, this must be Linda's krewe. I promised to come to see her. Red tractors pulled the floats along; scaffoldings creak, paper and canvas tremble. Linda, I think, is one of half a dozen shepherdesses dressed in short pleated skirts and mercury sandals with thongs criss-crossed up bare calves. But they are masked and I can't be sure. If she is, her legs are not so fine after all. All twelve legs are shivery and goosepimpled. A few businessmen stop to watch the girls and catch trinkets.

A warm wind springs up from the south piling up the clouds and bearing with it a far-off rumble, the first thunderstorm of the year. The street looks tremendous. People on the far side seem tiny and archaic, dwarfed by the great sky and the windy clouds like pedestrians in old prints. Am I mistaken or has a fog of uneasiness, a thin gas of malaise, settled on the street? The businessmen hurry back to their offices, the shoppers to their cars, the tourists to their hotels. Ah, William Holden, we already need you again. Already the fabric is wearing thin without you.

The mystery deepens. For ten minutes I stand talking to Eddie Lovell and at the end of it, when we shake hands and part, it seems to me that I cannot answer the simplest question about what has taken place. As I listen to Eddie speak plausibly and at length of one thing and another—business, his wife Nell, the old house they are redecorating—the fabric pulls together into one bright texture of investments, family projects, lovely old houses, little theater readings and such. It comes over me: this is how one lives! My exile in Gentilly has been the worst kind of self-deception.

Yes! Look at him. As he talks, he slaps a folded newspaper against his pants leg and his eye watches me and at the same time sweeps the terrain behind me, taking note of the slightest movement. A green truck turns down Bourbon Street; the eye sizes it up, flags it down, demands credentials, waves it on. A businessman turns in at the Maison Blanche building; the eye knows him, even knows what he is up to. And all the while he talks very well. His lips move muscularly, molding words into pleasing shapes, marshalling arguments, and during the slight pauses are held poised, attractively exerted in a Charles-Boyer pout—while a little web of saliva gathers in a corner like the clear oil of a good machine. Now he jingles the coins deep in his pocket. No mystery here!—he is as cogent as a bird dog quartering a field. He understands everything out there and everything out there is something to be understood.

Eddie watches the last float, a doubtful affair with a squashed cornucopia.

"We'd better do better than that."

"We will."

"Are you riding Neptune?"

"No."

I offer Eddie my four call-outs for the Neptune ball. There is always the problem of out-of-town clients, usually Texans, and especially their wives. Eddie thanks me for this and for something else.

"I want to thank you for sending Mr Quieulle to me. I really appreciate it."

"Who?"

"Old man Quieulle."

"Yes, I remember." Eddie has sunk mysteriously into himself, eyes twinkling from the depths. "Don't tell me—"

Eddie nods.

"—that he has already set up his trust and up and died?"

Eddie nods, still sunk into himself. He watches me carefully, hanging fire until I catch up with him.

"In Mrs Quieulle's name?"

described a Louisiana governor as a peckerwood son of a bitch;
Dr Wills, the lion-headed one, the rumpled country genius
who developed a gut anastomosis still in use; and Alex, serene
in his dream of youth and of his hero's death to come. But my
father is not one of them. His feet are planted wide apart, arms
locked around an alpenstock behind him; the katy is pushed
back releasing a forelock. His eyes are alight with an expression
I can't identify; it is not far from what his elders might have
called smart-alecky. He is something of a dude with his round
head and tricky tab collar. Yet he is, by every right, one of them.
He was commissioned in the RCAF in 1940 and got himself
killed before his country entered the war. And in Crete. And
in the wine dark sea. And by the same Boche. And with a copy
of *The Shropshire Lad* in his pocket. Again I search the eyes,
each eye a stipple or two in a blurred oval. Beyond a doubt
they are ironical.

"Does you, Mister Jack?" asks Mercer, still in limbo, one
foot toward the fire, the other on its way out.

"Yes, I do. Unilateral disarmament would be a disaster."

"What drivel." My aunt comes in smiling, head to one side,
hands outstretched, and I whistle with relief and feel myself
smiling with pleasure as I await one of her special kind of
attacks, attacks which are both playful and partly true. She
calls me an ingrate, a limb of Satan, the last and sorriest scion
of a noble stock. What makes it funny is that this is true. In a
split second I have forgotten everything, the years in Gentilly,
even my search. As always we take up again where we left off.
This is where I belong after all.

My aunt has done a great deal for me. When my father was
killed, my mother, who had been a trained nurse, went back
to her hospital in Biloxi. My aunt offered to provide my education. As a consequence much of the past fifteen years has
been spent in her house. She is really my great aunt. Yet she
is younger by so many years than her brothers that she might
easily be my father's sister—or rather the daughter of all three
brothers, since it is as their favorite and fondest darling that
she still appears in her own recollection, the female sport of
a fierce old warrior gens and no doubt for this reason never
taken quite seriously, even in her rebellion—as when she left
the South, worked in a settlement house in Chicago and, like

many well-born Southern ladies, embraced advanced political ideas. After years of being the sort of "bird" her brothers
indulged her in being and even expected her to be—her career
reached its climax when she served as a Red Cross volunteer
in the Spanish civil war, where I cannot picture her otherwise
than as that sort of fiercely benevolent demoniac Yankee lady
most incomprehensible to Spaniards—within the space of six
months she met and married Jules Cutrer, widower with child,
settled down in the Garden District and became as handsome
and formidable as her brothers. She is no longer a "bird." It is
as if, with her illustrious brothers dead and gone, she might
now at last become what they had been and what as a woman
had been denied her: soldierly both in look and outlook. With
her blue-white hair and keen quick face and terrible gray eyes,
she is somehow at sixty-five still the young prince.

It is just as I thought. In an instant we are off and away
down the hall and into her office, where she summons me for
her "talks." This much is certain: it is bad news about Kate. If
it were a talk about me, my aunt would not be looking at me.
She would be gazing into the hive-like recesses of her old desk,
finger pressed against her lip. But instead she shows me something and searches my face for what I see. With her watching
me, it is difficult to see anything. There is a haze. Between us
there is surely a carton of dusty bottles—*bottles*?—yes, surely
bottles, yet blink as I will I can't be sure.

"Do you see these whisky bottles?"

"Yes ma'am."

"And this kind?" She gives me an oblong brown bottle.

"Yes."

"Do you know where they came from?"

"No'm."

"Mercer found them on top of an armoire. That armoire."
She points mysteriously to the very ceiling above us. "He was
setting out rat poision."

"In Kate's room?"

"Yes. What do you think?"

"Those are not whisky bottles."

"What are they?"

"Wine. Gypsy Rose. They make wine bottles flat like that."

"Read that." She nods at the bottle in my hand.

"Sodium pentobarbital. One and one half grains. This is a wholesaler's bottle."

"Do you know where we found that?"

"In the box?"

"In the incinerator. The second in a week."

I am silent. Now my aunt does take her seat at the desk.

"I haven't told Walter. Or Jules. Because I'm not really worried. Kate is just fine. She is going to come through with flying colors. And she and Walter are going to be happy. But as time grows short, she is getting a little nervous."

"You mean you think she is afraid of another accident?"

"She is afraid of a general catastrophe. But that is not what worries me."

"What worries you?"

"I don't want her moping around the house again."

"She's not working downtown with you?"

"Not for two weeks."

"Does she feel bad?"

"Oh no. Nothing like that. But she's a little scared."

"Is she seeing Dr Mink?"

"She refuses. She thinks that if she goes to see a doctor she'll get sick."

"What do you want me to do?"

"She will not go to the ball. Now that's all right. But it is very important that she not come to the point where it becomes more and more difficult to meet people."

"She's seen no one?"

"No one but Walter. Now all in the world I want you to do is take her to the Lejiers and watch the parade from the front porch. It is not a party. There will be no question of making an entrance or an exit. There is nothing to brace for. You will drop in, speak or not speak, and leave."

"She is that bad?"

"She is not bad at all. I mean to take care that she won't be."

"What about Walter?"

"He's krewe captain. He can't possibly get away. And I'm glad he can't, to tell the truth. Do you know what I really want you to do?"

"What?"

"I want you to do whatever it was you did before you walked

out on us, you wretch. Fight with her, joke with her—the child doesn't laugh. You and Kate always got along, didn't you? Sam too. You knew Sam will be here Sunday to speak at the Forum?"

"Yes."

"I want Sam to talk to Kate. You and Sam are the only people she'd ever listen to."

My aunt is generous with me. What she really means is that she is sure Sam can set things right and that she hopes I can hold the fort till Sam arrives.

3

It is a surprise to find Uncle Jules at lunch. Last fall he suffered a serious heart attack from which, however, he recovered so completely that he has dispensed with his nap since Christmas. He sits between Kate and Walter and his manner is so pleasant and easy that even Kate is smiling. It is hard to believe anything is wrong; the bottles, in particular, seem grotesque. Uncle Jules is pleased to see me. During the past year I discovered my sole discernible talent: the trick of making money. I manage to sell a great many of the stocks which Uncle Jules underwrites. He is convinced, moreover, that I predicted the January selloff and even claims that he advanced a couple of issues on my say-so. This he finds pleasing, and he always greets me with a tremendous wink as if we were in cahoots and might get caught any minute.

He and Walter talk football. Uncle Jules' life ambition is to revive the fortunes of the Tulane football team. I enjoy the talk because I like football myself and especially do I like to hear Uncle Jules tell about the great days of Jerry Dalrymple and Don Zimmerman and Billy Banker. When he describes a goal-line stand against L.S.U. in 1932, it is like King Arthur standing fast in the bloodred sunset against Sir Modred and the traitors. Walter was manager of the team and so he and Uncle Jules are thick as thieves.

Uncle Jules is as pleasant a fellow as I know anywhere. Above his long Creole horseface is a crop of thick gray hair cut short as a college boy's. His shirt encases his body in a way that pleases me. It fits him so well. My shirts always have something wrong with them; they are too tight in the collar or too loose around

I walked home with him after he had been tapped for Golden Fleece—which was but the final honor of a paragraph of honors beneath his picture in the annual. "Binx," he said—with me he had at last dropped his sour-senseless way of talking. "I'll let you in on a secret. That business back there—believe it or not, that doesn't mean anything to me." "What does, Walter?" He stopped and we looked back at the twinkling campus as if the cities of the world had been spread out at our feet. "The main thing, Binx, is to be humble, to make Golden Fleece and be humble about it." We both took a deep breath and walked back to the Delta house in silence.

When I was a freshman, it was extremely important to me to join a good fraternity. But what if no fraternity invited me to join? During rush week I was invited to the Delta house so the brothers could look me over. Another candidate, Boylan "Sockhead" Bass from Bastrop, and I sat together on a leather sofa, hands on our knees while the brothers stood around courting us like virgins and at the same time eyeing us like heifers. Presently Walter beckoned to me and I followed him upstairs where we had a confidential talk in a small bedroom. Walter motioned to me to sit on the bed and for a long moment he stood, as he is standing now: hands in pockets, rocking back on his heels and looking out the window like Samuel Hinds in the movies. "Binx," he said. "We know each other pretty well, don't we?" (We'd both gone to the same prep school in New Hampshire.) "That's right, Walter," I said. "You know me well enough to know I wouldn't hand you the usual crap about this fraternity business, don't you?" "I know you wouldn't, Walter." "We don't go in for hot boxes around here, Binx. We don't have to." "I know you don't." He listed the good qualities of the SAEs, the Delta Psis, the Dekes, the KAs. "They're all good boys, Binx. I've got friends in all of them. But when it comes to describing the fellows here, the caliber of the men, the bond between us, the meaning of this little symbol—" he turned back his lapel to show the pin and I wondered if it was true that Deltas held their pins in their mouths when they took a shower—"there's not much I can say, Binx." Then Walter took his hat off and stood stroking the tricornered peak. "As a matter of fact, I'm not going to say anything at all. Instead, I'll ask you a single question and then we'll go down. Did you or did you not feel a unique something when you walked into this house? I won't attempt to describe it. If you felt it, you already know exactly what I mean. If you didn't—!" Now Walter stands over me, holding his hat over his heart. "Did you feel it, Binx?" I told him straight off that nothing would make me happier than to pledge Delta on the spot, if that was what he was getting at. We shook hands and he called in some of the brothers. "Fellows, I want you to meet Mister John Bickerson Bolling. He's one of those broken-down Bollings from up in Feliciana Parish—you may have heard the name. Binx is a country boy and he's full of hookworm but he ought to have some good stuff in him. I believe he'll make us a good man." We shook hands all around. They were good fellows.

As it turned out, I did not make them a good man at all. I managed to go to college four years without acquiring a single honor. When the annual came out, there was nothing under my picture but the letters ΔΨΔ—which was appropriate since I had spent the four years propped on the front porch of the fraternity house, bemused and dreaming, watching the sun shine through the Spanish moss, lost in the mystery of finding myself alive at such a time and place—and next to ΔΨΔ my character summary: "Quiet but a sly sense of humor." Boylan Bass of Bastrop turned out to be no less a disappointment. He was a tall farm boy with a long neck and an Adam's apple who took pharmacy and for four years said not a word and was not known even to his fraternity brothers. His character line was: "A good friend."

Walter is at ease again. He turns away from the window and once more stands over me and inclines his narrow hollowed-out temple.

"You know most of the krewe, don't you?"

"Yes. As a matter of fact I still belong—"

"It's the same bunch that go down to Tigre au Chenier. Why didn't you come down last month?"

"I really don't like to hunt much."

Walter seems to spy something on the table. He leans over and runs a thumb along the grain. "Just look at that wood. It's all one piece, by God." Since his engagement, I have noticed that Walter has begun to take a proprietary interest in the house, tapping on walls, measuring floorboards, hefting vases.

He straightens up. "I don't know what's gotten into you. All I can figure is that you've got me on your list."

"It's not that."

"What is it then?"

"What is what?"

"Why in the hell don't you give me a call some time?"

"What would we talk about?" I say in our sour-senseless style of ten years ago.

Walter gives my shoulder a hard squeeze. "I'd forgotten what a rare turd you are. No, you're right. What would we talk about," says Walter elegiacally. "Oh Lord. What's wrong with the goddamn world, Binx?"

"I am not sure. But something occurred to me this morning. I was sitting on the bus—"

"What do you do with yourself out there in Gentilly?" People often ask me what is wrong with the world and also what I do in Gentilly, and I always try to give an answer. The former is an interesting question. I have noticed, however, that no one really wants to listen to an answer.

"Not much. Sell mutual funds to widows and dagos."

"Is that right?" Walter drops his shoulder and feels the muscle in his back. Squatting down on his heels, he runs an eye along the baseboard calculating the angle of settle.

After the war some of us bought a houseboat on Vermilion Bay near Tigre au Chenier. Walter got everything organized. It was just like him to locate a cook-caretaker living right out there in the swamp and to line up some real boogalee guides. But to me the venture was not a success. It was boring, to tell the truth. Actually there was very little fishing and hunting and a great deal of poker and drinking. Walter liked nothing better than getting out in that swamp on week-ends with five or six fellows, quit shaving and play poker around the clock. He really enjoyed it. He would get up groaning from the table at three o'clock in the morning and pour himself a drink and, rubbing his beard, stand looking out into the darkness. "God-damn, this is all right, isn't it? Isn't this a terrific set-up, Binx? Tomorrow we're going to have duck Rochambeau right here. Tell me honestly, have you ever tasted better food at Gala-toire's?" "No, it's very good, Walter." "Give me your honest opinion, Binx." "It's very good." He got Jake the caretaker out of trouble once and liked having him around. Jake would sit in close to the poker game. "Jake, what do you think of that fellow over there?" Walter would ask him, nodding toward me or one of the others. He liked to think that Negroes have a sixth sense and that his Negro had an extra good one. Jake would cock his head as if he were fathoming me with his sixth sense. "You got to watch *him*! That Mister Binx is all right now!" And in some fashion, more extraordinary than a sixth sense, Jake would manage to oblige Walter without disobliging me. The houseboat seemed like a good idea, but as it worked out I became depressed. To tell the truth I like women better. All I could think about in that swamp was how much I'd like to have my hands on Marcia or Linda and be spinning along the Gulf Coast.

To tell the absolute truth, I've always been slightly embarrassed in Walter's company. Whenever I'm with him, I feel the stretch of the old tightrope, the necessity of living up to the friendship of friendships, of cultivating an intimacy beyond words. The fact is we have little to say to each other. There is only this thick sympathetic silence between us. We are comrades, true, but somewhat embarrassed comrades. It is probably my fault. For years now I have had no friends. I spend my entire time working, making money, going to movies and seeking the company of women.

The last time I had friends was eight years ago. When I returned from the Orient and recovered from my wound, I took up with two fellows I thought I should like. I did like them. They were good fellows both. One was an ex-Lieutenant like me, a University of Cal man, a skinny impoverished fellow who liked poetry and roaming around the countryside. The other was a mad eccentric from Valdosta, a regular young Burl Ives with beard and guitar. We thought it would be a good thing to do some hiking, so we struck out from Gatlinburg in the Smokies, headed for Maine on the Appalachian Trail. We were all pretty good drinkers and talkers and we could spiel about women and poetry and Eastern religion in pretty good style. It seemed like a fine idea, sleeping in shelters or under the stars in the cool evergreens, and later hopping freights. In fact this was what I was sure I wanted to do. But in no time at all I became depressed. The times we did have fun, like

sitting around a fire or having a time with some girls, I had the
feeling they were saying to me: "How about this, Binx? This
is really it, isn't it, boy?", that they were practically looking up
from their girls to say this. For some reason I sank into a deep
melancholy. What good fellows they were, I thought, and how
much they deserved to be happy. If only I could make them
happy. But the beauty of the smoky blue valleys, instead of
giving us joy, became heartbreaking. "What's the matter with
you, Binx?" they said at last. "My dear friends," I said to them.
"I will say good-by and wish you well. I think I will go back to
New Orleans and live in Gentilly." And there I have lived ever
since, solitary and in wonder, wondering day and night, never
a moment without wonder. Now and then my friends stop by,
all gotten up as young eccentrics with their beards and bicycles,
and down they go into the Quarter to hear some music and
find some whores and still I wish them well. As for me, I stay
home with Mrs Schexnaydre and turn on TV. Not that I like
TV so much, but it doesn't distract me from the wonder. That
is why I can't go to the trouble they go to. It is distracting,
and not for five minutes will I be distracted from the wonder.

4

Walter offers to drive Uncle Jules to town. Through the liv-
ing-room doors I can see my aunt sitting by the fire, temple
propped on her fingers. The white light from the sky pours into
her upturned face. She opens her eyes and, seeing me, forms a
soundless word with her lips.

I find Kate in the ground-level basement, rubbing an iron
fireplace. Since Christmas she and Walter have taken to cleaning things, removing a hundred years' accumulation of paint
from old walls and cupboards to expose the cypress and brick
underneath. As if to emphasize her sallowness and thinness,
she has changed into shirt and jeans. She is as frail as a ten year
old, except in her thighs. Sometimes she speaks of her derrière,
sticks it out Beale Street style and gives it a slap and this makes
me blush because it is a very good one, marvellously ample and
mysterious and nothing to joke about.

To my relief she greets me cheerfully. She clasps one leg,
rests her cheek on a knee and rubs an iron welt with steel wool.

She has the advantage of me, sitting at her ease in a litter of summers past, broken wicker, split croquet balls, rotting hammocks. Now she wipes the welt with solvent; it begins to turn pale. "Well? Aren't you supposed to tell me something?"

"Yes, but I forget what it was."

"Binx Binx. You're to tell me all sorts of things."

"That's true."

"It will end with me telling you."

"That would be better."

"How do you make your way in the world?"

"Is that what you call it? I don't really know. Last month I made three thousand dollars—less capital gains."

"How did you get through a war without getting killed?"

"It was not through any doing of yours."

"Anh anh anh." It is an old passage between us, more of a joke now than a quarrel. "And how do you appear so reasonable to Mother?"

"I feel reasonable with her."

"She thinks you're one of her kind."

"What kind is that?"

"A proper Bolling. Jules thinks you're a go-getter. But you don't fool me."

"You know."

"Yes."

"What kind?"

"You're like me, but worse. Much worse."

She is in tolerable good spirits. It is not necessary to pay too much attention to her. I spy the basket-arm of a broken settee. It has a presence about it: the ghost of twenty summers in Feliciana. I perch on a bony spine of wicker and prop hands on knees.

"I remember what I came for. Will you go to Lejiers and watch the parade?"

Kate stretches out a leg to get at her cigarettes. Her ritual of smoking stands her in good stead. She extracts the wadded pack, kneads the warm cellophane, taps a cigarette violently and accurately against her thumbnail, lights it with a Zippo worn smooth and yellow as a pocket watch. Pushing back her shingled hair, she blows out a plume of gray lung smoke and plucks a grain from her tongue. She reminds me of college girls before the war, how they would sit five and six in a convertible, seeming old to me and sullen-silent toward men and toward their own sex, how they would take refuge in their cigarettes: the stripping of cellophane, the clash of Zippos, the rushing plume of lung smoke expelled up in a long hissing sigh.

"Her idea?"

"Yes."

Kate begins to nod and goes on nodding. "You must have had quite a powwow."

"Not much of one."

"You've never understood Mother's dynamics."

"Her dynamics?"

"What do you suppose she and I talk about?"

"What?"

"You. I'm sick of talking about you."

Now I do look at her. Her voice has suddenly taken on its "objective" tone. Since she started her social work, Kate has spells of talking frankly in which she recites case histories in a kind of droning scientific voice: "—and all the while it was perfectly obvious that the poor woman had never experienced an orgasm." "Is such a thing possible!" I would cry and we would shake our heads in the strong sense of our new camaraderie, the camaraderie of a science which is not too objective to pity the follies and ignorance of the world.

There is nothing new in her tack against her stepmother. Nor do I object, to tell the truth. It seems to serve her well enough, this discovery of the possibilities of hatred. She warms under its influence. It serves to make the basement a friendlier place. Her hatred is a consequence of a swing of her dialectic. She has, in the past few months, swung back to her father (the basement is to be a TV room for him). In the beginning she had been her father's child. Then, as a young girl, the person of her stepmother, this quick, charming and above all intelligent woman, had appeared at a critical time in her rebellion. Her stepmother became for her the rallying point of all those forces which, until then, had been hardly felt as more than formless discontents. If she hadn't much use for her father's ways, his dogged good nature, his Catholic unseriousness, his little water closet jokes, his dumbness about his God, the good Lord; the everlasting dumb importuning of her just to be good, to mind the sisters, and to go his way, his dumb way of inner faith and outer good spirits—if she hadn't much use for this, she hardly knew how little until she found herself in the orbit of this enchanting person. Her stepmother had taken her in charge and set her free. In the older woman, older than a mother and yet something of a sister, she found the blithest gayest fellow rebel and comrade. The world of books and music and art and ideas opened before her. And if later her stepmother was to take alarm at Kate's political activities—a spiritual rebellion was one thing, the soaring of the spirit beyond the narrow horizons of the parochial and into the lofty regions of Literature and Life; nor was there anything wrong with the girlish socialism of Sarah Lawrence; but political conspiracy here and now in New Orleans with the local dirty necks of the bookshops and a certain oracular type of social worker my aunt knew only too well—that was something else. But even so, now that it was in the past, it was not really so bad. In fact, as time went on, it might even take on the flavor of one's *Studententage*. How well I remember, her stepmother told her, the days when we Wagnerians used to hiss old Brahms—O for the rapturous rebellious days of youth. But now it is she, my aunt herself, who falls prey to Kate's dialectic of hatreds. It was inevitable that Kate should catch up with and "see into" her stepmother, just as she caught up with her father, and that she should, in the same swing of the dialectic, rediscover her father as the authentic Louisiana businessman and, if not go to Mass with him, build him a TV room. It was inevitable that she should give up the Philharmonic upstairs and take up the Gillette Cavalcade in the basement. It is, as I say, all the same to me which parent she presently likes or dislikes. But I am uneasy over the meagerness of her resources. Where will her dialectic carry her now? After Uncle Jules what? Not back to her stepmother, I fear, but into some kind of dead-end where she must become aware of the dialectic. "Hate her then," I feel like telling her, "and love Jules. But leave it at that. Don't try another swing."

I say: "Then you're not going to the Lejiers."

She puts her cigarette on a potsherd and goes back to her rubbing.

"And you're not going to the ball?" I ask.

"No."

kidney stones or not (they didn't, incidentally), compared to
the mystery of those summer afternoons. I asked Harry if he
would excuse me. He was glad enough to, since I was not much
use to him sitting on the floor. I moved down to the Quarter
where I spent the rest of the vacation in quest of the spirit of
summer and in the company of an attractive and confused girl
from Bennington who fancied herself a poet.

But I am mistaken. My aunt is not suggesting that I go into
research.

"I want you to think about entering medical school this fall.
You know you've always had it in the back of your mind. Now
I've fixed up your old garçonnière in the carriage house. Wait
till you see it—I've added a kitchenette and some bookshelves.
You will have absolute privacy. We won't even allow you in the
house. No—it is not I doing something for you. We could use
you around. Kate is going through something I don't understand. Jules, my dear Jules won't even admit anything is wrong.
You and Sam are the only ones she'd ever listen to."

We come to the corner of the gallery and a warm spray blows
in our faces. One can smell the islands to the south. The rain
slackens and tires hiss on the wet asphalt.

"Here's what we'll do. As soon as hot weather comes, we'll
all go up to Flat Rock, the whole family, Walter included. He's
already promised. We'll have a nice long summer in the mountains and come back here in September and buckle down to
work."

Two cars come racing abreast down Prytania; someone
shouts an obscenity in a wretched croaking voice. Our footsteps echo like pistol shots in the basement below.

"I don't know."

"You think about it."

"Yes ma'am."

She does not smile. Instead she stops me, holds me off.

"What is it you want out of life, son?" she asks with a sweetness that makes me uneasy.

"I don't know'm. But I'll move in whenever you want me."

"Don't you feel obliged to use your brain and to make a
contribution?"

"No'm."

She waits for me to say more. When I do not, she seems to

forget about her idea. Far from holding my refusal against me, she links her arm in mine and resumes the promenade.

"I no longer pretend to understand the world." She is shaking her head yet still smiling her sweet menacing smile. "The world I knew has come crashing down around my ears. The things we hold dear are reviled and spat upon." She nods toward Prytania Street. "It's an interesting age you will live in—though I can't say I'm sorry to miss it. But it should be quite a sight, the going under of the evening land. That's us all right. And I can tell you, my young friend, it is evening. It is very late."

For her too the fabric is dissolving, but for her even the dissolving makes sense. She understands the chaos to come. It seems so plain when I see it through her eyes. My duty in life is simple. I go to medical school. I live a long useful life serving my fellowman. What's wrong with this? All I have to do is remember it.

"—you have too good a mind to throw away. I don't quite know what we're doing on this insignificant cinder spinning away in a dark corner of the universe. That is a secret which the high gods have not confided in me. Yet one thing I believe and I believe it with every fibre of my being. A man must live by his lights and do what little he can and do it as best he can. In this world goodness is destined to be defeated. But a man must go down fighting. That is the victory. To do anything less is to be less than a man."

She is right. I will say yes. I will say yes even though I do not really know what she is talking about.

But I hear myself saying: "As a matter of fact I was planning to leave Gentilly soon, but for a different reason. There is something—" I stop. My idea of a search seems absurd.

To my surprise this lame reply is welcomed by my aunt.

"Of course!" she cries. "You're doing something every man used to do. When your father finished college, he had his *Wanderjahr*, a fine year's ramble up the Rhine and down the Loire, with a pretty girl on one arm and a good comrade on the other. What happened to you when you finished college? War. And I'm so proud of you for that. But that's enough to take it out of any man."

Wanderjahr. My heart sinks. We do not understand each other after all. If I thought I'd spent the last four years as a *Wanderjahr*, before "settling down," I'd shoot myself on the spot.

"How do you mean, take it out of me?"

"Your scientific calling, your love of books and music. Don't you remember how we used to talk—on the long winter evenings when Jules would go to bed and Kate would go dancing, how we used to talk! We tired the sun with talking and sent him down the sky. Don't you remember discovering Euripides and Jean-Christophe?"

"You discovered them for me. It was always through you that—" All at once I am sleepy. It requires an effort to put one foot in front of the other. Fortunately my aunt decides to sit down. I wipe off an iron bench with my handkerchief and we sit, still arm in arm. She gives me a pat.

"Now. I want you to make me a promise."

"Yes ma'am."

"Your birthday is one week from today."

"Is that right?"

"You will be thirty years old. Don't you think a thirty year old man ought to know what he wants to do with his life?"

"Yes."

"Will you tell me?"

"Then?"

"Yes. Next Wednesday afternoon—after Sam leaves. I'll meet you here at this spot. Will you promise to come?"

"Yes ma'am." She expects a great deal from Sam's visit.

Pushing up my sleeve to see my watch, she sucks in her breath. "Back to the halt and the lame and the generally no 'count."

"Sweetie, lie down first and let me rub your neck." I can tell from her eyes when she has a headache.

Later, when Mercer brings the car around to the front steps, she lays a warm dry cheek against mine. "m-M! You're such a comfort to me. You remind me so much of your father."

"I can't seem to remember him."

"He was the sweetest old thing. So gay. And did the girls

fall over him. And a mind! He had a mind like a steel trap, an analytical mind like yours." (She always says this, though I have never analyzed anything.) "He had the pick of New Orleans."

(And picked Anna Castagne.)

Mercer, who has changed to a cord coat and cap, holds the door grudgingly and cranes up and down the street as much as to say that he may be a chauffeur but not a footman.

She has climbed into the car but she does not release my hand.

"He would have been much happier in research," she says and lets me go.

6

The rain has stopped. Kate calls from under the steps.

She is in the best of spirits. She shows me the brick she found under linoleum and the shutters Walter bought in a junkyard. It bothers her that when the paint was removed the shutters came somewhat frayed from the vat. "They will form a partition here. The fountain and planter will go out here." By extending the partition into the garden, a corner of the wall will be enclosed to form a pleasant little nook. I can see why she is so serious: truthfully it seems that if she can just hit upon the right *place*, a shuttered place of brick and vine and flowing water, her very life can be lived. "I feel wonderful."

"What made you feel wonderful?"

"It was the storm." Kate clears the broken settee and pulls me down in a crash of wicker. "The storm cut loose, you and Mother walked up and down, up and down, and I fixed myself a big drink and enjoyed every minute of it."

"Are you ready to go to Lejiers?"

"Oh I couldn't do that," she says, plucking her thumb. "Where are you going?" she asks nervously, hoping that I will leave.

"To Magazine Street." I know she isn't listening. Her breathing is shallow and irregular, as if she were giving thought to each breath. "Is it bad this time?"

She shrugs.

"As bad as last time?"

Kate. Kate seems better and my aunt is pleased and gives me the credit. She has made an appointment for Kate with Dr Mink and Kate has consented to go. When Kate calls me, she takes her analytic tone. It is something of a strain for both of us. For some reason or other she feels obliged to keep one jump ahead of the conventional. When I answer the phone, instead of hearing "Hello, this is Kate," there comes into my ear a low-pitched voice saying something like: "Well, the knives have started flying," which means that she and her mother have been aggressive toward each other; or: "What do you know? I'm celebrating the rites of spring after all," which turns out to mean that she has decided, in her ironic and reflected way, to attend the annual supper given for former queens of the Neptune ball. This is something of a strain for both of us, as I say, but I am glad to hear from her. To tell the truth, I am somewhat worried about her, more so than her stepmother is. Kate is trapping herself too often: hitting upon a way out, then slamming the door upon herself. She has broken her engagement with Walter. But her stepmother understands, and Walter too, it seems. He stands by loyally to do what he can—it is none other than Walter, in fact, who will drive her to the hotel for the queens' supper. All seems well, but Kate is uneasy. "They think they're helping me, but they aren't," comes the low voice in my ear. "How much better it would be if they weren't so damn understanding—if they kicked me out of the house. To find yourself out in the street with two dollars to your name, to catch the streetcar downtown and get a job, perhaps as an airline stewardess. Think how wonderful it would be to fly to Houston and back three times a week for the next twenty years. You think I'm kidding? I'm not. It would be wonderful." "Then why don't you walk out of the house and get yourself a job?" I ask her. There comes a silence, then a click. But this doesn't mean anything. Abrupt hang-ups are a part of our analytic way of talking.

Sharon seems to pay no attention to these alexandrine conversations, even though we occupy the same small office and she is close enough to touch. Today she wears a sleeveless dress of yellow cotton; her arms come out of the armholes as tenderly as a little girl's. But when she puts her hand to her hair, you see that it is quite an arm. The soft round muscle goes slack of its own weight. Once she slapped a fly with her bare hand and set my Artmetal desk ringing like a gong. Her back is turned to me, but obliquely, so that I can see the line of her cheek with its whorl of down and the Slavic prominence under the notch of her eye and the quick tender incurve, shortening her face like a little mignon. There is on her desk a snapshot of her father and it is this very crowding of the cheekbone into the eye socket, narrowing the eye into a squint-eyed almost Chinese treacherousness, which is so ugly in him and so beautiful in her. As she types, the little kidney-shaped cushion presses against the small of her back in a nice balance of thrusts.

I am in love with Sharon Kincaid. She knows nothing of this, I think. I have not asked her for a date nor even been specially friendly. On the contrary: I have been aloof and correct as a Nazi officer in occupied Paris. Yet when she came in this morning unshouldering her Guatemalan bag and clearing her hair from her short collar, I heard a soughing sound in my ears like a desert wind. The Guatemalan bag contains *Peyton Place*, I happen to know. She had it when she applied for the job, a drugstore-library copy which she held under her purse. Ever since, the bag has been heavy with it—I can tell by the swing of it. She reads it at her lunch in the A & G cafeteria. Her choice in literature I took to be a good omen at the time, but I have changed my mind. My Sharon should not read this kind of stuff.

Her person has acquired a priceless value to me. For the first time I understand the conceits of the old poets: how I envy thee, little kidney-shaped cushion! Oh, to take thy place and press in thy stead against the sweet hollow of her back, etc. The other day Frank Hebert from Savings & Loan next door was complaining about his overhead: his rent was so much, his office girl such and such. To think of it: Sharon Kincaid as an item on a list, higher than the janitor, lower than the rent. Yet I dare not raise her salary, though before long I shall and with reason. She is a first-class secretary, quicker to learn than either Marcia or Linda. Only this much do I know from the interview: she comes from Barbour County, Alabama; she attended Birmingham Southern for two years; her mother and father left the farm and are divorced; her mother sells Real Silk hosiery and often visits Sharon but does not live with her.

Sharon lives in a rooming house on Esplanade. Her roommate works for Alcoa. One night I drove by the house, a tall narrow pile with blue windows and a display of plumbing fixtures on the ground floor.

Toward her I keep a Gregory Peckish sort of distance. I am a tall black-headed fellow and I know as well as he how to keep to myself, make my eyes fine and my cheeks spare, tuck my lip and say a word or two with a nod or two.

It is just as well I keep my distance. Today it is louder than ever, this mistral whistling in my ears. I am nearly sick with it. Desire for her is like a sorrow in my heart. Ten minutes ago she rolled backwards in her little chair to hand me a letter and did not even touch me, but there singing about me was Rosenkavalier and here was the yellow-cotton smell of her and of the summer to come. Once she did touch my hand with the warm ventral flesh of her forearm: sparks flew past the corner of my eye and I actually became dizzy.

Today I read *Arabia Deserta* enclosed in a Standard & Poor binder. She conceals *Peyton Place*; I conceal *Arabia Deserta*.

> Pleasant, as the fiery heat of the daylight is done, is our homely evening fire. The sun goes down upon a highland steppe of Arabia, whose common altitude is above three thousand feet, the thin dry air is presently refreshed, the sand is soon cold; wherein yet at three fingers' depth is left the sunny warmth of the past day's heat until the new sunrise. After a half hour it is the blue night, and a clear hoary starlight in which there shines the girdle of the milky way, with a marvellous clarity. As the sun is setting, the nomad housewife brings in a truss of sticks and dry bushes, which she has pulled or hoed with a mattock (a tool they have seldom) in the wilderness; she casts down this provision by our hearthside, for the sweet-smelling evening fire.

There was a time when this was the last book on earth I'd have chosen to read. Until recent years, I read only "fundamental" books, that is, key books on key subjects, such as *War and Peace*, the novel of novels; *A Study of History*, the solution of the problem of time; Schroedinger's *What is Life?*, Einstein's

The Universe as I See It, and such. During those years I stood outside the universe and sought to understand it. I lived in my room as an Anyone living Anywhere and read fundamental books and only for diversion took walks around the neighborhood and saw an occasional movie. Certainly it did not matter to me where I was when I read such a book as *The Expanding Universe*. The greatest success of this enterprise, which I call my vertical search, came one night when I sat in a hotel room in Birmingham and read a book called *The Chemistry of Life*. When I finished it, it seemed to me that the main goals of my search were reached or were in principle reachable, whereupon I went out and saw a movie called *It Happened One Night* which was itself very good. A memorable night. The only difficulty was that though the universe had been disposed of, I myself was left over. There I lay in my hotel room with my search over yet still obliged to draw one breath and then the next. But now I have undertaken a different kind of search, a horizontal search. As a consequence, what takes place in my room is less important. What is important is what I shall find when I leave my room and wander in the neighborhood. Before, I wandered as a diversion. Now I wander seriously and sit and read as a diversion.

Sharon turns not one hair as I talk with my aunt about Kate in our old Feliciana style of talking and as I talk to Kate in our analytic style of talking. Yet she recognizes each voice and passes the phone back with a "Miz Cutrer" or a "Miss Cutrer." Now, as she answers the phone again, it crosses my mind that she may not be entirely unselfconscious: she tilts her head and puts her pencil to her cheek like the secretary in the Prell commercial. She presses the mouthpiece against her chest.

"Mr Sartalamaccia called earlier. I forgot."

"Is that he?"

She nods. Her agate eyes watch me. I think it over Gregory-Peckishly and hold out a hand with no time for her.

It is a matter of no importance. Mr Sartalamaccia wants to buy some land, my patrimony in fact, a worthless parcel of swamp in St Bernard Parish. He offers eight thousand dollars. It is enough to say yes here and now, but a Gregorish Peckerish idea pops into my head. I propose to Mr Sartalamaccia that he meet me on the site at ten thirty tomorrow morning. He sounds disappointed.

"Miss Kincaid, I'll want you to come down with me to St Bernard Parish tomorrow and copy a title in the courthouse." In truth it would be interesting to see how much my father paid for it. Any doings of my father, even his signature, is in the nature of a clue in my search.

"St Bernard Parish?" To my Sharon, fresh from Eufala, I might just as well have said Mont Saint Michel.

"We'll be back here by one."

"Just as long as I get back uptown by seven thirty tomorrow night."

Now I am Gregory-grim and no fooling this time. What the devil. Three weeks in New Orleans and she's already having dates?

2

Customers come in after hours and it is late evening when I leave the office. Unlike the big downtown brokers, most of our clients are storekeepers and employed people. It is a source of satisfaction to me to make money. Not even Sharon or *Arabia Deserta* interferes with this. Another idea occurred to me yesterday as I read about Khalil in the high plateau country of the Negd. What gives it merit is that it should not only make money; it should also bring me closer to Sharon. I shall discuss it with her tomorrow. My first idea was the building itself. It looks like a miniature bank with its Corinthian pilasters, portico and iron scrolls over the windows. The firm's name, Cutrer, Klostermann & Lejier is lettered in Gothic and below in smaller letters, the names of the Boston mutual funds we represent. It looks far more conservative than the modern banks in Gentilly. It announces to the world: modern methods are no doubt excellent but here is good old-fashioned stability, but stability with imagination. A little bit of old New England with a Creole flavor. The Parthenon façade cost twelve thousand dollars but commissions have doubled. The young man you see inside is clearly the soul of integrity; he asks no more than to be allowed to plan your future. This is true. This is all I ask.

The sun has set but the sky is luminous and clear and apple green in the east. Nothing is left of the smog but a thumb-smudge over Chef Menteur. Bullbats hawk the insects in the warm air next to the pavement. They dive and utter their thrumming *skonk-skonk* and go sculling up into the bright upper air. I stop at the corner of Elysian Fields to buy a paper from Ned Daigle. Ned is a former jockey and he looks quite a bit like Leo Carroll but older and more dried-up. "What seh, Jackie," he calls in his hoarse bass, as hoarse as the bullbats, and goes humping for the cars, snapping the papers into folds as he goes. He catches the boulevard traffic at the stoplight and often sells half a dozen papers before the light changes. Ned knows everybody at the Fairgrounds including all the local hoods and racketeers. During racing season he often brings them around to my office. For some reason or other he thinks my brokerage business is a virtuous and deserving institution, something like a church. The gangsters too; quite a few of them buy growth funds for their children. Uncle Jules would be astonished if he knew some of his customers who own Massachusetts Investors Trust.

"Is it going to be clear for Carnival, Jackie?"

We stand on the concrete island between the double streams of traffic. The light changes and off Ned goes again.

Evening is the best time in Gentilly. There are not so many trees and the buildings are low and the world is all sky. The sky is a deep bright ocean full of light and life. A mare's tail of cirrus cloud stands in high from the Gulf. High above the Lake a broken vee of ibises points for the marshes; they go suddenly white as they fly into the tilting salient of sunlight. Swifts find a windy middle reach of sky and come twittering down so fast I think at first gnats have crossed my eyelids. In the last sector of apple green a Lockheed Connie lowers from Mobile, her running lights blinking in the dusk. Station wagons and Greyhounds and diesel rigs rumble toward the Gulf Coast, their fabulous tail-lights glowing like rubies in the darkening east. Most of the commercial buildings are empty except the filling stations where attendants hose down the concrete under the glowing discs and shells and stars.

On the way home I stop off at the Tivoli. It is a Jane Powell picture and I have no intention of seeing it. However, Mr

Kinsella the manager sees me and actually pulls me in by the coatsleeve for a sample look. He says it is a real pleaser and he means it. There go Jane and some fellow walking arm in arm down the street in a high wide and handsome style and doing a wake up and sing number. The doorman, the cop on the corner, the taxi driver, each sunk in his own private misery, smile and begin to tap their feet. I am hardly ever depressed by a movie and Jane Powell is a very nice-looking girl, but the despair of it is enough to leave you gone in the stomach. I look around the theater. Mr Kinsella has his troubles too. There are only a few solitary moviegoers scattered through the gloom, the afternoon sort and the most ghostly of all, each sunk in his own misery, Jane or no Jane. On the way out I stop at the ticket window and speak to Mrs de Marco, a dark thin worried lady who has worked here ever since I moved to Gentilly. She does not like the movies and takes no pleasure in her job (though she could see most of the last show every night). I tell her that it is a very fine job and that I would like nothing better than sitting out here night after night and year after year and watch the evenings settle over Elysian Fields, but she always thinks I am kidding and we talk instead about her son's career in the air force. He is stationed in Arizona and he hates the desert. I am sorry to hear this because I would like it out there very much. Nevertheless I am interested in hearing about it. Before I see a movie it is necessary for me to learn something about the theater or the people who operate it, to touch base before going inside. That is the way I got to know Mr Kinsella: engaging him in conversation about the theater business. I have discovered that most people have no one to talk to, no one, that is, who really wants to listen. When it does at last dawn on a man that you really want to hear about his business, the look that comes over his face is something to see. Do not misunderstand me. I am no do-gooding José Ferrer going around with a little whistle to make people happy. Such do-gooders do not really want to listen, are not really selfish like me; they are being nice fellows and boring themselves to death, and their listeners are not really cheered up. Show me a nice Jose cheering up an old lady and I'll show you two people existing in despair. My mother often told me to be unselfish, but I have become suspicious of the advice. No, I do it for my own selfish reasons. If I did not talk to the theater owner or the ticket seller, I should be lost, cut loose metaphysically speaking. I should be seeing one copy of a film which might be shown anywhere and at any time. There is a danger of slipping clean out of space and time. It is possible to become a ghost and not know whether one is in downtown Loews in Denver or suburban Bijou in Jacksonville. So it was with me.

Yet it was here in the Tivoli that I first discovered place and time, tasted it like okra. It was during a re-release of *Red River* a couple of years ago that I became aware of the first faint stirrings of curiosity about the particular seat I sat in, the lady in the ticket booth . . . As Montgomery Clift was whipping John Wayne in a fist fight, an absurd scene, I made a mark on my seat arm with my thumbnail. Where, I wondered, will this particular piece of wood be twenty years from now, 543 years from now? Once as I was travelling through the Midwest ten years ago I had a layover of three hours in Cincinnati. There was time to go see Joseph Cotten in *Holiday* at a neighborhood theater called the Altamont—but not before I had struck up an acquaintance with the ticket seller, a lady named Mrs Clara James, and learned that she had seven grandchildren all living in Cincinnati. We still exchange Christmas cards. Mrs James is the only person I know in the entire state of Ohio.

When I get back to my apartment, the first thing I see is a letter from my aunt stuck behind the aluminum seagull on the screen door. I know what it is. It is not a letter actually but a memo. Often when we have had one of our serious talks, she has second thoughts which she is anxious to communicate. Sometimes I get a memo out of a clear sky. She takes a great deal of trouble with me. I wish I were able to please her better.

But before I can read the letter, Mrs Schexnaydre comes down and lends me her copy of *Reader's Digest*.

Mrs Schexnaydre is a vigorous pony-size blond who wears sneakers summer and winter. She is very good to me and sees to it that everything is kept spick-and-span. The poor woman is quite lonely; she knows no one except the painters and carpenters and electricians who are forever working on her house. She has lived in New Orleans all her life and knows no one. Sometimes I watch television with her and share a bottle of Jax and

talk about her years at MacDonough No. 6 school, the happiest
period of her life. It is possible to do this because her television
will bring in channel 12 and mine won't. She watches the quiz
programs faithfully and actually feels she knows the contestants. Sometimes I even persuade her to go to the movies with
me. Her one fear in life is of Negroes. Although one seldom
sees Negroes in this part of Gentilly, our small yard is enclosed
by a hurricane fence eight feet high; every window is barred.
Over the years she has acquired three dogs, each for the reason
that it had been reputed to harbor a special dislike for Negroes.
I have no particular objection to this trait in a dog—for all I
know, Mrs Schexnaydre's fears may be quite justified. However,
these are miserable curs and to make matters worse, they also
dislike me. One I especially despise, an orange-colored brute
with a spitz face and a plume of a tail which curves over his back
exposing a large convoluted anus. I have come to call him old
Rosebud. He is usually content to eye me and raise his lip, but
one foggy night he slipped out of an azalea bush and sank his
teeth in my leg. Now and then when I know Mrs Schexnaydre
is out, I will give him a tremendous kick in the ribs and send
him yowling.

"I marked a real cute article for you," she says briskly and
makes a point of leaving immediately to show she is not one of
those landladies who intrude upon their tenants.

I am happy to have the magazine. The articles are indeed
cute and heart-warming. People who are ordinarily understood
to dislike each other or at least to be indifferent toward each
other discover that they have much in common. I seem to recall
an article about a subway breaking down in New York. The
passengers who had their noses buried in newspapers began
to talk to each other. They discovered that their fellow passengers were human beings much like themselves and with
the same hopes and dreams; people are much the same the
world over, even New Yorkers, the article concluded, and given
the opportunity will find more to like than to dislike about
each other. A lonely old man found himself talking excitedly
to a young girl about his hobby of growing irises in a window
box, she to him about her hopes and dreams for a career in
art. I have to agree with Mrs Schexnaydre: such an episode is

indeed heart-warming. On the other hand, it would make me nervous to be present at such a gathering. To tell the truth, if I were a young girl, I would have nothing to do with kindly old philosophers such as are portrayed by Thomas Mitchell in the movies. These birds look fishy to me.

But I can't read the article now. My aunt's letter makes a stronger demand upon me. She thinks constantly of other people—she is actually unselfish, the only person I know who is. When she reads something or thinks of something which may be useful to others, she is likely as not to write it down on the spot and mail it to them. Yes, it is a memo. There is no salutation or signature, only a single fat paragraph in a bold backslanted hand.

> Every moment think steadily as a Roman and a man, to do what thou hast in hand with perfect and simple dignity, and a feeling of affection and freedom and justice. These words of the Emperor Marcus Aurelius Antoninus strike me as pretty good advice, for even the orneriest young scamp.

My apartment is as impersonal as a motel room. I have been careful not to accumulate possessions. My library is a single book, *Arabia Deserta*. The television set looks as if it took coins. On the wall over the bed hang two Currier and Ives prints of ice-skaters in Central Park. How sad the little figures seem, skimming along in step! How sad the city seems!

I switch on television and sit directly in front of it, bolt upright and hands on knees in my ladder-back chair. A play comes on with Dick Powell. He is a cynical financier who is trying to get control of a small town newspaper. But he is baffled by the kindliness and sincerity of the town folk. Even the editor whom he is trying to ruin is nice to him. And even when he swindles the editor and causes him to have a heart attack from which he later dies, the editor is as friendly as ever and takes the occasion to give Powell a sample of his homespun philosophy. "We're no great shakes as a town," says the editor on his deathbed, teetering on the very brink of eternity. "But we're friendly." In the end Powell is converted by these good folk and instead of trying to control the paper, applies to the editor's daughter for the job of reporter so he can fight against political corruption.

It is time to pick up Kate.

3

Tonight, Thursday night, I carry out a successful experiment in repetition.

Fourteen years ago, when I was a sophomore, I saw a western at a movie-house on Freret Street, a place frequented by students and known to them as the Armpit. The movie was *The Oxbow Incident* and it was quite good. It was about this time of year I saw it, for I remember the smell of privet when I came out and the camphor berries popping underfoot. (All movies smell of a neighborhood and a season: I saw *All Quiet on the Western Front*, one of my first, in Arcola, Mississippi in August of 1941, and the noble deeds were done, not merely fittingly but inevitably, in the thick singing darkness of Delta summer and in the fragrance of cottonseed meal.) Yesterday evening I noticed in the *Picayune* that another western was playing at the same theater. So up I went, by car to my aunt's house, then up St Charles in a streetcar with Kate so we can walk through the campus.

Nothing had changed. There we sat, I in the same seat I think, and afterwards came out into the smell of privet. Camphor berries popped underfoot on the same section of broken pavement.

A successful repetition.

What is a repetition? A repetition is the re-enactment of past experience toward the end of isolating the time segment which has lapsed in order that it, the lapsed time, can be savored of itself and without the usual adulteration of events that clog time like peanuts in brittle. Last week, for example, I experienced an accidental repetition. I picked up a German-language weekly in the library. In it I noticed an advertisement for Nivea Creme, showing a woman with a grainy face turned up to the sun. Then I remembered that twenty years ago I saw the same advertisement in a magazine on my father's desk, the same woman, the same grainy face, the same Nivea Creme. The events of the intervening twenty years were neutralized, the thirty million deaths, the countless torturings, uprootings and wanderings to and fro. Nothing of consequence could have happened because Nivea Creme was exactly as it was before. There remained only time itself, like a yard of smooth peanut brittle.

How, then, tasted my own fourteen years since *The Oxbow Incident*?

As usual it eluded me. There was this: a mockery about the old seats, their plywood split, their bottoms slashed, but enduring nevertheless as if they had waited to see what I had done with my fourteen years. There was this also: a secret sense of wonder about the enduring, about all the nights, the rainy summer nights at twelve and one and two o'clock when the seats endured alone in the empty theater. The enduring is something which must be accounted for. One cannot simply shrug it off.

"Where to now?" asks Kate. She stands at my shoulder under the marquee, plucking at her thumb and peering into the darkness.

"Wherever you like."

"Go on about your business."

"Very well."

She saw Merle Mink this afternoon and seems to feel better for it. He approved her breaking her engagement with Walter and set up a not very rigorous schedule of office visits. Most important, she no longer feels she is coming near the brink of an abyss. "But the trouble is," she said gloomily as we sat in the theater waiting for the lights to go out, "I am always at my best with doctors. They are charmed with me. I feel fine when I'm sick. It is only when I'm well that—" Now in the shadow of the camphor tree she stops suddenly, takes my arm in both hands. "Have you noticed that only in time of illness or disaster or death are people real? I remember at the time of the wreck—people were so kind and helpful and *solid*. Everyone pretended that our lives until that moment had been every bit as real as the moment itself and that the future must be real too, when the truth was that our reality had been purchased only by Lyell's death. In another hour or so we had all faded out again and gone our dim ways."

We wander along the dark paths of the campus and stop off at my weedy stoop behind the laboratory. I sit on the concrete step and think of nothing. Kate presses her bleeding thumb to her mouth. "What is this place?" she asks. A lamp above the path makes a golden sphere among the tree-high shrubs.

"I spent every afternoon for four years in one of those laboratories up there."

"Is this part of the repetition?"

"No."

"Part of the search?"

I do not answer. She can only believe I am serious in her own fashion of being serious: as an antic sort of seriousness, which is not seriousness at all but despair masquerading as seriousness. I would as soon not speak to her of such things, since she is bound to understand it as a cultivated eccentricity, like the eccentricity of the roommate she used to talk about: "A curious girl, BoBo. Do you know what she liked to do? Collect iron deer. She located every iron deer in Westchester County and once a month she'd religiously make her rounds and pay them a visit—just park and look at them. She had names for each one: Tertullian, Archibald MacLeish, Alf Landon—she was quite serious about it." I have no use at all for girls like BoBo nor for such antic doings as collecting iron deer in Westchester County.

"Why don't you sit down?" I ask her irritably.

"Now the vertical search is when—"

(Am I irritable because, now that she mentions it, I do for a fact sound like BoBo and her goddamn iron deer?)

"If you walk in the front door of the laboratory, you undertake the vertical search. You have a specimen, a cubic centimeter of water or a frog or a pinch of salt or a star."

"One learns general things?"

"And there is excitement to the search."

"Why?" she asks.

"Because as you get deeper into the search, you unify. You understand more and more specimens by fewer and fewer formulae. There is the excitement. Of course you are always after the big one, the new key, the secret leverage point, and that is the best of it."

"And it doesn't matter where you are or who you are."

"No."

"And the danger is of becoming no one nowhere."

"Never mind."

Kate parses it out with the keen male bent of her mind and yet with her woman's despair. Therefore I take care to be no more serious than she.

"On the other hand, if you sit back here and take a little carcass out of the garbage can, a specimen which has been used and discarded, there remains something left over, a clue?"

"Yes, but let's go."

"You're a cold one, dear."

"As cold as you?"

"Colder. Cold as the grave." She walks about tearing shreds of flesh from her thumb. I say nothing. It would take very little to set her off on an attack on me, one of her "frank" appraisals. "It is possible, you know, that you are overlooking something, the most obvious thing of all. And you would not know it if you fell over it."

"What?"

She will not tell me. Instead, in the streetcar, she becomes gay and affectionate toward me. She locks her arms around my waist and gives me a kiss on the mouth and watches me with brown eyes gone to discs.

4

It is two o'clock before I get back to Gentilly. Yet sometime before dawn I awake with a violent start and for the rest of the night lie dozing yet wakeful and watchful. I have not slept soundly for many years. Not since the war when I was knocked out for two days have I really lost consciousness as a child loses consciousness in sleep and wakes to a new world not even remembering when he went to bed. I always know where I am and what time it is. Whenever I feel myself sinking toward a deep sleep, something always recalls me: "Not so fast now. Suppose you should go to sleep and it should happen. What then?" What is this that is going to happen? Clearly nothing. Yet there I lie, wakeful and watchful as a sentry, ears tuned to the slightest noise. I can even hear old Rosebud turning round and round in the azalea bushes before settling down.

At dawn I dress and slip out so quietly that the dogs do not stir. I walk toward the lake. It is almost a summer night. Heavy warm air has pushed up from the Gulf, but the earth has memories of winter and lies cold and sopping wet from dew.

It is good to walk in the suburbs at this hour. No one ever uses the sidewalks anyhow and now there are not even children on tricycles and miniature tractors. The concrete is virginal, as grainy as the day it was poured; weeds sprout in the cracks.

The closer you get to the lake, the more expensive the houses are. Already the bungalows and duplexes and tiny ranch houses are behind me. Here are the fifty and sixty thousand dollar homes, fairly big moderns with dagger plants and Australian pines planted in brick boxes, and reproductions of French provincials and Louisiana colonials. The swimming pools steam like sleeping geysers. These houses look handsome in the sunlight; they please me with their pretty colors, their perfect lawns and their clean airy garages. But I have noticed that at this hour of dawn they are forlorn. A sadness settles over them like a fog from the lake.

My father used to suffer from insomnia. One of my few recollections of him is his nighttime prowling. In those days it was thought that sleeping porches were healthful, so my father stuck one onto the house, a screen box with canvas blinds that pulled up from below. Here Scott and I slept on even the coldest nights. My father had trouble sleeping and moved out with us. He tossed like a wounded animal, or slept fitfully, his breath whistling musically through the stiff hairs of his nose—and went back inside before morning, leaving his bed tortured and sour, a smell which I believed to be caused by a nasal ailment known then as "catarrh." The porch did not work for him and he bought a Saskatchewan sleeping bag from Abercrombie and Fitch and moved out into the rose garden. Just at this hour of dawn I would be awakened by a terrible sound: my father crashing through the screen door, sleeping bag under his arm, his eyes crisscrossed by fatigue and by the sadness of these glimmering dawns. My mother, without meaning to, put a quietus on his hopes of sleep even more effectively than this forlorn hour. She had a way of summing up his doings in a phrase that took the heart out of him. He dreamed, I know, of a place of quiet breathing and a deep sleep under the stars and next to the sweet earth. She agreed. "Honey, I'm all for it. I think we all ought to get back to nature and I'd be right with you, Honey, if it wasn't for the chiggers. I'm chigger bait." She made him out to be another Edgar Kennedy (who was making shorts then) thrashing around in the bushes with his newfangled camping equipment. To her it was better to make a joke of it than be defeated by these chilly dawns. But after that nothing more was said about getting back to nature.

He made a mistake. He was trying to sleep. He thought he had to sleep a certain number of hours every night, breathe fresh air, eat a certain number of calories, evacuate his bowels regularly and have a stimulating hobby (it was the nineteen thirties and everybody believed in science and talked about "ductless glands"). I do not try to sleep. And I could not tell you the last time my bowels moved; sometimes they do not move for a week but I have no interest in such matters. As for hobbies, people with stimulating hobbies suffer from the most noxious of despairs since they are tranquillized in their despair. I muse along as quietly as a ghost. Instead of trying to sleep I try to fathom the mystery of this suburb at dawn. Why do these splendid houses look so defeated at this hour of the day? Other houses, say a 'dobe house in New Mexico or an old frame house in Feliciana, look much the same day or night. But these new houses look haunted. Even the churches out here look haunted. What spirit takes possesion of them? My poor father. I can see him, blundering through the patio furniture, the Junior Jets and the Lone Ranger pup tents, dragging his Saskatchewan sleeping bag like the corpse of his dead hope.

When I return, the sun is warm on my back. I stretch out in a snug little cul de sac between the garage and the house, under the insolent eye of Rosebud, and doze till nine o'clock when the market opens.

5

Awakened by Rosebud's growling. It is the postman. Rosebud feels my eye on him, cocks an eyebrow around to see me and is discomfited to meet my eye; he looks away, pretends to settle his mouth, but his lip is dry and snags high on a tooth. Now he is actively embarrassed.

School children across the street line up in ragged platoons before the storklike nuns, the girls in little blue bell-shaped skirts and suspenders, the boys a bit dreary in their khaki. In they march, under the schematic dove. The morning sunlight winks on the polished metal of ocean wave and the jungle gym. How shiny and strong and well-set are the steel pipes, polished to silver by thousands of little blue-skirted and khaki-clad butts.

The postman has a letter from Harold Graebner in Chicago. It is a note and a birth announcement. Harold asks me to be godfather to his new baby. The enclosed card announces the birth in the following way:

1 C.O.D. PACKAGE
SHIPPING WEIGHT: 7 LB. 4 OZ.
HANDLE WITH TENDER LOVING CARE, ETC.

Harold Graebner probably saved my life in the Orient and for this reason he loves me. When I get a letter, it is almost certain to be from Harold Graebner. I no longer write or receive letters, except Harold's. When I was in the army I wrote long, sensitive and articulate letters to my aunt, giving my impressions of countries and peoples. I wrote such things as

Japan is lovely this time of year. How strange to think of going into combat! Not so much fear—since my chances are very good—as wonder, wonder that everything should be so full of expectancy, every tick of the watch, every rhododendron blossom. Tolstoy and St Exupery were right about war, etc.

A regular young Rupert Brooke was I, "—full of expectancy." Oh the crap that lies lurking in the English soul. Somewhere it, the English soul, received an injection of romanticism which nearly killed it. That's what killed my father, English romanticism, that and 1930 science. A line for my notebook:

Explore connection between romanticism and scientific objectivity. Does a scientifically minded person become a romantic because he is a left-over from his own science?

I must reply to Harold, but it is almost more than I can do to write two sentences in a row. The words are without grace.

Dear Harold: Thank you for asking me to be godfather to your baby. Since, however, I am not a practical Catholic, I doubt if I could. But I certainly appreciate—

Certainly appreciate. Tear it up.

6

An odd thing. Ever since Wednesday I have become acutely aware of Jews. There is a clue here, but of what I cannot say. How do I know? Because whenever I approach a Jew, the Geiger counter in my head starts rattling away like a machine gun; and as I go past with the utmost circumspection and with every sense alert—the Geiger counter subsides.

There is nothing new in my Jewish vibrations. During the years when I had friends my Aunt Edna, who is a theosophist, noticed that all my friends were Jews. She knew why moreover: I had been a Jew in a previous incarnation. Perhaps that is it. Anyhow it is true that I am Jewish by instinct. We share the same exile. The fact is, however, I am more Jewish than the Jews I know. They are more at home than I am. I accept my exile.

Another evidence of my Jewishness: the other day a sociologist reported that a significantly large percentage of solitary moviegoers are Jews.

Jews are my first real clue.

When a man is in despair and does not in his heart of hearts allow that a search is possible and when such a man passes a Jew in the street, he notices nothing.

When a man becomes a scientist or an artist, he is open to a different kind of despair. When such a man passes a Jew in the street, he may notice something but it is not a remarkable encounter. To him the Jew can only appear as a scientist or artist like himself or as a specimen to be studied.

But when a man awakes to the possibility of a search and when such a man passes a Jew in the street for the first time, he is like Robinson Crusoe seeing the footprint on the beach.

7

A beautiful Friday morning and a successful excursion into St Bernard Parish with Sharon.

Sharon eyes my MG narrowly. After she has gotten in, she makes it plain that MG or no MG there is to be no monkey business. How does she make such a thing plain and in an MG sitting thigh to thigh and knee to knee? By her Southern female trick of politeness. "This is the cutest little *car*!" she sings and goes trailing off in a fit of absent-mindedness, hands to the nape of her neck and tilting her head forward so that she surveys the street through her eyebrows and with a cold woman's eye; then seeming to rouse herself apologetically: "This sure beats typing. Mhm-M!"—as singsongy and shut off to herself as her mammy in Eufala. Southern girls learn a lot from their nurses.

We meet Mr Sartalamaccia and a queer thing happens.

First, some kind of reversal takes place and it becomes natural for Mr Sartalamaccia to show me the place he wants to buy. He becomes the guide to my property and even points out the good features. A far cry from a duck club now, my patrimony is hemmed in on one side by a housing development and on the other by a police pistol range. In fact, my estate puts me in mind of the pictures in detective magazines of the scene where a crime was committed: a bushy back lot it is, tunnelled through by hog trails and a suspicious car track or two. Every inch of open ground sprouts new green shoots and from the black earth there seems to arise a green darkness. It is already like summer here. Cicadas drone in the weeds and the day seems long.

We leave the MG in a glade (a good hard-used creature of red metal and fragrant worn leather; I run a hand over its flank of stout British steel as if it were a mare) and stand on a hummock with Mr Sartalamaccia between us; Mr Sartalamaccia: wagging a limp panama behind him and giving off a bitter cotton smell. He is less an Italian than a Southern country man, haggard and clean as an Alabama farmer come to church.

"The lodge was here, Roaring Camp they called it," I tell Sharon. She stands blinking and inviolate, a little rared back and entrenched within herself. Not for her the thronging spirit-presence of the place and the green darkness of summer come back again and the sadness of it. She went to Eufala High School and it is all the same to her where she is (so she might have stood in the Rotunda during her school trip to Washington) and she is right, for she is herself sweet life and where is the sadness of that? "I came here once with my father and great uncle. They wouldn't have beds, so we slept on the floor. I slept between them and I had a new Ingersoll watch and when I went to bed, I took it out and put it on the floor beside my head. During the night my uncle rolled over on it and broke it. It became a famous story and somehow funny, the way he rolled over on my watch, and they would all laugh—haw haw haw—like a bunch of Germans. Then at Christmas he gave me another watch which turned out to be a gold Hamilton." Sharon stands astraddle, as heavy of leg as a Wac. "I remember when my father built the lodge. Before that he had read the works of Fabre and he got the idea of taking up a fascinating scientific hobby. He bought a telescope and one night he called us outside and showed us the horsehead nebula in Orion. That was the end of the telescope. After that he began to read Browning and saw himself in need of a world of men. That was when he started the duck club."

"Grow old along with me

The best is yet to be," says Sharon.

"That's right."

Mr Sartalamaccia has become restless; he works his hat behind him. His fingernails are large and almost filled with white moons. "Your father didn't build it. Judge Anse was the one that built it."

"Is that right? You knew them? I didn't know you—"

Mr Sartalamaccia tells it forlornly, without looking up—knowing no more than the facts pure and simple and hardly believing that we don't know. Everybody knows. "I built it for him."

"How did you know him?"

"I didn't. One morning before Christmas I was just about finished with my store over there and Judge Anse come in and started talking to me. He said—uh—" Mr Sartalamaccia smiles a secret little smile and his head sinks even lower as he makes bold to recall the very words. "—what's your name? Yes:

what's your name? I told him. He said—uh: *you built this store?*
I said, yessir. We talked. So he looked at me and he said—uh:
I'm going tell you what I want you to do. He writes this check.
He said—uh: *Here's a check for a thousand dollars. I want you
to build me a lodge and come on, I'll show you where.* So I said,
all right. So he said—uh—" Mr Sartalamaccia waits until the
words, the very words, speak themselves—"*Let's go, Vince*, like
him and me, we were going to have us a big time. He never
saw me before in his life and he walks in my store and writes
me a check on the Canal Bank for a thousand dollars. And he
didn't come back for six weeks."

"Did he like the lodge?"

"I mean he liked it."

"I see." I see. There was such a time and there were such
men (and Mr Sartalamaccia smiles to remember it), men who
could say to other men, *here do this*, and have it done and
done with pleasure and remembered with pleasure. "Have you
always been here?"

"Me?" Mr Sartalamaccia looks up for the first time. "I had
only been here three weeks! Since November."

"Where are you from?"

"I was raised in Ensley, near Birmingham, but in nineteen thirty-two times was so hard I started moving around.
I visited forty-six states, all but Washington and Oregon, just
looking around and I never went hungry. In nineteen thirty
four I come to stay with my brother in Violet and started
trapping."

It turns out that Mr Sartalamaccia is a contractor and owns
the housing development next door. He has done well and he
wants my duck club for an addition. I ask about the houses.

"You want to see one?"

We follow him along a hog trail to a raw field full of pretty
little flat-topped houses. He must show us one abuilding. I take
pleasure in watching him run a thumb over the sawn edges of
the sheathing. Sharon does not mind. She stands foursquare,
eyes rolled back a little, showing white. She is sleepy-eyed and
frumpy; she looks like snapshots of Ava Gardner when she was
a high school girl in North Carolina.

"You know what's in this slab?" The concrete is smooth as
silk.

"No."

"Chance number six copper pipe. Nobody will ever know it's there but it will be there a long time." I see that with him it is not purely and simply honesty; it is his own pleasure at thinking of good pipe in a good slab.

Back at the hummock, Mr Sartalamaccia takes me aside and holds his hat away to the east. "You see that ditcher and doozer?"

"Yes."

"You know what that's going to be?"

"No."

"That's the tidewater canal to the Gulf. You know how much our land is going to be worth?"

"How much?"

"Fifty dollars a foot." Mr Sartalmaccia draws me close. Again he tells it as the veriest piece of news. Deal or no deal, this is a piece of news that bears telling.

Later Sharon tells me I was smart to trick him into revealing the true value of my duck club. But she is mistaken. It came about from the moment I met him that thenceforward it pleased him to speak of the past, of his strange odyssey in 1932 when he gazed at Old Faithful in Yellowstone Park and worked on the causeway to Key West and did not go hungry— it pleased him to speak with me of the past and to connive with me against the future. He speaks from his loneliness and together we marvel at the news of the canal and enjoy the consolation of making money. For money is a great joy.

Mr Sartalamaccia has become possessed by a secret hilarity. He gives me a poke in the ribs. "I'll tell you what we can do, Mr Bolling. You keep your land! I'll develop it for you. You make the offsite improvements. I'll build the houses. We'll make us some money." He shrinks away in some kind of burlesque.

"How much do you think we can make?"

"Well I don't know. But I can tell you this." Mr Sartalamaccia is hopping in a sort of goat dance and Sharon stands dreaming in the green darkness of the glade. "I'll give you fifteen thousand for it right now!"

Our name is Increase.

*

Sharon and I spin along the River Road. The river is high and the booms and stacks of ships ride up and down the levee like great earth engines.

In the Shell station and in a drift of honeysuckle sprouting through the oil cans and standing above Sharon with a coke balanced on her golden knee, I think of flattening my hummock with bulldozers and it comes back to me how the old Gable used to work at such jobs: he knew how to seem to work and how to seem to forget about women and still move in such a way as to please women: stand asweat with his hands in his back pockets.

It is a great joy to be with Sharon and to make money at it and to seem to pay no attention to her. As for Sharon: she finds nothing amiss in sitting in the little bucket seat with her knees doubled up in the sunshine, dress tucked under. An amber droplet of Coca-Cola meanders along her thigh, touches a blond hair, distributes itself around the tiny fossa.

"Aaauugh," I groan aloud.

"What's the matter?"

"It is a stitch in the side." It is a sword in the heart.

Sharon holds a hand against the sun to see me. "Mr Bolling?"

"Yes."

"Do you remember the price Mr Sartalamaccia first mentioned?"

"Eight thousand dollars."

"He was really gon mess you up."

"No he wasn't. But if it hadn't been for you, I'd have taken the eight thousand."

"Me?"

"You got me to come down here."

She assents doubtfully, casting back in her mind with one eye screwed up.

"Do you know how much you saved me, or rather made for me? At least seven thousand dollars and probably a great deal more. I'm obliged to give you ten percent."

"You're not giving me any money, son."

I have to laugh. "Why not?"

"Ain't nobody giving me any money." (Now she catches herself and speaks broadly on purpose.) "I got plenty money."

"How much money do you have?"

"Ne'mind."

By flexing her leg at a certain angle, she can stand the coke on a facet of her knee. What a structure it is, tendon and bone, facet and swell, and gold all over.

I go home as the old Gable, asweat and with no thought for her and sick to death with desire. She is pleased because, for one thing, she can keep quiet. I notice that it makes her uneasy to keep up a conversation.

She says only one more thing, tilting her head, eyes alight. "What about the court house?"

"It's too late. You didn't have to come. I'm sorry."

"Listen!" she cries, as far away as Eufala itself. "I had a wonderful time!"

8

Once a week, on Fridays, all Cutrer salesmen return to the main office for a lunch conference with the staff. The week's business is reviewed, sales reports made, talks given on market conditions and coming issues presented by the underwriter. But today there is not much talk of business. Carnival is in full swing. Parades and balls go on night and day. A dozen krewes have already had their hour, and Proteus, Rex and Comus are yet to come. Partners and salesmen alike are red-eyed and abstracted. There is gossip about the identity of the king and queen of Iberia tonight (most of the staff of Cutrer, Klostermann and Lejier are members either of the Krewe of Neptune or the Krew of Iberia). It is generally conceded that the king of Iberia will be James (Shorty) Jones, president of Middle Gulf Utilities, and the queen Winky Ouillibert, the daughter of Plauche Ouillibert of Southern Mutual. The choice is a popular one—I can testify that both men are able, likable and unassuming fellows.

Some Fridays, Uncle Jules likes to see me in his office after lunch. When he does, he so signifies by leaving his door open to the corridor so that I will see him at his desk and naturally stop by to say hello. Today he seems particularly glad to see me. Uncle Jules has a nice way of making you feel at home. Although he has a big office with an antique desk and a huge portrait of Aunt Emily, and although he is a busy man, he makes you feel as if you and he had come upon this place in your wanderings; he is no more at home than you. He sits everywhere but in his own chair and does business everywhere but at his own desk. Now he takes me into a corner and stands feeling the bones of my shoulder like a surgeon.

"Ravaud came in to see me this morning." Uncle Jules falls silent and throws his head straight back. I know enough to wait. "He said, Jules, I've got a little bad news for you—you know the convention of the open-ends, the one you never miss? I said, sure, I know about it." Now Uncle Jules puts his head down to my chest as if he were listening to my heart. I wait. "Do you know when it is? Why yes, along about the middle of March, I told him. Along about Tuesday, says Ravaud. Carnival day." Uncle Jules presses my shoulder to keep me quiet. "Is that right, Ravaud? Oh, that reminds me. Here are your tickets. Have a good trip." Uncle Jules is bent way over and I can't tell whether he is laughing, but his thumb presses deep into the socket of my shoulder.

"That's pretty good."

"But then he said something that stuck in my mind. He said, I don't mind going if you want me to, Jules, but you got the man right in your own family. Why that scoun'l beast Jack Bolling knows more about selling open-ends than anybody on Carondelet Street. So. You don't really care about Carnival, do you?" He does not really believe I do not. As for himself, he could not conceive being anywhere on earth Mardi Gras morning but the Boston Club.

"No sir."

"So. You take the ten-thirty plane Tuesday morning," says Uncle Jules in his gruff way of conferring favors.

"Where to?"

"Where to! Why goddam, Chicago!"

Chicago. Misery misery son of a bitch of all miseries. Not in a thousand years could I explain it to Uncle Jules, but it is no small thing for me to make a trip, travel hundreds of miles across the country by night to a strange place and come out where there is a different smell in the air and people have a different way of sticking themselves into the world. It is a small thing to him but not to me. It is nothing to him to close his eyes in New Orleans and wake up in San Francisco and think the same thoughts on Telegraph Hill that he thought on Carondelet Street. Me, it is my fortune and misfortune to know how the spirit-presence of a strange place can enrich a man or rob a man but never leave him alone, how, if a man travels lightly to a hundred strange cities and cares nothing for the risk he takes, he may find himself No one and Nowhere. Great day in the morning. What will it mean to go moseying down Michigan Avenue in the neighborhood of five million strangers, each shooting out his own personal ray? How can I deal with five million personal rays?

"I want you to make a few more contacts." Uncle Jules lays back his head and we wait ten seconds. "Then when you get back, I think we might have something for you downtown." The gruffest voice and so the greatest favor of all.

"Yes sir," say I, looking pleased as punch and even prickling in the hairline to do justice to his gruffest favor. Oh sons of all bitches and great beast of Chicago lying in wait. There goes my life in Gentilly, my Little Way, my secret existence among the happy shades in Elysian Fields.

9

For some time now the impression has been growing upon me that everyone is dead.

It happens when I speak to people. In the middle of a sentence it will come over me: yes, beyond a doubt this is death. There is little to do but groan and make an excuse and slip away as quickly as one can. At such times it seems that the conversation is spoken by automatons who have no choice in what they say. I hear myself or someone else saying things like: "In my opinion the Russian people are a great people, but—" or "Yes, what you say about the hypocrisy of the North is unquestionably true. However—" and I think to myself: this is death. Lately it is all I can do to carry on such everyday conversations, because my cheek has developed a tendency to twitch of its own accord. Wednesday as I stood speaking to Eddie Lovell, I felt my eye closing in a broad wink.

After the lunch conference I run into my cousin Nell Lovell on the steps of the library—where I go occasionally to read liberal and conservative periodicals. Whenever I feel bad, I go to the library and read controversial periodicals. Though I do not know whether I am a liberal or a conservative, I am nevertheless enlivened by the hatred which one bears the other. In fact, this hatred strikes me as one of the few signs of life remaining in the world. This is another thing about the world which is upsidedown: all the friendly and likable people seem dead to me; only the haters seem alive.

Down I plunk myself with a liberal weekly at one of the massive tables, read it from cover to cover, nodding to myself whenever the writer scores a point. Damn right, old son, I say, jerking my chair in approval. Pour it on them. Then up and over to the rack for a conservative monthly and down in a fresh cool chair to join the counterattack. Oh ho, say I, and hold fast to the chair arm: that one did it: eviscerated! And then out and away into the sunlight, my neck prickling with satisfaction.

Nell Lovell, I was saying, spotted me and over she comes brandishing a book. It seems she has just finished reading a celebrated novel which, I understand, takes a somewhat gloomy and pessimistic view of things. She is angry.

"I don't feel a bit gloomy!" she cries. "Now that Mark and Lance have grown up and flown the coop, I am having the time of my life. I'm taking philosophy courses in the morning and working nights at Le Petite Theatre. Eddie and I have re-examined our values and found them pretty darn enduring. To our utter amazement we discovered that we both have the same life-goal. Do you know what it is?"

"No."

"To make a contribution, however small, and leave the world just a little better off."

"That's very good," I say somewhat uneasily and shift about on the library steps. I can talk to Nell as long as I don't look at her. Looking into her eyes is an embarrassment.

"—we gave the television to the kids and last night we turned on the hi-fi and sat by the fire and read *The Prophet* aloud. I don't find life gloomy!" she cries. "To me, books and people and things are endlessly fascinating. Don't you think so?"

"Yes." A rumble has commenced in my descending bowel, heralding a tremendous defecation.

Nell goes on talking and there is nothing to do but shift

around as best one can, take care not to fart, and watch her in a general sort of way: a forty-year-old woman with a good open American face and another forty years left in her; and eager, above all, eager, with that plaintive lost eagerness American college women get at a certain age. I get to thinking about her and old Eddie re-examining their values. Yes, true. Values. Very good. And then I can't help wondering to myself: why does she talk as if she were dead? Another forty years to go and dead, dead, dead.

"How is Kate?" Nell asks.

I jump and think hard, trying to escape death. "To tell you the truth, I don't know."

"I am so devoted to her! What a grand person she is."

"I am too. She is."

"Come see us, Binx!"

"I will!"

We part laughing and dead.

10

At four o'clock I decide it is not too early to set in motion my newest scheme conceived in the interests of money and love, my love for Sharon. Everything depends on a close cooperation between business and love. If ever my business should suffer because of my admiration for Sharon, then my admiration for Sharon would suffer too. Never never will I understand men who throw over everything for some woman. The trick, the joy of it, is to prosper on all fronts, enlist money in the service of love and love in the service of money. As long as I am getting rich, I feel that all is well. It is my Presbyterian blood.

At four fifteen I sit on the edge of her desk, fold my arms and look troubled.

"Miss Kincaid. I have a favor to ask of you."

"Yes sir, Mr Bolling."

As she looks up at me, I think how little we know each other. She is really a stranger. Her yellow eyes are quite friendly and opaque. She is very nice and very anxious to be helpful. My heart sinks. Love, the very possibility of love, vanishes. Our sexes vanish. We are a regular little team.

"Do you know what these names are?"

"Customers' files."

"They are also portfolios, individual listings of stocks and bonds and so forth. Now I tell you what we do every year about this time. In a few weeks income taxes must be filed. Now we usually mail our customers a lot of booklets and charts and whatnot to help them with their returns. This year we're going to do something different. I'm going to go through each portfolio myself, give the tax status of each transaction and make specific recommendations to every customer in a personal letter, recommendations about capital gains, and losses, stock rights and warrants, dates of involuntary conversions, stock dividends and so on. You'd be amazed how many otherwise shrewd businessmen will take long term gains and losses the same year."

She listens closely, her yellow eyes snapping with intelligence.

"Now I'm already familiar with the accounts, so that's no problem. But it's going to mean a lot of letters. And we don't have much time." Why I must have been crazy; this girl is a good little sister.

"When would we start?"

"Can you work an hour later this afternoon and Saturday morning?"

"I'd like to make a phone call," she says in the brusque-kindly manner of country folk who grant favors with an angry willingness.

A moment later she is standing at my desk stroking the beige plastic with two scarlet nails.

"Is it all right for someone to pick me up at five for a few minutes?"

Someone. How ancient is her wisdom. I am nothing to her, yet by the surest of instincts she labels her date a neuter person. She knows I do not believe there is such a person. But she knows what she does. Despite myself I believe a someone will pick her up, a shadowy and inconsequential person of neuter gender.

"I hope I'm not interfering with anything too serious."

"Are you kidding?"

"Why no."

She surprises me. I said "serious" ambiguously and perhaps purposely so. But she is quick to give it its courtship meaning.

Here is an unexpected advantage. It could be useful to me to see what sort of fellow her friend is. But I needn't worry about managing a glimpse of him. A few minutes before five he walks right into the office. He is much to my liking—I could throw my arms around him. A sharp character—no youth as I feared—a Faubourg Marigny type, Mediterranean, big-nosed, lumpy-jawed, a single stitched-in wrinkle over his eyebrows from just above which there springs up a great pompadour of wiry bronze hair. His face aches with it. He has no use for me at all. I nod at him with the warmest feelings, and he appears to nod at me but keeps on nodding, nods past me and at the office as if he were appraising it. Now and then his lip draws back along his teeth admitting a suck of air as sharp as a steam blast. As he waits for Sharon, he swings his fist into an open hand and snaps his knee back and forth inside his wide pants.

The Faubourg Marigny fellow leaves at last and we work steadily until seven. I dictate some very sincere letters. Dear Mr Hebert: I happened to be looking over your portfolio this morning and it occurred to me that you might realize a substantial tax saving by unloading your holding of Studebaker-Packard. Naturally I am not acquainted with your overall tax picture, but if you do have a problem taxwise, I suggest taking a capital loss for the following reasons . . .

It is good to have both Mr Hebert and Sharon on my mind. To be thinking of only one of them would make me nervous.

We work hard and as comrades, swept along by a partnership so strong that the smallest overture of love would be brushed aside by either of us as foolishness. *Peyton Place* would embarrass both of us now.

By six o'clock I become aware that it is time to modulate the key ever so slightly. From now on everything I do must exhibit a certain value in her eyes, a value, moreover, which she must begin to *recognize.*

Thus we send out for sandwiches and drink coffee as we work. Already the silences between us have changed in character, become easier. It is possible to stand at the window, loosen my collar and rub the back of my neck like Dana Andrews. And to become irritable with her: "No no no no, Kincaid, that's not what I meant to say. Take five." I go to the cooler, take two aspirins, crumple the paper cup. Her friend, old "someone," turns out to be invaluable. In my every tactic he is the known quantity. He is my triangulation point. I am all business to his monkey business.

Already she has rolled a fresh sheet into the platen. "Try it again," and she looks at me ironically and with lights in her eyes.

I stretch out both hands to her desk, put my head down between my arms.

"All right. Take it this way . . . " O Rory Rory Rory.

She is getting it. She is alert: there is something afoot. Now when she looks up between sentences, it is through her eyebrows and with her head cocked and still, still as a little partridge.

She watches closely now, her yellow agate-eyes snapping with interest. We are, all at once, on our way. We are like two children lost in a summer afternoon who, hardly aware of each other, find a door in a wall and enter an enchanted garden. Now we might join hands. She is watchful to see whether I see this too.

But this is no time to take chances. Although Baron Ochs' waltz sings in my ears and although I could grab her up out of her chair and kiss her smack on the mouth—we go back to work.

"Dear Mr Fontenot: Glancing over your portfolio, it struck me that you are not in the best position to take advantage of the dawning age of missiles . . ."

The Faubourg Marigny fellow does not return and at seven thirty it seems natural for me to drive Sharon home.

A line of squalls is due from Texas and we drive down to Esplanade in a flicker of summer lightning. The air presses heavily over Elysian Fields; earlier in the evening lake swallows took alarm and went veering away to the swamps. The Quarter is teeming. It is good to put behind us the green fields and the wide sky of Gentilly and to come into a narrow place pressed in upon by decrepit buildings and filled by man-smells and man-sounds. No thrush flutings and swallow cries in here. At twilight it is good to come away from the open sky and into a yellow-lit place and sit next to a warm thigh. I almost violate my resolution and ask Sharon if she will have a drink. But I

don't. Instead I watch her up into her house. She ascends a
new flight of concrete steps which soars like a gangplank into
a dim upper region.

II

Tonight is Kate's supper with the queens and I shall not see
her. I drink beer and watch television, but every minute or so
thoughts of Sharon, my big beautiful majorette from Alabama,
come crowding into my head and my hands begin to sweat.
The air is heavy and still. It is a time to be on guard. At such
times there is the temptation to behave without prudence, to
try to see Sharon tonight, or even park on Esplanade and spy
on her and run the risk of ruining everything. Then at last the
storm breaks, a real Texas rattler. Gradually the malaise lets
up and it becomes possible to sit without perturbation and at
heart's ease, hands on knees in my ladderback chair and watch
television.

The marshal traps some men in an Indian hogan. The squaw
has been killed, leaving a baby. In an unexpected turn of events
the killers get the upper hand and hold the marshal in a line
shack as a hostage. The marshal reminds them of the baby in
the hogan. This is no ordinary marshal. He is also a humanist.
"It ain't nothing but a stinking Indian," says one of the killers.
"You're wrong," says the marshal. "It is a human being." In
the end he prevails upon the killers to spare the baby and even
to have it baptized. The killers go out in a gruff manner and
fetch the padre, a fellow who looks as much like the late H. B.
Warner as it is possible for a man to look.

I go to bed cozy and dry in the storm, snug as a larva in a
cocoon, wrapped safe and warm in loving Christian kindness.
From chair to bed and from TV to radio for one little nightcap
of a program. Being a creature of habit, as regular as a monk,
and taking pleasure in the homeliest repetitions, I listen every
night at ten to a program called This I Believe. Monks have
their compline, I have This I Believe. On the program hundreds
of the highest-minded people in our country, thoughtful and
intelligent people, people with mature inquiring minds, state
their personal credos. The two or three hundred I have heard
so far were without exception admirable people. I doubt if any

other country or any other time in history has produced such thoughtful and high-minded people, especially the women. And especially the South. I do believe the South has produced more high-minded women, women of universal sentiments, than any other section of the country except possibly New England in the last century. Of my six living aunts, five are women of the loftiest theosophical panBrahman sentiments. The sixth is still a Presbyterian.

If I had to name a single trait that all these people shared, it is their niceness. Their lives are triumphs of niceness. They like everyone with the warmest and most generous feelings. And as for themselves: it would be impossible for even a dour person not to like them.

Tonight's subject is a playwright who transmits this very quality of niceness in his plays. He begins:

> I believe in people. I believe in tolerance and understand-
> ing between people. I believe in the uniqueness and the
> dignity of the individual—

Everyone on This I Believe believes in the uniqueness and the dignity of the individual. I have noticed, however, that the believers are far from unique themselves, are in fact alike as peas in a pod.

> I believe in music. I believe in a child's smile. I believe in
> love. I also believe in hate.

This is true. I have known a couple of these believers, human-ists and lady psychologists who come to my aunt's house. On This I Believe they like everyone. But when it comes down to this or that particular person, I have noticed that they usually hate his guts.

I did not always enjoy This I Believe. While I was living at my aunt's house, I was overtaken by a fit of perversity. But instead of writing a letter to an editor, as was my custom, I recorded a tape which I submitted to Mr Edward R. Murrow. "Here are the beliefs of John Bickerson Bolling, a moviegoer living in New Orleans," it began, and ended, "I believe in a good kick in the ass. This—I believe." I soon regretted it, however, as what my grandfather would have called "a smart-alecky stunt" and I was relieved when the tape was returned. I have listened faithfully to This I Believe ever since.

I believe in freedom, the sacredness of the individual and the brotherhood of man—

concludes the playwright.

I believe in believing. This—I believe.

All my shakiness over Sharon is gone. I switch off my radio and lie in bed with a pleasant tingling sensation in the groin, a tingling for Sharon and for all my fellow Americans.

12

Sometime during the night and at the height of the storm the telephone rings, a dreadful summons, and I find myself in the middle of the floor shaking like a leaf and wondering what is amiss. It is my aunt.

"What's that?" The telephone crackles with static. I listen so hard I can't hear.

My aunt tells me that something has happened to Kate. When Uncle Jules and Walter arrived at the hotel from the Iberia ball, Kate was not to be found. Nell Lovell, herself a former queen, told them that Kate had left abruptly sometime before eleven o'clock. That was three hours ago and she had not come home. But Nell wasn't worried. "You know as well as I do what she's doing, Cousin Em," she told my aunt. "You remember my Christmas party at Empire when she took out up the levee and walked all the way to Laplace? That Kate." But my aunt has her doubts. "Listen to this," she says in a peculiar voice—it is the dry litigious way of speaking of closely knit families in times of trouble: one would imagine she was speaking of a stranger. "Here is the last entry in her diary: Tonight will tell the story—will the new freedom work—if not, no more tight ropes for me, thank you. Now you recall her tight rope."

"Yes." "Tight rope" is an expression Kate used when she was sick the first time. When she was a child and her mother was alive, she said, it used to seem to her that people laughed and talked in an easy and familiar way and stood on solid ground, but now it seemed that they (not just she but everybody) had become aware of the abyss that yawned at their feet even on the most ordinary occasions—especially on the most ordinary occasions. Thus, she would a thousand times rather find herself in the middle of no man's land than at a family party or luncheon club.

"Now I'm not really worried about her," my aunt declares briskly. There is a silence and the wire crackles. Strange to say, my main emotion is a slight social embarrassment. I cast about for something to say. "After all the girl is twenty-five years old," says my aunt.

"That's true."

Lightning strikes somewhere close, a vicious bolt. The clap comes hard upon it, in the very whitening, and shakes the house.

"—finally reached him in his hotel room in Atlanta."

"Who?"

"Sam. He's flying down first thing in the morning, instead of Sunday. He was quite excited."

"About what?"

"He said he had the most extraordinary piece of news. He wouldn't tell me what it was. It seems that by the eeriest sort of coincidence two things happened this very day with a direct bearing on Kate. Anyhow."

"Yes ma'am?"

"I have a hunch she'll wander out your way. If she does, will you drive her home?"

"Yes."

"It isn't as if Kate were another Otey Ann," says my aunt after a moment.

"No, it isn't." She is thinking of two things: one, an acquaintance from Feliciana named Otey Ann Aldridge who went crazy and used to break out of the state hospital in Jackson and come to New Orleans and solicit strangers on Bourbon Street; two, she is thinking of the look in Nell Lovell's eye, the little risible gleam, even as she reassured my aunt.

*

I awake with a start at three o'clock, put on a raincoat and go outside for a breath of air.

The squall line has passed over. Elysian Fields is dripping and still, but there is a commotion of winds high in the air where the cool heavy front has shouldered up the last of the fretful ocean air. The wind veers around to the north and blows away the storm until the moon swims high, moored like a kite and darting against the fleeing shreds and ragtags of cloud.

I sit in the shelter outside Mrs Schexnaydre's chain link fence. Opposite the school, it is used by those children who catch buses toward the lake. The streetlight casts a blueblack shadow. Across the boulevard, at the catercorner of Elysian Fields and Bons Enfants, is a vacant lot chest high in last summer's weeds. Some weeks ago the idea came to me of buying the lot and building a service station. It is for sale, I learned, for twenty thousand dollars. What with the windfall from Mr Sartalamaccia, it becomes possible to think seriously of the notion. It is easy to visualize the little tile cube of a building with its far flung porches, its apron of silky concrete and, revolving on high, the immaculate bivalve glowing in every inch of its pretty styrene (I have already approached the Shell distributor).

A taxi pulls up under the streetlight. Kate gets out and strides past the shelter, hands thrust deep in her pockets. Her eyes are pools of darkness. There is about her face the rapt almost ugly look of solitary people. When I call out to her, she comes directly over with a lack of surprise, with a dizzy dutiful obedience, which is disquieting. Then I see that she is full of it, one of her great ideas, the sort that occur to people on long walks.

"What a fool I've been!" She lays both hands on my arm and takes no notice of the smell of the hour. She is nowhere; she is in the realm of her idea. "Do you think it is possible for a person to make a single mistake—not do something wrong, you understand, but make a miscalculation—and ruin his life?"

"Why not?"

"I mean after all. Couldn't a person be miserable because he got one thing wrong and never learned otherwise—because the thing he got wrong was of such a nature that he could not be told because the telling itself got it wrong—just as if you had landed on Mars and therefore had no way of knowing that a Martian is mortally offended by a question and so every time you asked what was wrong, it only grew worse for you?" Catching sight of my sleeve, she seizes it with a curious rough gesture, like a housewife fingering goods. "My stars, pajamas," she says offhandedly. "Well?" She searches my face in the violet shadow.

"I don't know."

"But I do know! I found out, Binx. None of you could have told me even if you wanted to. I don't even know if you know."

I wait gloomily. Long ago I learned to be wary of Kate's revelations. These exalted moments, when she is absolutely certain what course to take for the rest of her life, are often followed by spells of the blackest depression. "No, I swear I don't believe you do," says Kate, peering into my face, into one eye and then the other, like a lover. "And my telling you would do no good."

"Tell me anyhow."

"I am free. After twenty-five years I am free."

"How do you know?"

"You're not surprised?"

"When did you find out?"

"At four thirty this afternoon, yesterday afternoon."

"At Merle's?"

"Yes. I was looking up at his bookshelf and I hadn't said anything for a long time. I saw his book, a book with a sort of burlap cover that always struck me unpleasantly. Yet how hard I had tried to live up to him and his book, live joyfully and as oneself etcetera. There were days when I would come in as nervous as an actress and there were moments when I succeeded—in being myself and brilliantly (look at me, Merle, I'm doing it!), so brilliantly that I think he loved me. Poor Merle. You see, there is nothing he can say. He can't tell me the secret even if he knew it. Do you know what I did? After a minute or so he asked me: what comes to mind? I sat up and rubbed my eyes and then it dawned on me. But I couldn't believe it. It was too simple. My God, can a person live twenty-five years, a life of crucifixion, through a *misunderstanding*? Yes! I stood up. I had discovered that a person does not have to *be* this or *be* that or be anything, not even oneself. One is free. But even if Merle knew this and told me, there is no way in the world I could have taken his advice. How strange to think that you cannot pass along the discovery. So again Merle said: what comes to mind? I got up and told him good-by. He said, it's only four thirty; the hour is not yet over. Then he understood I was leaving. He got interested and suggested we look into the reasons. I said, Merle, how I wish you were right. How good to think that there are reasons and that if I am silent, it means I am hiding something. How happy I would be to be hiding something. And how proud I am when I do find secret reasons for you, your own favorite reasons. But what if there is nothing? That is what I've been afraid of until now—being found out to be concealing nothing at all. But now I know why I was afraid and why I needn't be. I was afraid because I felt that I must *be* such and such a person, even as good a person as your joyous and creative person (I read your articles, Merle). What a discovery! One minute I am straining every nerve to be the sort of person I was expected to be and shaking in my boots for fear I would fail—and the next minute to know with the calmest certitude that even if I could succeed and become your joyous and creative person, that it was not good enough for me and that I had something better. I was free. Now I am saying good-by, Merle. And I walked out, as free as a bird for the first time in my life, twenty-five years old, healthy as a horse, rich as cream, and with the world before me. Ah, don't disapprove, Binx. Binx, Binx. You think I should go back! Oh I will, no doubt. But I know I am right or I would not feel so wonderful."

She will not feel wonderful long. Already the sky over the Chef is fading and soon the dawn will glimmer about us like the bottom of the sea. I know very well that when the night falls away into gray distances, she will sink into herself. Even now she is overtaking herself: already she is laboring ever so slightly at her exaltation.

I take her cold hands. "What do you think of this for an idea?" I tell her about the service station and Mr Sartalamaccia. "We could stay on here at Mrs Schexnaydre's. It is very comfortable. I may even run the station myself. You could come sit with me at night, if you liked. Did you know you can net over fifteen thousand a year on a good station?"

"You sweet old Binx! Are you asking me to marry you?"

"Sure." I watch her uneasily.

"Not a bad life, you say. It would be the best of all possible lives." She speaks in a rapture—something like my aunt. My heart sinks. It is too late. She has already overtaken herself.

"Don't—worry about it."

"I won't! I won't"—as enraptured and extinguished in her soul, gone, as a character played by Eva Marie Saint. Leaning over, she hugs herself.

"What's the matter?"

"Ooooh," Kate groans, Kate herself now. "I'm so afraid."

"I know."

"What am I going to do?"

"You mean right now?"

"Yes."

"We'll go to my car. Then we'll drive down to the French Market and get some coffee. Then we'll go home."

"Is everything going to be all right?"

"Yes."

"Tell me. Say it."

"Everything is going to be all right."

Three

SATURDAY MORNING at the office is dreary. The market is closed and there is nothing to do but get on with the letter writing. But this is no more than I expected. It is a fine day outside, freakishly warm. Tropical air has seeped into the earth and the little squares of St Augustine grass are springy and turgid. Camphor berries pop underfoot; azaleas and Judas trees are blooming on Elysian Fields. There is a sketch of cloud in the mild blue sky and the high thin piping of waxwings comes from everywhere.

As Sharon types the letters, I stand hands in pockets looking through the gold lettering of our window. I think of Sharon and American Motors. It closed yesterday at 30¼.

At eleven o'clock it is time to speak.

"I'm quitting now. I've got sixty miles to go before lunch."

"Wherebouts you going?"

"To the Gulf Coast."

The clatter of the typewriter does not slacken.

"Would you like to go?"

"M-hm"—absently. She is not surprised. "It just so happens I got work to do."

"No, you haven't. I'm closing the office."

"Well I be dog." There is still no surprise. What I've been waiting to see is how she will go about shedding her secretary manner. She doesn't. The clatter goes on.

"I'm leaving now."

"You gon let me finish this or not!" she cries in a scolding voice. So this is how she does it. She feels her way into familiarity by way of vexations. "You go head."

"Go?"

"I'll be right out. I got to call somebody."

"So do I." I call Kate. Mercer answers the phone. Kate has gone to the airport with Aunt Emily. He believes she is well.

Sharon looks at me with a yellow eye. "Is Miss Cutrer any kin to you?" she cries in her new scolding voice.

"She is my cousin."

90

"Some old girl told me you were married to her. I said nayo indeed."

"I'm not married to anyone."

"I said you weren't!" She tilts her head forward and goes off into a fit of absent-mindedness.

"Why did you want to know if I was married?"

"I'll tell you one thing, son. I'm not going out with any married man."

But still she has not come to the point of waiting upon my ministrations—like a date. Still very much her own mistress, she sets about tidying up her desk. When she shoulders her Guatemalan bag and walks briskly to the door, it is for me to tag along behind her. Now I see how she will have it: don't think I'm standing around waiting for you to state your business—you said you were closing the office—very well, I am leaving.

I jump ahead of her to open the door.

"Do you want to go home and let me pick you up in half an hour? Put your suit on under your clothes."

"All right!" But it isn't all right. Her voice is a little too bright.

"Meanwhile I'll go get my car and my suit."

"All right." She is openly grudging. It is not right at all! She is just like Linda.

"I have a better idea. Come on and walk home with me to get my car and then I'll take you to your house."

"All right." A much better all right. "Now you wait right here. This won't take me long."

When she comes out, her eyes are snapping.

"Is everything all right?"

"You mighty right it is"—eyes flashing. Uh oh. The boy friend has torn it.

"I hope you brought your suit down from Eufala."

"Are you kidding?"

"Why no."

"It's some suit. Just an old piece of a suit. I was going to get me one at Maison Blanche but I didn't think I'd be going swimming in March."

"Do you like to swim?"

"Are you kidding?"

"No."

"I'd rather swim than eat. I really would. Where're we going?"

"To the ocean."

"The ocean! I never knew there was an ocean anywhere around here."

"It's the open Gulf. The same thing."

When I put her in the car, she addresses an imaginary third person. "Now this is what I call real service. Your boss not only lets you off to go swimming—he takes you to the beach."

On these terms we set forth: she the girl whose heart's desire is to swim; I, her generous employer, who is nice enough to provide transportation.

Early afternoon finds us spinning along the Gulf Coast. Things have not gone too badly. As luck would have it, no sooner do we cross Bay St Louis and reach the beach drive than we are involved in an accident. Fortunately it is not serious. When I say as luck would have it, I mean good luck. Yet how, you might wonder, can even a minor accident be considered good luck?

Because it provides a means of winning out over the malaise, if one has the sense to take advantage of it.

What is the malaise? you ask. The malaise is the pain of loss. The world is lost to you, the world and the people in it, and there remains only you and the world and you no more able to be in the world than Banquo's ghost.

You say it is a simple thing surely, all gain and no loss, to pick up a good-looking woman and head for the beach on the first fine day of the year. So say the newspaper poets. Well it is not such a simple thing and if you have ever done it, you know it isn't—unless, of course, the woman happens to be your wife or some other everyday creature so familiar to you that she is as invisible as you yourself. Where there is chance of gain, there is also chance of loss. Whenever one courts great happiness, one also risks malaise.

The car itself is all-important, I have discovered. When I first moved to Gentilly, I bought a new Dodge sedan, a Red Ram Six. It was a comfortable, conservative and economical two-door sedan, just the thing it seemed to me, for a young Gentilly businessman. When I first slid under the wheel to drive it, it

seemed that everything was in order—here was I, a healthy
young man, a veteran with all his papers in order, a U.S. citizen
driving a very good car. All these things were true enough, yet
on my first trip to the Gulf Coast with Marcia, I discovered
to my dismay that my fine new Dodge was a regular incubator
of malaise. Though it was comfortable enough, though it ran
like a clock, though we went spinning along in perfect comfort
and with a perfect view of the scenery like the American couple
in the Dodge ad, the malaise quickly became suffocating. We
sat frozen in a gelid amiability. Our cheeks ached from smiling. Either would have died for the other. In despair I put my
hand under her dress, but even such a homely little gesture as
that was received with the same fearful politeness. I longed
to stop the car and bang my head against the curb. We were
free, moreover, to do that or anything else, but instead on we
rushed, a little vortex of despair moving through the world
like the still eye of a hurricane. As it turned out, I should have
stopped and banged my head, for Marcia and I returned to
New Orleans defeated by the malaise. It was weeks before we
ventured out again.

This is the reason I have no use for cars and prefer buses and
streetcars. If I were a Christian I would make a pilgrimage by
foot, for this is the best way to travel. But girls do not like it.
My little red MG, however, is an exception to the rule. It is a
miserable vehicle actually, with not a single virtue save one: it
is immune to the malaise. You have no idea what happiness
Marcia and I experienced as soon as we found ourselves spinning along the highway in this bright little beetle. We looked
at each other in astonishment: the malaise was gone! We sat
out in the world, out in the thick summer air between sky
and earth. The noise was deafening, the wind was like a hurricane; straight ahead the grains of the concrete rushed at us
like mountains.

It was nevertheless with some apprehension that I set out
with Sharon. What if the malaise had been abated simply by
the novelty of the MG? For by now the MG was no novelty.
What if the malaise was different with every girl and needed
a different cure? One thing was certain. Here was the acid
test. For the stakes were very high. Either very great happiness
lay in store for us, or malaise past all conceiving. Marcia and

Linda were as nothing to this elfin creature, this sumptuous elf from Eufala who moved like a ballerina, hard-working and docile, dreaming in her work, head to the side, cheek downy and spare as a boy's. With her in the bucket seat beside me I spin along the precipice with the blackest malaise below and the greenest of valleys ahead. One great advantage is mine: her boy friend, the Faubourg Marigny character. The fellow has no better sense than to make demands on her and she has no use for him. Thank God for the macaroni.

Indeed as we pass through the burning swamps of Chef Menteur, it seems to me that I catch a whiff of the malaise. A little tongue of hellfire licks at our heels and the MG jumps ahead, roaring like a bomber through the sandy pine barrens and across Bay St Louis. Sharon sits smiling and silent, her eyes all but closed against the wind, her big golden knees doubled up against the dashboard. "I swear, this is the cutest little car I ever saw!" she yelled at me a minute ago.

By some schedule of proprieties known to her, she did not become my date until she left her rooming house where she put on a boy's shirt and black knee britches. Her roommate watched us from an upper window. "Wave to Joyce," Sharon commands me. Joyce is leaning on the sill, a brown-haired girl in a leather jacket. She has the voluptuous look of room-mates left alone. It becomes necessary to look a third time. Joyce shifts her weight and beyond any doubt a noble young ham hikes up under the buckskin. A sadness overtakes me. If only— If only what? If only I could send Sharon on her way and go straight upstairs and see Joyce, a total stranger? Yes. But not quite. If only I could be with both of them, with a house full of them, an old Esplanade rooming house full of strapping American girls with their silly turned heads and their fine big bottoms. In the last split-second I could swear Joyce knows what I am thinking, for she gives me a laughing naughty-you look and her mouth forms oh-*ho!* Sharon comes piling into the car and up against me. Now she can touch me.

"Where is Joyce from?"

"Illinois."

"Is she nice?"

"Joyce is a good old girl."

"She seems to be. Are you all good friends?"

"Are you kidding?"

"No."

"Lordy lord, the crazy talks we have. If people could hear us, they would carry us straight to Tuscaloosa."

"What do you talk about?"

"Everybody."

"Me?"

"Why sure."

"What do you say?"

"Do you really want to know?"

"Yes."

"Well I can tell you one thing, son."

"What's that?"

"You're surely not gon find out from me."

"Why not?"

"Larroes catch medloes."

Out Elysian Fields we go, her warm arm lying over mine. All at once she is free with herself, flouncing around on the seat, bumping knee, hip, elbow against me. She is my date (she reminds me a little of a student nurse I once knew: she is not so starchy now but rather jolly and horsy). The MG jumps away from the stop signs like a young colt. I feel fine.

Yes, she is on to the magic of the little car: we are earthbound as a worm, yet we rush along at a tremendous clip between earth and sky. The heavy fragrant air pushes against us, a square hedge of pyrocantha looms dead ahead, we flash past and all of a sudden there is the Gulf, flat and sparkling away to the south.

We are bowling along below Pass Christian when the accident happens. Just ahead of us a westbound green Ford begins a U-turn, thinks it sees nothing, creeps out and rams me square amidships. Not really hard—it makes a hollow metal bang *b-rramp!* and the MG shies like a spooked steer, jumps into the neutral ground, careens into a drain hole and stops, hissing. My bad shoulder has caught it. I think I pass out for a few seconds, but not before I see two things: Sharon, she is all right; and the people who hit me. It is an old couple, Ohio plates. I swear I almost recognize them. I've seen them in the motels by the hundreds. He is old and lean and fit, with a turkey throat and a baseball cap; she is featureless. They are on their way to Florida. He gives me a single terrified look as we buck over the grass, appeals to his wife for help, hesitates, bolts. Off he goes, bent over his wheel like a jockey.

Sharon hovers over me. She touches my chin as if to get my attention. "Jack?"

The pain in my shoulder was past all imagining but is already better.

"How did you know my name was Jack?"

"Mr Daigle and Mr Hebert call you Jack."

"Are you all right?"

"I think so."

"You look scared."

"Why that crazy fool could have killed us."

The traffic has slowed, to feast their eyes on us. A Negro sprinkling a steep lawn under a summer house puts his hose down altogether and stands gaping. By virtue of our misfortune we have become a thing to look at and witnesses gaze at us with heavy-lidded almost seductive expressions. But almost at once they are past and those who follow see nothing untoward. The Negro picks up his hose. We are restored to the anonymity of our little car-space.

Love is invincible. True, for a second or so the pain carried me beyond all considerations, even that of love, but for no more than a second. Already it has been put to work and is performing yeoman service, a lovely checker in a lovely game.

"But what about you?" Sharon asks, coming close. "Honey, you look awful pale."

"He bumped my shoulder."

"Let me see." She comes around and helps me take off my shirt, but the T-shirt is too tight and I can't raise my arm. "Wait." She goes after her Guatemalan bag and finds some cuticle scissors and cuts the sleeve through the neck. I feel her stop.

"That's not—"

"Not what?"

"Not from this wreck."

"Sure."

"You got a handkerchief." She runs down to the beach to wet it in salt water. "Now. We better find a doctor."

I was shot through the shoulder—a decent wound, as decent

as any ever inflicted on Rory Calhoun or Tony Curtis. After all it could have been in the buttocks or genitals—or nose. Decent except that the fragment nicked the apex of my pleura and got me a collapsed lung and a big roaring empyema. No permanent damage, however, except a frightening-looking scar in the hollow of my neck and in certain weather a tender joint.

"Come on now, son, where did you get that?" Cold water runs down my side.

"That Ford."

"Why that's terrible!"

"Can't you tell it's a scar?"

"Where did you get it?"

"My razor slipped."

"Come on now!"

"I got it on the Chongchon River."

"In the war?"

"Yes."

"Oh."

O Tony. O Rory. You never had it so good with direction. Nor even you Bill Holden, my noble Will. O ye morning stars together. Farewell forever, malaise. Farewell and good luck, green Ford and old Ohioan. May you live in Tampa happily and forever.

And yet there are fellows I know who would have been sorry it happened, who would have had no thought for anything but their damned MG. Blessed MG.

I am able to get out creakily and we sit on the grassy bank. My head spins. That son of a bitch really rocked my shoulder. The MG is not bad: a dented door.

"And right exactly where you were sitting," says Sharon holding the handkerchief to my shoulder. "And that old scoun'l didn't even stop." She squats in her black pants like a five year old and peers at me. "Goll—! Didn't that *hurt*?"

"It was the infection that was bad."

"I'll tell you one dang thing."

"What?"

"I surely wouldn't want anybody shooting at me."

"Do you have an aspirin in your bag?"

"Wait."

When she returns, she gives me the aspirin and holds my

ruined shoulder in both hands, as if the aspirin were going to hurt.

"Now look behind the seat and bring me the whisky." She pours me a thumping drink into a paper cup, also from the Guatemalan bag. The aspirin goes down in the burning. I offer her the bottle.

"I swear I believe I will." She drinks, with hardly a face, hand pressed to the middle of her breastbone. We pull on my shirt by stages.

But the MG! We think of her at the same time. What if she suffered a concussion? But she starts immediately, roaring her defiance of the green Ford.

I forget my whisky bottle and when I get out to pick it up, I nearly fall down. She is right there to catch me, Rory. I put both my arms around her.

"Come on now, son, put your weight on me."

"I will. You're just about the sweetest girl I ever knew."

"Ne'mind that. You come on here, big buddy."

"I'm coming. Where're we going?"

"You sit over here."

"Can you drive?"

"You just tell me where to go."

"We'll get some beer, then go to Ship Island."

"In this car?"

"In a boat."

"Where is it?"

"There." Beyond the waters of the sound stretches a long blue smudge of pines.

The boat ride is not what I expected. I had hoped for an empty boat this time of year, a deserted deck where we might stretch out in the sun. Instead we are packed in like sardines. We find ourselves sitting bolt upright on a bench in the one little cabin surrounded by at least a hundred children. It is, we learn, a 4-H excursion from Leake County, Mississippi. A dozen men and women who look like Baptist deacons and deaconesses, red-skinned, gap-toothed, friendly—decent folk they are—are in charge. We sit drenched in the smell of upcountry Mississippi, the smell of warm white skins under boiled cotton underwear. How white they are, these farm children, milk white. No sign of sun here, no red necks; not pale are they but white, the rich damp white of skin under clothes.

Out we go like immigrants in the hold, chuffing through the thin milky waters of Mississippi Sound.

The only other couple on the boat is a Keesler Field airman and his girl. His fine silky hair is cropped short as ermine, but his lip is pulled up by the tendon of his nose showing two chipmunk teeth and giving him a stupid look. The girl is a plump little Mississippi armful, fifteen or sixteen; she too could be a Leake County girl. Though they sit holding hands, they could be strangers. Each stares about the cabin as if he were alone. One knows that they would dance and make love the same way, not really mindful of each other but gazing with a mild abiding astonishment at the world around. Surely I have seen them before too, at the zoo or Marineland, him gazing at the animals or fishes noting every creature with the same slow slack wonderment, her gazing at nothing in particular but not bored either, enduring rather and secure in his engrossment.

We land near the fort, a decrepit brick silo left over from the Civil War and littered with ten summers of yellow kodak boxes and ticket stubs and bottle caps. It is the soul of dreariness, this "historic site" washed by the thin brackish waters of Mississippi Sound. The debris of summers past piles up like archeological strata. Last summer I picked up a yellow scrap of newspaper and read of a Biloxi election in 1948, and in it I caught the smell of history far more pungently than from the metal marker telling of the French and Spanish two hundred years ago and the Yankees one hundred years ago. 1948. What a faroff time.

A plank walk leads across some mudholes and a salt marsh to an old dance pavilion. As we pass we catch a glimpse of the airman and his girl standing bemused at a counter and drinking RC Cola. Beyond, a rise of sand and saw grass is creased by a rivulet of clear water in which swim blue crabs and cat-eye snails. Over the hillock lies the open sea. The difference is very great: first, this sleazy backwater, then the great blue ocean. The beach is clean and a big surf is rolling in; the water in the middle distance is green and lathered. You come over the hillock and your heart lifts up; your old sad music comes into the major.

We find a hole in the rivulet and sink the cans of beer and

go down the beach a ways from the children, to a tussock of sand and grass. Sharon is already in, leaving her shirt and pants on the beach like a rag. She wades out ahead of me, turning to and fro, hands outstretched to the water and sweeping it before her. Now and then she raises her hands to her head as if she were placing a crown and combs back her hair with the last two fingers. The green water foams at her knees and sucks out ankle deep and swirling with sand. Out she goes, thighs asuck, turning slowly and sweeping the water before her. How beautiful she is. She is beautiful and brave and chipper as a sparrow. My throat catches with the sadness of her beauty. Son of a bitch, it is enough to bring tears to your eyes. I don't know what is wrong with me. She smiles at me, then cocks her head.

"Why do you look at me like that?"

"Like what?"

"What's the matter with you?"

"I don't know."

"Come on, son. I'm going to give you some beer."

Her suit is of a black sheeny stuff like a swim-meet suit and skirtless. She comes out of the water like a spaniel, giving her head a flirt which slaps her hair around in a wet curl and stooping, brushes the water from her legs. Now she stands musing on the beach, leg locked, pelvis aslant, thumb and forefinger propped along the iliac crest and lightly, propped lightly as an athlete. As the salt water dries and stings, she minds herself, plying around the flesh of her arm and sending fingers along her back.

Down the beach the children have been roped off into two little herds of girls and boys. They wade—evidently they can't swim—in rough squares shepherded by the deacons who wear black bathing suits with high armholes and carry whistles around their necks. The deaconesses watch from bowers which other children are busy repairing with saw grass they have gathered from the ridge.

We swim again and come back to the tussock and drink beer. She lies back and closes her eyes with a sigh. "This really beats typing." Her arm falls across mine and she gives me an affectionate pat and settles herself in the sand as if she really meant to take a nap. But her eyes gleam between her eyelids and I bend to kiss her. She laughs and kisses me back with a friendly passion. We lie embracing each other.

"Whoa now, son," she says laughing.

"What's the matter?"

"Right here in front of God and everybody?"

"I'm sorry."

"Sorry! Listen, you come here."

"I'm here."

She makes a movement indicating both her friendliness and the limit she sets to it. For an hour we swim and drink beer. Once when she gets up, I come up on my knees and embrace her golden thighs, such a fine strapping armful they are.

"What do you think you're doing, boy?"

"Honey, I've been waiting three weeks to grab you like this."

"Well now that you've grabbed me you can turn me loose."

"Sweetheart, I'll never turn you loose." Mother of all living, what an armful.

"All right now, son—"

"What?"

"You can turn me loose."

"No."

"Listen, big buddy. I'm as strong as you are."

"No, you're not."

"I may not be as big as you are—"

"You are here."

"—but I'm just as strong."

"Not really."

"All right, you watch here." She balls up her fist like a man's and smacks me hard on the arm.

"That hurts."

"Then quit messing with me."

"All right. I won't mess with you."

"Hit me."

"What?"

"You heard me. Hit me." She holds her elbow tight against her body. "Come on, boy."

"What are you talking about? I'm not going to hit you."

"Come on hit me. I'm not kidding. You can't hurt me."

"All right." I hit her.

"Na. I don't mean just playlike. Really hit me."

"You mean it?"

"I swear before God."

I hit her just hard enough to knock her over.

"Got dog." She gets up quickly. "That didn't hurt. I got a good mind to hit you right in the mouth, you jackass."

"I believe you," I say laughing. "Now you come here."

"What for? All right now!" She cocks her fist again. "What do you think you're doing?"

"I just want to tell you what's on my mind."

"What?"

"You. You and your sweet lips. Sweetheart, before God I can't think about anything in the world but putting my arms around you and kissing your sweet lips."

"O me."

"Do you care if I do?"

"I don't care if you do."

I hold springtime in my arms, the fullness of it and the rinsing sadness of it.

"I'll tell you something else."

"What?"

"Sweetheart, I can't get you out of my mind. Not since you walked into my office in that yellow dress. I'm crazy about you and you know it, don't you?"

"O me."

I sit back to see her and take her hands. "I can't sleep for thinking of you."

"You swear?"

"I swear."

"We made us some money, didn't we?"

"We sure did. Don't you want some money? I'll give you five thousand dollars."

"No, I don't want any money."

"Let's go down the beach a ways."

"What for?"

"So they can't see us."

"What's the matter with them seeing us?"

"It's all right with me."

"Ho now, you son."

"You're my sweetheart. Do you care if I love you?"

"Nayo indeed. But you're not getting me off down there with those rattlesnakes."

"Rattlesnakes!"

"No sir. We gon stay right here close to those folks and you gon behave yourself."

"All right." I clasp my hands in the hollow of her back. "I'll tell you something else."

"Uh oh." She rears back, laughing, to see me, a little embarrassed by our closeness. "Well you got me."

"I'm sorry you work for me."

"Sorry! Listen, son. I do my work."

"I wouldn't want you to think I was taking advantage of you."

"Nobody's taking advantage of me," she says huffily.

I laugh at her. "No, I mean our business relationship." We sit up and drink our beer. "I have a confession to make to you. I've been planning this all week."

"What?"

"This picnic."

"Well I be dog."

"Don't kid me. You knew."

"I swear I didn't."

"But it's the business part of it that worries me—"

"Business and pleasure don't have to mix."

"Well, all I wanted you to know was that when I acted on impulse—"

"I always act on impulse. I believe in saying what you mean and meaning what you say."

"I can see that."

"You just ask Joyce what I said about you."

"Joyce?"

"My roommate."

"What did you say?"

"You just ask her."

I look up and down the beach. "I don't see her."

"I don't mean now, you jackass."

We swim and lie down together. The remarkable discovery forces itself upon me that I do not love her so wildly as I loved her last night. But at least there is no malaise and we lie drowsing in the sun, hands clasped in the other's back, until the boat whistle blows.

Yet loves revives as we spin homewards along the coast through the early evening. Joy and sadness come by turns, I know now. Beauty and bravery make you sad, Sharon's beauty and my aunt's bravery, and victory breaks your heart. But life goes on and on we go, spinning along the coast in a violet light, past Howard Johnson's and the motels and the children's carnival. We pull into a bay and have a drink under the stars. It is not a bad thing to settle for the Little Way, not the big search for the big happiness but the sad little happiness of drinks and kisses, a good little car and a warm deep thigh.

"My mother has a fishing camp at Bayou des Allemands. Would you like to stop there?"

She nods into my neck. She has become tender toward me and now and then presses my cheek with her hand.

Just west of Pearl River a gravel road leaves the highway and winds south through the marshes. All at once we are in the lonely savannah and the traffic is behind us. Sharon still hides her face in my neck.

A lopsided yellow moon sheds a feeble light over the savannah. Faraway hummocks loom as darkly as a flotilla of ships. Awkwardly we walk over and into the marsh and along the boardwalk. Sharon cleaves to me as if, in staying close, she might not see me.

I cannot believe my eyes. It is difficult to understand. We round a hummock and there is the camp ablaze like the *Titanic*. The Smiths are home.

2

My half brothers and sisters are eating crabs at a sawbuck table on the screened porch. The carcasses mount toward a naked light bulb.

They blink at me and at each other. Suddenly they feel the need of a grown-up. A grown-up must certify that they are correct in thinking that they see me. They all, every last one, look frantically for their mother. Thèrése runs to the kitchen doorway.

"Mother! Jack is here!" She holds her breath and watches her mother's face. She is rewarded. "Yes, Jack!"

"Jean-Paul ate some lungs." Mathilde looks up from directly under my chin.

My half brother Jean-Paul, the son of my mother, is a big fat yellow baby piled up like a buddha in his baby chair, smeared with crab paste and brandishing a scarlet claw. The twins goggle at us but do not leave off eating.

Lonnie has gone into a fit of excitement in his wheelchair. His hand curls upon itself. I kiss him first and his smile starts his head turning away in a long trembling torticollis. He is fourteen and small for his age, smaller than Clare and Donice, the ten year old twins. But since last summer when Duval, the oldest son, was drowned, he has been the "big boy." His dark red hair is nearly always combed wet and his face is handsome and pure when it is not contorted. He is my favorite, to tell the truth. Like me, he is a moviegoer. He will go see anything. But we are good friends because he knows I do not feel sorry for him. For one thing, he has the gift of believing that he can offer his sufferings in reparation for men's indifference to the pierced heart of Jesus Christ. For another thing, I would not mind so much trading places with him. His life is a serene business.

My mother is drying her hands on a dishcloth.

"Well well, look who's here," she says but does not look.

Her hands dry, she rubs her nose vigorously with her three middle fingers held straight up. She has hay fever and crabs make it worse. It is a sound too well known to me to be remembered, this quick jiggle up and down and the little wet wringing noises under her fingers.

We give each other a kiss or rather we press our cheeks together, Mother embracing my head with her wrist as if her hands were still wet. Sometimes I feel a son's love for her, or something like this, and try to give her a special greeting, but at these times she avoids my eye and gives me her cheek and calls on me to notice this about Mathilde or that about Thérèse.

"Mother, I want you to meet Sharon Kincaid."

"Well now!" cries Mother, turning away and inserting herself among the children, not because she has anything against Sharon but because she feels threatened by the role of hostess. "There is nobody here but us children," she is saying.

Sharon is in the best of humors, rounding her eyes and laughing so infectiously that I wonder if she is not laughing at me. From the beginning she is natural with the children. Linda, I remember, was nervous and shifted from one foot to the other and looked over their heads, her face gone heavy as a pudding. Marcia made too much over them, squatting down and hugging her knees like Joan Fontaine visiting an orphanage.

Mother does not ask how I happen to be here or give a sign that my appearance is in any way remarkable—though I have not seen them for six months. "Tessie, tell Jack about your class's bus trip."—and she makes her escape to the kitchen. After a while her domesticity will begin to get on my nerves. By the surest of instincts she steers clear of all that is exceptional or "stimulating." Any event or idea which does not fall within the household regimen, she stamps at once with her own brand of the familiar. If, as a student, I happened to get excited about Jackson's Valley Campaign or Freud's *Interpretation of Dreams*, it was not her way to oppose me. She approved it as a kind of wondrous Rover boy eccentricity: "Those? Oh those are Jack's books. The stacks and stacks of books that boy brings home! Jack, do you know everything in those books?" "No'm." Nevertheless I became Dick Rover, the serious-minded Rover boy.

It is good to see the Smiths at their fishing camp. But not at their home in Biloxi. Five minutes in that narrow old house and dreariness sets into the marrow of my bones. The gas logs strike against the eyeballs, the smell of two thousand Sunday dinners clings to the curtains, voices echo round and round the bare stairwell, a dismal Sacred Heart forever points to itself above the chipped enamel mantelpiece. Everything is white and chipped. The floors, worn powdery, tickle the nostrils like a schoolroom. But here on Bayou des Allemands everybody feels the difference. Water laps against the piling. The splintered boards have secret memories of winter, the long dreaming nights and days when no one came and the fish jumped out of the black water and not a soul in sight in the whole savannah; secrets the children must find out and so after supper they are back at their exploring, running in a gang from one corner to another. Donice shows me a muskrat trap he had left last August and wonder of wonders found again. They only came down this morning, Mother explains, such a fine day it was, and since the children have a holiday Monday, will stay through Mardi Gras if the weather holds. With Roy away, Mother is a member of the gang. Ten minutes she will spend in the kitchen working with her swift cat-efficiency, then out and away with the children, surging to and fro in their light inconstant play, her eyes fading in a fond infected look.

Thèrése is telling about her plans to write her Congressman about the Rivers and Harbors bill. Thèrése and Mathilde are something like Joan and Jane in the Civics reader.

"Isn't that Tessie a *case*?" my mother cries as she disappears into the kitchen, signifying that Tessie is smart but also that there is something funny about her precocity.

"Where's Roy? We didn't see a car. We almost didn't walk over."

"Playing poker!" they all cry. This seems funny and everybody laughs. Lonnie's hand curls. If our arrival had caused any confusion, we are carried quickly past by the strong current of family life.

"Do you have any more crabs, Mother?"

"Any more crabs! Ask Lonnie if we weren't just wondering what to do with the rest. You haven't had your supper?"

"No'm."

Mother folds up the thick layer of newspapers under the crab carcasses, making a neat bundle with her strong white hands. The whole mess comes away leaving the table dry and clean. Thèrése spreads fresh paper and Mathilde fetches two cold bottles of beer and two empty bottles for hammering the claws and presently we have a tray apiece, two small armies of scarlet crabs marching in neat rows. Sharon looks queer but she pitches in anyhow and soon everybody is making fun of her. Mathilde shows her how to pry off the belly plate and break the corner at the great claw so that the snowy flesh pops out in a fascicle. Sharon affects to be amazed and immediately the twins must show her how to suck the claws.

Outside is the special close blackness of night over water. Bugs dive into the tight new screen and bounce off with a guitar thrum. The children stand in close, feeling the mystery of the swamp and the secrecy of our cone of light. Clairain presses his stomach against the arm of my chair. Lonnie tries to tune his transistor radio; he holds it in the crook of his wrist, his hands bent back upon it. Once his lip falls open in the most ferocious leer. This upsets Sharon. It seems to her that a crisis is at hand, that Lonnie has at last reached the limit of his endurance. When no one pays any attention to him, she grows fidgety—why doesn't somebody help him?—then, after an eternity, Mathilde leans over carelessly and tunes in a station loud and clear. Lonnie turns his head, weaving, to see her, but not quite far enough.

Lonnie is dressed up, I notice. It turns out that Aunt Ethel, Roy's sister, was supposed to take him and the girls to a movie. It was not a real date, Mother reminds him, but Lonnie looks disappointed.

"What is the movie?" I ask him.

"*Fort Dobbs.*" His speech is crooning but not hard to understand.

"Where is it?"

"At the Moonlite."

"Let's go."

Lonnie's head teeters and falls back like a dead man's.

"I mean it. I want to see it."

He believes me.

I corner my mother in the kitchen.

"What's the matter with Lonnie?"

"Why nothing."

"He looks terrible."

"That child won't drink his milk!" sings out my mother.

"Has he had pneumonia again?"

"He had the five day virus. And it was bad bad bad bad bad. Did you ever hear of anyone with virus receiving extreme unction?"

"Why didn't you call me?"

"He wasn't in danger of death. The extreme unction was his idea. He said it would strengthen him physically as well as spiritually. Have you ever heard of that?"

"Yes. But is he all right now?"

She shrugs. My mother speaks of such matters in a light allusive way, with the overtones neither of belief nor disbelief but rather of a general receptivity to lore.

everything. The pleasant man in the bow is taken by surprise and knocked off balance as the boat skews against the dock. But now the boat seeks open water and the fishermen sit quickly about and settle themselves, their faces serene now and full of hope. Roy Smith is seen to be a cheerful florid man, heavy-set but still youngish. The water of the bayou boils up like tea and disgorges bubbles of smoke. The hull disappears into a white middle distance and the sound goes suddenly small as if the boat had run into cotton.

A deformed live oak emerges from the whiteness, stands up in the air, like a tree in a Chinese print. Minutes pass. An egret lets down on his light stiff wings and cocks one eye at the water. Behind me the screen door opens softly and my mother comes out on the dock with a casting rod. She props the rod against the rail, puts down a wax-paper bundle, scratches both arms under the sleeves and looks about her, yawning. "Hinh-honh," she says in a yawn-sigh as wan and white as the morning. Her blouse is one of Roy's army shirts and not much too big for her large breasts. She wears blue Keds and ladies' denims with a flyless front pulled high over her bulky hips. With her baseball cap pressed down over her wiry hair she looks like the women you see fishing from highway bridges.

Mother undoes the bundle, takes out a scout knife and pries loose the frozen shrimp. She chops off neat pink cubes, slides them along the rail with her blade, stopping now and then to jiggle her nose and clear her throat with the old music. To make sure of having room, she goes out to the end of the dock, lays back her arm to measure, and casts in a big looping straight-arm swing, a clumsy yet practiced movement that ends with her wrist bent in in a womanish angle. The reel sings and the lead sails far and wide with its gyrating shrimp and lands with hardly a splash in the light etherish water. Mother holds still for a second, listening intently as if she meant to learn what the fishes thought of it, and reels in slowly, twitching the rod from time to time.

I pull on my pants and walk out barefoot on the dock. The sun has cleared the savannah but it is still a cool milky world. Only the silvery wood is warm and raspy underfoot.

"Isn't it mighty early for you!" Her voice is a tinkle over the water.

My mother is easy and affectionate with me. Now we may speak together. It is the early morning and our isolation in the great white marsh.

"Can I fix you some breakfast?"

"No'm. I'm not hungry." Our voices go ringing around the empty room of the morning.

Still she puts me off. I am only doing a little fishing and it is like any other day, she as much as says to me, so let us not make anything remarkable out of it. She veers away from intimacy. I marvel at her sure instinct for the ordinary. But perhaps she knows what she is doing.

"I *wish* I had known you were going to get up so early," she says indignantly. "You could have gone over to the Rigolets with Roy and Kinsey. The reds are running."

"I saw them."

"Why didn't you go!"—in the ultimate measure of astonishment.

"You know I don't like to fish."

"I had another rod!"

"It's just as well."

"That's true," she says after a while. "You never did. You're just like your father." She gives me a swift look, which is unusual for her. "I noticed last night how much you favor him." She casts again and again holds still.

"He didn't like to fish?"

"He thought he did!"

I stretch out at full length, prop my head on a two-by-four. It is possible to squint into the rising sun and at the same time see my mother spangled in rainbows. A crab spider has built his web across a finger of the bayou and the strands seem to spin in the sunlight.

"But he didn't really?"

"Unh un—" she says, dragging it out to make up for her inattention. Every now and then she wedges the rod between her stomach and the rail and gives her nose a good wringing.

"Why didn't he?"

"Because he didn't. He would say he did. And once he did! I remember one day we went down Little Bayou Sara. He had been sick and Dr Wills told him to work in the morning and take off in the afternoons and take up fishing or an interesting hobby. It was the prettiest day, I remember, and we found a hole under a fallen willow—a good place for *sac au lait* if ever I saw one. So I said, go ahead, drop your line right there. Through the *tree*? he said. He thought it was a lot of humbug—he wasn't much of a fisherman; Dr Wills and Judge Anse were big hunters and fishermen and he pretended he liked it but he didn't. So I said, go ahead, right down through the leaves—that's the way you catch *sac au lait*. I be John Brown if he didn't pull up the fattest finest *sac au lait* you ever saw. He couldn't believe his eyes. Oh he got himself all wound up about it. Now isn't this an ideal spot, he would say over and over again, and: Look at such and such a tree over there, look how the sunshine catches the water in such and such a way—we'll have to come back tomorrow and the next day and all summer—that's all we have to do!" My mother gives her rod a great spasming jerk, reels in quickly and frowns at the mangled shrimp. "Do you see what that scoun'l beast—! Do you know that that ain't anything in the world but some old hardhead sitting right on the bottom."

"Did he go back the next day?"

"Th. No indeed. No, in, deed," she says, carving three cubes of shrimp. Again she lays back her arm. The shrimp gyrates and Mother holds still. "What do you think he says when I mention *sac au lait* the next morning?"

"What?"

"'Oh no. Oh no. You go ahead.' And off he goes on his famous walk."

"Walk?"

"Up the levee. Five miles, ten miles, fifteen miles. Winter or summer. I went with him one Christmas morning I remember. Mile after mile and all of it just the same. Same old brown levee in front, brown river on one side, brown fields on the other. So when he got about a half a mile ahead of me, I said, shoot. What am I doing out here humping along for all I'm worth when all we going to do is turn around and hump on back? So I said, good-by, Mister, I'm going home—you can walk all the way to Natchez if you want to." It is my mother's way to see life, past and present, in terms of a standard comic exaggeration. If she had spent four years in Buchenwald, she would recollect it so: "So I said to him: listen, Mister, if you think I'm going to eat this stuff, you've got another think coming."

The boards of the dock, warming in the sun, begin to give off a piney-winey smell. The last tendril of ground fog burns away, leaving the water black as tea. The tree is solitary and mournful, a poor thing after all. Across the bayou the egret humps over, as peaked and disheveled as a buzzard.

"Was he a good husband?" Sometimes I try, not too seriously, to shake her loose from her elected career of the commonplace. But her gyroscope always holds her on course.

"Good? Well I'll tell you one thing—he was a good walker!"

"Was he a good doctor?"

"Was he! And what hands! If anyone ever had the hands of a surgeon, he did." My mother's recollection of my father is storied and of a piece. It is not him she remembers but an old emblem of him. But now something occurs to her. "He was smart, but he didn't know it all! I taught him a thing or two once and I can tell you he thanked me for it."

"What was that?"

"He had lost thirty pounds. He wasn't sick—he just couldn't keep anything down. Dr Wills said it was amoeba (that year he thought everything was amoeba; another year it was endometritis and between you and me he took out just about every uterus in Feliciana Parish). At the breakfast table when Mercer brought in his eggs and grits, he would just sit there looking at it, white as a sheet. Me, it was all I could do not to eat, my breakfast and his. He'd put a mouthful of grits in his mouth and chew and chew and he just couldn't swallow it. So one day I got an idea. I said listen: you sat up all night reading a book, didn't you? Yes, I did, he said, what of it? You enjoyed it, didn't you? Yes, I did. So I said: all right. Then we'll read it. The next morning I told Mercer to go on about his business. I had my breakfast early and I made his and brought it to him right there in his bed. I got his book. I remember it—it was a book called *The Greene Murder Case*. Everybody in the family read it. I began to read and he began to listen, and while I read, I fed him. I told him, I said, you can eat, and I fed him. I put the food in his mouth and he ate it. I fed him for six months and he gained twenty five pounds. And he went back to work. Even when he ate by himself downstairs, I had to read to him. He would get downright mad at me if I stopped. 'Well go on!' he would say."

I sit up and shade my eyes to see her.

Mother wrings her nose. "It was because—"

"Because of what?" I spit over into the water. The spit unwinds like a string.

She leans on the rail and gazes down into the tea-colored bayou. "It was like he thought eating was not—*important* enough. You see, with your father, everything, every second had to be—"

"Be what, Mother?"

This time she gives a real French shrug. "I don't know. Something."

"What was wrong with him?"

"He was overwrought," she replies at once and in her regular mama-bee drone and again my father disappears into the old emblem. I can hear echoes of my grandfather and grandmother and Aunt Emily, echoes of porch talk on the long summer evenings when affairs were settled, mysteries solved, the unnamed named. My mother never got used to our porch talk with its peculiar license. When someone made a spiel, one of our somber epic porch spiels, she would strain forward in the dark, trying to make out the face of the speaker and judge whether he meant to be taken as somberly as he sounded. As a Bolling in Feliciana Parish, I became accustomed to sitting on the porch in the dark and talking of the size of the universe and the treachery of men; as a Smith on the Gulf Coast I have become accustomed to eating crabs and drinking beer under a hundred and fifty watt bulb—and one is as pleasant a way as the other of passing a summer night.

"How was he overwrought?"

She plucks the hook clean, picks up a pink cube, pushes the barb through, out, and in again. Her wrists are rounded, not like a young girl's but by a deposit of hard fat.

"It was his psychological make-up."

Yes, it is true. We used to talk quite a bit about psychological make-ups and the effect of glands on our dismal dark behavior. Strangely, my mother sounds more like my aunt than my aunt herself. Aunt Emily no longer talks of psychological make-ups.

"His nervous system was like a high-powered radio. Do you know what happens if you turn up the volume and tune into WWL?"

"Yes," I say, unspeakably depressed by the recollection of the sad little analogies doctors like to use. "You mean he wasn't really cut out to be an ordinary doctor, he really should have been in research."

"That's right!" My mother looks over in surprise, but not much surprise, then sends her lead off like a shot. "Now Mister—!" she addresses an unknown fish and when he does not respond, falls to musing. "It's peculiar though. You're so much like your father and yet so different. You know, you've got a little of my papa in you—you're easy-going and you like to eat and you like the girls."

"I don't like to fish."

"You're too lazy, if you ask me. Anyhow, Papa was not a fisherman, as I have told you before. He owned a fleet of trawlers at Golden Meadow. But did he love pretty girls. Till his dying day."

"Does it last that long?"

"Anh anh anh anh anh!" In the scandal of it, Mother presses her chin into her throat, but she does not leave off watching her float. "Don't you get risque with me! This is your mother you're talking to and not one of your little hotsy-totsies."

"Hotsy-totsies!"

"Yes."

"Don't you like Sharon?"

"Why yes. But she's not the one for you." For years my mother has thrown it out as a kind of proverb that I should marry Kate Cutrer, though actually she has also made an emblem out of Kate and does not know her at all. "But do you know a funny thing?"

"What?"

"It's not you but Mathilde who is moody like your father. Sister Regina says she is another Alice Eberle."

"Who is Alice Eberle?"

"You know, the Biloxi girl who won the audition with Horace Heidt and His Musical Knights."

"Oh."

Mother trills in her throat with the old music. I squint up at her through the rainbows.

"But when he got sick the next time, I couldn't help him."

"Why not?"

She smiles. "He said my treatment was like horse serum: you can only use it once."

"What did happen?"

"The war came."

"That helped?"

"He helped himself. He had been in bed for a month, up in your room—you were off at school. He wouldn't go to the clinic, he wouldn't eat, he wouldn't go fishing, he wouldn't read. He'd just lie there and watch the ceiling fan. Once in a while he would walk down to the Chinaman's at night and eat a po-boy. That was the only way he could eat—walk down to the Chinaman's at midnight and eat a po-boy. That morning I left him upstairs as usual. I sent Mercer up with his paper and his tray and called Clarence Saunders. Ten minutes later I look up and here he comes, down the steps, all dressed up. He sits himself down at the dining room table as if nothing had happened, orders breakfast and eats enough to kill a horse—all the while reading his paper and not even knowing he was eating. I ask him what has happened. What has happened! Why, Germany has invaded Poland, and England and France have declared war! I'm here to tell you that in thirty minutes he had eaten his breakfast, packed a suitcase and gone to New Orleans."

"What for?"

"To see the Canadian consul."

"Yes, I remember him going to Windsor, Ontario."

"That was two months later. He gained thirty pounds in two months."

"What was he so excited about?"

"He knew what it meant! He told us all at supper: this is it. We're going to be in it sooner or later. We should be in it now. And I'm not waiting. They were all so proud of him—and especially Miz Cutrer. And when he came home that spring in his blue uniform and the gold wings of a flight surgeon, I swear he was the best looking man I ever saw in my life. And so—cute! We had the best time."

Sure he was cute. He had found a way to do both: to please them and please himself. To leave. To do what he wanted to do and save old England doing it. And perhaps even carry off the grandest coup of all: to die. To win the big prize for them and for himself (but not even he dreamed he would succeed not only in dying but in dying in Crete in the wine dark sea).

"Then before that he was lazy too."

"He was not!"

"It is not laziness, Mother. Partly but not all. I'll tell you a strange thing. During the war a bad thing happened to me. We were retreating from the Chongchon River. We had stopped the Chinese by setting fire to the grass with tracer bullets. What was left of a Ranger company was supposed to be right behind us. Or rather we thought we were retreating, because we got ambushed on the line of retreat and had to back off and head west. I was supposed to go back to the crossroad and tell the Ranger company about the change. I got back there and waited half an hour and got so cold I went to sleep. When I woke up it was daylight."

"And you didn't know whether the Rangers had come by or not?"

"That wasn't it. For a long time I couldn't remember anything. All I knew was that something was terribly wrong."

"Had the Rangers gone by during the night?" asks my mother, smiling and confident that I had played a creditable role."

"Well no, but that's not—"

"What happened to them?"

"They got cut off."

"You mean they were all killed?"

"There wasn't much left to them in the first place."

"What a terrible thing. We'll never know what you boys went through. But at least your conscience was clear."

"It was not my conscience that bothered me. What I am trying to tell you is that nothing seemed worth doing except something I couldn't even remember. If somebody had come up to me and said: if you will forget your preoccupation for forty minutes and get to work, I can assure you that you will find the cure of cancer and compose the greatest of all symphonies—I wouldn't have been interested. Do you know why? Because it wasn't good enough for me."

"That's selfish."

"I know."

"I'll tell you one thing. If they put me up there and said,

Anna, you hold your ground and start shooting, you know what I would do?"

"What?"

"I'd be long gone for the rear."

I summon up the vision of my mother in headlong retreat before the Chinese and I have to laugh.

"We'll never know what it was like though," Mother adds, but she is not paying much attention, to tell the truth. I really have to laugh at her. She kneads a pink cube so the fish can smell it. "You know what, Jack?" Her eyes brim with fondness, a fondness carefully guarded against the personal, the heartfelt, a fondness deliberately rendered trite. "It's funny you should mention that. Believe it or not, Roy and I were talking the other day and Roy, not me, said you would be wonderful in something like that."

"Like what?"

"Cancer research."

"Oh."

Fishing is poor. The egret pumps himself up into the air and rows by so close I can hear the gristle creak in his wings.

5

After breakfast there is a commotion about Mass. The Smiths, except Lonnie, would never dream of speaking of religion— raising the subject provokes in them the acutest embarrassment: eyes are averted, throats are cleared, and there occurs a murmuring for a minute or two until the subject can be changed. But I have heard them argue forty-five minutes about the mechanics of going to Mass and with all the ardor of relief, as if in debating the merits of the nine o'clock Mass in Biloxi as against the ten thirty in Bay St Louis they were indeed discussing religion and who can say they weren't? But perhaps they are right: certainly if they spoke to me of God, I would jump into the bayou.

I suggest to Roy Smith, who has just returned from the Rigolets, that Sharon and I stay home and mind Jean-Paul. "Oh no," says my mother under drooping lids. "Jean-Paul can go. We'll all go. Sharon's going too, aren't you, Sharon?" Sharon laughs and says she will. They've been talking together.

The church, an old one in the rear of Biloxi, looks like a post office. It is an official-looking place. The steps are trodden into scallops; the brass rail and doorplate are worn bright as gold from hard use. We arrive early so Lonnie can be rolled to a special place next to a column. By the time Mass begins we are packed in like sardines. A woman comes up the aisle, leans over and looks down our pew. She gives me an especially hard look. I do not budge. It is like the subway. Roy Smith, who got home just in time to change to a clean perforated shirt, gives up his seat to a little girl and kneels in the aisle with several other men, kneels on one knee like a tackle, elbow propped on his upright knee, hands clasped sideways. His face is dark with blood, his breath whistles in his nose as he studies the chips in the terrazzo floor.

Sharon is good: she has a sweet catholic wonder peculiar to a certain type of Protestant girl—once she is put at her ease by the heroic unreligiousness of the Smiths (what are they doing here? she thinks); she gazes about yellow-eyed. (She thinks: how odd they all are, and him too—all that commotion about getting here and now that they are here, it is as if it were over before it began—each has lapsed into his own blank-eyed vacancy and the priest has turned his back.)

When the bell rings for communion, Roy gets heavily to his feet and pilots Lonnie to the end of the rail. All I can see of Lonnie is a weaving tuft of red hair. When the priest comes to him, Roy holds a hand against Lonnie's face to steady him. He does this in a frowning perfunctory way, eyes light as an eagle's.

6

The women are in the kitchen, my mother cleaning redfish and Sharon sitting at a window with a lapful of snapbeans. The board sash opens out over the swamp where a flock of redwings rattle like gourds and ride down the cattails, wings sprung out to show their scarlet epaulets. Jean-Paul swings over the floor, swiveling around on his fat hip, his sharklike flesh whispering over the rough boards, and puts his finger into the cracks to get at the lapping water. There comes to me on the porch the voices of the morning, the quarreling late eleven o'clock sound of the redwings and the talk of the women, easy in its silences, come together, not in their likenesses (for how different they are: Sharon's studied upcountry exclamations—"I surely didn't know people ate crawfish!"—by which she means that in Eufala only Negroes eat crawfish; and my mother's steady catarrhal hum—"If Roy wants bisque this year, he'd better buy it—do you know how long it takes to make bisque?") but come together rather in their womanness and under the easy dispensation of the kitchen.

The children are skiing with Roy. The blue boat rides up and down the bayou, opening the black water like a knife. The gear piled at the end of the dock, yellow nylon rope and crimson lifebelt, makes aching phosphor colors in the sunlight.

Lonnie finds me and comes bumping his chair into my cot. On Sundays he wears his suit and his snapbrim felt hat. He has taken off his coat but his tie is still knotted tightly and fastened by a chain-and-bar clasp. When Lonnie gets dressed up, he looks like a little redneck come to a wedding.

"Do you want to renew your subscriptions?"

"I might. How many points do you have?"

"A hundred and fourteen."

"Doesn't that make you first?"

"Yes, but it doesn't mean I'll stay first."

"How much?"

"Twelve dollars, but you don't have to renew."

The clouds roll up from Chandeleur Island. They hardly seem to move, but their shadows come racing across the grass like a dark wind. Lonnie has trouble looking at me. He tries to even his eyes with mine and this sets his head weaving. I sit up.

Lonnie takes the money in his pronged fingers and sets about putting it into his wallet, a bulky affair with an album of plastic envelopes filled with holy cards.

"What is first prize this year?"

"A Zenith Trans-World."

"But you have a radio."

"Standard band." Lonnie gazes at me. The blue stare holds converse, has its sentences and periods. "If I get the Zenith, I won't miss television so much."

"I would reconsider that. You get a great deal of pleasure from television."

Lonnie appears to reconsider. But he is really enjoying the talk. A smile plays at the corner of his mouth. Lonnie's monotonous speech gives him an advantage, the same advantage foreigners have: his words are not worn out. It is like a code tapped through a wall. Sometimes he asks me straight out: do you love me? and it is possible to tap back: yes, I love you.

"Moreover, I do not think you should fast," I tell him.

"Why not?"

"You've had pneumonia twice in the past year. It would not be good for you. I doubt if your confessor would allow it. Ask him."

"He is allowing it."

"On what grounds?"

"To conquer an habitual disposition." Lonnie uses the peculiar idiom of the catechism in ordinary speech. Once he told me I needn't worry about some piece of foolishness he heard me tell Linda, since it was not a malicious lie but rather a "jocose lie."

"What disposition is that?"

"A disposition to envy."

"Envy who?"

"Duval."

"Duval is dead."

"Yes. But envy is not merely sorrow at another's good fortune: it is also joy at another's misfortune."

"Are you still worried about that? You accused yourself and received absolution, didn't you?"

"Yes."

"Then don't be scrupulous."

"I'm not scrupulous."

"Then what's the trouble?"

"I'm still glad he's dead."

"Why shouldn't you be? He sees God face to face and you don't."

Lonnie grins at me with the liveliest sense of our complicity: let them ski all they want to. We have something better. His expression is complex. He knows that I have entered the argument as a game played by his rules and he knows that I know it, but he does not mind.

"Jack, do you remember the time Duval went to the field meet in Jackson and won first in American history and the next day made all-state guard?"

"Yes."

"I hoped he would lose."

"That's not hurting Duval."

"It is hurting me. You know what capital sin does to the life of the soul."

"Yes. Still and all I would not fast. Instead I would concentrate on the Eucharist. It seems a more positive thing to do."

"That is true." Again the blue eyes engage mine in lively converse, looking, looking away, and looking again. "But Eucharist is a sacrament of the living."

"You don't wish to live?"

"Oh sure!" he says laughing, willing, wishing even, to lose the argument so that I will be sure to have as much fun as he.

It is a day for clouds. The clouds come sailing by, swelled out like clippers. The creamy vapor boils up into great thundering ranges and steep valleys of cloud. A green snake swims under the dock. I can see the sutures between the plates of its flat skull. It glides through the water without a ripple, stops mysteriously and nods against a piling.

"Jack?"

"Yes?"

"Are we going for a ride?"

For Lonnie our Sundays together have a program. First we talk, usually on a religious subject; then we take a ride; then he asks me to do him like Akim.

The ride is a flying trip over the boardwalk and full tilt down the swamp road. Lonnie perches on the edge of his chair and splits the wind until tears run out of his eyes. When the clouds come booming up over the savannah, the creatures of the marsh hush for a second then set up a din of croaking and pumping.

Back on the porch he asks me to do him like Akim. I come for him in his chair. It has to be a real beating up or he won't be satisfied. During my last year in college I discovered that I was picking up the mannerisms of Akim Tamiroff, the only useful thing, in fact, that I learned in the entire four years.

"I must get those plans."

"Come on now Jack don't." Lonnie shrinks back fearfully-joyfully. His hand curls like a burning leaf.

My mother sticks her head out of the kitchen.

"Now aren't those two a case?" She turns back to Sharon. "I'll tell you, that Lonnie and Jack are one more *case*."

After I kiss him good-by, Lonnie calls me back. But he doesn't really have anything to say.

"Wait."

"What?"

He searches the swamp, smiling.

"Do you think that Eucharist—"

"Yes?"

He forgets and is obliged to say straight out: "I am still offering my communion for you."

"I know you are."

"Wait."

"What?"

"Do you love me?"

"Yes."

"How much?"

"Quite a bit."

"I love you too." But already he has the transistor in the crook of his wrist and is working at it furiously.

7

On its way home the MG becomes infested with malaise. It is not unexpected, since Sunday afternoon is always the worst time for malaise. Thousands of cars are strung out along the Gulf Coast, whole families, and all with the same vacant headachy look. There is an exhaust fume in the air and the sun strikes the water with a malignant glint. A fine Sunday afternoon, though. A beautiful boulevard, ten thousand handsome cars, fifty thousand handsome, well-fed and kind-hearted people, and the malaise settles on us like a fall-out.

Sorrowing, hoping against hope, I put my hand on the thickest and innerest part of Sharon's thigh.

She bats me away with a new vigor.

"Son, don't you mess with me."

"Very well, I won't," I say gloomily, as willing not to mess with her as mess with her, to tell the truth.

"That's all right. You come here."

"I'm here."

She gives me a kiss. "I got your number, son. But that's all right. You're a good old boy. You really tickle me." She's been talking to my mother. "Now you tend to your business and get me on home."

"Why?"

"I have to meet someone."

Four

S AM YERGER is waiting for me on the sidewalk, bigger than life. Really his legs are as big and round as an elephant's in their heavy cylindrical linens and great flaring brogues. Seeing him strikes a pang to the marrow; he has the urgent gentle manner of an emissary of bad news. Someone has died.

Beyond a doubt he is waiting for me. At the sight of my MG, he makes an occult sign and comes quickly to the curb.

"Meet me in the basement," he actually whispers and turns and goes immediately up the wooden steps, his footsteps echoing like pistol shots.

Sam looks very good. Though he is rumpled and red-eyed, he is, as always, of a piece, from his bearish-big head and shoulders and his soft collar riding up like a ruff into the spade of hair at the back of his neck to his elephant legs and black brogues. It would be a pleasure to be red-eyed and rumpled if one could do it with Sam's style. His hair makes two waves over his forehead in the Nelson Eddy style of a generation ago.

Sam Yerger's mother, Aunt Mady, was married to Judge Anse's law partner, old man Ben Yerger. After college in the East, Sam left Feliciana Parish for good and worked on the old New Orleans *Item*. In the nineteen thirties he wrote a humorous book about the French-speaking Negroes called *Yambilaya Ya-Ya* which was made into a stage show and later a movie. During the war Sam was chief of the Paris bureau of a wire service. I remember hearing a CBS news analyst call him "an able and well-informed reporter." For a while he was married to Joel Craig, a New Orleans beauty (Joel's voice, a throaty society voice richened, it always seemed to me, cured, by good whisky—took on for me the same larger-than-life plenitude as Sam himself). They lived first in the Quarter and then in the Mexican state of Chiapas, where I visited them in 1954. There he wrote a novel called *The Honored and the Dishonored* which dealt, according to the dust jacket, with "the problem of evil and the essential loneliness of man." Sam broke his leg in search of some ruins in a remote district and nearly died before

128

some Indians found the two of them. He and Joel were very fond of each other and liked to joke in a way that at first seemed easy-going. For example, Sam liked to say that Joel was just the least little bit pregnant, and before they were married Joel liked to say that she was sick and tired of being Sam's bawd; I liked hearing her say *bawd* in that big caramel voice. She liked to call me Leftenant: "Leftenant, it has at long last dawned on me what it is about you that attracts me." "What?" I asked, shifting around uneasily. "You've got dignidad, Leftenant." It was not a good thing to say because thereafter I could never say or do anything without a consciousness of my dignity. When I visited them in Mexico, each spoke highly of the other and in the other's presence, which was slightly embarrassing. "He's quite a guy," Joel told me. "Do you know what he told me after lying under a cliff for thirty six hours with two inches of his femur sticking out? He said: Queenie, I think I'm going to pass out and before I do, I'm going to give you a piece of advice— God, I thought he was going to die and knew and was telling me what to do with his book—and he said quite solemnly: Queenie, always stick to Bach and the early Italians—and passed out cold as a mackerel. And by God, it's not bad advice." Sam would say of Joel: "She's a fine girl. Always cherish your woman, Binx." I told him I would. That summer I had much to thank him for. At the City College of Mexico I had met this girl from U.C.L.A. named Pat Pabst and she had come down with me to Chiapas. "Always cherish your woman," Sam told me and stomped around in very good style with his cane. I looked over at Pat Pabst who, I knew, was in Mexico looking for the Real Right Thing. And here it was: old Sam, a regular bear of a writer with his black Beethoven face, pushing himself around with a stoic sort of gracefulness; and I in my rucksack and with just the hint of an old Virginian voice. It was all her little California heart desired. She clave to me for dear life. After leaving Mexico—he had been overtaken by nostalgia, the characteristic mood of repetition—Sam returned to Feliciana where he wrote a nostalgic book called *Happy Land* which was commended in the reviews as a nice blend of a moderate attitude toward the race question and a conservative affection for the values of the agrarian South. An earlier book, called *Curse upon the Land*, which the dust jacket described as "an

impassioned plea for tolerance and understanding," had not
been well received in Feliciana. Now and then Sam turns up in
New Orleans on a lecture tour and visits my aunt and horses
around with Kate and me. We enjoy seeing him. He calls me
Brother Andy and Kate Miss Ruby.

"We've got to get Kate out of here and to do it, I need your
help."

Sam comes bursting through Kate's new shutters and starts
pacing up and down the tiny courtyard where I sit hunched
over and bemused by the malaise. I notice that Kate has begun
peeling plaster from the wall of the basement, exposing more
plantation brick. "Here's the story. She's going to New York
and you're going to take her there. Take her there today and
wait for me—I'll be back in ten days. She is to see Étienne
Suë—you know who he is: one of those fabulous continental
geniuses who is as well known for his work in Knossan antiqui-
ties as his clinical researches. The man is chronically ill himself and sees no more than a handful of patients, but he'll see
Kate. I've already called him. But here is the master stroke. I've
already made arrangements for her to stay with the Princess."

"The Princess?"

There is a noise above us. I blink up into the thin sunlight.
Bessie Coe—so called to distinguish her from Bessie Baham
the laundress—a speckle-faced Negress with a white lip, leans
out from the servant's walk to shake a mop. Since she is kitchen
help, she can allow herself to greet me in the old style. "Mist
Binx," she declares hoarsely, hollering it out over my head
to the neighborhood in a burlesque of a greeting yet good-
naturedly and even inviting me to join in the burlesque.

"She is seventy five years old, a little bitty dried-up old thing
and next to Em the most charming, the wittiest and the wisest
woman I ever knew. She has been of more service to us in the
U.N. than the entire American delegation. Her place is always
electric with excitement. Kate—who in my opinion is already a
great lady—would find herself for the first time. The long and
the short of it is she needs a companion. The very night I left
New York she said to me: now you listen here—while you are
in your American South, you make it your business to find me
a nice Southern girl—you know the kind I have in mind. Of
course the kind she had in mind is the Southerner who is so

curiously like the old-style Russian gentry. I thought no more about it until last night as I watched Kate go up the steps. My God, I said, there goes Natasha Rostov. Have you ever noticed it?"

"Natasha?" I say blinking. "What has happened? Has something happened to Kate?"

"I am not sure what happened." Sam places heel to toe and, holding his elbow in his hand and his arm straight up and down in front of him—himself gathered to a point, aimed— puffs a cigarette. "Certainly there was nothing wrong when Kate went to bed at two o'clock this morning. On the contrary. She was exalted. We had had, she and I and Em, four hours of the best talk I ever had anywhere. She was the most fascinating woman in New Orleans and she damn well knew it."

(Aye, sweet Kate, and I know too. I know your old upside-down trick: when all is lost, when they despair of you, then it is, at this darkest hour, that you emerge as the gorgeous one.)

"Emily and I talked for a little while longer and went up to bed. It was not later than two thirty. At four o'clock something woke me. What it was I can't for the life of me recall but I awoke with the most importunate sense of something wrong. I went into the hall. There was a light under Kate's door but I heard nothing. So I went back to bed and slept until eight." Sam speaks in a perfunctory voice, listing items rapidly and accurately in a professional style. "When Kate had not appeared for breakfast by ten o'clock, Emily sent Mercer up with a tray. Meanwhile Jules had left for church. Mercer knocked at Kate's door and called out loudly enough to be heard downstairs and received no answer. Now Emily was visibly alarmed and asked me to come up with her. For ten minutes we knocked and called (do you know how very long ten minutes is?). So what the hell, I kicked the door down. Kate was in bed and deeply asleep, it seemed to me. But her breathing was quite shallow and there was a bottle of capsules open on the table. But it was by no means empty—I judge that it was just over one third filled. Anyhow, Emily could not wake her up. Whereupon she, Emily, became extremely agitated and asked me to call Dr Mink. By the time he arrived, of course, Kate had waked up and was lashing out with a particularly malevolent and drunken sort of violence. Toward Emily she exhibited a cold fury which was actually frightening. When she told us to get the hell out, I can assure you that I obeyed at once. Dr Mink lavaged her stomach and gave her a stimulant—" Sam looks at his watch, "—that was an hour ago. Now that fellow has pretty good nerve. He wouldn't put her in the hospital which would have been the cagey thing to do. Emily asked him what he proposed to do. He said Kate had promised to see him Monday and that was good enough for him—and as for the pentobarbital, no one could really keep anybody else from swallowing any number any time he wanted to. He's a great admirer of Suë, by the way. We did manage to get the bottle, however—"

"Sam!" My aunt's voice, low and rich in overtones of meaning, comes down to us.

Sam looks down past his arm to see that his heel is aligned properly. I start up nervously, uneasy that Sam might have missed the warning in my aunt's voice.

"One more thing. Oscar and Edna are here. Now wouldn't you know they'd be? But perhaps it is just as well. For it is an awkward moment for Kate. The trick is for her to show herself. Here's what we hit upon: you show up, knowing nothing, come looking for her and fetch her down to dinner."

My aunt catches my eye from the dining room and I go in to kiss her and speak to the Oscar Bollings. Things seem calm enough. Uncle Jules is laughing with Aunt Edna about something. Though Aunt Emily is abstracted, temple propped on three fingers, she speaks cheerfully, and I can't help but wonder if Sam's story is not exaggerated. Uncle Oscar and Aunt Edna have come down from Feliciana Parish for Carnival and the Spring Pilgrimage, an annual tour of old houses and patios. Aunt Edna is a handsome stoutish woman with snapping black eyes and a near-mustache. Though she is at least sixty five, her hair is still black and loops back over her ears in a way that makes me think of "raven tresses." Uncle Oscar is all dressed up, but you can tell he is countrified. The fourth of the elder Bolling brothers, he elected to be neither soldier nor lawyer nor doctor but storekeeper—that is, until his recent success in exhibiting Lynwood to tourists at a dollar a head. In certain quirks of expression and waggings of head, he is startlingly like Judge Anse, but there is a flattening of the nosebridge and a softening of the forehead and a giddy light-blue amiability about the eyes. Upon the death of the brothers and the emigration of the girls, Uncle Oscar and Aunt Edna fell heir to the old place. It is not much of a showplace, to be honest (it never occurred to anyone to give it a name until Aunt Edna thought of Lynwood), being a big old rambling pile and having no special virtue save only its deep verandas and its avenue of oaks. But Uncle Oscar and Aunt Edna managed to fix it up wonderfully well and even win a permanent place on the Azalea Trail. Strangely enough, it was not Uncle Oscar, the old settler, who restored the house in the best Natchez style—adding a covered walk to the out-kitchen, serving mint juleps where the Bollings had never drunk anything but toddies, and even dressing up poor old Shad in a Seagram's butler suit and putting him out on the highway with a dinner bell—it was not Uncle Oscar but Aunt Edna, the druggist's daughter from upstate New York whom Uncle Oscar met and married while he was training at Plattsburg in the first world war.

When I bend to kiss her, my aunt gives me no sign whatever, beyond her usual gray look and the usual two quick pats on the cheek—no sign, unless it is a certain depth of irony, a gray under gray.

There comes to me in the ascent a brief annunciatory syllable in the throat stopped in the scrape of a chair as if, having signaled me and repenting of it, it had then to pass itself off as but one of the small day noises of the house. Off the landing is a dark little mezzanine arranged as a room of furniture. It is a place one passes twenty times a day and no more thinks of entering than of entering a picture, nor even of looking at, but having entered, enters with all the oddness of entering a picture, a tableau in depth wherein space is untenanted and wherefrom the view of the house, the hall and dining room below, seems at once privileged and strange. Kate is there in the shadows. She sits beside the porcelain fireplace with its glassed-in cases of medals and tufted Bohemian slippers and gold-encrusted crystal and the ambrotype of Captain Alex Bolling of the 2nd Louisiana Infantry not merely locked in but sealed in forever by glass set into the wall, an immurement which used to provoke in me the liveliest speculation by virtue of its very permanence—to think of the little objects closeted away forever in the same sequestered air of 1938—Kate sits, herself exempt from the needs and necessaries of all passers-by, and holds her arms in her hands and cheerfully makes room for me in the love seat. Not until later do I think why it is she looks so well: she is all dressed up, for the first time since Christmas. It is the scent of her perfume, her nylon-whispering legs, the white dress against her dark skin, a proper dress fluted and flounced and now gathered by her and folded away from me.

The angle is such that we can see the dining room and its company, except my aunt. There is only her right wrist and hand curving out and under the chair arm to rub the lion's face with its cloven leprous nose.

"Tell Mother that I am fine and that I will be down later. I am not hungry." Then I will indeed be fine, Kate as good as says. It is her sense of their waiting upon her and that alone that intrudes itself into her mezzanine.

When I return (my aunt received me with a single grave nod), Kate is smoking, inhaling deeply and blowing plumes of lung smoke into the air. Her knees are crossed and she swings her leg and holds her Zippo and pack in her lap.

"Have you seen Sam?" she asks me.

"Yes."

"What did he tell you?"

"That you had a bad night and that Merle had been here." I tell her the truth because I have not the wit to tell her anything else. Kate knows it: I am the not-quite-bright one whom grown-ups take aside to question.

"Hm. Do you want to know the truth? I had a very good night. Possibly the best night of my life."

Sam touches knife to goblet. As is his custom, he speaks down the table to my aunt but with a consciousness of the others as listeners-in. At his right, Uncle Jules is content to listen in and look on with an expression of almost besotted amiability. This is one of Em's "dinners," Sam is speaking at the Forum, Em is president. Long ago he, Uncle Jules, and with the same shrewdness with which recognizes signs of corporate illness and corporate health, made out a certain pattern in Emily's lecturers. Persons of the most advanced views on every subject and of the most exquisite sensitivity to minorities (except Catholics, but this did not bother Uncle Jules), they were nevertheless observed by him to observe the same taboos and celebrate the same rites. Not so Uncle Oscar. Sitting there rared back and gazing up at the chandelier, he too is aware that he has fallen in with pretty high-flown company, but he will discover no such thing; any moment now he will violate a taboo and blaspheme a rite by getting off on niggers, Mrs Roosevelt, dagos and Jews, and all in the same breath. But Uncle Jules will neither trespass nor be trespassed upon. His armor is his unseriousness. It would never occur to him to take their, Aunt Emily's lecturers', irreverent sallies as an assault upon his own deep dumb convictions. The worst they can do is live up to themselves, behave just as he has come to expect "Em's people" to behave.

Sam tolls his goblet. "Last Thursday, Em, Eric got back from Geneva and I met him at the airport. His face was white as chalk—"

Kate, who has been sitting back and peering down her cheek at Sam like a theater-goer in the balcony, begins smoothing out the cellophane of her cigarette pack.

"We talked like that last night. I was very happy—"

Aunt Edna leans out to intercept Sam's monologue. She has not yet caught on to Sam's way of talking, so she is upset. "But what can a person *do*?"—and she actually wrings her hands. Aunt Edna is as nice as can be, but she is one of our kinfolks I avoid. Her soul is in her eyes and when we meet, she shoots me deep theosophical soul-glances, and though I shoot them back and am quite sympathetic on the whole, it is an uneasy business.

"Sam is a very gentle person and a very kind person," says Kate.

"I know."

"He is very fond of you. Are you going to hear his lecture?"

"I would like to, but I have to get up early tomorrow morning and go to Chicago."

"What for?"

"Business."

"We had a wonderful evening, but when I went to bed, I was somewhat apprehensive. You know how you have to guard against Sam's flights?"

"Yes."

"Whatever goes up must come down and I was ten miles high."

"I know."

"But I was on guard and I did not fall. I went straight to bed and to sleep. Then some hours later I awoke suddenly. There was nothing wrong. I was wide awake and completely alert. I thought about your proposal and it seemed to me that it might be possible after all. If only I did not ruin everything."

Mercer passes a dish of sweet potatoes. At each place he stops breathing, head thrown back and eyes popping out, then lets out his breath with a strangling sound.

Uncle Oscar has hiked an arm back over his chair and says something to Sam. I can't make it out but I recognize the voice, the easy garrulity wheezing off into a laughter which solicits your agreement and threatens reprisal if you withhold it. Yet I used to like Uncle Oscar's store in Feliciana—to hear his voice now is almost to smell the floorboards soured by wet Growena. But even then, to be there and to be solicited by him was a perilous thing. It was a perilous thing to see him do battle in the deadly arena of a country store, see him gird himself to annihilate his opponent and, to insure himself against counterattack, go wheezing off into easy laughter and so claim the victory.

"Oscar!" cries Aunt Edna, pretending to be in a buzzing good humor. Already she can hear Sam in Dallas: "I heard a delightful commentary on the mind of the South last week—" Leaning over, she gives Uncle Oscar a furious affectionate pat which signifies that he is a good fellow and we all love him. It also signifies that he can shut up.

"There was no question of sleep," says Kate. "I came downstairs and found one of Father's mysteries and went back to bed and read the whole thing. It was about some people in Los Angeles. The house was dark and still and once in a while a boat whistle blew on the river. I saw how my life could be—living as a neat little person like Della Street, doing my stockings every night. But then I remembered what happened in Memphis. Did you know I lived in Memphis once?"

My aunt pays as little attention to Uncle Oscar as to Sam.

Her thumbnail methodically combs the grooves which represent the lion's mane.

"It was in 1951—you were in the army. Father and I were warring over politics. Come to think of it, I might actually have been kicked out of the house. Anyhow Mother suggested it might be a good thing if I went to visit an old classmate of hers in Memphis, a lady named Mrs Boykin Lamar. She was really quite a person, had sung in the Civic Opera in New York and wrote quite a funny book about her travels in Europe as a girl. They were as kind to me as anyone could be. But no one could think of anything to say. Night after night we sat there playing operas on the phonograph and dreading the moment when the end came and someone had to say something. I became so nervous that one night I slipped on the hearth and fell into the fire. Can you believe it was a relief to suffer extreme physical pain? Hell couldn't be fire—there are worse things than fire. I moved to a hotel and for a while I was all right. I had a job doing case work and I had plenty of dates. But after a while the room began to reproach me. When I came home from work every afternoon, the sun would be setting across the river in Arkansas and every day the yellow light became sadder and sadder. And Arkansas over there in the yellow West—O my God, you have no idea how sad it looked. One afternoon I packed my suitcase and caught the Illinois Central for home."

Sam is spieling in pretty good style, all the while ironing out the tablecloth into shallow gutters with the blade of his knife. A new prefatory note creeps into his voice. It is like a symphony when the "good" part is coming, and I know that Sam is working up to one of his stories. These stories of Sam used to arouse in me an appreciation so keen and pleasurable that it bordered on the irritable. On the dark porch in Feliciana he told us once of the time when he made a journey up the headwaters of the Orinoco and caught a fever and lay ill for weeks. One night he heard an incredibly beautiful voice sing the whole of *Winterreise*. He was sure it was delirium until the next morning when he met the singer, an Austrian engineer who sang lieder better than Lotte Lehmann, etc. When he finished I was practically beside myself with irritable pleasure and became angry with the others because they were not sufficiently moved by the experience.

"Emily, do you remember the night we saw *There Shall Be No Night* and you were so moved that you insisted on walking all the way back to the Carlyle?"

But Kate pays no attention. She holds her feathered thumb to the light and inspects it minutely. "Last night everything was fine until I finished the book. Then it became a matter of waiting. What next, I thought. I began to get a little scared—for the first time I had the feeling of coming to the end of my rope. I became aware of my own breathing. Things began to slip a little. I fixed myself a little drink and took two nembutals and waited for the lift."

It is the first time she has spoken of her capsules. My simple-mindedness serves her well.

"You know what happened then? What did Sam say? Never mind. Did you see Merle? No? Hm. What happened was the most trivial thing imaginable, nothing grand at all, though I would like to think it was. I took six or eight capsules altogether. I knew that wouldn't kill me. My Lord, I didn't want to die—not at that moment. I only wanted to—break out, or off, off dead center— Listen. Isn't it true that the only happy men are wounded men? Admit it! Isn't that the truth?" She breaks off and goes off into a fit of yawning. "I felt so queer. Everything seemed so—no 'count somehow, you know?" She swings her foot and hums a little tune. "To tell you the truth, I can't remember too well. How strange. I've always remembered every little thing."

"—and you spoke to me for the first time of your messianic hopes?" Sam smiles at my aunt. In Feliciana we used to speculate on the new messiah, the scientist-philosopher-mystic who would come striding through the ruins with the *Gita* in one hand and a Geiger counter in the other. But today Sam miscalculates. My aunt says nothing. The thumbnail goes on combing the lion's mane.

Dinner over, Uncle Oscar waits in the dining room until the others have left, then seizes his scrotum and gives his leg a good shake.

I rise unsteadily, sleepy all at once to the point of drunkenness.

"Wait." Kate takes my arm urgently in both hands. "I am going with you."

"All right. But first I think I'll take a little nap on the porch."

"I mean to Chicago."

"Chicago?"

"Yes. Do you mind if I go?"

"No."

"When are you leaving?"

"Tomorrow morning."

"Could you change it to tonight and get two tickets on the train?"

"Why the train?" I begin to realize how little I have slept during the past week.

"I'll tell you what. You go lie down and I'll take care of it."

"All right."

"After Chicago do you think there is a possibility we might take a trip out west and stay for a while in some little town like Modesto or Fresno?"

"It is possible."

"I'll fix everything." She sounds very happy. "Do you have any money?"

"Yes."

"Give it to me."

It is a matter for astonishment, I think drowsily in the hammock, that Kate should act with such dispatch—out she came, heels popping, arm in arm with her stepmother, snapped her purse and with Sam looking on, somewhat gloomily it struck me, off she went in her stiff little Plymouth—and then I think why. It is trains. When it comes to a trip, to the plain business of going, just stepping up into the Pullman and gliding out of town of an evening, she is as swift and remorseless as Della Street.

Now later, on Prytania, Uncle Oscar hands Aunt Edna into the station wagon—they are bound for their Patio-by-Candlelight tour—and goes huffing around to his door, rared back and with one hand pressed into his side. Sam tiptoes to the screen. "Well now look ahere, Brother Andy. Ain't that the Kingfish and Madame Queen? Sho 'tis."

In this vertigo of exhaustion, laughter must be guarded against like retching.

"Brother Andy, is you getting much?"

"No." My stomach further obliges Sam with a last despairing heave. Oh Lord.

Later there seems to come into my hand—and with it some instructions from Sam of which there is no more to be remembered than that they were delivered in the tone of one of my aunt's grand therapeutic schemes—a squarish bottle, warmed by Sam's body and known to my fingers through the ridge of glass left by the mold and the apothecary symbol *oz* or 3 or ℥.

2

Sure enough, three hours later we are rocking along an uneven roadbed through the heart of the Ponchitoula swamp.

No sooner do we open the heavy door of Sieur Iberville and enter the steel corridor with its gelid hush and the stray voices from open compartments and the dark smell of going high in the nostrils—than the last ten years of my life take on the shadowy aspect of a sojourn between train rides. It was ten years ago that I last rode a train, from San Francisco to New Orleans, and so ten years since I last enjoyed the peculiar gnosis of trains, stood on the eminence from which there is revealed both the sorry litter of the past and the future bright and simple as can be, and the going itself, one's privileged progress through the world. But trains have changed. Gone are the uppers and lowers, partitions and cranks, and the green velour; only the porter remains, the same man, I think, a black man with palms the color of shrimp and a neck swollen with dislike. Our roomettes turn out to be little coffins for a single person. From time to time, I notice, people in roomettes stick their heads out into the corridor for some sight of human kind.

Kate is affected by the peculiar dispensation of trains. Her gray jacket comes just short of her wide hips and the tight skirt curves under her in a nice play on vulgarity. On the way to the observation car she pulls me into the platform of the vestibule and gives me a kiss, grabbing me under the coat like a waitress. In celebration of Mardi Gras, she has made up her eyes with

a sparkle of mascara and now she looks up at me with a black
spiky look.

"Are we going to live in Modesto?"

"Sure," I say, uneasy at her playfulness. She is not as well as
she makes out. She is not safe on a train after all; it is rather
that by a kind of bravado she can skim along in the very face
of the danger.

The observation car is crowded, but we find seats together
on a sofa where I am jammed against a fellow reading a newspaper. We glide through the cottages of Carrollton cutting off
back yards in odd trapezoids, then through the country clubs
and cemeteries of Metaire. In the gathering dusk the cemeteries look at first like cities, with their rows of white vaults,
some two- and three-storied and forming flats and tenements,
and the tiny streets and corners and curbs and even plots of
lawn, all of such a proportion that in the very instant of being
mistaken and from the eye's own necessity, they set themselves
off into the distance like a city seen from far away. Now in the
suburbs we ride at a witch's level above the gravelly roofs.

It gradually forces itself upon me that a man across the aisle
is looking at me with a strange insistence. Kate nudges me. It is
Sidney Gross and his wife, beyond a doubt bound also for the
convention. The son of Sidney Gross of Danziger and Gross,
Sidney is a short fresh-faced crinkle-haired boy with the bright
beamish look Southern Jews sometimes have. There has always
been a special cordiality between us. He married a pretty Mississippi girl; she, unlike Sidney, is wary of such encounters—she
would know which of us spoke first at our last encounter—so
she casts sleepy looks right past us, pausing, despite herself on
Kate's white face and black spiky eyes. But Sidney hunches over
toward us, beaming, a stalwart little pony back with his head
well set on his shoulders and his small ears lying flat.

"Well well well. Trader Jack. So you slipped up on your plane
reservations too."

"Hello, Sidney, Margot. This is Kate Cutrer."

Margot becomes very friendly, in the gossipy style of the
Mississippi Delta.

"So you forgot about it being Mardi Gras and couldn't get
a plane."

"No, we like the train."

Sidney is excited, not by the trip as I am, but by the convention. Leaning across the aisle with a program rolled up in his hand, he explains that he is scheduled for a panel on tax relief for bond funds. "What about you?"

"I think I am taking part in something called a Cracker Barrel Session."

"You'll like it. Everybody talks right off the top of their head. You can take your coat off, get up and stretch. Anything. Last year we had this comical character from Georgia." Sidney casts about for some way of conveying just how comical and failing, passes on without minding. "What a character. Extremely comical. What's the topic?"

"Competing with the variable endowments."

"Oh yass," says Sidney with a wry look of our trade. "I don't worry about it." He slides the cylinder of paper to and fro. "Do you?"

"No."

Sidney suggests a bridge game, but Kate begs off. The Grosses move to a table in the corner and start playing gin rummy.

Kate, who has been fumbling in her purse, becomes still. I feel her eyes on my face.

"Do you have my capsules?"

"What?"

"My capsules."

"Why yes, I do. I forgot that I had them."

Not taking her eyes from my face, she receives the bottle, puts it in her purse, snaps it.

"That's not like you."

"I didn't take them."

"Who did?"

"Sam gave them to me. It was while I was in the hammock. I hardly remember it."

"He took them from my purse?"

"I don't know."

For a long moment she sits, hands in her lap, fingers curling up and stirring a little. Then abruptly she rises and leaves. When she returns, her face is scrubbed and pale, the moisture still dark at the roots of her hair. What has upset her is not the incident of the capsules but meeting the Grosses. It spoils everything, this prospect of making pleasant talk, of having a delightful time, as Sidney would put it ("There we were moping over missing the plane, when Jack Bolling shows up and we have ourselves a ball")—when we might have gone rocking up through dark old Mississippi alone together in the midst of strangers. Still she is better. Perhaps it is her reviving hope of losing the Grosses to gin rummy or perhaps it is the first secret promise of the chemicals entering her blood.

Now, picking up speed, we gain the swamp. Kate and I sway against each other and watch the headlights of the cars on the swamp road, winking through the moss like big yellow lightning bugs.

The drowsiness returns. It is unwelcome. I recognize it as the sort of fitful twilight which has come over me of late, a twilight where waking dreams are dreamed and sleep never comes.

The man next to me is getting off in St Louis. When the conductor comes to collect our tickets, he surrenders a stub: he is going home. His suit is good. He sits with his legs crossed, one well-clad haunch riding up like a ham, his top leg held out at an obtuse angle by the muscle of his calf. His brown hair is youthful (he himself is thirty-eight or forty) and makes a cowlick in front. With the cowlick and the black eyeglasses he looks quite a bit like the actor Gary Merrill and has the same certified permission to occupy pleasant space with his pleasant self. In ruddy good health, he muffles a hearty belch in a handkerchief. This very evening, no doubt, he has had an excellent meal at Galatoire's, and the blood of his portal vein bears away a golden harvest of nutrient globules. When he first goes through his paper, he opens it like a book and I have no choice but to read the left page with him. We pause at an advertisement of a Bourbon Street nightclub which is a picture of a dancer with an oiled body. Her triceps arch forward like a mare's. For a second we gaze heavy-lidded and pass on. Now he finds what he wants and folds his paper once, twice and again, into a neat packet exactly two columns wide, like a subway rider in New York. Propping it against his knee, he takes out a slender gold pencil, makes a deft one-handed adjustment, and underlines several sentences with straight black lines (he is used to underlining). Dreaming at his shoulder, I can make out no more than

In order to deepen and enrich the marital—

It is a counseling column which I too read faithfully.

The train sways through the swamp. The St Louisan, breathing powerfully through the stiff hairs of his nose, succeeds in sitting in such a manner, tilted over on his right hip and propped against himself, that his thigh forms a secure writing platform for the packet.

The voices in the car become fretful. It begins to seem that the passengers have ridden together for a long time and have developed secret understandings and old grudges. They speak crossly and elliptically to each other.

Staying awake is a kind of sickness and sleep is forever guarded against by a dizzy dutiful alertness. Waking wide-eyed dreams come as fitfully as swampfire.

Dr and Mrs Bob Dean autograph copies of their book *Technique in Marriage* in a Canal Street department store. A pair of beauties. I must have come in all the way from Gentilly, for I stand jammed against a table which supports a pyramid of books. I cannot take my eyes from the Deans: an oldish couple but still handsome and both, rather strangely, heavily freckled. As they wait for the starting time, they are jolly with each other and swap banter in the professional style of show people (I believe these preliminaries are called the warm-up). "No, we never argue," says Bob Dean. "Because whenever an argument starts, we consult the chapter I wrote on arguments." "No, dear," says Jackie Dean. "It was I who wrote the chapter—" etc. Everyone laughs. I notice that nearly all the crowd jamming against me are women, firm middle-aged one-fifty pounders. Under drooping lids I watch the Deans, peculiarly affected by their routine which is staged so effortlessly that during the exchange of quips, they are free to cast business-like looks about them as if no one were present. But when they get down to business, they become as sober as Doukhobors and effuse an air of dedicated almost evangelical helpfulness. A copy of the book lies open on the table. I read: "Now with a tender regard for your partner remove your hand from the nipple and gently manipulate—" It is impossible not to imagine them at their researches, as solemn as a pair of brontosauruses, their heavy old freckled limbs twined about each other, hands probing skillfully for sensitive zones, pigmented areolas, out-of-the-way mucous glands, dormant vascular nexuses. A wave of prickling passes over me such as I have never experienced before.

My head, nodding like a daffodil, falls a good three inches toward the St Louisan before it jerks itself up. Kate sits shivering against me, but the St Louisan is as warm and solid as roast beef. As the train rocks along on its unique voyage through space-time, thousands of tiny thing-events bombard us like cosmic particles. Lying in a ditch outside is a scrap of newspaper with the date May 3, 1954. My Geiger counter clicks away like a teletype. But no one else seems to notice. Everyone is buried in his magazine. Kate is shaking like a leaf because she longs to be an anyone who is anywhere and she cannot.

The St Louisan reads a headline

SCIENTIST PREDICTS FUTURE IF
NUCLEAR ENERGY IS NOT MISUSED

Out comes the gold pencil to make a neat black box. After reading for a moment he comes back to the beginning and is about to make a second concentric box, thinks better of it, takes from his pocket a silver knife, undoes the scissors and clips the whole article, folds it and places it in his wallet. It is impossible to make out any of the underlined passages except the phrase: "the gradual convergence of physical science and social science."

A very good phrase. I have to admire the St Louisan for his neat and well-ordered life, his gold pencil and his scissors-knife and his way of clipping articles on the convergence of the physical sciences and the social sciences; it comes over me that in the past few days my own life has gone to seed. I no longer eat and sleep regularly or write philosophical notes in my notebook and my fingernails are dirty. The search has spoiled the pleasure of my tidy and ingenious life in Gentilly. As late as a week ago, such a phrase as "hopefully awaiting the gradual convergence of the physical sciences and the social sciences" would have provoked no more than an ironic tingle or two at the back of my neck. Now it howls through the Ponchitoula Swamp, the very sound and soul of despair.

Kate has stopped shivering and when she lights up and starts smoking, I am certain she is better. But I am mistaken. "Oooh," she says in a perfunctory workaday voice and starts forward again. The car lurches and throws her against Sidney's chair; there the train holds her fast: for three seconds she might be taken for a rapt onlooker of the gin-rummy game. Sidney rocks the deck against the polished wood until the cards are perfectly aligned. The gold ring on his little finger seems to serve as a device, a neat little fastening by means of which his hand movements are harnessed and made trim.

Half an hour passes and Kate does not return. I find her in her roomette, arms folded and face turned to the dark glass. We sit knee to knee.

"Are you all right?"

She nods slowly to the window, but her cheek is against me. Outside a square of yellow light flees along an embankment, falls away to the woods and fields, comes roaring back good as new. Suddenly a perky head pops up. Kate is leaning forward hugging herself.

"I am all right. I am never too bad with you."

"Why?"

"No thanks to you. On the contrary. The others are much more sympathetic than you, especially Mother and Sam."

"What about Merle?"

"Merle! Listen, with Merle I could break wind and he would give me that same quick congratulatory look. But you. You're nuttier than I am. One look at you and I have to laugh. Do you think that is sufficient ground for marriage?"

"As good as any. Better than love."

"Love! What do you know about love?"

"I didn't say I knew anything about it."

She is back at her window, moving her hand to see it move in the flying yellow square. We hunch up knee to knee and nose to nose like the two devils on the Rorschach card. Something glitters in the corner of her eye. Surely not a tear.

"Quite a Carnival. Two proposals in one Mardi Gras."

"Who else?"

"Sam."

"No kidding."

"No kidding. And I'll tell you something else. Sam is quite a person behind that façade. An essentially lonely person."

"I know."

"You're worse than Sam." She is angry.

"How?"

"Sam is a schemer. He also likes me. He knows that someday I will be quite rich. But he also likes me. That isn't so bad. Scheming is human. You have to be human to be a schemer. Whenever I see through one of Sam's little schemes, I feel a sensation of warmth. Ah ha, think I to myself, so it must have been in the world once—men and women wanting something badly and scheming away like beavers. But you—"

"Yes?"

"You're like me. So let us not deceive one another."

Her voice is steadier. Perhaps it is the gentle motion of the train with which we nod ever so slightly, yes, yes, yes.

She says: "Can't you see that for us it is much too late for such ingenious little schemes?"

"As marrying?"

"The only way you could carry it off is as another one of your ingenious little researches. Admit it."

"Then why not do it?"

"You remind me of a prisoner in the death house who takes a wry pleasure in doing things like registering to vote. Come to think of it, all your gaiety and good spirits have the same death house quality. No thanks. I've had enough of your death house pranks."

"What is there to lose?"

"Can't you see that after what happened last night, it is no use. I can't play games now. But don't you worry. I'm not going to swallow all the pills at once. Losing hope is not so bad. There's something worse: losing hope and hiding it from yourself."

"Very well. Lose hope or not. Be afraid or not. But marry me anyhow, and we can still walk abroad on a summer night, hope or no hope, shivering or not, and see a show and eat some oysters down on Magazine."

"No no."

"I don't understand—"

"You're right. You don't understand. It is not some one thing, as you think. It is everything. It is all so monstrous."

"What is monstrous?"

"I told you," she says irritably. "Everything. I'm not up to it. Having a little hubby—you would be hubby, dearest Binx, and that is ridiculous—did I hurt your feelings? Seeing hubby off in the morning, having lunch with the girls, getting tight at Eddie's and Nell's house and having a little humbug with somebody else's hubby, wearing my little diaphragm and raising my two lovely boys and worrying for the next twenty years about whether they will make Princeton."

"I told you we would live in Gentilly. Or Modesto."

"I was being ingenious like you."

"Do you want to live like Sam and Joel?"

"Binx Binx. You're just like your aunt. When I told her how I felt, she said to me: Katherine, you're perfectly right. Don't ever lose your ideals and your enthusiasm for ideas—she thought I was talking about something literary or political or Great Books, for God's sake. I thought to myself: is that what I'm doing?—and ran out and took four pills. Incidentally they're all wrong about that. They all think any minute I'm going to commit suicide. What a joke. The truth of course is the exact opposite: suicide is the only thing that keeps me alive. Whenever everything else fails, all I have to do is consider suicide and in two seconds I'm as cheerful as a nitwit. But if I could *not* kill myself—ah then, I would. I can do without nembutal or murder mysteries but not without suicide. And that reminds me." And off she goes down the steel corridor, one hand held palm out to the wall.

None of this is new, of course. I do not, to tell the truth, pay too much attention to what she says. It is her voice that tells me how she is. Now she speaks in her "bold" tone and since she appears more composed, to the point of being cheerful, than her words might indicate, I am not seriously concerned about her.

But the roomette soon becomes suffocating and, not feeling up to talking business with Sidney Gross, I head in the opposite direction, stop in the first vestibule and have a long drink from my Mardi Gras bottle. We must be pulling into Jackson.

The train screeches slowly around a curve and through the back of town. Kate comes out and stands beside me without a word. She smells of soap and seems in vaulting good spirits.

"Have a drink?"

"Do you remember going up to Baton Rouge on the train to see the football games?"

"Sure." Balancing there, her oval face aglow in the dark vestibule, hair combed flat on her head and down into the collar of her suit, she looks like a college girl. She drinks, pressing fingers to her throat. "Lord, how beautiful."

The train has stopped and our car stands high in the air, squarely above a city street. The nearly full moon swims through streaming ragtags of cloud and sheds a brilliant light on the Capitol dome and the spanking new glass-and-steel office buildings and the empty street with its glittering streetcar track. Not a soul is in sight. Far away, beyond the wings of the Capitol building stretch the dark tree-covered hills and the twinkling lights of the town. By some trick of moonlight the city seems white as snow and never-tenanted; it sleeps away on its hilltop like the holy city of Zion.

Kate shakes her head slowly in the rapt way she got from her stepmother. I try to steer her away from beauty. Beauty is a whore.

"You see that building yonder? That's Southern Life & Accident. If you had invested a hundred dollars in 1942, you'd now be worth twenty five thousand. Your father bought a good deal of the original stock." Money is a better god than beauty.

"You don't know what I *mean*," she cries in the same soft rapture.

I know what she means all right. But I know something she doesn't know. Money is a good counterpoise to beauty. Beauty, the quest of beauty alone, is a whoredom. Ten years ago I pursued beauty and gave no thought to money. I listened to the lovely tunes of Mahler and felt a sickness in my very soul. Now I pursue money and on the whole feel better.

"I see how I could live in a city!" Kate cries. She turns to face me and clasps her hands behind my waist.

"How?"

"Only one way. By your telling me what to do. It is as simple as that. Why didn't I see it before?"

"That I should tell you what to do?"

"Yes. It may not be the noblest way of living, but it is one way. It is my way! Oh dear sweet old Binx, what a joy it is to discover at last what one is. It doesn't matter what you are as long as you *know*!"

"What are you?"

"I'll gladly tell you because I just found out and I never want to forget. Please don't let me forget. I am a religious person."

"How is that?"

"Don't you see? What I want is to believe in someone completely and then do what he wants me to do. If God were to tell me: Kate, here is what I want you to do; you get off this train right now and go over there to that corner by the Southern Life and Accident Insurance Company and stand there for the rest of your life and speak kindly to people—you think I would not do it? You think I would not be the happiest girl in Jackson, Mississippi? I would."

I have a drink and look at her corner. The moonlight seems palpable, a dense pure matrix in which is embedded curbstone and building alike.

She takes the bottle. "Will you tell me what to do?"

"Sure."

"You can do it because you are not religious. God is not religious. You are the unmoved mover. You don't need God or anyone else—no credit to you, unless it is a credit to be the most self-centered person alive. I don't know whether I love you, but I believe in you and I will do what you tell me. Now if I marry you, will you tell me: Kate, this morning do such and such, and if we have to go to a party, will you tell me: Kate, stand right there and have three drinks and talk to so and so? Will you?"

"Sure."

Kate locks her arms around my chest, wrist in hand, and gives me a passionate kiss.

Later, just as I knew it would, her precious beauty leaves her flat and she is frightened. Another trip to the washroom and now she stands swaying against me as Sieur Iberville rocks along through north Mississippi. We leave spring behind. The moon hangs westering and yellow over winter fields as blackened and ancient and haunted as battlegrounds.

"Oh oh oh," Kate moans and clings to me. "I feel awful. Let's go to your roomette."

"It's been made up."

"Then we'll lie down."

We have to lie down: the door opens onto the bed. Feeling tender toward her, I embrace her and tell her that I love her.

"Oh no," says Kate and takes hold of me coarsely. "None of that, bucko."

"None of what?"

"No love, please."

I misunderstand her and pull away.

"No no. Don't leave either," she says, holding me and watching me still.

"All right."

"Just don't speak to me of love, bucko."

"All right, but don't call me bucko."

Her black spiky eyes fall full upon me, but not quite seeing, I think. Propped on one hand, she bites her lip and lets the other fall on me heavily, as if I were an old buddy. "I'll tell you something."

"What?"

"The other day I said to Merle." Again the hand falls heavily and takes hold of me. "What would you say to me having a little fling? He misunderstood me and gave me the business about a mature and tender relation between adults etcetera etcetera—you know, I said, no no, Merle, you got it wrong. I'm talking about some plain old monkey business—" she gives me a shake, "—like a comic book one of your aunt's maids showed me last week in which Tillie the Toiler and Mac—not the real Tillie, you understand, but a Frenchy version of Tillie—go to an office party and Tillie has a little set-to with Mac in the stockroom and gets caught by Whipple. I told Merle about it and said: that's what I mean, Merle, how about that?"

"What did Merle say?"

Kate doesn't seem to hear. She drums her fingers on the sill and gazes out at the rushing treetops.

"So—when all is said and done, that is the real thing, isn't it? Admit it. You and the little Hondurian on the second floor with her little book, in the morning, in the mid-morning, and there in the linen closet with the mops and pails—"

"It is your Hondurian and your comic book—"

"Now I'll tell you what you can do, Whipple. You get out of here and come back in exactly five minutes. Oh you're a big nasty Whipple and you're only fit for one thing."

I'll have to tell you the truth, Rory, painful though it is. Nothing would please me more than to say that I had done one of two things. Either that I did what you do: tuck Debbie in your bed and, with a show of virtue so victorious as to be ferocious, grab pillow and blanket and take to the living room sofa, there to lie in the dark, hands clasped behind head, gaze at the ceiling and talk through the open door of your hopes and dreams. Or—do what a hero in a novel would do: he too is a seeker and a pilgrim of sorts and he is just in from Guanajuato or Sambuco where he has found the Real Right Thing or from the East where he apprenticed himself to a wise man and became proficient in the seventh path to the seventh happiness. Yet he does not disdain this world either and when it happens that a maid comes to his bed with a heart full of longing for him, he puts down his book in a good and cheerful spirit and gives her as merry a time as she could possibly wish for. Whereupon, with her dispatched into as sweet a sleep as ever Scarlett enjoyed the morning of Rhett's return, he takes up his book again and is in an instant ten miles high and on the Way.

No, Rory, I did neither. We did neither. We did very badly and almost did not do at all. Flesh poor flesh failed us. The burden was too great and flesh poor flesh, neither hallowed by sacrament nor despised by spirit (for despising is not the worst fate to overtake the flesh), but until this moment seen through and canceled, rendered null by the cold and fishy eye of the malaise—flesh poor flesh now at this moment summoned all at once to be all and everything, end all and be all, the last and only hope—quails and fails. The truth is I was frightened half to death by her bold (not really bold, not whorish bold but theorish bold) carrying on. I reckon I am used to my blushing little Lindas from Gentilly. Kate too was scared. We shook like leaves. Kate was scared because it seemed now that even Tillie the Toiler must fail her. I never worked so hard in my life, Rory. I had no choice: the alternative was unspeakable. Christians talk about the horror of sin, but they have overlooked some-thing. They keep talking as if everyone were a great sinner, when the truth is that nowadays one is hardly up to it. There is very little sin in the depths of the malaise. The highest moment of a malaisian's life can be that moment when he manages to sin like a proper human (Look at us, Binx—my vagabond friends as good as cried out to me—we're sinning! We're succeeding! We're human after all!).

"Good night, sweet Whipple. Now you tuck Kate in. Poor Kate." She turns the pillow over for the cool of the underside. "Good night, sweet Whipple, good night, good night, good night."

3

It turns out that my misgivings about Chicago were justified. No sooner do we step down from the train than the genie-soul of Chicago flaps down like a buzzard and perches on my shoulder. During the whole of our brief sojourn I am ridden by it—brief sojourn, I say, briefer even than it was planned to be, since it was cut abruptly short by the catastrophe Monday night, the very night of our arrival. All day long before the castastrophe I stand sunk in thought, blinking and bemused, on street corners. Kate looks after me. She is strangely at home in the city, wholly impervious to the five million personal rays of Chicagoans and the peculiar smell of existence here, which must be sniffed and gotten hold of before taking a single step away from the station (if only somebody could tell me who built the damn station, the circumstances of the building, details of the wrangling between city officials and the railroad, so that I would not fall victim to it, the station, the very first crack off the bat. Every place of arrival should have a booth set up and manned by an ordinary person whose task it is to greet strang-ers and give them a little trophy of local space-time stuff—tell them of his difficulties in high school and put a pinch of soil in their pockets—in order to insure that the stranger shall not become an Anyone). Oh son of a bitch but I am in a sweat. Kate takes charge with many a cluck and much fuss, as if she had caught sight in me of a howling void and meant to conceal it from the world. All of a sudden she is a regular city girl not distinguishable from any other little low-browed olive-skinned big-butted Mediterranean such as populates the streets and subways of the North.

I am consoled only to see that I was not mistaken: Chicago is just as I remembered it. I was here twenty five years ago. My father brought me and Scott up to see the Century of Progress and once later to the World Series. Not a single thing do I remember from the first trip but this: the sense of the place, the savor of the genie-soul of the place which every place has or else is not a place. I could have been wrong: it could have been nothing of the sort, not the memory of a place but the memory of being a child. But one step out into the brilliant March day and there it is as big as life, the genie-soul of the place which, wherever you go, you must meet and master first thing or be met and mastered. Until now, one genie-soul and only one ever proved too strong for me: San Francisco—up and down the hills I pursued him, missed him and was pursued, by a presence, a powdering of fall gold in the air, a trembling brightness that pierced to the heart, and the sadness of coming at last to the sea, the coming to the end of America. Nobody but a Southerner knows the wrenching rinsing sadness of the cities of the North. Knowing all about genie-souls and living in haunted places like Shiloh and the Wilderness and Vicksburg and Atlanta where the ghosts of heroes walk abroad by day and are more real than people, he knows a ghost when he sees one, and no sooner does he step off the train in New York or Chicago or San Francisco than he feels the genie-soul perched on his shoulder.

Here is Chicago. Now, exactly as twenty five years ago, the buildings are heavy and squarish and set down far apart and at random like monuments on a great windy plain. And the Lake. The Lake in New Orleans is a backwater glimmering away in a pleasant lowland. Not here. Here the Lake is the North itself: a perilous place from which the spirit winds come pouring forth all roused up and crying out alarm.

The wind and the space—they are the genie-soul. Son of a bitch, how can I think about variable endowments, feeling the genie-soul of Chicago perched on my shoulder?

But the wind and the space, they are the genie-soul. The

wind blows in steady from the Lake and claims the space for its own, scouring every inch of the pavements and the cold stony fronts of the buildings. It presses down between buildings, shouldering them apart in skyey fields of light and air. The air is windpressed into a lens, magnifying and sharpening and silencing—everything is silenced in the uproar of the wind that comes ransacking down out of the North. This is a city where no one dares dispute the claim of the wind and the skyey space to the out-of-doors. This Midwestern sky is the nakedest loneliest sky in America. To escape it, people live inside and underground. One other thing I remember: my father took me down into one of these monuments to see the pool where Tarzan-Johnnie-Weissmuller used to swim—an echoing underground place where a cold gray light filtered down from a three-story skylight and muscular men wearing metal discs swam and shouted, their voices ringing against the wet tile walls.

Some years later, after Scott's death, we came my father and I to the Field Museum, a long dismal peristyle dwindling away into the howling distance, and inside stood before a tableau of Stone Age Man, father mother and child crouched around an artificial ember in postures of minatory quiet—until, feeling my father's eye on me, I turned and saw what he required of me—very special father and son we were that summer, he staking his everything this time on a perfect comradeship—and I, seeing in his eyes the terrible request, requiring from me his very life; I, through a child's cool perversity or some atavistic recoil from an intimacy too intimate, turned him down, turned away, refused him what I knew I could not give.

Prepared then for the genie-soul of Chicago, we take the city in stride at first and never suffer two seconds of malaise. Kate is jolly. Straight to the Stevens to register for rooms and the Cracker Barrel—there is Sidney standing by the reception table, princely-looking in his way of standing not like the others in friendly head-down-to-listen attitudes, but rared back in his five and a half feet, hand in pocket and coat hiked open at the vent, forehead faceted and flashing light.

Sidney fastens a plastic name card to my lapel and, before I know it, has hustled me off upstairs to a blue ballroom, leaving Kate and Margot to trail along, somewhat stony-faced, behind us.

"What is this, Sidney?" I say dismayed and hanging back. I begin to sweat and can only think of hitting the street and having three drinks in the first bar. Trapped in this blue cave, the genie-soul of Chicago will surely catch up with us. "I didn't think there were any doings till tomorrow."

"That's right. This is only the Hot Stove League."

"Oh Lord, what is that?" I say sweating.

"We get acquainted, talk over last year's business, kick around the boners of the funds. You'll like it."

Sure enough, there in the middle of the floor is a ten-foot potbellied stove made of red cellophane. Waiters pass by with trays of martinis and a salon orchestra plays "Getting to Know You."

The delegates are very decent fellows. I find myself talking to half a dozen young men from the West Coast and liking them very much—one in particular, a big shy fellow from Spokane named Stanley Kinchen, and his wife, a fine-looking woman, yellow-haired and bigger than Sharon, lips curling like a rose petal, head thrown back like a queen and a tremendous sparkle in the eye. What good people they are. It is not at all bad being a businessman. There is a spirit of trust and cooperation here. Everyone jokes about such things, but if businessmen were not trusting of each other and could not set their great projects going on credit, the country would collapse tomorrow and be no better off than Saudi Arabia. It strikes me that Stanley Kinchen would actually do anything for me. I know I would for him. I introduce Kate as my fiancée and she pulls down her mouth. I can't tell whether it is me she is disgusted with or my business colleagues. But these fellows: so friendly and—? What, dejected? I can't be sure.

Kinchen asks me if I am going to be in the Cracker Barrel. He is very nervous: it seems he is program chairman and somebody defected on him. He takes me aside.

"Would you do me a favor? Would you kick off with a ten minute talk on Selling Aids?"

"Sure."

We shake hands and part good comrades.

But I have to get out of here, good fellows or no good fellows. Too much fellow feeling makes me nervous, to tell the truth. Another minute and the ballroom will itself grow uneasy. Already the cellophane stove has begun to glow ominously.

"I have to find Harold Graebner," I tell Kate.

I grab her hand and slip out and away into the perilous out-of-doors, find the tiniest bar in the busiest block of the Loop. There I see her plain, see plain for the first time since I lay wounded in a ditch and watched an Oriental finch scratching around in the leaves—a quiet little body she is, a tough little city Celt; no, more of a Rachel really, a dark little Rachel bound home to Brooklyn on the IRT. I give her a pat on the leg.

"What?" she says, hardly paying attention—she is busy finding Harold's address on the map and adding up the bar bill. I never noticed how shrewd and parsimonious she is—a true Creole.

"Sweet Kate," say I patting her.

"All right, let's go." But she does not leave immediately. We have six drinks in two bars, catch buses, cross a hundred miles of city blocks, pass in the neighborhood of millions of souls, and come at last to a place called Wilmette which turns out not to be a place at all since it has no genie, where lives Harold Graebner the only soul known to me in the entire Midwest. Him, one soul in five million, we must meet and greet, wish good luck and bid farewell—else we cannot be sure we are here at all—before hopping off again into the maze of a city set down so unaccountably under the great thundering-lonesome Midwestern sky.

Off the bus and hopping along Wilmette happy as jaybirds, pass within a few feet of noble Midwestern girls with their clear eyes and their splendid butts and never a thought for them. What an experience, Rory, to be free of it for once. Rassled out. What a sickness it is, Rory, this latter-day post-Christian sex. To be pagan it would be one thing, an ease-ment taken easily in a rosy old pagan world; to be Christian it would be another thing, fornication forbidden and not even to be thought of in the new life, and I can see that it need not be thought of if there were such a life. But to be neither pagan nor Christian but this: oh this is a sickness, Rory. For it to be longed after and dreamed of the first twenty years of one's life, not practiced but not quite prohibited; simply longed after, longed after as a fruit not really forbidden but mock-forbidden and therefore secretly prized, prized first last and always by the cult of the naughty nice wherein everyone is nicer than Christians and naughtier than pagans, wherein there are dreamed not one but two American dreams: of Ozzie and Harriet, nicer-than-Christian folks, and of Tillie and Mac and belly to back.

We skip on by like jaybirds in July.

Harold lives in a handsome house in a new suburb back of Wilmette. His father left him a glass business in South Chicago and Harold has actually gotten rich. Every Christmas he sends a card with a picture of his wife and children and a note something like: "Netted better than thirty five thou this year—now ain't that something?" You would have to know Harold to understand that this is not exactly a boast. It is a piece of cheerful news from a cheerful and simple sort of a fellow who can't get over his good fortune and who therefore has to tell you about it. "Now ain't that something, Rollo?" he would say and put up his hands in his baby-claw gesture. I know what he means. Every time American Motors jumps two dollars, I feel the same cheerful and expanding benevolence.

Since Kate and I can hardly wait to be back on our rambles, we visit with Harold about twenty minutes. As I said before, Harold loves me because he saved my life. I love him because he is a hero. I have a boundless admiration for heroes and Harold is the real thing. He got the DSC for a patrol action in the Chongchon Valley. Another lieutenant leading the fix patrol—I, you may as well know—got himself hung up; Lieutenant Graebner, who had the support patrol, came roaring up through the mortar fire like old Pete Longstreet himself and, using his three five rocket launcher like a carbine, shot a hole through the concertina (we were hung up on a limestone knob encircled by the concertina) and set fire to an acre or so of Orientals. When I say he is an unlikely hero, I don't mean he is a modest little fellow like Audie Murphy—Audie Murphy is a hero and he looks like a hero. Harold is *really* unheroic—to such a degree that you can't help but feel he squanders his heroism. Not at all reticent about the war, he speaks of it in

such a flat unlovely way that his own experiences sound disap-
pointing. With his somewhat snoutish nose and his wavy hair
starting half way back on his head and his sing-songy way of
talking, he reminds me of a TV contestant:

M.C.: Lieutenant, I bet you were glad to see the fog roll in
    that particular night.

HAROLD: (unaccountably prissy and sing-songy): Mr
    Marx, I think I can truthfully say that was one time I
    didn't mind being in a fog about something (looking
    around at the audience).

M.C.: Hey! I'm supposed to make the jokes around here!

Harold's wife is a thin hump-shouldered girl with a beautiful face. She stands a ways off from us holding her baby, my
godson, and hesitates between a sort of living room and a peninsula bar; she seems on the point of asking us to sit down in
one place or the other but she never does. I keep thinking she
is going to get tired herself, holding the big baby. Looking at
her, I know just how Harold sees her: as beeyoutiful. He used
to say that so-and-so, Veronica Lake maybe, was beeyoutiful—
Harold is orginally from Indiana and he called me peculiar
Midwestern names like "heller" and "turkey"—and his wife
is beautiful in just the same way: blond hair waving down her
cheeks like a madonna, heavenly blue eyes, but stooped so that
her shoulder-blades flare out in back like wings.

Harold walks up and down with both hands lifted up in the
baby-claw gesture he uses when he talks, and there stands his
little madonna-wife sort of betwixt and between us and the kids
around the TV. But Harold is glad to see me. "Old Rollo," he
says, looking at the middle of my chest. "This is great, Rollo,"
and he is restless with an emotion he can't identify. Rollo is
a nickname he gave me in the Orient—it evidently signifies
something in the Midwest which is not current in Louisiana.
"Old Rollo"—and he would be beside himself with delight at
the aptness of it. Now it comes over him in the strongest way:
what a good thing it is to see a comrade with whom one has
suffered much and endured much, but also what a wrenching

thing. Up and down he goes, arms upraised, restless with it and not knowing what it is.

"Harold, about the baby's baptism—"

"He was baptized yesterday," says Harold absently.

"I'm sorry."

"You were godfather-by-proxy."

"Oh."

The trouble is there is no place to come to rest. We stand off the peninsula like ships becalmed—unable to move.

Turning my back on Harold, I tell Kate and Veronica how Harold saved my life, telling it jokingly with only one or two looks around at him. It is too much for Harold, not my gratitude, not the beauty of his own heroism, but the sudden confrontation of a time past, a time so terrible and splendid in its arch-reality; and so lost—cut adrift like a great ship in the flood of years. Harold tries to parse it out, that time and the time after, the strange ten years intervening, and it is too much for him. He shakes his head like a fighter.

We stand formally in the informal living area.

"Harold, how long have you been here?"

"Three years. Look at this, Rollo." Harold shoves along the bar-peninsula a modernistic horsehead carved out of white wood, all flowing mane and arching neck. "Who do you think made it?"

"It's very good."

"Old Rollo," says Harold, eying the middle of my chest. Harold can't parse it out, so he has to do something. "Rollo, how tough are you? I bet I can take you." Harold wrestled at Northwestern. "I could put you down right now." Harold is actually getting mad at me.

"Listen, Harold," I say, laughing. "Do you go into the city every day?"

Harold nods but does not raise his eyes.

"How did you decide to live here?"

"Sylvia's family live in Glencoe. Rollo, how do you like it way down yonder in New Orleens?"

Harold would really like to wrestle and not so playfully either. I walked in and brought it with me, the wrenching in the chest. It would be better for him to be rid of it and me.

Ten minutes later he lets us out at the commuter station and tears off into the night.

"What a peculiar family," says Kate, gazing after the red turrets of Harold's Cadillac.

Back to the Loop where we dive into the mother and Urwomb of all moviehouses—an Aztec mortuary of funeral urns and glyphs, thronged with the spirit-presences of another day, William Powell and George Brent and Patsy Kelly and Charley Chase, the best friends of my childhood—and see a movie called *The Young Philadelphians*. Kate holds my hand tightly in the dark.

Paul Newman is an idealistic young fellow who is disillusioned and becomes cynical and calculating. But in the end he recovers his ideals.

Outside, a new note has crept into the wind, a black williwaw sound straight from the terrible wastes to the north. "Oh oh oh," wails Kate as we creep home to the hotel, sunk into ourselves and with no stomach even for hand-holding. "Something is going to happen."

Something does. A yellow slip handed across the hotel desk commands me to call operator three in New Orleans.

This I accordingly do, and my aunt's voice speaks to the operator, then to me, and does not change its tone. She does not bother to add a single overtone of warmth or cold, love or hate, to the monotone of her notification—and this is more ominous than ten thousand williwaws.

"Is Kate with you?"

"Yes ma'am."

"Would you like to know how we found you?"

"Yes."

"The police found Kate's car at the terminal."

"The police?"

"Kate did not tell anyone she was leaving. However, her behavior is not unexplainable and therefore not inexcusable. Yours is."

I am silent.

"Why didn't you tell me?"

I think. "I can't remember."

4

It is impossible to find a seat on a flight to New Orleans the night before Mardi Gras. No trains are scheduled until Tuesday morning. But buses leave every hour or so. I send my aunt a telegram and call Stanley Kinchen and excuse myself from the talk on Selling Aids—it is all-right: the original speaker had recovered. Stanley and I part even more cordially than we met. It is a stratospheric cordiality such as can only make further meetings uneasy. But I do not mind. At midnight we are bound for New Orleans on a Scenicruiser which takes a more easterly course than the Illinois Central, down along the Wabash to Memphis by way of Evansville and Cairo.

It is good to be leaving; Chicago is fit for no more than a short rotation. Kate is well. The summons from her stepmother has left her neither glum nor fearful. She speaks at length to her stepmother and, with her sure instinct for such matters, gets her talking about canceling reservations and return tickets, wins her way, decides we'll stay, then changes her mind and insists on coming home to ease their minds. Now she gazes curiously about the bus station, giving way every few seconds to tremendous face-splitting yawns. Once on the bus she collapses into a slack-jawed oblivion and sleeps all the way to the Ohio River. I doze fitfully and wake for good when the dawn breaks on the outskirts of Terre Haute. When it is light enough, I take out my paper-back *Arabia Deserta* and read until we stop for breakfast in Evansville. Kate eats heartily, creeps back to the bus, takes one look at the black water of the Ohio River and the naked woods of the bottom lands where winter still clings like a violet mist, and falls heavily to sleep, mouth mashed open against my shoulder.

Today is Mardi Gras, fat Tuesday, but our bus has left Chicago much too late to accommodate Carnival visitors. The passengers are an everyday assortment of mothers-in-law visiting sons-in-law in Memphis, school teachers and telephone operators bound for vacations in quaint old Vieux Carré. Our upper deck is a green bubble where, it turns out, people feel themselves dispensed from the conventional silence below as if, in mounting with others to see the wide world and the green sky, they had already established a kind of freemasonry and

spoken the first word among themselves. I surrender my seat to
Kate's stretchings out against me and double up her legs for her
and for the rest of the long day's journey down through Indiana and Illinois and Kentucky and Tennessee and Mississippi
hold converse with two passengers—the first, a romantic from
Wisconsin; the second, a salesman from a small manufacturing
firm in Murfreesboro, Tennessee who wrecked his car in Gary.

Now in the fore seat of the bubble and down we go plunging
along the Illinois bank of the Mississippi through a region of
sooty glens falling steeply away to the west and against the
slope of which are propped tall frame houses with colored windows and the spires of Polish churches. I read:

> We mounted in the morrow twilight; but long after day-
> break the heavens seemed shut over us, as a tomb, with
> gloomy clouds. We were engaged in horrid lava beds.

The romantic sits across the aisle, slumped gracefully, one foot
propped on the metal ledge. He is reading *The Charterhouse of
Parma*. His face is extraordinarily well-modeled and handsome
but his head is too small and, arising as it does from the great
collar of his car coat, it makes him look a bit dandy and dudish.
Two things I am curious about. How does he sit? Immediately
graceful and not aware of it or mediately graceful and aware of
it? How does he read *The Charterhouse of Parma*? Immediately
as a man who is in the world and who has an appetite for the
book as he might have an appetite for peaches, or mediately as
one who finds himself under the necessity of sticking himself
into the world in a certain fashion, of slumping in an acceptable
slump, of reading an acceptable book on an acceptable bus? Is
he a romantic?

He is a romantic. His posture is the first clue: it is too good
to be true, this distillation of all graceful slumps. To clinch
matters, he catches sight of me and my book and goes into a
spasm of recognition and shyness. To put him out of his misery,
I go over and ask him how he likes his book. For a tenth of
a second he eyes me to make sure I am not a homosexual;
but he has already seen Kate with me and sees her now, lying
asleep and marvelously high in the hip. (I have observed that
it is no longer possible for one young man to speak unwarily

to another not known to him, except in certain sections of the South and West, and certainly not with a book in his hand.) As for me, I have already identified him through his shyness. It is pure heterosexual shyness. He is no homosexual, but merely a romantic. Now he closes his book and stares hard at it as if he would, by dint of staring alone, tear from it its soul in a word. "It's—very good," he says at last and blushes. The poor fellow. He has just begun to suffer from it, this miserable trick the romantic plays upon himself: of setting just beyond his reach the very thing he prizes. For he prizes just such a meeting, the chance meeting with a chance friend on a chance bus, a friend he can talk to, unburden himself of some of his terrible longings. Now having encountered such a one, me, the rare bus friend, of course he strikes himself dumb. It is a case for direct questioning.

He is a senior at a small college in northern Wisconsin where his father is bursar. His family is extremely proud of the educational progress of their children. Three sisters have assorted PhDs and MAs, piling up degrees on into the middle of life (he speaks in a rapid rehearsed way, a way he deems appropriate for our rare encounter, and when he is forced to use an ordinary word like "bus"—having no other way of conferring upon it a vintage flavor, he says it in quotes and with a wry expression). Upon completion of his second trimester and having enough credits to graduate, he has lit out for New Orleans to load bananas for a while and perhaps join the merchant marine. Smiling tensely, he strains forward and strikes himself dumb. For a while, he says. He means that he hopes to find himself a girl, the rarest of rare pieces, and live the life of Rudolfo on the balcony, sitting around on the floor and experiencing soul-communions. I have my doubts. In the first place, he will defeat himself, jump ten miles ahead of himself, scare the wits out of some girl with his great choking silences, want her so desperately that by his own peculiar logic he can't have her; or having her, jump another ten miles beyond both of them and end by fleeing to the islands where, propped at the rail of his ship in some rancid port, he will ponder his own loneliness.

In fact, there is nothing more to say to him. The best one can do is deflate the pressure a bit, the terrible romantic pressure, and leave him alone. He is a moviegoer, though of course he does not go to movies.

The salesman has no such trouble. Like many businessmen, he is a better metaphysician than the romantic. For example, he gives me a sample of his product, a simple ell of tempered and blued steel honed to a two-edged blade. Balancing it in his hand, he tests its heft and temper. The hand knows the blade, practices its own metaphysic of the goodness of the steel.

"Thank you very much," I say, accepting the warm blade.

"You know all in the world you have to do?"

"No."

"Walk into the office—" (He sells this attachment to farm implement stores) "—and ask the man how much is his bush hog blade. He'll tell you about nine and a half a pair. Then all you do is drop this on his desk and say thirty five cents and you can't break it."

"What does it do?"

"Anything. Clears, mulches, peas, beans, saplings so big, anything. That little sombitch will go now." He strikes one hand straight out past the other, and I have a sense of the storied and even legendary properties of the blade, attested in the peculiar Southern esteem of the excellence of machinery: the hot-damn beat-all risible accolade conferred when some new engine sallies forth in its outlandish scissoring side-winding foray.

We sit on the rear seat, the salesman with his knee cocked up, heel under him, arm levered out over his knee. He wears black shoes and white socks for his athlete's foot and now and then sends down a finger to appease the itching. It pleases him to speak of his cutter and of his family down in Murfreesboro and speak all the way to Union City and not once to inquire of me and this pleases me since I would not know what to say. Businessmen are our only metaphysicians, but the trouble is, they are one-track metaphysicians. By the time the salesman gets off in Union City, my head is spinning with facts about the thirty five cent cutter. It is as if I had lived in Murfreesboro all my life.

Canal Street is dark and almost empty. The last parade, the Krewe of Comus, has long since disappeared down Royal

Street with its shuddering floats and its blazing flambeau. Street cleaners sweep confetti and finery into soggy heaps in the gutters. The cold mizzling rain smells of sour paper pulp. Only a few maskers remain abroad, tottering apes clad in Spanish moss, Frankenstein monsters with bolts through their necks, and a neighborhood gang or two making their way arm in arm, wheeling and whip-popping, back to their trucks.

Kate is dry-eyed and abstracted. She stands gazing about as if she had landed in a strange city. We decide to walk up Loyola Avenue to get our cars. The romantic is ahead of us, at the window of a lingerie shop, the gay sort where black net panties invest legless torsos. Becoming aware of us before we pass and thinking to avoid the embarrassment of a greeting (what are we to say, after all, and suppose the right word fails us?), he hurries away, hands thrust deep in his pockets, his small well-modeled head tricking to and fro above the great collar of his car coat.

Five

"I AM NOT SAYING that I pretend to understand you. What I am saying is that after two days of complete mystification it has at last dawned on me what it is I fail to understand. That is at least a step in the right direction. It was the novelty of it that put me off, you see. I do believe that you have discovered something new under the sun."

It is with a rare and ominous objectivity that my aunt addresses me Wednesday morning. In the very violence of her emotion she has discovered the energy to master it, so that now, in the flush of her victory, she permits herself to use the old forms of civility and even of humor. The only telltale sign of menace is the smile through her eyes, which is a bit too narrow and finely drawn.

"Would you verify my hypothesis? Is not that your discovery? First, is it not true that in all of past history people who found themselves in difficult situations behaved in certain familiar ways, well or badly, courageously or cowardly, with distinction or mediocrity, with honor or dishonor. They are recognizable. They display courage, pity, fear, embarrassment, joy, sorrow, and so on. Such anyhow has been the funded experience of the race for two or three thousand years, has it not? Your discovery, as best as I can determine, is that there is an alternative which no one has hit upon. It is that one finding oneself in one of life's critical situations need not after all respond in one of the traditional ways. No. One may simply default. Pass. Do as one pleases, shrug, turn on one's heel and leave. Exit. Why after all need one act humanly? Like all great discoveries, it is breathtakingly simple." She smiles a quizzical-legal sort of smile which reminds me of Judge Anse.

The house was no different this morning. The same chorus of motors, vacuum cleaners, dishwasher, laundromat, hum and throb against each other. From an upper region, reverberating down the back stairwell, comes the muted hollering of Bessie Coe, as familiar and querulous a sound as the sparrows under the eaves. Nor was Uncle Jules different, except only in his slight embarrassment, giving me wide berth as I passed him on the porch and saying his good morning briefly and sorrowfully as if the farthest limit of his disapproval lay in the brevity of his greeting. Kate was nowhere to be seen. Until ten o'clock my aunt, I know, is to be found at her roll-top desk where she keeps her "accounts." There is nothing to do but go directly in to her and stand at ease until she takes notice of me. Now she looks over, as erect and handsome as the Black Prince.

"Yes?"

"I am sorry that through a misunderstanding or thoughtlessness on my part you were not told of Kate's plans to go with me to Chicago. No doubt it was my thoughtlessness. In any case I am sorry and I hope that your anger—"

"Anger? You are mistaken. It was not anger. It was discovery."

"Discovery of what?"

"Discovery that someone in whom you had placed great hopes was suddenly not there. It is like leaning on what seems to be a good stalwart shoulder and feeling it go all mushy and queer."

We both gaze down at the letter opener, the soft iron sword she has withdrawn from the grasp of the helmeted figure on the inkstand.

"I am sorry for that."

"The fact that you are a stranger to me is perhaps my fault. It was stupid of me not to believe it earlier. For now I do believe that you are not capable of caring for anyone, Kate, Jules, or myself—no more than that Negro man walking down the street—less so, in fact, since I have a hunch he and I would discover some slight tradition in common." She seems to notice for the first time that the tip of the blade is bent. "I honestly don't believe it occurred to you to let us know that you and Kate were leaving, even though you knew how desperately sick she was. I truly do not think it ever occurred to you that you were abusing a sacred trust in carrying that poor child off on a fantastic trip like that or that you were betraying the great trust and affection she has for you. Well?" she asks when I do not reply.

I try as best I can to appear as she would have me, as being, if not right, then wrong in a recognizable, a right form of wrongness. But I can think of nothing to say.

"Do you have any notion of how I felt when, not twelve hours after Kate attempted suicide, she vanishes without a trace?"

We watch the sword as she lets it fall over the fulcrum of her forefinger; it goes *tat't't* on the brass hinge of the desk. Then, so suddenly that I almost start, my aunt sheathes the sword and places her hand flat on the desk. Turning it over, she flexes her fingers and studies the nails, which are deeply scored by longitudinal ridges.

"Were you intimate with Kate?"

"Intimate?"

"Yes."

"Not very."

"I ask you again. Were you intimate with her?"

"I suppose so. Though intimate is not quite the word."

"You suppose so. Intimate is not quite the word. I wonder what is the word. You see—" she says with a sort of humor, "—there is another of my hidden assumptions. All these years I have been assuming that between us words mean roughly the same thing, that among certain people, gentlefolk I don't mind calling them, there exists a set of meanings held in common, that a certain manner and a certain grace come as naturally as breathing. At the great moments of life—success, failure, marriage, death—our kind of folks have always possessed a native instinct for behavior, a natural piety or grace, I don't mind calling it. Whatever else we did or failed to do, we always had that. I'll make you a little confession. I am not ashamed to use the word class. I will also plead guilty to another charge. The charge is that people belonging to my class think they're better than other people. You're damn right we're better. We're better because we do not shirk our obligations either to ourselves or to others. We do not whine. We do not organize a minority group and blackmail the government. We do not prize mediocrity for mediocrity's sake. Oh I am aware that we hear a great many flattering things nowadays about your great common man—you know, it has always been revealing to me that he is perfectly content so to be called, because that is exactly what he is: the common man and when I say common I mean common as hell. Our civilization has achieved a distinction of sorts. It will be remembered not for its technology nor even its wars but for its novel ethos. Ours is the only civilization in history which has enshrined mediocrity as its national ideal. Others have been corrupt, but leave it to us to invent the most undistinguished of corruptions. No orgies, no blood running in the street, no babies thrown off cliffs. No, we're sentimental people and we horrify easily. True, our moral fiber is rotten. Our national character stinks to high heaven. But we are kinder than ever. No prostitute ever responded with a quicker spasm of sentiment when our hearts are touched. Nor is there anything new about thievery, lewdness, lying, adultery. What is new is that in our time liars and thieves and whores and adulterers wish also to be congratulated and are congratulated by the great public, if their confession is sufficiently psychological or strikes a sufficiently heartfelt and authentic note of sincerity. Oh, we are sincere. I do not deny it. I don't know anybody nowadays who is not sincere. Didi Lovell is the most sincere person I know: every time she crawls in bed with somebody else, she does so with the utmost sincerity. We are the most sincere Laodiceans who ever got flushed down the sinkhole of history. No, my young friend, I am not ashamed to use the word class. They say out there we think we're better. You're damn right we're better. And don't think they don't know it—" She raises the sword to Prytania Street. "Let me tell you something. If he out yonder is your prize exhibit for the progress of the human race in the past three thousand years, then all I can say is that I am content to be fading out of the picture. Perhaps we are a biological sport. I am not sure. But one thing I am sure of: we live by our lights, we die by our lights, and whoever the high gods may be, we'll look them in the eye without apology." Now my aunt swivels around to face me and not so bad-humoredly. "I did my best for you, son. I gave you all I had. More than anything I wanted to pass on to you the one heritage of the men of our family, a certain quality of spirit, a gaiety, a sense of duty, a nobility worn lightly, a sweetness, a gentleness with women—the only good things the South ever had and the only things that really matter in this life. Ah well. Still you can tell me one thing. I know you're not a bad boy—I wish you were. But how did it happen that none of this ever meant anything to you? Clearly it did not. Would you please tell me? I am genuinely curious."

I cannot tear my eyes from the sword. Years ago I bent the tip trying to open a drawer. My aunt looks too. Does she suspect?

"That would be difficult for me to say. You say that none of what you said ever meant anything to me. That is not true. On the contrary. I have never forgotten anything you ever said. In fact I have pondered over it all my life. My objections, though they are not exactly objections, cannot be expressed in the usual way. To tell the truth, I can't express them at all."

"I see. Do you condone your behavior with Kate?"

"Condone?" Condone. I screw up an eye. "I don't suppose so."

"You don't suppose so." My aunt nods gravely, almost agreeably, in her wry legal manner. "You knew that Kate was suicidal?"

"No."

"Would you have cared if Kate had killed herself?"

"Yes."

After a long silence she asks: "You have nothing more to say?"

I shake my head.

Mercer opens the door and sticks his head in, takes one whiff of the air inside, and withdraws immediately.

"Then tell me this. Yes, tell me this!" my aunt says, brightening as, groping, she comes at last to the nub of the matter. "Tell me this and this is all I shall ever want to know. I am assuming that we both recognize that you had a trust toward Kate. Perhaps my assumption was mistaken. But I know that you knew she was taking drugs. Is that not correct?"

"Yes."

"Did you know that she was taking drugs during this recent trip?"

"Yes."

"And you did what you did?"

"Yes."

"That is all you have to say?"

I am silent. Mercer starts the waxer. It was permission for this he sought. I think of nothing in particular. A cry goes up in the street outside, and there comes into my sight the Negro my aunt spoke of. He is Cothard, the last of the chimney sweeps, an outlandish blueblack Negro dressed in a frock coat and bashed-in top hat and carrying over his shoulder a bundle of palmetto leaves and broom straw. The cry comes again. "*R-r-r-ramonez la chiminée du haut en bas!*"

"One last question to satisfy my idle curiosity. What has been going on in your mind during all the years when we listened to music together, read the *Crito*, and spoke together—or was it only I who spoke—good Lord, I can't remember—of goodness and truth and beauty and nobility?"

Another cry and the *ramoneur* is gone. There is nothing for me to say.

"Don't you love these things? Don't you live by them?"

"No."

"What do you love? What do you live by?"

I am silent.

"Tell me where I have failed you."

"You haven't."

"What do you think is the purpose of life—to go to the movies and dally with every girl that comes along?"

"No."

A ledger lies open on her desk, one of the old-fashioned kind with a marbled cover, in which she has always kept account of her properties, sundry service stations, Canadian mines, patents—the peculiar business accumulation of a doctor—left to her by old Dr Wills. "Well." She closes it briskly and smiles up at me, a smile which, more than anything which has gone before, marks an ending. Smiling, she gives me her hand, head to one side, in her old party style. But it is her withholding my name that assigns me my new status. So she might have spoken to any one of a number of remotely connected persons, such as a Spring Fiesta tourist encountered by accident in her own hall.

We pass Mercer who stands respectfully against the wall. He murmurs a greeting which through an exquisite calculation expresses his affection for me and at the same time declares his allegiance to my aunt. Out of the corner of my eye, I see him hop nimbly into the dining room, full of fizzing good spirits. We find ourselves on the porch.

"I do thank you so much for coming by," says my aunt, fingering her necklace and looking past me at the Vaudrieul house.

*

Kate hails me at the corner. She leans into my MG, tucking her blouse, as brisk as a stewardess.

"You're stupid stupid stupid," she says with a malevolent look.

"What?"

"I heard it all, you poor stupid bastard." Then, appearing to forget herself, she drums her nails rapidly upon the windshield. "Are you going home now?"

"Yes."

"Wait for me there."

2

It is a gloomy day. Gentilly is swept fitfully by desire and by an east wind from the burning swamps at Chef Menteur.

Today is my thirtieth birthday and I sit on the ocean wave in the schoolyard and wait for Kate and think of nothing. Now in the thirty-first year of my dark pilgrimage on this earth and knowing less than I ever knew before, having learned only to recognize merde when I see it, having inherited no more from my father than a good nose for merde, for every species of shit that flies—my only talent—smelling merde from every quarter, living in fact in the very century of merde, the great shithouse of scientific humanism where needs are satisfied, everyone becomes an anyone, a warm and creative person, and prospers like a dung beetle, and one hundred percent of people are humanists and ninety-eight percent believe in God, and men are dead, dead, dead; and the malaise has settled like a fall-out and what people really fear is not that the bomb will fall but that the bomb will not fall—on this my thirtieth birthday, I know nothing and there is nothing to do but fall prey to desire.

Nothing remains but desire, and desire comes howling down Elysian Fields like a mistral. My search has been abandoned; it is no match for my aunt, her rightness and her despair, her despairing of me and her despairing of herself. Whenever I take leave of my aunt after one of her serious talks, I have to find a girl.

Fifty minutes of waiting for Kate on the ocean wave and I

am beside myself. What has happened to her? She has spoken to my aunt and kicked me out. There is nothing to do but call Sharon at the office. The little pagoda of aluminum and glass, standing in the neutral ground of Elysian Fields at the very heart of the uproar of a public zone, is trim and pretty on the outside but evil-smelling within. Turning slowly around, I take note of the rhymes in pencil and the sad cartoons of solitary lovers; the wire thrills and stops and thrills and in the interval there comes into my ear my own breath as if my very self stood beside me and would not speak. The phone does not answer. Has she quit?

Some children have come into the playground across the street; two big boys give them a ride on the ocean wave. Ordinarily the little children ride only the merry-go-round which is set close to the ground and revolves in a fixed orbit.

I've got to find her, Rory. It is certain now that my aunt is right and that Kate knows it and that nothing is left but Sharon. The east wind whistles through the eaves of my pagoda and presses the glass against its fittings. I try the apartment. She is out. But Joyce is there, Joyce-in-the-window, Joyce of the naughty-you mouth and the buckskin jacket.

"This is Jack Bolling, Joyce," says a voice from old Virginia.

"Well well."

"Is Sharon there?"

"She is out with her mother and Stan." Joyce's voice has a Middle West snap. Moth-errr, she says and: we-ull we-ull. "I don't know when shill be back." She sounds like Pepper Young's sister.

"Who is Stan?"

"Stan Shamoun, her fiancé."

"Oh yes, that's right." What's right? She's not only quit. She's marrying the macaroni. "What about you? Are you getting married?"

"What's that?"

"I've been wanting to meet you for some time."

"I just thot of something."

"What?"

"The Lord of Misrule reigned yesterday—"

"Who?" Is she starting out on some sort of complicated

Midwestern joke? Grinning like a lunatic, I hold on for dear life.

Joyce goes on talking in a roguish voice about the Lord of Misrule and a fellow down from Purdue, a dickens if she ever saw one.

The two big boys on the playground have got the ocean wave going fast enough so they can jump on and keep up speed by kicking the ground away on the low passes. *Iii-oorrr iii-oorrr* goes the dry socket on its pole in a faraway childish music and the children embrace the iron struts and lay back their heads to watch the whirling world.

"Joyce, I wonder if I may be frank with you"—the voice comes into my ear and I myself am silent.

"Please do. I like frank people."

"I thought you were that kind of person—" Old confederate Marlon Brando—a reedy insinuating voice, full of winks and leers and above all pleased with itself. What a shock. On and on it goes. "—I know some folks might think it was a little unconventional but I'm gon tell you anyway. I know you don't remember it but I saw you last Saturday—" It is too much trouble to listen.

"I remember!"

Round and round goes the ocean wave screeching out its Petrouchka music *iii-oorrr iii-oorrr* and now belling out so far that the inner bumper catches the pole and slings around in a spurt so outrageously past all outrage that the children embrace the iron struts for dear life.

"I'm only home for lunch," says Joyce. "But why don't you come over Saturday night. Some of the kids will be there. Praps we could all go to Pat O'Brien's." Joyce makes herself out to be a big girl child, one of the kids, and all set for high jinks.

"No praps about it."

A watery sunlight breaks through the smoke of the Chef and turns the sky yellow. Elysian Fields glistens like a vat of sulfur; the playground looks as if it alone had survived the end of the world. At last I spy Kate; her stiff little Plymouth comes nosing into my bus stop. There she sits like a bomber pilot, resting on her wheel and looking sideways at the children and not seeing, and she could be I myself, sooty eyed and nowhere.

Is it possible that— For a long time I have secretly hoped for the end of the world and believed with Kate and my aunt and Sam Yerger and many other people that only after the end could the few who survive creep out of their holes and discover themselves to be themselves and live as merrily as children among the viny ruins. Is it possible that—it is not too late?

Iii-oorrr goes the ocean wave, its struts twinkling in the golden light, its skirt swaying to and fro like a young dancing girl.

"I'd like to very much, Joyce. May I bring along my own fiancée, Kate Cutrer? I want you and Sharon to meet her."

"Why shore, why shore," says Joyce in a peculiar Midwest take-off of her roommate Sharon and sounding somewhat relieved, to tell the truth.

The playground is deserted. I notice that the school itself is locked and empty. Traffic goes hissing along Elysian Fields and the jaybirds jeer in the camphor trees. People turn in now and then at the school gate but they make for the church next door. At first I suppose it is a wedding or a funeral, but they leave by twos and threes and more arrive. Then, as a pair of youths come ambling along the sidewalk, I catch sight of the smudge at the hair roots. Of course. It is Ash Wednesday. Sharon has not quit me. All Cutrer branch offices close on Ash Wednesday.

We sit in Kate's car, a 1951 Plymouth which, with all her ups and downs, Kate has ever cared for faithfully. It is a tall gray coupe and it runs with a light gaseous sound. When she drives, head ducked down, hands placed symmetrically on the wheel, the pale underflesh of her arms trembling slightly, her paraphernalia—straw seat, Kleenex dispenser, magnetic tray for cigarettes—all set in order about her, it is easy to believe that the light stiff little car has become gradually transformed by its owner until it is hers herself in its every nut and bolt. When it comes fresh from the service station, its narrow tires still black and wet, the very grease itself seems not the usual muck but the thrifty amber sap of the slender axle tree.

"Why didn't you tell her about our plans?" Kate still holds the steering wheel and surveys the street. "I was in the library and heard every word. You *idiot*."

Kate is pleased. She is certain that I have carried off a grand
stoic gesture, like a magazine hero.

"Did you tell her?" I ask.

"I told her we are to be married."

"Are we?"

"Yes."

"What did she say to that?"

"She didn't. She only hoped that you might come to see her
this afternoon."

"I have to anyway."

"Why?"

"I promised her one week ago I would tell her what I planned
to do."

"What do you plan to do?"

I shrug. There is only one thing I can do: listen to people,
see how they stick themselves into the world, hand them along
a ways in their dark journey and be handed along, and for
good and selfish reasons. It only remains to decide whether this
vocation is best pursued in a service station or—

"Are you going to medical school?"

"If she wants me to."

"Does that mean you can't marry me now?"

"No. You have plenty of money."

"Then let us understand each other."

"All right."

"I don't know whether I can succeed."

"I know you don't."

"It seems the wildest sort of thing to do."

"Yes."

"We had better make it fast."

"All right."

"I am so afraid."

Kate's forefinger begins to explore the adjacent thumb, test-
ing the individual spikes of the feathered flesh. A florid new
Mercury pulls up behind us and a Negro gets out and goes up
into the church. He is more respectable than respectable; he is
more middle-class than one could believe: his Archie Moore
mustache, the way he turns and, seeing us see him, casts a
weather eye at the sky; the way he plucks a handkerchief out of

his rear pocket with a flurry of his coat tail and blows his nose in a magic placative gesture (you see, I have been here before: it is a routine matter).

"If I could be sure you knew how frightened I am, it would help a great deal."

"You can be sure."

"Not merely of marriage. This afternoon I wanted some cigarettes, but the thought of going to the drugstore turned me to jelly."

I am silent.

"I am frightened when I am alone and I am frightened when I am with people. The only time I'm not frightened is when I'm with you. You'll have to be with me a great deal."

"I will."

"Do you want to?"

"Yes."

"I will be under treatment a long time."

"I know that."

"And I'm not sure I'll ever change. Really change."

"You might."

"But I think I see a way. It seems to me that if we are together a great deal and you tell me the simplest things and not laugh at me—I beg you for pity's own sake never to laugh at me—tell me things like: Kate, it is all right for you to go down to the drugstore, and give me a kiss, then I will believe you. Will you do that?" she says with her not-quite-pure solemnity, her slightly reflected Sarah Lawrence solemnity.

"Yes, I'll do that."

She has started plucking at her thumb in earnest, tearing away little shreds of flesh. I take her hand and kiss the blood.

"But you must try not to hurt yourself so much."

"I will try! I will!"

The Negro has already come outside. His forehead is an ambiguous sienna color and pied: it is impossible to be sure that he received ashes. When he gets in his Mercury, he does not leave immediately but sits looking down at something on the seat beside him. A sample case? An insurance manual? I watch him closely in the rear-view mirror. It is impossible to say why he is here. Is it part and parcel of the complex business of coming up in the world? Or is it because he believes that

God himself is present here at the corner of Elysian Fields and Bons Enfants? Or is he here for both reasons: through some dim dazzling trick of grace, coming for the one and receiving the other as God's own importunate bonus?

It is impossible to say.

Epilogue

S O ENDED my thirtieth year to heaven, as the poet called it.
In June Kate and I were married. It was practicable to
wind up my business affairs in Gentilly and to accompany my
aunt to North Carolina sooner than I expected, since Sharon,
now Mrs Stanley Shamoun, had become so competent that
she was able to transact the light summer business without
assistance, at least until my replacement could be found. In
August Mr Sartalamaccia purchased my duck club for twenty
five thousand dollars. When medical school began in September, Kate found a house near her stepmother, one of the very
shotgun cottages done over by my cousin Nell Lovell and very
much to Kate's taste with its saloon doors swinging into the
kitchen, its charcoal-gray shutters and its lead St Francis in the
patio.

My aunt has become fond of me. As soon as she accepted
what she herself had been saying all those years, that the Bolling family had gone to seed and that I was not one of her
heroes but a very ordinary fellow, we got along very well. Both
women find me comical and laugh a good deal at my expense.

On Mardi Gras morning of the next year, my Uncle Jules
suffered a second heart attack at the Boston Club, from which
he later died.

The following May, a few days after his fifteenth birthday,
my half-brother Lonnie Smith died of a massive virus infection
which was never positively identified.

As for my search, I have not the inclination to say much on
the subject. For one thing, I have not the authority, as the great
Danish philosopher declared, to speak of such matters in any
way other than the edifying. For another thing, it is not open
to me even to be edifying, since the time is later than his, much
too late to edify or do much of anything except plant a foot
in the right place as the opportunity presents itself—if indeed
asskicking is properly distinguished from edification.

Further: I am a member of my mother's family after all and
so naturally shy away from the subject of religion (a peculiar

THE LAST GENTLEMAN

FOR BUNT

If a man cannot forget, he will never amount to much.

Søren Kierkegaard, *Either/Or*

. . . We know now that the modern world is coming to an end . . . at the same time, the unbeliever will emerge from the fogs of secularism. He will cease to reap benefit from the values and forces developed by the very Revelation he denies . . . Loneliness in faith will be terrible. Love will disappear from the face of the public world, but the more precious will be that love which flows from one lonely person to another . . . the world to come will be filled with animosity and danger, but it will be a world open and clean.

Romano Guardini, *The End of the Modern World*

The characters in this novel are fictional. No real persons are portrayed. The places do not necessarily correspond to geography. That is to say, New York is New York, but localities in Alabama, Mississippi, and Louisiana have been deliberately scrambled. For example, the Southern city herein set forth bears certain resemblances to Birmingham. But the nearby university is more like the state institution in Mississippi. The town of Shut Off, Louisiana, is not across the Mississippi River from Vicksburg. These liberties are taken as a consequence of my impression that this region as a whole, comprising parts of Alabama, Mississippi, and Louisiana, shares certain traits which set it apart from much of the United States and even from the rest of the South.

But before he could think what to do, his love had finished her sandwich, wiped her mouth with Kleenex, and vanished. By the time he reached the alp, there was no sign of her.

Taking the gravel path which skirts the pond, he crossed Central Park West, entered the Y.M.C.A., and went straight up to his room, which was furnished with a single bed and a steel desk varnished to resemble wood grain. Carefully stowing away his telescope under the Val-Pak which hung in the closet, he undressed to his shorts and lay on the bed. After gazing at the ceiling for some minutes, he fell asleep and slept soundly for five hours.

2.

He was a young man of a pleasant appearance. Of medium height and exceedingly pale, he was nevertheless strongly built and quick and easy in his ways. Save for a deafness in one ear, his physical health was perfect. Handsome as he was, he was given to long silences. So girls didn't know what to make of him. But men liked him. After a while they saw that he was easy and meant no harm. He was the sort whom classmates remember fondly; they liked to grab him around the neck with an elbow and cuff him around. Good-looking and amiable as he was, however, he did not strike one as remarkable. People usually told him the same joke two or three times.

But he looked better than he was. Though he was as engaging as could be, something was missing. He had not turned out well. There is a sort who does well in school and of whom much is heard and expected and who thereafter does less and less well and of whom finally is heard nothing at all. The high tide of life comes maybe in the last year of high school or the first year of college. Then life seems as elegant as algebra. Afterwards people ask, what happened to so and so? And the answer is a shrug. He was the sort who goes away.

Even now he made the highest possible scores on psychological aptitude tests, especially in the area of problem-solving and goal-seeking. The trouble was he couldn't think what to do between tests.

New York is full of people from small towns who are quite content to live obscure lives in some out-of-the-way corner of the city. Here there is no one to keep track. Though such a person might have come from a long line of old settlers and a neighborhood rich in memories, now he chooses to live in a flat on 231st Street, pick up the paper and milk on the doorstep every morning, and speak to the elevator man. In Southern genealogies there is always mention of a cousin who went to live in New York in 1922 and not another word. One hears that people go to New York to seek their fortunes, but many go to seek just the opposite.

In his case, though, it was part of a family pattern. Over the years his family had turned ironical and lost its gift for action. It was an honorable and violent family, but gradually the violence had been deflected and turned inward. The great grandfather knew what was what and said so and acted accordingly and did not care what anyone thought. He even wore a pistol in a holster like a Western hero and once met the Grand Wizard of the Ku Klux Klan in a barbershop and invited him then and there to shoot it out in the street. The next generation, the grandfather, seemed to know what was what but he was not really so sure. He was brave but he gave much thought to the business of being brave. He too would have shot it out with the Grand Wizard if only he could have made certain it was the thing to do. The father was a brave man too and he said he didn't care what others thought, but he did care. More than anything else, he wished to act with honor and to be thought well of by other men. So living for him was a strain. He became ironical. For him it was not a small thing to walk down the street on an ordinary September morning. In the end he was killed by his own irony and sadness and by the strain of living out an ordinary day in a perfect dance of honor.

As for the present young man, the last of the line, he did not know what to think. So he became a watcher and a listener and a wanderer. He could not get enough of watching. Once when he was a boy, a man next door had gone crazy and had sat out in his back yard pitching gravel around and hollering out to his enemies in a loud angry voice. The boy watched him all day, squatted down and watched him, his mouth open and drying. It seemed to him that if he could figure out what was wrong with the man he would learn the great secret of life.

Like many young men in the South, he became overly subtle and had trouble ruling out the possible. They are not like an immigrant's son in Passaic who decides to become a dentist and that is that. Southerners have trouble ruling out the possible. What happens to a man to whom all things seem possible and every course of action open? Nothing of course. Except war. If a man lives in the sphere of the possible and waits for something to happen, what he is waiting for is war—or the end of the world. That is why Southerners like to fight and make good soldiers. In war the possible becomes actual through no doing of one's own.

But it was worse than this in his case. It was more than being a Southerner. For some years he had had a nervous condition and as a consequence he did not know how to live his life. As a child he had had "spells," occurrences which were nameless and not to be thought of, let alone mentioned, and which he therefore thought of as lying at the secret and somehow shameful heart of childhood itself. There was a name for it, he discovered later, which gave it form and habitation. It was *déjà vu*, at least he reckoned it was. What happened anyhow was that even when he was a child and was sitting in the kitchen watching D'lo snap beans or make beaten biscuits, there came over him as it might come over a sorrowful old man the strongest sense that it had all happened before and that something else was going to happen and when it did he would know the secret of his own life. Things seemed to turn white and dense and time itself became freighted with an unspeakable emotion. Sometimes he "fell out" and would wake up hours later, in his bed, refreshed but still haunted.

When he was a youth he had lived his life in a state of the liveliest expectation, thinking to himself: what a fine thing it will be to become a man and to know what to do—like an Apache youth who at the right time goes out into the plains alone, dreams dreams, sees visions, returns and knows he is a man. But no such time had come and he still didn't know how to live.

To be specific, he had now a nervous condition and suffered spells of amnesia and even between times did not quite know what was what. Much of the time he was like a man who has just crawled out of a bombed building. Everything looked strange. Such a predicament, however, is not altogether a bad thing. Like the sole survivor of a bombed building, he had no secondhand opinions and he could see things afresh.

There were times when he was as normal as anyone. He could be as objective-minded and cool-headed as a scientist. He read well-known books on mental hygiene and for a few minutes after each reading felt very clear about things. He knew how to seek emotional gratifications in a mature way, as they say in such books. In the arts, for example. It was his custom to visit museums regularly and to attend the Philharmonic concerts at least once a week. He understood, moreover, that it is people who count, one's relations with people, one's warmth toward and understanding of people. At these times he set himself the goal and often achieved it of "cultivating rewarding interpersonal relationships with a variety of people"—to use a phrase he had come across and not forgotten. Nor should the impression be given that he turned up his nose at religion, as old-style scientists used to do, for he had read widely among modern psychologists and he knew that we have much to learn from the psychological insights of the World's Great Religions.

At his best, he was everything a psychologist could have desired him to be. Most of the time, however, it was a different story. He would lapse into an unproductive and solitary life. He took to wandering. He had a way of turning up at unlikely places such as a bakery in Cincinnati or a greenhouse in Memphis, where he might work for several weeks assaulted by the *déjà vus* of hot growing green plants.

A German physician once remarked that in the lives of people who suffer emotional illness he had noticed the presence of *Lücken* or gaps. As he studied the history of a particular patient he found whole sections missing, like a book with blank pages.

Most of this young man's life was a gap. The summer before, he had fallen into a fugue state and wandered around northern Virginia for three weeks, where he sat sunk in thought on old battlegrounds, hardly aware of his own name.

3.

A few incidents, more or less as he related them to his doctor, will illustrate the general nature of his nervous condition.

His trouble came from groups. Though he was as pleasant and engaging as could be, he had trouble doing what the group expected him to do. Though he did well at first, he did not for long fit in with the group. This was a serious business. His doctor spoke a great deal about the group: what is your role in the group? And sure enough that was his trouble. He either disappeared into the group or turned his back on it.

Once when he was a boy his father and stepmother put him in a summer camp and went to Europe. Now here was one group, the campers, he had no use for at all. The games and the group activities were a pure sadness. One night as the tribe gathered around the council fire to sing songs and listen to the director tell stories and later ask everyone to stand up then and there and make a personal decision for Christ, he crept out of the circle of firelight and lit out down the road to Asheville, where he bought a bus ticket which carried him as far as his money, to Cedartown, Georgia, and hitchhiked the rest of the way home. There he lived with his aunts for several weeks and with the help of a Negro friend built a tree house in a tall sycamore. They spent the summer aloft, reading comics while the tree house tossed like a raft in a sea of dappled leaves.

Later there was trouble with another group. Like his father and grandfather and all other male forebears, save only those who came of age during the Civil War, he was sent up to Princeton University. But unlike them he funked it. He did very well in his studies, joined a good club, made the boxing team, but funked it nevertheless. It happened this way. One beautiful fall afternoon of his junior year, as he sat in his dormitory room, he was assaulted by stupefying *déjà vus*. An immense melancholy overtook him. It was, he knew, the very time of life one is supposed to treasure most, a time of questing and roistering, the prime and pride of youth. But what a sad business it was for him, this business of being a youth at college, one of many generations inhabiting the same old buildings, joshing with the same janitors who had joshed with the class of '37. He envied the janitors. How much better it would be to be a janitor and go home at night to a cozy cottage by the railroad tracks, have a wee drop with one's old woman, rather than sit here solemn-and-joyous, *feierlich*, in these honorable digs. On this afternoon, some of his classmates were standing just outside in the hall, a half dozen young Republicans from Bronxville and Plainfield and Shaker Heights. They too knew it was the best years of their lives and they were enjoying themselves accordingly. They had a certain Princeton way of talking, even the ones from Chicago and California, and a certain way of sticking their hands in their pockets and settling their chins in their throats. They were fine fellows, though, once you got used to their muted Yankee friendliness. Certainly this was the best of times, he told himself with a groan. Yet, as he sat at his desk in Lower Pyne, by coincidence in the very room occupied by his grandfather in 1910, he said to himself: what is the matter with me? Here I am surrounded by good fellows and the spirit of Old Nassau and wishing instead I was lying in a ditch in Wyoming or sitting in a downtown park in Toledo. He thought about his father and grandfather. They had been very fond of their classmates, forming relationships which lasted through the years. One had only to mention the names, Wild Bill (each had a Wild Bill in his class), the Dutchman, Froggie Auchincloss the true frog the blue frog the unspeakably parvenu frog, and his father would smile and shake his head fondly and stick his hands in his pockets in a certain way and rock back on his heels in the style of the class of '37.

His classmates used words in a distinctive way. That year they called each other "old buddy" long before this expression was heard at Tulane or Utah State, and they used the words "hack" and "go" in an obscure but precise way: if you made a good run in touch football, somebody might say to you, "What a hack." At other times and out of a clear sky, even in the middle of a sentence, somebody might say to you, "Go!", a command not to be confused with the argot of disc jockeys but intended rather as an ironic summons to the speaker to go forth. It was a signal to him that he was straying ever so slightly from the accepted way of talking or acting, perhaps showing unseemly enthusiasm or conviction. "Go!" he would be told in the obscure but exact sense of being sent on a mission.

The fall afternoon glittered outside, a beautiful bitter *feierlich* Yankee afternoon. It was the day of the Harvard–Princeton game. He felt as if he had seen them all. The ghost of his grandfather howled around 203 Lower Pyne. He knew his grandfather occupied room 203 because he had seen the number written in the flyleaf of Schiller's *Die Räuber*, a dusty yellow book whose pages smelled like bread. After a moment the young Southerner, who still sat at his desk, tried to get up, but his limbs were weighed down by a strange inertia and he moved like a sloth. It was all he could do to keep from sinking to the floor. Walking around in old New Jersey was like walking on Saturn, where the force of gravity is eight times that of earth. At last, and despite himself, he uttered a loud groan, which startled him and momentarily silenced his classmates. "Hm," he muttered and peered at his eyeballs in the mirror. "This is no place for me for another half hour, let alone two years."

Forty minutes later he sat on a bus, happy as a lark, bound for New York, where he lived quite contentedly at the Y.M.C.A.

The following summer, in deference to the wishes of his father, who hoped to arouse in him a desire to complete his education and particularly to awaken a fondness for the law, he worked as a clerk in the family law firm. There was no place to sit but the library, a dusty room with a large oval table of golden oak which also served as a conference room and a place to read wills and pass acts of sale. The fragrant summer air thrust in at the window and the calfskin of the law books crumbled and flew up his nostrils. Beyond the glittering street, the oaks of the residential section turned yellow with pollen, then a dark lustrous green, then whitened with dust. He contracted dreadful hay fever and sat all summer, elbows propped on the conference table, tears running down his cheeks. His nose swelled up like a big white grape and turned violet inside. Through the doorway, opened at such an angle that he might overhear without being seen, he heard his father speak with his clients, a murmurous sound compounded of grievance and redress. As the summer wore on, it became more and more difficult to distinguish the words from the sound, until finally they merged with the quarrels of the sparrows under the window sill and the towering sound of the cicadas that swelled up from the vacant lots and filled the white sky. The other members of the firm were cordial enough, but he could not get on any other

footing with them save that of the terrific cordiality of their
first greetings, to which he responded as best he could while
holding his great baboon's nose in a handkerchief.

At the end of summer his father died. Though his death was
sudden, people were less surprised than they might have been,
since it was well known that in this particular family the men
died young, after short tense honorable lives, and the women
lived another fifty years, lived a brand new life complete with a
second girlhood, outings with other girls, 35,000 hearty meals,
and a long quarrelsome senescence.

For another month or so the young man, whose name was
Williston Bibb Barrett or Will Barrett or Billy Barrett, sat rocking on the gallery with six women: one, his stepmother, who
was a good deal older than his father, was nice enough but
somewhat abstracted, having a way of standing in the pantry
for minutes at a time and whistling the tunes of the Hit Parade;
three aunts; a cousin; and a lady who was called aunt but was
not really kin—all but one over seventy and each as hale as a
Turk. He alone ailed, suffering not only from hay fever but
having fallen also into a long fit of melancholy and vacancy
amounting almost to amnesia. It was at that time that he came
near joining the ranks of the town recluses who sit dreaming
behind their shutters thirty or forty years while the yard goes
to jungle and the bugs drone away the long summer days.

Managing to revive himself, however, he concluded his
father's affairs, sold the law library to the surviving members of
the firm, reapportioned the rooms of the house in the fashion
best calculated to minimize quarrels, had drawn in his favor a
letter of credit in the amount of $17,500, his inheritance—and,
again losing the initiative, sat rocking on the gallery with his
aunts. He considered farming. But all that remained of Hampton, the family plantation, was two hundred acres of buckshot
mud long since reclaimed by canebrakes.

As it turned out, his mind was made up for him, for he was
drafted shortly thereafter. He put Hampton in the soil bank
and served two years in the United States Army, where he took
a large number of courses in electronics and from which he was
honorably and medically discharged when he was discovered
totally amnesic and wandering about the Shenandoah Valley

He began to get things backward. He felt bad when other people felt good and good when they felt bad. Take an ordinary day in New York. The sun is shining, people live well, go about satisfying their needs and achieving goals, work at creative jobs, attend cultural attractions, participate in interesting groups. This is, by every calculation, as it should be. Yet it was on just such a day as this, an ordinary Wednesday or Thursday, that he felt the deepest foreboding. And when his doctor, seeking to reassure him, suggested that in these perilous times a man might well be entitled to such a feeling, that only the insensitive did not, etc., it made him feel worse than ever. The analyst had got it all wrong. It was not the prospect of the Last Day which depressed him but rather the prospect of living through an ordinary Wednesday morning.

Though science taught that good environments were better than bad environments, it appeared to him that the opposite was the case.

Take hurricanes, for example, certainly a bad environment if ever there was one. It was his impression that not just he but other people too felt better in hurricanes—though it must be admitted that he had studied only four people and one hurricane, evidence hardly adequate to support a scientific hypothesis. One real robin does suggest a spring, however.

The summer before, he had got caught in hurricane Donna. A girl named Midge Auchincloss, none other in fact than the daughter of his father's old friend, had invited him to drive her up to a jazz festival in Newport. During the same weekend a small hurricane was beating up along the coast but giving every sign of careening off into the North Atlantic. Nobody took much notice of it. Friday afternoon, nothing was very different. The old Northeast smelled the same, the sky was hazed over, and things were not worth much. The engineer and his friend Midge behaved toward each other in their customary fashion. They did not have much to say, not as a consequence of a breakdown in communications such as one often hears about nowadays, but because there was in fact not much to say. Though they liked each other well enough, there was nothing to do, it seemed, but press against each other whenever they were alone. Coming home to Midge's apartment late at night, they would step over the sleeping Irishman, stand in the elevator and press against each other for a good half hour, each gazing abstractedly and dry-eyed over the other's shoulder.

But a knoll of high pressure reared up in front of Donna and she backed off to the west. On the way home from Newport, the Auchinclosses' Continental ran into the hurricane in Connecticut. Searching for Bridgeport and blinded by the rain, which hit the windshield like a stream from a firehose, the engineer took a wrong exit off the turnpike and entered upon a maze of narrow high-crowned blacktops such as crisscross Connecticut, and got lost. Within a few minutes the gale winds reached near-hurricane strength and there was nothing to do but stop the car. Feeling moderately exhilarated by the uproar outside and the snugness within, dry as a bone in their cocoon of heavy-gauge metal and safety glass, they fell upon one another fully clothed and locked in a death grip. Strange Yankee bushes, perhaps alder and dogbane, thrashed against the windows. Hearing a wailing sound, they sat up and had the shock of their lives. There, standing in the full glare of the headlights, or rather leaning against the force of the hurricane, was a child hardly more than a babe. For a long moment there was nothing to do but gaze at him, so wondrous a sight it was, a cherub striding the blast, its cheeks puffed out by the four winds. Then he was blown away. The engineer went after him, backing up on all fours, butt to wind like a range pony, reached the ditch and found him. Now with the babe lying as cold as lard between them and not even shivering, the engineer started the Continental and crept along, feeling the margin of the road under his tire like a thread under the fingertip, and found a diner, a regular old-style streetcar of a restaurant left over from the days before the turnpikes.

For two hours they sat in a booth and cared for the child, fed him Campbell's chicken-and-rice soup and spoke to him. He was not hurt but he was round-eyed and bemused and had nothing to say. It became a matter of figuring out what to do with him. The phone was dead and there was no policeman or anyone at all except the counterman, who brought a candle and joined them. The wind shrieked and the streetcar swayed and thrummed as if its old motors had started up. A window broke. They helped the counterman board it up with Coca-Cola crates. Midge and the counterman, he noticed, were very happy. The hurricane blew away the sad, noxious particles which befoul the sorrowful old Eastern sky and Midge no longer felt obliged ot keep her face stiff. They were able to talk. It was best of all when the hurricane's eye came with its so-called ominous stillness. It was not ominous. Everything was yellow and still and charged up with value. The table was worth $200. The unexpected euphoria went to the counterman's head and he bored them with long stories about his experiences as a bus boy in a camp for adults (the Southerner had never heard of such a thing) somewhere in the Catskills.

Even the problem of the lost child turned into a pleasure instead of a chore, so purgative was the action of the hurricane. "Where in the world do you come from?" Midge asked him. The child did not answer and the counterman did not know him. At last Midge turned up a clue. "What a curious-looking ring," she said, taking the child's hand.

"That's not a ring, that's a chickenband," said the counterman.

"Is there a chicken farm near here?" the engineer asked him.

There was, and it was the right place. When they delivered the babe an hour later, wonder of wonders, he had not even been missed. Ten children were underfoot and Dad and Mom were still out in the chickenhouses, and sister, a twelve-year-old who was also round-eyed and silent, received the prodigal as if it were nothing out of the way. This was the best of all, of course, returning the child before it was missed, him not merely delivered from danger but the danger itself cancelled, like Mr. Magoo going his way through the perilous world, stepping off the Empire State building onto a girder and never seeing the abyss.

Breakfast in the diner and back to the turnpike and on their way again. Down and out of the storm and into the pearly light of morning, another beautiful day and *augh* there it was again: the Bronx all solid and sullen from being the same today as yesterday, full of itself with lumpish Yankee fullness, the bricks coinciding with themselves and braced against all comers. Gravity increased.

Down into the booming violet air of Park Avenue they crept, under the selfsame canopy and into the selfsame lobby and over the sleeping Irishman and into the elevator where they strove against each other like wrestlers, each refusing to yield an inch.

5.

One day the next week, a rainy Thursday afternoon, he stood in a large room in the Metropolitan Museum of Art. Somewhere in the heights a workman was rattling the chain of a skylight. Happy people were worse off in their happiness in museums than anywhere else, he had noticed sometime ago. In here the air was thick as mustard gas with ravenous particles which were stealing the substance from painting and viewer alike. Though the light was technically good, illuminating the paintings in an unexceptional manner, it nevertheless gave the effect of descending in a dismal twilight from a vast upper region which roared like a conch shell. Here in the roaring twilight the engineer stationed himself and watched people watch the paintings. Sometime ago he had discovered that it is impossible to look at a painting simply so: man-looking-at-a-painting, *voilà!*—no, it is necessary to play a trick such as watching a man who is watching, standing on his shoulders, so to speak. There are several ways of getting around the ravenous particles.

Today the paintings were there, yes, in the usual way of being there but worse off than ever. It was all but impossible to see them, even when one used all the tricks. The particles were turning the air blue with their singing and ravening. Let everything be done properly: let one stand at the correct distance from a Velázquez, let the Velázquez be correctly lighted, set the painting and viewer down in a warm dry museum. Now here comes a citizen who has the good fortune to be able to enjoy a cultural facility. There is the painting which has been bought at great expense and exhibited in the museum so that millions can see it. What is wrong with that? Something, said the engineer, shivering and sweating behind a pillar. For the paintings were encrusted with a public secretion. The harder one looked, the more invisible the paintings became. Once again the force of gravity increased so that it was all he could do to keep from sinking to all fours.

entertained, royally it is true and getting paid for the privilege besides, but entertained nevertheless. Trophies they were sure enough, these dazzling wares offered every day, trophies to put him off the scent while the patient got clean away. Sourer still was the second suspicion that even the patient's dreams and recollections, which bore out the doctor's theories, confirmed hypotheses right and left, were somehow or other a performance too, the most exquisite of courtesies, as if the apple had fallen to the ground to please Sir Isaac Newton. Charged accordingly, the patient of course made an equally charming confession, exhibited heroic sweats and contortions to overcome his bad habits, offered crabbed and meager dreams, and so made another trophy of his disgrace.

The last year of the analysis the doctor had grown positively disgruntled. This one was a Southern belle, he decided, a good dancing partner, light on his feet and giving away nothing. He did not know how not to give away nothing. For five years they had danced, the two of them, the strangest dance in history, each attuned to the other and awaiting his pleasure, and so off they went crabwise and nowhere at all.

The doctor didn't like his patient much, to tell the truth. They were not good friends. Although they had spent a thousand hours together in the most intimate converse, they were no more than acquaintances. Less than acquaintances. A laborer digging in a ditch would know more about his partner in a week than the doctor had learned about this patient in a year. Yet outwardly they were friendly enough.

The engineer, on the other hand, had a high opinion of his analyst and especially liked hearing him speak. Though Dr. Gamow was a native of Jackson Heights, his speech was exotic. He had a dark front tooth, turned on its axis, and he puckered his lips and pronounced his *r*'s almost like *w*'s. The engineer liked to hear him say *neu-wosis*, drawing out the second syllable with a musical clinical Viennese sound. Unlike most Americans, who speak as if they were sipping gruel, he chose his words like bonbons, so that his patients, whose lives were a poor meager business, received the pleasantest sense of the richness and delectability of such everyday things as words. Unlike some analysts, he did not use big words or technical words; but the small ordinary words he did use were invested with a peculiar luster. "I think you are pretty unhappy after all," he might say, pronouncing *prĕtty* as it is spelled. His patient would nod gratefully. Even unhappiness is not so bad when it can be uttered so well. And in truth it did seem to the engineer, who was quick to sniff out theories and such, that people would feel better if they could lay hold of ordinary words.

At five o'clock, the Southerner's hour, the office smelled of the accumulated misery of the day, an ozone of malcontent which stung the eyes like a Lionel train. Some years ago the room had been done in a Bahama theme, with a fiber rug and prints of hummingbirds and Negresses walking with baskets on their heads, but the rug had hardened and curled up at the corners like old skin. Balls of fluff drifted under the rattan table.

"I—suggest—that if it is all right with you—" began Dr. Gamow, jotting a note on a smooth yellow pad with a gold pencil (this is all you really need to set your life in order, the patient was thinking, a good pad and pencil), "—we'll change Monday from five to five thirty. How is that for you, bad, eh?"

"No, it's not bad at all."

Dr. Gamow pricked up his ears. "Did you say mad?"

"No, I believe I said bad: it's not bad at all."

"It seemed to me that at first you said mad."

"It's possible," said the agreeable patient.

"I can't help wondering," said Dr. Gamow shyly, "who is mad at who." Whenever he caught his patient in a slip, he had a way of slewing his eyes around as shyly as a young girl. "Now what might it be that you are mad about?"

"I'm not really."

"I detected a little more *m* than *b*. I think maybe you are a little mad at me."

"I don't—" began the other, casting back in his mind to the events of the last session, but as usual he could remember nothing. "You may well be right, but I don't recall anything in particular."

"Maybe you think I'm a little mad at you."

"I honestly don't know," said the patient, pretending to rack his brain but in fact savoring the other's words. *Maybe*, for example, was minted deliberately as a bright new common coin *mebbe* in conscious preference to *perhaps*.

Dr. Gamow put his knees exactly together, put his head to one side, and sighted down into the kneehole of his desk. He might have been examining a bank of instruments. His nostril curved up exposing the septum of his nose and imparting to him a feral winged look which served to bear out his reputation of clinical skill. His double-breasted suit had wide lapels and it was easy to believe that, sitting as he did, hunched over and thick through the chest, his lapels bowed out like a cuirass, his lips pursed about the interesting reed of a tooth, that he served his patients best as artificer and shaper, receiving the raw stuff of their misery and handing it back in a public and acceptable form. "It does sound to me as if you've had a prětty bad time. Tell me about it." And the unspeakable could be spoken of.

He told Dr. Gamow he had reached a decision. It seemed plain to him that he had exhausted the resources of analysis—not that he had not benefited enormously—and in the future he thought he might change places with the analyst, making a little joke of it, heh-heh. After spending almost five years as an object of technique, however valuable, he thought maybe he'd go over to the other side, become one of them, the scientists. He might even have an idea or two about the "failure of communication" and the "loss of identity" in the modern world (at it again, throwing roses in the path, knowing these were favorite subjects of Dr. Gamow's). Mebbe he should strike out on his own.

For another thing, said he, he had run out of money.

"I see that after all you are a little mad at me," said Dr. Gamow.

"How's that?" said the patient, appearing to look caught out.

"Perhaps it might be worthwhile to look into whatever it is you are mad about."

"All right," said the patient, who would as soon do one thing as another.

"Yesterday," said the analyst, leafing back through his pad, "we were talking about your theory of environments. I believe you said that even under ideal conditions you felt somewhat— hollow was the word I think you used."

"Yes." He was genuinely surprised. He had forgotten that he had spoken of his new theory.

"I wondered out loud at the time what you meant by hollow—whether it referred to your body or perhaps an organ, and it seemed to me you were offended by the suggestion."

"Yes."

He remembered now that he had been offended. He had known at the time that Dr. Gamow had thought he meant that he had felt actually hollowed out, brain or spleen emptied of its substance. It had offended him that Dr. Gamow had suggested that he might be crazy.

"I then made the suggestion that mebbe that was your way of getting rid of people, literally 'hollowing them out,' so to speak. A pretty thoroughgoing method of execution."

"That is possible."

"Finally, you may recall, you made a little slip at the end of the hour. You said you had to leave early—you had jumped up, you may recall—saying that you had to attend a meeting at the store, but you said 'beating.'"

"Yes."

"I couldn't help but wonder who the beating was intended for. Was it you who got the beating from me yesterday? Or am I getting a beating from you today?"

"You could be right," said the other, trying to straighten the ambiguous chair and face the doctor. He meant to signify that he wished to say something that should be listened to and not gotten at. "Nevertheless I have decided on a course of action and I think I'd better see it through." For some reason he laughed heartily. "Oh me," he said with a sigh.

"Hnhnhn," said Dr. Gamow. It was an ancient and familiar sound, so used between them, so close in the ear, as hardly to be a sound at all.

The Southerner leaned back and looked at the print of hummingbirds. They symbolized ideas, Dr. Gamow had explained jokingly, happy ideas which he hoped would fly into the heads of his patients. One bird's gorget did not quite fit; the print had been jogged in the making and the gorget had slipped and stuck out like a bib. For years the patient had gazed at this little patch of red, making a slight mental effort each time to put it back in place.

"I notice now that you use the phrase 'run out'—'I have run out of money'," said Dr. Gamow. Lining up his feet again, he sighted along his knee like an astronaut. "The idea suggests itself that you literally ran out of your own money—"

"Figuratively," murmured the other.

"Leaving it behind? I could not help but notice you seem to have acquired what seems to be a very expensive possession."

"What is that?"

"The handsome leather case." Dr. Gamow nodded toward the reception room. "Camera? Microscope?"

"Telescope," he said. He had forgotten his recent purchase! He was, moreover, obscurely scandalized that the doctor should take account of something out in the waiting room.

"A telescope," mused the analyst, sighting into the farthest depths of the desk. "Do you intend to become a seer?"

"A seer?"

"A see-er. After all a seer is a see-er, one who can see. Could it be that you believe that there is some ultimate hidden truth and that you have the magical means for obtaining it?"

"Ha-ha, there might be something in that. A see-er. Yes."

"So now it seems you have spent your money on an instrument which will enable you to see the truth once and for all?"

The patient shrugged affably.

"It would be pretty nice if we could find a short cut and get around all this hard work. Do you remember, the last time you left you stood up and said: 'Look here now, this analysis is all very well but how about telling me the truth just between ourselves, off the record, that is, what am I *really* supposed to do?' Do you remember that?"

"Yes."

"And do you still think that I am spoofing you?" Dr. Gamow, who liked to be all things to all men, had somewhere got the notion that in the South you said "spoofing" a great deal.

The patient nodded.

"You also recall that this great thirst for the 'answer,' the key which will unlock everything, always overtakes you just before the onset of one of your fugue states?"

"Not always."

"Always in the past."

"Not this time."

"How much did it cost you?"

"What?"

"The telescope."

"Nineteen hundred dollars."

"Nineteen hundred dollars," repeated the analyst softly.

"Which leaves me with the sum of fifty-eight dollars and thirty cents," said the patient. "According to my calculations, I owe you for eight sessions this month, including this one." And arising from the ambiguous chair, he placed two twenties and a ten on the desk. "Now I owe you one fifty. I'll pay you at the end of the month."

Dr. Gamow gazed at the money. "May I review for you one or two facts. Number one, you have had previous fugue states. Number two, you give every indication of having another. You always quit the analysis and you always buy something expensive before taking off. The last time it was a Corvette. You still have a defective ego structure, number three. Number four, you develop ideas of reference. This time it is hollow men, noxious particles, and ultimate truths."

It always seemed strange to hear Dr. Gamow speak of him clinically. Once, when the analyst was called away from the office, he had ventured out of the ambiguous chair and stolen a glance at the file which lay open on the blotter. ". . . a well-developed and nourished young white male," he read, "with a pleasing demeanor, dressed in an unusual raglan jacket." (This description must have been written at the time he had fallen in with the Ohioans, become one himself, and bought a raglan jacket so that he could move his shoulders around freely.) "When asked why he had chosen this particular article of apparel, he replied that 'it made me feel free.'"

Seeing himself set down so, in a clinical quotation, gave him a peculiar turn. His scalp bristled.

But now he nodded equably and, leaning back, gazed at the dusty little hummingbird.

"Very well," said Dr. Gamow when he did not answer. "You have made your decision. The question is, what is to be done next."

"Yes sir."

"May I make a suggestion?"

"Certainly."

"Next week I am starting a new group in therapy. It will be

limited to ten persons. It is a very good group and my feeling is that you could profit by the experience. They are people like yourself who are having difficulty relating to other people in a meaningful way. Like yourself they find themselves in some phase or other of an identity crisis. There is—let me see—a novelist who is blocked, an engineer like yourself who works with digital computers and who feels somewhat depersonalized. There is an actress you will recognize instantly, who has suddenly begun forgetting her lines. There is a housewife with a little more anxiety than she can handle, psychiatrically oriented but also success-oriented. There is an extremely sensitive Negro who is *not* success-oriented—a true identity problem there. And four social workers from White Plains. It's a lot better than the last group you were in—these are some very highflying folks and I don't think you'll be able to snow them quite as successfully."

That's what you think, said the Southerner to himself; these are just the kind of folks I snow best.

"We shall meet here three times a week. The fee is nominal, five dollars."

"I certainly do appreciate it," said the other earnestly. "It does indeed sound like an interesting group, but for the present my salary will not permit it. Perhaps when my soil-bank check comes through—"

"From the old plantation?" asked Dr. Gamow.

"Yes. But I assure you I feel quite well."

"Euphoric, in fact," said Dr. Gamow ironically.

He grinned. "Mebbe I could join y'all later."

"This is not a catfish fry," said the analyst testily.

At the end of the hour they arose and shook hands pleasantly. The patient took a last look at the dusty hummingbird which had been buzzing away at the same trumpet vine for five years. The little bird seemed dejected. The bird, the print, the room itself had the air of things one leaves behind. It was time to get up and go. He was certain that he would never see any of them again.

Before leaving, he obtained from Dr. Gamow a prescription for the little blue spansules which he saved for his worst times. They did not restore his memory, but when he was at his hollowest, wandering about some minor battlefield in Tennessee, he could swallow a spansule, feel it turn warm, take root, and flower under his ribs.

So it was that Williston Bibb Barrett once again set forth into the wide world at the age of twenty-five, Keats's age at his death, in possession of $8.35, a Tetzlar telescope, an old frame house, and a defunct plantation. Once again he found himself alone in the world, cut adrift from Dr. Gamow, a father of sorts, and from his alma mater, sweet mother psychoanalysis.

Though it may have been true that he gave every sign of a relapse of his nervous condition, of yet another spell of forgetfulness and of wandering about the U.S. and peering into the faces of Georgians and Indianians, for the present at least he was in the best possible humor and alert as a cat. In the elevator he set down the telescope and threw a few punches: his arm was like a young oak, he could have put his fist right through the steel of the Otis cab. Each of his five senses was honed to a razor's edge and attuned like the great Jodrell Bank antenna to the slightest signal of something gone amiss.

I am indeed an engineer, he thought, if only a humidification engineer, which is no great shakes of a profession. But I am also an engineer in a deeper sense: I shall engineer the future of my life according to the scientific principles and the self-knowledge I have so arduously gained from five years of analysis.

Chapter Two

IT WAS THE DAY after he broke off his analysis that the engineer received a sign: he set up his telescope in the park to photograph the peregrine and had instead and by the purest chance witnessed the peculiar behavior of the Handsome Woman and her beautiful young friend. Every morning thereafter the engineer returned to the park and took his position beside the same outcropping of rock.

The peregrine returned to his perch. Every morning he patrolled the cornice, making an awkward sashay in his buff pants, cocked a yellow eye at the misty trees below, and fell like a thunderbolt, knocking pigeons out of the air in all directions. The engineer took a dozen photographs at magnification one fifty, trusting that at least one would catch the fierce eclipsed eye of the falcon.

Every morning after work he set up his Tetzlar. After taking his two bearings, one on the eyrie of the peregrine, the other on the park bench, he had then only to lock the positions into the celestial drive, press a button, and the instrument would swing in its mount and take aim like a Navy rifle.

The Handsome Woman came four days later, left a note, but the girl did not come. Again he prized open the semicircle of tin and again he found a verse.

> *From you have I been absent in the spring,*
> *When proud-pied April, dressed in all his trim,*
> *Hath put a spirit of youth in every thing;*
> *That heavy Saturn laugh'd and leap'd with him.*

After that, neither one came.

At night he sat at his desk in the Y.M.C.A. casting about in his mind and drumming his fingernails on the steel top, which had been varnished to represent wood grain.

For two weeks he spent every spare moment at his vigil, coming to the park directly from work, forgetful of all else, sometimes forgetting to change his engineer's smock.

What had become of his love?

Emerging one morning from Macy's sub-basement, the engineer stood blinking in the sunlight at Nedick's corner. It was the most valuable spot on the entire earth, having been recently appraised, he had read in *The Times*, at ninety dollars per cubic inch. It gave him pleasure to stand in Nedick's and think about the cubic inch of space at the tip of his nose, a perfect little jewel of an investment.

For a minute or so he stood watching the bustle of traffic, garment porters pushing trucks of dresses, commuters from Penn Station pouring down Thirty-fourth Street.

Then, and for several mornings running, he experienced a hallucination which, however, he did not entirely recognize as such, a bad enough sign in itself. When he got sick, his sense of time went out of kilter, did not quite coincide with the ongoing present moment, now falling behind, now speeding ahead: a circumstance that no doubt accounted for the rich harvest of *déjà vus*. Now, as he stood in Nedick's, it seemed to him that the scene which took place before his eyes was happening in a time long past. The canyon of Seventh Avenue with the smoking rays of sunlight piercing the thundering blue shadow, the echoing twilight spaces as dim and resounding as the precipice air of a Western gorge, the street and the people themselves seemed to recede before his gaze. It was like watching a film of bygone days in which, by virtue merely of the lapsed time, the subject is invested with an archaic sweetness and wholeness all the more touching for its being exposed as an illusion. People even walked faster, like the crowds in silent films, surging to and fro in a wavelike movement, their faces set in expressions of serious purpose so patent as to be funny and tender. Everyone acted as if he knew exactly what he was doing and this was the funniest business of all. It reminded him of a nurse he had in the South. Once his father took some movies of him and his nurse in a little park. Ten years later, when on Christmas Eve the film was shown and D'lo, passing in the hall behind the projector, stood for a moment to see herself with the others, the black nurses whose faces were underexposed and therefore all the more inscrutable but who nevertheless talked and moved and cocked a head with the patent funniness of lapsed time—D'lo let out a shriek and, unable to bear the sight of herself, threw her apron over her head. It was, he reckoned, the drollness of the past which struck her, the perky purpose of the people who acted for all the world as if they knew what they were doing, had not a single doubt.

Still no sign of the women in the park, and he cut short his vigil, watching only during the noon hour. There was more time now to attend to his physical health. He took pains to eat and sleep regularly and to work out in the Y.M.C.A. gym. He punched a sandbag an hour a day, swam forty laps in the pool, or, on cool days, jogged three times around the reservoir in the park. After a cold shower and a supper of steak, milk, vegetables, and wheat germ, he allowed himself a half hour of television and spent the remaining three hours before work seated bolt upright at his desk trying to set his thoughts in order.

He began the day by reading a few lines from *Living*, a little volume of maxims for businessmen which he had come across in Macy's book department. It made him feel good to read its crisp and optimistic suggestions.

> On your way to work, put aside your usual worries. Instead keep your mind both relaxed and receptive—and playful. The most successful businessmen report that their greatest ideas often come to them in such intervals.

Yes. And it was in fact very pleasant walking up Broadway instead of riding the subway every morning, one's mind wiped clean as a blackboard (not that it was necessary for him to try to "put aside your usual worries," since he forgot everything anyhow, worries included, unless he wrote them down).

Cheerful and sensible though his little book of maxims was, it was no match for the melancholy that overtook him later in the day. Once again he began to feel bad in the best of environments. And he noticed that other people did too. So bad did they feel, in fact, that it took the worst of news to cheer them up. On the finest mornings he noticed that people in the subway looked awful until they opened their newspapers and read of some airliner crashing and killing all hundred and seven passengers. Where they had been miserable in their happiness, now as they shook their heads dolefully at the tragedy they became happy in their misery. Color returned to their cheeks and they left the train with a spring in their step.

Every day the sky grew more paltry and every day the ravening particles grew bolder. Museums became uninhabitable. Concerts were self-canceling. Sitting in the park one day, he heard a high-pitched keening sound directly over his head. He looked up through his eyebrows but the white sky was empty.

That very night as he sat at his console under Macy's, his eye happened to fall upon the Sunday *Times*, which lay in a corner. There on the front page of an inner section was a map of Greater New York which was overlaid by a series of concentric circles rippling out to Mamaroneck in the north, to Plainfield in the south. He picked it up. It was one of those maps illustrating the effects of the latest weapon, in this case some kind of nerve gas. The innermost circle, he noted idly, called the area of irreversible axon degeneration, took in Manhattan Island and Brooklyn as far as Flatbush, Queens as far as Flushing, and the lower Bronx. The next circle was marked the zone of "fatty degeneration of the proximal nephrone," and the third that of "reversible cortical edema."

He frowned at the flickering lights of the console. Was it possible, he wondered, that—that "It" had already happened, the terrible event that everyone dreaded. He smiled and socked his head: he was not yet so bad off as to believe that he was being affected by an invisible gas.

Then, after looking at the map another ten minutes, he saw it at last, and his heart gave a big bump in his neck. Like a funnel, the circles carried his eye plunging down into the heart of Manhattan Island to—there, just inside the southeast corner of Central Park; there the point of the compass had been stuck while the pen swiveled, there just north of the little amoeba of the Pond.

The bench, where the Handsome Woman had sat, was exactly at ground zero.

He smiled again. It was a sign. He knew he would see the two women again.

He resolved to resume his vigil.

2.

He needn't have bothered. The very next morning, an unmemorable day neither cloudy nor clear, hot or cold, the engineer, who had emerged from Macy's only to plunge immediately underground again, caught sight of the Handsome Woman on the subway level of Pennsylvania Station. It was not even necessary to follow her. She took his train. When she did not get up at Columbus Circle, he stayed on too.

The train burrowed deep into the spine of the island and began a long climb up into Washington Heights, where they emerged, she taking an elevator and he a flight of steps (but why? she didn't know him from Adam), into a gray warren of a place which descended in broken terraces to the Hudson River. From the moraine of blackened gravel which covered the rooftops below, there sprouted a crooked forest of antennae and branching vent pipes. A perpetual wind pushed up the side streets from the river, scouring the gutters and forcing the denizens around into the sunny lee of Broadway with its sheltered bars and grills and kosher groceries and Spanish hairdressers.

He followed the Handsome Woman into a great mauve pile of buildings. Inside he took a sniff: hospital.

This time, when he saw her bound for an elevator, he entered beside her and swung around behind her as she turned. Now, eight inches in front of him, she suddenly looked frail, like a dancer who leaves the stage and puts on a kimono. There arose to his nostrils the heavy electric smell of unperfumed hair.

She got off at the tenth floor, so up he went to the eleventh and back down the steps in time to catch a glimpse of her foot and leg disappearing through a doorway. He kept on his way, past the closed door and other doors, past a large opening into a ward, and to the end of the corridor, where he cocked a foot on a radiator, propped his mouth on a knuckle, and looked out a sooty window. As usual, he had forgotten to put on his jacket when he left Macy's, and his tan engineer's smock gave him the look, if not of a doctor, at least of a technician of sorts.

Directly a man came out of the room into which the Handsome Woman had disappeared, and, to the engineer's astonishment, made straight for him.

At first he was certain he had been found out and someone had been sent to deal with him. His imagination formed the picture of a precinct station where he was charged with a misdemeanor of a vaguely sexual nature, following a woman on a subway. His eyes rolled up into his eyebrows.

But the stranger, an old man, only nodded affably. Lining up beside him, he rubbed himself against the vanes of the radiator and began to smoke a cigar with great enjoyment. He cradled one elbow in the crook of the other arm and rocked to and fro in his narrow yellow shoes.

"It looks like Dr. Calamera is running late." The stranger screwed up an eye and spoke directly into the smoke. He was a puckish-looking old fellow who, the engineer soon discovered, had the habit of shooting his arm out of his cuff and patting his gray hair.

"Who?" murmured the engineer, also speaking straight ahead since he was not yet certain he was being addressed.

"Aren't you assisting him in the puncture?"

"Sir?"

"You're not the hematologist?"

"No sir."

"They suspect a defect in the manufacture of the little blood cells in the marrow bones, like a lost step," said the stranger cheerfully, rocking to and fro. "It don't amount to much."

Two things were instantly apparent to the sentient engineer, whose sole gift, after all, was the knack of divining persons and situations. One was that he had been mistaken for a member of the staff. The other was that the stranger was concerned about a patient and that he, the stranger, had spent a great deal of time in the hospital. He had the air of one long used to the corridor, and he had developed a transient, fabulous, and inexpert knowledge of one disease. It was plain too that he imputed to the hospital staff a benevolent and omniscient concern for the one patient. It amounted to a kind of happiness, as if the misfortune beyond the door must be balanced by affectionate treatment here in the corridor. In hospitals we expect strangers to love us.

An intern passed, giving them a wide berth as he turned into the ward, holding out his hand to fend them off good-naturedly.

"Do you know him?" asked the old man.

"No sir."

"That's Dr. Moon Mullins. He's a fine little fellow."

The illness must be serious, thought the engineer. He is too fond of everyone.

The stranger was so wrapped up in cigar smoke and the loving kindness of the hospital that it was possible to look at him. He was old and fit. Ruddy sectors of forehead extended high into iron-colored hair. Though he was neatly dressed, he needed a shave. The stubble which covered his cheeks had been sprinkled with talcum powder and was white as frost. His suit, an old-fashioned seersucker with a broad stripe, gave off a fresh cotton-and-ironing-board smell that pierced the engineer's memory. It reminded him of something but he could not think what.

The engineer cleared his throat.

"Excuse me, sir, but are you from Alabama?" He had caught a lilt in the old man's speech, a caroling in the vowels which was almost Irish. And the smell. The iron-washpot smell. No machine in the world had ever put it there and nobody either but a colored washwoman working in her own back yard and sprinkling starch with a pine switch.

"I was." The old man took a wadded handkerchief from his pocket and knocked it against his nose.

"From north Alabama?"

"I was." His yellow eye gleamed through the smoke. He fell instantly into the attitude of one who is prepared to be amazed. There was no doubt in his mind that the younger man was going to amaze him.

"Birmingham? Gadsden?"

"Halfway between," cried the old man, his eye glittering like an eagle's. "Wait a minute," said he, looking at the engineer with his festive and slightly ironic astonishment. "Don't I know you? Aren't you—" snapping his finger.

"Will Barrett. Williston Bibb Barrett."

"Over in—" He shook his hand toward the southwest.

"Ithaca. In the Mississippi Delta."

"You're Ed Barrett's boy."

"Yes sir."

"Lawyer Barrett. Went to Congress from Mississippi in nineteen and forty." Now it was his turn to do the amazing. "Trained pointers, won at Grand Junction in—"

"That was my uncle, Fannin Barrett," murmured the engineer.

"Fannin Barrett," cried the other, confirming it. "I lived in Vicksburg in nineteen and forty-six and hunted with him over in Louisiana."

"Yes sir."

"Chandler Vaught," said the old man, swinging around at him. The hand he gave the engineer was surprisingly small and dry. "I knew I'd seen you before. Weren't you one of those fellows that ate over at Mrs. Hall's in Hattiesburg?"

"No sir."

"Worked for the highway department?"

"No sir."

"How did you know I wasn't from Georgia? I spent many a year in Georgia."

"You don't sound like a Georgian. And north Alabama doesn't sound like south Alabama. Birmingham is different from Montgomery. We used to spend the summers up in Mentone."

"Sho. But now you don't talk like—"

"No sir," said the engineer, who still sounded like an Ohioan. "I've been up here quite a while."

"So you say I'm from somewhere around Gadsden and Birmingham," said the old man softly in the way the old have of conferring terrific and slightly spurious honors on the young. "Well now I be damn. You want to know exactly where I come from?"

"Yes sir."

"Anniston."

"Yes sir."

"He don't even act surprised," the old man announced to the hospital at large. "But hail fire, I left Anniston thirty years ago."

"Yes sir. Did you know my father?" asked the engineer, already beginning to sound like an Alabamian.

"*Know* him! What are you talking about?"

"Yes sir."

"We used to hunt together down at Lake Arthur," he cried
as if he were launching into a reminiscence but immediately fell
silent. The engineer guessed that either he did not really know
his father or they were on different sides of the political fence.
His cordiality was excessive and perfunctory. "I got my young-
est boy in there," he went on in the same tone. "He got sick
just before his graduation and we been up here ever since. You
know Jamie?" For all he knew, the engineer knew everything.
    "No sir."
    "Do you know Sutter, my oldest boy? He's a doctor like
you."
    "I'm not a doctor," said the engineer, smiling.
    "Is that so," said the other, hardly listening.
    Now, coming to himself with a start, Mr. Vaught took hold
of the engineer's arm at the armpit and the next thing the latter
knew he had been steered into the sickroom where Mr. Vaught
related his "stunt," as he called it.
    It seemed to be a roomful of women. There were only three,
he determined later, but now with Mr. Vaught gripping him
tight under the armpit and five pairs of eyes swinging round
to him and shooting out curious rays, he felt as if he had been
thrust onto a stage.
    "And listen to this," said Mr. Vaught, still holding him
tightly. "He didn't say Gadsden and he didn't say Birmingham,
he said halfway between."
    "Actually I didn't say that," began the engineer.
    "This is Ed Barrett's boy, Mama," he said after pointing the
engineer in several different directions.
    A pince-nez flashed at him. There was a roaring in his ears.
"Lord, I knew your mother, Lucy Hunicutt, the prettiest little
thing I ever saw!"
    "Yes ma'am. Thank you."
    The women were taken up for a while with tracing kinships.
(Again he caught a note of rueful eagerness in their welcome:
were they political enemies of his father?) Meantime he could
catch his breath. It was a longish room and not ordinarily used,
it seemed, for patients, since one end was taken up with medical appliances mounted on rubber casters and covered by plastic
envelopes. At the other end, between the women, a youth lay
in bed. He was grinning and thrashing his legs about under

the covers. The Handsome Woman stood at his bedside, eyes vacant, hand on his pillow. As the engineer looked at her he became aware of a radiance from another quarter, a "certain someone" as they used to say in old novels. There was the same dark-browed combed look he remembered. Again a pang of love pierced his heart. Having fallen in love, of course, he might not look at her.

"—my wife, Mrs. Vaught," Mr. Vaught was saying, aiming him toward the chunky little clubwoman whose pince-nez flashed reflections of the window. "My daughter, Kitty—" Then Kitty was his love. He prepared himself to "exchange glances" with her, but woe: she had fallen into a vacant stare, much like the Handsome Woman, and even had the same way of rattling her thumbnail against her tooth. "And my daughter-in-law, Rita." The Handsome Woman nodded but did not take her eyes from the patient. "And here all piled up in the bed is my bud, Jamie." The patient would have been handsome too but for a swollen expression, a softening, across the nosebridge, which gave his face an unformed look. Jamie and Kitty and Mrs. Vaught were different as could be, yet they had between them the funded look of large families. It was in their case no more than a blackness of brow, the eyebrows running forward in a jut of bone which gave the effect of setting the eye around into a profile, the clear lozenge-shaped Egyptian eye mirroring the whorled hair of the brow like a woods creature.

He sized them up as Yankee sort of Southerners, the cheerful, prosperous go-getters one comes across in the upper South, in Knoxville maybe, or Bristol.

"Where're you from," cried Mrs. Vaught in a mock-accusatory tone he recognized and knew how to respond to.

"Ithaca," he said, smiling. "Over in the Delta." He felt himself molt. In the space of seconds he changed from a Southerner in the North, an amiable person who wears the badge of his origin in a faint burlesque of itself, to a Southerner in the South, a skillful player of an old play who knows his cues and waits smiling in the wings. You stand in the posture of waiting on ladies and when one of them speaks to you so, with mock-boldness and mock-anger (and a bit of steel in it too), you knew how to take it. They were onto the same game. Mrs. Vaught feasted her eyes on him. He was *nice*. (She, he saw at once, belonged to an older clan than Mr. Vaught; she knew ancient cues he never heard of.) She could have married him on the spot and known what she was getting.

It was just as well he hadn't pretended to be a doctor, for presently two doctors came in. One, a gaunt man with great damp hands and coiling veins, took the patient's arm and began massaging it absently. The doctor gave himself leave not to talk and not to focus his eyes. The hand was absent-minded too, felt its way into the boy's armpit, touched the angle of his jaw. What I am doing is of no importance, said the hand. Nothing was important but an unfocused fondness which seemed to hum and fill the room. Now, while the hand went its way, browsing past bone and artery and lymph node, the doctor leaned over to read the title of the book the boy had closed on his finger.

"Tractatus Log—" he began, and exchanged glances with his assistant, a chesty little house physician with a mustache and a row of gleaming pencils and penlights clipped in his pocket. The doctors gazed at each other with thunderstruck expressions which made everybody laugh. Again the youth's eyes narrowed and his legs began to thrash about. Again the big damp hand went about its business, this time gliding to the youth's knee and quieting him. Why, he's seriously ill, thought the sentient engineer, watching the monitory hand.

"It's not too hard to read," said the patient, his voice all squeaks and horns. "Sutter gave it to me," he told the Hand-some Woman, who was still gazing dry-eyed and had taken no notice even of the doctors.

"What a wonderful man," cried the engineer when the doctors left. "I envy you," he told the patient.

"You wouldn't envy me if you had to live in this room for five weeks."

"I wouldn't mind at all," said the engineer earnestly.

They looked at him. "How long have you been up here?" Mrs. Vaught asked.

"Five years. Seven, including my two years at Princeton. All my immediate family are dead. Do you know this is the first time I have talked to a, ah, family in years. I had forgotten—" he broke off and rubbed his forehead. He saw that he was expected to give an account of himself. "No, really. I don't think it is bad to be here. It reminds me of a time I was in the hospital—for three months—and it wasn't bad at all! In fact I felt better in the hospital than anywhere else."

"What was the matter with you?" Jamie asked him.

"I had a nervous condition, nothing very serious, an episode of amnesia, if you want to know the truth."

"Amnesia," said Kitty, looking at him for the first time.

"Yes. I didn't know my own name, but I knew enough to put myself in the hospital. It was caused by a toxic condition."

"You committed yourself," said Mrs. Vaught.

"Yes ma'am. I went to a very expensive place in Connecticut and was soon much better."

"How did you recover your memory?" Kitty asked him curiously.

"That was the strangest thing of all. For two months I remembered nothing. During this time I had gotten into the habit of playing Chinese checkers with another patient, a girl with a more serious condition than mine. She had not spoken to anyone for two years—she had not uttered a single word—even though she had received shock treatment. There was something familiar about her. Perhaps that was why I was attracted to her—that and the fact that I too was shy about talking and since she—"

They all laughed and he looked startled. "Yes, it's true. I was shy! I don't know why I'm not shy now. Anyhow she said nothing and I remembered nothing, and so it wasn't bad. You asked me how my memory came back. It was very simple. One night as we played Chinese checkers I looked at her and remembered who she was. 'Aren't you Margaret Rich?' I asked her. She said nothing. 'Didn't your family have the cottage next to ours in Monteagle ten years ago?' (That was before we started going to Mentone.) Still she said nothing. 'Why, I remember the dress you wore to a dance,' I told her (I always remember the remote past first). 'It was an orange-colored cotton twill sort of material.' 'That was my piqué,' says she as normally as you please." For some reason he flushed and fell silent.

"Do you mean that she spoke normally after that?" asked Kitty presently. She had swung around and was searching his face with her bold brown eyes.

"No, not normally, but it was a beginning," he said, frowning, feeling irritated with himself for being garrulous.

"I don't understand why she didn't speak before," said Jamie, thrashing his legs.

"I understand it!" cried Kitty. But then she blushed and turned away.

The others were not as amazed by the engineer's somewhat disconnected story as one might expect. For, strange to say, it was understood that it was open to him at that moment to spin just such a yarn, half-serious and curious.

"Yes, I know why your stay in the hospital was not so bad," said Jamie. "You weren't really sick."

"I'll trade with you any time," said the engineer. "Believe me, it is a very uncomfortable experience to have amnesia."

At that moment the Handsome Woman whispered something to Kitty and the two of them kissed the patient, said their goodbyes and left. He waited for another brown-eyed look but Kitty had lapsed into vacancy again and did not seem to notice him. The talkative engineer fell silent.

Presently he roused himself and took his leave. The patient and his mother asked him to come back. He nodded absently. Mr. Vaught followed him into the hall and steered him to the window, where they gazed down on the sooty moraine of Washington Heights.

"You come on up here and see Jamie again, you heanh me," he said, drawing him close and exhaling his old-man smell of fresh cotton and sour breath.

"Yes sir. Sir?"

"What's that?" said the old man, giving him a hairy convoluted ear.

"The lady who just left. Now is that Mrs. Rita Sutter or Miss—"

"Mrs. Mrs. Rita Vaught. She married my oldest boy, Sutter Vaught. Dr. Vaught. They're divorced. But I'm going to tell you, we're closer to her than to Sutter, my own flesh and blood. Oh, she's a fine woman. Do you know what that woman did?"

"No sir," said the engineer, cupping a hand to his good ear and straining every nerve to get the straight of it.

"Why, she's the one who went up to his school when he got

sick this time and got him into the hospital. When there was no room. That's not even a regular hospital room!"

"And, ah, Kitty?"

"Kitty is Jamie's sister. You want to know what she's done for Kitty?"

"Yes sir."

"She invites Kitty to come up here to New York not for a week but a year, to take ballet. She's taking her to Europe next month! And she's not even kin! What are you going to do with a woman like that," cried the old man, taking the engineer by the blade of muscle at his shoulder and squeezing it hard.

"All right," said the engineer, nodding and wincing.

"And she's second in command to the third largest foundation in the world!"

"Foundation," said the engineer vaguely.

"She's executive secretary. She can pick up the telephone and spend five million dollars this afternoon."

"Is that right?"

"You come on up here in the morning and see Jamie."

"Yes sir."

3.

He did go see Jamie but Kitty was not there.

"What about Kitty?" he asked Mr. Vaught in the hall. It was not really a bold question since Mr. Vaught had once again set a tone of antic confidence, as much as to say: here we are two thousand miles from home, so it's all right for me to tell you about my family.

"Do you know what they've had that girl doing eight hours a day as long as I can remember?"

"No sir." The other, he noticed, pronounced "girl" as "gull," a peculiarity he last remembered hearing in Jackson, Mississippi.

"Ballet dancing. She's been taking ballet since she was eight years old. She hopes to try out for the New York City Center Ballet Company."

"Very good."

"Lord, they've had her studying up here, in Chicago, Cleveland, everywhere."

The engineer wondered who "they" were. Mrs. Vaught? "She must be very good."

"Good? You should see her prizes. She won first prize two years in a row at the Jay Cee Festival. Last year her mama took her up to Cleveland to study with the world's most famous ballet teacher. They lived in a hotel for nine weeks."

"It must require a great deal of self-sacrifice."

"Sacrifice? That's all she does." The other's eye glittered through the billowing smoke. Yet there was something unserious, even farcical, about his indignation.

"Even now?"

"I mean all. She dudn't go out to parties. She dudn't have, just as to say, dates. If a young man paid a call on her, I swear I don't think she'd know what to do."

"Is that right," said the engineer thoughtfully.

"I don't think it's worth it, do you?"

"No sir," he said absently. He rose. "I think I'll go in and see Jamie. Excuse me, sir."

"That's all right!"

4.

Without quite knowing why he did so—for now he had the Handsome Woman's name and had looked her up in the telephone book and now knew where Kitty lived—he kept up his vigil in the park.

Once he went to look at the house they lived in. They had, Kitty and Rita, a charming cottage in a mews stuck away inside a city block in the Village. He had not imagined there could be such a place in New York, that the paltry particles, ravening and singing, could be so easily gotten round. But they were gotten round, by making things small and bright and hiding them away in the secret sunny center of a regular city block. Elsewhere in New York—wherever one stood—there was the sense of streets running a thousand miles in either direction, clear up to 302nd Street and petering out in some forlorn place above Yonkers or running clean to Ontario, for all he knew. They, Kitty and Rita, got out of the wind, so to speak, found a sunny lee corner as sheltered as a Barbados Alley.

Then why not pick up the telephone and call her up and

say, what about seeing you? Well, he could not exactly say why except that he could not. The worst way to go see a girl is to go see her. The best way is not to go see her but to come upon her. Having a proper date with a girl delivers the two of you into a public zone of streets and buildings where every brick is turned against you.

The next day Rita came to the bench and Kitty joined her. It was not until he saw them through the telescope that he knew why he had kept up his vigil: it was because he did not know enough about Kitty.

When they left, they turned west. He waited. After five or six minutes they came through the maples and crossed the meadow toward the Tavern-on-the-Green. There they sat not half a mile away but twenty feet, outlined in rainbows and drifting against each other weightless and soundless like mermaids in the shallow ocean depths. Packing his telescope, he walked south past the restaurant and turned back. He found a table against a peninsula of open brickwork where by every calculation—yes: through a niche he caught a glimpse of the gold chain clasping the hardy structures of Kitty's ankle. He ordered a beer.

Like all eavesdroppers, he felt as breathless as if the future of his life might depend on what was said. And perhaps, he being what he was, it did.

"It's no use," Kitty was saying.

"It is use," said Rita. Her hair stirred. She must be turning her head to and fro against the bricks.

"What do you think is the matter with me, Ree?"

"Nothing that is not the matter with all of us."

"I am not what I want to be."

"Then accept yourself as you are."

"I do!" Kitty had a trick of ending her sentences with a lilt like a question. It was a mannerism he had noticed in the younger actresses.

"What is it?"

"Everything."

"Ah."

"What's wrong with me?"

"Tell me," said Rita, turning her head to and fro.

"Do you want to know?"

"Yes."

"The truth is, I'm stupid. I'm the stupidest person in the world."

"I see."

"That doesn't help."

"What would help?"

"I'm serious. Val and Jamie and you and Sutter are all so smart."

"You're the best of the lot," said Rita idly, turning her head against the bricks.

"Sometimes I think other people know a secret I don't know."

"What secret?"

"The way they talk—"

"People, what people? Do you mean a man and a woman?"

"Well, yes."

"Ah."

"Do you know, before I meet somebody—"

"Somebody? Who is somebody?"

"Before I meet them—if I know I'm going to meet them—I actually have to memorize two or three things to say. What a humiliating confession. Isn't that awful. And it is getting worse. Why am I like that?"

"Why say anything?"

"I keep thinking that it must be possible to be with a person with things natural between us."

"A person? What person? I'm a person. Aren't things easy between us?"

"Yes—because you've spoiled me."

"Like hell. Finish your sandwich and get back to work."

"Ree, I'm not even a good dancer."

"You're good, but you're lazy."

"No, Can Can." Or did she say *QuinQuin*?

"So now I'm getting old."

"No, Ree. But in a particular relationship do you think it is one's attitude or the other person who counts?"

"Who is this other person?"

"Do you remember what Will said yesterday?"

"Will?"

"Will Barrett? You know, the boy Poppy brought in."

"So now it's Will."

"Didn't you like him?"

"You make him sound like Cousin Will from Savannah."

"Well."

"Honey, I've got news for you."

"What?"

"That boy is not well."

"Not really."

"Really. And I can assure you there is nothing romantic about mental illness."

"But he isn't—"

"Wait. I suddenly begin to get it. I do believe that it is his symptoms which interest you."

"No, I think he's very nice."

"Yes, I see it! You're the girl who can't talk. And he can't remember. That makes you a pair."

"No."

"So you're going to remember for him and he's going to talk for you."

"No."

"Only it's more than that, isn't it? You also believe you can help him."

"Help him? Why does he need help?"

Rita's reply was not audible. They had gotten up and were moving away.

He sat deep in thought until he finished his beer. My need for eavesdropping is legitimate enough, he said to himself, screwing up an eye. What with the ravening particles and other noxious influences, when one person meets another in a great city, the meeting takes place edge on, so to speak, each person so deprived of his surface as to be all but invisible to the other. Therefore one must take measures or else leave it to luck. Luck would be this: if he saw her snatch a purse, flee into the park pursued by the cops. Then he would know something and could do something. He could hide her in a rocky den he had discovered in a wild section of the park. He would bring her food and they would sit and talk until nightfall, when they could slip out of the city and go home to Alabama. Such a turn of events was unlikely, however.

5.

The Vaughts liked the engineer very much, each feeling that he
was his or her special sort of person. And he was.

Each saw him differently.

Mr. Vaught was certain he was a stout Southern lad in the
old style, wellborn but lusty as anyone, the sort who knows
how to get along with older men. Back home he would have
invited the younger man on a hunt or to his poker club, where
he was certain to be a favorite. The second time Mr. Vaught
saw him, he took him aside ceremoniously and invited him to
Jamie's birthday party.

Jamie—who, he was told, had a severe and atypical mono-
nucleosis—saw him as a fellow technician, like himself an initi-
ate of science, that is, of a secret, shared view of the world, a
genial freemasonry which sets itself apart from ordinary folk
and sees behind appearances. He lent the engineer a tattered
offprint of a scientific article which was written by his brother
and which he kept under his pillow. It was titled *The Incidence
of Post-orgasmic Suicide in Male University Graduate Students*,
and divided into two sections, the first subtitled "Genital
Sexuality as the Sole Surviving Communication Channel
between Transcending-Immanent Subjects," and the second,
"The Failure of Coitus as a Mode of Reentry into the Sphere
of Immanence from the Sphere of Transcendence." The engineer read the article twice and could not make head or tail of
it, except a short description of technical procedure in which
Dr. Sutter, following some hunch or other, had examined the
urethral meatus of some thirty male suicides for the presence
of spermatozoa.

To Mrs. Vaught elder he was as nice as he could be. His
manners were good without being too ceremonial. There was
a lightness in him: he knew how to fool with her. They could
even have a fuss. "Now you listen to me, Billy Barrett, it's
time you buckled down," etc. So acute was his radar that neither Mrs. Vaught nor her husband could quite get it into their
heads that he did not know everything they knew. He *sounded*
like he did. She would speak allusively of six people utterly
unknown to him—"So I took one look at her when she got

home from school and of course her face was all broken out
and I said-ho-*ho*—"

"Who is that now?" asked the engineer, cupping a hand to
his good ear and straining every nerve.

"Sally, Myra's oldest."

"Myra?"

"My stepdaughter."

She was much as he remembered other ladies at home,
companionable and funny, except when she got off on her pet
subject, fluoridation or rather the evils of it, which had come
in her mind to be connected with patriotic sentiments. Then
her voice became sonorous and bell-like. She grew shorter than
ever, drew into herself like a fort, and fired in all directions. She
also spoke often of the "Bavarian Illuminati," a group who, in
her view, were responsible for the troubles of the South. They
represented European and Jewish finance and had sold out the
Confederacy.

"You know the real story of Judah P. Benjamin and John
Slidell, don't you?" she asked him, smiling.

"No ma'am," he said, looking at her closely to see if she was
serious. She was. In her smiling eyes he caught sight of fiery
depths.

Rita, however, paid no attention to him. She looked through
him.

Kitty? Twice she was in Jamie's room when he came up,
but she seemed abstracted and indifferent. When he asked
her if she wanted a Coke (as if they were back in high school
in Atlanta), she put her head down and ducked away from
him. He couldn't understand it. Had he dreamed that he had
eavesdropped?

On his fourth visit to Jamie he had a small amnesic fit, the first
in eighteen months.

As he climbed into the thin watery sunlight of Washington
Heights, the look and smell of the place threw him off and he
slipped a cog. He couldn't remember why he came. Yonder
was a little flatiron of concrete planted with maybe linden trees
like a park in Prague. Sad-looking Jewish men walked around
with their hands in their pockets and hair growing down their

necks. It was as far away as Lapland. A sign read: *Washington Heights Bar and Grill*. Could George Washington have set foot here? Which way is Virginia?

He sat down under a billboard of Johnnie Walker whose legs were driven by a motor. He put his hands on his knees and was careful not to turn his head. It would happen, he knew, that if he kept still for a while he could get his bearings like a man lost in the woods. There was no danger yet of slipping: jumping the tracks altogether and spending the next three months in Richmond.

It was then that he caught sight of Kitty coming from the hospital, head down, bucking the eternal gale of the side streets. He knew only that he knew her. There were meltings of recognition about his flank and loin. He wished now that he had looked in his wallet, to make sure of his own name and maybe find hers.

"Wait," he caught her four steps down the IRT.

"What? Oh." She smiled quickly and started down again.

"Wait a minute."

"I've got to *go*," she said, making a grimace by way of a joke.

"Please come over here for a moment. I have something to tell you." He knew that he could speak to her if he did not think about it too much.

She shrugged and let him guide her to the bench.

"What?"

"I, ah, thought you might do me a favor." He looked at her hard, groping for himself in her eyes. If he could not help her, hide her in Central Park, then she could help him.

"Sure, what?"

"You're going in the subway?"

"Yes."

"I just came out. To see, ah—" He knew he would know it as soon as she thought it. She thought it. "—Jamie."

"Good. He'll be glad to see you." She eyed him, smiling, not quite onto whatever roundabout joke he was playing and not liking it much.

"I changed my mind and decided to go back downtown."

"All right." But it was not all right. She thought he was up to some boy-girl business. "What's the favor?"

"That I ride with you and that you give me a punch if I miss my station."

"What?"

"Do you know where I live?"

"Yes. At—"

He touched her arm. "Don't tell me. I want to see if I know when I get there."

"What's the matter—oh"—all joking aside now, eyes black as shoe buttons. She saw he was sweating.

Oddest of all: strange as he felt, having slipped six cogs, the engineer knew nevertheless that it was a negotiable strangeness. He could spend some on her. "Nothing much. Will you do as I say?"

"Yes."

Above them, Johnnie Walker's legs creaked like ship's rigging.

"Let's go." He started straight out, not waiting on her.

"That's the wrong subway," she said, catching up with him. "I'm taking the IRT."

"Right." It was like a *déjà vu*: he knew what she was going to say as soon as she said it.

They rode in silence. When the train came to the first lights of the Columbus Circle platform, he rose. "This is it," he said.

"Yes," she said, watching him sloe-eyed.

"Thank you," he said, taking her hand like a man's, and left quickly.

He stopped at a gum-machine mirror to see how he looked. There was nothing much wrong. His face was pale but intact. But when he straightened, his knee gave way and he stumbled to the edge of the platform. The particles began to sing.

A hand took his. "This way," said Kitty. Her hand was warm and grubby from riding subways.

She led him to a bench on an arc of the Circle. It is strange, he thought, musing, but love is backwards too. In order to love, one has not to love. Look at her. Her hand was on his thigh, rough as a nurse. She made herself free of him, peering so close he could smell her breath.

"Are you all right?"

"Yes."

"You're pale. Your hand is so cold." She made a slight move-ment and checked it. He knew she had meant to warm his hand in her lap.

"As long as you are here, will you go over there and buy me a glass of orange juice?"

She watched him drink the juice. "Have you eaten anything today?"

"No."

"Did you have supper last night?"

"I don't remember."

"You don't remember to eat?"

"I eat when I get hungry. I don't remember that I have eaten."

"Are you hungry now?"

"Yes."

They walked to the automat on Fifty-seventh Street. While she drank coffee, he ate four dollars' worth of roast beef and felt much better. I'm in love, he thought as he drank his third glass of milk.

I don't think there is anything wrong with you," she said when he finished.

"That's right."

"What will you do now?"

"Go home and go to bed."

"You work at night?"

"Yes."

"Oh, for heaven's sake."

"There's one more thing—" he said.

"What?"

"Write your name and telephone number on this."

She smiled and did so but when she looked up and saw him she grew serious. "Oh."

"Yes, I need somebody to call. Is that all right with you?"

"Yes."

The sicker I am, the more I know, he thought. And the more she loves me. "Suppose I need to call you at three o'clock in the morning and say come to Weehawken."

"Call me." Her face clouded. "What about next month?"

"What about it?"

"I'll be in Spain. In Torremolinos."

"Write it down." After she wrote it, he asked her. "Now what if I call you over there?"

She looked at him, taking a tuck of lip between her teeth. "Do you mean it?"

"I mean it. You're the one I'm going to call."

"Why me?"

He drew his chair closer to the corner of the table and put his hand in her lap. "I'm in love."

"You are," she said. "Oh."

"I've never been in love before."

"Is that right?" Keeping a wary eye on him, she turned her head toward the empty automat.

"Hold still," he said, and leaning forward put his mouth on hers before she closed it. She held still from the habit of ministering to him. She was helping him. But hold on!

"Good Lord," she said presently and to no one.

"I never thought it would be so simple," said he, musing.

"Simple?" She was caught, betwixt and between being a girl full of stratagems and a rough and ready nurse.

"That you are in love and that there is time for it and that you take the time."

"I see."

"Let's go to your house."

"What for?"

He kissed her again.

She tucked the corner of her mouth and began to nod and slap the table softly.

What he wanted to tell her but could not think quite how was that he did not propose country matters. He did not propose to press against her in an elevator. What he wanted was both more and less. He loved her. His heart melted. She was his sweetheart, his certain someone. He wanted to hold her charms in his arms. He wanted to go into a proper house and shower her with kisses in the old style.

"What do you do when you also have breakfast?" she asked him.

"What? Oh," he said, seeing it was a joke. "Well, I'm not joking." He'd as soon she didn't make Broadway jokes, gags.

"I see you're not."

"I love you."

"You do." The best she could do was register it.

"Let's go to your house."

"You said you worked last night and were going to bed."

"I'm not sleepy."

"I think you need some sleep."

"I need very little sleep."

"You're pretty tough."

"Yes, I'm very strong. I can press 250 pounds and snatch 225. I can whip every middleweight at Princeton, Long Island University, and the Y.M.C.A."

"Now you're joking."

"Yes, but it's true."

"You weren't so strong in the subway."

"I blacked out for a second."

"Do you think you're going to have another spell of amnesia?"

"I don't think so. But I'd like to have you around if I do."

"For how long?"

"Let's begin with the weekend. How strange that it is Friday afternoon and that we are together now and can be together the whole weekend."

"This all seems like a conclusion you have reached entirely on your own. What about me?"

"What about you?"

"Oh boy," she said and commenced nodding and slapping again. "I don't know."

"Where do you want to go?"

"Go?"

"Now. For the weekend."

"You don't fool around, do you?"

"Don't talk like that."

"Why?"

"Because you know it's not like that."

"What is it like?"

"Where then?"

"I'm sorry," she said and put her hand on his, this time a proper girl's hand, not a nurse's. "Rita and I are going to Fire Island."

"Let Rita go and we'll stay home."

"I can't."

"Why not?"

"Rita is very dear to me. I can't hurt her feelings."

"Why is she dear to you?"

"What right have you to ask?"

"Now I'm sorry."

"No, I'll tell you. For one thing, Rita has done so much for us, for me, and we have done so badly by her."

"What has she done?"

"Oh Lord. I'll tell you. You hear about people being unselfish. She actually is—the only one I know. The nearest thing to it is my sister Val, who went into a religious order, but even that is not the same because she does what she does for a reason, love of God and the salvation of her own soul. Rita does it without having these reasons."

"Does what?"

"Helps Jamie, helps me—"

"How did she help you?"

"Mama took me up to Cleveland but I became terribly depressed and went home. I went to work in Myra's real-estate office for a while, then came up here to school—and got horribly lonely and depressed again. It was then that Rita grabbed me by the scruff of the neck and began to put the pieces back together—in spite of what my brother did to her."

"What did he do to her?"

"Oh," she shrugged. "It's a long story. But what a horrible mess. Let's just say that he developed abnormal psychosexual requirements."

"I see." He frowned. He didn't much like her using the word "psychosexual." It reminded him of the tough little babes of his old therapy group, who used expressions like "mental masturbation" and "getting your jollies." It had the echo of someone else. She was his sweetheart and ought to know better. None of your smart-ass Fifty-seventh Street talk, he felt like telling her. "I was wondering," he said.

"What?"

"I love you. Do you love me?"

"If you don't kill me. I swear to goodness."

He fell to pondering. "This is the first time I've been in

love," he said, almost to himself. He looked up, smiling. "Now that I think of it, I guess this sounds strange to you."

"Not strange at all!" she cried with her actress's lilt.

He laughed. Presently he said, "I see now that it could be taken in the sense that I say it without meaning it."

"Yes, it could be taken in that sense."

"I suppose in fact that it could even be something one commonly says. Men, I mean."

"Yes, they do."

"Did you take me to mean it like that?"

"No, not you."

"Well?"

"It's time for me to leave."

"You're going to Fire Island?"

"Yes, and you're sleepy."

All of a sudden he was. "When will I see you?"

"Aren't you coming to my birthday party Monday?"

"Oh yes. In Jamie's room. I thought it was Jamie's birthday."

"We're two days apart. Monday falls between. I'll be twenty-one and Jamie sixteen."

"Twenty-one." His eyes had fallen away into a stare.

"Go to bed."

"Right." Twenty-one. The very number seemed hers, a lovely fine come-of-age adult number faintly perfumed by her, like the street where she lived.

6.

When his soil-bank check arrived on Friday, he, the strangest of planters, proprietor of two hundred acres of blackberries and canebrakes, was able to pay his debt to Dr. Gamow. Having given up his checking account, he cashed the check at Macy's and dropped off the money at Dr. Gamow's office on his way home Monday morning.

Sticking his head through Dr. Gamow's inner door at nine o'clock, he caught a glimpse of the new group seated around a new table. It didn't take twenty seconds to hand over the bills, but that was long enough. In an instant he sniffed out the special group climate of nurtured hostilities and calculated affronts. Though they could not have met more than two or three times, already a stringy girl with a shako of teased hair (White Plains social worker?) was glaring at a little red rooster of a gent (computer engineer?). She was letting him have it: "Don't act out at me, Buster!" The old virtuoso of groups heaved a sigh. And even though Dr. Gamow opened the door another notch by way of silent invitation, he shook his head and said goodbye. But not without regret. It was like the great half-back George Gipp paying a final visit to Notre Dame stadium.

But that left him $34.54 to buy presents for Kitty and Jamie and to eat until payday Saturday. Sunday night he sat at his console under Macy's racking his brain. What to give these rich Texas-type Southerners who already had everything? A book for Jamie? He reckoned not, because not even Sutter's book held his attention for long. It was felt, fingered, flexed, but not read. His choice finally was both easy and audacious. Easy because he could not really afford to buy a gift and himself owned a single possession. Then why not lend it to Jamie: his telescope. The money went for Kitty's present, a tiny golden ballet slipper from Tiffany's for her charm bracelet.

"I don't have any use for it right now," said he to Jamie as he clamped the Tetzlar to the window sill. "I thought you might get a kick out of it." Not for one second did he, as he fiddled with the telescope, lose sight of Kitty, who was unwrapping the little jewel box. She held up the slipper, gave him her dry sideways Lippo Lippi look, tucked in the corner of her mouth, and nodded half a millimeter. His knee leapt out of joint. What was it about this splendid but by no means extraordinary girl which knocked him in the head and crossed his eyes like Woody Woodpecker?

Jamie's bed was strewn with neckties and books—three people had given him the same funny book entitled *So You're a Crock*. The nurses bought a Merita cake and spelled out "Happy Birthday" in chart paper. The internes made a drink of laboratory alcohol and frozen grapefuit juice, as if they were all castaways and had to make do with what they had. From an upper Broadway novelty shop Mr. Vaught had obtained a realistic papier-mâché dogturd which he slipped onto the bed under the very noses of the nurses. As the latter spied it and let out their screams of dismay, the old man charged fiercely about the room, peering under appliances. "I saw him in here, a little feist dog!"

Screwing in the terrestrial ocular fitted with a prism, and focusing quickly on the Englewood cliffs, the engineer stepped aside. The patient had only to prop himself on an elbow and look down into the prism. A little disc of light played about his pupil. The engineer watched him watch: now he, Jamie, would be seeing it, the brilliant theater bigger and better than life. Picnickers they were, a family deployed on a shelf of granite above the Hudson. The father held a can of beer.

Once Jamie looked up for a second, searched his face for a sign: did he really see what he saw? The engineer nodded. Yes, he saw.

"What kind of beer is he drinking?" he asked Jamie.

"Rheingold," said Jamie.

The others took their turn, all but Rita, then Moon Mullins, who swung the Tetzlar around to the nurses' dormitory. There was no talking to Jamie this morning. He must watch the tugs on the river, the roller coaster at Palisades Park, the tollhouse on the George Washington Bridge, two housewives back-fencing in Weehawken. Now it was Jamie who became the technician, focusing on some bit of New Jersey and leaning away to let the doctors look.

Mrs. Vaught elder couldn't get over it. Her pince-nez flashed in the light and she took the engineer's arm. "Would you look at the color in that child's face!" She made her husband take a look through the telescope, but he pretended he couldn't see.

"I can't see a thing!" he cried irritably, jostling his eye around the ocular.

Presently Kitty left with Rita, giving him as she left a queer hooded brown-eyed-susan look. He sat down dizzily and blew out his lips. Why couldn't he leave with them? But when he jumped up, Mr. Vaught took him high by the arm and steered him out into the hall. He faced the younger man into a corner and for a long time did not speak but stood with his head down, nodding. The engineer thought the other was going to tell him a joke.

"Bill." The nodding went on.

"Yes sir."

"How much did that thing cost you?"

"The telescope? Nineteen hundred and eight dollars."

"How much do you make a week?"

"I take home one forty-eight."

"Did your father leave you anything?"

"Not much. An old house and two hundred acres of buckshot."

The engineer was sure he was in for a scolding—all at once the telescope seemed folly itself. But Mr. Vaught only took out his fried-up ball of a handkerchief and knocked it against his nose.

"Bill."

"Yes sir."

"How would you like to work for me?"

"I'd like it fine, sir, but—"

"We have a garage apartment, which Mrs. Vaught did over completely. You'd be independent."

"Well, I really appreciate it, but—"

"You're Ed Barrett's boy," began Mr. Vaught in an enumerating voice.

"Yes sir."

"Dolly knew your mother and said she was the sweetest little lady in the world."

"Yes sir."

"Your mother and daddy are dead and here you are up here fooling around and not knowing what in the hail you are doing. Isn't that so?"

"Well, sir, I'm a humidification engineer."

"What in the woerrrld is that?" asked the other, his mouth gone quirky and comic.

The engineer explained.

"Why, hailfire, man, you mean you're the janitor," cried Mr. Vaught, falling back and doing a jaunty little step. For the first time the engineer caught a glimpse of the shrewdness behind the old man's buffoonery.

"I guess I am, in a way."

"Tell me the truth now. You don't know what—in—the—woerrrld you are doing up here, do you?"

"Well now—" began the engineer, intending to say something about his scientific theories. But instead he fell silent.

"Where did you go to college?"

"Princeton."

"What's your religion?"

"Episcopalian," said the engineer absently, though he had never given the matter a single thought in his entire life.

"Man, there's nothing wrong with you."

"No sir."

But if there is nothing wrong with me, he thought, then there is something wrong with the world. And if there is nothing wrong with the world, then I have wasted my life and that is the worst mistake of all. "However, I do have a nervous condition—"

"Nervous! Hell, I'd be nervous too if I lived up here with all these folks." He nodded down at the moraine of Washington Heights. "All huddled up in the Y in the daytime and way up under a store all night. And peeping at folks through a spyglass. Shoot, man!"

The engineer had to laugh. Moreover, suggestible as he was, he began to think it mightn't be a bad idea to return to the South and discover his identity, to use Dr. Gamow's expression. "What would you want me to do, Mr. Vaught?"

"All right. Here's what you do. You come on down with us. Spend a year with Jamie. This will give you time to finish school if that's what you want to do, or look around for what kind of work you want. Whatever you want to do."

"I still don't exactly know what it is you want—"

"Bill, I'm going to tell you something." Mr. Vaught drew him close enough to smell his old man's sourness and the ironing-board smell of seersucker. "I need somebody to help me out. I'm taking Jamie *home*"—somebody didn't want him to!—"and I want you to come down with me."

"Yes sir. And then?"

"Jamie likes you. He dudn't like anybody else at home but he likes you. (He likes Sutter, but that sapsucker—never mind.) He's been up here four years and he's smart as a whip about some things but he doesn't know enough to come out of the rain about some others. He can't drive a car or shoot a gun!

You know what he and Kitty do at home? Nothing! Sit in the pantry and pick their noses."

"How do you know I won't do the same thing?" asked the engineer, smiling.

"Do it! But also show him how folks act. I just saw what effect you had on him. That's the first time I've seen that boy perk up since I been up here. Can you drive?"

"Yes sir."

"Do you have a driver's license?"

"Yes sir." He got one to drive the Auchinclosses' Continental.

"What do you say?"

"Do I understand that you would want me to be a kind of tutor or companion?"

"Don't have to be anything. Just be in the house."

"As a matter of fact, I've had some experience along these lines," said the engineer and told him about his tutoring stints with his young Jewish charges.

"You see there! We have some of the finest Jewish people at home you'll ever find," he added, as if the engineer were himself Jewish. "Right now the main thing we need is somebody to help me drive home."

The proposal was not quite as good as it sounded. Mr. Vaught, he early perceived, was the sort of man who likes to confide in strangers. And the farther he got from home, one somehow knew, the more confidential he became. He was the sort to hold long conversations with the porter on train trips, stand out with him on dark station platforms. "How much do you make, Sam?" he might ask the porter. "How would you like to work for me?"

"I had this boy David drive us up, ahem," said Mr. Vaught, clearing his throat diffidently. "I didn't know we were going to be up here this long, so I sent him home on the bus. He couldn't drive either. He like to have scared me to death."

The engineer nodded and asked no questions, since he understood that the "boy" was a Negro and Mr. Vaught was embarrassed lest it should appear that the engineer was being offered a Negro's job.

"Mrs. Vaught is certain you'll be comfortable in Sutter's old apartment," he added quickly (you see it's not a Negro's job).

For the first time the engineer began to wonder if the proposal might not be serious. "Come on, let's go get us a Coke."

7.

He followed the older man to a niche off the corridor which had been fitted out as a tiny waiting room with a chrome sofa, a Coke machine, and a single window overlooking the great plunging battleship of Manhattan.

Mr. Vaught put his hand on the younger man's knee and gave it a shake. "Son, when you reach my age I hope you will not wake up to find that you've gone wrong somewhere and that your family have disappointed you."

"I hope so too, sir." He was sure he would not. Because he had lived a life of pure possibility, the engineer, who had often heard older people talk this way, always felt certain he would not repeat their mistakes.

"It's something when the world goes to hell and your own family lets you down, both," said Mr. Vaught, but not at all dolefully, the engineer noticed. His expression was as chipper as ever.

The tiny room soon became so thick with cigar smoke that the engineer's eyes began to smart. Yet, as he sat blinking, hands on knees, he felt quite content.

"Ah, Billy, there's been a loss of integrity in the world, all the things that made this country great."

"Yes sir."

"But the bitterest thing of all is the ingratitude of your own children."

"It must be."

Mr. Vaught sat on the very edge of the sofa and turned around and looked back through the smoke. "Rita's the only one that's worth a damn and she's not even kin."

"Sutter's the oldest," said the engineer, nodding.

"The oldest and the smartest and still isn't worth a damn. Never was and never will be."

"He wrote some very learned articles."

"I'll tell you what he did. He went to the bad on liquor and women."

"Is that so?" All his life the engineer had heard of men who "went to the bad" on women, but he still didn't quite know what it meant. "Isn't he a good doctor?" he asked the older man.

"He had the best education money could buy and you know what he does?"

"No sir."

"He went to Harvard Medical School and made the second highest grades ever made there. After that he interned at Massachusetts General Hospital. Came home. Practiced four years with wonderful success. Was doing people a world of good. Then he quit. Do you know what he does now?!"

"No sir."

"He's assistant coroner. He makes five hundred dollars a month cutting on dead people in the daytime and chases women all night. Why, he's not even the coroner. He's the assistant. He works at the hospital but he doesn't practice. What he is is an interne. He's a thirty-four-year-old interne."

"Is that right?"

"You know that boy in there," Mr. Vaught nodded toward the room.

"Yes sir."

"He is evermore crazy about his big brother and I be dog if I know why. And smart!"

"Which one?"

"Both."

"——"

"I'll tell you what happened, though."

"What?"

"I made a mistake. Three years ago, when my other daughter Val had her twenty-first birthday, I got the idea of giving each of my children a hundred thousand dollars if they hadn't smoked till they were twenty-one. Why not enjoy your money while you're living?"

"That's true," said the engineer, who owned $7.

"Anyway I didn't want to have to look at the bunch of them tippy-toeing around and grinning like chess cats, waiting for me to die. You know what I mean."

"Yes sir," said the other, laughing.

"So what do you think happens? Sutter is older, so he gets

his check the same time as Val. So Sutter, as soon as he gets his money, quits practicing medicine, goes out West, and buys a ranch and sits down and watches the birdies. And when he spends the money, do you know what he does? He takes a job at a dude ranch, like a ship's doctor, only he's taking care of five hundred grass widows. Oh, I really did him a favor. Oh, I really did him a big favor. Wait. I want to show you something. Today, you know, is Kitty's and Jamie's birthday. Kitty is twenty-one and Jamie is only sixteen, but I'm going to give him his money now."

The engineer looked at the other curiously, but he could fathom nothing.

"Maybe you and Jamie would like to take a trip around the world," said Mr. Vaught without changing his expression. He was fumbling in the back pocket of his seersucker pants and now took out a wallet as rounded off and polished as a buckeye. From it he plucked two checks and handed them to the engineer, watching him the while with a brimming expectation. They were stiff new checks, as rough as a cheese grater, bristling with red and black bank marks and punch-holes and machine printing. A row of odd Q-shaped zeros marched to the east.

"This one must be for Kitty," he said, reading the word *Katherine*. "One hundred thousand dollars." It seemed to be what the old man expected, for he nodded.

"You give it to one, you got to give it to all. I hope she didn't mess me up too."

"Did Val mess you up?"

"Val? She was the worst. And yet she was my girlie. I used to call her that, girlie. When she was little, she used to have growing pains. I would hold her in my lap and rock her in the rocking chair, for hours."

"What did she do?"

"With the money? Gave it to the niggers."

"Sir?"

"That's what I'm telling you. She gave it to the niggers."

"But—" began the engineer, who had formed a picture of a girl standing on the front porch handing out bills to passing Negroes. "I thought Kitty told me she went into a, ah, convent."

"She did," cried the old man, peering back through the smoke.

"Then how—"

"Now she's begging from niggers. Do you think that is right?"

"I don't know, sir."

"Let me ask you something. Do you think the good Lord wants us to do anything unnatural?"

"I don't know, sir," said the engineer warily. He perceived it was an old argument and a sore subject.

"Or leave your own kind?"

"Sir?"

"I mean to go spend the rest of your life not just with niggers but with Tyree niggers—do you think that is natural?"

"I don't know, sir."

"You've heard your daddy talk about Tyree niggers?"

"I don't remember."

"Not even niggers have anything to do with Tyree niggers. Down there in Tyree County they've got three different kinds of schools, one for the white folks, one for niggers, and a third for Tyree niggers. They're speckled-like in the face and all up in the head. Some say they eat clay. So where do you think Val goes?"

"Yes sir," said the engineer.

"She went to Agnes Scott, then to Columbia and was just about to get her master's."

The engineer perceived that here was one of those families, more common in the upper South, who set great store by education and degrees.

"So what do I do? Two weeks before graduation I give her her money. So what does she do?"

"Gave it to the Tyree niggers?"

"Man, I'm telling you."

An easy silence fell between them. Mr. Vaught crossed his legs and pulled one ankle above the other with both hands. The little lobby, now swirling with cigar smoke, was something like an old-style Pullman smoker where men used to sit talking by night, pulling their ankles above their knees, and leaning out to spit in the great sloshing cuspidor.

"Let's get us another Coke, Bill."

"I'll get them, sir."

Mr. Vaught drank his Coke in country style, sticking out a little finger and swigging it off in two swallows. "Now. Here's what we'll do. The doctors say Jamie can travel in a week or so. I aim to start home about Thursday week or Friday. Mama wants to go by Williamsburg and Charleston. Now you going to quit all this foolishness up here and come on home with us. What I'm going to do is get you and Jamie a little bitty car—you know I'm in the car business. Do you play golf?"

"Yes sir."

"Hell, man, we live on the golf links. Our patio is twenty feet from number 6 fairway. You like to sail? The Lil' Doll is tied up out at the yacht club and nobody will sail her. You'd be doing me a great favor."

The engineer wished he would mention a salary.

"You and Jamie can go to college—or go round the world! Now isn't that better than being a janitor?"

"Yes sir."

"You think about it."

"I will. Sir?"

"What?"

"Here—I'm going to write down my number here in New York." Meaning, he hoped: you didn't mention a figure and when you want to, it is for you to call me.

"Sho now," said Mr. Vaught absently, and shoved the slip of paper into the side pocket of his seersucker, a bad enough sign in itself.

8.

He stayed only long enough to watch the presentation of the checks. Kitty was back and without Rita!

Standing between Jamie and Kitty, Mr. Vaught crossed his arms, a check in each hand.

"When was your last cigarette?" he asked Jamie.

"There was no last cigarette," said Jamie, grinning and thrashing.

"Your last drink?"

"There was no last drink."

"Then go buy yourself a drink."

"Yes sir," said Jamie, taking his check.

"Kitty?"

"No cigarette and no drink."

"Then go buy yourself one!"

"I might," said Kitty, laughing.

"I mean it! They're certified. You can cash it right down there at the bar on the corner."

"Thank you, Poppy," said Kitty, kissing him.

The checks were passed around among family, nurses, and internes.

Once again Kitty left and once again the engineer tried to follow her, but Jamie stopped him.

"Bill."

"Yes?"

"Come here."

"What?"

"Did Poppy speak to you?" he whispered.

"Yes."

"What did you say?"

"We didn't get down to terms."

"That's Poppy. But what do you say in general?"

"I say O.K., if I can be of use to you."

"Where do you want to go?"

"Where do *I* want to go?"

Jamie waved the check. "Name it."

"No sir. You name it. And I think you'd better name a school."

"O.K.," said Jamie immediately and cheerfully.

9.

During the next week he set about putting his life in order. He ate and slept regularly, worked out every day, went down to Brooks Brothers like his father and grandfather before him and bought two ten-dollar pullover shirts with a tuck in the back and no pocket in the front, socks, ties, and underwear, and dressed like a proper Princetonian. At work he read business maxims in *Living*.

*

The only way people are defeated by their problems is by refusing to face them.

One day, some years ago, a now famous industrial counselor walked into the office of a small manufacturing concern. "How would you like to increase sales 200% the first year?" he asked the president. The latter of course tried to get rid of him. "O.K., I'm leaving," said the counselor. "But first lend me your scratch pad." He wrote a few lines and handed the pad to the executive. "Read this. Think about it. If you put it into practice, send me a check a year from now for what it was worth to you." One year later the counselor received a check in the mail for $25,000.

The counselor had written two sentences:
(1) Make a list of your problems, numbering them in the order of priority.
(2) Devote *all* your time, one day, one month, however long it takes, to disposing of *one* problem at a time. Then go to the next.

Simple? Yes. But as a result this executive is now president of the world's third largest corporation and draws a salary of $400,000 a year.

It was no more nor less than true. You do things by doing things, not by not doing them. No more crazy upsidedownness, he resolved. Good was better than bad. Good environments are better than bad environments. Back to the South, finish his education, make use of his connections, be a business or professional man, marry him a wife and live him a life. What was wrong with that? No more pressing against girls, rassling around in elevators and automobiles and other similar monkey business such as gives you stone pains and God knew what else. What was wrong with a good little house in a pretty green suburb in Atlanta or Birmingham or Memphis and a pretty little wife in a brand-new kitchen with a red dress on at nine o'clock in the morning and a sweet good-morning kiss and the little ones off to school and a good old mammy to take care of them? The way to see Kitty is not not to see her but to see her.

But it didn't work. Kitty's phone didn't answer. Outside in the park the particles were ravening and singing. Inside he went careening around the dark Aztec corridors of the Y.M.C.A. wringing out his ear and forgetting which floor he lived on. When he lay in bed, one leg defied gravity and rose slowly of itself. His knee began to leap like a fish.

Once when he called Kitty, someone did pick up the telephone but did not speak. "Hello, hello," he said. "Who's there?" But there came only the sound of breathing and of the crepitation of skin on plastic. Presently the telephone was replaced softly.

Nor did he hear from Mr. Vaught. He went once more to visit Jamie and, coming face to face with the older man, waited upon him smilingly. But the old man pulled out his gold watch, mumbled an excuse, and was off down the hall like the white rabbit.

Very well then, said he to himself, good day. If they wanted him, let them send for him.

Wednesday when he came home from work he was handed a message with his key. It was from Kitty. Meet me in the park, at the zoo, at four thirty. He went and waited until five thirty. She did not come.

Meanwhile he was getting worse. Thursday morning he slipped another cog. It came, he hoped, from working a double shift and not eating. The day man, a fellow named Perlmutter who had a sick wife, did not show. Like an idiot, he offered to stay on, figuring, what with his new plans and his expenses at Brooks Brothers, that he needed the money.

After sixteen hours underground he came staggering out into the gorge air of Seventh Avenue. For some ten minutes he stood, finger to nose, in the thunderous blue shadow of Pennsylvania Station. A bar turned in his head. Now let me see, said he, and taking out *Living* from his pocket, read a few maxims. Hmm. The thing to do is make a list.

Somewhere in the smoky vastness of the station lanced through with late slanting cathedral beams of sunlight—late or early? was it evening or morning—and haunted by old *déjà vus* of Here-I-am-up-from-Charlotte-or-Chattanooga-or-Tuscaloosa-and-where-do-I-go-from-here, he got turned around good and proper and came down on the wrong platform, headed in the wrong direction, and took the wrong train. He must have dozed off, for when he woke up he was in New Lots Avenue, or perhaps it was Far Rockaway.

What woke him? Something. His heart was thumping, making a regular commotion. Now he knew! A pair of eyes had been looking at him, gazing into his even as he slept with eyes open. Who? Rita. Or did he dream it? The train had stopped. He looked around but there was no one. Yet somebody was following him. He knew that. Goofy as he was, his radar still swung free and there was a prickling between his shoulder blades. Somewhere in Brooklyn he changed to an old local with straw seats and came out at a seaside station.

It was dark. He found himself in a long street which was nearly black between the yellow street lights at the corners. The sea was somehow close. There was a hint of an uproar abroad in the night, a teeming in the air and the sense of coming closer with each step to a primal openness. He walked six blocks in the empty street and there it was. But it was nothing like Wrightsville or Myrtle Beach or Nag's Head, lonesome and wide and knelling. It was domesticated. There were notion shops right up to the sand and the surf was poky, came snuffling in like lake water and collapsed *plaush* on a steep little old brown beach.

He looked behind him. No one followed him in the street. The drowsiness came again. He had to sleep then and there. He lay down in the warm black sand of a vacant lot and slept two hours without moving a muscle. He woke in his right mind and went back to the Y.

10.

Jogging home from the reservoir the next morning, he spotted Rita two hundred yards away, sitting on a bench next to the milk-fund booth, the toilet-shaped telescope case under her hand. All at once he knew everything: she had come to get rid of him. She hoped he would take his telescope and go away.

But she was, for the first time, as pleasant as could be and patted the bench next to her. And when he sat down, she came sliding smack up against him, a bit too close for comfort. He humped himself over in his sweat suit and tried to smell as good as he could.

Her fist came softly down on his knee; she looked him in the eye and spoke not eight inches away. He couldn't hear for listening.

"But you and I know better," she was saying. "He's got no business going home."

"Jamie?"

Looking into her eyes was something of a shock. Every line of her face was known to him. Yet now, with her eyes opening into his, she became someone else. It was like watching a picture toy turned one degree: the black lines come and the picture changes. Where before her face was dark and shut off as a gypsy, now her eyes opened into a girlishness.

"Bill—"

"Yes ma'am."

"Oh, come *on*. Rita."

"O.K., Rita."

Again the fist came down softly on his knee.

"I want you to do something for me."

"What?"

"The Vaughts are very fond of you."

"I'm glad to hear it."

"The extraordinary part of it is that though you are a new friend—perhaps because you are a new friend—you have more influence with them than anyone else."

"I doubt it. I haven't heard from them in several days."

"Oh, they carry on about you something awful. They plan to take you home with them, don't they?"

"When did you hear that?"

"Yesterday."

"Did Mr. Vaught tell you?"

"Yes."

"I'm glad to hear it."

"But never mind about Poppy. Right now it's Jamie who needs us." As gravely as she spoke, he noticed that she cast her eyes about, making routine surveys of Eighth Avenue. There was about her the air of a woman who keeps busy in a world of men. Her busyness gave her leave to be absent-minded. She was tired, but she knew how to use her tiredness.

"Why?"

"Jamie can't go home, Bill."

"Why not?"

"Let me tell you something."

"All right."

"First—how much do you care for Jamie?"

"Care for him?"

"Would you do something for him?"

"Yes."

"Would you do anything for him?"

"What do you mean?"

"If he were in serious trouble, would you help him?"

"Of course."

"I knew you would."

"What is it?" he asked after a moment.

Rita was smoothing out her skirt until it made a perfect membrane across her thighs. "Our Jamie is not going to make it, Bill," she said in a low thrilling voice and with a sweetness that struck a pang to the marrow.

There passed between them the almost voluptuous intercourse of bad news. Why is it, thought he, hunkering over and taking his pulse, I cannot hear what people say but only the channel they use?

"So it's not such a big thing," she said softly. "One small adolescent as against the thirty thousand Japanese children we polished off."

"How's that?" said the engineer, cupping his good ear.

"At Hiroshima and Nagasaki."

"I don't, ah—"

"But this little guy happens to be a friend of mine. And yours. He has myelogenous leukemia, Bill."

Oh, and I'm sick too, he thought anxiously, looking at his hands. Why is it that bad news is not so bad and good news not so good and what with the bad news being good, aye that is what makes her well and me sick? Oh, I'm not well. He was silent, gazing at his open hands on his knees.

"You don't seem surprised," said Rita after a moment.

"I knew he was sick," he murmured.

"What's that?" she asked quickly. He saw she was disappointed by his listlessness. She had wanted him to join her, stand beside her and celebrate the awfulness.

"Why shouldn't he go home?" he asked, straightening up.

"Why shouldn't he indeed? A very good question: because just now he is in a total remission. He feels fine. His blood's as normal as yours or mine. He's out of bed and will be discharged tomorrow."

"So?"

"So. He'll be dead in four months."

"Then I don't see why he shouldn't go home or anywhere else."

"There is only one reason. A tough little bastard by the name of Larry Deutsch up at the Medical Center. He's got a drug, a horrifyingly dangerous drug, which incidentally comes from an herb used by the Tarahumaras."

To his relief, Rita started on a long spiel about Jamie's illness. He knew the frequency of her channel, so he didn't have to listen.

"—so Larry said to me in the gentlest voice I ever heard: 'I think we're in trouble. Take a look.' I take a look, and even knowing nothing whatever about it, I could see there was something dreadfully wrong. The little cells were smudged—they looked for all the world like Japanese lanterns shining through a fog. That was over a year ago—"

Instead he was thinking of wars and death at home. On the days of bad news there was the same clearing and sweetness in the air. Families drew closer. Azaleas could be seen. He remembered his father's happiness when he spoke of Pearl Harbor—where he was when he heard it, how he had called the draft board the next morning. It was not hard to see him walking to work on that Monday. For once the houses, the trees, the very cracks in the sidewalk had not their usual minatory presence. The dreadful threat of weekday mornings was gone! War is better than Monday morning.

As his sweat dried, the fleece began to sting his skin.

"—fact number two. Jamie has the best mind I ever encountered. Better even than Sutter, my charming ex-husband. It's really quite funny. His math teacher in New Hampshire was glad to get rid of him. 'Get him out of here,' he told me. 'He wants to argue about John von Neumann's *Theory of Games*—'"

It was her silences, when they came, that he attended.

"So what is the problem?" he asked.

"He's remitted on prednisone. Poppy and Dolly refuse to admit that he is going to die. Why not give him another pill, they say. Well, there are no more pills. He's been through them all."

He was silent.

She regarded him with a fond bright eye.

"Somehow you remind me of the lance corporal in *Der Zauberberg*. Do you mind if I call you lance corporal?"

"No ma'am."

"What would you like to do if you had your choice?"

"I do have my choice. Go with Jamie."

"No, I mean if Jamie hadn't showed up."

"Oh, I'd go see Kitty."

"Leave all of us out of it. And suppose, too, money is no object."

"I guess I'd finish my education."

"In what?"

"Oh, metallurgy, I expect."

"What school would you pick?"

"Colorado School of Mines."

"You'd like to go out there?"

He shrugged. "Why not?"

"Suppose Jamie would want to go too."

"That's up to him."

"Take a look at this."

He found himself gazing at a curled-up Polaroid snapshot of a little white truck fitted with a cabin in its bed. The truck was parked on a stretch of meager shingly beach. Kitty, in long shorts, leaned against the cabin, wide-brimmed hat in hand in a burlesque of American-lady-on-safari.

"What is this?"

"Ulysses."

"Ulysses?"

"He was meant to lead us beyond the borders of the Western world and bring us home."

"I see."

"But seriously now, here's the proposition," she said. And he found that when she gave him ordinary directions he could hear her. "As of this moment you are working for me as well as for Poppy. Perhaps for both of us but at least for me. Keep Jamie up here long enough for Larry to give him a course of huamuratl. You two rascals take my apartment here in the city and here are the keys to the shack on Fire Island. Now when you get through with Larry, take Ulysses and take off. Go home. Go to Alaska. In any event, Ulysses is yours. He has been three hundred miles, cost me seven thousand dollars, and is as far as I'm concerned a total loss. Here is the certificate of ownership, which I've signed over to you and Jamie. It will cost you one dollar. Jamie has coughed up. She held out her hand. "I'll take my money, please."

"I don't have a dollar."

The articles, papers, keys, photograph she lined up on his thigh. He looked closely at the snapshot again.

"What did you get it for?" he asked her.

"To camp in Europe. Isn't that stupid? Considering that I'd have to buy gas for that monster Ulysses by the liter."

"You've already told Jamie?"

"Yes."

"And Mr. Vaught agrees to this?"

"He will if you ask him."

"What about Kitty?"

"My friend, allow me to cue you in. Perhaps you have not noticed it, but our young friend Jamie is sick to death of the women in the family. Including me. Kitty and I made him the same deal: the three of us for Long Island and the camper (it sleeps three) and he laughed in our faces and I can't say I blame him. Let me put it to you straight out."

"All right."

"Just suppose you asked him—you said, Jamie, I got Ulysses parked outside in the street—come on now, let's me and you hit the road. What would he say?"

"He wouldn't like the Ulysses part."

"Dear God, you're right." Her fist came down on his knee and stayed there. "You're right. You see, you *know*. All right, leave out the word 'Ulysses.' What then? What would he do?"

"He'd go."

"You know something: you're quite a guy."

"Thank you." He plucked at his sweat suit. It came away from him like old skin. "Then you mean Kitty will go to Europe, after all?"

"My dear young friend, hear this. I do believe you underestimate yourself. I do not believe you realize what a hurricane you've unleashed and how formidable you yourself are. You've got our poor Kitty spinning like a top. Not that I blame her. Why is it some men can sit like Achilles sat and some men can't? But I propose to you, my lordly young sir, that we give our young friend her year abroad, which is the only one she'll ever have. Seriously, Kitty saved my life. She is the sister of that son of a bitch I married. She bucked me up when I needed it and by God I'm returning the favor. Do you have any idea what it would be like to be raised by Poppy and Dolly, who are in their own way the sweetest people in the world, but I mean—God. You have no idea what it's like down there these days, the poor bloody old South. I'll tell you what. Give her her year in Florence and then if *you* haven't forgotten all about her, I'll send her home as fast as her little legs will carry her. Or better still, when you and Jamie get through with Larry, come on over and join us!"

The next thing he knew, she was thrusting something into his pocket, but he didn't have a pocket, then inside the drawstring of his sweat suit, tucked it with a fierce little tuck like an aunt at Christmas. "Your first month's salary in advance," she said, and was on her way.

Taking the check from his loin, he read it several times. It seemed to be postdated. He scratched his head. On the other hand, what was today's date?

II.

It was the first hot night. There were signs of summer. Fires had broken out in Harlem. Twice there were gunshots as close as Seventieth or Eightieth Street. Police cars raced north along Central Park West. But the park was quiet. Its public space, paltry by day, was leafed out in secrecy and darkness. Lamps made gold-green spaces in the rustling leaves.

He strolled about the alp at the pond, hands in pockets and

brow furrowed as if he were lost in thought. It was a dangerous place to visit by night, but he paid no attention. He felt
irritable and strong and wouldn't have minded a fistfight. A
few minutes earlier a damp young man had fallen in step on
his deaf side.

"Didn't we take philosophy together at the Y?" the stranger
murmured, skipping nimbly to get in step.

"What's that," said the engineer absently.

"I thought it unconscionably bad," murmured the other.

"Eh?" The engineer cupped his good ear.

"Are you interested in the Platonic philosophy?" the other
asked him.

"In *what*," said the engineer, stopping and swinging around
to hear better but also bending upon the other such an intent,
yet unfocused gaze that he melted into the night.

Strong and healthy as he felt, he was, if the truth be known,
somewhat dislocated. The sudden full tide of summer sent him
spinning. The park swarmed with old *déjà vus* of summertime.
It put him in mind of something, the close privy darkness
and the black tannin smell of the bark and the cool suspiring vapors of millions of fleshy new leaves. From time to time
there seemed to come to him the smell of Alabama girls (no,
Mississippi), who bathe and put on cotton dresses and walk
uptown on a summer night. He climbed the alp dreamily and
stooped over the bench. The cul-de-sac held the same message
it had held for days, a quotation from Montaigne. He read it
under a lamp:

> Man is certainly stark mad. He can't make a worm, but he
> makes gods by the dozens.

No one had picked it up. Nor was it very interesting, for that
matter: when he sniffed it, it smelled not of Montaigne but of
a person who might quote Montaigne on such a night as this,
an entirely different matter.

"Wait—" he stopped in a dapple of light and leaves and
snapped his fingers softly. That was what his father used to say.
He too quoted Montaigne on a summer night but in a greener,
denser, more privy darkness than this. The young man in the
park snapped his fingers again. He stood a full minute, eyes

closed, swaying slightly. He raised a hand tentatively toward the West.

Yonder was not the alp but the levee, and not the lamp in the trees but the street light at Houston Street and De Ridder. The man walked up and down in the darkness under the water oaks. The boy sat on the porch steps and minded the Philco, which clanked and whirred and plopped down the old 78's and set the needle hissing and voyaging. Old Brahms went abroad into the summer night. West, atop the levee, couples sat in parked cars. East, up De Ridder, from the heavy humming ham-rich darkness of the cottonseed-oil mill there came now and then the sound of Negro laughter.

Up and down the man walked and spoke to the boy when he passed the steps. More cars came nosing discreetly up the levee, lights out and appearing to go by paws, first left then right. The man grew angry.

"The prayer meeting must be over," said the man ironically.

Out poured old Brahms, the old spoiled gorgeous low-German music but here at home surely and not in Hamburg.

"What do they expect," said the man now, westbound. He took his turn under the street light and came back.

"Now they," he went on, nodding to the east. "They fornicate and the one who fornicates best is the preacher."

The Great Horn Theme went abroad, the very sound of the ruined gorgeousness of the nineteenth century, the worst of times.

"But they," he said to the levee—"they fornicate too and in public and expect *them* back yonder somehow not to notice. Then they expect their women to be respected."

The boy waited for the scratch in the record. He knew when it was coming. The first part of the scratch came and he had time to get up and hold the tone arm just right so the needle wouldn't jump the groove.

"Watch them."

"Yes sir."

"You just watch them. You know what's going to happen?"

"No sir."

"One will pick up the worst of the other and lose the best of himself. Watch. One will learn to fornicate in public and the other will end by pissing in the street. Watch."

The man stayed, so the boy said, "Yes sir."

"Go to whores if you have to, but always remember the difference. Don't treat a lady like a whore or a whore like a lady."

"No sir, I won't."

The record ended but the eccentric groove did not trip the mechanism. The boy half rose.

"If you do one, then you're going to be like them, a fornicator and not caring. If you do the other, you'll be like them, fornicator and hypocrite."

He opened his eyes. Now standing in the civil public darkness of the park, he snapped his fingers softly as if he were trying to remember something.

Then what happened after that? After he—

Leaning over, he peered down at the faint dapple on the path. After a long moment he held up his watch to the lamplight. After a look around to get his bearings, he walked straight to the corner of the park and down into the BMT subway.

Yet he could scarcely have been in his right mind or known exactly where he was, for what he did next was a thing one did at home but never did here. He dropped in. He walked up to Rita's apartment in the Mews and knocked on the door at eight thirty in the evening.

Kitty answered the door. Her mouth opened and closed. She could not believe her eyes. He defied the laws of optics.

"Oh," she said, fearing either to look at him or to take her eyes from him.

"Let's walk up the street," he said. "It's a nice night."

"Oh, I'd love to," she cried, "but I can't. Give me a rain check." She was managing somehow both to stand aside and to block the doorway.

"Let's go ride the ferry to Staten Island."

"Oh, I can't," she wailed like an actress.

"Aren't you going to ask me in," he said after a moment.

"What? Oh. *Oh.*" But instead of standing aside she put her head over coquettishly. *Tock*, she said, clicking her tongue and eyeing the darkness behind him. They were having a sort of date here in the doorway.

"There is something I wanted to ask you. It will not take long. Your phone didn't answer."

"It didn't?" She called something over her shoulder. It seemed that here was the issue: the telephone. If this issue could be settled, it seemed, he would take his leave like a telephone man. But it allowed her to admit him: she stood aside.

So it was at last that he found himself in the living room standing, in a kind of service capacity. He had come about the telephone. The two women smiled up at him from a low couch covered with Navaho blankets. No, only Kitty smiled. Rita eyed him ironically, her head appearing to turn perpetually away.

It was not a Barbados cottage after all but an Indian hogan. Rita wore a Chamula huipil (Kitty was explaining nervously) of heavy homespun. Kitty herself had wound a white quexquemetl above her Capri pants. Brilliant quetzals and crude votive offerings painted on tin hung from the walls.

They were drinking a strong-smelling tea.

"I've been unable to reach you by phone," he told Kitty.

The two women looked at him.

"I may as well state my business," said the engineer, still more or less at attention, though listing a bit.

"Good idea," said Rita, taking a swig of the tea, which smelled like burnt corn. He watched as the muscular movement of her throat sent the liquid strumming along.

"Kitty, I want to ask you something."

"What?"

"Could I speak to you alone?"

"You're among friends, ha-ha," said Kitty laughing loudly.

"Very well. I wanted to ask you to change your mind about going to Europe and instead go south with Jamie and me." Until the moment he opened his mouth, he had no idea what he wished to ask her. "Here is your check, Mrs. Vaught. I really appreciate it, but—"

"Good grief," said Kitty, jumping to her feet as if she had received an electric shock. "Listen to the man," she cried to Rita and smacked her thigh in a Jewish gesture.

Rita shrugged. She ignored the check.

The engineer advanced and actually took Kitty's hand. For a second her pupils enlarged and she was as black-eyed as an Alabama girl on a summer night. Then she gaped at her own hand in stupefaction: it could not be so! He was holding her hand! But instead of snatching it away, she pulled him down on the couch.

"Here. Try some hikuli tea."

"No thanks." As he lay back among the pillows, his eye fell upon a votive painting. It showed a man who had been thrown from a motorcycle and now lay in a ditch. He had apparently suffered internal injuries, for blood spurted from his mouth like a stream from a garden hose.

"That's my favorite," said Kitty. "Isn't it wonderful?"

"I guess so."

"He was cured miraculously by the Black Virgin."

"Is that right?"

As Kitty went on, no longer so nervous now but seeming rather to have hit upon a course she might steer between the two of them, he noticed a spot of color in her cheek. There was a liquid light, not a tear, in the corner of her eye.

"Ree's been giving me the most fascinating account of the hikuli rite which is practiced by the Huichol Indians. The women are absolved from their sins by tying knots in a palm-leaf string, one knot for each lover. Then they throw the string into Grandfather Fire. Meanwhile the men—Ree was just getting to the men. What do the men do, Ree?"

"I really couldn't say," said Rita, rising abruptly and leaving the room.

"Tie a knot for me," said the engineer.

"*What*," cried Kitty, craning her neck and searching the horizon like a sea bird. "Oh."

"Let us now—" he began and sought dizzily to hold her charms in his arms.

"Ah," said the girl, lying passive, eyes full of light.

"I've reached a decision," he said and leaned back uncomfortably among the pillows, head in the air.

"What is that?"

"Now you know that I need you."

"You do?"

"And that although I will be all right eventually, I still have a nervous condition, and that for some time to come I'll need you to call upon."

"You will?"

"I've loved you ever since I saw you in Central—that is, in Jamie's room."

"Ah."

Love, he thought, and all at once the word itself went opaque and curious, a little howling business behind the front teeth. Do I love her? I something her. He felt his nose.

"Let's go home, either to your home or mine, and be married."

"Married," said Kitty faintly.

Dander from the old blankets was beginning to bother his nose. "Would you mind taking this off," he asked her presently and took hold of her quexquemetl. "Aren't you hot?"

"Are you out of your mind," she whispered fiercely.

"I'm sorry. I didn't mean—" He hadn't meant to undress her but only to get her out of these prickly homespuns and back into decent Alabama cotton.

Kitty sat up. Her eyes were fixed in a stare upon a bowl of tiny cactus plants. "The Huichol believe that things change forms, that one thing can become another thing. An hour ago it sounded like nonsense."

"Is that right?" He had heard it before, this mythic voice of hers. One of his aunts lived in Cuernavaca.

"The hikuli plant *is* the deer. The deer *is* the corn. Look at that."

"What?"

"That color."

He looked down at the blanket between them where forked Navaho lightning clove through an old brown sky, brown as old blood.

"What about it?"

"Do you see the depths opening into depths?"

"No." He tried to blow his nose but the mucous membranes had swelled against each other like violet eiderdowns. "I think I'll be going."

"Wait," she called from the doorway as he walked rapidly off into the night, forgetful of summer now, head ducked, shouldering as if he were still bucking the winter gales. He waited.

"All right," she said. "Where do you want to go?"

He gazed vaguely about at the shuttered shops and dark brownstones.

"We can't go back there," she said. Her pale face loomed unsteadily in the darkness. He was thinking about the reciprocal ratio of love: was it ever so with the love of women that they held out until the defeat of one's first fine fervor, not merely until one feigned defeat but rather until one was in truth defeated, had shrugged and turned away and thought of other matters—and now here they came, all melts and sighs, breathing like a furnace. Her lips were parted slightly and her eyes sparkled. His nose was turning to concrete.

"And we can't go to the Y." She had taken his arm. He felt importunate little tugs at his elbow as if he were a blind man and she wanted him to cross the street.

She pulled him close. "Do you notice anything?"

"No."

"The lampposts."

"What about them?"

"They seem alive and ominous."

He was displeased with her. Was it then the case with love that lovers must alternate, forever out of phase with one another? It did not suit her to be fanciful. Was she drunk? She gave him a kiss tasting of burnt corn. He wished she would chew Juicy Fruit like a proper Alabama girl.

"I do know a place," he said finally. "But it won't do at night."

"Why not?"

"It's in the park."

"Wait," she said and flew back to the cottage. He waited, listing at a ten-degree angle. Had he, empathic as ever, got dizzy from her dizziness?

When she returned, she wore a skirt and blouse instead of pants and quexquemetl. "Take this." She pressed something into his hand.

"What's this for?" It was a small revolver, a police special, with hardly a quarter inch of barrel.

"For the park. My brother gave it to me as a going-away present when I came to New York."

"Sutter?"

"Yes. He's a police surgeon."

He stuck the pistol into his coat pocket and allowed himself to be nudged toward the subway.

They walked from the Broadway subway exit to the park. Fifty blocks north there were more fires in Harlem and the sense of faraway soundless tumult. Police sirens kicked out, subsided to a growl.

He hesitated. "I don't know."

Again the nudge at his elbow. "Don't worry. They're all up there."

He shrugged and took her into the Ramble, a densely wooded stretch. Holding her behind him, he walked swiftly along a path, stooped and holding the girl's head down, turned into a thicket of privet whose bitter bark smelled like the dry rain gutters of his own house. Dark as it was, with no more light than a sinking gibbous moon, it didn't matter. He knew the southwest quadrant of the park as he knew his own back yard. (Though he could not see them, he knew when he passed the Disney statuettes, could have put out a hand and touched Dopey.)

The place was down a ravine choked with dogbane and whortleberry and over a tumble of rocks into a tiny amphitheater, a covert so densely shaded that its floor was as bare as cave's dirt. By day it looked very like the sniper's den on Little Round Top which Brady photographed six weeks after the battle: the sniper was still there! a skeleton in butternut, his rifle propped peaceably against the rocks.

He set the police special in the dust beside him and drew Kitty down on the other side. They leaned into the curve of a shallow overhang of smooth rock facing the cleft where they entered. There was no sound of traffic or sight of the lighted windows of the apartment houses along Central Park West, or any sign of the city at all except, when he moved his head slightly, a chink of red sky over 110th Street.

"My Lord," said Kitty. "How could anybody find us here. I can't even see you." Her fingers brushed clumsily across his face.

He kissed her with an amiable passion, mainly concerned now to bear with her, serve her anticness as gracefully as he could. He aimed to guard her against her own embarrassment. His nose was no better.

"To answer your question," she said softly, "Yes."

"Fine," he said, nodding in the dark. What question?

"Dearest," she breathed, holding her hand to his cheek with a tenderness that struck dismay to his heart.

The puzzle is: where does love pitch its tent? in the fine fervor of a summer night, in a jolly dark wood wherein one has a bit o' fun as the English say? or in this dread tenderness of hers?

"Don't go away, darling," she whispered. "I'll be right back."

"All right."

She moved away. As he traced a finger in the dust, drawing the old Northern Pacific yin-yang symbol, he heard the rustling of clothes and the singing of zippers. She returned without a sound. He embraced her and was enveloped in turn by the warm epithelial smell of her nakedness. What a treasure, he thought, his heart beating as rapidly and shallowly as a child's. What suppleness.

"Hold me," whispered Kitty with her dismaying tenderness. "My precious."

"Right." Now holding her charms in his arms at last, he wondered if he had ever really calculated the terrific immediacy of it.

"Why don't you—" she said.

"What? Oh. Pardon," said the courtly but forgetful engineer and blushed for his own modesty, clad as he was from head to toe in Brooks Bros.' finest. Making haste to sit up, he began to unbutton his shirt.

"Now. Oh, my darling, do you love me?"

"Oh yes," said the engineer, swinging her forty-five degrees in the dust so that he could look past her toward the opening of the covert. The sky was redder. From the same direction there came a faint crepitant sound like crumpled newspaper. The cops and the Negroes were shooting it out in Harlem.

"Will you cherish me?"

"Yes, certainly," said the engineer.

"I don't mean just now. I want to be protected always. I want to be cherished."

"I will," he assured her.

"Do you know what matters most of all?"

"What?"

"Love."

"Right."

"Love is everything."

"Yes."

"Rita asked me what I believed in. I said I believed in love."

"Me too."

"Besides which I want to prove something to myself," said the girl, almost to herself.

"Prove what?"

"A little experiment by Kitty for the benefit of Kitty."

"What experiment is that?"

"Let me tell you, there is nothing wrong with Kitty," she said.

"I didn't say there was."

Holding her, he couldn't help thinking of Perlmutter, his young fresh-eyed colleague at Macy's. Though he was from Brooklyn, Perlmutter looked like an Indiana farm boy. Perlmutter spoke of his wife with a lack of reserve, though not of respect, which was startling. Making love to his wife, Perlmutter said, was like "being in heaven." Now he understood. Kitty too, he would have to say, was an armful of heaven. The astounding immediacy of her. She was more present, more here, than he could ever have calculated. She was six times bigger and closer than life. He scarcely knew whether to take alarm or to shout for joy, hurrah!

"Never mind. What about you, you big geezer?"

Geezer, thought the engineer. "What about me?"

"You were the one who was always sweeping Kitty off her feet before! What happened?" She even socked him, jokingly but also irritably. The poor girl could not get the straight of it: the engineer's alternating fits of passion and depression.

He was wondering: had the language of women, "love" and "sweeping one off one's feet," and such, meant this all along, the astounding and terrific melon immediacy of nakedness. Do women know everything?

"What about it, friend?" asked Kitty, heaving up, her pale face swimming above him. "Kitty wants to know."

"Know what?"

"Is this the same Will Barrett who swept Kitty off her feet in the automat?"

"No, but it's just as well," he said dryly.

"Tell Kitty why."

"Kitty might be too attractive," said the chivalrous but wry engineer. "So attractive that it is just as well I don't feel too well—for one thing, my sinuses are blocked—"

"Oh that's sweet," said Kitty in as guttural, as ancient and risible and unbuttoned an Alabama voice as Tallulah Bankhead. Did he know anything about women?

"Do you feel bad," she asked suddenly and touched his face. "If it is not possible now to—" she broke off.

He felt just bad enough—his head was caulked, the pressure turning him ever away into a dizzy middle distance—and so it was just possible.

"Lover," said Kitty as they hugged and kissed.

"Darling," said the engineer, not to be surpassed—was this it at last, the august secret of the Western world?

"My sweet," said Kitty, patting his cheek at the corner of his mouth.

But is love a sweetnesse or a wantonnesse, he wondered.

Yet when at last the hard-pressed but courteous and puissant engineer did see the way clear to sustaining the two of them, her in passing her test, him lest he be demoralized by Perlmutter's heaven, too much heaven too soon, and fail them both—well, I do love her, he saw clearly, and therefore I shall—it was too late.

"Dear God," said the girl to herself, even as he embraced her tenderly and strongly—and fell away from him.

"What's the matter?"

"I'm so sick," she whispered.

"Oh, that's too bad," he said, shaking his head dolefully. Even their sicknesses alternated and were out of phase.

She went to the farthest corner of the sniper's den and began to retch. The engineer held her head. After a moment she asked in a dazed voice. "What happened?"

"I think it was that tea you were drinking."

"You are so smart," she said faintly.

What with her swaying against him, he was having a hard time finding her clothes. It was too much for a man to follow, he mused, these lightning hikuli-transformations from Kitty as

great epithelial-warm pelvic-upcurving-melon-immediate Maja
to Kitty as waif, huddled under his arm all ashiver and sour
with gastric acid. But when they were dressed, they felt better.
Now trousered, collared, buttoned up, he at least was himself
again. There is a great deal to be said for clothes. He touched
Kitty to place her, like a blind man. To his relief she sat hugging
her decent skirted knees like a proper Georgia coed.

"Do you feel better?" he asked her.

"Yes," she said, hardly audibly. "But talk to me."

"What about?"

"Anything. Anything that comes into your head."

"All right." After all, this was one thing he was good at. "I
was thinking about the summer of 1864," said the engineer,
who always told the truth. "My kinsman took part in the siege
of Richmond and later of Petersburg. We have a letter he wrote
his mother. He was exactly my age and a colonel in the infantry.
Petersburg was a rats' war, as bad as Stalingrad. But do you
know that even at the worst the officers would go to balls and
cotillions? In the letter he thanks his mother for the buttermilk
cookies and says: 'Met Miss Sally Trumbull last night. She said
I danced tolerably well. She gave me her handkerchief.' He was
killed later on in the Crater."

"Would you take me to a dance?" asked Kitty, her head
turned away.

"Sure. But what is curious is that—"

"I've been dancing five hours a day for years and I can't
remember the last dance I went to."

"—he did not feel himself under the necessity, almost moral,
of making love—"

"I love to dance."

"—in order that later things be easy and justified between
him and Miss Trumbull, that—"

"My grandmother composed the official ATO waltz at
Mercer," said Kitty.

"—that even under the conditions of siege he did not feel
himself under the necessity, or was it because it was under the
conditions of siege that—"

"You're so smart," said Kitty, shivering and huddling against
him. "Oh, I'm so cold."

"I must speak to your father," said the engineer absently.

The girl started nervously and stopped shivering. "What for?"

"To ask your hand in marriage," said the engineer somewhat formally.

"You know everything," said Kitty, commencing to shiver again. "You're so smart."

"No, but I know one thing."

"Tell Kitty."

"I know what you fear most."

"What?"

"People, and that is the trouble. The source of your happiness is also the source of your nightmares."

"That's true."

Even now he was at it again, scheming, establishing his credentials. Like all women, she was, he knew, forever attuned to fortunetelling, soothsaying, and such. If he told her something, she might tell him. For there was something he wanted to know.

"I know who you like to be with."

"Who?"

"Rita and me."

"That's right. Why is that?"

"You like Rita because she is among other things a woman and no threat to you. You like me and that would be enough to put you off ordinarily because I am a man but you know something is wrong with me and that neutralizes the threat."

"Yes," said the girl gloomily. "Oh, dear. I really don't feel well."

"What about Rita?"

"What about her?" He could scarcely hear her.

"What about the notes, verses, and so on, she leaves in the park for you?" He had calculated correctly. Knowing as much as he did about her, he judged that in her eyes it must appear he might know everything. She would not think to ask how he knew about the notes. For all she knew, Rita could have told him.

"The notes in the bench, yes. It is not quite what you think." Was she now smiling down at her crossed legs?

12.

Kitty said:

The notes. You know, I have a confession to make. I led her on. It's my fault.

Here it comes again, he thought, *the sweet beast of catastrophe. Am I not like Rita after all and do I not also live by catastrophe? I can smell it out every time. Show me a strange house and I can walk straight to the door where the bad secrets are kept. The question is: is it always here that one seeks one's health, here in the sweet, dread precincts of disaster? Strange: that her disaster now enables me, that now I could love her again and more easily from the pity of it.*

No, no, no, Kitty said, I don't mean there was anything really wrong. Nothing has ever happened, not the least thing. But what I don't know is whether from the very beginning I didn't know in my heart of hearts what I was doing—the way a child knows nothing and yet knows everything. I've often wondered whether a person who found herself for the first time in her life really and truly liked by another person and having the power for the first time to make another person like her, would she not use that power every time? Rita is a remarkable person and, wonder of wonders, she liked me. I had never dreamed that anybody would like me. And I knew exactly how to make her like me! This whole thing started last summer. The notes? They're notes, that's all. Poems.

Everything happened last summer in one week. Do you think there are times like that when everything comes to a head for several people and after that their lives take a different turning? Jamie and I had gone out to see Sutter and Rita in Tesuque. Val came out a little later. A few days later and everybody had gone off in different directions. First, I think Sutter found out that something was wrong with Jamie. Sutter could look at you and tell what was wrong with you—he's about shot now—but I remember he did take Jamie to the laboratory. Then he and Jamie went out into the desert and got lost etcetera etcetera. After that Val left to become a postulant or something. Then I came to New York with Rita. She and Sutter had already separated. I had never met anybody like

Rita. My own life had been abnormal. I had polio as a little girl and was crippled and overcame it with ten years of toe dancing (like Glenn Cunningham, Poppy said). I had tutors and Poppy sent me to a school in Switzerland—now you talk about something peculiar: those girls were a mess. I came home. My life at home. Do you know what everybody does? We live in a country club; we are not just members, we live right there on the golf links along with a hundred other houses. The men make money and watch pro football. The women play golf and bridge at the club. The children swim in meets. The mothers of the losers hate the mothers of the winners. At night Mama always gets mad at Huntley–Brinkley, turns off the TV and gets off on the Negroes and the Jews and the Federal Reserve Bank. Sunday we go to church. That's what we do at home. Then all of a sudden I found myself with Rita. She showed me something I never dreamed existed. Two things. First, the way she devoted herself to the Indians. I never saw anything like it. They adored her. I saw one child's father try to kneel and kiss her foot. Then she showed me how a thing can be beautiful. She kept Shakespeare's sonnets by her bed. And she actually read them. Listen to this, she would say, and she would read it. And I could hear it the way she heard it! Bare ruin'd choirs, where late the sweet birds sang. Poetry: who'd have thought it? We went for walks. I listened to her but then (is this bad?) I began to see how much she was enjoying teaching me. We went to corn dances in the pueblos. I said I had a confession. My confession is this: that even though I knew Rita and Sutter were estranged, or at least were having trouble, and although I knew exactly what effect our own friendship was having, I knew how to make Rita like me and I did it. Finally when Jamie and Sutter came back there was a scene between Val and Rita and everything blew up. At the time Val was fretting about whether to go into this religious order and she was not very stable. But everybody was unstable. Anyhow Val accused Rita of destroying Carlos's faith—

Carlos?

A Zuñi boy who was Rita's servant and protégé. (I beat him too. Rita liked him but she soon liked me better.) He was her prize pupil and she'd got him into Harvard on a scholarship. She was having Carlos and me dance the Ahaiyute myths.

Carlos was the Beast God and I was the Corn Woman. Val told Carlos he was trading his birthright for a mess of pottage. Rita asked her what mess of pottage she meant, the Ahaiyute myths or Harvard? This—this idolatry, said Val. But Val dear, said Rita, this *is* his birthright, the Zuñis had the Ahaiyute myths for hundreds of years before the Spanish priests came. Val stormed out. She never liked Rita.

What did Sutter say?

Nothing. Or rather he laughed. But it was then that Val made up her mind too. She came back the same night and apologized. She told Rita: "It is you who are doing the work and I who am being hateful and doing nothing. Is it possible to come to believe in Christ and the whole thing and afterwards to be more hateful than before? But at least now I know what to do, and I thank you for it, Rita." And so around she goes to each of us, kissing us and asking us to forgive her (it was that kind of summer).

What did Sutter say to that?

Oh, he said something about: now I don't know, Val, maybe there is something to be said nowadays for a theology of hatred—you know Sutter. No, you don't. But then I came on to New York with Rita. The poems in the park? They're just that. She likes to show me her favorites—she knows I can see them as she sees them. I have to get up earlier than she does and we have different lunch hours. So if she reads something the night before—she reads at all hours—she'll put it in the bench for me to read during my lunch. I owe her a great deal. Now she wants me to go to Europe with her. I owe her the pleasure she will take in showing it to me. But first I have to make sure of my own motives. I wrote Sutter that. I conceal nothing from him.

What did he say?

Nothing. He's entirely too selfish to write a letter. If Rita is the most unselfish person I know, Sutter is the most selfish. That was the real trouble all along, that Rita did all the giving and Sutter did all the taking. Do you know what he said to me? "Blankety-blank on unselfishness," said he. "I agree with Val and the Christers, it's a fornication of spirit." But that's not right either. That's not what Christ said.

Blankety-blank?

Crap.
Don't talk like that.
I'm sick. Take me home.

13.

The next morning he called Kitty from Macy's. "Today," he told her, "I've got to get this business settled one way or the other."

"Don't speak to me," she said, her voice faint and cold.

"Eh?"

"You know what I'm talking about."

"No, I don't." But he thought he did—though, as it turned out, he was wrong.

"You took advantage of me."

"Ah, dearest—" he began. His heart sank: she was right.

But she broke in quickly (he was not right). "I have been out of my mind with worry the last few days, about this whole business, Jamie and Europe and everything. Then on top of everything I was allergic to the paint fumes and it was too much."

"Paint fumes," said the engineer. He looked up in time to see his old friends the Ohioans punching in at the time clock, bound for sportswear and lingerie, a lusty clear-eyed crew who had no trouble understanding each other.

"We painted Rita's attic yesterday and I turned out to be allergic to the benzene or whatever it was. I went completely out of my head. What did I say?"

"Nothing much."

"But I remember enough to know that you took advantage of me, barging in like that."

"Barging in?"

"Rita tells me that you didn't call her, you just showed up."

"Yes," he said contritely, willing, anxious to be convicted of a lesser crime. What foulness had he committed? It was not enough to lie with Kitty in Central Park like a common sailor: he must also take his pleasure, or almost take his pleasure, with a nice girl rendered defenseless by paint fumes.

"I really think it put me in a terrible position for you to come to Rita's like that. You know better than that! And then to leave without so much as a fare-you-well to Rita and walking me clear to New Jersey or wherever it was."

"Yes."

"What do you want?"

"What?"

"You called me, remember?"

"Oh yes," said the engineer, shaking his head to clear the cobwebs. "I've got to, ah, get this business settled." But he had lost his resolution.

"What business?" said Kitty coldly.

"Whether I am working for Rita or your father. But in either case—"

"Working for Rita?" she asked sharply.

"Rita wants me and Jamie to take the camper while you all go to Europe."

"I see."

"The point is," he said, gathering strength, collecting his wits at last, "I don't want you to go."

"Oh, you don't want me to go."

"No, I want you to stay here and either go south with Jamie and me or—"

"You've got your nerve."

"Kitty."

"What?"

"Do you remember that I asked you to marry me last night?"

"Oh Lord," said the girl nervously and hung up, not so much, he thought, on him as on herself.

Later, after shower and breakfast, he called Jamie from the Y.M.C.A. It was time to settle things one way or another.

Jamie surprised him by answering the phone himself.

"Why didn't you keep the telescope?" the engineer asked him.

"We're leaving, aren't we? Thanks, by the way."

"Rita spoke to me today. Do you know what she wants us to do?"

"Yes."

"Is that what you want to do?"

Again he heard the slight break in breathing, the little risible and incredulous sound he seemed to call forth from people.

"What would you do?" asked Jamie after a silence.

"I'd do what the doctor said."

"Me too. But in any case you're going to bum around with me for a while?"

"Sure."

"Then call Poppy and see what's what. After all, he's the boss."

"You're right. I will. Where is he?"

"At the Astor."

"How extraordinary."

"It was the only hotel they knew."

"Yello, yello." Mr. Vaught answered the telephone as eccentrically and routinely as a priest reciting the rosary.

"Sir, this is Bill Barrett."

"Who? Billy boy!"

"Yes sir. Sir—"

"Yayo."

"I would like to know exactly where we stand."

"You ain't the only one."

"Sir?"

"What is it you want to know, Bill?"

"I would like to know, sir, whether I am working for you or working for Rita or for both or for neither."

"You want to know something, Bill."

"Yes sir."

"It would be a crying shame if you didn't turn out to be a lawyer. You sound just like your daddy."

"Yes sir. But—"

"Listen to me, Bill."

"I will," said the engineer, who had learned to tell when the old man was not fooling.

"You got your driver's license?"

"Yes sir."

"All right. You be standing outside on the sidewalk at nine o'clock in the morning. We'll pick you up. Then we'll see who's going where."

"Yes sir."

"All yall be ready," he said, like Kitty, somewhat aside from the telephone, to the world around.

It was not a good sign, thought the engineer as he hung up slowly, that Mr. Vaught spoke both broadly and irritably.

14.

The next morning he resigned his position at Macy's—the chief engineer, who had heard this before and was something of a psychologist himself, nodded gravely and promised the job would be waiting for him when he felt better—checked out of the Y.M.C.A. and sat on his telescope at the curb for three hours. No one came to pick him up. Once he went inside to call the hospital, the hotel, and Kitty. Had he got the directions wrong? Jamie had been discharged, the Vaughts had left the hotel, and Kitty's telephone did not answer.

Only then, three hours later, did it occur to him that there must be a message for him. He climbed the steps again. Already the Y reentered was like a place he had lived in long ago with its special smell of earnestness and breathed air and soaped tile, the smell, as he had always taken it but only just now realized, of Spanish Protestantism. Two yellow slips were handed him across the desk. Superstitiously, he took pains to return to his perch on the street corner before reading either. The first was a garbled note, evidently from Mr. Vaught. "If plans are not finalized and you change your mind a job is always waiting. S. Vote." "Vote" could only be Vaught.

The second was from Kitty and he couldn't see for looking. "Europe out," he finally made out. "Jamie more important. Please change your mind and catch up with us at Coach-and-Four Motel, Williamsburg. Know you had cause to lose patience but please change your mind. Did you mean what you said? Kitty."

Change my mind? Mean what I said? What did I say, asked the engineer aloud. He blinked into the weak sunlight. Screwing up an eye, he tried mightily to get the straight of it. It follows, said he, diagramming a syllogism in the air, that they think I changed my mind about going with them. But I told them no such thing. Then it follows someone else did.

Another twenty minutes of squatting and musing on the telescope, not so much addled as distracted by the curiousness of sitting in the street and having no address, and he jumped suddenly to his feet.

Why, they have all left, thought he, socking himself with amazement: the whole lot of them have pulled out.

Early afternoon found him on a southbound bus counting his money. He bought a ticket as far as Metuchen. The bus was a local, a stained old Greyhound with high portholes. The passengers sat deep in her hold, which smelled of the 1940's and many a trip to Fort Dix. Under the Hudson River she roared, swaying like a schooner, and out onto old US 1 with its ancient overpasses and prehistoric Sinclair stations. The green sky filtered through the high windows. In Elizabeth, when the door opened, he fancied he heard a twittering, ravening noise high in the green sky.

When the bus got clear of the factories and overpasses, he pulled the cord and alighted on the littered highway. On the corner stood a blackened stucco dollhouse with a pagoda roof, evidently a subdivision field office left over from the period between the great wars.

It began to rain, a fine dirty Jersey mizzle, and he took refuge in the pagoda, which was empty but for scraps of ancient newspapers, a sepia rotogravure section depicting Lucky Lindy's visit to Lakehurst in 1928.

The drizzle stopped but it was a bad place to catch a ride. There were few cars. The concrete underfoot trembled like an earthquake as the great tankers and tractors rolled by. Yet prudence had not failed him. Against such an occasion he had obtained certain materials in Penn Station, and, returning to the pagoda, he lettered a sign which he propped against his telescope: PRINCETON STUDENT SEEKS RIDE SOUTH.

And now once again, not entirely aware that he did so, he stuck his hands in his pockets a certain way and carried his chin in his throat. In the end he even took off his Macy's jacket (which looked more like Ohio State than Princeton), uncovering his shirt with the tuck in back and no pocket in front.

Chapter Three

FOR AN HOUR and a half the great trucks rolled past, shaking the earth and exhaling clouds of blue headache smoke. Was it possible that his Princeton placard did more harm than good? He had in fact given up, counted his money for the third time, and resolved to ride the bus and waive eating; had even picked up telescope but not, fortunately, Val-pak, which supported the placard, when a bottle-green Chevrolet, an old '58 Junebug, passed and hesitated, the driver's foot lifting and the carburetor sucking wind, speeded up and hesitated again. As the engineer watched politely lest he presume upon fortune, the Chevrolet pulled off the highway and sat interestingly on the shoulder a good hundred yards to the south. At last it came, the sign, a hand beckoned to him importunately and in a single swoop he caught up Val-pak and telescope and left placard behind.

Already, even as he stooped, smiling, to stow his gear through the back door, which had been opened for him, he had registered his benefactor without quite looking at him. The driver was a light-colored high-stomached Negro dressed in a good brown suit, no doubt a preacher or a teacher. Now sitting beside him and taking note of the other's civil bald bun-shaped head, of the sharp knees and thin ankles clad in socks-with-clocks, he was sure of it: here was the sort to hold converse at a lofty level with instant and prodigious agreement on all subjects. He would belong to a committee on Religion and Mental Health.

As it turned out, the driver spoke not of religion or mental health but of Princeton and Einstein. The placard *had* worked.

"There was a quality of simplicity about him," said the driver, turning his head and not his eyes sociably toward his passenger, and launched at once into his own pet theory. It was his conviction that there was a balance in nature which was upset by man's attempt to improve upon it.

The engineer agreed and, casting his eye about the ruinous

289

New Jersey flats, cited an article he had read about rivers in this very neighborhood which fairly foamed with detergents and chemical wastes.

"No no," said the driver excitedly. He explained that he was not speaking of ordinary pollution but of a far more fundamental principle. Rather was it his conviction that man's very best efforts to improve his environment, by air-conditioning and even by landscaping, upset a fundamental law which it took millions of years to evolve. "You take your modern office building, as tastefully done as you please. What does it do to a man to uproot him from the earth? There is the cause of your violence!"

"Yes," said the sentient engineer, frowning thoughtfully. Something was amiss here. He couldn't quite get hold of this bird. Something was out of kilter. It was his speech, for one thing. The driver did not speak as one might expect him to, with a certain relish and a hearkening to his own periods, as many educated Negroes speak. No, his speech was rapid and slurred, for all the world like a shaky white man's.

Obligingly, however, the engineer, who had become giddy from hunger and his long wait, set forth his own ideas on the subject of good environments and bad environments—without mentioning the noxious particles.

"Yes!" cried the driver in his damped reedy voice. He was tiring and excited and driving badly. The passenger became nervous. If only he would ask me to drive, he groaned, as the Chevy nearly ran under a great Fruehauf trailer. "That's your reaction to artificial environments in general! Wonderful! Don't you see how it dovetails?"

The engineer nodded reluctantly. He did not see. Back-to-nature was the last thing he had in mind. "Except—ahem—" said he, feeling his own voice go a bit reedy. "Except I would suspect that even if one picked out the most natural surroundings he might carry his own deprivation with him."

"Capital," cried the driver and smote the steering wheel.

The engineer could all but feel the broad plastic knurls between his knuckles. I could make this old Junebug take off, he thought. But the driver was slowing down again, row-boating badly as he did so.

"Now isn't this something," he said. "Here we are, total

strangers, talking like this—" He was fairly jumping out of his skin in his nervous elation.

They passed an abandoned miniature golf links, the ancient kind with asbestos greens and gutter pipes which squirt out the ball. But no sooner had they entered the countryside of middle Jersey than the driver pulled off the highway and stopped. The hitchhiker sat as pleasant as ever, hands on knees, nodding slightly, but inwardly dismayed.

"Do you mind if I ask a question," said the driver, swinging over a sharp, well-clad knee.

"Why, no."

"I like to know what a man's philosophy is and I want to tell you mine."

Uh-oh, thought the engineer gloomily. After five years of New York and Central Park and the Y.M.C.A., he had learned to be wary of philosophers.

With his Masonic ring winking fraternally, the dignified colored man leaned several degrees nearer. "I have a little confession to make to you."

"Certainly," said the courteous engineer, cocking a weather eye at his surroundings. All around them stretched a gloomy cattail swamp which smelled like a crankcase and from which arose singing clouds of mosquitoes. A steady stream of Fruehauf tractor-trailers rumbled past, each with a *no-rider* sign on the windshield.

"I'm not what you think I am," the driver shouted above the uproar.

"You're not," said the pleasant, forward-facing engineer.

"What do you think I am? Tell me honestly."

"Um. I'd guess you were a minister or perhaps a professor."

"What *race?*"

"Why, um, colored."

"Look at this."

To the hitchhiker's astonishment, the driver shucked off his coat and pushed a jeweled cuff up a skinny arm.

"Ah," said the engineer, nodding politely, though he couldn't see much in the gathering darkness.

"Well?"

"Sir?"

"Look at that patch."

"Then you're not—?"

"I'm not a Negro."

"Is that right?"

"My name is not Isham Washington."

"No?"

"It's Forney Aiken."

"Is that so," said the interested engineer. He could tell that the other expected him to be surprised, but it was not in him to be surprised because it was no more surprising to him when things did not fall out as they were supposed to than when they did.

"Does that name ring a bell?"

"It does sound familiar," said the engineer truthfully, since his legions of *déjà vus* made everything sound familiar.

"Do you remember a picture story that appeared in July '51 *Redbook* called 'Death on the Expressway'?"

"I'm not sure."

"It was reprinted by the National Safety Council, ten million copies."

"As a matter of fact, I think I do—"

"Do you remember the fellow who interviewed Jafsie Condon in the cemetery?"

"Who?"

"Or the article in *Liberty*: 'I Saw Vic Genovese'? For forty-eight hours I was the only man alive in contact with both the F.B.I. and Vic Genovese."

"You're Forney Aiken the—"

"The photographer."

"Yes, I think I do," said the engineer, nodding but still wary. This fellow could still be a philosopher. "Anyhow I certainly do appreciate the ride." The singing hordes of mosquitoes were coming ever nearer. He wished Forney would get going.

"Forney," cried the other, holding out a hand.

"Will. Will Barrett."

The green Chevrolet resumed its journey, taking its place shakily among the Fruehauf tractors. Breathing a sigh of relief, the engineer spoke of his own small efforts in photography and took from his wallet a color snapshot of the peregrine falcon, his best.

"Tremendous," cried the photographer, once again beside

himself with delight at having fallen in with such a pleasant and ingenious young man. In return he showed his passenger a tiny candid camera concealed under his necktie whose lens looked like the jewel of a tie clasp.

It, the candid camera, was essential to his present assignment. The photographer, it turned out, was setting forth on an expedition this very afternoon, the first he had undertaken in quite awhile. It was something of a comeback, the engineer surmised. He had the shaky voice and the fitful enthusiasms of a man freshly sober.

The nature of his new project accounted for his extraordinary disguise. He wished to do a series on behind-the-scene life of the Negro. The idea had come to him in the middle of the night: why not *be* a Negro? To make a long story short, he had persuaded a dermatologist friend to administer an alkaloid which simulates the deposit of melanin in the skin, with the difference that the darkening effect could be neutralized by a topical cream. Therefore the white patch on his forearm. To complete the disguise, he had provided himself with the personal papers of one Isham Washington, an agent for a burial insurance firm in Pittsburgh.

This very afternoon he had left the office of his agent in New York, tonight would stop off at his house in Bucks County, and tomorrow would head south, under the "cotton curtain," as he expressed it.

The pseudo-Negro was even more delighted to discover that his passenger was something of an expert on American speech. "You were my first test and I passed it, and you a Southerner."

"Well, not quite," replied the tactful engineer. He explained that for one thing you don't say in*sur*-ance but *in*-surance or rather *in*-shaunce.

"Oh, this is marvelous," said the pseudo-Negro, nearly running under a Borden tanker.

You don't say that either, *mah*velous, thought the engineer, but let it go.

"What do you think of the title 'No Man an Island'?"

"Very good."

Tomorrow, the pseudo-Negro explained, he planned to stop in Philadelphia and pick up Mort Prince, the writer, who planned to come with him and do the text.

"But hold on," exclaimed the driver, smacking the steering wheel again. "How stupid can you get."

For the third time in a month the engineer was offered a job. "Why didn't I think of it before! Why don't you come with us? You know the country and you could do the driving. I'm a lousy driver." He was. His driving was like his talking. He was alert and chipper and terrified. "Do you drive?"

"Yes sir."

But the engineer declined. His services were already engaged, he explained, by a family who was employing him as tutor-companion to their son.

"Ten dollars a day plus keep."

"No sir. I really can't."

"Plus a piece of the royalties."

"I certainly appreciate it."

"You know Mort?"

"Well, I've heard of him and read some of his books."

"You know, it was Mort and I who first hit on the idea of the Writers' and Actors' League for Social Morality."

The engineer nodded agreeably. "I can certainly understand it, considering the number of dirty books published nowadays. As for the personal lives of the actors and actresses—"

The pseudo-Negro looked at him twice. "Oh-*ho*. Very good! Very ironical! I like that. You're quite a character, Barrett."

"Yes sir."

"Joking aside, though, it was our idea to form the first folk theater to travel through the South. Last summer it played in over a hundred towns. Where are you from—I bet it played there."

The engineer told him.

"My God." The pseudo-Negro ran off the road in his excitement. The hitchhiker put a discreet hand on the wheel until the Chevy was under control. "That's where we're having our festival this fall. Some of the biggest names in Hollywood and Broadway are coming down. What it is, is like the old morality plays in the Middle Ages."

"Yes sir."

"Is that where you're from?"

"Yes sir."

"Then you've got to come with us."

The engineer managed to decline, but in the end he agreed to drive the other as far as Virginia and the "cotton curtain." When they stopped the second time to change drivers, he was glad enough to add the two ten-dollar bills, which the pseudo-Negro made a great show of paying him in advance, to his flattened wallet and to sprint around and hop into the driver's seat.

2.

Under the engineer's steady hand, the Chevrolet fairly sailed down US 1. In short order it turned onto a great new westering turnpike and swept like a bird across the Delaware River not far from the spot where General Washington crossed nearly two hundred years ago.

Forney Aiken's stone cottage was also standing at the time of the crossing. Some years ago, he told the engineer, he and his wife had left New York and beat a more or less disorderly retreat to Bucks County. She was an actor's agent and had to commute. He was trying to quit drinking and thought it might help to live in the country and do chores, perhaps even farm. When farming didn't work, he took to making things, the sort of articles, firkins and sisal tote bags, which are advertised in home magazines. But this was not as simple as it looked either. There was more to it than designing an ad for a magazine. You have to have your wholesale outlet.

There were some people sitting around a lighted pool in an orchard when they arrived. The travelers skirted them in a somewhat ambiguous fashion, not quite ignoring them and not quite stopping to speak but catching a few introductions on the fly, so to speak. Mrs. Aiken looked after them with an expression which gave the engineer to understand that the photographer often showed up with strangers and skirted the pool. Even though it was dark, the photographer insisted on showing the engineer the orchard and barn. It was a pity because the engineer recognized one of the guests, a nameless but familiar actor who took the part of a gentle, wise doctor on the daytime serial which it was his habit to watch for a few minutes after lunch in the Y. But he must be shown on to the barn instead, which was stacked to the rafters with cedar firkins, thousands of them. For some eighteen months the barn had served as a firkin factory. But of the eight or nine thousand manufactured, only five hundred had been sold. "Take your pick," his host urged him, and the engineer was glad enough to do so, having a liking for well-wrought wooden things. He chose a stout two-gallon firkin of red-and-white cedar bound in copper and fitted with a top. It would be a good thing to carry country butter in or well water or just to sit on between rides.

Later he did meet the poolside group. The actor was a cheerful fellow, not at all like the sad doctor he played, even though his face had fallen into a habitual careworn expression after years in the part. But he had a thick brown merry body and a good pelt on his chest, upon which he rested his highball. No one paid any attention to Forney's disguise. They treated him with the tender apocalyptic cordiality and the many warm hugs of show-business people. Though he knew nothing about show biz, the sentient engineer had no trouble translating their tender regard for their host. It clearly signified: Forney, you're dead, done for, that's why we love you. Forney was as abrupt with them as they were tender with him. He had the manner of one going about his business. To the others, it seemed to the sentient engineer, the expedition was "something Forney was doing" and something therefore to be treated with a mournful and inattentive sympathy which already discounted failure. A rangy forty-five-year-old couple with muscular forty-five-year-old calves, burnt black as Indians, found the engineer and asked him who he was. When he told them he came with Forney, they went deaf and fond. "Forney's got more talent in his little finger than anybody here," cried the man both privately and loudly, like a proverb, and hurried away.

Though he had not eaten or slept since the day before, he drank two drinks and went swimming. Soon he was treading water in the deep dark end of the pool with Forney's daughter, the only other young person present. Everyone called her Muzh or Moosh. She had the fitful and antic manner of one used to the company of her elders. In no time the two of them had their heads together, snuffling the water like seals. It was understood between them that they were being the young folk. Muzh had just returned from her college year abroad. Her shoulders were strong and sloping from bicycling around youth hostels. In the clear yellow water her strong legs bent like pants.

She told him about the guests. Her way of speaking was rapid and confidential as if they had left off only a short time earlier. She rattled off some recent history. "Coop over there—" she spoke into the lambent water, nodding toward a distinguished silver-haired gent, "—is just out of the Doylestown jail, where he served six months for sodomy, though Fra says sodomy rates two to ten." Who was Fra? (As usual, strangers expected him to know their, the strangers', friends.) And had she, for a fact, said sodomy? He wrung out his ear. Unfortunately she was at that moment on his deaf side.

She dawdled toward him, working the water to and fro through the sluice of her shoulder. On she went about the guests in her rapid, cataloguing voice, bent toward him, the waterline at his mouth, while he grew ever fainter with hunger and more agitated. As her knees brushed against his and she spoke of having transcended Western values, he seized her through the thick parts, fell upon her as much from weakness as desire, fainted upon her, the fine brown berry of a girl she was. "Zut alors," she cried softly, and now perfunctorily, unsurprised, keeping herself flexed and bent away from him, she asked him about the transvaluation of values. "I couldn't say," he replied, disappointed. He had heard enough about values from Dr. Gamow. "No, really," she said. "I am in something of a value crisis and so I'm deeply concerned. What can we do?" "Let's go over yonder," he replied, fainting with hunger and desire, and nodded to the dark polygon of the barn. "Zut," she cried, but idly, and swam away. As he stood slack in the water, both lustful and shrunken with cold, she made forays in the water around him, flexing like a porpoise, came under him in the shallows, put him astride and unhorsed him in bluff youth-hostel style. "See you later," she said at last and went away, but how said she it?

Coming to himself all at once, he socked himself in the head. Swine, said he, staggering about in the shallows, white trash. Here you are in love with a certain person and bound south as a gentleman like Rooney Lee after a sojourn in the North, and at it again: pressing against girls like a horny dolphin and abusing your host besides. No more humbuggery! Leaping from the pool, he ran to the room Forney had shown him and, starved or not, threw a hundred combination punches and did thirty minutes of violent isomorphics until he dripped with sweat, took an ice-cold shower and read two pages of *Living*. Saints contemplated God to be rid of concupiscence; he turned to money. He returned to the pool, exhausted, ravenous, but in his right mind.

"I apologize," he told Muzh formally as they stood in line for cold cuts. "As a matter of fact I've been, ahem, in something of a value crisis myself and have not eaten or slept in quite a while. I apologize for being forward with you."

"Good God," said Muzh, brushing against him with several dorsal surfaces. "Don't," she whispered.

"Don't what?"

She didn't answer.

Damn, thought he, and had to thrust his hand through his pocket to keep his knee from leaping.

He ate three helpings of turkey and ham and rye bread and sat slack and heavy with his blood singing in his ears. Fortunately his host was brimming with plans for the morrow and put him to work after supper toting paraphernalia, cameras and insurance manuals, to the Chevrolet. Later he showed him the house.

"You're going to like Mort Prince. He's our kind of folks." They had reached the cellar, which the engineer looked at and sniffed with interest because at home the ground was too low for cellars and he'd never seen one before. "He's a sweet guy," said Forney.

"Yes sir."

"Have you read his stuff?"

"A couple of novels quite a while ago."

"You haven't read *Love*?"

"His latest? No."

"I'll get you a copy tonight."

"Thank you, but I'm very sleepy. I think I'll go to bed."

Forney came closer. "You know what that guy told me with a straight face. I asked him what this book was going to be about and he said quite seriously: it was about —ing. And in a sense it is!" They were by now back at poolside and within earshot of others, including Muzh. It made the engineer nervous. "But it is a beautiful piece of work and about as pornographic as Chaucer. Indeed it is deeply religious. I'll get you a copy."

The engineer groaned. What the devil does he mean telling me it's about —ing? Is —ing a joking matter? Am I to understand I am free to — his daughter? Or do we speak of —ing man to man, jokingly, literarily, with no thought of —ing anyone in the vicinity? His radar boggled.

"It is essentially a religious book, in the sense of being a yea-saying rather than a nay-saying," Forney went on. "Mort has one simple credo: saying Yes to Life wherever it is found."

"Yes sir," said the engineer, rising unsteadily. "I think I'll go to bed."

But no sooner had he fallen into the four-poster than a knock came at the door. It was Muzh in a shorty nightgown delivering *Love*. "You talk about randy," said she and smote her brow. "Sheesh!"

"Thank you," said the engineer, laughing heartily, and when she had left went reeling about the room like Rooney Lee after the battle of Seven Days. What saved him in the end was not only Southern chivalry but Yankee good sense. Muzh he saw all at once and belatedly, as she might have been seen by her classmates, as a horsy, good-natured, sisterly sort. She was, as they say in the North, a good kid. And so it was permitted him to leave her alone and to excuse himself. What a relief. He wiped his brow.

Worse luck, though, sleep deserted him, left him half dead from lack of it and wide awake. There was nothing to do but read *Love*. He read it straight through, finishing at three o'clock.

Love was about orgasms, good and bad, some forty-six. But it ended, as Forney had said, on a religious note. "And so I humbly ask of life," said the hero to his last partner with whose assistance he had managed to coincide with his best expectations, "that it grant us the only salvation, that of one human being discovering himself through another and through the miracle of love."

The poor engineer arose, faint with fatigue, and threw a few final combination punches to clear his head. But when he got back in bed he found himself lying at attention, his feet sticking up, his left leg tending to rise of itself. There was nothing to do but swallow two of Dr. Gamow's spansules, which induced sleep only indirectly by inhibiting the cortical influence on the midbrain—even though he knew that his sense of time and place would suffer in consequence. Though he might not know where he was tomorrow or what year it was, at least he'd feel better than this.

At any rate he went fast asleep and woke in midmorning, somewhat disoriented but feeling quite cheerful and well.

3.

Early afternoon found him driving like a cat. The bottle-green Chevrolet went roaring and banking around the many ramps and interchanges of eastern Pennsylvania. The pseudo-Negro sat beside him as alert and jumpy as ever. Presently they left the expressway and went among the sooty little hill towns. *Déjà vus* stole alongside and beckoned at the corner of his eye. How familiar were these steep streets and old 1937 brick-and-limestone high schools and the sooty monkey Pullman smell. Surely I attended that very one, he told himself, where I recall taking mechanical drawing in the basement. Two girls in summer school sat on the school steps, dumb pretty Pennsylvania girls. He waved. They waved back. Oh girls I love you. Don't let anybody mess with you till I get back because I've been here before. Where is this place? "Where is this?" he asked so abruptly that the pseudo-Negro jumped a good inch.

The pseudo-Negro kept harping on Mort Prince, whom they were presently to pick up. The writer, it seemed, had astonished his friends by moving to Levittown. He had inherited the house from an aunt and, instead of selling it, had sold his farm in Connecticut and moved in more or less, as the pseudo-Negro expressed it, for the simple heck of it. "Imagine going from Fiesole to Levittown," he said, shaking his head. The engineer could very well imagine it.

He began to look forward to meeting Mort Prince. Some years ago he had read two of his novels and remembered them perfectly—he could remember perfectly every detail of a book he had read ten years ago or a conversation with his father fifteen years ago; it was the day before yesterday that gave him trouble. After a war novel which made him famous, Mort Prince wrote a novel about a young veteran who becomes disillusioned with the United States and goes to Italy in quest of his own identity. It is in Europe that he discovers he is an American after all. The book ended on a hopeful note. Mark comes home to visit his dying father, who is a judge in Vermont. The judge is a Yankee in the old style, a man of granite integrity. Now he too, Mark, knows who he is, what he must do, and that all men are his brothers. In the last chapter he climbs High Tor overlooking the valley. If a man does nothing else in life, said Mark to himself, he can at least tell one other man (that all men are brothers) and he another and he in turn another until at last amid the hatred and the dying all men shall one day hear and hearing understand and understanding believe. Mark had come home. Arising from High Tor, he picked up his coat and turned his face to the city.

After his first return to the United States, the pseudo-Negro was saying, Mort Prince had married a hometown girl and moved to Connecticut. It was at this time, as the engineer recalled it, that he had read *The Farther Journey*, a novel about a writer who lives in Connecticut and enters into a sexual relationship with a housewife next door, not as a conventional adultery, for he was not even attracted to her, but rather as the exercise of that last and inalienable possession of the individual in a sick society, freedom. In the words of one reviewer, it was "the most nearly absolutely gratuitous act since Lafcadio pushed Fleurissoire out of the railway carriage in *Les Caves du Vatican*."

Following his divorce and his latest trip to Italy the writer, according to the pseudo-Negro, had felt the strongest compulsion to return to the United States, seek out the most commonplace environment, and there, like Descartes among the Burghers of Amsterdam, descend within himself and write the first real war novel, an absolutely unvarnished account of one day's action of one infantry platoon. When his aunt died and left him a house, he took off from Fiesole by the first plane.

The attentive engineer, at this moment skillfully piloting the green Chevrolet into the pleasant maze of Levittown, understood perfectly. If his aunt had left him such a house, he'd have moved in too and settled down in perfect contentment.

They entered Levittown. The freshly sprinkled lawns sparkled in the sunlight, lawns as beautiful as Atlanta lawns but less spectral and Druidic. Chipper little Swiss swales they were and

no Negroes to cut the grass but rather Mr. Gallagher and Mr.
Shean cranking up their Toros and afterward wisecracking over
the fence. Here, he reckoned, housewives ran into each other's
kitchens to borrow a cup of Duz. Not a bad life! Really he
would like it very much. He could live here cheerfully as a Swiss
with never a care for the morrow. But a certain someone was
already in Old Virginny by now and his heart pressed south.

But even as they began to circle the blocks and search for
house numbers, the sentient engineer began to detect unpleasant radiations. While the pseudo-Negro gabbled away and
noticed nothing, it struck the engineer that more people than
one might expect were standing about on their lawns and sidewalks. Indeed he could swear that some of them were shooting
hostile glances in the direction of the Chevrolet! Recollecting
Dr. Gamow's strong hints about certain delusions of persecution, he tried to pay no attention. But they were at it again!
One group of householders in particular he noticed and one
man in particular, a burly fellow with a small mustache who
wore a furry alpine hat which was too small for him.

"What number did you say it was?" he asked the pseudo-
Negro.

"One forty-two."

"Then here it is," said the engineer, circling the block a
second time and pulling up at the same group of householders. He followed the pseudo-Negro up the walk, the latter as
garrulous and shaky as ever and noticing nothing, his nerve
ends firing at the slightest breeze, even nodding to the householders on the next lawn, whom he fancied to be well-wishers
of some sort. They were not well-wishers. They stood about
silently, hands in pockets, and kicking the turf. Next to the
burly alpiner the engineer spied trouble itself: a thin fierce-eyed
damp-skinned woman whose hair was done up in plastic reels,
a regular La Pasionaria of the suburbs. He ventured another
look. Beyond a doubt, she was glaring straight at him, the
engineer!

Mort Prince met them in the deep-set cathedral door, beer
in hand, a pleasant slightish fellow with twirling black hair
which flew away in a banner of not absolutely serious rebellion.
He wore a black leather wristlet and, as he talked, performed a
few covert isometrics on the beer can. The engineer liked him

at once, perceiving that he was not the mighty fornicator of his novels but a perky little bull-shooter of a certain style, the sort who stands in the kitchen during parties, suspended from himself so-to-speak, beer can in hand and matter forming at the corner of his mouth, all the while spieling off some very good stuff and very funny. One would like to get him going (and the engineer was just the one).

One glance past him into the house and he knew also how it stood with the house and how the writer lived in it. Their voices echoed on bare parquet floors. There was no furniture except a plastic dinette and an isomorphic bar in a doorway. So that was how he did it, standing clear of walls suspended within himself and disdaining chairs because chairs were for sitting and therefore cancelled themselves.

He shook hands with the engineer with a strong wiry grip, pronating his elbow.

"This is the guy that's going with us," said the pseudo-Negro, linking arms with them. "He knows everybody down there and the ones he doesn't know he's kin to."

"No," said the engineer, frowning and blushing.

"You from down South," asked Mort Prince, squeezing the beer can and not quite looking at him.

"Yes." Though the pseudo-Negro had led him to believe that Mort Prince would welcome him with open arms, he couldn't help noticing that the writer wore an indifferent, if not unfriendly, expression.

"Tell him where you're from."

The engineer told him.

But Mort Prince seemed abstracted and gloomy and did not respond. He said nothing and went back to pressing the beer can.

"That's where the festival is," said the pseudo-Negro, giving the writer several meaningful nudges.

"No, I'm sorry," said the engineer, looking at his watch. He was anxious to be on his way. He didn't like the look of things. Through the open doorway—Mort had not quite invited them in and they were standing barely beyond the sill—the engineer noticed that the householders were closer. Yes, beyond a doubt they were bearing down upon Mort Prince's house.

"I really appreciate it but as I told Mr. Aiken—" began the

engineer, already nodding to the new arrivals to prepare Mort Prince and the pseudo-Negro—but it was too late.

"Hey, you," called the burly man in the alpine hat, pointing with his chin and resting his hands lightly on his hips.

The engineer looked at him twice. Beyond any question, the stranger was addressing him. His heart gave a single dread leap. Adrenalin erected his hair roots, could it have come at last, a simple fight, with the issue clear beyond peradventure? "Are you speaking to me?"

"You from Haddon Heights?"

"Sir?" The engineer cupped a hand to his ear. The burly man's T-shirt had the legend *Deep Six* printed on it. No doubt he belonged to a bowling league. He reminded the engineer of the fellows he used to see around bowling alleys in Long Island City.

"You heard me."

"Sir, I don't believe I like your tone," said the engineer, advancing a step with his good ear put forward. Perhaps the time had come again when you could be insulted, hear it aright, and have it out then and there as his grandfather used to have it out. But there must be no mistake. "You were speaking to me?" he asked again, straining every nerve to hear, for nothing is worse than being an honorable deaf man who can't be certain he is insulted.

The alpiner turned to Mort Prince. "Mae here sawr him in Haddon Heights. Her brother-in-law lives in Haddonfield."

"Haddon Heights? Haddonfield? I've never heard of either place," said the bemused engineer. "In any case I don't care for this fellow's tone." It had happened again, he knew, he had been mistaken for someone else.

The next thing he knew, another man came crowding in, a fair-skinned oldish man with a gray crew cut and tabs on his elbows like Jiggs.

"He's a Jersey agent, Mr. Prince," said the newcomer.

"What's all this about?" asked the writer, feeling his wristlet uneasily. The engineer perceived that the other set great store by getting along with his neighbors—like Descartes—and so was in a quandary.

"That's a fact, Mr. Prince," said the burly man, who had

decided to take a neighborly tone toward the writer. "That's the way they do it, they come over here from Jersey like him and his friend there and they ride around the block slow like them, looking. You saw them! But we're not worried about you, Mr. Prince. I was just telling Whitey here that Mr. Prince wasn't about to sell his house."

"I'm not a Jersey agent, whatever that is," said the engineer, noticing that the pseudo-Negro was smiling a brilliant nervous rueful smile and was opening his hands first to one side and then the other.

"Fellows," the pseudo-Negro appealed to all parties, calling heaven to witness the follies and misunderstandings of men. "This is ridiculous," he cried, opening his hands, "believe me."

The engineer flushed angrily. "And furthermore I've never heard of Haddon Heights," he told them. Yet strive as he might to keep his anger pure and honorable, it was no use. The alpiner had detached himself somewhat and stood apart with an ironic expression like a man who has been in a wreck and is embarrassed by passers-by. And the engineer, up to his old tricks despite himself, began to tune him in to see how it stood with him. Damnation, he swore to himself. To make matters worse, his hay fever had returned, his nose swelled up and began to run, and he had left his handkerchiefs in the firkin. Rage leaked away.

But he had not reckoned with the woman.

"Faggot!" she cried, rushing past Jiggs and thrusting her face within inches of the engineer's. She wore a black bolero jacket over her bowling-league skirt. Her bare arms were moist and muscular like a man's.

"Faggot?" repeated the puzzled engineer, feeling his nose.

"You work for Oscar Fava, don't you?" she asked, both malignant and triumphant.

"I do not." He glanced at her uneasily. What to do with a maniac of a woman?

"As a matter of fact, I do have the place for sale," said Mort Prince, who had decided to be irritated with his neighbors after all.

"Did you sign any papers?" asked the burly man, his good nature beginning to stick in his throat.

"What is it to you?"

"Could I see the papers, Mr. Prince?" He pronounced it päpers.

"They can't break a block without you let them," said Jiggs, his face beginning to mottle Irish red and white.

"Get the hell out of my house," said Mort Prince, although the householders had not crossed the threshold. Everyone still stood in the cathedral doorway.

"Fink," said the woman, who had not taken her eyes from the engineer's face. As he watched incredulously, she balled up her fist like a man, thumb out of the way, and cocked it back.

"Hold on," said the engineer—she could hit him! And at the same moment from the corner of his eye he saw the burly man advance upon the writer, hand outstretched, perhaps for the "papers," perhaps to shake hands, but advancing nevertheless. Two other householders, he noticed for the first time, were standing in the background, speaking in low tones and swinging their arms briskly in the manner of bystanders.

"Excuse me," said the engineer to the woman, squeezing past her as if she were an irate shopper in Macy's basement. On the way he brushed against Jiggs, who immediately fell back and began to crouch and wave him in with his fingertips.

"Come on, come on," said Jiggs.

But it was the pseudo-Negro who caught his attention. He had come between the engineer and Jiggs and shook his head sadly and good-naturedly. "Hold on, fellows," he said, undoing his cuff link. "I'm afraid there's been a rather pathetic misunderstanding here—a sad commentary in fact on the frailty of us all. Fellows—"

"No," cried the engineer angrily. "Don't roll up your sleeve."

"Go ahead and roll up your sleeve," cried Jiggs, misunderstanding, dancing ominously and now waving the pseudo-Negro into him.

The engineer groaned. "No. I—" he began, taking another step toward the grinning alpiner. Here was the villain!

But in that instant, even as he was passing the woman, whom he had forgotten, she drew back her fist clear to her earlobe and, unleashing a straight whistling blow, struck the engineer on the fleshy part of his nose, which was already swollen and tender from hay fever.

Oh, hideous exploding humiliating goddamnable nose pain, the thump-thud of woe itself. Oh, ye bastards all together. "Come here," he thought he heard himself say as he struggled to get at the alpiner—did he hit him?—but the next thing he knew he was sitting on the front steps enveloped by the dreadful cordiality of misunderstandings cleared away, of debits to be balanced. The bastards, friends and foe, were all apologizing to each other. As he held his nose, he saw the pseudo-Negro rolling his sleeve down. He had shown them his white patch.

Only Mort Prince was still angry. "That's not the point," he was saying furiously to the householders, who, the engineer perceived instantly, were anxious for him to score his point. They were allowing him his anger. Everyone felt bad. The engineer groaned.

"I thought they were blockbusters, for Christ's sake," Jiggs was telling a newcomer. "They been here," he assured Mort Prince. "And they come from Jersey."

"I just want to make it damn clear I'm selling to anyone I please, regardless of race, creed, or national origin."

"Me too! That's just what I was telling Lou here."

"And hear this," said the writer, massaging his wristlet grimly. "If there is any one thing that pisses me off, it's bigotry."

"You're right," cried Jiggs. "Mr. Prince, if Mae and I didn't have our savings in our house—listen, let me tell you!" But though everyone listened, he fell silent.

"We keep the lawr, Mr. Prince," said the alpiner earnestly. Then, seeing a chance to put a good face on the whole affair, he laughed and pointed his chin toward the engineer. "Tiger over there though, he was coming for me. Did you see him? I'm telling you, he was coming and I was getting out of his way. Tiger." Hand outstretched, he crossed to the engineer.

The engineer held his nose and looked at the hand. He had had enough of the whole crew.

"You not from Jersey, fella?" asked the alpiner, for some reason taking off his hat. "Mae here said—now isn't that something!" He called upon the neighborhood to witness the human comedy.

The engineer did not answer.

"You don't work for Oscar Fava?" cried the tall woman, meaning the question for the engineer, but not quite bringing herself to look at him. "You know Fava's real estate over there, next to Pik-a-Pak," she asked Jiggs and when he nodded she offered it to the engineer as a kind of confirmation, perhaps even an apology. "Over in Haddon Heights."

"I thought it was in Haddonfield," said Jiggs. They argued the point as another earnest of their good faith. "You never been over to Tammy Lanes in Haddonfield?" Jiggs asked him.

The engineer shook his head.

"Wasn't that Oscar Fava come over last night?" Jiggs asked Mae.

"And *he* was with him," said the woman. "Him or his twin brother."

"You know what I wish he would do," the alpiner told the other householders, presuming to speak of the engineer fondly—a true character was he, this engineer, another five minutes and they'd call him Rocky. "I wish he'd come on down to Tammy with us tonight, just to bug Oscar." Again he held out a hand to the engineer. "Come on down just for laughs."

"No, thank you," said the latter gloomily. He rose. "I've got to be on my way." He looked around for the pseudo-Negro, who had vanished. Most of all he wanted to get away from Mort Prince, who was still trying to hit upon some way to use his anger, a special delayed Hemingway writer's sort of anger. It was embarrassing. This was the age of embarrassment, thought the engineer, of unspendable rage. Who to hit? No one. Mort Prince took the engineer by the arm and pulled him inside. The best Mort could do was slam the door on the householders, catching Jiggs in midsentence:

"Any time any of youse want to come down—"

Reviving now, the writer opened a fresh beer and hung suspended from himself, free and clear of the refrigerator, while he told them: "I've got it, by God. I'm going to call up this guy Oscar Fava and let him sell it. Stick around for laughs," he told the engineer.

"No, thanks," said the engineer, who was sick of them and their laughs.

Fetching his firkin, in which he had packed his medicines, he took three Chlortrimeton tablets for his hay fever and rubbed his nose with an ice cube.

"Bill," said the pseudo-Negro earnestly, "if I can't persuade you to make the tour with us, at least promise me you'll come as far as Virginia."

"No, thanks," said the engineer, politely now. "I've really got to be going. I'd be obliged if you'd take me to the bus station."

"Very well," said the pseudo-Negro, as formally as the other. Shaky as he was, he was as sentient as anyone. He knew there were times for staying and times for leaving, times for sitting and times for standing. He stood up.

"Perhaps it would be possible for us to meet you in your hometown later this summer," he said.

"Perhaps," said the engineer and picked up his firkin.

4.

A white misty morning in northern Virginia found a young man, pleasant of mien and moderately disoriented, dressed neatly and squatting on a stout cedar firkin beside a highway which ran between a white-oak swamp on one side and a foggy hill, flattened on top like a mesa, on the other. He sat on the firkin and counted his money several times, reviewed the contents of a notebook, and from time to time read a page or two from a small red volume. Then he unfolded an Esso map of Virginia and spread it out on an expensive case of blue leather. Opening the firkin, which was as cedarous and cool inside as a springhouse, he took out a round molding of sweet butter, a box of Ritz crackers, a plastic knife, and a quart of buttermilk. As he ate his breakfast he traced the red and blue lines on the map with his gold pencil.

Where could he have spent the night? Not even he was certain, but he must have spent it tolerably well because his Brooks Brothers shirt was still fresh, his Dacron suit unwrinkled, and his cheek smooth and fragrant with soap. Another fact may be pertinent. An hour or so earlier, a Mayflower van with two riders had turned off the highway onto the gravel road directly behind him and pulled up at a farmhouse nestled at the foot of the foggy hill. Mayflower vans, he had learned recently and already forgotten, are owned by their drivers, who usually drive them home after finishing a haul.

The sun came up and warmed his back. Sapsuckers began

yammering in the swamp. He gazed at the network of red and blue lines and with his pencil circled a tiny pair of crossed swords marking a battlefield. As best he could determine, his present location lay somewhere near Malvern Hill and the James River. No doubt he was correct, because he was experiencing the interior dislocations which always afflicted him on old battlegrounds. His nose was better and he could smell. He sniffed the morning. It was white and dim and faraway as Brooklyn but it was a different sort of whiteness and dimness. Up yonder was a faraway Lapland sort of dimness, a public wheylike sunlight, where solitary youths carrying violin cases wait at bus stops. Here the dimness was private and one's own. He may not have been here before but it seemed to him that he had. Perhaps it was the place of his father's childhood and he had heard about it. From the corner of his eye he took note of the green confettilike plant which floated on the black water, of the fluted trunks and bald red knees of the cypress, of the first fall specklings of the tupelo gums.

He studied his map. He reckoned he could not be more than twenty miles from Richmond. Richmond. Yes, had he not passed through it last night? As he ate Ritz crackers and sweet butter, he imagined how Richmond might be today if the war had ended differently. Perhaps Main Street would be the Wall Street of the South, and Broad might vie with New Orleans for opera and theater. Here in the White Oak Swamp might be located the great Lee-Randolph complex, bigger than GM and making better cars (the Lee surpassing both Lincoln and Cadillac, the Lil' Reb outselling even Volkswagens). Richmond would have five million souls by now, William and Mary be as good as Harvard and less subverted. In Chattanooga and Mobile there would be talk of the "tough cynical Richmonders," the Berliners of the hemisphere.

When he finished his breakfast, he took a steel mirror from his Val-Pak and examined his nose in the morning sunlight. It was within bounds, though still lilac inside. His face reassured him. It was all of a piece, an equable lower-South Episcopal face. He began to feel better and, standing up, threw a few combinations at the rising sun. My name is Williston Bibb Barrett, he said aloud, consulting his wallet to make sure, and

I am returning to the South to seek my fortune and restore the good name of my family, perhaps even recover Hampton plantation from the canebrakes and live out my days as a just man and little father to the faithful Negroes working in the fields. Moreover, I am in love with a certain someone. Or I shall marry me a wife and live me a life in the lovely green environs of Atlanta or Memphis or even Birmingham, which, despite its bad name, is known to have lovely people.

Hitchhiking in Virginia was better than New Jersey; within half an hour he had been picked up and now went roaring down historic old US 60 in a noble black Buick, a venerable four-holer. His father used to drive one and it summoned up many a *déjà vu* to hear once again the old loose-meshed roaring runaway sound of the Dynaflow transmission. It was a carful of ladies, so crowded that he had to put his Val-Pak and firkin in the trunk. Rejoicing, he climbed in and held his telescope on his lap: what good fortune to be picked up by a bevy of Virginia noblewomen. Nor did he mind when they turned out to be Texans, golfers from a Fort Worth club, fortyish and firm as India rubber and fairly bursting their seersuckers. They had just played in a tournament at Burning Tree and were out for a good time sightseeing. They laughed all the way to Williamsburg. He too. Once he caught sight of himself in the sunshade mirror grinning like a forty-pounder. They told stories on each other, on one in particular, the lady on his left, a good-looking younger one who was subject to blushing.

"Grace settin' up there," said one lady in the back seat, "acting like she's crowded and can't stand it."

"She can stand it, hooo," said another and they all hooted with laughter.

Another one said: "I peep out of my door last night and here comes Grace tippy-toeing down the hall with this little bitty man and I say what is this: look like Grace got a little blister, the way she walking."

For some reason the word "blister" set them off again. It even seemed to the engineer to mean six different things. "Hooo, she got a little blister!" The most ordinary words and objects like zippers and golf tees brought on more hoots and jabs in the ribs. Although the engineer did not quite know what the joke was—it had something to do with the good-looking one sitting next to him—he couldn't help being tickled and in fact laughed like a maniac. By the time the old howling Dynaflow Buick reached Williamsburg, his sides ached.

Though he had planned to go into town and there collect his thoughts and begin his sleuthing, it turned out not to be necessary. As the Buick sailed past the Coach-and-Four Motel on the outskirts, he spotted the two vehicles and recognized both, though he had seen neither before: the Trav-L-Aire, glittering and humped up and practical, yet somehow airy and light on its four brand-new Goodyear jumbo treads; cheek to jowl with a squirrel-gray Cadillac which was mean and low and twenty feet long. He hollered to the driver but she wouldn't let him out. When at last she did stop and he asked them to wait until he could get his firkin from the trunk, they began to hoot again, positively rolling about on the seats. He had a six-block walk back to the motel.

There was nobody in sight but a pair of listless slothlike children worming over the playground equipment. He had time to take a good look at the Trav-L-Aire. She was all she might be, a nice balance of truck heaviness, steel and stout below and cabined aluminum lightness above. She had just the faintest and rightest quilted look, her metal skin tucked down by rivets like an airplane wing. Vents and sockets and knobs made discreet excrescences, some faired against the wind, others propped out to scoop the wind. The step was down and the back door ajar and he had a peep inside: the coziest little caboose imaginable, somehow larger inside than out, yet all compact of shelf, bunk, galley, and sink.

Now here surely is a good way to live nowadays, said he and sat down on the firkin: mobile yet at home, compacted and not linked up with the crumby carnival linkage of a trailer, in the world yet not of the world, sampling the particularities of place yet cabined off from the sadness of place, curtained away from the ghosts of Malvern Hill, peeping out at the doleful woods of Spotsylvania through the cheerful plexiglass of Sheboygan.

"Hullo!"

It was Mr. Vaught. He had come out of his motel room,

scratched his seat, shot his cuff, and, spying the engineer, hailed him over as if he were just the man he was looking for.

"Got dog, man," said the old man, cocking his head direfully. "So you thought better of it."

"Thought better of what?"

"You decided to come after all."

"Sir," said the engineer, blinking. Was this the plan all along, that he was to meet them here?

"You want to see something fine?"

"Yes sir."

Mr. Vaught unlocked the trunk of the Cadillac and showed him a vast cargo of food, Quaker jams, Shaker jellies, Virginia hams. He began to give an account of each package.

"Excuse me, sir," said the engineer, interrupting him.

"Yace."

"Excuse me but I can't help but think that explanations are in order. For my part I can say—"

"That's all right," cried the old man hastily. He was actually blushing. "I'm just tickled to death to have you aboard!"

"Thank you, sir. But I think we'd better clear this up." He heard himself speak without consulting his memory. His voice had a memory of its own. "My understanding was yall were going to pick me up. I waited for three hours."

"No," cried the old man and coming close seized him under the armpit and took him aside. "Take this apple jelly."

"Thank you."

"Son, look. If it was a question of money, why didn't you say so? I'll tell you this where I wouldn't just as to say tell most folks: I got more damn money than I know what to do with and if I don't give it to you the government's going to get it anyway."

"Money," said the engineer, screwing up an eye.

"Rita said she asked you to come with us and you refused."

"No sir," he said, remembering. "What she asked was whether I wanted to be employed by her or—"

"Naturally, when I didn't hear from you to the contrary, I assumed you didn't want the job."

"No sir!"

"Son, you know what we really thought? We thought you

didn't want to come with either one of us but that you would be nice enough *to* come if we asked you, just to help us, and I wasn't going to do that. Look," cried the old man joyfully.

"What?"

"It's better this way!"

"How is that, sir?"

"Now we know where we stand. Now I believe you want to come with us."

"Yes sir, that is true," said the engineer dryly. "I desire now only to have the same assurance from you."

"What! Oh! By George," said the other, shooting his cuff and calling on the high heavens. "If you're not your daddy all over again."

"Yes sir," said the engineer gloomily, wondering if the old man was slipping away again like the white rabbit. But this time Mr. Vaught took out his buckeye wallet and counted out five $100 bills, like crisp suède, freshly pollinated from the mint, into the other's hand. "One month's salary in advance. Do we understand each other now?"

"Yes sir."

"I'll tell you what we're going to do."

"What's that?"

"Rita will drive us in the Cadillac. You and Jamie take that thing." He nodded toward the camper.

"All right, sir."

"Now you and Jamie get on down the road. We'll see you at home." He counted out two more bills. "Expenses."

"Do you mean you want us to leave now and—"

But before he could finish, the rest of the family came swarming out half a dozen doors and bore down upon him. His natural shyness was almost made up for by the pleasant sensation of reunion. Perhaps he belonged here after all!

"Look who's here!"—"What in the woerrld—!"—"Well I'll be damned—!" they cried.

The side of his face was also being looked at by a pair of roguish eyes.

"Look at him blush," cried Mrs. Vaught.

For some reason his being there, hands in pockets and eyes rolled up to the eyebrows, began to be funny. They were all laughing at him. All but Kitty. She came close and touched him but at the same time it was as if she couldn't stand the sight of him. She turned him roughly by the shoulder as if she was another boy.

"What happened to your *nose*?" she asked angrily. It was somehow shameful to her that a misfortune should have befallen his *nose*.

He waved a hand vaguely toward the north. "A white lady up in New Jersey—" he began.

"*What*," Kitty cried incredulously, curling her lip and calling the others to witness. "What happened?"

"A lady from Haddon Heights hit me on the nose."

The others laughed and the engineer too. Only Kitty went on curling her lip in the most sensual and angry way. Rita laughed but her eyes were wary. She was handsome!

Jamie stood a little above them, on the motel walk, grinning and shaking his head. He looked brown and fit but a bit sooty-eyed.

"Wait a minute, Kitty," said the engineer as the girl turned away.

"What now?"

"Hold on! Don't leave."

"All right, what?"

"It seems I have not been able to make myself understood," he told them all, "or at least to prevent misunderstandings. I want to be very certain that everybody understands me now."

"I told you he wanted to come with us," said Mrs. Vaught to her husband, her pince-nez flashing.

"In any case," said the engineer, "let me state my intentions once and for all, particularly with regard to Jamie and, ah, Kitty." He almost said Miss Kitty.

"My God," said Kitty, turning red as a beet. "What is the man talking about?" She besought Rita, who in turn was watching the engineer like a hawk, her eyes wary and fine.

"I want to make clear what apparently I failed to make clear in New York, that from the beginning I accepted Mr. Vaught's offer with great pleasure and that I shall be happy to go to school with Jamie or anywhere else he wants to go."

Kitty seemed both relieved and irritated. "That's why he was fixing to take off for Colorado," she said loudly to Rita, and hollowed out her cheek with her tongue.

"What's that," asked the engineer quickly.

"He wants to know whose idea Colorado was," she said, still addressing Rita. She actually jerked a thumb at him, angry as an umpire. What had happened to his love?

Rita shrugged.

"Have you already forgotten what you told Rita?" asked the girl, meeting his eye.

"That's possible," said the engineer slowly. The worst of it was that he could have forgotten. "Since it was Rita I told, maybe she could refresh my memory."

"Glad to, Lance Corporal," she said, shrugging and smiling. "Though it is nothing we all don't already know. What you told me, if you recall, was that what you really wanted to do was attend the Colorado School of Mines."

"Without Kitty," said Kitty.

"No," said the engineer.

"Yes," said Rita. "Don't you remember the day I returned the telescope?"

"Why yes," said the engineer, remembering something, "but I certainly did not mean that I wasn't ready and anxious to join the Vaughts. Besides that, I had already committed myself to Mr. Vaught and I always honor my obligations."

"So now we're an obligation," said Kitty, addressing all Virginia. Her eyes flashed. It crossed his mind that she was what used to be called a noble high-spirited girl.

"No no, Kitty," said the poor engineer.

"You may recall, Lance Corporal," said Rita dryly, "that I asked you straight out which of us you wanted to work for, me or Poppy. You were unable to give a clear answer and spoke instead of Colorado. Knowing that you were a gentleman and did not like wrangling with women (I don't blame you), I did not press the issue. Perhaps I was wrong."

The trouble was he could not be sure and she knew it. And as he gazed at her he fancied he caught a gleam in her eye. She was skirting with him the abyss within himself and not doing it ill-naturedly: I know, said the gleam, and you know that I know and that you are not quite sure and that I might even be right.

"Anyhow Poppy is right," said Rita, rubbing her hands briskly. "We are all here and that is what counts. Why don't we hit the road?"

They were all leaving that very day, it turned out. Another two hours and he'd have missed them.

Mrs. Vaught and Kitty had one more room in the Governor's Palace to see, one more pewter candle-snuffer to buy. The engineer stayed at the motel to help Jamie pack. But Jamie was tired and went to lie down; the engineer packed for him. Rita found him sitting on the back step of the camper counting his money.

"You can keep that," she said. He had come to her postdated check.

"No, thanks," he said and handed it over. Now it was he who eyed her warily, but not disagreeably.

"Believe it or not, I'm very happy things worked out as they have."

"You are?"

"I'm afraid I was the cause of the misunderstanding."

He shrugged.

"Anyhow you passed your test by ordeal and here is your prize." For the second time she handed him a little hexagonal General Motors key.

"Thank you."

"You want to know why I'm glad you're here? Because you're the only one who can help Jamie. If only you will. You know sometimes I have the feeling, Lance Corporal, that you are onto all of us, onto our most private selves. Or perhaps it is rather that it is you and I who know, who really know; and perhaps it is the nature of our secret that we cannot tell our friends or even each other but must rather act for the good of our friends."

The engineer was silent. From force of habit, he looked as if he knew what she was talking about, what their "secret" was, though in truth he had not the least idea.

"Bill."

"Yes?"

"Take Jamie and get the hell out of here. Take Ulysses and go while the going is good. Go roam the byways and have a roistering good time of it. Find yourselves a couple of chicks. You're two good-looking fellows, you know!"

"Thank you," said the engineer politely.

"Drink and love and sing! Do you know what I thought as I was standing in the governor's bedroom yesterday?"

"No."

"Jamie was standing in front of me in the lovely, careless way he gets from you or from somebody, like young golden-haired Sir Tristram, leaning on his sword, and all at once the dreadful thought occurred to me: what must it be like to live and die without ever having waked in the morning and felt the warm mouth of one's beloved on his?"

"I couldn't say," said the engineer, who had never waked in the morning and found anybody's warm mouth on his.

"Bill, have you ever been to the Golden Isles of Georgia?"

"No."

"That's where we're headed. You can meet us there or not, as you like. And if you two bums want to detour through Norfolk, that's all right too."

"O.K."

5.

They didn't, the engineer and Jamie, quite cut loose after all, or detour through Norfolk (did Rita mean he should take Jamie to a whorehouse?) or feel any beloveds' warm mouths on theirs. But they had a good time and went their own way for a day or two at a time, wandering down the old Tidewater, sleeping in the piney woods or along the salt marshes and rendezvousing with the Cadillac in places like Wilmington and Charleston.

The camper was everything he had hoped for and more. Mornings on the road, the two young men sat together in the cab; afternoons the engineer usually drove alone. Well as he looked, Jamie tired easily and took to the bunk in the loft over the cab and either read or napped or watched the road unwind. They stopped early in the evening and went fishing or set up the telescope on a lonesome savanna and focused on the faraway hummocks where jewel-like warblers swarmed about the misty oaks.

Nights were best. Then as the thick singing darkness settled about the little caboose which shed its cheerful square of light on the dark soil of old Carolina, they might debark and, with the pleasantest sense of stepping down from the zone of the possible to the zone of the realized, stroll to a service station or fishing camp or grocery store, where they'd have a beer or fill the tank with spring water or lay in eggs and country butter and grits and slab bacon; then back to the camper, which they'd show off to the storekeeper, he ruminating a minute and: all I got to say is, don't walk off and leave the keys in it—and so on in the complex Southern tactic of assaying a sort of running start, a joke before the joke, ten assumptions shared and a common stance of rhetoric and a whole shared set of special ironies and opposites. He was home. Even though he was hundreds of miles from home and had never been here and it was not even the same here—it was older and more decorous, more tended to and adream with the past—he was home.

A *déjà vu*: so this is where it all started and which is not quite like home, what with this spooky stage-set moss and Glynn marshes but which is familiar nevertheless. It was familiar and droll and somehow small and curious like an old house revisited. How odd that it should have persisted so all this time and in one's absence!

At night they read. Jamie read books of great abstractness, such as *The Theory of Sets*, whatever a set was. The engineer, on the other hand, read books of great particularity, such as English detective stories, especially the sort which, answering a need of the Anglo-Saxon soul, depict the hero as perfectly disguised or perfectly hidden, holed up maybe in the woods of Somerset, actually hiding for days at a time in a burrow of ingenious construction from which he could notice things, observe the farmhouse below. Englishmen like to see without being seen. They are by nature eavesdroppers. The engineer could understand this.

He unlimbered the telescope and watched a fifty-foot Chris-Craft beat up the windy Intercoastal. A man sat in the stern reading the *Wall Street Journal*. "Dow Jones, 894—" read the engineer. What about cotton futures, he wondered.

He called Jamie over. "Look how he pops his jaw and crosses his legs with the crease of his britches pulled out of the way."

"Yes," said Jamie, registering and savoring what the engineer registered and savored. *Yes, you and I know something the man in the Chris-Craft will never know.* "What are we going to do when we get home?"

He looked at Jamie. The youth sat at the picnic table where the telescope was mounted, stroking his acne lightly with his fingernails. His whorled police-dog eye did not quite look at the engineer but darted close in a gentle nystagmus of recognitions, now focusing upon a mote in the morning air just beside the other's head, now turning inward to test what he saw and heard against his own private register. This was the game they played: the sentient tutor knowing quite well how to strike the dread unsounded chords of adolescence, the youth registering, his mouth parted slightly, fingernails brushing backward across his face. *Yes, and that was the wonder of it, that what was private and unspeakable before is speakable now because you speak it.* The difference between me and him, thought the engineer and noticed for the first time a slight translucence at the youth's temple, is this: like me he lives in the sphere of the possible, all antenna, ear cocked and lips parted. But I am conscious of it, know what is up, and he is not and does not. He is pure aching primary awareness and does not even know that he doesn't know it. Now and then he, the engineer, caught flashes of Kitty in the youth, but she had a woman's knack of cutting loose from the ache, putting it out to graze. She knew how to moon away the time; she could doze.

"Why don't we go to college?" he said at last.

"It's forty miles away," said Jamie, almost looking at him.

"We can go where we please, can't we? I mean, do you want to live at home?"

"No, but—"

Ah, it's Sutter he has in mind, thought the engineer. Sutter's at home.

"We could commute," said the engineer.

"Then you'll go?"

"Sure. We'll get up early in the morning."

"What will you take?"

"I need some mathematics. What about you?"

"Yes, me too," nodded the youth, eyes focused happily on the bright mote of agreement in the air between them.

It suited them to lie abed, in the Trav-L-Aire yet also in old Carolina, listening to baseball in Cleveland and reading about set theory and an Englishman holed up in Somerset. Could a certain someone be watching the same Carolina moon?

Or they joined the Vaughts, as they did in Charlestown, where they visited the gardens even though there was nothing

in bloom but crape myrtle and day lilies. Evil-tempered mock-
ingbirds sat watching them, atop tremendous oily camellias.
Sprinklers whirled away in the sunlight, leaving drops sparkling in the hairy leaves of the azaleas. The water smelled bitter
in the hot sun. The women liked to stand and talk and look at
houses. They were built for standing, pelvises canted, and they
more or less leaning on themselves. When the men stood still
for thirty minutes, the blood ran to their feet. The sun made
the engineer sick. He kept close to the women, closed his eyes,
and took comfort in the lady smell of hot fragrant cotton. A
few years from now and we'll be dead, he thought, looking at
tan frail Jamie and nutty old Mr. Vaught, and they, the women,
will be back here looking at "places."

It was like home here, but different too. At home we have
J.C. Penney's and old ugly houses and vacant lots and new ugly
houses. Here were pretty, wooden things, old and all painted
white, a thick-skinned decorous white, thick as ship's paint,
and presided over by the women. The women had a serious cus-
todial air. They knew the place was theirs. The men were not
serious. They all but wore costumes. They plied their trades,
butcher, baker, lawyer, in period playhouses out in the yard.

Evenings the Vaughts sat around the green chloriniferous
pools of the California motels, Rita and Kitty swimming and
minding their bodies, Mr. Vaught getting up often to monkey
with his Cadillac (he had installed a top-oiler and claimed
he got the same mileage as a Chevrolet), Mrs. Vaught always
dressed to the nines and rocking vigorously in the springy
pool chair and bathing her face with little paper pads soaked
in cologne. When she was lucky, she found some lady from
Moline who shared her views of fluoridation.

Kitty avoided him. He sought her out, but she damped him
down. She must think badly of him, he decided, and quick as
he was to see as others saw, was willing to believe she was right.
Was it simply that she took the easy way: she was with Rita and
not with him and that was that? At any rate, if she didn't love
him, he discovered he loved her less.

When they met by chance in motel passageways they angled
their shoulders and sidled past like strangers. At Folly Beach
they collided at the ice dispenser. He stood aside and said nothing. But when she filled her pitcher, she propped it on the rim

of her pelvis and waited for him, a somewhat abstracted Rachel at the well.

"It's a lovely night," she said, stooping to see the full moon through the cloister of the Quality Court.

"Yes," he said politely. He didn't feel much like waiting upon her. But he said, "Would you like to take a walk?"

"Oh yes."

They put their pitchers in the chest and walked on the beach. The moonlight curled along the wavelets. She put her hand in his and squeezed it. He squeezed back. They sat against a log. She took her hand away and began sifting sand; it was cool and dry and left not a grain on the skin.

He sat with his hands on his knees and the warm breeze flying up his pants leg and thought of nothing.

"What's the matter, Bill?" Kitty leaned toward him and searched his face.

"Nothing. I feel good."

Kitty shifted closer. The sand under her sheared against itself and made a musical sound. "Are you mad at me?"

"No."

"You act mad."

"I'm not."

"Why are you different then?"

"Different from what?"

"From a certain nut who kissed a very surprised girl in the automat."

"Hmm."

"Well?"

"I'm different because you are different," said the engineer, who always told the exact truth.

"*Me!* How?"

"I had looked forward to being with you on this trip. But it seems you prefer Rita's company. I had wanted to be with you during the ordinary times of the day, for example after breakfast in the morning. I did not have any sisters," he added thought-fully. "So I never knew a girl in the morning. But instead we have become like strangers. Worse, we avoid each other."

"Yes," she said gravely, conscious, he could not help but notice, of saying it so: gravely. "Don't you know why?" she said at last.

"No."

She sifted the cool discrete sand into her palm, where it made a perfect pyramid, shedding itself. "You say you never had sisters. Well, I never had a date, boyfriends—except a few boys in my ballet class who had foreheads this low. Rita and I got used to living quietly."

"And now?"

"I guess I'm clinging to the nest like a big old cuckoo. Isn't that awful?"

He shrugged.

"What do you want me to do?" she asked him.

"What do I want you to do?"

"Tell me."

"How do you feel?"

"How do *you* feel? Do you still love me?"

"Yes."

"Do you? Oh, I love you too."

Why did this not sound right, here on Folly Beach in old Carolina in the moonlight?

One thing I'm sure of, thought he as he held her charms in his arms: I shall court her henceforth in the old style. I shall press her hand. No more grubby epithelial embraces in dogbane thickets, followed by accusing phone calls. Never again! Not until we are in our honeymoon cottage in a cottage small by a waterfall.

But when he kissed her and there she was again looking at him from both sides at once, he had the first inkling of what might be wrong. She was too dutiful and athletic. She worked her mouth against his (is this right, she as good as asked).

"Wonderful," she breathed, lying back. "A perfect setting."

Why is it not wonderful, he wondered, and when he leaned over again and embraced her in the sand, he knowing without calculating the exact angle at which he might lie over against her—about twenty degrees past the vertical—she miscalculated, misread him and moved slightly, yet unmistakably to get plainly and simply under him, then feeling the surprise in him stopped almost before she began. It was like correcting a misstep in dancing.

"What is it?" she whispered presently.

"Nothing," he said, kissing her tenderly and cursing himself.

His heart sank. Was it not that she was right and that he made too much of it? What it was, though, was that this was the last thing he expected. It was part of his expectations of the life which lay before him that girls would be girls just as camellias were camellias. If he loved a girl and walked with her on Folly Beach by moonlight, kissed her sweet lips and held her charms in his arms, it should follow that he would be simply he and she she, she as complete as a camellia with her corolla of reticences and allurements. But she, Kitty, was no such thing. She didn't know any better than he. Love, she, like him, was obliged to see as a naked garden of stamens and pistils. But what threw him off worst was that, sentient as always, he found himself catching onto how it was with her: he saw that she was out to be a proper girl and taking every care to do the right wrong thing. There were even echoes of a third person: what, you worry about the boys as good a figure as you have, etc. So he was the boy and she was doing her best to do what a girl does. He sighed.

"What?" she asked again.

"Nothing," he said, kissing her eyes, which were, at any rate, like stars.

He sighed again. Very well, I'll be both for you, boyfriend and girlfriend, lover and father. If it is possible.

They stirred in the musical sand. "We'd better go back," said the gentlemanly engineer and kissed her somewhat lewdly so she wouldn't feel she had failed. It seemed to be his duty now to protect her non-virtue as best he could. After all, he mused, as he reckoned girls must have mused in other ages, if worst comes to worst and all else fails I can let her under me—I shan't begrudge her the sacrifice. What ailed her, him, them, he wondered. Holding her hand as they returned to the Quality Court, he flexed his wrist so that he could count his pulse against her bone.

Mainly their trouble—or good fortune, as the case might be—was that they were still out of phase, their fervors alternating and jostling each other like bad dancers. For now, back at the cooler and she then going ahead of him with her pitcher on the rim of her pelvis, desire like a mighty wind caught him from behind and nearly blew him down. He almost fainted with old motel lewd-longing. "Wait," he whispered—oh, the piercing sorrow of it, this the mortal illness of youth like death to old age. "Wait." He felt his way along the blotting-paper wall like a blind man. She took his outstretched hand.

"What is it, dearest?"

"Let's go in here," he said, opening the door to a closet which housed a giant pulsing Fedders.

"What for?" she asked. Her eyes were silvery and turned in.

"Let us go in the service room." For it is here and not by moonlight—he sighed. Her willingness and nurse-tenderness were already setting him at naught again.

"There you are," said Rita, opening the door opposite. "Where in the world was the ice machine?"

And off he went, bereft, careening down the abstract, decent, lewd Quality corridor.

The next day they went their separate ways as before, he moon-ing off with Jamie in the Trav-L-Aire, keeping the days empty and ears attuned to the secret sounds of summer. They met again in Beaufort. Kitty and Rita filled the day with small rites. They both took Metrecal and made a ceremony of it at every stop, lining up the wafers on a Sèvres dish, assembling a miniature stove from Lewis and Conger to heat the water for their special orange-flavored tea. Or if Kitty had a hangnail, the afternoon was spent rounding up Q-tips, alcohol, cuticle scissors.

6.

One hot night they stopped at a raw red motel on a raw red hillside in Georgia. The women had got tired of the coast and took to the upcountry in search of hooked rugs and antiques. And the engineer had to admit that it was the pleasantest of prospects: to buy a five-dollar chiffonier and come down through six layers of paint to old ribby pine from the days of General Oglethorpe.

The two youths had dawdled as usual and it was almost midnight when the Trav-L-Aire came groaning up the hill, bucket swinging under her like a Conestoga wagon, and crept into a pine grove bursting with gouts of amber rosin still fra-grant from the hot afternoon. It was too hot to sleep. Jamie sat in the cab and read his *Theory of Sets*. The engineer strolled over to the cinder-block porch of the motel, propped his chair against the wall, and watched a construction gang flattening a hill across the valley. They were making a new expressway, he reckoned. The air throbbed with the machinery, and the floodlights over the hill spoiled the night like a cast in a black eye. He had noticed this about the South since he returned. Along the Tidewater everything was pickled and preserved and decorous. Backcountry everything was being torn down and built anew. The earth itself was transformed overnight, gouged and filled, flattened and hilled, like a big sandpile. The whole South throbbed like a diesel.

"—but here am I, Ree, twenty-one and never been to college!"

"Then go to a good one."

He knew now why he had left the camper. It had come over him again, the old itch for omniscience. One day it was longing for carnal knowledge, the next for perfect angelic knowledge. Tonight he was not American and horny but English and eavesdropper. He had to know without being known.

Not ten feet behind him and through the open window, Rita and Kitty lay in their beds and talked. The Trav-L-Aire had crept up the hill with its lights out—had he planned it even then? He had come onto the porch as silently as an Englishman entering his burrow in Somerset.

"Have I told you what I want to be?"

"I'm afraid you have."

"I want to be an ordinary silly girl who has dates and goes to dances."

"You're in a fair way to do it."

"I love to dance."

"Then work harder at it. You're lazy."

"You know what I mean. I mean dancing cheek to cheek. I want to be broken in on."

"They don't dance like that now."

"I want to have beaus."

"You can have beaus in Tesuque or in Salamanca and not ruin your mind while you do it."

"I want to be Tri Delt."

"Good God!"

"I want to go to dances and get a tremendous rush. That's what my grandmother used to say: I went to such and such a dance and got a tremendous rush. Did you know my grandmother composed the official ATO waltz at Mercer?"

"Yes, you told me."

"I want to talk the foolishness the girls and boys at home talk."

"You're on your way."

"I want to go to school. I want to buy new textbooks and a binder full of fresh paper and hold my books in my arms and walk across the campus. And wear a sweater."

"Very well."

"I want to go to the Sugar Bowl."

"Christ."

"But you're going to stay with us! I need you!"

Rita was silent.

"Remember our bargain, Ree."

"What bargain?" said Rita in a muffled voice. She had turned away from the window.

"That you stay till Christmas. By then I'll know. I could easily have flunked out by then just as I flunked out before. But even if I don't, I'll know. I'll know whether to go with you or not."

"We'll see," said Rita absently.

7.

They reached the Golden Isles of Georgia in time for the first tropical storm of the year. The wind whipped over the gray ocean, out of kilter with the slow rhythm of the waves, tore up patches of spume, and raised a spindrift. Georgians had sense enough to go home and so the Vaughts had the hotel to themselves, an honorable old hacienda of wide glassed-in vestibules opening into conservatories and recreation rooms, and rows of brass pots planted with ferns, great cretaceous gymnosperms from the days of Henry Grady, dry and dusty as turkey wings. They looked at stuffed birds and group photographs of Southern governors and played mahjong.

A hundred servants waited on them, so black and respectful, so absolutely amiable and well-disposed that it was possible to believe that they really were. One or two of them were by way of being characters and allowed themselves to get on a footing with you. In a day's time they had a standing joke going as if you had been there a month. One bold fellow noticed the engineer take out his red book and read a few maxims as he waited for the elevator. "Now he's gon' be the *smart* one!" he announced to the hotel and later meeting him in the hall would therefore holler: "You got your book with you?" with a special sort of boldness, even a recklessness, which he took to be his due by virtue of the very credential of his amiability. The engineer laughed politely and even cackled a bit in order to appear the proper damn fool they would have him be.

By four o'clock the afternoon had turned yellow and dark. The engineer and Jamie found some rook cards and played a game in the conservatory, which still had a magic lantern from the days when lectures were delivered to vacationers on birds and sea shells. When the wind picked up, the engineer decided to go see to the Trav-L-Aire. Jamie wouldn't come. He went out of his way to tell the engineer he was going to telephone his sister Val.

"What for?" the engineer asked him, seeing that the other wanted him to ask.

"When I feel bad, I call her and she makes me feel better."

"Is she the sister who joined the religious order?"

"Yes."

"Are you religious?"

"No."

"Then what good can she do you?" They had fallen into the abrupt mocking but not wholly unserious way of talking which people who spend a lot of time together get into.

"She is not religious either, at least not in the ordinary sense."

"What is she doing in a religious order?"

"I don't know. Anyhow that is not what I'm interested in."

"What are you interested in?" asked the engineer, sniffing the old rook cards. They smelled like money.

"I thought she might give me a job."

"Doing what?"

"Anything. Teaching, minor repairs. I am feeling very good physically."

"I'm sure it's a wonderful work she is doing."

"I'm not interested in that either," said Jamie irritably. "I'm not interested in the Negroes."

"What are you interested in?"

"Anything she wants me to do. Her place is down in Tyree County in the piney woods, ten miles from nowhere. I thought it wouldn't be bad to live there as we have been living, in the camper. We could teach, give her a hand. You may not want to. But I am feeling very strong. Feel my grip."

"Very good."

"I can put you down hand-wrestling."

"No, you can't."

"Let's see."

The engineer, who never faked with Jamie, put him down quickly. But Jamie was surprisingly strong.

"Why don't we work out together, Bill?"

"O.K."

"What do you think of going down to Tyree County?" asked Jamie, hiding behind his rook cards.

"I thought you wanted to go to college."

"What I don't want is to go back home to the same thing, see Mother and Poppy every morning, watch the same golfers pass on number 6 fairway."

"O.K." Then he's changed his mind about Sutter, thought the engineer.

"O.K. what? You mean you'll go?"

"Sure," said the engineer, who in truth saw how it stood with Jamie and did not think it such a bad idea himself, going to the end of nowhere, parking in the pines and doing a few humble tasks.

Jamie laughed. "You mean it, don't you? You're telling the truth, you're ready to go."

"Sure. Why shouldn't I tell the truth?"

"I don't know," said Jamie, laughing at him.

Before he left the hotel, he picked up an old crime-club selection in the library, *The Murder of Roger Ackroyd*, a light pulpy book gnawed by silverfish and smelling of the summer of 1927. Kitty saw him and wanted to go to the camper with him. He saw that she was exhilarated by the storm, and since she was, he was not. No more for him the old upside-down Manhattan monkey business of rejoicing in airplane crashes and staggering around museums half out of his head and falling upon girls in hurricanes. Henceforth, he resolved, he would do right, feel good when good was called for, bad when bad. He aimed to take Kitty to a proper dance, pay her court, not mess around.

Accordingly he proposed that they stay in the bird room and play mahjong with Poppy and Jamie and Rita but she wouldn't hear of it.

Once they were outside in the storm, however, he felt better despite himself, though he had sworn not to feel good in bad environments. It was going to be a bad storm. Under the dirty low-flying clouds the air was as yellow as electric light. His spirits rose, he told himself, because it might be possible for them to enter here and now into a new life. If they were trapped by the storm in the Trav-L-Aire, they could sit at the dinette and play gin rummy, snug as children, very like many another young couple who came down here in the days of the great Bobby Jones and had a grand time. Sit face to face and deal the cards and watch the storm, like a chapter from Mary Roberts Rinehart entitled "Trapped in the Storm: Interesting Developments"; perhaps even steal a kiss or two.

The camper was hove to in a hollow of the dunes. He had snugged her down with a hundred feet of Nylon rope which he wound around cabin and axle and lashed to iron rings set in some broken beachworks. Inside the cabin he pumped up the butane tank and lit the little ashen mantles. Soon the camper leapt against its tether; the wind sang like a harp in her rigging. She creaked in every joint like the good prairie schooner she was and wouldn't leak a drop. The sand scoured the aluminum skin like birdshot.

He got Kitty across the table fairly enough but she was not onto the game he wanted to play. Instead of dealing the ancient honorable Bicycle cards he'd brought from the hotel and playing gin rummy in good faith for itself (That was it! Ordinary things such as gin rummy had lost weight, been evacuated. Why?) and worrying about the storm in good faith and so by virtue of the good faith earning the first small dividends of courtship, a guarding of glances, a hand upon the deck and a hand upon the hand—most happy little eight of clubs to be nestled so in the sweet hollow of her hand, etc—instead she gazed boldly at him and used up their common assets, spent everything like a drunken sailor. She gazed like she kissed: she came on at him like a diesel locomotive.

"Oh me," he sighed, already in a light sweat, and discarded the jack of clubs.

"Aren't you picking up jacks?" he reminded her.

"Am I?" she said ironically but not knowing the uses of irony.

Look at her, he thought peevishly. She had worn leotards so many years she didn't know how to wear a dress. As she sat, she straddled a bit. Once in a Charleston restaurant he had wanted to jump up and pull her dress down over her knees.

Abruptly she put her cards down and knocked up the little Pullman table between them. "Bill."

"Yes."

"Come here."

"All right."

"Am I nice?"

"Yes."

"Am I pretty?"

"Sure."

"I mean, how would I look to you if you saw me in a crowd of girls?"

"Fine. The best, in fact."

"Why don't I think so?"

"I don't know."

She stretched out her leg, clasping her dress above the knee. "Is that pretty?"

"Yes," he said, blushing. It was as if somehow it was his leg she was being prodigal with.

"Not crippled?"

"No."

"Not muscle-bound?"

"No."

"I worry about myself."

"You don't have to."

"What do you really think of me? Tell me the literal truth."

"I love you."

"Besides that."

"I couldn't say."

"Oh darling, I didn't mean that. I mean, do you also *like* me? As a person."

"Sure."

"Do you think other boys will like me?"

"I don't know," said the engineer, sweating in earnest. Great Scott, he thought in dismay. Suppose she does have a date with another "boy."

"I mean like at a dance. If you saw me at a dance, would you like to dance with me?"

"Sure."

"Do you know that I've danced all my life and yet I've never been to a regular dance?"

"You haven't missed much," said the engineer, thinking of the many times he had stood around picking his nose at Princeton dances.

"Do you realize that I've hardly ever danced with a boy?"

"Is that right?"

"What does it feel like?"

"Dancing with a boy?"

"Show me, stupid."

He switched on the Hallicrafter and between storm reports they danced to disc-jockey music from Atlanta. There was room for three steps in the camper. Even though they were sheltered by the dunes, now and then a deflected gust sent them stumbling.

She was not very good. Her broad shoulders were shy and quick under his hand, but she didn't know how close to hold herself and so managed to hold herself too close or too far. Her knees were both workaday and timid. He thought of the long hours she had spent in dusty gymlike studios standing easy, sister to the splintery wood. She was like a boy turned into a girl.

"Will I do all right?"

"Doing what?"

"Going to dances."

"Sure." It was this that threw him off, her having to aim to be what she was.

"Tell me."

"Tell you what?"

"How to do right."

"Do right?" How to tell the sweet Georgia air to be itself?

"Do you love me?" she asked.

"Yes."

The storm crashed around them. Kitty drew him down to the lower bunk, which was like the long couch in an old-style Pullman drawing room. "Hold me tight," she whispered.

He held her tight.

"What is it?" she asked presently.

"I was thinking of something my father told me."

"What?"

"When my father reached his sixteenth birthday, my grand-father said to him: now, Ed, I'm not going to have you worry-ing about certain things—and he took him to a whorehouse in Memphis. He asked the madame to call all the girls in and line them up. O.K., Ed, he told my father. Take your pick."

"Did he?"

"I guess so."

"Did your father do the same for you?"

"No."

"I didn't know until this minute that it was hore. I thought it was whore."

"No."

"My poor darling," said Kitty, coming so close that her two eyes fused into one. "I think I understand what you mean. You've been brought up to think it is an ugly thing whereas it should be the most beautiful thing in the world."

"Ah."

"Rita says that anything two people do together is beautiful if the people themselves are beautiful and reverent and unself-conscious in what they do. Like the ancient Greeks who lived in the childhood of the race."

"Is that right?"

"Rita believes in reverence for life."

"She does?"

"She says—"

"What does Sutter say?"

"Oh, Sutter. Nothing I can repeat. Sutter is an immature

person. In a way it is not his fault, but nevertheless he did something dreadful to her. He managed to kill something in her, maybe even her capacity to love."

"Doesn't she love you?"

"She is terrified if I get close to her. Last night I was cutting my fingernails and I gave her my right hand to cut because I can't cut with my left. She gave me the most terrible look and went out. Can you understand that?"

"Yes."

"Very well. I'll be your whore."

"Hore."

"Hore."

"I know," said the engineer gloomily.

"Then you think I'm a whore?"

"No." That was the trouble. She wasn't. There was a lumpish playfulness, a sort of literary gap in her whorishness.

"Very well. I'll be a lady."

"All right."

"No, truthfully. Love me like a lady."

"Very well."

He lay with her, more or less miserably, kissed her lips and eyes and uttered sweet love-murmurings into her ear, telling her what a lovely girl she was. But what am I, he wondered: neither Christian nor pagan nor proper lusty gentleman, for I've never really got the straight of this lady-and-whore business. And that is all I want and it does not seem too much to ask: for once and all to get the straight of it.

"I love you, Kitty," he told her. "I dream of loving you in the morning. When we have our house and you are in the kitchen in the morning, in a bright brand-new kitchen with the morning sun streaming in the window, I will come and love you then. I dream of loving you in the morning."

"Why, that's the sweetest thing I ever heard in my life," she said, dropping a full octave to her old unbuttoned Tallulah-Alabama voice. "Tell me some more."

He laughed dolefully and would have but at that moment, in the storm's lull, a knock rattled the louvers of the rear door.

It was Rita, looking portentous and solemn and self-coinciding. She had a serious piece of news. "I'm afraid something has come up," she said.

They sat at the dinette, caressing the Formica with their fingertips and gazing at the queer yellow light outside. The wind had died and the round leaves of the sea grapes hung still. Fiddler crabs ventured forth, fingered the yellow decompressed air, and scooted back to their burrows. The engineer made some coffee. Rita waited, her eyes dry and unblinking, until he came back and she had her first swallow. He watched as the muscles of her throat sent the liquid streaming along.

"I'm afraid we're in for it, kids," she told them.

"Why is that," the engineer asked since Kitty sat silent and sullen.

"Jamie has telephoned Sutter," Rita told Kitty.

Kitty shrugged.

The engineer screwed up an eye. "He told me he was going to call his sister Val."

"He couldn't reach Val," said Rita flatly.

"Excuse me," said the engineer, "but what is so alarming about Jamie calling his brother?"

"You don't know his brother," said Rita trying to exchange an ironic glance with Kitty. "Anyhow it was what was said and agreed upon that was alarming."

"How do you know what was said?" asked Kitty, so disagreeably that the engineer frowned.

"Oh, Jamie makes no bones about it," Rita cried. "He's going to move in with Sutter."

"You mean downtown," Kitty asked quickly.

"Yes."

"I don't understand," said the engineer.

"Let me explain, Bill," said Rita. "Sutter, my ex, and Kitty and Jamie's brother, lives in a dark little hole next to the hospital. The plan of course had been for you and Jamie to take the garage apartment out in the valley."

The engineer shrugged. "I can't see that it's anybody's loss but mine if Jamie would rather live with his brother. In fact, it sounds quite reasonable."

Again Rita tried to enlist Kitty in some kind of exchange but the girl was hulkish and dull and sat gazing at the sea grapes.

"It's like this, Lance Corporal," said Rita heavily. "Kitty here can tell you how it was. I saved the man once. I loved him and pulled him out of the gutter and put him back together. And

I still think he's the greatest diagnostician since Libman. Do you know what I saw him do? Kitty was there. I saw him meet a man in Santa Fe, at a party, speak with him five minutes—a physicist—ask him two questions, then turn to me and say: that man will be dead of malignant hypertension inside a year."

"Was he?" asked the engineer curiously. "Dead, I mean?"

"Yes, but that's neither here nor there."

"How did Sutter, Dr. Vaught, know that?"

"I have no idea, but that's not what concerns us now."

"What were the two questions?"

"Ask him yourself. What is important now is what's in store for Jamie."

"Yes."

"Here again Kitty will bear me out. If not, I shall be glad to be corrected. It is not that Sutter is an alcoholic. It's not that he is a pornographer. These traits, charming as they are, do not in themselves menace Jamie, or you or me—no matter what some people may say. I flatter myself that all of us are sufficiently mature. No, what concerns me is Sutter's deep ambivalence toward Jamie himself."

"What do you mean?" asked the engineer, straining his good ear. The storm had begun banging away again.

"He has every right to make away with himself but he can damn well leave Jamie alone."

"I don't believe that," said Kitty. "I mean, I don't believe he tried to harm Jamie."

"It is not a question of belief," said Rita. "It is a question of facts. Do you deny the facts?"

Kitty was silent.

"It was an experiment," she said presently.

"Some experiment. What do you think of this as an experiment, Lance Corporal. Last summer, shortly after Sutter learned of Jamie's illness, he took him camping in the desert. They were lost for four days. Even so, it was not serious because they had plenty of water. On the fourth day the canteens were found mysteriously emptied."

"How did they get out?"

"By pure freakish chance. Some damn fool shooting coyotes from an airplane spotted them."

"He meant no harm to Jamie," said Kitty dully.

"What did he mean?" said Rita ironically.

"Val said it was a religious experience."

"Thank you all the same, but if that is religion I'll stick to my ordinary sinful ways."

"What do you mean, he is a pornographer?" the engineer asked her.

"Nothing out of the ordinary," said Rita calmly. "He likes fun and games, picture books, and more than one girl at a time."

"I don't think it's pornography," said Kitty.

"This time, by God, I know wherof I speak. I was married to him. Don't tell me."

"My brother," said Kitty solemnly to the engineer, "can only love a stranger."

"Eh?"

"It is a little more than that," said Rita dryly. "But have it any way you please. Meanwhile let us do what we can for Jamie."

"You're right Ree," said Kitty, looking at her for the first time.

"What do you want me to do?" the engineer asked Rita.

"Just this. When we get home, you grab Jamie, throw him in this thing and run for your life. He'll go with you!"

"I see," said the engineer, now falling away like Kitty and turning mindless and vacant-eyed. "Actually we have a place to go," he added. "He wants either to go to school or visit his sister Val. He asked me to go with him."

Rita looked at him. "Are you going?"

"If he wants me to."

"Fair enough."

Presently he came to himself and realized that the women had left in the storm. It was dark. The buffeting was worse. He made a plate of grits and bacon. After supper he climbed into the balcony bunk, turned up the hissing butane lamp, and read *The Murder of Roger Ackroyd* from cover to cover.

Chapter Four

THE SOUTH he came home to was different from the South he had left. It was happy, victorious, Christian, rich, patriotic and Republican.

The happiness and serenity of the South disconcerted him. He had felt good in the North because everyone else felt so bad. True, there was a happiness in the North. That is to say, nearly everyone would have denied that he was unhappy. And certainly the North was victorious. It had never lost a war. But Northerners had turned morose in their victory. They were solitary and shut-off to themselves and he, the engineer, had got used to living among them. Their cities, rich and busy as they were, nevertheless looked bombed out. And his own happiness had come from being onto the unhappiness beneath their happiness. It was possible for him to be at home in the North because the North was homeless. There are many things worse than being homeless in a homeless place—in fact, this is one condition of being at home, if you are yourself homeless. For example, it is much worse to be homeless and then to go home where everyone is at home and then still be homeless. The South was at home. Therefore his homelessness was much worse in the South because he had expected to find himself at home there.

The happiness of the South was very formidable. It was an almost invincible happiness. It defied you to call it anything else. Everyone was in fact happy. The women were beautiful and charming. The men were healthy and successful and funny; they knew how to tell stories. They had everything the North had and more. They had a history, they had a place redolent with memories, they had good conversation, they believed in God and defended the Constitution, and they were getting rich in the bargain. They had the best of victory and defeat. Their happiness was aggressive and irresistible. He was determined to be as happy as anyone, even though his happiness before had come from Northern unhappiness. If folks down here are happy and at home, he told himself, then I shall be happy and at home too.

As he pressed ever farther south in the Trav-L-Aire, he passed more and more cars which had Confederate plates on the front bumper and plastic Christs on the dashboard. Radio programs became more patriotic and religious. More than once Dizzy Dean interrupted his sportscast to urge the listener to go to the church or synagogue of his choice. "You'll find it a rich and rewarding experience," said Diz. Several times a day he heard a patriotic program called "Lifelines" which praised God, attacked the United States government, and advertised beans and corn.

What was wrong with a Mr. and Mrs. Williston Bibb Barrett living in a brand-new house in a brand-new suburb with a proper address: 2041 Country Club Drive, Druid Hills, Atlanta, Georgia?

Nothing was wrong, but he got worse anyway. The happiness of the South drove him wild with despair.

What was wrong with marrying him a wife and living a life, holding Kitty's charms in his arms the livelong night?

Nothing, but his memory deteriorated and he was assaulted by ghostly legions of *déjà vus* and often woke not knowing where he was. His knee leapt like a fish. It became necessary to unravel the left pocket of his three pairs of pants in order to slip a hand down and keep his patella in place.

It was unsettling, too, coming among a people whose radars were as sensitive as his own. He had got used to good steady wistful post-Protestant Yankees (they were his meat, ex-Protestants, post-Protestants, para-Protestants, the wistful ones who wanted they knew not what; he was just the one to dance for them) and here all at once he found himself among as light-footed and as hawk-eyed and God-fearing a crew as one could imagine. Everyone went to church and was funny and clever and sensitive in the bargain. Oh, they were formidable, born winners (how did they lose?). Yet his radar was remarkable, even for the South. After standing around two or three days, as queer and nervous as a Hoosier, he quickly got the hang of it. Soon he was able to listen to funny stories and tell a few himself.

The Vaughts liked him fine of course and did not notice that he was worse. For he was as prudent and affable as ever and mostly silent, and that was what they expected of him. All but Sutter. He had not yet met Sutter. But one day he saw his car, as he and Jamie were sitting in the sunny quarter of the golf shelter just off number 6 fairway in front of the Vaughts' house.

Jamie was still reading *The Theory of Sets*. The engineer was pondering, as usual, the mystery of the singularity of things. This was the very golf links, he had reason to believe, where his grandfather had played an exhibition round with the great Bobby Jones in 1925 or thereabouts. It was an ancient sort of links, dating from the golden age of country clubs, with sturdy rain shelters of green-stained wood and old-fashioned ball-washers on each tee and soft rolling bunkers as peaceful as an old battlefield. Deep paths were worn through the rough where caddies cut across from green to fairway. The engineer's amnesia was now of this order: he forgot things he had seen before, but things he had heard of and not seen looked familiar. Old new things like fifty-year-old golf links where Bobby Jones played once were haunted by memory.

How bad off was he, he wondered. Which is better, to walk the streets of Memphis in one's right mind remembering everything, what one has done yesterday and must do tomorrow—or to come to oneself in Memphis, remembering nothing?

Jamie had asked him what he was thinking about. When he told him, Jamie said: "You sound like Sutter."

"Have you seen him?"

"I went to see him yesterday. Yonder he goes now."

But he saw no more than the car, a faded green Edsel which swung out of the steep driveway and disappeared down the links road. Jamie told him that Sutter drove an Edsel to remind him of the debacle of the Ford Motor Company and to commemorate the last victory of the American people over marketing research and opinion polls. The engineer wasn't sure he liked the sound of this. It had the sound of a quixotic type who admires his own gestures.

2.

The Vaughts lived in a castle fronting on a golf links. It was an old suburb set down in a beautiful green valley across a ridge from the city. There were other ridges, the last wrinkles of the Appalachians, which formed other valleys between them, and newer suburbs and newer country clubs.

The houses of the valley were built in the 1920's, a time when rich men still sought to recall heroic ages. Directly opposite the castle, atop the next ridge to the south, there stood a round, rosy temple. It was the dwelling of a millionaire who had admired a Roman structure erected by the Emperor Vespasian in honor of Juno and so had reproduced it in good Alabama red brick and Georgia marble. At night a battery of colored floodlights made it look redder still.

The Vaught castle was made of purplish bricks which had been broken in two and the jagged side turned out. It had beam-in-plaster gables and a fat Norman tower and casement windows with panes of bottle glass. Mr. Vaught, it turned out, was richer even than the engineer had supposed. He had made his first fortune by inventing and manufacturing a new type of journal box for coal cars. After the second war he branched out into insurance companies, real estate, and auto dealerships. Now he owned and operated the second largest Chevrolet agency in the world. His talent, as the engineer divined it, was the knack of getting onto the rhythm of things, of knowing when to buy and sell. So that was the meaning of his funny way of hopping around like a jaybird with his ear cocked but not really listening to anybody! Rather was he tuned in to the music and rhythm of ventures, himself poised and nodding, like a schoolboy waiting to go into a jump rope. The engineer soon learned to pay no attention to him either: his talk was not talk at all, one discovered, that is, a form of communication to be attended to, but rather a familiar hum such as Lugurtha the cook made when she was making beaten biscuits.

There were other persons living in the castle. The "Myra" of whom Mrs. Vaught often spoke to the engineer as if he knew her, turned out to be Myra Thigpen, Mr. Vaught's stepdaughter by an earlier marriage. The Thigpens were staying in the Vaught castle while their own house was being built across the golf links. Lamar Thigpen worked for Mr. Vaught as personnel manager. Myra ran a real-estate agency. A handsome woman with strong white arms and a cloud of heavy brown hair, she reminded the engineer of the Business and Professional

Women he had seen turning out for luncheons at Holiday Inns from Charleston to Chattanooga. If Mrs. Vaught had thrown him off earlier by acting as if he ought to know whom she was talking about, Myra dislocated him now by acting as if she had known him all along. Had she? "You remember that old boy Hoss Hart from Greenwood who went to Mississippi State and later moved to Ithaca?" she asked him. "You mean Mr. Horace Hart who used to sell for Checkerboard Feed?" asked the engineer, who did in fact perfectly remember such a person, having heard his name once or twice fifteen years ago. "I saw him the other day," Myra went on, "selling fruitcake for Civitan over at Boys' State. He told me about when you and he and your daddy went duck-hunting on a houseboat on the White River." "The White River?" The engineer scratched his head. Had Hoss Hart remembered something he had forgotten? "When you see Hoss," said Myra, giving him a sisterly jostle such as coeds at Mississippi State give you, "just ask him if he remembers Legs." "Yes ma'am." "Don't say Miss Homecoming of 1950, just say Legs and see what he says." "Yes ma'am, I will."

Sutter was nowhere to be seen, but the engineer made sure he would see him when he did come—as he was told Sutter occasionally did to spend the night. Sutter's old apartment was next to the quarters assigned to the two young men, on the second floor above the great four-car garage. Not two hours passed after his arrival before he explored the apartment and discovered two things. One was a bottle of three-dollar whiskey in the cupboard of the kitchenette between the two apartments. The other thing was a knothole in the wall of his closet which looked straight into Sutter's bedroom. He hung his Val-Pak over the hole.

I'm not well, reflected the engineer, and therefore it is fitting that I should sit still, like an Englishman in his burrow, and see what can be seen.

It was a good place to live and collect one's thoughts. In the daytime the valley echoed with the faint far-off cries of the golfers. At night a yellow harvest moon hung over the ridge and the floodlights played on the fat rosy temple of Juno. His duties were light. Indeed he had no duties. Nothing more was

said after Sea Island about Jamie's plans to go live with his
sister in the pine barrens or with his brother in the city. The
sick youth seemed content to move into the garage apartment.
Within three weeks of their arrival the two young men and
Kitty had registered at the university forty miles away and two
weeks later the engineer and Jamie had pledged Phi Nu and
learned the grip. Kitty realized her ambition and became not
a Tri Delt but a Chi Omega.

On the morning of registration they had set out for the
university, the three of them, the engineer driving, Kitty in
the middle, in Mrs. Vaught's Lincoln, and came home early
enough to sit on the garden grass and leaf through their brand-
new textbooks with the glazed glittering pages and fragrant
fresh print. The engineer, who had just received his October
check from Mr. Vaught, bought a $25 slide rule as thick and
slick as a mahjong tile and fitted at the rear with a little window.

Later in the afternoon he played golf, borrowing Jamie's
clubs and making a foursome with Mr. Vaught and two pleasant fellows, Lamar Thigpen and a man from the agency. The
engineer's skill at golf stood him in good stead. (Golf he was
good at, it was living that gave him trouble. He had caddied for
his father and broke eighty when he was thirteen.) It was not
that he was so much better than the others but rather that he
was strong and had a good swing. So that when the old man,
who somehow knew this, had mumbled something about "my
potner" and got his bets down and waved him onto the first
tee, after he and Justin and Lamar had driven, he had happened
to hit a dandy. The driver sang in the air and the ball went
chack, flattening, it seemed like, and took off low, then went
high and overdrove the par four green. The two opponents
exchanged great droll thunderstruck comical mid-South looks.

"Well now, what is this," said Justin, the agency man, who
was a big slow easy fellow, the sort referred to in these parts as
a good old boy.

"Looka here now," said Lamar.

"Sho," said Mr. Vaught, already striking out down the fairway. "Come on, potner."

He hit five more towering drives and scored a lucky-after-
the-layoff 36.

"Well now goddamn," said Lamar.

They called him Bombo, the son of Tarzan, and Mr. Clean. The engineer had to laugh. They were good fellows and funny.

The sixth hole fairway of the second nine ran in front of the castle. It had got to be the custom after teeing off to mark the balls and veer over to the patio, where David, the butler, had toddies ready. Custom also required that the talk, unlike other occasions, be serious, usually about politics but sometimes even about philosophical questions. The tone of the sixth-hole break was both pessimistic and pleasurable. The world outlook was bad, yes, but not so bad that it was not a pleasant thing to say so of a gold-green afternoon, with a fair sweat up and sugared bourbon that tasted as good as it smelled. Over yonder, a respectful twenty yards away, stood the caddies, four black ragamuffins who had walked over the ridge from the city and now swung the drivers they took from the great compartmented, zippered, pocketed, studded, bonneted golf bags.

The golfers gazed philosophically into their whiskey and now and then came out with solemn *Schadenfreude* things, just like four prosperous gents might have done in old Virginny in 1774.

"The thing is, you just don't get integrity where you need it most," said Lamar Thigpen, a handsome fellow who sat slapping his bare brown arm and looking around. He was maybe forty-five and just going slack and he worried about it, pushing his sleeve up and hardening his biceps against his chest.

"I'm going to tell yall the truth," Justin might say. "If they want the country all that bad, I'm not all that much against letting them have it."

But even these dire things were not said in ill humor.

"Ain't nobody here but us niggers anyway," somebody else would say finally. "Let's play golf."

They would get up a little creakily, their sweat having cooled and muscles stiffened, and walk to their lies. Mr. Vaught always took his second shot first because he seldom drove over a hundred yards but that always straight down the middle. And now he wound up with his brassie, drawing back slowly and swaying backward too and with a ferocious deliberation; then, for all the world as if he had been overtaken by some dread mishap, went into a kind of shiver and spasm and, like a toy wound too tight and shooting its springs, came down on the ball from all directions—Poppy drives, Lamar told Justin, like a man falling out of a tree—uttering at the end of it, as he always did, a little cry both apologetic and deprecating: "Voop!", calculated to conjure away all that was untoward and out of the ordinary—and off he would march, hopping along like a jaybird.

3.

Living as he did in the garage apartment and hanging out as he did in the pantry and not with Mrs. Vaught's coterie of patriots and anti-fluoridationists who kept to the living room, the engineer met the servants first of all. Met, not got to know. The engineer was the only white man in the entire South who did not know all there was to know about Negroes. He knew very little about them, in fact nothing. Ever since he was a child and had a nurse, he had been wary of them and they of him. Like many others, he had had a little black boy for a friend, but unlike the others, who had enjoyed perfect love and understanding with their little black friends, he had been from the beginning somewhat fuddled and uneasy. At the age of thirteen he was avoiding Negroes like a queasy middle-aged liberal.

No doubt these peculiar attitudes were a consequence of his nervous condition. Anyhow it was the oddest encounter imaginable, that between him and the Vaught servants. He baffled the Negroes and they him. The Vaught servants were buffaloed by the engineer and steered clear of him. Imagine their feeling. They of course lived by their radars too. It was their special talent and it was how they got along: tuning in on the assorted signals about them and responding with a skill two hundred years in the learning. And not merely responding. Not merely answering the signals but providing home and sustenance to the transmitter, giving him, the transmitter, to believe that he dwelled in loving and familiar territory. He must be made to make sense, must the transmitter; must be answered with sense and good easy laughter: sho now, we understand each other. But here came this strange young man who transmitted no signal at all but who rather, like them, was all ears and eyes and antennae. He actually looked at them. A Southerner looks at a Negro twice: once when he is a child and sees his nurse for the first time; second, when he is dying and there is a Negro with him to change his bedclothes. But he does not look at him during the sixty years in between. And so he knows as little about Negroes as he knows about Martians, less, because he knows that he does not know about Martians.

But here come this strange young man who act' like one of them but look at you out of the corner of his eye. What he waiting for? They became nervous and jumped out of the way. He was like a white child who does not grow up or rather who grows up in the kitchen. He liked to sit in the pantry and watch them and talk to them, but they, the Negroes, didn't know what to do with him. They called him "he," just as they used to call the madam of the house "she." "Where he is?" one might say, peeping out of the kitchen door and as often as not look straight into his eyes. "Uh-oh."

"He," the engineer, usually sat in the pantry, a large irregular room with a single bay window. It was not properly a room at all but rather the space left over in the center of the house when the necessary rooms had been built. Mr. Vaught, who also did not know what he did not know, had been his own architect. The ceiling was at different levels; many doors and vestibules opened into the room. David usually sat at one end, polishing silver in the bay. The dark end of the room let into the "bar," a dusty alcove of blue mirrors and buzzing fluorescent lights and chrome stools. It was one of the first of its kind, hailing from the 1920's and copied from the swanky bars used by Richard Barthelmess and William Powell in the movies. But it had not been used as such for years and now its mirror shelves were lined with Windex bottles, cans of O-Cedar and Bab-O and jars of silver polish stuffed with a caked rag. It fell out somehow or other that both Negro and white could sit in the pantry, perhaps because it was an intermediate room between dining room and kitchen, or perhaps because it was not, properly speaking, a room at all.

David Ross was different from the other Negroes. It was as if he had not caught onto either the Negro way or the white way. A good-humored seventeen-year-old, he had grown too fast and was as raw as any raw youth. He was as tall as a basketball player and wore summer and winter the same pair of heavy damp tweeds whose cuffs were swollen as if they had a chronic infection. He was supposed to be a butler and he wore a butler's jacket with little ivory fasten-on buttons but his arms stuck out a good foot from the sleeves. He was always polishing silver, smiling as he did so a great white smile, laughing at everything (when he did not laugh, his face looked naked and strange) a hissing laugh between his teeth, *ts-ts-ts.* Something about him irritated the engineer, though. He was not cunning enough. He, the engineer, was a thousand times more cunning and he didn't have to be. He, David, was too raw. For example, he was always answering advertisements in magazines, such as *Learn Electronics! Alert Young Men Needed! Earn Fifty Dollars a Day! Send for Selling Kit!* And the selling kit would come and David would show it to everybody, but his long black-and-pink fingers could never quite work the connections and the soldering iron. He was like a rich man's son! The engineer would never have dreamed of spending such money ($10 for a selling kit!). Hell no, David, the engineer told him, don't send off for that. Damnation, why didn't he have better sense? He should either be cunning with a white man's cunning or cunning with a black man's cunning. As it was, he had somehow managed to get the worst of each; he had both white sappiness and Negro sappiness. Why doesn't somebody tell him? One day he did tell him. "Damnation, David," said he as David showed him a selling kit for an ice-cube dispenser which was supposed to fit any kind of refrigerator. "Who do you think you're going to sell that to?"

"All the folks around here," cried David, laughing *ts-ts-ts* and waving a great limp hand in the direction of the golf links. "Folks out here got plenty money and ain't one in ten got a dispenser-type box" (he'd been reading the brochure). "It only come with GE and Servel!"

"Well, what in the world do they want it for," moaned the flabbergasted engineer.

"When the he'p gone in the evenings and folks want to fix they drinks! They ain't going to want to fool with no old-fashioned knuckle-bruising trays" (more from the brochure). "It's not S.E. on the other boxes."

"S.E.?" asked the engineer.

"Standard Equipment."

"Oh. Then you're just going to walk up to some lady's house at ten o'clock in the morning and ring the doorbell and when she comes to the door you're going to ask her to let you show this ice dispenser."

"Sho," said David and began laughing at the sour-looking engineer, *ts-ts-ts*.

"Well, you're not," the engineer would groan. Damnation, David couldn't even polish silver. There was always silver cream left in the grooves. Still, the engineer liked to watch him at work. The morning sunlight fell among the silver like fish in the shallows. The metal was creamy and satiny. The open jar of silver cream, the clotted rag, the gritty astringent smell of it, put him in mind of something but he couldn't say what.

But damn this awful vulnerability of theirs, he ranted, eyes fixed on the glittering silver. It's going to ruin us all, this helplessness. Why, David acted as if everybody was going to treat him well! If I were a Negro, I'd be tougher than that. I'd be steadfast and tough as a Jew and I'd beat them. I'd never rest until I beat them and I could. I should have been born a Negro, for then my upsidedownness would be right side up and I'd beat them and life would be simple.

But Oh Christ, David, this goddamn innocence, it's going to ruin us all. You think they're going to treat you well, you act like you're baby brother at home. Christ, they're not going to treat you well. They're going to violate you and it's going to ruin us all, you, them, us. And that's a shame because they're not that bad. They're not bad. They're better than most, in fact. But you're going to ruin us all with your vulnerability. It's God's terrible vengeance upon us, Jamie said Val said, not to loose the seven plagues upon us or the Assyrian or even the Yankee, but just to leave you here among us with this fearful vulnerability to invite violation and to be violated twenty times a day, day in and day out, our lives long, like a young girl. Who would not? And so the best of us, Jamie said she said, is only good the way a rapist is good later, for a rapist can be good later and even especially good and especially happy.

But damn him, he thought, him and his crass black inept baby-brother vulnerability. Why should I, for Christ's sake, sit here all asweat and solicitous of his vulnerability. Let him go sell his non-knuckle-bruising ice trays and if he gets hurt: well, I'm not well myself.

David's mother, Lugurtha Ross, was cook. She was respectable and black as black, with a coppery highlight, and had a straight Indian nose. She wanted no trouble with anybody. All she wanted in the world was to find fervent areas of agreement. She spoke to you only of such things as juvenile delinquency. "Chirren don't have any respect for their parents any more," she would cry. "You cain't even correck them!"—even though David was her only living child and it was impossible to imagine him as a delinquent. She made it sound as if everybody were in the same boat; if only children would have more respect, our troubles would be over. She often made beaten biscuits in the evening, and as she sifted flour on the marble and handled the mitt of dough, she sang in a high decorous deaconess voice, not spirituals but songs she made up.

> *Up in an airplane*
> *Smoking her sweet cigarette*
> *She went way up in an airplane*
> *Smoking her sweet cigarette*

John Houghton, the gardener, lived in a room under the engineer's apartment. An ancient little Negro with dim muddy eyes and a face screwed up like a prune around a patch of bristling somewhere near the middle of which was his mustache, he was at least sixty-five and slim and quick as a boy. He had come from the deep country of south Georgia and worked on the railroad and once as a hod carrier forty years ago when they built the dam at Muscle Shoals. He had been night watchman for the construction company when Mr. Vaught built his castle. Mr. Vaught liked him and hired him. But he was still a country Negro and had country ways. Sometimes Jamie and David would get him in a card game just to see him play. The only game he knew was a strange south Georgia game called pitty-pat. You played your cards in turn and took tricks but there was not much rhyme or reason to it. When John Houghton's turn came, he always stood up, drew back, and slapped the card down with a tremendous *ha-a-a-umph!*, just as if he were swinging a sledge hammer, but pulling up at the last second and setting the card down soft as a feather. David couldn't help laughing *ts-ts-ts*. "What game we gon' play, John," he would ask the gardener to get him to say pitty-pat. "Lessus have a game of pitty-pat," John Houghton would say, standing up also to shuffle the cards, which he did by chocking them into each other, all the while making terrific feints and knee-bends like a boxer. "*Pitty-pat*," cried David and fell out laughing. But John Houghton paid no attention and told them instead of his adventures in the city, where, if the police caught you playing cards, they would sandbag you and take you to jail.

"What do you mean, sandbag?" asked the puzzled engineer.

"That's what I mean!" cried John Houghton. "I mean they sandbag you."

Of an evening John Houghton would don his jacket, an oversize Marine drawstring jacket with deep patch pockets, turn the collar up around his ears so that just the top of his gnarled puckered head showed above it, thrust his hands deep into the patch pockets, and take a stroll down the service road which wound along the ridge behind the big houses. There he met the maids getting off work.

At night and sometimes all night long there arose from the room below the engineer's the sounds of scuffling and, it seemed to him, of flight and pursuit; of a chair scraped back, a sudden scurry of feet and screams, he could have sworn more than one voice, several in fact, screams both outraged and risible as pursuer and quarry rounded the very walls, it seemed like.

4.

They sat in the garden, the three students, on the last day of summer and leafed through their new textbooks. The white-throat sparrows had come back early and were scratching in the sour leaves. The October sunlight was blinding on the white glazed pages, which smelled like acetate and the year ahead. The chemistry text seemed to exhale the delicate effluvium of new compounds. From the anthology there arose a subtler smell, both exotic and businesslike, of the poet's disorder, his sweats and scribblings, and of the office order of the professor and the sweet ultimate ink. By contrast, everything else seemed untidy, the summer past, the ruined garden, one's own life. Their best hope lay in the books themselves, the orderly march of chapter and subheading, the tables, the summaries, the index, the fine fat page of type.

The old spurious hope and elegance of school days came back to him. How strange it was that school had nothing whatever to do with life. The old talk of school as a preparation for life—what a bad joke. There was no relation at all. School made matters worse. The elegance and order of school had disarmed him for what came later.

Jamie had a queer-looking physical-chemical reference, as stubby and thick as a German handbook. Hefting it, you felt like a German: a whole body of knowledge, a *Wissenschaft*, here in your hand, a good chunky volume. Kitty had a great $15 atlas-size anthology of World Literature from Heraclitus to Robert Frost—the whole works. The engineer was content with a thin tight little volume, *The Theory of Large Numbers*, that and his slide rule, which he wore in a scabbard like a dagger. Sitting in the funky tannin smell of the fall garden, he slid the window of his rule and read off cube roots and cosines. He for artifacts, bright pretty useful objects like slide rules, and you can have your funky gardens and jaybirds crying down October.

Each believed privately that he was taking the best course, had hit on the real thing, the meat of the university, and that the other two were deceiving themselves. Imagine what a chemistry student thinks of an anthology.

Son Junior, Lamar Thigpen's son, came out to join them and stood around fiddling with his Thunderbird keys, but they didn't like him much and nobody spoke to him and at last he went away. He was a pale glum sophomore who lived at the university and drove home to the castle on weekends. Yet strangely enough, glum as he was, he had many friends at the university who liked him despite his sullen ways. He brought them over to the castle before football games, and while everyone had a good time drinking in the pantry, he stood off and fiddled with his car keys.

The engineer, if the truth be told, was in a bad way, having been seriously dislocated by his first weeks at the university.

Now feeling all at once knocked in the head, bumbly and sleepy, he excused himself and crept off to a sunny corner of the garden wall, where he curled up and went to sleep. The sparrows eyed him and hopped around in the dry crape myrtle leaves, which curled like orange peelings and seemed to burn with a clear flame in the sunlight.

What had happened was that the university had badly thrown him off with its huge pleasantness. Powerful friendship radiations came at him from all directions. It was enough to make one uneasy. By ten o'clock on the first morning he was fairly jumping with nervousness. He did believe that the campus was the pleasantest place he had ever seen. Everyone he met was happy and good-looking and victorious and kindly and at-one with themselves, and here he was, solitary and goofy and shut up in himself, eyeballs rolled up in his eyebrows. Perfect strangers in shirtsleeves spoke to him on the paths. Beautiful little flatfooted girls swinging along in fresh cotton skirts called out to him: hi! His knee leapt. The boys said: what say! and the girls said: hi! He had of course got into the Yankee way of not speaking to anyone at all. In New York it is gradually borne in upon one that you do not speak to strangers and that if you do, you are fairly taken for a homosexual. Indeed he had noticed that Northern college boys worry about being mistaken for homosexuals and take trouble to demonstrate that they are not. At Princeton one not only did not speak to strangers on the paths; one also took care which acquaintances one acknowledged. There were those, in fact, who measured their own worth by the number of people one could afford to cut in public. That was how he nearly got into a fistfight and came to take up boxing. Still used to Southern ways, he spoke to a fellow coming toward him on the path, a cool, pipe-smoking gent (it was raining and he smoked his pipe upside-down) he had been introduced to not thirty minutes earlier at an eating club. "What say," said the engineer and the fellow looked straight through him, snuffled in his pipe, and cut him dead. Now the engineer was not nearly as tense and honorable as his father but was still fairly tense and honorable and unused to slights, and after all his grandfather had been a great one for face-to-face showdowns in the street ("I told you, you bed-sheeted Ku Klux cowardly son of a bitch, to be out of town by four o'clock," etc.). Before he knew it or even thought what he was doing, he had turned back, grabbed the other by his elbow, and spun him around. "Excuse me," said the courteous engineer, "but I was introduced to you not thirty minutes ago and just now I spoke to you and furthermore I saw that you saw me speak to you and that you chose not to acknowledge my greeting. I suggest now that you do so acknowledge it." Or some such of the formal goofy language he used with strangers. "Pardon," said the other, looking at him for the maniac that he was. "I s'pose I was completely lost in my thots." And off he went, snuffling in his pipe. Later the engineer observed that he smoked the pipe upsidedown even on clear days. He was a Choate man. Evidently he had discovered that the engineer graduated from Ithaca High School. Thought the latter to himself: if I'm going to be challenging these fellows on the paths, I'd better be in shape to do it. You can run into a tartar, a sure-enough thick-legged gent. And what a sad business that would be, to challenge some fellow and then get the living hell beat out of you. So he went out for boxing, became a demon middle-weight and had no more trouble with Choate snobs or anyone else for that matter.

But now it was he who had learned Yankee ways. He took to eyeing people on the path to see when they would speak. He judged the distance badly and said his "hi" and "what say" too soon. His face ached from grinning. There was something to be said after all for the cool Yankee style of going your own way and paying no attention to anyone. Here for God's sake the air fairly crackled with kinship radiations. That was it. These beautiful little flatfooted girls greeted you like your own sister! What do you do about that? He had forgotten. It made him blush to think of laying hands on them. Then he remembered: that was how you did lay hands on them!—through a kind of sisterly-brotherly joshing, messing around it was called. Everybody was wonderful and thought everybody else was. More than once he overheard one girl tell another: "She's the most wonderful girl I ever knew!"

That was how they treated the courses too: they cancelled out the whole academic side by honorifics. "Professor so-and-so? He's the second smartest professor in the United States!" "Ec 4? Universally recognized as the hardest course ever given on the subject!" Etc. And poof! out the window went the whole intellectual business, kit and caboodle, cancelled out, polished off, even when you made straight A's. Especially when you made straight A's.

Naturally in such an intersubjective paradise as this, he soon got the proper horrors. He began to skid a little and catch up with himself like a car on ice. His knee leapt so badly that he had to walk like a spastic, hand thrust through pocket and poking patella with each step. Spotting oncomers, fifty, sixty, seventy feet away, he began grinning and composing himself for the encounter. "Hi!" he hollered, Oh Lord, a good twenty feet too soon.

Under the crape myrtle in the garden the song sparrow scratched like a chicken, one foot at a time, and the yellow leaves curled in a clear flame. Close by, John Houghton trimmed the brick border with an old-fashioned spring blade. *Snick, snick snee*, went the blade scissoring along the bricks.

He was dreaming his old dream of being back in high school and running afoul of the curriculum, wandering up and down the corridors past busy classrooms. Where was his class? He couldn't find it and he had to have the credit to graduate.

Someone kissed him on the mouth, maybe really kissed him as he lay asleep, for he dreamed a dream to account for the kiss, met Alice Bocock behind the library stacks and gave her a sweet ten-o'clock-in-the-morning kiss.

There was a step behind him and presently voices. He cracked an eyelid. The song sparrow was scratching, kicking leaves and looking around like a chicken. Fireballs danced on his lashes, broke into bows and sheaves of color.

"Very well, little Hebe. Be Betty coed and have your little fun on Flirtation Walk—"

"Flirtation *Walk*!"

"And all the warm dalliance you want to. Drain your cup, little Hebe, then let me know when you want to get down to business."

"What in the world are you *talking* about?"—delivered in Kitty's new ironclad coed style, for crying out loud, her head tilted at an angle signifying mock-incredulity, eyes inattentive and going away.

Englishman that he was, he woke in his burrow without a commotion. Though his cheek was pressed into the leaves and was stinging, he did not move. The sunlight fell upon a loose screen of sasanqua. He could not see them, but he heard Kitty and Rita talking a few feet away, where they must be sitting on the grass.

A movement caught his eye. Some thirty feet away and ten feet above him a balcony of the garage overhung the garden, not a proper balcony, but just enough ledge to break the ugly wall and give a pleasant cloistered effect to the garden; not for standing on, but there stood a man anyhow, with his hands in his pockets, looking down into the garden.

He was a Vaught, with the black brow and the high color and the whorled police-dog eye, but a very finely drawn Vaught. Motionless as he was, he gave the effect of restiveness and darting. He was both merry and haggard. Sutter, the engineer was to learn, always looked as if he had just waked up, with one side of his face flushed and creased and his hair brushed up against the grain by the pillow. There was something old-fashioned about him. Perhaps it was his clothes. He was in shirtsleeves, but his shirt and pants were the kind you wear with a suit. They could be the trousers of a $35 Curlee suit. One knew at once that he would never wear slacks and a sport shirt. He put one in mind of a bachelor of the 1940's come home to his quarters and putting on a regular white shirt and regular suit pants and stepping out to take the air of an evening. Most notable was his thinness. He was thin as a child is thin, with a simple scanting of flesh on bones. The shirt, still starched and stuck together on one side, did not lay hold of his body. It was the sort of thinness a young man worries about. But this man did not. He was indifferent to his thinness. He did not hold himself in such a way as to minimize it.

Sutter's hands moved in his pockets as he watched Rita and Kitty.

"What's the story?" Rita was saying. "Why the headlong rush for anonymity?"

Kitty did not reply. The engineer could hear her hand moving against the nap of the freshly cut grass.

"Mmm?" said Rita, questioning softly.

"Nothing is *changed*, Ree," caroled Kitty.

Sutter turned his head. There was something wrong with his cheek, a shadowing, a distinguished complication like a German saber scar.

"On your way, Minnie cat," said Rita, and the women arose, laughing.

Before they could turn, Sutter, still fingering the change in his pocket, ducked through the open window. Rita looked up quickly, holding her hand against the sun.

5.

"A pretty links, isn't it? You know, I was one of the first people to be brought up in a suburb. Aren't you Will Barrett?"

He had been watching the golfers from the patio and he turned around quickly, irritably, not liking to be surprised. There stood a woman he first took to be a Salvation Army lass and he was about to refuse her alms even more irritably. But then he noticed she was a Vaught. She must be Val.

"In the past," she went on before he could answer, "people have usually remembered their childhood in old houses in town or on dirt farms back in the country. But what I remember is the golf links and the pool. I spent every warm day of my girlhood at the pool, all day every day, even eating meals there. Even now it doesn't seem right to eat a hamburger without having wrinkled fingers and smelling chlorine." She didn't laugh but went on gazing past him at the golfers. Her musing absent-mindedness, he reckoned, was one of the little eccentricities nuns permitted themselves. He had never spoken to a nun. But perhaps she was not a proper nun after all, wearing as she did not a proper habit but a black skirt and blouse and a little cap-and-veil business. But beyond a doubt she was a Vaught, though a somewhat plumpish bad-complexioned potato-fed Vaught. Her wrist was broad and white as milk and simple: it was easy for him to imagine that if it was cut through it would show not tendon and bone but a homogenous nun-substance.

"I've been looking for you, Barrett. Once I heard your father make a speech to the D.A.R. on the subject of *noblesse oblige* and our duty to the Negro. A strange experience and a strange bunch of noblewomen. Not that I know much about *noblesse oblige*, but he gave them proper hell. He was right about one thing, of course, character. You don't hear much about that either nowadays."

"Is that why you became a nun?" he asked politely.

"Partly, I suppose. I drove up to see Jamie and now I want to see you."

"Yes ma'am."

"Jamie looks awful."

"Yes." He was about to enter with her onto the mournful ground of Jamie's illness, but she fell away again. John Houghton's scissors came snickersneeing along the brick walk behind her and flushed a towhee out of the azaleas, a dandy little cock in tuxedo-black and cinnamon vest. She gazed down at the bird with the same mild distracted eye.

"Does John Houghton still run after schoolgirls?"

"Ma'am? Oh. Well, yes."

Now freed by her preoccupation with the forgotten trophies of her past, the sentient engineer swung full upon her. What to make of it, this queer casualness of hers? Was it Catholic, a species of professional unseriousness (death and sin are our affair, so we can make light of them), almost frivolity, like electricians who make a show of leaning on high-voltage wires? Or was it an elaborate Vaught dialectic, thus: Rita and the rest of you are going to be so serious about Jamie, therefore I am not, etc. His radar boggled and couldn't get hold of her. He was obscurely scandalized. He didn't like her much.

"How long does Jamie have?"

"Eh? To live— Oh, Rita said months, four months I think she said. But I think longer. Actually he is much better."

"Jamie tells me you and he are good friends." Her gaze was still fixed on the tiny amber eye of the towhee, which crouched with its head cocked, paralyzed.

"Yes."

"He says that you and he may go somewhere together."

"Jamie changes his mind about that. He was talking earlier about living with Sutter or going down to stay with you."

"Well, now he wants to go somewhere with you."

"Do you mean, leave school?"

"Yes."

"He knows I'm ready to go any time." Presently he added: "I can understand him wanting to go away."

"Yes. That was what I want to speak to you about."

He waited.

"Mr. Barrett—"

"Yes ma'am."

"It may well happen that it will be you and not one of us who will be with Jamie during the last days of his life and even at his death."

"I suppose that is true," said the engineer, taking note of a warning tingle between his shoulder blades.

"Everyone thinks very highly of you—though for strangely diverse, even contradictory reasons. I can't help noticing. You are evidently quite a fellow. That's hardly surprising, considering whose son you are."

"Ah—" began the engineer, frowning and scratching his head.

"Though I can't say that I agree with your father on his reasons for treating Negroes well rather than beating them up, still I'd rather that he'd won over the current scoundrels even if he'd won for the wrong reasons."

"Perhaps," said the engineer uneasily, not wanting to discuss either his father's "reasons" or her even more exotic reasons.

"But in any case I too can perceive that you are a complex and prescient young man."

"I certainly appreciate—" began the engineer gloomily.

"Clearly you would do right by Jamie even if you had no affection for him, which I have reason to believe you do have."

"Yes," said the other warily. It was still impossible to get a fix on her. He had known very few Catholics and no nuns at all.

"Mr. Barrett, I don't want Jamie to die an unprovided death."

"Unprovided?"

"I don't want him to die without knowing why he came here, what he is doing here, and why he is leaving."

"Ma'am?" The engineer felt like wringing out his ear but he did not.

"It may fall to you to tell him."

"Tell him what?"

"About the economy of salvation."

"Why don't you tell him?" He was watching her as intently

as the towhee watched her. There was no telling what she might
do.

She sighed and sat down. The towhee, released from its spell,
flew away. "I have told him."

The engineer, though standing erect, began to lean about
five degrees away from her.

"It is curious, Mr. Barrett, but what I told him was absolutely the last thing on earth he would listen to. It was not
simply one of a great number of things he might have listened
to more or less indifferently. It was, of all things, absolutely the
last thing. Doesn't that strike you as strange?"

"I couldn't say. But if you can't tell him what you believe,
you his sister, how do you expect me to tell him what I don't
believe?"

But she was at it again, her trick of engaging him then slipping away. "They didn't ride in carts the last time I was here,"
she said, gazing past him at the golfers. Do all nuns banter
about salvation? "And yet, there he was, reading all that guff
with relish."

"What guff?"

"That book about radio noise from the galaxies, noise which
might not be noise. Did you give it to him?"

"No."

She ignored his irritation. "I've noticed," she said gloomily
and not especially to him, "that it is usually a bad sign when
dying people become interested in communication with other
worlds, and especially when they become spiritual in a certain
sense."

"Don't you believe in other worlds and, ah, spirits?"

"It is strange, but I've always distrusted so-called spiritual
people," she muttered, mostly ruminating with herself. "You
know how women talk about such and such a priest being
spiritual?"

"No." How could he know any such thing?

"I always steer clear of those birds. But no, actually I owe
spiritual people, ladies, a great deal—they're very generous
with me when I beg from them. It's a strange business, isn't it?
The most unlikely people are generous. Last week I persuaded
the local Klonsul of the Klan to give us a Seven-Up machine.

Do you think it is possible to come to Christ through ordinary dislike before discovering the love of Christ? Can dislike be a sign?"

"I couldn't say," said the sleepy engineer.

She brought herself up and looked at him for the first time. "Mr. Barrett, Jamie's salvation may be up to you."

"Eh? Excuse me, but apart from the circumstance that I do not know what the word 'salvation' means, I would refuse in any case to accept any such commission, Miss, ah—, that is, Sister—"

"Val."

"Sister Val."

"No," she said laughing. "Just Val. I am Sister Johnette Mary Vianney."

"Is that right?"

His refusal, he noticed, was delivered with a tingle of pleasure, both perverse and familiar. Familiar because—yes, he remembered his father refusing a priest and taking some satisfaction in it even though he, his father, took the Catholics' side in their troubles with the Klan. "Mr. Barrett," the priest asked him with the same jolly gall, "I don't think you realized it but you just fired one of my parishioners, heh-heh, and I want to ask you if you will take her back. She has a family and no husband—" "And who could that be," said his father, his voice ominously civil. "Souella Johnson." Souella Johnson, who, being not merely a winehead but, failing to find Gallo sherry in the house, had polished off as a poor substitute some six cases of twenty-year-old bourbon over the years. "I will not, sir," said his father and bang, down went the telephone.

"I will not," he told Val with the same species of satisfaction. Perhaps we are true Protestants despite ourselves, he mused, or perhaps it is just that the protest is all that is left of it. For it is in stern protest against Catholic monkey business that we feel ourselves most ourselves. But was her request true Catholic gall, the real article, or was it something she had hit upon through a complicated Vaught dialectic? Or did she love her brother?

He read in her eyes that he looked odd. "What is it," she asked him smiling. For a split second he saw in her his Kitty, saw it in her lip-curling bold-eyed expression. It was as if his

Kitty, his golden girl of summertime and old Carolina, had come back from prison where she had got fat and white as white and bad-complexioned.

"What," she asked again.

"I was wondering," said the engineer, who always told the truth, "how you manage to come to the point where you feel free to make requests of people."

She laughed again. "Jamie was right. You're a good companion. Well, I can ask you, can't I?"

"Sure."

"It's like the story about the boy who got slapped by quite a few girls but who—well. But it's extraordinary how you can ask the most unlikely people—you can ask them straight out: say, look, I can see you're unhappy; why don't you stop stealing or abusing Negroes, go confess your sins and receive the body and blood of Our Lord Jesus Christ—and how often they will just look startled and go ahead and do it. One reason is that people seldom ask other people to do anything."

"I see."

"Now I have to go see Sutter."

"Yes ma'am."

He began nodding in ancient Protestant fuddlement and irony, not knowing whether to bow, shake hands, or look down his nose. But it didn't matter. She had left without noticing.

6.

Jamie was not in the apartment. There were voices in the room next door. That would be Sutter and Val, he calculated, and perhaps Jamie. The old itch for omniscience came upon him— lost as he was in his own potentiality, having come home to the South only to discover that not even his own homelessness was at home here—but he resisted the impulse to eavesdrop. I will not overhear nor will I oversee, he said, and instead threw a dozen combination punches, for henceforth I shall be what I am no matter how potential I am. Whereupon he dismounted the telescope through which he and Jamie had studied the behavior of golfers who hooked their drives from number 5 tee into the creek. Some cheated. It was with a specific, though unidentified pleasure that one watched the expressions of the men who stood musing and benign and Kiwanian while one busy foot nudged the ball out of the water.

He lay on the bed, feet sticking straight up, and broke out in a cold sweat. What day is this, he wondered, what month, and he jumped up to get his Gulf calendar card from his wallet. The voices in the next room murmured away. A chair scraped back. The vacuum of his own potentiality howled about him and sucked him toward the closet. He began to lean. Another few seconds, and he was holed up as snug as an Englishman in Somerset, closet door closed behind him, Val-Pak on his back like a chasuble.

The hole commanded perhaps a 100 degree view of Sutter's room. It was furnished in rancho style with a maple couch and chair with wagonwheel arms. There were pictures of famous moments of medical history: First Use of Anesthesia, Dr. Lister Vaccinates, Tapping Ascites. Mrs. Vaught, he remembered, had fixed up the room for Sutter when he was in school.

Sutter was sitting in the wagonwheel chair, idly brandishing an automatic pistol, aiming it here and there, laying the muzzle against his cheek. Val was leaving: he caught no more than a flurry of black skirt and a shoe of cracked leather. At close range Sutter did not look so youthful. His olive skin had a yellowish cast. The high color of his cheeks resolved into a network of venules. His fingertips were wrinkled and stained by chemicals.

"—found him in New York," Val was saying. "He's Ed Barrett's son. Have you met him?"

"I saw him in the garden." Sutter aimed the pistol at something over the engineer's head.

"What did you think of him?"

Sutter shrugged. "You know. He is—" His free hand, held forth like a blade, moved back and forth across the vertical.

"Yes," said Val.

"—nice," ended Sutter with six overtones in his voice, "you know."

"Yes."

My God, thought the closeted Englishman, they already knew what he was, agreed on it, and communicated their complex agreement with hardly a word!

"Put that thing up," said Val.

"Why?"

"Some day you're going to blow your fool head off—by accident."

"That would offend you more than if I did it deliberately, wouldn't it?"

"And it would please you, wouldn't it, to die absurdly?"

The engineer heard no more. He had become extremely agitated, whether by their reference to him or by the sight of the pistol, he could not have said, but he left the closet and paced up and down the bedroom. He took his pulse: 110. A door closed and the stairs creaked under a heavy step. For some minutes he stood listening. A car started below. He went to the window. It was a Volkswagen microbus painted a schoolbus yellow and stained with red dust.

He had already started for the door, blood pounding in his ears, when the shot rang out. It was less a noise than a heavy concussion. Lint flew off the wall like a rug whipped by a broom. His ears rang. Now, hardly knowing how he came here, he found himself standing, heart pounding in his throat, outside Sutter's door on the tiny landing. Even now, half out of his mind, his first thought was of the proprieties. It had seemed better to go to Sutter's outside door than directly through the kitchenette, which with the closet separated the apartments. And now, standing at the door, knuckles upraised, he hesitated. Does one knock after a shot. With a sob of dismay, dismay less for Sutter than himself, he burst into the room.

The wagonwheel chair was empty. He went lunging about.

"You must be Barrett."

Sutter stood at a card table, almost behind the door, cleaning the pistol with a flannel disk soaked in gun oil.

"Excuse me," said the reeling engineer. "I thought I heard a noise."

"Yes."

"It sounded like a shot."

"Yes."

He waited but Sutter said no more.

"Did the pistol go off accidentally?"

"No. I shot him."

"Him?" The engineer suddenly feared to turn around.

Sutter was nodding to the wall. There hung yet another medical picture, this of The Old Arab Physician. The engineer

had not seen it because his peephole was some four inches
below the frame. Moving closer, he noticed that the Arab,
who was ministering to some urchins with phials and flasks,
was badly shot up. Only then did it come over him that his
peephole was an outlying miss in the pattern of bullet holes.

"Why him?" asked the engineer, who characteristically,
having narrowly escaped being shot, dispatched like Polonius
behind the arras, had become quite calm.

"Don't you know who that is?"

"No."

"That's Abou Ben Adhem."

The engineer shook his head impatiently. "Now that I'm
here I'd like to ask you—"

"See the poem? There in a few short, badly written lines is
compressed the sum and total of all the meretricious bullshit
of the Western world. And lo! Ben Adhem's name led all the
rest. Why did it lead all the rest?"

"I don't know," said the engineer. His eyes were fixed
vacantly on the dismantled gun barrel. The fruity steel smell
of Hoppe's gun oil put him in mind of something, but he
couldn't think what.

"There it is," said Sutter, loading the clip, "the entire melancholy procession of disasters. First God; then a man who is
extremely pleased with himself for serving man for man's sake
and leaving God out of it; then in the end God himself turned
into a capricious sentimental Jean Hersholt or perhaps Judge
Lee Cobb who is at first outraged by Abou's effrontery and
then thinks better of it: by heaven, says he, here is a stout fellow
when you come to think of it to serve his fellow man with no
thanks to me, and so God swallows his pride and packs off the
angel to give Abou the good news—the new gospel. Do you
know who did the West in?"

"No."

"It wasn't Marx or immorality or the Communists or the
atheists or any of those fellows. It was Leigh Hunt."

"Who?" repeated the engineer absently, eyes glued forever
to the Colt Woodsman.

"If I were a Christian, I shouldn't hesitate to identify the
Anti-Christ. Leigh Hunt."

"Leigh Hunt," said the engineer, rubbing his eyes.

"I'm glad you came down with Jimmy," said Sutter. "Come sit over here."

"Yes sir." Still not quite able to rouse himself, he allowed Sutter to lead him to the wagonwheel chair. But before he could sit down, Sutter turned him into the light from the window.

"What's the matter with you?"

"I feel all right now. I was quite nervous a few minutes ago. I've had a nervous condition for some time." He told Sutter about his amnesia.

"I know. Jimmy told me. Are you going into a fugue now?"

"I don't know. I thought perhaps that you—"

"Me? Oh no. I haven't practiced medicine for years. I'm a pathologist. I study the lesions of the dead."

"I know that," said the engineer, sitting down wearily. "But I have reason to believe you can help me."

"What reason?"

"I can tell when somebody knows something I don't know."

"You think I know something?"

"Yes."

"How can you tell?"

"I don't know how but I can. I had an analyst for five years and he was very good, but he didn't know anything I didn't know."

Sutter laughed. "Did you tell him that?"

"No."

"You should have. He could have done a better job."

"I'm asking you."

"I can't practice. I'm not insured."

"Insured?"

"The insurance company cancelled my liability. You can't practice without it."

"I'm not asking you to practice. I only want to know what you know."

But Sutter only shrugged and turned back to the Colt.

"Why did they cancel your insurance?" the engineer asked desperately. There was something he wanted to ask but he couldn't hit on the right question.

"I got the idea of putting well people in the hospital and sending the truly sick home."

"Why did you do that," asked the engineer, smiling slightly. He was not yet certain when the other was joking.

Again Sutter shrugged.

The engineer was silent.

Sutter rammed a wad through the barrel. "I had a patient once who lived under the necessity of being happy. He almost succeeded but did not quite. Since he did not, he became depressed. He became very unhappy that he was not happy. I put him in the terminal ward of the hospital, where he was surrounded by the dying. There he soon recovered his wits and became quite cheerful. Unfortunately—and by the purest bad luck—he happened to suffer a serious coronary before I sent him home. As soon as it became apparent that he was going to die, I took it upon myself to remove him from his oxygen tent and send him home to his family and garden. There he died. The hospital didn't like it much. His wife sued me for a half a million dollars. The insurance company had to pay."

The engineer, still smiling faintly, was watching the other like a hawk. "Dr. Vaught, do you know what causes amnesia?"

"Causes it? Like a virus causes chicken pox?"

"Have you seen many cases?"

"Do you regard yourself as a case?"

"I would like to know."

"You are a very persistent young man. You ask a great many questions."

"And I notice you don't answer them."

The pistol was assembled. Sutter sat down, shoved in the clip, pulled back the breech and rang up a bullet. He clicked the safety and took aim at the Arab physician. The engineer screwed up one eye against the shot, but Sutter sighed and set the pistol down.

"All right, Barrett, what's wrong?"

"Sir?"

"I'm listening. What's wrong?"

Now, strangely, the engineer fell silent for a good twenty seconds.

Sutter sighed. "Very well. How old are you?"

"Twenty-five."

Sutter was like an unwilling craftsman, the engineer perceived, a woodworker who has put on his coat and closed up shop. Now a last customer shows up. Very well, if you insist. He takes the wood from the customer, gives it a knock with his knuckles, runs a thumb along the grain.

"Are you a homosexual?"

"No."

"Do you like girls much?"

"Yes."

"How much?"

"Very much."

"Do you have intercourse with girls?"

The engineer fell silent.

"You don't like to speak of that?"

He shook his head.

"Did you speak of it with your psychiatrist?"

"No."

"Do you mean that for five years you never told him whether you had intercourse with girls?"

"No."

"Why not?"

"It was none of his business."

Sutter laughed. "And none of mine. Did you tell him that?"

"No."

"You were not very generous with him."

"Perhaps you are right."

"Do you believe in God?"

The engineer frowned. "I suppose so. Why do you ask?"

"My sister was just here. She said God loves us. Do you believe that?"

"I don't know." He stirred impatiently.

"Do you believe that God entered history?"

"I haven't really thought about it."

Sutter looked at him curiously. "Where are you from?"

"The Delta."

"What sort of man was your father?"

"Sir? Well, he was a defender of the Negroes and—"

"I know that. I mean what sort of man was he? Was he a gentleman?"

"Yes."

"Did he live in hope or despair?"

"That is hard to say."

"What is the date of the month?"

"The nineteenth."

"What month is it?"

The engineer hesitated.

"What is the meaning of this proverb: a stitch in time saves nine?"

"I would have to think about it and tell you later," said the engineer, a queer light in his eye.

"You can't take time off to tell me now?"

"No."

"You really can't tell me, can you?"

"No."

"Why can't you?"

"You know why."

"You mean it is like asking a man hanging from a cliff to conjugate an irregular verb?"

"No. I'm not hanging from a cliff. It's not that bad. It's not that I'm afraid."

"What is it then?"

The engineer was silent.

"Is it rather that answering riddles does not seem important to you? Not as important as—" Sutter paused.

"As what?" asked the engineer, smiling.

"Isn't that for you to tell me?"

The engineer shook his head.

"Do you mean you don't know or you won't tell me?"

"I don't know."

"All right. Come here."

Sutter took a clean handkerchief from his pocket and for the second time turned the other into the light. "You won't feel this." He twisted a corner of the handkerchief and touched the other's cornea. "O.K.," said Sutter and sitting down fell silent for a minute or two.

Presently the engineer spoke. "You seem to have satisfied yourself of something."

Sutter rose abruptly and went into the kitchenette. He returned with half a glass of the dark brown bourbon the engineer had noticed earlier.

"What is it?" the latter asked him.

"What is what?"

"What did you satisfy yourself about?"

"Only that you were telling the truth."

"About what?"

"About when you believe someone has something to tell you, you will then believe what he tells you. I told you you would not feel the handkerchief, so you didn't. You inhibited your corneal reflex."

"Do you mean that if you tell me to do something I will do it?"

"Yes."

The engineer told him briefly of his *déjà vus* and of his theory about bad environments. The other listened with a lively expression, nodding occasionally. His lack of surprise and secret merriment irritated the engineer. He was even more irritated when, as he finished his account, the other gave a final nod as much as to say: well, that's an old story between us—and spoke, not of him, the engineer, but of Val. Evidently her visit had made a strong impression on him. It was like going to a doctor, hurting, and getting harangued about politics. Sutter was more of a doctor than he knew.

"Do you know why Val came up here? This concerns you because it concerns Jimmy."

"No, I don't," said the engineer gloomily. Damnation, if I am such an old story to him, why doesn't he tell me how the story comes out?

"She wanted me to promise her something," said Sutter, keeping a bright non-medical eye on the other. "Namely, that if she were not present I would see to it that Jimmy is baptized before he dies. What do you think of that?"

"I couldn't say."

"It happened in this fashion," said Sutter, more lively than ever. "My father was a Baptist and my mother an Episcopalian. My father prevailed when Jamie was born and he wasn't baptized. You know of course that Baptist children are not baptized until they are old enough to ask for it—usually around twelve or thirteen. Later my father became an Episcopalian and so by the time Jamie came of age there was no one to put the question to him—or he didn't want it. To be honest, I think everybody was embarrassed. It is an embarrassing subject nowadays, even slightly ludicrous. Anyhow Jamie's baptism got lost in the shuffle. You might say he is a casualty of my father's ascent in status."

"Is that right," said the engineer, drumming his fingers on his knees. He was scandalized by Sutter's perky, almost gossipy interest in such matters. It reminded him of something his father said on one of his nocturnal strolls. "Son," he said through the thick autumnal web of Brahms and the heavy ham-rich smell of the cottonseed-oil mill. "Don't ever be frightened by priests." "No sir," said the startled youth, shocked that his father might suppose that he could be frightened by priests.

"Well," he said at last and arose to leave. Though he could not think what he wanted to ask, he was afraid now of overstaying his welcome. But when he reached the door it came to him. "Wait," he said, as though it was Sutter and not he who might leave. "I know what I want to ask."

"All right." Sutter drained off the whiskey and looked out the window.

The engineer closed the door and, crossing the room, stood behind Sutter. "I want to know whether a nervous condition could be caused by not having sexual intercourse."

"I see," said the other and did not laugh as the engineer feared he might. "What did your analyst say?" he asked, without turning around.

"I didn't ask him. But he wrote in his book that one's needs arise from a hunger for stroking and that the supreme experience is sexual intimacy."

"Sexual intimacy," said Sutter thoughtfully. He turned around suddenly. "Excuse me, but I still don't quite see why you single me out. Why not ask Rita or Val, for example?"

"I'm asking you."

"Why?"

"I don't know why, but I know that if you tell me I will believe you. And I think you know that."

"Well, I will not tell you," said Sutter after a moment.

"Why not?"

Sutter flushed angrily. "Because for one thing I think you've come to me because you've heard something about me and you already know what I will say—or you think you know. And I think I know who told you."

"No sir, that's not true," said the engineer calmly.

"I'll be goddamned if I'll be a party to any such humbug."

"This is not humbug."

"I will not tell you."

"Why not?"

"Who do you think I am, for Christ's sake? I am no guru and I want no disciples. You've come to the wrong man. Or did you expect that?" Sutter looked at him keenly. "I suspect you are a virtuoso at this game."

"I was, but this time it is not a game."

Sutter turned away. "I can't help you. Fornicate if you want to and enjoy yourself but don't come looking to me for a merit badge certifying you as a Christian or a gentleman or whatever it is you cleave by."

"That's not why I came to you."

"Why then?"

"As a matter of fact, to ask what it is *you* cleave by."

"Dear Jesus, Barrett, have a drink."

"Yes sir," said the engineer thoughtfully, and he went into the kitchenette. Perhaps Kitty and Rita were right, he was thinking as he poured the horrendous bourbon. Perhaps Sutter is immature. He was still blushing from the word "fornicate." In Sutter's mouth it seemed somehow more shameful than the four-letter word.

7.

"I've got to go," said Jamie.

"O.K. When?"

After leaving Sutter, the engineer had read a chapter of Freeman's *R. E. Lee* and was still moving his shoulders in the old body-English of correcting the horrific Confederate foul-ups, in this case the foul-up before Sharpsburg when Lee's battle orders had been found by a Union sergeant, the paper wrapped around three cigars and lying in a ditch in Maryland. I'll pick it up before he gets there, thought the engineer and stooped slightly.

"I mean leave town," said Jamie.

"Very well. When?"

"Right now."

"O.K. Where are we going?"

"I'll tell you later. Let's go."

From the pantry he could look into the kitchen, which was filled with a thick ticking silence; it was the silence which comes late in the evening after the cook leaves.

But at that moment David came over for the usual game of hearts. Rita had taken David aside for an earnest talk. In the last few days David had decided he wanted to be a sportscaster. The engineer groaned aloud. Sportscaster for Christ's sake; six feet six, black as pitch, speech like molasses in the mouth, and he wanted to be a sportscaster.

"No," he told David when he heard it. "Not a sportscaster."

"What I'm going to do!" cried David.

"Do like me," said the engineer seriously. "Watch and wait. Keep your eyes open. Meanwhile study how to make enough money so you don't have to worry about it. In your case, for example, I think I'd consider being a mortician."

"I don't want to be no mortician."

He was David sure enough, of royal lineage and spoiled rotten. He wouldn't listen to you. Be a sportscaster then.

Now he couldn't help overhearing Rita, who was telling David earnestly about so-and-so she knew at CBS, a sweet wonderful guy who might be able to help him, at least suggest a good sportscasting school. Strangest of all, the sentient engineer could actually see how David saw himself as a sportscaster: as a rangy chap (he admired Frank Gifford) covering the Augusta Masters (he had taken to wearing a little yellow Augusta golf cap Son Junior gave him).

Jamie wore his old string robe which made him look like a patient in the Veterans Hospital. While Rita spoke to David, Son Junior told the engineer and Kitty about rumors of a Negro student coming on campus next week. It was part of the peculiar dispensation of the pantry that Son Junior could speak about this "nigger" without intending an offense to David. Rita looked sternly at Son—who was in fact dull enough to tell David about the "nigger."

Sutter sat alone at the blue bar. The engineer had come in late and missed whatever confrontation had occurred between Sutter and Rita. Now at any rate they sat thirty feet apart, and Rita's back was turned. Sutter appeared to take no notice and sat propped back in a kitchen chair, whiskey in hand and face livid in the buzzing blue light. The family did not so much avoid Sutter as sequester him in an enclave of neutral space such as might be assigned an afflicted member. One stepped around him, though one might still be amiable. "What you say, Sutter," said Lamar Thigpen as he stepped up to the bar to fix a drink.

Kitty got Son off the subject by asking him what band would play for the Pan-Hellenic dance. Later Kitty whispered to the engineer, "Are you going to take me?"

"Take you to what?"

"The Pan-Hellenic."

"When is it?"

"Saturday night after the Tennessee game."

"What day is this?"

"Thursday, stupid."

"Jamie wants to go somewhere." He was thinking gloomily of standing around at a dance for seven hours drinking himself cross-eyed while Kitty danced the night away. "Where do you want to go, Jamie?"

But Jamie wouldn't tell Kitty.

"Son asked me to go with him," said Kitty.

"Isn't he your nephew?"

"Not really. Myra is no kin. She is Poppy's stepdaughter by another marriage."

"You still can't go with Son."

"Why not!" she cried, widening her eyes. Since she had become a coed, Kitty had given up her actress's lilt for a little trite sorority cry which was made with her eyes going away. She wore a cashmere sweater with a tiny gold sorority dagger pinned over her breast.

"I'm telling you, you can't." It actually made him faint to think of Kitty going anywhere with Son Junior, who was a pale glum fornicator, the type who hangs around the men's room at a dance, patting himself and talking about poontang.

"Why *not*?"—eyes going away again but not before peeping down for a glimpse of her pin.

"He's a bastard."

"Shh! He likes you."

He did. Son had discovered through intricate Hellenistic channels that the engineer had been a collegiate middleweight and had not lost a fight. "We're strong in everything but boxing," he had told the engineer, speaking of the Phi Nu's campus reputation. The engineer agreed to go out for boxing and golf. And during some hazing horseplay Son had told one of the brothers to take it easy with this one—"he can put your ass right on the Deke front porch with a six-inch punch." And so he had attached himself to the engineer with a great glum Greek-letter friendship.

Now once again Son came close, sidling up and speaking at length while he twirled his Thunderbird keys. It was the engineer's bad ear, but as best he could tell, Son was inviting him to represent the pledge class at a leadership conference next summer at the fraternity headquarters in Columbus, Ohio. "They always have outstanding speakers," Son told him. "This year the theme is Christian Hellenism."

"I really appreciate it, Son," said the engineer.

"Look, Kitty," he said when Son drifted off. He took off his own pledge pin. "Why don't you wear mine?" It was a great idea. He had only recently discovered that being pinned was a serious business at the university, the next thing to an engagement ring. If she wore his pin, Son wouldn't take her to the dance.

"Will you take me to the dance?"

"Yes. If Jamie doesn't veto it. I promised to go with him."

"Don't worry about Jamie."

As he watched, she pinned his gold shield to the same lovely soft blue mount, oh for wantonnesse and merrinesse, thought he tenderly and crossed his good knee over bad lest it leap through the card table.

Jamie punched him. He was angry because they were not paying attention to the game of hearts (here is my heart, thought the engineer sentimentally). "What do you say," whispered the youth fiercely. "Are you ready to go?"

"Yes."

"O.K. What do you think of this? We'll drive to the coast and—"

But before Jamie could tell him, the engineer caught sight of Mrs. Vaught beckoning to him from the dark doorway of the dining room. The engineer excused himself.

Mrs. Vaught had a book for him. "I saw what you were

reading this afternoon in the garden!" She waggled her finger at him.

"Ma'am. Oh." He remembered the *R. E. Lee* and saw at once that the sight of it had set Mrs. Vaught off on some gambit or other.

"Here's a book on the same subject that I'm sure you'll find fascinating," she said, laughing and making rueful fun of herself, which was a sure sign she was proselytizing.

"Yes ma'am. Thank you very much. Is it about the Civil War?"

"It's the real story behind the so-called official version of General Kirby Smith's surrender at Shreveport. It's the story behind the story. We all think that General Kirby Smith wanted to surrender."

"Yes ma'am. That is true."

"No, it isn't. He was holding out until he could make a deal with the Rothschilds and the international bankers in Mexico to turn over Texas and Louisiana to Maximilian's Jewish republic."

"Ma'am?" He wrung out his good ear.

"Here's proof," she said, taking back the book and thumbing through it, still laughing ruefully at herself. She read: "At a meeting of the Rothschilds in London in 1857, Disraeli jumped to his feet and announced: 'We'll divide the United States into two parts, one for you, James Rothschild, and the other for you, Lionel Rothschild. Napoleon III will do what I tell him to do.'"

The engineer rubbed his forehead and tried to concentrate. "But don't I recall that Kirby Smith did in fact surrender at Shreveport?"

"He didn't want to! His men surrendered, fortunately for us."

She got off on the Bavarian Illuminati and he leaned down to her so he needn't look at her, looking instead at his shoes, lined up carefully with the sill of the dining-room door.

"Excuse me, Mother," said Jamie, plucking at the engineer's sleeve. Evidently he was so used to his mother's opinions that he paid no attention.

"You read this!" Again she thrust the book on him, shaking her head at her own zeal.

"Yes ma'am."

"Bill," said Jamie.

"What?"

"Let's go."

"All right. Where do you want to go?"

"Let's take the camper down to the Gulf Coast and live on the beach. Just for the weekend."

"You don't want to see the Tennessee game?"

"No."

"You mean leave after classes tomorrow?"

"No, I meant—well, all right."

"O.K."

They were headed back to the hearts game but Lamar Thigpen caught them. "Did you ever hear about this alligator who went into a restaurant?" He took them by the neck and drew them close as lovers.

"No, I didn't," said the courteous engineer, though he had. Jokes always made him nervous. He had to attend to the perilous needs of the joke-teller. Jamie dispensed himself and paid no attention: I'm sick and I don't have to oblige anybody.

"The waitress came over and brought him a menu. So this alligator says to her: do yall serve niggers in here? She says yes, we do. So he says, O.K. I'll take two."

"What about leaving tonight, Bill?" said Jamie.

"That's all right, Mr. Thigpen," said the engineer while the other held him close as a lover and gazed hungrily at his cheek. Rita had been watching Jamie and she knew something was wrong. The engineer, diverted by Lamar's terrible needs, only realized it when he heard Rita's hearty no-nonsense tone.

"Come on over here, Tiger." She took the youth's arm. Jamie flung her off angrily. He looked dog-faced. He plucked his thumb and pretended to muse.

"Hold it, Tiger," said Rita, now managing to draw him down in David's chair but not looking at him because he was close to tears.

Jamie looked sternly about but his eyes shone and there was heat and vulnerability in the hollow of his neck. The engineer wished that Son Junior would go away. In every such situation, he had noticed, there is always one person who makes things worse.

David left quickly. Dull in some ways, he was as quick as any Negro to know when white people had white troubles. Rita drew Jamie down in David's chair.

"I can't wait for the game," cried Kitty. "You coming to see me work, Jimbo?" In the past month she had metamorphosed from ballerina to cheerleader. "We're number one! We're number one!" she would chant and set her white skirt swirling about her legs so cunningly that the engineer almost fell out of the grandstand, overcome by pride and love.

"No, it's not the game," said Rita, gazing steadfastly away but patting Jamie's arm with hard steady pats. Kitty's gambit didn't work, she was saying. But hers didn't either.

"Jamie and I are planning to go down to the Coast this weekend," said the engineer.

Everyone looked at Jamie, but he could not bring himself to say anything.

"You don't mean this weekend," cried Kitty.

"I'm going," said Jamie in a loud voice, all squeaks and horns.

"I'm with you, Tiger," said Rita, still patting.

Damn, don't pat him, thought the engineer.

Rita ran a hand through Jamie's hair (like my mother, thought the engineer in a sudden *déjà vu*, ruffling my hair for the photographer so it would look "English" and not slicked down). "Val was here today and she upset him with some of her—ideas."

"It's not that," said Jamie, losing control of his voice again.

"I think he really wants to go down to Tyree County and clear things up and I don't blame him."

"I don't."

"You said you did."

"That was before."

"Don't misunderstand me," said Rita, speaking for some reason to the engineer. "I think Val is doing a magnificent job down there. I happen to know a little about such things, having worked with Indian kids, who are just as bad off. No, my hat's off to her. But to come up here cold, so to speak, after making herself scarce for the past year as far as Jamie is concerned and to seriously propose to this guy here who despite the fact that he is a wretch and a no-good-bum"—she ruffled Jamie's hair—"nevertheless pulled down first place in the National Science competition—that a rather stupid Irishman in a black skirt pour water over his head while uttering words in a dead language (and uttering them in atrocious ecclesiastical Latin besides)—excuse me, but I think the whole affair is exceedingly curious. Though I'm frank to say I don't know why it upsets you. But listen now: if you want to go down there, Tiger, I'll drive the car for you and hold the ewer or whatever it is."

"I am *not* going there," said Jamie through his teeth. "And if I were, that would *not* be the reason." The engineer sighed with relief. Jamie's anger had got the better of his tears.

"I'm Baptist and DeMolay myself," said Son Junior, twirling his keys glumly. He had not quite got the straight of it but did perceive that the subject of religion had come up.

"That's not the point," cried Jamie, in anguish again. "I'm not interested in either—"

Mr. Vaught, who couldn't stay put anywhere for long and so made a regular tour of the house, shuttling back and forth between the pantry and the living room, where Mrs. Vaught and Myra Thigpen usually sat, happened at that moment to be circling the wall of the pantry.

"We all headed for the same place and I don't think the good Lord cares how we get there," he cried, shot his cuff, and went on his way.

"The Bible says call no man father," said Lamar Thigpen sternly, looking around for the adversary.

Sutter, whom the engineer had not for one second lost sight of, sighed and poured another glass of dark brown bourbon.

Jamie groaned and the engineer reflected that there were no clear issues any more. Arguments are spoiled. Clownishness always intervenes.

Rita waited until the Thigpens drifted away and then pulled the card players closer. "If you want to know what sets my teeth on edge and I strongly suspect Jamie here might be similarly affected"—she spoke in a low voice—"it is this infinitely dreary amalgam of Fundamentalism and racism."

"No, no, no," groaned Jamie loudly, actually holding his head. "What do I care about that. That's not it." He glared at Rita angrily, embarrassing the engineer, who was aware of Rita's strong bid for low-pitched confidential talk and didn't mind obliging her. "This is all irrelevant," cried Jamie, looking behind him as if he was expecting someone. "I just don't care about that."

"What do you care about?" asked Rita after a moment.

"It's just that—I can't explain."

"Jamie wants to get away," said the engineer. "He would like to spend some time in a new place and live a simple life without the old associations—such as, for example, parking the camper on a stretch of beach."

"That is correct," said Jamie instantly and soberly.

"Listen who's telling me that," said Rita. "What in the world have I been saying all summer?" She spoke to them earnestly. Why didn't they finish the semester and join her in her house in Tesuque? Better still, she and Kitty could go now, since credit hours were more important to men than women—everyone made a fuss over Jamie's credit hours—get the place ready and the two young men could join them later. "I'm calling your bluff, Tiger. You can kill two birds with one stone. You can have your new life and you can get out of the closed society at the same time."

Jamie frowned irritably. He opened his mouth.

"Ah, that's fine, Rita," said the engineer. "That really sounds wonderful. But I think Jamie has in mind something right away, now, this minute." He rose. "Jamie."

"Now wait a minute," said Kitty, smoothing down her sweater, taking a final peep at the two pins (to think she is mine! rejoiced the engineer, all her sweet cashmered self!). "Whoa now. Not so fast. I think yall are all crazy. I'm going to the game and I'm going to the dance and I'm going to school tomorrow morning." She rose. "I'll meet yall in the garage at six thirty."

To the engineer's surprise, Jamie made no protest. Something had mollified him. At any rate he said no more about leaving and presently rose wearily and invited the engineer to the apartment for a bedside game of gin rummy. It pleased him to play a single snug game, pull the beds together and direct a small disk of light upon the tray between them where the cards were stacked.

Son Junior and his father started their favorite argument about Big Ten versus Southeastern Conference football.

"The Big Ten on the whole is better," said Son glumly. "You have your ten teams, one as good as any other."

"Yes," said Lamar, "but there are always two or three teams in the Southeast which could take any of them. And don't you think the Big Ten doesn't know it. I happen to know that both Alabama and Ole Miss have been trying for years to schedule Ohio State and Michigan. Nothing doing and I don't blame them."

At that moment Myra, Lamar's wife, came into the pantry and the engineer was glad to have an excuse to leave. She would, he knew, do one of two things. Both were embarrassing. She would either quarrel with her husband or make up to Rita, whom she admired. It was a dread performance in either case, one from which, it is true, a certain amount of perverse skin-prickling pleasure could be taken, but not much.

Here she came toward Rita and as certain as certain could be she would make a fool of herself. Something about Rita made her lose her head. The night before, Kitty and Rita were talking, almost seriously, of going to Italy instead of New Mexico. Rita had lived once in Ferrara, she said, in a house where one of Lucrezia's husbands was said to have been murdered. Oh yes, broke in Myra, she knew all about Lucrezia Bori, the woman who had started St. Bartholomew's Massacre. And on and on she went with a mishmash about the Huguenots—her mother's family were Huguenots from South Carolina, etc. She had not the means of stopping herself. The engineer lowered his eyes.

"Pardon me," said Rita at last. "Who is it we are talking about? Lucrezia Bori, the opera singer, the Duchess of Ferrara, Lucrezia Borgia, or Catherine de' Medici?"

"I too often get the two of them mixed up," said the poor sweating engineer.

"But not the three," said Rita.

Why did she have to be cruel, though? The engineer sat between the two, transfixed by a not altogether unpleasant horribleness. He couldn't understand either woman: why one should so dutifully put her head on the block and why the other should so readily chop it off. And yet, could he be wrong or did he fancy that Rita despite her hostility felt an attraction for Myra? There was a voluptuousness about these nightly executions.

But tonight he wasn't up to it and he left with Jamie. He was careful not to forget his book about General Kirby Smith's surrender at Shreveport in 1865. He was tired of Lee's sad fruitless victories and would as soon see the whole thing finished off for good.

8.

The man walked up and down in the darkness of the water oaks, emerging now and then under the street light, which shed a weak yellow drizzle. The boy sat on the steps between the azaleas and watched. He always imagined he could see the individual quanta of light pulsing from the filament.

When the man came opposite the boy, the two might exchange a word; then the man would go his way, turn under the light, and come back and speak again.

"Father, you shouldn't walk at night like this."

"Why not, son?"

"Father, they said they were going to kill you."

"They're not going to kill me, son."

The man walked. The youth listened to the music and the hum of the cottonseed-oil mill. A police car passed twice and stopped; the policeman talked briefly to the man under the street light. The man came back.

"Father, I know that the police said those people had sworn to kill you and that you should stay in the house."

"They're not going to kill me, son."

"Father, I heard them on the phone. They said you loved niggers and helped the Jews and Catholics and betrayed your own people."

"I haven't betrayed anyone, son. And I don't have much use for any of them, Negroes, Jews, Catholics, or Protestants."

"They said if you spoke last night, you would be a dead man."

"I spoke last night and I am not a dead man."

Through an open window behind the boy there came the music of the phonograph. When he looked up, he could see the Pleiades, which seemed to swarm in the thick air like lightning bugs.

"Why do you walk at night, Father?"

"I like to hear the music outside."

"Do you want them to kill you, Father?"

"Why do you ask that?"

"What is going to happen?"

"I'm going to run them out of town, son, every last miserable son of a bitch."

"Let's go around to the garden, Father. You can hear the music there."

"Go change the record, son. The needle is stuck in the groove."

"Yes sir."

The engineer woke listening. Something had happened. There was not a sound, but the silence was not an ordinary silence. It was the silence of a time afterwards. It had been violated earlier. His heart beat a strong steady alarm. He opened his eyes. A square of moonlight lay across his knees.

A shot had been fired. Had he dreamed it? Yes. But why was the night portentous? The silence reverberated with insult. There was something abroad.

Nor had it come from Sutter's room. He waited and listened twenty minutes without moving. Then he dressed and went outside into the moonlight.

The golf links was as pale as lake water. To the south Juno's temple hung low in the sky like a great fiery star. The shrubbery, now grown tall as trees, cast inky shadows which seemed to walk in the moonlight.

For a long time he gazed at the temple. What was it? It alone was not refracted and transformed by the prism of dreams and memory. But now he remembered. It was fiery old Canopus, the great red star of the south which once a year reared up and hung low in the sky over the cottonfields and canebrakes.

Turning at last, he walked quickly to the Trav-L-Aire, got his flashlight from the glove compartment, cut directly across the courtyard and entered the back door of the castle; through the dark pantry and into the front hall, where he rounded the newel abruptly and went up the stairs. To the second and then the third floor as if he knew exactly where he was, though he had only once visited the second floor and not once been above it. Around again and up a final closeted flight of narrow

wooden steps and into the attic. It was a vast unfinished place
with walks of lumber laid over the joists. He prowled through
the waists and caverns of the attic ribbed in the old heart pine
of the 1920's. The lumber was still warm and fragrant from
the afternoon sun. He shone the flashlight into every nook
and cranny.

When he heard the sound behind him, he slid the switch of
the flashlight and stepped four feet to the side (out of the line
of fire?) and waited.

"Bill?"

A wall switch snapped on, lighting a row of bulbs in the peak
of the roof. The girl, hugging her wrap with both arms, moved
close to him and peered into his face. Her lips, scrubbed clean
of lipstick, were slightly puffed and showed the violet color of
blood.

"Are you all right?"

"Yes."

"I saw you outside."

He didn't answer.

"What are you looking for?"

"I heard something."

"You heard something up here from the garage?"

"I didn't know where it came from. I thought it might be
from the attic."

"Why?"

"Is there a room up here?"

"A room?"

"A room closed off from the rest of the attic?"

"No. This is all."

He said nothing.

"You don't know where you are, do you?"

"Where I am?"

"Where are you?"

"I know." He did know now but he didn't mind her thinking
he didn't. She was better, more herself, when he was afflicted.

"You were sleepwalking, I think."

"It's possible."

"Come on. I'll take you back."

"You don't have to."

"I know I don't."

He made her stay in the pantry. She was sweet and loving and not at all antic. It is strange, he thought as he stood in his own and Jamie's room a few minutes later: we are well when we are afflicted and afflicted when we are well. I can lie with her only if she tends my wounds.

"Was there a shot?" he asked her as he left.

She had shaken her head but smiled, signifying she liked him better for being mistaken.

The square of moonlight had moved onto Jamie's face. Arms folded, the engineer leaned against his bed and gazed down at the youth. The eye sockets were pools of darkness. Despite the strong black line of the brow, the nose and mouth were smudged and not wholly formed. He reminded the engineer of the graduates of Horace Mann, their faces quick and puddingish and acned, whose gift was the smart boy's knack of catching on, of hearkening: yes, I see. If Jamie could live, it was easy to imagine him for the next forty years engrossed and therefore dispensed and so at the end of the forty years still quick and puddingish and childlike. They were the lucky ones. Yet in one sense it didn't make much difference, even to Jamie, whether he lived or died—if one left out of it what he might "do" in the forty years, that is, add to "science." The difference between me and him, he reflected, is that I could not permit myself to be so diverted (but diverted from what?). How can one take seriously the Theory of Large Numbers, living in this queer not-new not-old place haunted by the goddess Juno and the spirit of the great Bobby Jones? But it was more than that. *Something is going to happen*, he suddenly perceived that he knew all along. He shivered. It is for me to wait. Waiting is the thing. Wait and watch.

Jamie's eyes seemed to open in their deep sockets. But they gazed back at him, not with their usual beamish expression, casting about for recondite areas of agreement in the space between them, but mockingly: ah, you deceive yourself, Jamie seemed to say. But when the engineer, smiling and puzzled, leaned closer, he saw that the eyes had not opened.

A bar of yellow light fell across the room. A figure was outlined in the doorway of the kitchenette. It beckoned to him.

It was Rita.

As soon as he was inside the tiny room, she closed the door and whispered: "Is Jamie asleep?"

"Yes."

Sutter stood gazing into the sink. The sink was dusty and still had a paper sticker in the basin.

"We want you to settle a little point," said Rita.

Sutter nodded. The engineer sniffed. The kitchenette had the close expired air of impasse. Now as if they were relieved by the diversion, its occupants turned toward him with a mild, unspecified interest.

"I want to know whether you are still prepared to go somewhere with Jamie," Rita said.

The engineer rubbed his forehead. "What time is it?" he asked no one in particular. Was this the true flavor of hatred, he wondered, this used, almost comfortable malice sustained between them, with its faint sexual reek? They turned as fondly to him as spent lovers greeting a strange child.

"Two thirty," said Sutter.

"What about it, Bill?" asked Rita crisply.

"What? Oh, Jamie," he repeated, aware that Sutter watched him. "Why, yes. But you knew all along that I would go with him. Why do you ask?"

"I have reason to believe that Jamie is getting restless and that he may ask Sutter to go off somewhere with him. I think this is too much to ask of Sutter."

He stole a glance at Sutter, but the latter's expression was still fond and inattentive.

"You are very much in demand, Bill," said he at last. "Jimmy wants you, not me."

"Then what's the difficulty?" asked the bemused engineer, feeling their apathy steal into his bones.

"The difficulty," said Sutter, "is that Rita wants to make sure Jimmy doesn't go anywhere with me."

"Why not?"

"That's a good question, isn't it, Rita," said Sutter, but still not quite looking at her (couldn't they stand the sight of each other?). "Why don't you want Jimmy to go with me?"

"Because of your deliberate cultivation of destructiveness, of your death-wish, not to mention your outhouse sexuality," said Rita, still smiling, and addressing Sutter through the engineer. "Every man to his own taste but you can bloody well leave Jamie out of it."

"What do you think I would do?" Sutter asked.

"I know what you have done."

"Jamie also spoke of going down to Val's," said the engineer for reasons of his own. He could not quite make this pair out and wished to get another fix on them. Val was his triangulation point.

"Val," said Rita nodding. "Yes, between the two of you, Sutter and Val, you could dispose of him very nicely. You'd kill him off in three weeks and Val would send his soul to heaven. If you don't mind I shall continue to minister to the living."

"Kill him off?" Sutter frowned but still could not tear his vacant eye from the engineer. "I understood he was in a remission."

"He was."

"What's his white count?"

"Eighteen thousand."

"How many immature forms?"

"Twenty percent."

"What's he on?"

"Prednisone."

"Wasn't he on Aminopterin?"

"That was a year ago"

"What's his red count?"

"Just under three million."

"Is his spleen palpable?"

"That's what I like about you and your sister," said Rita.

"What's that?"

"Your great concern for Jamie, one for his body, the other for his soul. The only trouble is your interest is somewhat periodic."

"That's what interests me," said Sutter. "Your interest, I mean."

"Put up your knife, you bastard. You no longer bother me."

They quarreled with the skillful absent-minded malice of married couples. Instead of taking offense, they nodded sleepily and even smiled.

"What is it you want this young man to do?" Sutter asked, shaking his head to rouse himself.

"My house in Tesuque is open," said Rita. "Teresita is there to cook. The Michelins are next door. I have even determined that they could transfer to the college in Santa Fe without loss of credit—at the end of this semester."

"Who are the Michelins?" asked the engineer.

"A duo piano team," said Sutter. "Why don't you take him out yourself, Rita?"

"You persuade him to go and I will," said Rita listlessly.

"Rita," said Sutter in the same mild temper which the engineer had not yet put down to ordinary friendliness or pluperfect malice, "what do you really care what happens to Jimmy?"

"I care."

"Tell me honestly what difference it makes to you whether Jimmy lives or dies."

The engineer was shocked but Rita replied routinely. "You know very well there is no use in my answering you. Except to say that there is such a thing as concern and there is such a thing as preference for life over death. I do not desire death, mine, yours, or Jamie's. I do not desire your version of fun and games. I desire for Jamie that he achieve as much self-fulfillment as he can in the little time he has. I desire for him beauty and joy, not death."

"That is death," said Sutter.

"You see, Bill," said Rita, smiling but still unfocused.

"I'm not sure," said the engineer, frowning. "But mainly what I don't understand is what you are asking me to do since you already know I will go anywhere Jamie wants to go and anytime."

"I know, Bill," said Rita mournfully. "But apparently my former husband thinks you have reasons for staying."

"What reasons?" he asked Sutter.

"He cannot conceive that everyone is not as self-centered as he is," Rita put in before Sutter could reply.

"No, I can't, that's true," said Sutter. "But as to reasons, Bill, I know you are having some difficulties and it was my impression you wanted me to help you." Sutter was opening and closing cabinet doors, searching for the bottle which was in plain sight on the counter. The engineer handed it to him.

"What's number two?"

"Number two: I would not suppose that you were anxious to leave Kitty."

"Kitty?" The engineer's heart gave a queer extra thump.

"I could not help but observe her kissing you in the garden as you lay under a Governor Mouton."

He stopped his hand, which had started up to touch his lips. Then someone had kissed him, not Alice Bocock in his dream but Kitty herself, warm and flushed from the sun, tiny points of sweat glistening in the down of her lip. He shrugged. "I don't see what that has to do—"

"The question is not whether you would stay but whether Kitty would go with you."

"I don't think so," said the engineer, blushing with pleasure at the prospect. It had not occurred to him.

"The further question is, ahem, whether in case all three of you go, Rita might not go along with you after all."

"You can't reach me any more, you bastard," said Rita, but not, it seemed, angrier than before.

"You're right, of course," said Sutter cheerfully and earnestly, facing her for the first time over his drink. "You were right before and I was wrong. I couldn't stand prosperity. We were good, you and I, as good as you wanted us to be, and in the end I couldn't stand it. You were productive and so, for the first time in years, was I, and thanks to you. As you say, we were self-actualizing people and altogether successful, though somewhat self-conscious, in our cultivation of joy, zest, awe, freshness, and the right balance of adult autonomous control and childlike playfulness, as you used to call it. Though I don't mind telling you that I never really approved your using technical terms like 'penis envy' in ordinary conversation—"

"Excuse me," said the engineer, setting a foot toward the door. But Rita was squarely in the way and gave no sign of seeing him.

"I confess," Sutter went on, "that in the end it was I who collapsed. Being geniuses of the orgasm is the hardest of tasks, far more demanding than Calvinism. So I couldn't stand prosperity and had to mess around with Teresita. I longed for old-fashioned humbug in the same way other men long for the dear sights of home. You never really forgave me. And yet, now at this moment I forgive you for—"

"*Don't you dare,*" said Rita in a strangled whisper, advancing upon Sutter and at the same time, fortuitously, upon the engineer, who saw his chance and made his escape. As he left he heard Sutter say:

"You always said I knew you backwards. Well, I'm telling you now that you are wrong about yourself and wrong about what you think you want. There is nothing wrong with you beyond a certain spitefulness and pride and a penchant for a certain species of bullshit. You're a fine girl, a fine Georgia girl—did you know Rita was from Georgia, Bill?—who got too far from home. Georgia girls have no business at Lake Chapala. Come on here—"

"Oh foul, foul, foul—" said Rita as he shut the door.

It is proof that the engineer was not in any ordinary sense an eavesdropper or a Peeping Tom that not only did he not head for the closet when he reached his room but instead closed the closet door and jumped into bed and pulled the pillow over his head so he could not hear a door close and so could not tell whether Rita stayed or left.

9.

On the way to school Friday morning, Jamie leaned over and began to fiddle with the ashtray of the Lincoln. "I—ah—" said he, smiling a bit—they hardly ever spoke during this hour, the engineer drove, brother and sister watched the road as they would have from a schoolbus—"I've decided to quit school and go out west. Or rather transfer."

"How soon would you like to go?" asked the engineer.

"I'm ready now."

"Have you asked if it is all right with your parents?"

"Yes."

It was a dewy bright haunted October morning. The silvery old Rock City barns leaned into the early sunlight. Killdeers went crying along the fallow fields where tough shallow spiderwebs were scattered like saucers. Now and then the Lincoln crossed deep railroad cuts filled with the violet light of ironweed.

"Then it would be in June," said Kitty carelessly, putting her chin back to catch sight of the pledge pins on her cashmere sweater. "Could I go with you? Let's open up Rancho Merced," she cried, but in a standard coed cry, eyes going away.

But the engineer was already turning the Lincoln around. It was Mrs. Vaught's car, a good solid old glossy black four-door, rounded fore and aft in the style of the fifties and smelling inside of wax like a ship's saloon.

"What in the world," cried Kitty. "Where are you going?"

"Back to get the camper."

"The camper. What for?"

"Jamie said he wanted to go out west. The camper would be better than this car."

"My God, he didn't mean now!"

"I thought he did."

They had gotten as far as Enfield. Even after the few weeks of their commuting, every inch of the way had become as familiar to them as their own back yard: this was the place where they always ran afoul of an unlucky traffic light which detained them at an empty crossing for an endless forty-five seconds. Always when they passed at this hour a line of sunlight and shade fell across the lettering of an abandoned storefront, SALOMON, whose middle o had fallen off, leaving its outline on the brick. Enfield was a defunct coal depot on the L & N Railroad.

"Jamie, tell him to turn around. I have an eight o'clock and so do you."

But Jamie only went on with his smiling and his fiddling with the ashtray.

The engineer was smiling too, but from the pleasure of having her next to him and touching him at arm, hip, and calf. What a lovely fine fragrant Chi Omega she was in her skirt and sweater. A beautiful brown-kneed cheerleader and it was cheer to sit beside her. She saved them both from this decrepit mournful countryside. Without her he'd have jumped straight into one of these lonesome L & N gorges where old train whistles from the 1930's still echoed.

"The Tennessee game is tomorrow," she said laughing, truly shaken because now she believed them. Overnight she had turned into a fierce partisan for the Colonels, who were now ranked number two in the United States. "Tennessee is number four and if we beat them—"

"That's right," said Jamie, who, now that it was settled, sat back and took notice of the countryside. It was very different now, fifteen minutes later and what with them not going but returning with the sun in their faces. The hamlets seemed to be stirring with ordinary morning enterprise.

"How long will it take you to get ready?" Jamie asked him.

"I can have the camper stocked in thirty minutes!"

"O.K."

"I have never in my life," said Kitty, tapping her Scripto pencil on the world anthology.

He saw that she was angry. If Jamie had not been with them, he would have stopped then and there and kissed her pretty pouting lips and pressed her lovely cashmered person against him, Chi O pin and all. It was the sisterly aspect of her which excited him, big sister sweetheart at eight o'clock in the morning, her mouth not yet cleared of breakfast butter and molasses.

"Of course you're going with us," he said to her, sending the Lincoln swooping along on its limber old springs.

"Hah. Not me, boy," she cried, casting about her huffy coed glances.

"I'm serious."

"I'm serious too."

"Is it all right with you, Jamie, if your sister goes?"

"I don't care who goes. But I'm going."

"Why for God's sake?" For the first time she spoke directly to her brother.

"What do you mean, why?" he asked her irritably. "Does there have to be a why?"

When Kitty did not answer and in fact began to blink back tears Jamie said: "I am not interested in seeing the Tennessee game."

"And I happened to know how much you like Chem 2. Bubba Ray Ross was telling me. I'll bet you've heard too, haven't you Billy?"

"No."

"I am not interested in Chem 2," Jamie said, "or 3 or 4."

"Well, what in the world are you interested in?" Kitty was

smiling angrily and busily tucking her skirt under her knee and squaring away the world anthology on her lap.

"I—ah. I just want to take this trip. No, to tell you the truth I'm going to transfer. I've already spoken to—it can be done."

"Transfer! Where? Where're yall going to live—in the camper?"

"I know this boy who goes to school in Albuquerque. In fact I heard from him yesterday. I correspond with him quite a bit. I could live with him, in fact." After a moment he added: "His father has a shop of some sort. Out on the highway."

"Oh, for heaven's sake. Tell him, Billy."

"All I want Jamie to tell me is whether he has made arrangements to live with somebody or whether he wants me to go with him."

"Well, I mean, if you want to."

"O.K."

"Do yall mean to tell me that you're going to jump in that little truck and go out there and park it somewhere and just start going to school?"

Jamie smiled and leaning forward spoke to both of them in a different voice. "I remember reading this novel in school last year, by a Russian writer. I think his name was Goncharov, or something like that, but he is a wonderful writer. Do you know him?"

"No," said the engineer. Kitty did not answer.

"He's really a good writer," said Jamie, going back to his ashtray. "At least in this novel. It was about this young man who was a refugee or a prisoner, I forget which. He was traveling the whole length of Russia in a cattle car, along with hundreds of others. He was sick with brain fever, whatever that is, I have only come across brain fever in Russian novels. It was summer and they were crossing Siberia, day after day, weeks even. The car was crowded and he had one tiny corner and a bit of straw and that was all. And though he was quite ill and even delirious at times, the strange thing about it was that it wasn't so bad. Through the slats of the car he could see the fields, which were covered by a little blue flower. And of course the sky. The train stopped often and peasant women would bring him bowls of blueberries and fresh warm milk—that was the peculiar thing about it, that even though he knew no one and the train only stopped for a few minutes at a time, somehow news of this young man traveled ahead of the train and they expected him. And though everybody else on the train became exhausted by the hardships of the trip, he actually got better! It was really good. I think it's the best novel I ever read."

"That's fine, Jamie, that's fine and I agree with you," said Kitty peevishly. "But I still don't see why—"

The engineer interrupted her. "Are you coming?"

"Me? No, indeed."

They were silent when the Lincoln turned up the links road. When Jamie got out into the garage, which smelled of wet concrete from David's hosing, the engineer held Kitty.

"What?" she said, still turned away and not quite managing a look back at him.

"I want to tell you something."

"What?"

"Or rather ask you something."

"What?"

"I want you to come with us."

"Are you kidding?"

"No, I want you to marry me."

"In the next thirty minutes?"

"Look. Jamie wants to go and I think we ought to go with him."

"*Why* does he want to go?" She was peevish still, but there was a settling under her peevishness. Though one foot was still out of the car and her books cradled in her arm, she had settled back half a millimeter.

"We can be married in Louisiana tomorrow."

"Now I have heard it all. I don't mind saying that I have heard it *all*."

"Put your book down."

"*What?*"

"Give me your book."

"What for?"

But she gave it to him and he threw it into the back seat and took hold of her while the warm Lincoln ticked away in the resounding garage. Oh, damnable straight upstanding Lincoln seat. He was almost beside himself with tenderness at the eight o'clock splendor of her. "I'm in love," he said, kissing her and taking hold of the warm pad back of her knee, which he loved best of all when she was leading cheers. But the angles were bad and contrived against him.

"Good God," cried Kitty, breaking free. "What in the world has happened to you and Jamie this morning! You're crazy!"

"Come here and let me hold you tight."

"Hold me tight, my foot."

"You didn't answer my question."

"What question?"

"Will you marry me?"

"Jeezum," she said in a new expression of hers, something she got from the Chi O's. And retrieving her world anthology from the back seat, she left him alone in the garage.

10.

Jamie became cheerful and red-cheeked as they fitted out the Trav-L-Aire. While the engineer set about laying in his usual grits and buttermilk and slab bacon and filling the tank with the sweet artesian water of the valley against the day of the evil alkali water of the desert, Jamie staked out the upper forward bunk as his private domain. It was a broad bed lying athwart the trim ship, with a fine view forward over the top of the cab. There was a shelf for his radio, a recessed reading light something like the old Pullman upper berth. Jamie hit on the idea of replacing the mattress with a cot pad which not only gave him the narrow hard corner he wanted but left a gutter just wide enough to hold his books.

"Let's take plenty of fresh milk with us," said Jamie.

"O.K."

"I've drunk a lot of milk lately. I've gained three pounds."

"Good."

Jamie stretched out on the hard bed and watched the engineer store away the staples Lugurtha had given him from the kitchen. "You know I truly believe that if I could live a simple life, I could actually conserve my energy and therefore gain strength. I honestly think it's a question of living simply and conserving your energy. I'll live right here, get up, go to class, come back, get up, eat, come back, etcetera. Don't you agree?"

"Yes." To tell the truth, it didn't seem unreasonable.

"Are you really going to marry Kitty?"

"I asked her. But if I do and she does come along, it will be just the same for you. These are your quarters if we are married, yours and mine if we're not."

"What if she won't, ah—go? Will you still come?"

"If you want me to."

"O.K.," said Jamie and began to arrange his books in alphabetical order. "Where do you keep your telescope?"

"Here."

"Oh yes. I remember. Look. I'm bringing my Freylinghausen star charts along. I understand the atmosphere is a great deal clearer in New Mexico."

"That's right. Now, Jamie, I think you'd better go find your parents. It is not enough for you to tell me that you have their permission. They must tell me too."

"O.K."

"We'll drive till we get tired and start out again when we feel like it."

II.

It turned out to be a morning for dealing with practical matters. Two letters awaited him on the refectory table in the castle hall. He never received mail from anywhere. They had been written more than two weeks earlier and addressed to the Y.M.C.A. in New York, forwarded to General Delivery in Williamsburg and thence to the Vaughts' home address. Both had to do with money. One was from his Uncle Fannin, who lived in Shut Off, Louisiana. His uncle wrote to remind him that although the "place" had been sold many years ago, certain mineral rights had been retained, and that he had recently received a lease offer from Superior Oil Company of California. The rights, as he must know, were jointly owned by the two surviving male Barretts. Would he, the younger, signify his intention in this matter? He, the elder, would as soon accept the offer. The share of each would come to $8,300. The letter was written in neat pencil script on ruled paper which had been torn from a pad.

The other letter had also to do with money. The First National Bank of Ithaca wished to advise him of the existence of a savings account in his name, opened for him by his father in the year 1939. What with the compounding of interest, his balance now stood at $1,715.60. The occasion of this notice was the present reorganization of the bank. He pondered—1939. That was the year of his birth.

Jamie was delayed. His clothes still lay on the bed in the garage apartment. After waiting for him a good forty minutes, the engineer returned to the house. Lugurtha was making beaten biscuits for the football picnic tomorrow. On the marble slab sifted with flour, she rolled out a soft mitt of dough. Kitty met him in the pantry, in a secret glee, and hustled him into the "little" pantry, a dark cold closet where potatoes and onions were stored in bins. He peered at her.

"My darling," she whispered, giving him a passionate kiss and making herself free of him in an entirely new way, all joyous legs and arms. He felt a vague unease. "Guess what?"

"What?" Through two doorways he could see Lugurtha handle the dough up into the air, fingers dancing under it, giving way, yet keeping it up, setting gravity at nought.

"Jamie has decided not to go until after Christmas."

"Why?"

"Then he will have his semester credits and can transfer without losing a month's work."

"Where is he?"

"In the sun parlor. Darling, don't you see what this means?"

"Yes, but—"

"What's the matter?" Swaying, her hands clasped in the small of his back in a new conjugal way, like a French girl saying farewell to her *poilu*, she squeezed him close and leaned away from him.

"I am afraid he might be doing it for me. Us."

"He wants to!"

"I'm afraid you talked him into it."

"It was his idea!"

"Who talked to him?"

Her eyes sparkled triumphantly. "Rita!"

"Rita?" He pondered. "Did Rita know that you and I might be leaving with Jamie today?"

"Yes!" Swaying triumphantly.

"And she talked Jamie into staying?"

"She didn't talk him into anything. It was his idea. In fact, he wants more time to plan the trip." Her tongue hollowed out her cheek and made a roguish joke. "What a nut! Imagine the three of us wandering around Arkansas in the middle of the winter like a bunch of Okies." She shook her head at him fondly, wifely. "I've got news for you, you big dope."

"Eh?"

"You're among friends here, you know."

"Yes." What he could not tell her was: if I can marry, then you can travel. I can even stand this new horsy conjugal way, this sad *poilu* love with you, if you will hit the road with me. Jamie is dying, so he needs to go. But I need to go too. Now the pantry's got us, locked in, with a cold potato love, and you the chatelaine with the keys at your belt. "I'd better go see Jamie."

"He'll tell you. What's the matter?" Her fingers touched his sweating forehead.

"I'm hot."

"It's freezing in here."

His eyes were caught in a stare. Lugurtha's working of the biscuit dough, the quick kneading gathering movement of her hands against the sifted marble, put him in mind of something. She sang:

> *Up in an airplane*
> *Smoking her sweet cigarette*

Keeping his hand clasped in hers, Kitty led him to the sun parlor and showed, not him to them but them to him, as if they were trophies, the articles of her proof: Jamie stretched on the sofa with a wet handkerchief across his eyes; Mrs. Vaught waiting, hands outstretched to them: a new Mrs. Vaught, too, a genial little pony of a lady, head to one side, pince-nez flashing quick family love-flashes, Rita in a wide stance, back to the coal fire. Mrs. Vaught gave him a quick press of her hand and a kiss, a dismaying thing in itself. She said nothing, but there was an easement in the air, the tender settled sense of larger occasions.

The sun parlor itself was an unused ceremonial sort of place. He had only been inside it once before, when Mr. Vaught showed him his old Philco, a tall console glistening with O'Cedar. It had a tilted sounding board and it still worked.

Mr. Vaught turned it on and presently the tubes heated up and put out regular 1932 static and the smell of hot speaker-silk such as used to attend the broadcasts of Ben Bernie and Ruth Etting and the Chase & Sanborn hour.

The cold wind pressed against the old-style double-hung windows, leaked through and set dust devils whirling along the tile under the wicker. There were lacquered Chinese boxes and miniature chests of drawers, a mahjong set, and a large gonglike table; the brass coalbox was stamped with a scene of jolly Dutch burghers. The coal grate, which had not been used, gave off a smell of burnt varnish. In one corner stood a stork five feet tall with a hollow eye and a beak which cut off the ends of cigars.

Mrs. Vaught twined her arm in his and, rocking slightly, held the two of them by the fire. "Did I tell you that I knew your mother very well one summer?"

"No'm."

"It was at the old Tate Springs Hotel. Lucy Hunicutt was the prettiest little thing I have ever seen—all dark hair and big violet eyes. And beaus! They swarmed around her like flies. She was a demon tennis player and wore a little cap like Helen Wills. In fact, everyone called her 'Little Miss Poker Face.' But there was one boy who was hopelessly in love with her— Boylston Fisk from Chattanooga (Boylston is now chairman of the board of Youngstown and Reading)—and he was the handsomest man I ever saw. But he could never dance more than three steps with her before somebody would break. So she told him if he could ever find out the name of her favorite piece she would dance it with him. Well, somehow he did. It was 'Violets.' And don't you know, he asked the orchestra to play it, not during the dance but while everyone was still at dinner. And he came across the room to her table with every eye on him and bowed and said: Miss Hunicutt, I believe this is our dance. It was like a dare, don't you see, but she got up! And they danced the whole piece out on the floor by themselves. I swear it was the most romantic thing I ever saw in my life!"

It was as if the memory of this gentler age had dispensed Mrs. Vaught from the terrible quarrels of the present. She softened. His radar sensed it without quite defining it: the connection between the past time and the present insane quarrel over fluoridation. For him it was the other way around! It was the olden time with its sweetness and its great occasions which struck a dread to his heart! It was past fathoming.

Jamie lay with the handkerchief across his eyes and said nothing. When Mrs. Vaught let him go, the engineer went over and sat on the sofa beside him.

"What happened?"

"What do you mean what happened?" said Jamie irritably.

"I thought we were leaving."

"I don't mind waiting a while. After all, what's the big hurry?"

"But it was not your idea, the postponement."

"Sure it was!"

"I'm packed and ready to go."

"I know you are."

"If you want to go, all you have to do is to get up and we'll leave. And I think Kitty will go with us. But even if she doesn't, I'm ready."

"I know you are." Jamie looked at him curiously. The engineer blushed.

"If you are staying on my account, then I don't want it. I'd truly rather leave. You understand?"

"Yes."

"So I am putting you on your honor to say whether it is on my account or anyone's account that you are staying. If it is, then let's go."

Jamie took away the wet handkerchief and wiped his mouth but did not reply. As the engineer waited, the cold air seeped into his shoes. The jaybirds called in the ragged garden outside. Above the Philco hung a great gloomy etching of Reims cathedral depicting 1901 tourists with parasols and wide hats and bustles strolling about its portal. The three women in the parlor, he suddenly became aware, had fallen silent. Turning his head a degree, he saw that they were watching the two of them. But when he arose, Kitty and her mother had put their heads together and were talking in the most animated way, Mrs. Vaught counting off items on her fingers as if she were compiling a list of some sort. Jamie put the handkerchief across his eyes.

Rita still stood in front of the fire, feet wide apart, hands locked behind her. She watched ironically as the shivering engineer came up to get warm.

"What's the problem?"

"Ma'am?"

"You and Jamie don't seem to be very happy about things."

"Jamie told me this morning he wanted to take a trip out west—and leave immediately. I told him I would. Now I'm afraid he's delaying the trip on my account. Don't you think the trip would be a good idea?" He watched her closely.

She shrugged. "Oh, I don't know. How could a delay of a few weeks matter one way or another? Perhaps it would be better to wait at least until everyone knows what he and she really wants to do. Right now I can't help but detect a certain precipitousness in the air. I don't think it's a bad idea, once decisions are made, to live with them for a while, to see if perhaps they can be lived with."

As he watched, she set her jaw askew, made her eyes fine, and moved her chin to and fro in the web of her thumb. It was a gesture that reminded him strangely of his own father. Suddenly a thrill of recognition and of a nameless sweet horribleness ran like electricity down his spine and out along the nerves between his ribs. *She was daring him.* Very well, said the fine-eyed expression and the quirky (yes, legal) eyebrow. Let us see what we shall see. Perhaps I know something about you, you don't know. Let us see if you can do what you say you want to do, stay here and get married in the regular woman's way of getting married, marry a wife and live a life. Let us see. I dare you.

But was he being flattered or condemned? Was she saying you know better than to stay here or you don't have what it takes to stay? He cocked an eye at her and opened his mouth to say something, but at that moment Kitty plucked at his sleeve. "Let's go, Tiger."

"What?"

"I have a couple of calls to make. You want to come along?"

"Sure."

There had occurred between the people in the room, in the very air itself, a falling upward of things and into queer new place, like the patterns of a kaleidoscope. But it was his own Kitty who had been most mysteriously transformed. Her cheek was flushed and she swung her shoulders in her school blouse like a secretary sitting between three desks. She bustled. No longer was she the solitary girl on the park bench, as inward and watchful as he, who might wander with him through old green Louisiana, perch on the back step of the camper of an evening with the same shared sense of singularity of time and the excellence of place. No, she was Miss Katherine Gibbs Vaught and the next thing he knew she'd have her picture in the *Commercial Appeal.*

"Where're we going?" he asked her, trying to keep up as she sailed through the pantry.

"I am to deliver you to someone who wishes a word with you."

The next thing he knew, he was sitting in Kitty's tiny Sprite, his knees about his ears as they went roaring up and over the mountain and down into the city.

"What is this place?" he asked when they stopped in an acre or so of brand-new automobiles.

"The shop, crazy. Poppy wants to talk to you!"

He sat blinking around him, hands on his knees. The "shop" was Mr. Vaught's Confederate Chevrolet agency, the second largest in the world. Dozens of salesmen in Reb-colonel hats and red walking canes threaded their way between handsome Biscaynes and sporty Corvettes. By contrast with their jaunty headgear and the automobiles, which were as bright as tropical birds, the faces of the salesmen seemed heavy and anxious.

"Come on," cried Kitty, already on her way.

They found Mr. Vaught in a vast showroom holding another acre of Chevrolets. He was standing in a fenced-off desk area talking to Mr. Ciocchio, his sales manager. Kitty introduced him and vanished.

"You see this sapsucker," said Mr. Vaught to Mr. Ciocchio, taking the engineer by the armpit.

"Yes sir," said the other, responding with a cordial but wary look. The sales manager was a big Lombard of an Italian with a fine head of thick curly hair. In his Reb-colonel hat he looked like Garibaldi.

"Do you know what he can do?"

"No sir."

"He can hit a golf ball over three hundred yards and he is

studying a book by the name of *The Theory of Large Numbers.*
What do you think of a fellow like that?"

"That's all right." Mr. Ciocchio smiled and nodded as
cordially as ever. The engineer noticed that his eyes did not
converge but looked at him, one past each ear.

"He is evermore smart."

The engineer nodded grimly. This old fellow, his employer,
he had long since learned, had a good working blade of malice.
Was this not in fact his secret: that he had it in for everybody?

"Sir," he said, politely disengaging himself from Mr. Vaught's
master grip. "Kitty said you wished to see me. As a matter of
fact, I wanted to see you earlier. Jamie said he wanted to take
a trip out west. I told him I would take him if it met with your
approval."

Mr. Ciocchio, seeing his chance, vanished as quickly as Kitty
had.

"But now, it seems, plans have been changed. Jamie tells me
he wishes to postpone the trip. I might add too that I asked
Kitty to marry me. This seems as good a time as any to inform
you of my intentions and to ask your approval. I am here, however, at your request. At least, that is my understanding."

"Well now," said the old man, turning away and looking
back, eyeing him with his sliest gleam. Aha! At least he knows
I'm taking none of his guff, the engineer thought. "Billy boy,"
he said in a different voice and hobbled over to the rail with a
brand-new limp—oh, what a rogue he was. "Take a look at this
place. Do you want to know what's wrong with it?"

"Yes sir."

"Do you see those fellows out there?" He nodded to a half
dozen colonels weaving fretfully through the field of cars.

"Yes sir."

"I'll tell you a funny damn thing. Now there's not a thing in
the world wrong with those fellows except for one thing. They
want to sell. They know everything in the book about selling.
But there is one thing they can't do. They can't close."

"Close?"

"Close out. They can't get a man in here where those fellows
are." He pointed to more colonels sitting at desks in the fenced-
off area. "That's where we sign them up. But they can't get
them in here. They stand out there and talk and everybody is

nice and agreeable as can be. And the man says all right, thanks a lot, I'll be back. And he's gone. Now you know, it's a funny thing but that is something you can't teach a fellow—when the time has come to close. We need a coordinator."

"Sir?"

"We need a liaison man to cruise the floor, watch all the pots, see which one is coming to a boil. Do you understand me?"

"Yes sir," said the engineer gloomily.

"I'm going to tell you the plain truth, Billy," said the old man in a tone of absolute sincerity. "You can't hire a good man for love or money. I'd pay twenty thousand a year for just an ordinary good man."

"Yes sir."

"I can't understand it."

"What's that, sir?"

"What makes those fellows so mis'able? Look at them. They are the most mis'able bunch of folks I ever saw."

"You mean they're unhappy?"

"Look at them."

They were. "What makes them miserable?"

"You figure *that* out and I'll pay you twenty-five."

"Yes sir," said the engineer absently; he had caught sight of Kitty waiting for him in her Sprite.

"Listen son," said the old man, drawing him close again. "I'm going to tell you the truth. I don't know what the hell is going on out there with those women and Jamie and all. Whatever yall want to do is all right with me. And I'm tickled to death to hear about you and Kitty. More than delighted. I know that you and I understand each other and that I'm more than happy to have you with us here any time you feel like it."

"Yes sir," said the engineer glumly.

By evening the engineer felt as uncommonly bad as he had felt good when he had set out for the university early in the morning of the same day. His knee leapt. Once he thought he heard the horrid ravening particles which used to sing in the pale sky over New York and Jersey. To make matters worse, everyone else in the pantry felt better than ever. It was the night before the Tennessee game. There was a grace and a dispensation in the air, an excitement and hope about the game on the morrow and a putting away of the old sad unaccomplished past. Tomorrow our own lads, the good smiling easy youths one met on the campus paths, but on the gridiron a ferocious black-helmeted wrecking crew, collide with the noble old single-wing of Tennessee. A big game is more than a game. It allows the kindling of hope and the expectation of great deeds. One liked to drink his drink the night before and muse over it: what will happen?

Ordinarily he too, the engineer, liked nothing better than the penultimate joys of a football weekend. But tonight he was badly unsettled. The two brothers, Jamie and Sutter, had been deep in talk at the blue bar for a good half hour. And Rita had Kitty off in the bay, Rita speaking earnestly with her new level-browed legal expression, Kitty blossoming by the minute: a lovely flushed bride. Every few seconds her eyes sought him out and sent him secret shy Mary Nestor signals. Now it was she who was sending the signals and he who was stove up and cranky. Only once had she spoken to him and then to whisper: "It may be possible to swing a sweetheart ceremony with the Chi O's as maids. I'm working on it." "Eh? What's that," cocking his good ear and holding down his knee. But she was off again before he had a chance to discover what she meant. It left him uneasy.

Something else disturbed him. Son Thigpen had brought over a carload of classmates from the university. Son, as morose as he was, and devoted exclusively to his Thunderbird and the fraternity (not the brothers themselves but the idea, Hellenism, as he called it), had nevertheless the knack of attracting large numbers of friends, lively youths and maids who liked him despite his sallowness and glumness. Now, having delivered this goodly company, he stood apart and fiddled with his Thunderbird keys. His guests were Deltans, from the engineer's country, though he did not know them. But he knew their sort and it made him uneasy to see how little he was like them, how easy they were in their ways and how solitary and Yankeefied he was—though they seemed to take him immediately as one of them and easy too. The young men were Sewanee Episcopal types, good soft-spoken hard-drinking graceful youths, gentle with women and very much themselves with themselves, set,

that is, for the next fifty years in the actuality of themselves
and their own good names. They knew what they were, how
things were and how things should be. As for the engineer, he
didn't know. I'm from the Delta too, thought he, sticking his
hand down through his pocket, and I'm Episcopal; why ain't
I like them, easy and actual? Oh, to be like Rooney Lee. The
girls were just as familiar to him, though he'd never met them
either. Lovely little golden partridges they were, in fall field
colors, green-feathered and pollen-dusted. Their voices were
like low music and their upturned faces were like flowers. They
were no different at all from the lovely little bitty steel-hearted
women who sat at the end of the cotton rows and held the
South together when their men came staggering home from
Virginia all beaten up and knocked out of the war, who sat in
their rocking chairs and made everybody do right; they were
enough to scare you to death. But he for his Kitty, a little
heavy-footed, yes, and with a tendency to shoulder a bit like
a Wellesley girl and not absolutely certain of her own sex, a
changeling (she was flushed and high-colored now just because
she had found out what she was—a bride). For example, Kitty,
who had worked at it for ten years, was still a bad dancer, where
every last one of these Delta partridges was certain to be light
and air in your arms.

They were talking about politics and the Negro, who was
now rumored to be headed for the campus this weekend. "Do
yall know the difference between a nigger and an ape?" said
Lamar Thigpen, embracing all three Deltans. They're good
chaps, though, thought the engineer distractedly, and spying
Mr. Vaught circling the walls, thought of something he wanted
to ask him and took out after him, pushing his kneecap in with
each step like a polio victim. They're good chaps and so very
much at one with themselves and with the dear world around
them as bright and sure as paradise. The game was tomorrow
and they were happy about that; they knew what they wanted
and who they hated. Oh, why ain't I like them, thought the
poor engineer, who was by no means a liberal—never in fact
giving such matters a single thought—but who rather was so
mystified by white and black alike that he could not allow himself the luxury of hatred. Oh, but they were lordly in theirs, he

noticed, as he hobbled along. Then forgetting what he wanted to ask Mr. Vaught, he fetched up abruptly and took his pulse. "I'm not at all well," he said to himself.

"What's the matter," asked Sutter, who had been watching him from his kitchen chair at the blue bar. Jamie, the engineer noticed, had left.

"I don't feel well. Where's Jamie?"

"He went to bed."

"I wanted to ask him what his plans were."

"Don't worry about him. He's all right. What about you?"

"I think my nervous condition is worse. I feel my memory slipping."

"What was that book you were reading earlier?"

"Freeman's *R. E. Lee*."

"Are you still strongly affected by the Civil War?"

"Not as strongly as I used to be."

"How strongly was that?"

"When I was at Princeton, I blew up a Union monument. It was only a plaque hidden in the weeds behind the chemistry building, presented by the class of 1885 in memory of those who made the supreme sacrifice to suppress the infamous rebellion, or something like that. It offended me. I synthesized a liter of trinitrotoluene in the chemistry lab and blew it up one Saturday afternoon. But no one ever knew what had been blown up. It seemed I was the only one who knew the monument was there. It was thought to be a Harvard prank. Later, in New York, whenever there was a plane crash, I would scan the passenger list to see how many Southerners had been killed."

"And yet you are not one of them." Sutter nodded toward the Thigpens.

"No."

"Are your nationalistic feelings strongest before the onset of your amnesia?"

"Perhaps they are," said the engineer, gazing at himself in the buzzing blue light of the mirror. "But that's not what I'm interested in."

Sutter gazed at him. "What are you interested in?"

"I—" the engineer shrugged and fell silent.

"What is it?"

"Why do they feel so good," he nodded toward the Deltans, "and I feel so bad?"

Sutter eyed him. "The question is whether they feel as good as you think, and if they do, then the question is whether it is necessarily worse to feel bad than good under the circumstances."

"That doesn't mean anything to me," said the engineer irritably.

"One morning," said Sutter, "I got a call from a lady who said that her husband was having a nervous breakdown. I knew the fellow. As a matter of fact, they lived two doors down. He was a Deke from Vanderbilt, president of Fairfield Coke and a very good fellow, cheerful and healthy and open-handed. It was nine o'clock in the morning, so I walked over from here. His wife let me in. There he stands in the living room dressed for work in his Haspel suit, shaved, showered, and in the pink, in fact still holding his attaché case beside him. All in order except that he was screaming, his mouth forming a perfect O. His corgi was howling and his children were peeping out from behind the stereo. His wife asked me for an opinion. After quieting him down and having a word with him, I told her that his screaming was not necessarily a bad thing in itself, that in some cases a person is better off screaming than not screaming—except that he was frightening the children. I prescribed the terminal ward for him and in two weeks he was right as rain."

The engineer leaned a degree closer. "I understand that. Now what I want to know is this: do you mean that in the terminal ward he discovered only that he was not so bad off, or is there more to it than that?"

Sutter looked at him curiously but did not reply.

"Did you get in trouble with him too?"

Sutter shrugged. "It was a near thing. His wife, who was a psychiatrically oriented type, put him into analysis with an old-timey hard-assed Freudian—they're only to be found down here in the South now—and he went crazy. Of course I got the blame for not putting him into treatment earlier. But she didn't sue me."

The engineer nodded toward the Deltans. "What about them?"

"What about them?"

"Would you put them in the terminal ward?"

"They're not screaming."

"Should they be screaming?"

"I should not presume to say. I only say that if they were screaming, I could have helped them once. I cannot do even that now. I am a pathologist."

The engineer frowned. He felt a stirring of anger. There was something unpleasantly ironic about Sutter's wry rapid way of talking. It was easy to imagine him ten years from now haunting a barroom somewhere and pattering on like this to any stranger. He began to understand why others made a detour around him, so to speak, and let him alone.

12.

He couldn't sleep. As he lay at attention listening to the frolic in John Houghton's room below, he began to kid a little and not recollect exactly where he was, like a boy who wakes in a strange bed. In the next bed Jamie breathed regularly. By three o'clock in the morning he was worse off than at any time since Eisenhower was President when he had worked three months for a florist in Cincinnati, assaulted by the tremendous *déjà vus* of hot green growing things.

At last he went out to the landing and, seeing a light under Sutter's door, knocked. Sutter answered immediately. He was sitting in the wagonwheel chair, dressed in the same clothes, feet flat on the floor, arms lying symmetrically on the rests. There was no drink or book beside him.

At last Sutter turned his head. "What can I do for you?" The naked ceiling bulb cast his eye sockets into bluish shadow. The engineer wondered if Sutter had taken a drug.

"I have reason to believe I am going into a fugue," said the engineer matter-of-factly. He turned up the collar of his pajamas. It was cold in here. "I thought you might be able to help me."

"Jimmy is in there dying. Don't you think I should be more concerned with helping him?"

"Yes, but I am going to live, and according to you that is harder."

CHAPTER FOUR 409

Sutter didn't smile. "Why do you ask me?"

"I don't know."

"What do you want me to do?"

"Tell me what you know."

"Why don't you get married and live happily ever afterwards?"

"Why was that man screaming that you told me about? You never did say."

"I didn't ask him."

"But you knew why."

Sutter shrugged.

"Was it a psychological condition?" asked the engineer, cocking his good ear.

"A psychological condition," Sutter repeated slowly.

"*What was wrong with him, Dr. Vaught?*" The pale engineer seemed to lean forward a good ten degrees, like the clowns whose shoes are nailed to the floor.

Sutter got up slowly, scratching his hair vigorously with both hands.

"Come over here."

Sutter led him to the card table, which had been cleared of dirty swabs but which still smelled of fruity Hoppe's gun oil. He fetched two chrome dinette chairs and set them on opposite sides of the table.

"Sit down. Now. I think you should go to sleep."

"All right."

"Give me your hand." Sutter took his hand in the cross-palm grip of Indian wrestling. "Look at me."

"All right."

"Does it embarrass you to hold hands with a man and look at him?"

"Yes." Sutter's hand felt as dry and tendinous as broomstraw.

"Count to thirty with me. When we finish counting, you will then be able to do what I tell you."

"All right."

When they had finished counting, Sutter said: "You say you believe I know something about you. Now you will also do what I tell you."

"All right."

"When you leave this room, you will go to your room and sleep soundly for nine hours. Do you understand?"

"Yes."

"Now when you do get up tomorrow, something is going to happen. As a consequence, you are going to be in a better position to decide what you want to do."

"All right."

"For the next few days you may have a difficult time. Now I shall not tell you what to do, but I will tell you now that you will be free to act. Do you understand me?"

"Yes."

"If you find yourself in too tight a spot, that is, in a situation where it is difficult to live from one minute to the next, come and see me and I'll help you. I may not be here, but you can find me. Do you understand?"

"Yes."

"Very well. Good night." Sutter yawned, pushed back his chair, and began to scratch his head with both hands.

"Good night."

In his cold bed, the engineer curled up like a child and fell at once into a deep and dreamless sleep.

13.

He awoke to a cold diamond-bright morning. Jamie's bed was empty. When he crossed the courtyard, the Thigpens were leaving for the game. Lamar gave John Houghton a drink, which he drained off in one gulp, little finger stuck out. In return, John Houghton did a buck-and-wing, swooping down with tremendous swoops and fetching up light as a feather, clapping his hands not quite together but scuffing the horny parts past each other. The engineer, standing pale and blinking in the sunlight, was afraid Lamar was going to say "Get hot!" or something similar, but he didn't. In fact, as the little caravan got underway and the three servants stood waving farewell on the back steps, Lugurtha fluttering her apron, Lamar shook his head fondly. "There's nothing like the old-timey ways!" he said. The Vaught retainers seemed to remind Lamar of an earlier, more gracious time, even though the purple castle didn't look much like an antebellum mansion and the golf links even less like a cotton plantation.

Kitty was eating batter cakes in the pantry. She eyed him somewhat nervously, he thought. But when later he kissed her mouth, not quite cleared of Br'er Rabbit syrup, she kissed him back with her new-found conjugal passion, though a bit absent-mindedly.

"Rita wants to see you," she told him as she led him through the dark dining room. "Something has happened."

"Where's Jamie?"

"I'm afraid that's what it's about."

"Come over here a minute," he said, trying to pull her behind a screen of iridescent butterfly wings. He felt like a sleepy husband.

"Later, later," said Kitty absently. For the first time he saw that the girl was badly upset.

As they entered Rita's tower bedroom, Kitty, he noticed, became all at once pudding-faced and hangdog. She looked like Jamie. She hung back like a fourteen-year-old summoned to the principal's office. Her noble matutinal curves seemed to turn to baby fat.

Rita, dressed in a heavy silk kimono, lay propped on a large bed strewn with magazines, cigarettes, eyeglasses, and opened mail. She was reading a book, which she set face down on the bed. From force of habit and by way of getting at someone, he set his head over to see the title. It was *The Art of Loving*. The engineer experienced a vague disappointment. He too had read the book and, though he had felt very good during the reading, it had not the slightest effect on his life.

Getting quickly out of bed and holding an unlit cigarette to her lip, Rita strode back and forth between them. So formidable was it, this way she had of setting the side of her face into a single ominous furrow (something was up all right), that he forgot all about the book.

"Well, they've done it up brown this time," she said at last, stopping at the window and rubbing her chin in the web of her thumb. "Or rather *he* has."

"Who?" asked the engineer.

"Sutter," she said, turning to face him. Kitty stood beside

him as flat-footed and button-eyed as Betty Jo Jones in Ithaca Junior High. "Sutter has left and taken Jamie with him," said Rita quietly.

"Where, Ree?" Kitty cried, but somewhat rhetorically, her eyes in her eyebrows. The surprise was for his benefit.

Rita shrugged.

"I have an idea where they might be headed," said the engineer.

Rita rolled her eyes. "Then for pity's sake tell us."

"Jamie was determined to go either out west or to Val's."

"Then I suggest that you jump in your little truck without further ado and go get him."

"What I can't understand," said the engineer absently, putting his fist to his forehead as if to cudgel his poor wits, "is why Dr. Vaught left when he did. He told me— Well, I had no idea he was planning to make a change."

"It seems a change was made for him," said Rita dryly.

He became aware that Kitty was woolgathering. Something had happened and she knew about it.

"What change is that?" he asked.

"Sutter has been discharged from the hospital staff." Removing her glasses, she thrust them into the deep pocket of her kimono sleeve. Her pale rough face looked naked and serious and justified, like a surgeon who comes out of the operating room and removes his mask. "It was understood that if he left, he would not be prosecuted."

"Prosecuted for what?" Up to his usual tricks, the engineer took her import not from the words she said but from the signals. That the import was serious indeed was to be judged from her offhandedness, the license she allowed herself in small things. She lit a cigarette and with a serious sort of free-and-easiness cupped it inward to her palm like a Marine and hunkered over an imaginary campfire between the three of them.

"What were they going to prosecute him for?" asked the engineer again. Within himself he was fighting against the voluptuousness of bad news. Would the time ever come when bad was bad and good good and a man was himself and knew straight up which was which?

"Sutter," said Rita, warming her hands at the invisible

embers and stamping her feet softly, "persuaded a ward nurse to leave her patients, some of whom were desperately ill, and accompany him to an unoccupied room, which I believe is called the terminal room. There they were discovered in bed by the night supervisor, and surrounded by pictures of a certain sort. Wynne Magahee called me last night—he's chief of medicine. He told me, he said: 'Look, we wouldn't care less what Sutter does with or to the nurses on his own time, but hell, Rita, when it comes to leaving sick people—and to make matters worse, somebody on the ward found out about it and is suing the hospital.' I had to tell Wynne, 'Wynne it is not for you to make explanations to us but rather for us—'"

Beside him, Kitty had gone as lumpish and cheeky as a chipmunk. "They were *not* desperately ill, Ree," she said wearily as if it were an old argument. "It was a chronic ward."

"Very well, they were not desperately ill," said Rita, eyeing the engineer ironically.

Kitty's lower lip trembled. Poor Kitty, it remained to her, one of the last, to be afflicted. "Poor Sutter," she whispered, shaking her head. "But why in the world did he—"

"However unfortunate the situation might be," said Rita grimly, "Sutter's being discovered was not purely and simply a misfortune, that is to say, bad luck. As it happens, Sutter set the time for his rendezvous a few minutes before the night supervisor made her rounds."

"Do you mean Sutter wanted to get caught, Ree?" cried Kitty.

"There are needs, my dear," said Rita dryly, "which take precedence over this or that value system. I suspect, moreover, that our friend here knows a good deal more about the situation than we do."

But though Kitty turned to him, he felt fretful and sore and would not answer. Anyhow he didn't know what Rita was talking about. Instead he asked her: "When did this happen?"

"Thursday night."

"Then when I spoke to him last night, he already knew that he had been discharged?"

"Yes. And he also knew that he and Jamie were leaving this morning."

"But he told me I could find him if—" The engineer broke off and fell silent. Presently he asked: "Do Mr. and Mrs. Vaught know?"

"Yes."

"What did they say?"

"Poppy threw up his hands over his head, you know, and rushed out of the room. Dolly took to the bed."

He was silent.

"I had supposed that your responsibilities as his tutor companion might include a reasonable concern for his life. The last time he went off with Sutter he was nearly killed."

The hearty thrust of her malice made him want to grin. He thought of his aunts. Malice was familiar ground. It was like finding oneself amid the furniture of one's living room. He looked at his watch. "I can leave in ten minutes. If he's in Tyree County, I'll be back tomorrow. If they've gone to New Mexico, and I think they have, it'll take longer. I'll look in Santa Fe and Albuquerque. Kitty?" He waited in the doorway without looking at her.

When she did not move, he looked up. The girl was stricken. She was wringing the fingers of one hand. He had never seen anyone wring his hands.

"Are you coming with me?"

"I can't," she said, open-mouthed and soundless like a fourteen-year-old talking past the teacher.

"Why not?"

"Bill," said Rita, brow gone all quirky, "you can't ask this child to travel with you. Suppose you do have to go to New Mexico."

"We can be married in Louisiana tomorrow. My uncle lives there and can arrange it."

She shook her head fondly. "Listen, kids. Here's what you do. Bill, go find Jamie. Then stay with him or bring him home. In either case I guarantee this girl will come a-running as fast as her little legs will carry her. Kitty, I assure you he is coming back. Look at her, Lance Corporal."

But he looked at Rita instead.

She was daring him! If you leave, said the fine gray eyes, you know that I know that you won't come back. I dare you!

And Kitty: by some queer transformation the girl, his lordly lioness of a Kitty, had been turned into a twittering bird-girl with little bitty legs.

"Kitty, I have to go to my room for a minute. Then I'm leaving."

"*Wait.*" Soundless as a little dove, she flew up to him, and still could not speak.

"What?" he said, smiling.

Rita linked arms with them and drew them together. "If it is of any interest to you, dearie," she said to Kitty, "my money is on him. Lance Corporal?"

"What?" said the puzzled engineer.

"Idiot," said Rita, giving him a dig in the ribs with her silken elbow. "The poor girl is wondering whether you are coming back."

Then, registering as he did a fine glint of appraisal in Rita's eye, he saw the two of them, Kitty and Billy, as doll-like figures tumbling before the magic wand of an enchantress. Nor, and here was the strangest part of it, did he really mind.

A note was clipped with a bobby pin to the ignition switch of the Trav-L-Aire.

Meet me in one hour. Go out 81—
Did she mean north or south 81?
Turn right near top of ridge—
Lord, which ridge and which side of it?
Watch for For Sale *sign and Mickle mailbox—*
Before or after turning off?
Pull up out of sight of the highway and wait for me. K.
Who was she afraid of?

There was time then for a stop at Sutter's apartment. For two reasons: to make sure Sutter had in fact left (for Rita was a liar), and if he had, maybe to find a clue or sign (Sutter might just leave one for him).

Straight up and over the mountain and down through deserted streets—what day was this, a holiday? No, the game! Everybody had gone to the game or in to their TV's, and the streets and cars and the occasional loiterer had the look of *not* going to the game—to the Kenilworth Arms, an ancient blackened stucco battlement, relic of the baronial years of the twenties. He went up in an elevator with a ruby glass in the door and down a narrow tile corridor hollow as a gutter. The silence and emptiness of Sutter's apartment met him at the open door, which had also been fitted with a ruby window. The apartment had a sunken living room and looked like Thelma Todd's apartment in the Hollywood Hills of 1931. There was open on the floor an old black friable Gladstone bag with a freshly ruptured handle and in the bathroom a green can of Mennen's talc. In a bureau drawer he found enclosed in a steno pad an Esso map of the Southeastern United States. A light penciled line ran southwest to an X marked in the badlands just above the Gulf Coast, turned northwest, and ran off the map past Shreveport. He cranked open a casement window. The faint uproar of the city below filled the tiled room like a sea shell. He sat on the steps of the balcony foyer and looked down into the littered well of the living room. It had an unmistakably sexual flavor. The orange candle flame bulbs, the ruby glass, the very sconces on the walls were somehow emblems of sex but of a lapsed archaic monkey-business sort of sex. Here, he reckoned, one used to have parties with flappers and make whoopee. Why did Sutter pick such a place to live in, with its echoes of ancient spectral orgies? He was not, after all, of that generation. The engineer opened the steno pad. It seemed to be a casebook of some sort, with an autopsy protocol here and there and much scribbling in between.

Sutter wrote:

A w.d. and n. white male, circa 49.

Eyes, ears, nose, mouth: neg. (upper dentures).
Skin: 12 cm. contusion rt. occipital region
Pleura: Neg.
Lungs: Neg.
Pericardium: 10 cc. pink frothy fluid
Heart: infarcted anterior wall right ventricle; coronary artery: moderate narrowing, occasional plaque; recent occlusion anterior descending branch, right c.a.
Abdomen: neg. except moderate cirrhosis of L. with texture fibrous to slice; central areas of lobules visible macroscopically.

Police report: subject found rolled in room above Mamie's on 16th St. behind old L & N depot. Traced to Jeff Davis hotel. Here from Little Rock on opticians' convention. Traced from hotel to men's smoker in warehouse (girl performer plus film, neither on opticians' schedule), thence to Mamie's, thence to room upstairs, wherein slugged or rolled; but head injury not cause of death. Mamie off hook.

Lewdness = sole concrete metaphysic of layman in age of science = sacrament of the dispossessed. Things, persons, relations emptied out, not by theory but by lay reading of theory. There remains only relation of skin to skin and hand under dress. Thus layman now believes that entire spectrum of relations between persons (e.g., a man and woman who seem to be connected by old complexus of relations, fondness, fidelity, and the like, understanding, the comic, etc.) is based on "real" substratum of genital sex. The latter is "real," the former is not. (Cf. Whitehead's displacement of the Real)

Scientist not himself pornographer in the practice of his science, but the price of the beauty and the elegance of the method of science = the dispossession of layman. Lewdness = climate of the anteroom of science. Pornography stands in a mutual relation to science and Christianity and is reinforced by both.

Science, which (in layman's view) dissolves concrete things and relations, leaves intact touch of skin to skin. Relation of genital sexuality reinforced twice: once because it is touch, therefore physical, therefore "real"; again because it corresponds with theoretical (i.e., sexual) substrata of all other relations. Therefore genital sexuality = twice "real."

Christianity is still viable enough to underwrite the naughtiness which is essential to pornography (e.g., the pornography of the East is desultory and perfunctory).

The perfect pornographer = a man who lives both in anteroom of science (not in research laboratory) and who also lives in twilight of Christianity, e.g., a technician. The perfect pornographer = lapsed Christian Southerner (who as such retains the memory not merely of Christianity but of a region immersed in place and time) who presently lives in Berkeley or Ann Arbor, which are not true places but sites of abstract activity which could take place anywhere else, a map coordinate; who is perhaps employed as psychological tester or opinion sampler or computer programmer or other parascientific pursuit. Midwestern housewives, look out! Hand-under-dress of a total stranger is in the service both of the theoretical "real" and the physical "real."

I do not deny, Val, that a revival of your sacramental system is an alternative to lewdness (the only other alternative is the forgetting of the old sacrament), for lewdness itself is a kind of sacrament (devilish, if you like). The difference is that my sacrament is operational and yours is not.

The so-called sexual revolution is not, as advertised, a liberation of sexual behavior but rather its reversal. In former days, even under Victoria, sexual intercourse was the natural end and culmination of heterosexual relations. Now one begins with genital overtures instead of a handshake, then waits to see what will turn up (e.g., we might become friends later). Like dogs greeting each other nose to tail and tail to nose.

But I am not a pornographer, Val, like the optician, now a corpse, i.e., an ostensible liver of a "decent" life, a family man, who fancies conventions with smokers and call girls. I accept the current genital condition of all human relations and try to go beyond it. I may sniff like a dog but then I try to be human rather than masquerade as human and sniff like a dog. I am a sincere, humble, and even moral pornographer. I cultivate pornography in order to set it at naught.

Women, of course, are the natural pornographers today, because they are not only dispossessed by science of the complexus of human relations (all but the orgasm) but are also kept idle in their suburban houses with nothing to do but read pseudo-science articles in the Reader's Digest and dirty novels (one being the natural preamble of the other). U.S. culture is the strangest in history, a society of decent generous sex-ridden men and women who leave each other to their lusts, the men off to the city and conventions, abandoning their wives to the suburbs, which are the very home and habitation of lewd dreams. A dirty deal for women, if you ask me.

Don't be too hard on Rita. She is peeved, not perverted, (The major discovery of my practice: that there are probably no such entities as "schizophrenia" and "homosexuality," conceived as Platonic categories, but only peevishness, revenge, spitefulness, dishonesty, fear, loneliness, lust, and despair—which is not to say we don't need psychiatrists. You people don't seem to be doing too well, you know.)

The only difference between me and you is that you think that purity and life can only come from eating the body and drinking the blood of Christ. I don't know where it comes from.

The engineer rose unsteadily from the floor of the sunken living room, where he had been reading Sutter's casebook, and went into the bathroom. As he urinated he gazed down at the maroon toilet seat and the black tile floor. Once, he remembered, his father had visited the home of a rich Syrian to draw up a will. "They had black sheets on the bed," he confided to his son with a regular cackle. And in truth there seemed even now something Levantine and fancy about tampering with the decent white of bathrooms and bedsheets.

He folded the Esso map into the casebook and went down to the camper. Reading Sutter's casebook had a strange effect upon him. His mind, instead of occupying itself with such subjects as "American women" and "science" and "sexuality," turned with relief to the most practical matters. He drove into a filling station and while the motor was being serviced studied the Esso map, calculating almost instantly and clairvoyantly the distance to Jackson, New Orleans, and Shreveport. When the attendant brought over the dip stick, exhibiting its coating of good green Uniflow, slightly low, he savored the hot sane

smell of the oil and felt in his own muscles the spring of the
long sliver of steel.

14.

Sure enough, just over the saddle of the farthest ridge the last
wrinkle of the Applachians, which overlooked a raw new golf
links and a snowfield of marble-chip rooftops of five hundred
G.E. Gold Medallion Homes, he found the mailbox and driveway. Up the rocky slope swarmed the sturdy G.M.C., shouldering like a badger, and plunged into a thicket of rhododendron.
Thick meaty leaves swept along the aluminum hull of his ship
and slapped shut behind him. He took a turn in the woods
but there was no sign of Kitty. While he waited for her, he
lay in Jamie's bunk and again studied the map he had found
in Sutter's apartment. Sutter's casebook disturbed him; there
were no clues here. But the map, with its intersecting lines and
tiny airplanes and crossed daggers marking battlefields, was
reassuring. It told him where to go.

The towhees whistled in the rhododendron and presently
the branches thrashed. There stood Kitty in the doorway with
light and air going round her arm.

"Oh, I'm glad to see you," he cried, leaping up and grabbing
her, hardly able to believe his good fortune. "You are here!"
And here she was, big as life, smelling of dry goods and brand-
new chemical blue jeans. They were not quite right, the jeans,
too new and too tight in the thigh and too neatly rolled at the
cuff, like a Macy's girl bound for the Catskills, but it only made
his heart leap all the more. He laughed and embraced her, held
her charms in his arms.

"Whoa now," she cried, flushing.

"Eh?"

"Get the game on the radio."

"Game?"

"Tennessee is ahead."

"Right," he said and turned the game on but instead of
listening told her: "Now. I can tell you that I feel very good
about the future. I see now that while I was living with your
family I was trying too hard to adapt myself to my environment
and to score on interpersonal relationships."

"Darling," said Kitty, once again her old rough-and-ready and good-looking Wellesley self.

"Anyhow, here's what we'll do," said he, holding her on his lap and patting her. "We'll strike out for Ithaca and pick up my money, then we'll cross the mighty Mississippi and see my uncle, who lives near the town of Shut Off, Louisiana, transact another small piece of business, get married, and head west, locate Jamie in either Rita's house in Tesuque or Sutter's ranch near Santa Fe, and thereafter live in Albuquerque or perhaps Sante Fe, park the camper in an arroyo or dry wash and attend the University of New Mexico since there is bound to be such a place, and make ourselves available to Jamie in whatever way he likes. We might live at Sutter's old ranch and in the evenings sit, the three of us, and watch the little yellow birds fly down from the mountains. I don't mind telling you that I set great store by this move, for which I thank Jamie, and that I am happier than I can tell you to see that you are with me."

Kitty, however, seemed abstracted and was trying to hear the radio. But no, she changed her mind, and grabbing him, took him by her warm heavy hand and yanked him out of the Trav-L-Aire. The next thing he knew, she was showing him a house and grounds in the bustling style of a real-estate agent. "Myra gave me the key. Do you know she told me she would let me work for her! She makes piles of money." It was a regular rockhouse cantilevered out over the ridge and into the treetops. She unlocked the door.

"What is this place?" he asked, wringing out his ear. The red and blue lines of the Esso map were still glimmering on his retina and he was in no mood for houses. But they were already inside and she was showing him the waxed paving stones and the fireplace and the view of the doleful foothills and the snow-field of G. E. Gold Medallion homes.

"This is the Mickle place. Myra has it listed for thirty-seven five but she'll let it go to the family for thirty-two. Isn't it lovely? Look at the stone of this fireplace."

"Thirty-seven five," said the engineer vaguely.

"Thirty-seven thousand five hundred dollars. In the summer you can't see that subdivision at all."

She took him outside to a ferny dell and a plashy little brook with a rustic bridge. When she walked with him, she slipped her hand behind him and inside his belt in a friendly conjugal style, as one sees the old folks do, John Anderson my jo, John.

"Do you mean you want to come back here and live?" he asked her at last, looking around at the ferny Episcopal woods and the doleful view and thinking of feeding the chickadees for the next forty years.

"Not before we find Jamie," she cried. "Come on." She yanked him toward the Trav-L-Aire. "Wait till I get my hands on that sorry Jamie." But again she changed her mind. "Oh. I forgot to show you the foc'sle, as Cap'n Mickle used to call it, which is built into the cliff under the 'bridge.' It is soundproof and womanproof, even the doorknob pulls out, the very place for an old growl bear like you—you can pull the hole in after you for all I care."

"No, thanks. Let's be on our way," said the engineer, eyeing the Episcopal ivy which seemed to be twining itself around his ankles.

"Old Cap'n Andy," said Kitty, shaking her head fondly. "He was a bit eccentric but a dear. He used to stroll up and down the bridge, as he called it, with his telescope under his arm and peer out at the horizon and cry 'Ahoy there!'"

"Is that right," said the engineer gloomily, already seeing himself as a crusty but lovable eccentric who spied through his telescope at the buzzards and crows which circled above this doleful plain. "Come on," he said, now also eyeing her covertly. She was fond and ferocious and indulgent. It was as if they had been married five years. Ahoy there. He had to get out of here. But there would be the devil's own time, he saw clearly, in hemming her up in a dry wash in New Mexico. She was house-minded.

But he did get her in the camper at last and down they roared, down the last slope of the Appalachians, which was tilted into the autumn sun, down through the sourwood and the three-fingered sassafras.

"How much money do you have?" she asked.

He shrugged. "Somewhere around fifteen thousand—after I transact my business." A thought cheered him up. "Not nearly enough to buy Cap'n Andy's house, as good a bargain as it is."

"Will you take care of this for me?"

The Esso map was open on the dash. Squarely across old

Arkansas it fell, the check, or cheque it looked more like, machine-printed, certified, punched, computed, red-inked, hatched up rough as a cheese grater. The engineer nearly ran off the mountain. A little army of red Gothic noughts marched clean to Oklahoma, leaning into the wind. It looked familiar. Had he seen it before?

"You have seen it before. Remember?"

"Yes," said the engineer. "What's it for?"

"My dowry, crazy. Turn it over."

He pulled up at a G.E. model home—what's wrong with one of these—they were much more cheerful than that buzzard's roost up on the ridge, and read aloud the lavender script: "For deposit only, to the account of Williston Bibb Barrett."

"Do you know how I got the Bibb?"

"No."

"I got Jamie to peek in your wallet."

"What do you want me to do with it?"

"Keep it. Hand me your wallet. I'll put it in."

"All right."

"It's really insurance."

"What kind of insurance?"

"Against your running out on me. I know you wouldn't steal a girl's money. Would you?"

"No."

Already the carnivorous ivy was stealing down the mountainside. Quickly he put the G.M.C. in gear and sent the Trav-L-Aire roaring down the gloomy Piedmont.

"Do we go anywhere near school?"

"Yes."

"Could we stop and pick up my books?"

"All right. But why do you want your books?"

"We have a test in Comp Lit Wednesday."

"Wednesday."

A half hour later, as dusk fell in a particularly gloomy wood, she clapped her hand to her mouth. "Oh my Lord, we forgot about the game."

"Yes."

"Turn on the radio and see if you can get the score."

"All right."

15.

Traffic was heavy in both directions and it was night before they reached the campus. The engineer stopped the Trav-L-Aire under a street light and cocked an ear.

Something was wrong. Whether there was something wrong with the town or inside his own head, he could not say. But beyond a doubt, a queer greenish light flickered over the tree-tops. There were flat popping noises, unchambered, not like a shotgun but two-syllabled, ba-*rop*, ba-*rop*. In the next block an old car stopped and three men got out carrying shotguns and dove straight into the woods. They were not students. They looked like the men who hang around service stations in south Jackson.

"I wonder if Tennessee won," said Kitty. "Why are you stopping here?"

"I think I'll leave the camper here." His old British wariness woke in him. He backed the camper onto a vacant lot behind a billboard.

They separated at a fork in the campus walk, she bound for the Chi Omega house to fetch her books, he for his *Theory of Large Numbers*. "I'll meet you here in ten minutes," he told her uneasily.

Dark figures raced past him on the paths. From somewhere close at hand came the sound of running feet, the heavy direful sound of a grown man running as hard as he can. A girl, a total stranger, appeared from nowhere and taking him by the coat sleeves thrust her face within inches of his. "Hi," he said.

"He's here," she sobbed and jerked at his clothes like a ten-year-old: "Kill him! Kill him! Kill him!" she sobbed, jerking now at his lapels.

"Who?" he asked, looking around.

Searching his face and not finding what she wanted, she actually cast him from her and flew on her way.

"Who?" he asked again, but she was gone. Coming to a lamp, he took out his plastic Gulf Oil calendar card and held it up to see what day of the month it was. He had forgotten and it made him feel uneasy.

At the Confederate monument a group of students ran toward him in ragged single file. Then he saw why. They were carrying a long flagstaff. The flag was furled—he could not tell whether it was United States or Confederate. The youth in front was a sophomore named Bubba Joe Phillips. He was known as a "con," that is, one who knows how to make money from such campus goings-on as decorating the gym for dances. Ordinarily a smiling crinkled-haired youth, he strained forward, his eyes bulging and unseeing. He was beside himself, besotted, with either fear or fury, and did not see the engineer, though he almost ran into him.

"What yall say," said the engineer amiably and stepped nimbly to the side, thinking they meant to go past him and down the path whence he came. But when they came abreast of the Confederate monument they turned toward the lights and the noise. They cleared him easily but what he did not see and they did not care about was the dark flagstaff behind them, which as they turned swept out in a wider arc and yet which he nevertheless saw a split second before the brass butt caught him at the belt buckle. "Oof," he grunted, not hurt much and even smiling. He would have sat down but for the wire fencelet, which took him by the heel and whipped him backward. He was felled, levered over, and would have killed himself if his head had struck the corner of the monument base but it struck instead the slanting face of the old pocked Vermont marble and he was sent spinning into the soft earth under an arborvitae.

The dawn of discovery, the imminent sense of coming at last upon those secrets closest to one and therefore most inaccessible, broke over him. "But why is it—?" he asked aloud, already knocked cold but raising a forefinger nevertheless, then lay down under the dark shrubbery.

Chapter Five

HE AWOKE shortly after dawn but not under the arborvitae. Though he never found out how he came to be here—perhaps he had awakened earlier, remembered more, crawled over, and passed out again—here he was, lying in the cab of the Trav-L-Aire, asleep on his back like a truck driver. When he sat up, his head hurt. But he started the truck and crept out into the street and, without noticing that he did so, took a certain route through the back of town. The streets were littered with broken glass. One automobile had been set afire and burned to a cinder. He drove past an army truck and a police car and straight out into the countryside.

Presently he heard a siren. Down the highway roared the camper careening like a runaway Conestoga, then topping a rise and spying a picnic area, swerved into it and plumb through it and dove into a copse of wax myrtle. Presently a patrol car passed, then another, sirens lapsing to a growl.

He waited in the fragrant cave of myrtles until the sun came up and made a dapple on the good gray hood of the G.M.C. What is this place? Where am I going?—he asked himself, touching his bruised head, and, as soon as he asked himself, did not know. Noticing a map and notebook on the seat beside him, he opened the latter.

I am the only sincere American.

Where I disagree with you, Val, is in you people's emphasis on sin. I do not deny, as do many of my colleagues, that sin exists. But what I see is not sinfulness but paltriness. Paltriness is the disease. This, moreover, is not a mistake you are obliged to make. You could just as easily hold out for life and having it more abundantly as hold out against sin. Your tactics are bad. Lewdness is sinful but it derives in this case not from a rebellion against God (Can you imagine such a thing nowadays—I mean, who cares?)—but from paltriness.

Americans are not devils but they are becoming as lewd as devils. As for me, I elect lewdness over paltriness. Americans practice it with their Christianity and are paltry with both. Where your treasure is, there is your heart and there's theirs, *zwischen die Beinen.*

Americans are the most Christian of all people and also the lewdest. I am no match for them! Do you know why it is that the Russians, who are atheists, are sexually modest whereas Americans, the most Christian of peoples, are also the lewdest?

Main Street, U.S.A. = a million-dollar segregated church on one corner, a drugstore with dirty magazines on the other, a lewd movie on the third, and on the fourth a B-girl bar with condom dispensers in the gents' room. Delay-your-climax cream. Even our official decency is a lewd sort of decency.

Watch a soap opera on TV where everyone is decent (and also sad, you will notice, as sad as lewdness is sad; I am the only American who is both lewd and merry). Beyond any question, these people who sit and talk so sorrowfully and decently are fumbling with each other under the table. There is no other alternative for them.

Soap opera is overtly decent and covertly lewd. The American theater is overtly lewd and covertly homosexual. I am overtly heterosexual and overtly lewd. I am therefore the only sincere American.

Last night Lamar Thigpen called me un-American. That is a lie. I am more American than he is because I elect the lewdness which he practices covertly. I unite in myself the new American lewdness with the old American cheerfulness. All I lack is Christianity. If I were a Christian as well as being lewd and cheerful, I'd be the new Johnny Appleseed.

My God, what is all this stuff, thought the poor bemused shivering engineer and with a sob flung out of the cab and began running up and down and swinging his arms to keep warm when a great pain took him at the back of his head so suddenly that he almost fainted. He sat on a picnic bench and felt his skull. It had a sticky lump the size of a hamburger. "Oh, where is this place?" he groaned aloud, hoping that if he heard a question he might answer it. "Where am I bound and what is my name?" When no answer came, he reached for his wallet. But even before his hand arrived, he had felt the ominous airiness and thinness of fabric of his back pocket. It was empty and the flap unbuttoned. Jumping up, he began to slap his pockets as quickly as possible (to surprise the wallet ere it could lose itself). He searched the camper. Beyond a doubt the wallet was gone, lost or stolen. But there was $34.32 in his forward pocket. A textbook in the cabin disclosed what he seemed to know as soon as he saw it, his name.

Spying through the wax myrtles a big-shield US 87, he consulted his map. At least I am on course, he thought, noticing the penciled line. But hold! Something tugged at him, as unfinished and urgent a piece of business as leaving the bathtub running. There was something that had to be attended to RIGHT NOW. But what? He knocked his poor throbbing head on the steering wheel, but it was no use. The thing was too much in the front of his mind to be remembered, too close to be taken hold of, like the last wrenching moment of a dream.

No wonder he was confused. He had forgotten Kitty and left her at the university and now remembered nothing more than that he had forgotten. There was only the nameless tug pulling him back. But he had also forgotten what Sutter told him the night before—*come find me*—and recorded only the huge tug forward in the opposite direction. He shrugged: well, I'm not going back because I've been there.

There was nothing to do but go about his business. Taking care to remove the ignition key, he locked himself in the camper and lit the hot-water heater. After a shower in the tiny slot of the stall, he shaved carefully, took three aspirins for his headache, and two spansules for his dislocation. Then donning his Macy's slacks and Brooks Brothers shirt whose collar ran up into his hair, making him all of a piece, so to speak, and restoring his old Princeton puissance (for strangely he had forgotten the Vaughts and even the Y.M.C.A. and remembered

Princeton), he cooked and ate a great bowl of minute grits and a quarter pound of slab bacon.

When he started up the camper and backed out of the myrtle thicket and went his way down US 87, the G.M.C. faltered and looked back of its shoulder like a horse leaving the barn. "Not that way!—that's where I came from," said the rider angrily and kicked the beast in the flank.

For several hours he cruised south on 87, choosing this route as a consequence of the penciled line on the Esso map. He did not dare examine the contents of his pockets, for fear he would not recognize what he found there, or for fear rather that, confronted with positive proof of himself, he still would not know and would lose the tenuous connection he had. He was like a man shot in the bowels: he didn't dare look down.

It was a frosty morn. The old corn shucks hung like frozen rags. A killdeer went crying down a freshly turned row, its chevroned wing elbowing along the greasy disced-up gobbets of earth. The smell of it, the rimy mucous cold in his nostrils, and the blast of engine-warm truck air at his feet put him in mind of something—of hunting! of snot drying in your nose and the hot protein reek of fresh-killed quail.

In the late morning he slowed and, keeping a finger on the map, turned off the highway onto a scraped gravel road which ran for miles through a sparse woodland of post oaks and spindly pines infected with tumors. Once he passed through a town which had a narrow courthouse and an old boarded-up hotel on the square. There were still wrecks of rocking chairs on the gallery. Either I have been here before, he thought, perhaps with my father while he was trying a case, or else it was he with his father and he told me about it.

Beyond the town he stopped at the foot of a hill. A tall blackish building with fluted iron columns stood on top. He looked for a sign, but there was only an old tin arrow pointing north to: *Chillicothe Business College, Chillicothe, Ohio, 892 miles.* Halfway up the hill he stopped again and made out the letters on the pediment: *Phillips Academy.* Why, I know this place, he thought. Either I went to school here or my father did. It was one of the old-style country academies which had thirty or forty pupils and two or three teachers. Dr. so-and-so who taught Greek and Colonel so-and-so who taught military science. But perhaps it is only a *déjà vu*. But there is a way of finding out, considered the canny engineer. If he had really been here before, he should be able to recall something and then verify his recollection. Whereas a *déjà vu* only confers the semblance of memory. He put his forehead on the steering wheel and pondered. It seemed that there was a concrete slab, a court of sorts, behind the school.

But if there ever had been, there was not now. When he drove up the hill, he was disappointed to find instead a raw settlement of surplus army buildings, Quonset huts, and one geodesic dome, stretching out into the piney woods, each building fed by a silver butane sphere. It looked like a lunar installation. There was no one around, but at last he found a woman dressed in black, feeding entrails to a hawk in a chicken coop. She looked familiar. He eyed her, wondering whether he knew her.

"Aren't you—" he asked.

"Valentine Vaught," she said, continuing to feed the hawk. "How are you, Bill?"

"Not too good," he said, watching to see how she saw him. From his breast pocket he took Sutter's casebook and made a note of her name.

"Is that Sutter's?" she asked, but made no move to take it.

"I suppose it is," he said warily, "do you want it?"

"I've heard it all before, dear," she said dryly. "When he gets drunk he writes me letters. We always argued. I've stopped."

Tell me what is tugging at me, he wanted to say, but asked instead: "Isn't this old Phillips Academy?"

"Yes, it used to be. Did you go to school here?"

"No, it was my father. Or perhaps grandfather. Wasn't there at one time a tennis court over there or maybe an outdoor basketball court?"

"Not that I know of. I have a message for you."

"What?"

"Sutter and Jamie were here. They said I was to tell you they were headed for Santa Fe."

She seemed to expect him. Had he been on his way here? He took out the map. Who had marked the route?

"Sutter and Jamie," he repeated. Again it came over him, the terrific claim upon him, the tug of memory so strong that he broke into a sweat. "I've got to go," he muttered.

"To find Jamie?" she asked.

"I suppose," he said uneasily. But instead of leaving, he watched her. It came to him for the second time that he didn't like her, particularly her absorption with the hawk. It was a chicken hawk with an old rusty shoulder and a black nostril. She attended to the hawk with a buzzing antic manner which irritated him. It scandalized him slightly, like the Pope making a fuss over a canary. He was afraid she might call the hawk by some such name as Saint Blaise.

"This is a wonderful work you're doing here," he said, remembering a little more, then added, for what reason God alone knew: "I've always liked Catholics."

"I wish I could say the same," she said, feeding a kidney to the hawk.

The task, he mused, was to give shape and substance to time itself. Time was turned on and running between them like the spools of a tape recorder. Was that not the nature of his amnesia: that all at once the little ongoing fillers of time, the throat-clearings and chair-scrapings and word-mumblings, stopped and the tape ran silent?

"At any rate, your bishop is a very courageous man," he heard himself say even more recklessly because he didn't know her bishop from Adam.

"I think he is chicken-hearted."

"Well, I'll be going," he said, flushing angrily. Really, he had no use for this prankish perverse manner of hers. As suggestible as ever, he began to feel it take possession of him too, a buzzing glassy-eyed inwardness.

"Why are you writing everything down?" she asked, looking at him for the first time.

He frowned. "I may have told you before that I have a nervous condition which affects my memory. Anyhow I only wrote down your name." And suddenly he remembered her religious name as well: Johnette Mary Vianney: remembered it precisely because it was difficult and barbarous. Taking note of her costume again, he reckoned she must be some sort of off-brand nun, perhaps not yet certified by the higher-ups. That's why she did not like her bishop!—he hadn't given her her license or whatever.

"If you catch up with Jamie," she said, speaking again to the hawk, "give him a good shaking."

"Why?"

"He's feeling sorry for himself and has taken to reading Kahlil Gibran, a bad sign even in healthy people. Did you give it to him—I know Sutter wouldn't."

"Who? No." *If he needed a good shaking, Sister, you should have given it to him.* But he said: "Do you like your work here?" Without knowing that he did so, he was going through his pockets. Oh my, I'm sure I had something of great value.

"We are very poor here," she said, watching him with interest.

He blushed. "I'm sorry to say that my wallet has been lost or stolen. I—" he began, and felt his sore occiput. "Otherwise I'd like very much to make a small contribution to your work."

"Say a prayer for us," she said, he thought, absently.

"Yes. Where are they now?"

"Who? Oh. The pupils don't come on weekends."

"Of course not," he said heartily. He wondered whether it was Saturday or Sunday. Something else came back to him. "I've heard the poverty here in Tyree County is abject."

"It's not that so much," she said carelessly.

"Not that? What then?"

"The children are dumb. They can't speak."

"Ah, they are mentally retarded—pellagra, no doubt."

"No, I mean they're dumb, mute. Children eleven and twelve can't speak. It took me six months to find out why. They're brought up in silence. Nobody at home speaks. They don't know thirty words. They don't know words like pencil or hawk or wallet."

"What a rewarding experience it must be to teach them."

"Yes, very," she said, and not ironically, he thought.

A complex system of scoring social debts kept him from leaving. Since he couldn't give her money, ransom himself, he had to pay her out by listening to her, since, goofy as he was, he knew two things not many people know. He knew how to listen and he knew how to get at that most secret and aggrieved enterprise upon which almost everyone is embarked. He'd give her the use of his radar.

"Is that why you came here?" he asked her. "Because of the children, I mean."

"Why I came here," she said vaguely. "No, that wasn't the reason. Somebody asked me."

"Who asked you?" he bent upon the hawk the same smiling unseeing gaze as she.

"A woman in the library at Columbia."

"A woman in the library at Columbia asked you to come down here?"

"Not directly. That is not what she asked me at first."

"What did she ask you at first?"

"I was writing a paper on Pareto. This nun and I shared the same cubicle in the stacks. She was doing her doctorate on John Dewey, whom she admired greatly—you know how they've taken up with the very ones they despised a few years ago."

"No, I don't," said the engineer. His head was beginning to hurt again.

She paid no attention. "I was aware that she was eyeing me and that she had her hooks out. The strange thing was that I was not in the least surprised when she did speak." Again she lapsed.

"What did she say?" asked the engineer as gently as Dr. Gamow.

"She said, what's the matter with you? I said, what do you mean what's the matter with me? She said, you look half dead." She shook her head and fed the hawk an intricate packet of viscera.

"Yes," said the engineer after a long minute.

"I said yes, I am half dead. She said why? I said I don't know. She said how would you like to be alive. I said I'd like that. She said all right, come with me. That was it."

"That was what," asked the engineer, frowning. "What happened?"

"I went with her to her mother house, a hideous red brick building in Paterson, New Jersey."

"Then what?"

"That was it. I received instruction, made a general confession, was shriven, baptized, confirmed, and made my first

vows, all in the space of six weeks. They thought I was crazy.
The Bishop of Newark required that I get a statement from my
doctor that there was no insanity in the family. When all I'd
done was take them at their word. They were mostly third-generation Irish from places like Bridgeport and Worcester, Mass.
That's what they would say: I'm from Worcester, Mass.—never
Massachusetts. They called me Alabam. You know." Again she
fell silent.

"How did you get down here?"

"They asked me how I would like to work with Sister Clare
in their mission down in 'Bama. I think they wanted to get rid
of me. I kept telling them that I believed it all, the whole business. But try as I might, I couldn't remember the five proofs
of God's existence or the difference between a substance and
an accident. I flunked out. They didn't know what to do with
me, so they figured six months of Sister Clare down in 'Bama
would cure me. Sister Clare is a harridan, mean as hell."

"Is she here?"

"No. She had a nervous breakdown, she instead of me, as
they had expected. She was sent to our rest home in Topeka.
What they didn't know was that I am mean as hell too. I out-
lasted her. That's what I don't understand, you know: that I
believe the whole business: God, the Jews, Christ, the Church,
grace, and the forgiveness of sins—and that I'm meaner than
ever. Christ is my lord and I love him but I'm a good hater and
you know what he said about that. I still hope my enemies fry
in hell. What to do about that? Will God forgive me?"

"I don't know. Why did you stay?"

"That was a fluke too." She draped two feet of gut over
the perch and the hawk cocked his eye. The engineer thought
about the falcon in Central Park: I could see him better at one
mile than this creature face to face. Jesus, my telescope: is it
still in the camper? "I think I stayed not so much out of charity
as from fascination with a linguistic phenomenon—that was
my field, you know. It has to do with the children's dumbness.
When they do suddenly break into the world of language, it
is something to see. They are like Adam on the First Day.
What's that? they ask me. That's a hawk, I tell them, and they
believe me. I think I recognized myself in them. They were
not alive and then they are and so they'll believe you. Their

eyes fairly pop out at the Baltimore catechism (imagine). I tell them that God made them to be happy and that if they love one another and keep the commandments and receive the Sacrament, they'll be happy now and forever. They believe me. I'm not sure anybody else does now. I have more influence than the Pope. Of course I'm not even supposed to be here, since I haven't taken final vows. But they haven't sent for me."

"That certainly is interesting," said the engineer, who was now leaving, actually setting a foot toward the camper. He had done his duty and was ready to be on his way. He had a fix on her at last. She struck him as an enthusiast of a certain sort who becomes wry as a countermeasure to her own outlandishness, like a collector of 1928 Model-T radiator caps who exhibits his trophies with a wry, rueful deprecation of their very oddness. He understood this. And was it not also the case that her off-handedness was a tactic and that she had *her* hooks out for *him*? He didn't mind if she had, and was even prepared to put on a thoughtful expression, as much as to say: you do give me pause, Sister; that is something to think about. But he was ready to go.

He was not to escape so easily. Changing her manner completely, she became cordial and brisk and took him on the "ten-dollar tour" of her foundation. For some fifty minutes he was towed helplessly around the outbuildings scattered through the cancerous pines. More than ever, it reminded him of a lunar installation, with silvery globes supplying nourishment to each building, a place of crude and makeshift beginnings on some blasted planet. Later there remained in his poor addled memory only a blurred impression of Seven-Up machines, plastic crucifixes, and worn, gnawed-at woodwork such as is found in old gymnasiums. Life indeed, thought he. Another hour in this gloomy cancerous wood and I'd be laid out stiff as a corpse, feet sticking up.

But she would not let him go, and when for the second or third time she led him past the wooden privies and the last time opened the door of one so that he might catch a whiff of the acuteness of the need, he got the idea. With trembling fingers he thrust hand into pocket and brought forth a disorderly clutch of bills, leaving him, as he discovered later, $1.36 in silver. "A small donation for your building fund," he murmured, blushing.

"I'll pray for you," she said absently. "Will you pray for me to receive sufficient grace in order not to hate the guts of some people, however much they deserve it?"

"Certainly," said the engineer heartily, who would have consented to anything.

She took the money with only perfunctory gratitude and, slipping it skillfully into a black-leather pouch she wore at her belt, lapsed instantly into her old smiling thrumming Papal inwardness, wherein she dispensed herself so that she might take note of God's creatures, small objects, and such. She went back to the hawk and he left.

2.

Down flew the Trav-L-Aire into the setting sun, down and out of the last of the ancient and impoverished South of red hills and Cardui signs and God-is-Love crosses. Down through humpy sugarloaves and loess cliffs sliced through like pound-cake. Dead trees shrouded in kudzu vines reared up like old women. Down and out at last and onto the vast prodigal plain of the Delta, stretching away misty and fecund into the October haze. The land hummed and simmered in its own richness. Picking was still going on, great $25,000 McCormicks and Farmalls browsing up and down the cotton rows. Bugs zoomed and splashed amber against the windshield; the Trav-L-Aire pushed like a boat through the heavy air and the rich protein smells, now the sweet ferment of alfalfa, now the smell of cot-tonseed meal rich as ham in the kitchen. There had been the sense ever since leaving New York and never quite realized until now of tarrying in upland places and along intermediate slopes and way stations (My Lord, where had he stopped? Where had he spent the last month? He cudgeled his brain) and now at last of coming sock down to the ultimate alluvial floor, the black teeming Ur-plain. He stopped the Trav-L-Aire and got out. Buzzards circled, leaning into the heavy mothering air, three, four tiers of buzzards riding round a mile-high chimney of air. A shrike, the Negro's ghost bird, sat on a telephone wire and looked at him through its black mask. It was a heedless prodigal land, the ditches rank and befouled, weeds growing through the junk: old Maytags, Coke machines, and a Hudson

Super Six pushed off into a turnrow and sprouting a crop all its own. But across the ditches and over the turnrows—here they got down to business—stretched the furrows of sifted mealy earth clean as a Japanese garden but forty miles long and going away, straight as a ruler, into the smoky distance. The cotton leaves were a dusky gray-green, as dusky as new money. Cotton wagons were on the road and the gins were humming. The little towns were squalid and rich. From the storefronts, tin roofs sagged across the sidewalk to the muddy Cadillacs. Across the road from a decaying mustard-colored I.C. depot stretched a line of great glittering harvesters and pickers parked in echelon like a squadron of Sherman tanks.

Straight across the Delta he flew and down into the tongue of the Yazoo plain to Ithaca, so named by a Virginian who admired Pericles more than Abraham and who had had his fill of the Bethels and the Shilohs of the Scotch-Irish. Yonder in the haze rose the brownish back of the Chickasaw Bluffs, and just beyond, the old wormy concrete towers of the Vicksburg battlefield.

When he stopped at Roscoe's Servicenter, Roscoe spoke as if he had never been away.

"What you say there, Will?—" holding nozzle to spout and all the while taking in the Trav-L-Aire, acknowledging it with a quirk of his mouth but not willing to make a fuss over it or even to speak of it directly.

"All right. What you say, Roscoe."

"You been camping or going?"

"Camping? Oh, I'm going."

"Do you know those niggers over there?"

"Who? No."

"They seem to know you."

Beyond the pumps sat a bottle-green Chevrolet, a stout old Bel Aire two-door, round as a turtle and filled with Negroes and what appeared to be a couple of Syrians. Sure enough the driver, a stately bun-headed preacher-type Negro seemed to be making signs and grimaces at him. The courteous engineer, the last man on earth to inflict a snub, nodded and smiled in turn even though he didn't know them from Adam. Or did he? Ah, the dread tug of the past not quite remembered! Then, even as he nodded, an aching vista opened in his head and he remembered—not them but Kitty! The green Chevrolet sent his mind spinning back but there stood Kitty like a lion in the path. God in heaven, he groaned, I've left Kitty. Dear Jesus, he said, and began to slap his pocket again. The check for $100,000—I've lost it. Yet even as he groaned he was giving a final cheery nod and now he gunned the Trav-L-Aire out into traffic. Oh, my lovely strapping wealthy Chi O 'Bama bride, he thought, and gave his leaping knee a few hard socks. I must call her immediately.

But after half a dozen blocks he noticed that the green Chevrolet had drawn abreast of him on the left, the passengers on the front seat pressing back to clear a view for the driver, who was motioning frantically. "Barrett!" The Chevrolet began to yaw like a tender on the high seas. He still can't drive, thought the engineer, even though he did not yet know that he knew the pseudo-Negro. At the same moment he caught sight of a commotion in front of the new courthouse. Pickets bearing signs were marching on one side of the street and a crowd watched from the other. Troopers directed traffic with electric batons. Somewhere to his rear, a siren growled. Having had enough of ruckuses and police sirens and especially of this particular carload of importuning Negroes, he swung the Trav-L-Aire without slowing into a lane between Club 85 and Krystal Hamburgers. The cabin swayed dangerously, dishpans clattering into the sink. The lane was a segment of the abandoned river road which turned at this very point into the lee of the levee. Not hesitating a second, the sturdy G.M.C. swarmed straight up and over the levee out onto the batture and dove into a towhead of willows.

No one followed.

He waited in the cab until the sun set in Louisiana. When it grew dark, he walked to the highway with his firkin, emerging by dead reckoning at a haunted Piggly Wiggly and a new-old Rexall, new ten years ago and persisting stupendously in his absence.

My lovely Kitty coed, he groaned even as he stocked up on grits and buttermilk and bacon, I must call her now. The thought of her living under the same roof with Son Thigpen, a glum horny key-twiddler, set him off in a spasm of jealousy. Yet it fell out, strange to say, that when he did find himself in a phone booth, he discovered he had spent all but nine cents! Oh damnable stupidity and fiendish bad luck, but what are you going to do? I'll call her in the morning after I've been to the bank, where I will stop payment on the check, he told himself, and returned to the camper in a better humor than one might suppose.

After supper, as he lay in the balcony bunk listening to patriotic and religious programs, he heard a noise from the river, a mild sustained roar like a surf. He found a flashlight in the locker and went outside. Twenty feet away the willows were nodding and thrashing against the current. Flotsam and brown foam were caught in the leaves. He knelt and examined the thicker trunks. The water was high but falling. The sky was clear. He returned to his bunk and listened to Profit Research, a program which gave money tips for changing times, and read from Sutter's notebook:

Moderately obese young colored female, circa 13
Skin: vaccination l. thigh; stellate keloid scar under chin.
Head: massive cmpd depressed fracture right parietal and
    right zygomatic arch.
Brain: frank blood in subdural space, extensive laceration
    right cortex; brick shards.
Thorax: comminuted cmpd fractures, right ribs 1 through
    8; frank blood in pleural space; extensive lacerations
    RML, RLL, brick shards. Heart: neg.
Abdomen: neg. Gen.: neg.
Cops report subject discovered in basement toilet of
    Emmanuel Baptist Church following explosion. Church
    tower fell on her.

But never mind the South.

It is you who concerns me. You are wrong and you deceive yourself in a more serious way. Do you know what you have managed to do? You have cancelled yourself. I can understand what you did in the beginning. You opted for the Scandalous Thing, the Wrinkle in Time, the Jew-Christ-Church business, God's alleged intervention in history. You acted on it, left all and went away to sojourn among strangers. I can understand this even though I could never accept the propositions (1) that my salvation comes from the Jews, (2) that my salvation depends upon hearing news rather than figuring it out, (3) that I must spend eternity with Southern Baptists. But I understand what you did and even rejoiced in the scandal of it, for I do not in the least mind scandalizing the transcending scientific assholes of Berkeley and Cambridge and the artistic assholes of Taos and La Jolla.

But do you realize what you did then? You reversed your dialectic and cancelled yourself. Instead of having the courage of your scandal-giving, you began to speak of the glories of science, the beauty of art, and the dear lovely world around us! Worst of all, you even embraced, Jesus this is what tore it, the Southern businessman! The Southern businessman is the new Adam, you say, smart as a Yankee but a Christian withal and having the tragical sense, etc., etc., etc.—when the truth of it is, you were pleased because you talked the local Coca-Cola distributor into giving you a new gym.

But what you don't know is that you are cancelled. Suppose you did reconcile them all, the whites and the niggers, Yankees and the K.K.K., scientists and Christians, where does that leave you and your Scandalous Thing? Why, cancelled out! Because it doesn't mean anything any more, God and religion and all the rest. It doesn't even mean anything to your fellow Christians. And you know this: that is why you are where you are, because it means something to your little Tyree dummies (and ten years from now it won't even mean anything to them: either they'll be Muslims and hate your guts or they'll be middle-class and buggered like everybody else).

The reason I am more religious than you and in fact the most religious person I know: because, like you, I turned my back on the bastards and went into the desert, but unlike you I didn't come sucking around them later.

There is something you don't know. They are going to win without you. They are going to remake the world and go into space and they couldn't care less whether you and God approve and sprinkle holy water on them. They'll even let you sprinkle holy water on them and they'll even like you because they'll know it makes no difference any more. All you will succeed in doing is cancelling yourself. At least have the courage of your revolt.

Sutter's notebook had the effect of loosening his synapses, like a bar turning slowly in his brain. Feeling not unpleasantly dislocated, he turned off the light and went to sleep to the sound of the lashing willows and a Spanish-language broadcast to Cuban refugees from WWL in New Orleans.

3.

The next morning he walked the levee into Ithaca, curving into town under a great white sky. New grass, killed by the recent frost, had whitened and curled like wool. Grasshoppers started up at his feet and went stitching away. Below where the town was cradled in the long curving arm of the levee, the bumpy crowns of oaks, lobules upon lobules, were broken only by steeples and the courthouse cupola. There arose to him the fitful and compassed sound of human affairs, the civil morning sounds of tolerable enterprise, the slap of lumber, a back-door slam, the chunk of an engine, and the routine shouts of a work crew: ho; ho; *ho now!*

Here he used to walk with his father and speak of the galaxies and of the expanding universe and take pleasure in the insignificance of man in the great lonely universe. His father would recite "Dover Beach," setting his jaw askew and wagging his head like F.D.R.:

> *for the world which seems*
> *To lie before us like a land of dreams,*
> *So various, so beautiful, so new,*
> *Hath really neither joy, nor love, nor light,*
> *Nor certitude, nor peace, nor help for pain—*

or else speak of the grandfather and the days of great deeds: "And so he looked down at him where he was sitting in his barber chair and he said to him: 'I'm going to tell you one time, you son of a bitch, and that's all, so hear me well: If anything happens to Judge Hampton, I'm not asking any questions, I'm not calling the police, I'm coming to look for you, and when I find you I'm going to kill you.' Nothing happened to Judge Hampton."

Beyond the old brown roiled water, the bindings and lacings of water upon water, the Louisiana shore stretched misty and perfunctory. When he came abreast of the quarterboat of the U. S. Engineers, his knee began to leap and he sat down in the tall grass under a river beacon and had a little fit. It was not a convulsion, but his eyes twittered around under his eyeballs. He dreamed that old men sat in a circle around him, looking at him from the corners of their eyes.

"Who's that?" he cried, jumping to his feet and brushing off his Macy's Dacron. Someone had called to him. But there was no one and nothing but the white sky and the humpy lobuled oaks of the town.

He went down into Front Street, past the Syrian and Jewish dry goods and the Chinese grocery, and turned quickly into Market and came to the iron lion in front of the bank. It was a hollow lion with a hole between his shoulders which always smelled of pee.

Spicer CoCo and Ben Huger, two planters his own age, stood in line behind him at the teller's window and began to kid him in the peculiar reflected style of the deep Delta.

"Reckon he's going to get all his money out and go on back off up there?" said Spicer CoCo.

"I notice he got his box-back coat on. I think he be here *for a while*," said Ben Huger.

He had to grin and fool with them, fend them off, while he asked the teller about the check. "Doris," he said to the pretty plump brunette, remembering her before he could forget, "can I stop payment on a certified check?"

She gave him a form to fill in. "Hello, Will. It's good to see you."

"Just fine." He scratched his head. "No, ah— You see, it's not my check and it's not on this bank. It was a check endorsed to me. I—it was misplaced." He hoped he didn't have to tell the amount.

"Then have the payer make a stop-payment order," she said, gazing at him with an expression both lively and absent-minded. "How long ago did you lose it?"

"I don't remember—ah, two days."

"Same old Will."

"What?"

"You haven't changed a bit."

"I haven't?" he said, pleased to hear it. "I thought I was worse." I'll call Poppy then, he said to himself and fell to wondering: how strange that they seem to know me and that I never supposed they could have, and perhaps that was my mistake.

"You know why he taking his money out," said Spicer.

"No, why is that?" asked Ben.

The two were standing behind him, snapping their fingers and popping their knees back and forth inside their trousers. They were talking in a certain broad style which was used in Ithaca jokingly; it was something like Negro talk but not the same.

"He on his way to the game Saddy. You can tell he come into town to get his money—look, he done took off his regular walking shoes which he hid under a bridge and done put on his town slippers"—pointing down to the engineer's suède oxfords.

"That had slipped my notice," said Ben. "But look how he still th'ows his foot out like Cary Middlecoff, like he fixin' to hit a *long ball*."

"He come over here to draw his money out and make a bet on the game and take our money because he thinks we don't know they number one."

"What are you talking about," cried the engineer, laughing and shaking his head, all but overcome by an irritable sort of happiness—and all the while trying to tell Doris Mascagni about his savings account. "Yall are number one on the U.P." he told them, turning around nervously.

"What you say there, Will." They shook hands with him, still casting an eye about in the oblique Ithaca style.

What good fellows they were, he thought, as Doris counted out his money. Why did I ever go away? Ben Huger detained him and told a story about a man who bought a golf-playing gorilla. The gorilla had been taught to play golf by the smartest trainer in the world. This man who bought the gorilla was also a hard-luck gambler but for once he seemed to have hit on a sure thing. Because when he took the gorilla out to a driving range and handed him a driver and a basket of balls, each ball flew straight down the middle for five hundred yards. So he entered the gorilla in the Masters at Augusta. On the first tee, a par five hole, the gorilla followed Nicklaus and Palmer. He addressed his ball with assurance and drove the green four hundred and ninety yards away. Great day in the morning, thought the gambler, who was acting as the gorilla's caddy, I got it made this time for sure. Already he had plans for the P.G.A. and the the British Open after collecting his fifty thousand in first prize money. But when the threesome reached the green and the gambler handed the gorilla his putter to sink the one-footer, the gorilla took the same full, perfected swing and drove the ball another four hundred and ninety yards. Then—

Here's what I'll do, thought the engineer who was sweating profusely and was fairly beside himself with irritable delight. I'll come back here and farm Hampton, my grandfather's old place, long since reclaimed by the cockleburs, and live this same sweet life with these splendid fellows.

"You gon' be home for a while, Will?" they asked him.

"For a while," he said vaguely and left them, glad to escape this dread delight.

Hardly aware that he did so, he took Kemper Street, a narrow decrepit boulevard which ran as string to the bow of the river. It still had its dusty old crape myrtles and chinaberries and horse troughs and an occasional tile marker set in the sidewalk: *Travelers Bicycle Club 1903.* The street changed to a Negro district. The old frame houses gave way to concrete nightclubs and shotgun cottages, some of which were converted to tiny churches by tacking on two square towers and covering the whole with brick paper. He sat on a trough which was choked with dry leaves and still exhaled the faint sunny tart smell of summer, and studied the Esso map, peering closely at the Gulf Coast, New Orleans, Houston, and points west. It came over him suddenly that he didn't live anywhere and had no address. As he began to go through his pockets he spied a new outdoor phone in a yellow plastic shell—and remembered

Kitty. Lining up quarters and dimes on the steel shelf, he gazed down Kemper to the old city jail at the corner of Vincennes. Here on the top step stood his great-uncle the sheriff, or high sheriff, as the Negroes called him, on a summer night in 1928.

The telephone was ringing in the purple castle beside the golf links and under the rosy temple of Juno.

The sheriff put his hands in his back pockets so that the skirt of his coat cleared his pistol butt. "I respectfully ask yall to go on back to your homes and your families. There will be no violence here tonight because I'm going to kill the first sapsucker who puts his foot on that bottom step. Yall go on now. Go ahead on."

"Hello." It was David.

"Hello. David."

"Yes suh." He would be standing in the narrow hall between the pantry and the big front hall, the receiver held as loosely in his hand as if it had fallen into the crotch of a small tree.

"This is, ah, Will Barrett." It sounded strange because they didn't, the Negroes, know him by a name.

"Who? Yes *suh*! Mist' Billy!" David, feeling summoned, cast about for the right response—was it surprise? joy?—and hit instead on a keening bogus cheeriness, then, seeing it as such, lapsed into hilarity: "*Ts-ts-ts.*"

"Is Miss Kitty there?"

"No suh. She *been* gone."

"Where?" His heart sank. She and Rita had gone to Spain.

"School."

"Oh yes." Today was Monday. He reflected.

"Yes suh," mused David, politely giving shape and form to the silence. "I notice the little bitty Spite was gone when I got here. And I got here on time."

"Is anyone else there?"

"Nobody but Miss Rita."

"Never mind. Give Miss Kitty a message."

"Oh yes suh."

"Tell her I got hurt at the college, got hit in the head, and had a relapse. She'll understand. Tell her I've been sick but I feel better."

"Yes suh. I'll sho tell her. *Sick?*" David, aiming for the famous Negro sympathy, hit instead on a hooting incredulity.

David, David, thought the engineer, shaking his head, what is going to happen to you? You ain't white nor black nor nothing.

"I'm better now. Tell her I'll call her."

"Yes suh."

"Goodbye, David."

"Goodbye, Mist' Billy!" cried David, stifling his hilarity. He reached Mr. Vaught at Confederate Chevrolet.

"Billy boy!" cried the old fellow. "You still at school?"

"Sir? Well, no sir. I—"

"You all right, boy?"

"Yes sir. That is, I was hurt—"

"How bad is it down there now?"

"Down here?"

"How did you get out? They didn't want to let Kitty leave. I had to go get her myself last night. Why, they kept them down in the basement of the sorority house all night. Man, they got the army in there."

"Yes sir," said the engineer, understanding not a single word save only that some larger catastrophe had occurred and that in the commotion his own lapse had been set at nought, remitted.

"You sure you all right?"

"I was knocked out but I got away the next morning," said the engineer carefully. "Now I'm on my way to find—" He faltered.

"Jamie. Good."

"Yes. Jamie. Sir," he began again. This one thing he clearly perceived: the ruckus on the campus dispensed him and he might say what he pleased.

"Yes?"

"Sir, please listen carefully. Something has happened that I think you should know about and will wish to do something about."

"If you think so, I'll do it."

"Yes sir. You see, Kitty's check has been lost or stolen, check for one hundred thousand dollars."

"*What's that?*" Mr. Vaught's voice sounded as if he had crept into the receiver. All foolishness aside: this was money, Chevrolets.

The engineer had perceived that he could set forth any facts whatever, however outrageous, and that they would be attended to, acted upon and not held against him.

"My suggestion is that you stop payment, if it is possible."

"It is possible," said the old man, his voice pitched at perfect neutrality. The engineer could hear him riffling through the phone book as he looked up the bank's number.

"It was endorsed over to me, if that is any help."

"It was endorsed over to you," repeated the other as if he were taking it down. *Very well then, it is understood this time, what with one thing and another, that it is for you to tell me and for me to listen. This time.*

"I tried to reach Kitty but couldn't. Tell her that I'll call her."

"I'll tell her."

"Tell her I'll be back."

"You'll be back."

After he hung up, he sat gazing at the old jail and thinking about his kinsman, the high sheriff. Next to the phone booth was the Dew Drop Inn, a rounded corner of streaked concrete and glass brick, a place he knew well. It belonged to a Negro named Sweet Evening Breeze who was said to be effeminate. As he left and came opposite the open door, the sound came: *psssst!*—not four feet from his ear.

"Eh," he said, pausing and frowning. "Is that you, Breeze?" *"Barrett!"*

"What?" He turned, blinking. A pair of eyes gazed at him from the interior darkness.

"Come in, Barrett."

"Thank you all the same, but—"

Hands were laid on him and he was yanked inside. By the same motion a shutter of memory was tripped: it was not so much that he remembered as that, once shoved out of the wings and onto stage, he could then trot through his part perfectly well.

"Mr. Aiken," he said courteously, shaking hands with his old friend, the pseudo-Negro.

"Come in, come in, come in. Listen, I don't in the least blame you—" began the other.

"Please allow me to explain," said the engineer, blinking around at the watery darkness which smelled of sweet beer and hosed-down concrete—there were others present but he could not yet make them out. "The truth is that when I saw you yesterday I did not place you. As you may recall, I spoke to you last summer of my nervous condition and its accompanying symptom of amnesia. Then yesterday, or the day before, I received a blow on the head—"

"Listen," cried the pseudo-Negro. "Yes, right! You have no idea how glad I am to see you. Oh, boy. God knows you have to be careful!"

"No, you don't understand—"

"Don't worry about it," said the pseudo-Negro.

The engineer shrugged. "What you say, Breeze?" He caught sight of the proprietor, a chunky shark-skinned Negro who still wore a cap made of a Nylon stocking rolled and knotted.

"All right now," said Breeze, shaking hands but sucking his teeth, not quite looking at him. He could tell that Breeze remembered him but did not know what to make of his being here. Breeze knew him from the days when he, the engineer, used to cut through the alley behind the Dew Drop on his way to the country club to caddy for his father.

"Where's Mort?" asked the engineer, who began to accommodate to the gloom.

"Mort couldn't make it," said the pseudo-Negro in a voice heavy with grievance, and introduced him to his new friends. There were two men, a Negro and a white man, and a white woman. The men, he understood from the pseudo-Negro's buzzing excitement, were celebrities, and indeed even to the engineer, who did not keep up with current events, they looked familiar. The white man, who sat in a booth with a beautiful sullen untidy girl all black hair and white face and black sweater, was an actor. Though he was dressed like a tramp, he wore a stern haughty expression. A single baleful glance he shot at the engineer and did not look at him again and did not offer his hand at the introduction.

"This is the Merle you spoke of?" the actor asked the pseudo-Negro, indicating the engineer with a splendid one-millimeter theatrical inclination of his head.

"Merle?" repeated the puzzled engineer. "My name is not Merle." Though the rudeness and haughtiness of the actor made him angry at first, the engineer was soon absorbed in the other's mannerisms and his remarkable way of living from one moment to the next. This he accomplished by a certain inclination of his head and a hitching around of his shoulder while he fiddled with a swizzle stick, and a gravity of expression which was aware of itself as gravity. His lips fitted together in a rich conscious union. The sentient engineer, who had been having trouble with his expression today, now felt his own lips come together in a triumphant fit. Perhaps he should be an actor!

"You're here for the festival, the, ah, morality play," said the engineer to demonstrate his returning memory.

"Yes," said the pseudo-Negro. "Do you know the sheriff here?"

"Yes," said the engineer. They were standing at the bar under a ballroom globe which reflected watery specters of sunlight from the glass bricks. The pseudo-Negro introduced him to the other celebrity, a playwright, a slender pop-eyed Negro who was all but swallowed up by a Bulldog Drummond trenchcoat and who, unlike his white companion, greeted the engineer amiably and in fact regarded him with an intense curiosity. For once the engineer felt as powerful and white-hot a radar beam leveled at him as he leveled at others. This fellow was not one to be trifled with. He had done the impossible!—kept his ancient Negro radar intact and added to it a white edginess and res-tiveness. He fidgeted around and came on at you like a proper Yankee but unlike a Yankee had this great ear which he swung round at you. Already he was onto the engineer: that here too was another odd one, a Southerner who had crossed up his wires and was something betwixt and between. He drank his beer and looked at the engineer sideways. Where the actor was all self playing itself and triumphantly succeeding, coinciding with itself, the playwright was all eyes and ears and not in the least mindful of himself—if he had been, he wouldn't have had his trenchcoat collar turned up in great flaps around his cheeks. The Negro was preposterous-looking, but he didn't care if he was. The actor did care. As for the poor engineer, tuning in both, which was he, actor or playwright?

"You really did not remember him, did you?" the Negro asked the engineer.

"No, that's right."

"He's not conning you, Forney," the playwright told the pseudo-Negro.

"I knew that," cried the pseudo-Negro. "Barrett and I are old shipmates. Aren't we?"

"That's right."

"We went through the Philadelphia thing together, didn't we?"

"Yes." It seemed to the engineer that the pseudo-Negro said "Philadelphia" as if it were a trophy, one of a number of campaign ribbons, though to the best of the engineer's recollection the only campaign which had occurred was his getting hit on the nose by an irate housewife from Haddon Heights, New Jersey.

"Do you think you could prevail upon the local fuzz to do something for you?" the pseudo-Negro asked him.

"What?"

"Let Bugs out of jail."

"Bugs?"

"Bugs Flieger. They put him in jail last night after the festival, and our information is he's been beaten up. Did you know Mona over there is Bug's sister?"

"Bugs Flieger," mused the engineer.

The actor and the white girl looked at each other, the former popping his jaw muscles like Spencer Tracy.

"Tell—ah—Merle here," said the actor, hollowing out his throat, "that Bugs Flieger plays the guitar a little."

"Merle?" asked the mystified engineer, looking around at the others. "Is he talking to me? Why does he call me Merle?"

"You really never heard of Flieger, have you?" asked the playwright.

"No. I have been quite preoccupied lately. I never watch television," said the engineer.

"Television," said the girl. "Jesus Christ."

"What have you been preoccupied with?" the playwright asked him.

"I have recently returned to the South from New York where I felt quite dislocated as a consequence of a nervous condition," replied the engineer, who always told the truth. "Only to find upon my return that I was no less dislocated here."

"I haven't been well myself," said the playwright as amiably as ever and not in the least sarcastically. "I am a very shaky man."

"Could you speak to the sheriff?" the pseudo-Negro asked him.

"Sure."

Breeze brought more beer and they all sat in the round booth at the corner under the glass bricks.

"Baby, are you really from around here?" the playwright asked the engineer.

"Ask Breeze." The engineer scowled. Why couldn't these people call him by his name?

But when the playwright turned to Breeze the latter only nodded and shrugged. Breeze, the engineer perceived, was extremely nervous. His, the engineer's, presence, disconcerted him. He didn't know what footing to get on with the engineer, the old one, the old ironic Ithaca style: "Hey, Will, where you going?" "Going to caddy." "How come your daddy pays you five dollars a round?" "He don't pay no five dollars"—or the solemn fierce footing of the others. But finally Breeze said absently and to no one and from no footing at all: "This here's Will Barrett, Lawyer Barrett's boy. Lawyer Barrett help many a one." But it was more than that, the engineer then saw, something else was making Breeze nervous. He kept opening the door a crack and looking out. He was scared to death.

But the pseudo-Negro wanted to talk about more serious matters. He asked the others some interview-type questions about racial subjects, all the while snapping pictures (only the engineer noticed) from his tie-clasp camera.

"It's a moral issue," said the actor, breaking the swizzle stick between his fingers, breaking it the way actors break swizzle sticks and pencils. The pseudo-Negro explained that the actor had flown in from Hollywood with Mona his companion to assist in the present drive at great cost to himself, both financially and emotionally, the latter because he was embroiled in a distressing custody suit in the course of which his wife had broken into his bedroom and pulled Mona's hair.

"Of course it's a moral issue," said the playwright. Now the engineer remembered seeing one of his plays with Midge Auchincloss. It was about an artist who has gone stale, lost his creative powers, until he musters the courage to face the truth within himself, which is his love for his wife's younger brother.

He puts a merciful end to the joyless uncreative marriage in favor of a more meaningful relationship with his friend. The last scene shows the lovers standing in a window of the artist's Left Bank apartment looking up at the gleaming towers of Sacre-Coeur. "There has been a loss of the holy in the world," said the youth. "Yes, we must recover it," replies the artist. "It has fallen to us to recover the holy." "It has been a long time since I was at Mass," says the youth, looking at the church. "Let's have our own Mass," replies the artist as softly as Pelleas and, stretching forth a shy hand, touches the youth's golden hair.

Sweet Evening Breeze, the engineer noticed, was growing more nervous by the minute. His skin turned grayer and more sharklike and he had fallen into a complicated way of snapping his fingers. Once, after peering through the cracked door, he called the pseudo-Negro aside.

"Breeze says the fuzz is on its way over here," the pseudo-Negro told them gravely.

"How do you know?" the playwright asked Breeze.

"I know."

"How do they know we're here?"

"Ask Merle," said the actor.

"Don't be ridiculous," said the pseudo-Negro, frowning. "I pulled him in here, remember. Barrett's all right."

"The man done pass by here twice," said Breeze, rattling off a drumroll of fingersnaps. "The next time he's coming in."

"How do you know?" asked the pseudo-Negro with his lively reporter's eye.

"I knows, that's all."

"Wonderful," said the playwright. The playwright's joy, the engineer perceived, came from seeing life unfold in the same absurd dramatic way as a Broadway play—it was incredible that the one should be like the other after all.

"Bill," said the pseudo-Negro earnestly. "We've got to get Mona out of here. You know what will happen to her?"

The engineer reflected a moment. "Do you all want to leave town?"

"Yes. Our business here is finished except for Bugs."

"What about your Chevrolet?"

"They picked it up an hour ago."

"Why not get on a bus?"

"That's where they got Bugs, at the bus station."

"Here they come," said Breeze.

Sure enough, there was a hammering at the door. "Here's what you do," said the engineer suddenly. Upside down as always, he could think only when thinking was impossible. It was when thinking was expected of one that he couldn't think. "Take my camper. Here." He quickly drew a sketch of the highway and the old river road. "It's over the levee here. I'll talk to the police. Go out the back door. You drive," he said to Mona, handing her the key. The actor was watching him with a fine gray eye. "The others can ride in the back." The hammering became deafening. "Now if I don't meet you at the levee," shouted the engineer, "go to my uncle's in Louisiana. Cross the bridge at Vicksburg. Mr. Fannin Barrett of Shut Off. I'll meet you there." From his breast pocket he took out a sheaf of road maps, selected a Conoco state map, made an X, and wrote a name and gave it to Mona. "Who are they?" he asked Breeze, who stood rooted at the heaving door.

"That's Mist' Ross and Mist' Gover," said Breeze eagerly, as if he were already smoothing things over with the police.

"Do you know them, Merle?" asked the actor, with a new appraising glint in his eye.

"Yes."

"How are they?"

"Gover's all right."

"Open the door, Breeze." The voice came through the door.

"Yes suh."

"No, hold it—" began the engineer.

"The man said unlock it." It was too late. The doorway was first flooded by sunlight, then darkened by uniforms.

"What do you say, Beans. Ellis," said the engineer, coming toward them.

"Where's the poontang?" asked Beans Ross, a strong, tall, fat man with a handsome tanned face and green-tinted sunglasses such as highway police wear, though he was only a town deputy.

"This is Will Barrett, Beans," said the engineer, holding out his hand. "Mister Ed's boy."

"What," said Beans, shoving his glasses onto his forehead. He even took the other's hand and there was for a split second a chance of peace between them. "What the hell are you doing here?" Beans took from his pocket a small blackjack as soft and worn as skin.

"I'll explain, but meanwhile there is no reason to hit Breeze." He knew at once what Beans meant to do.

"All right, Breeze," said Beans in a routine voice, not looking at him.

Sweet Evening Breeze, knowing what was expected of him, doffed his stocking cap and presented the crown of his head. Hardly watching but with a quick outward flick of his wrist, Beans hit Breeze on the forehead with the blackjack. Breeze fell down.

"Goddamn it, Beans," said the engineer. "That's no way to act."

"You got something to say about it?"

"Yes."

"Where's the poontang?" asked Beans, and with a gesture at once fond and conspiratorial—enlisting him—and contemptuous, he leaned across and snapped his middle finger on the engineer's fly.

"Augh," grunted the engineer, bowing slightly and seeming to remember something. Had this happened to him as a boy, getting snapped on the fly? The humiliation was familiar.

"Don't do that, Beans," said Ellis Gover, coming between them and shaking his head. "This is a real good old boy."

By the time the engineer's nausea had cleared, Beans had caught sight of Mona in the booth. Without taking his eyes from her, he pulled Ellis close and began to whisper. The engineer had time to straighten himself and to brace his foot in the corner of the jamb and sill of the front door. For once in his life he had time and position and a good shot, and for once things became as clear as they used to be in the old honorable days. He hit Beans in the root of his neck as hard as he ever hit the sandbag in the West Side Y.M.C.A. Beans's cap and glasses flew off and he sat down on the floor. "Now listen here, Ellis," said the engineer immediately, turning to the tall, younger policeman. "Yall go ahead," he told the others casually, waving them over Beans's outstretched legs and out the front door. "Catch a Bluebird cab at the corner."

"Wait a minute," said Ellis, but he did not stop them.

"Don't worry about it, Ellis. They haven't done anything. They're leaving town and that's what you want."

"But, shit, man," said Ellis, who could not take his eyes from the fallen policeman. "You done hit Beans."

"I know, but look at Breeze," said the engineer by way of answer, and nodded to the Negro, who was laid out straight as a corpse. Standing next to Ellis, he took him by the elbow just as he used to touch him in a football huddle. Ellis was all-state halfback and the engineer, who was quarterback (not all-state), had called the plays in huddle. Ellis was a bit slow in catching the signals and the engineer used to squeeze him so, just above the elbow.

"Yeah, but hailfire, Will."

"Listen, Ellis," said the engineer, already moving. "You bring charges against me to clear yourself, do you understand? Tell Beans the others got in behind you. You got it?"

"Yeah, but—"

"Now give Beans a hand and tell him to come after me, O.K.?" He said this though Beans was still out cold, and giving Ellis a final huddle sort of squeeze and nod, the engineer walked quickly to the back door and out into Heck's Alley.

"Will," cried Ellis again, feeling that all was not well. But the other had already crossed the alley to a certain board in a fence which had been eroded into the shape of Illinois and which he knew, now fifteen years later, to swing free on a single nail, was through it and into Miss Mamie Billups' back yard. Miss Mamie was sitting on her side porch when he stooped to pass under her satsuma tree.

"How do you do, Miss Mamie," said the courteous engineer, bowing and putting his tie inside his coat.

"Who is that?" called out the old woman sharply. Everyone used to steal her satsumas.

"This is Will Barrett, Miss Mamie."

"Will Barrett! You come on up here, Will!"

"I can't right now, Miss Mamie," said the engineer, turning up Theard Street. "I'll be right back!"

4.

His friends waited for him but not long enough. By the time he rounded the lower curve of Milliken Bend, having walked the inner shoulder of the levee out of sight of highway and town, the Trav-L-Aire had already lumbered out of the willows and started up the levee—at an angle! The cabin teetered dangerously. He forgot to tell Mona not to do this. He covered his face with his hands: Mona, thinking to spare the G.M.C. the climb straight up, was in a fair way to turn her plumb over. When he looked up, however, the levee was clear.

It was two o'clock. He was hungry. At the levee end of Theard Street he bought a half dozen tamales from a street vendor (but not the same whose cry *Rayed hot!* used to echo up and down the summer night in the 1950's). Now finding a patch of waist-high elephant grass past the towhead and out of sight of anyone standing on the levee behind him, he rolled to and fro and made a hollow which was tilted like a buttercup into the westering sun. It was warm enough to take off his coat and roll up his sleeves. He ate the tamales carefully, taking care not to stain his clothes. The meat was good but his tooth encountered a number-eight shot: rabbit or possibly squirrel. Afterwards he washed his hands in river water, which still thrashed through the lower level of the towhead, and dried them with his handkerchief. Returning to his hollow, he sat cross-legged for a while and watched a towboat push a good half acre of sulphur barges up the dead water on the Louisiana side. Then he curled up and, using his coat folded wrong-side-out for a pillow, went to sleep.

Cold and stiffness woke him. It was a moonless overcast night, but he could make out Scorpio writhing dimly over Louisiana, convulsed around great bloody Antares. Buttoning all three buttons of his jacket, he ran along the inner shoulder of the levee, out of sight of town, until he got warm. When he came abreast of the stacks of the gypsum mill, he went quickly over and down into Blanton Street and took the Illinois Central tracks, which went curving away behind the high school. It was pitch dark under the stadium, but his muscles remembered the spacing of the ties. The open rear of the bleachers exhaled a faint odor of cellar earth and urine. At the Chinaman's he took the tangent of Houston Street, which ran through a better Negro neighborhood of neat shotgun cottages and flower gardens, into the heavy humming air and ham-rich smell of the cottonseed oil mill, and out at De Ridder.

He stood in the inky darkness of the water oaks and looked at his house. It was the same except that the gallery had been closed by glass louvers and a flagpole stuck out of a second-story window. His aunts were sitting on the porch. They had moved out, television and all. He came closer and stood amid the azaleas. They were jolly and fit, were the aunts, and younger than ever. Three were watching "Strike It Rich," two were playing canasta, and one was reading *Race and Reason* and eating Whitman's Sampler. He remembered now that Sophie wrote love letters to Bill Cullen. What a tough hearty crew they were! hearty as muzhiks, and good haters, yet not ill-natured—they'd be honestly and unaffectedly glad to see him walk in, would kiss him and hold him off and make over him—rosy-skinned, easy in their consciences, arteries as supple as a girl's husbands dead and gone these forty years, pegged out so long ago that he could not remember anyone ever speaking of them; Christian ladies every one, four Protestant, Presbyterian, and Scotch-Irish, two Catholic and Creole, but long since reconciled, ecumenized, by bon appétit and laughter and good hearty hatred.

It was here under the water oaks that his father used to stroll of a summer night, hands in his pockets and head down, sauntering along the sidewalk in his old Princeton style of sauntering, right side turning forward with right leg. Here under the water oaks or there under the street light, he would hold parley with passers-by, stranger and friend, white and black, thief and police. The boy would sit on the front steps, close enough to speak with his father and close enough too to service the Philco which played its stack of prewar 78's but always had trouble doing it. The mechanism creaked and whirred and down came the record plop and round it went for a spell, hissing under the voyaging needle. From the open window came Brahms, nearly always Brahms. Up and down the sidewalk went his father, took his turn under the street light sometimes with a client, sometimes alone. The clients, black and white and by and large the sorriest of crews but of course listening now with every eager effort of attention and even of a special stratospheric understanding. Between records the boy could hear snatches of talk: "Yassuh, that's the way it is now! I have notice the same thing myself!"—the father having said something about the cheapness of good intentions and the rarity of good character—"I'm sho gon' do like you say"—the passer-by working him of course for the fifty cents or five dollars or what, but working him as gracefully as anyone ever worked, they as good at their trade as he at his. The boy listening: what was the dread in his heart as he heard the colloquy and the beautiful terrible Brahms which went abroad into the humming summer night and the heavy ham-rich air?

The aunts let out a holler. Bill Cullen had given away a cabin cruiser to a lady from Michigan City, Indiana.

It was on such an evening—he passed his hand over his eyes and stretching it forth touched the sibilant corky bark of the water oak—that his father had died. The son watched from the step, old Brahms went abroad, the father took a stroll and spoke to a stranger of the good life and the loneliness of the galaxies. "Yes suh," said the stranger, "I have heard tell it was so" (that the closest star was two years away).

When the man came back the boy asked him:

"Father, why do you walk in the dark when you know they have sworn to kill you?"

"I'm not afraid, son."

To the west the cars of the white people were nosing up the levee, headlights switched first to parking, then out altogether. From the east, beyond the cottonseed-oil mill, came the sound of Negro laughter.

The man walked until midnight. Once a police car stopped. The policeman spoke to the man.

"You've won," said the youth when the man came back. "I heard the policeman. They've left town."

"We haven't won, son. We've lost."

"But they're gone, Father."

"Why shouldn't they leave? They've won."

"How have they won, Father?"

"They don't have to stay. Because they found out that we are like them after all and so there was no reason for them to stay."

"How are we like them, Father?"

"Once they were the fornicators and the bribers and the takers of bribes and we were not and that was why they hated us. Now we are like them, so why should they stay? They know they don't have to kill me."

"How do they know that, Father?"

"Because we've lost it all, son."

"Lost what?"

"But there's one thing they don't know."

"What's that, Father?"

"They may have won, but I don't have to choose that."

"Choose what?"

"Choose them."

This time, as he turned to leave, the youth called out to him. "Wait."

"What?"

"Don't leave."

"I'm just going to the corner."

But there was a dread about this night, the night of victory. (Victory is the saddest thing of all, said the father.) The mellowness of Brahms had gone overripe, the victorious serenity of the Great Horn Theme was false, oh fake fake. Underneath, all was unwell.

"Father."

"What?"

"Why do you like to be alone?"

"In the last analysis, you are alone." He turned into the darkness of the oaks.

"*Don't leave.*" The terror of the beautiful victorious music pierced his very soul.

"I'm not leaving, son," said the man and, after taking a turn, came back to the steps. But instead of stopping to sit beside the youth, he went up past him, resting his hand on the other's shoulder so heavily that the boy looked up to see his father's face. But the father went on without saying anything: went into the house, on through the old closed-in dogtrot hall to the back porch, opened the country food press which had been converted to a gun cabinet, took down the double-barrel twelve-gauge Greener, loaded it, went up the back stairs into the attic, and, fitting the muzzle of the Greener into the notch of his breastbone, could still reach both triggers with his thumbs. That was how it had to happen, the sheriff told the youth, that was the only way it could have happened.

The sound came crashing through the music, louder than twenty Philcos, a single sound, yet more prolonged and thunderous than a single shot. The youth turned off the Philco and went upstairs.

"—and Anacin does not upset your stummick," said Bill Cullen.

Again his hand went forth, knowing where it was, though he could not see, and touched the tiny iron horsehead of the hitching post, traced the cold metal down to the place where the oak had grown round it in an elephant lip. His fingertips touched the warm finny whispering bark.

Wait. While his fingers explored the juncture of iron and bark, his eyes narrowed as if he caught a glimmer of light on the cold iron skull. *Wait.* I think he was wrong and that he was looking in the wrong place. No, not he but the times. The times were wrong and one looked in the wrong place. It wasn't even his fault because that was the way he was and the way the times were, and there was no other place a man could look. It was the worst of times, a time of fake beauty and fake victory. *Wait.* He had missed it! It was not in the Brahms that one looked and not in solitariness and not in the old sad poetry but—he wrung out his ear—but here, under your nose, here in the very curiousness and drollness and extraness of the iron and the bark that—he shook his head—that—

The TV studio audience laughed with its quick, obedient and above all grateful Los Angeles laughter—once we were lonesome back home, the old sad home of our fathers, and here we are together and happy at last.

A Negro came whistling toward him under the street light, a young man his own age. Entering the darkness of the water oaks, the Negro did not at first see him (though it had been his, the Negro's, business, until now, to see him first), then did see him two yards away and stopped for a long half second. They looked at each other. There was nothing to say. Their fathers would have had much to say: "In the end, Sam, it comes down to a question of character." "Yes suh, Lawyer Barrett, you right about that. Like I was saying to my wife only this evening—" But the sons had nothing to say. The engineer looked at the other as the half second wore on. You may be in a fix and I know that but what you don't know and won't believe and must find out for yourself is that I'm in a fix too and you got to get where I am before you even know what I'm talking about and I know that and that's why there is nothing to say now. Meanwhile I wish you well.

It was only then, belatedly, and as if it were required of him, that the Negro shuddered and went his way.

As he watched his aunts, a squad car came slowly down De Ridder and stopped not twelve feet beyond the iron horse. A policeman, not Ross or Gover, went up to the porch and spoke to Aunt Sophie. She shook her head four or five times, hand to her throat, and when the policeman left, turned off the television and in her excitement stumbled a little as she told the others. Aunt Bootie forgot the Whitman's Sampler in her lap, stood up and scattered nougats and bird eggs in all directions. No one noticed.

Without taking much care about it, he walked through the azaleas and around to the back screen door, which was locked and which he opened, without knowing that he remembered, by wedging the door back against its hinges so that the bolt could be forced free of its worn wooden mortise, and went straight up the two flights to the attic and straight into the windowless interior room built into the peak of the house. His upraised hand felt for and found the string. The old clear-glass 25-watt bulb shed a yellow mizzling light, a light of rays, actual striae. The room had not been touched, they were still here; the grandfather's army blanket, Plattsburg issue, the puttees, a belt of webbing, the Kaiser Bill helmets, the five-pound binoculars with an artillery scale etched into one lens. He picked up the Greener, broke the breech and sighted at the yellow bulb. The bore was still speckled with powder grains. And the collapsible boat: an English contraption of silvery zeppelin fabric with varnished spruce spars to spring it into shape. It lay as it had lain ten years ago, half disassembled and hastily packed from a duck hunt he and his father had taken on the White River in the early fifties. Now, as if it were the very night of their return, he knelt absently and repacked the boat, remembering the feel and fit of the spar-ends and the brass sockets and even the goofy English directions: "—Don't be discouraged if spar L does not fit immediately into socket J—patience is required."

After he repacked the boat, he lay on the cot and, propping himself against the wall, drew the hard scratchy army blanket up to his armpits. For two hours he sat so, wakeful and alert, while his eyes followed the yellow drizzle of light into every corner of the attic room.

It was eight o'clock when he went downstairs, English boat slung over one shoulder, artillery binoculars over the other. The aunts had not gotten up. Hearing D'lo shuffling about the kitchen, he took care not to startle her: he slipped out the back door and came in noisily again.

"Law, if it ain't Mr. Billy," said D'lo, rolling her eyes conventionally and noticing the wall clock as she did so. She was no more surprised by the doings of white folks than he was.

D'lo stirred steaming boilers of grits and batter, fist sunk deep into her side, knees driven together by her great weight and bare heels ridden off her old pink mules and onto the floor. It crossed his mind that D'lo had somehow known he was here. He asked her not to tell his aunts.

"I ain't gon' tell them nothing!"

"I'm surprised you're still here."

"Where I'm going!"

"They still fight?"

"Fight! You don't know, fight."

"The police are looking for me."

"Uh-oh," said D'lo. This was serious. Yet he could not have sworn she did not know all about it.

D'lo found him his father's Rolls razor and, while he washed and shaved in the downstairs bathroom, fixed him a big breakfast of grits and sausage and batter cakes. When he left, he gave her twenty dollars.

"I thank you," said D'lo formally and twisted the bill into the stocking roll below her fat old knee, which curved out in six different arcs of rich cinnamon flesh.

A step creaked. "Here *she* come," said D'lo. Sophie was *she*, ole miss, the one who gave the orders.

"I'll be seeing you, D'lo," he said, shouldering the boat.

"All right now, Mist' Billy," she cried politely, socking down the grits spoon on the boiler and curling her lip in a rich and complex acknowledgment of his own queerness and her no more than mild sympathy and of the distance between them, maybe not even sympathy but just a good-humored letting him be. (All right now, you was a good little boy, but don't mess with me too much, go on, get out of my kitchen.)

Ten minutes later he was up and over the levee and down into the willows, where he assembled the boat and the two-bladed paddle. It was a sparkling day. The river was ruffled by glittering steel wavelets like a northern lake. Shoving off and sitting buttoned up kayak style in the aft hole, he went dropping away in the fast water, past the barrow pits and blue holes, and now beginning to paddle, went skimming over the wide river, which seemed to brim and curve up like a watchglass from the great creamy boils that shed tons of cold bottom water, down past old Fort Ste. Marie on the Louisiana side, its ramparts gone back to blackberries and honeysuckle. He knew every tunnel, embrasure, magazine room, and did not bother to look. Two Negroes in a skiff were running a trotline under the caving bank. They watched him a second longer than they might have. Now they were watching him again, under their arms as they handed the line along. He frowned, wondering how he looked in the face, then recollected himself: it was after all an uncommon sight, a man fully dressed in coat and necktie and buttoned up in a tiny waterbug of a boat and at nine o'clock of a Tuesday morning. They could not encompass him; he was beyond their reckoning. But hold on, something new! As he drifted past the fort, he rubbed his eyes. A pennant fluttered from the parapet, the Stars and Bars! And the entire fort was surrounded by a ten-foot-high hurricane fence. But of course! This very month marked the hundredth anniversary of the reduction of the fort by Admiral Foote's gunboats. It was part of the preparation for the Centennial! No doubt they would, at the proper time, imprison the "Confederates" behind the fence.

But as he dropped past the fort, he was surprised to see "sentinels" patrolling the fence and even a few prisoners inside, but as unlikely a lot of Confederates as one could imagine—men and women! the men bearded properly enough, but both sexes blue-jeaned and sweat-shirted and altogether disreputable. And Negroes! And yonder, pacing the parapet—Good Lord!—was Milo Menander, the politician, who was evidently playing the role of Beast Banks, the infamous federal commandant of the infamous federal prison into which the fort was converted after its capture. Capital! And hadn't he got himself up grandly for the occasion: flowing locks, big cigar, hand pressed Napoleonically into his side, a proper villainous-looking old man if ever there was one.

But hold on! Something was wrong. Were they not two years late with their celebration? The fort was captured early in the war, and here it was 19— What year was this? He wrang out his ear and beat his pockets in vain for his Gulf calendar card. Another slip: if Beast Banks had reduced and occupied the fort, why was the Stars and Bars still flying?

It was past figuring even if he'd a stomach for figuring. Something may be amiss here, but then all was not well with him either. Next he'd be hearing singing ravening particles. Besides, he had other fish to fry and many a mile to travel. British wariness woke in him and, putting his head down, he dropped below the fort as silently as an Englishman slipping past Heligoland.

He put in at the old ferry landing, abandoned when the bridge at Vicksburg was built and now no more than a sloughing bank of mealy earth honeycombed by cliff swallows. Disassembling and packing his boat, he stowed it in a cave-in and pulled dirt over it and set out up the sunken ferry road, which ran through loess cuts filled now as always with a smoky morning twilight and the smell of roots (here in Louisiana across the river it was ever a dim green place of swamps and shacks and Negro graveyards sparkling with red and green medicine bottles; the tree stumps were inhabited by spirits), past flooded pin-oak flats where great pileated woodpeckers went ringing down the smoky aisles. Though it was only two hundred yards from home, Louisiana had ever seemed misty and faraway, removed in time and space. Over yonder in the swamps lived the same great birds Audubon saw. Freejacks, Frenchmen, and river rats trapped muskrat and caught catfish. It was a place of small and pleasant deeds.

*

"Hey, Merum!"

Uncle Fannin was walking up and down the back porch, his face narrow and dark as a piece of slab bark, carrying in the crook of his arm the Browning automatic worn to silver, with bluing left only in the grooves of the etching. The trigger guard was worn as thin as an old man's wedding ring.

"Mayrom! Where's that Ma'am?"

He was calling his servant Merriam but he never called him twice by the same name.

It was characteristic of the uncle that he had greeted his nephew without surprise, as if it were nothing out of the ordinary that he should come hiking up out of nowhere with his artillery binoculars, and after five years. He hardly stopped his pacing.

"We're fixing to mark some coveys up on Sunnyside," he said, as if it were he who owed the explanations.

The engineer blinked. They might have been waiting for him.

The Trav-L-Aire was nowhere in sight and Uncle Fannin knew nothing about it or any company of "actors," as the engineer called them (calculating that a mixture of blacks and whites was somehow more tolerable if they were performers).

Merriam came round the corner of the house with two pointers, one an old liver-and-white bitch who knew what was what and had no time for foolery, trotting head down, dugs rippling like a curtain; the other pointer was a fool. He was a young dog named Rock. He put his muzzle in the engineer's hand and nudged him hard. His head was heavy as iron. There were warts all over him where Uncle Fannin had shot him for his mistakes. Merriam, the engineer perceived, was partial to Rock and was afraid the uncle was going to shoot him again. Merriam was a short heavy Negro whose face was welted and bound up through the cheeks so that he was muffle-jawed in his speech. Blackness like a fury seemed to rush forward in his face. But the engineer knew that the fury was a kind of good nature. He wore a lumpy white sweater with stuffing sticking out of it like a scarecrow.

It was not a real hunt they were setting out on. Uncle Fannin wanted to mark coveys for the season. Later in the fall, businessmen would come down from Memphis and up from New

Orleans and he would take them out. The engineer refused the gun offered to him, but he went along with them. They drove into the woods in an old high-finned De Soto whose back seat had been removed to make room for the dogs. A partition of chicken wire fenced off the front seat. The dogs stuck their heads out the windows, grinning and splitting the wind, their feet scrabbling for purchase on the metal seat bed. The car smelled of old bitter car metal and croker sacks and the hot funky firecracker smell of dry bird dogs.

Merriam sat with the two Barretts on the front seat, but swiveled around to face them to show he was not sitting with them, not quite on or off the seat, mostly off and claiming, in a nice deprecation, not more than an inch of seat, not through any real necessity but only as the proper concession due the law of gravity. It was not hard to believe that Merriam could have sat in the air if it had been required of him.

The De Soto plunged and roared, crashing into potholes not with a single shock but with a distributed and mediated looseness, a shambling sound like throwing a chain against a wall, knocking the dogs every whichway. When Uncle Fannin slammed on the brakes, the dogs were thrust forward, their chins pushing against the shoulders of the passengers, but already back-pedaling apologetically, their expressions both aggrieved and grinning.

They hunted from an old plantation dike long since reclaimed by the woods and now no more than a high path through thickets. The engineer, still dressed in Dacron suit and suède oxfords, followed along, hands in pockets. Rock got shot again, though with bird shot and from a sufficient distance so that it did no more harm than raise a new crop of warts.

"Meroom!"

"Yassuh."

Merriam was carrying a brand-new single-shot nickel-plated sixteen-gauge from Sears Roebuck which looked like a silver flute.

"Look at that son of a bitch."

"I see him."

Below and ahead of them the bitch Maggie was holding a point, her body bent like a pin, tail quivering. Rock had swung wide and was doubling back and coming up behind her, bounding up and down like a springbok to see over the grass. He smelled nothing.

"He's sho gon' run over her," said the uncle.

"No suh, he ain't," said Merriam, but keeping a fearful weather eye on Rock.

"What's he doing then?"

The engineer perceived that the uncle was asking the question ironically, taking due notice of the magic and incantatory faculty that Negroes are supposed to have—they know what animals are going to do, for example—but doing it ironically.

"Goddamn, he *is* going to run over her!"—joking aside now.

"He ain't stuttn it," said Merriam.

Of course Rock, damn fool that he was, did run over Maggie, landing squarely in the middle of the covey and exploding quail in all directions—it coming over him in mid-air and at the last second, the inkling of what lay below, he braking and back-pedaling wildly like Goofy. Uncle Fannin shot three times, twice at quail and once at Rock, and, like all dead shots, already beginning to talk as he shot as if the shooting itself were the least of it. "Look at that cock, one, two, and—" *Wham.* He got three birds, one with one shot and two crossing with the other shot. The third shot hit Rock. The engineer opened his mouth to say something but a fourth shot went off.

"Lord to God," groaned Merriam. "He done shot him again." Merriam went to look after Rock.

The uncle didn't hear. He was already down the levee and after a single who had gone angling off into the woods, wings propped down, chunky, teetering in his glide. Uncle Fannin went sidling and backing into the underbrush, reloading as he went, the vines singing and popping around his legs. When he couldn't find the single, even though they had seen where he landed, Merriam told the two Barretts that the quail had hidden from the dogs.

"Now how in the hell is he going to hide from the dogs," said the disgusted uncle.

"He hiding now," said Merriam, still speaking to the engineer. "They has a way of hiding so that no dog in the world can see or smell them."

"Oh, Goddamn, come on now. You hold that dog."

"I seen them!"

"How do they hide, Merriam?" the engineer asked him.

"They hits the ground and grab ahold of trash and sticks with both feets and throws theyselfs upside down with his feets sticking up and the dogs will go right over him ever' time."

"Hold that goddamn dog now, Mayrim!"

After supper they watched television. An old round-eyed Zenith and two leatherette recliners, the kind that are advertised on the back page of the comic section, had been placed in a clearing that had been made long ago by pushing Aunt Felice's good New Orleans furniture back into the dark corners of the room. Merriam watched from a roost somewhere atop a pile of chairs and tables. The sentient engineer perceived immediately that the recliner he was given was Merriam's seat, but there was nothing he could do about it. Uncle Fannin pretended the recliner had been brought out for the engineer (how could it have been?) and Merriam pretended he always roosted high in the darkness. But when they, Uncle Fannin and Merriam, talked during the programs, sometimes the uncle, forgetting, would speak to the other recliner:

"He's leaving now but he be back up there later, don't worry about it."

"Yes suh," said Merriam from the upper darkness.

"He's a pistol ball now, ain't he?"

"I mean."

"But Chester, now. Chester can't hold them by himself."

"That Mist' Chester is all right now," cried Merriam.

"Shoot."

Whenever a commercial ended, Uncle Fannin lifted himself and took a quick pluck at his seat by way of getting ready.

"That laig don't hold him!"

"It ain't his leg that's holding him now," said the uncle, and, noticing that it was his nephew who sat beside him, gave him a wink and a poke in the ribs to show that he didn't take Merriam seriously.

Merriam didn't mind. They argued about the Western heroes as if they were real people whose motives could be figured out. During a commercial, Merriam told the engineer of a program they had seen last week. It made a strong impression on him because the hero, their favorite, a black knight of a man, both gentleman and brawler, had gotten badly beat up. It was part one of a series and so he was still beat up.

"I told Mist' Fanny"—Merriam spoke muffle-jawed and all in a rush as if he hoped to get the words out before they got bound up in his cheeks—"that the onliest way in the world they can catch him is to get in behind him. Mist' Fanny, he say they gon' stomp him. I say they got to get in behind him first. What happened, some man called his attention, like I say 'look here!' and he looked and they did get in behind him and Lord, they stomped him, bad, I mean all up in the head. He lay out there in the street two days and folks scared to help him, everybody scared of this one man, Mister errerr—, errerr—" Merriam snapped his fingers. "It slips my mind, but he was a stout man and low, lower than you or Mist' Fanny, he brush his hair up in the front like." Merriam showed them and described the man so that the engineer would recognize him if he happened to see him. "They taken his money and his gun and his horse and left him out there in the sun. Then here come this other man to kill him. And I said to Mist' Fanny, there is one thing this other man don't know and that is he got this little biddy pistol on him and they didn't take it off him because he got it hid in his bosom."

"Man, how you going to go up against a thirty-thirty with a derringer," said the uncle disdainfully, yet shyly, watchful of the engineer lest he, the engineer, think too badly of Merriam. His uncle was pleading with him!

"I'd like to see how that comes out," said the engineer. "Is the second part coming on tonight?" he asked Merriam.

"Yessuh."

"That fellow's name was Bogardus," said the uncle presently. "He carried a carbine with a lever action and he can work that lever as fast as you can shoot that automatic there."

"Yessuh," said Merriam, but without conviction.

Still no sign of the Trav-L-Aire, and at midnight the engineer went to bed—without taking thought about it, going up to the second-floor room he used to have in the summertime, a narrow cell under the eaves furnished with an armoire, a basin and ewer and chamber pot, and an old-style feather bed with bolster. The skull was still there on the shelf of the armoire, property of his namesake, Dr. Williston Barrett, the original misfit, who graduated from old Jefferson Medical College, by persuasion an abolitionist but who nevertheless went to fight in Virginia and afterwards having had enough, he said, of the dying and the dead and the living as well, the North and the South, of men in sum, came home to the country and never practiced a day in his life, took instead to his own laudanum and became a philosopher of sorts, lived another sixty years, the only long-lived Barrett male. The skull had turned as yellow as ivory and was pencil-marked by ten generations of children; it was sawed through the dome and the lid securely fastened by silver hinges; undo that and the brain pan was itself sectioned and hinged, opening in turn into an airy comb of sinus cells.

It was cold but he knew the feather bed, so he stripped to his shorts, and after washing his T-shirt in the ewer and spreading it on the marble stand to dry, he climbed into bed. The warm goosedown flowed up around him. It was, he had always imagined, something like going to bed in Central Europe. He pulled the bolster up to his shoulders and propped Sutter's casebook on its thick margin.

R.R., white male, c. 25, well-dev. but under-nour. 10 mm entrance wound in right temporal, moderate powder tattooing and branding, right exophthalmus and hematoma; stellate exit wound left mastoidal base, approx. 28 mm diam. Cops say suicide.

From Lt. B.'s report: R.R., b. Garden City, Long Island; grad LIU and MIT last June. Employed Redston Arsenal since June 15. Drove here after work yesterday, July 3, purchased S & W .38 rev. from Pioneer Sports, rented room at Jeff D. Hotel, found on bed clothed 9 a.m., approx time of death, 1 a.m., July 4.

Lt. B.: "His life before him, etc." "One of the lucky ones, etc." "No woman trouble, liquor or drugs or money, etc." "? ? ?"

Suicide considered as consequence of the spirit of abstraction and of transcendence; lewdness as sole portal of reentry into world demoted to immanence; reentry into

immanence via orgasm; but post-orgasmic transcendence
7 devils worse than first.

Man who falls victim to transcendence as the spirit of
abstraction, i.e., elevates self to posture over and against
world which is *pari passu* demoted to immanence and
seen as examplar and specimen and coordinate, and who
is not at same time compensated by beauty of motion of
method of science, has no choice but to seek reentry into
immanent world *qua* immanence. But since no avenue of
reentry remains save genital and since reentry cotermi-
nus $\bar{c}$ orgasm, post-orgasmic despair without remedy. Of
my series of four suicides in scientists and technicians,
3 post-coital (spermatozoa at meatus), 2 in hotel room.
Hotel room = site of intersection of transcendence and
immanence: room itself, a triaxial coordinate ten floors
above street; whore who comes up = pure immanence
to be entered. But entry doesn't avail: one skids off
into transcendence. *There is no reentry from the orbit of
transcendence.*

Lt. B.: "Maybe they're so shocked by what they've turned
loose on the world—" Pandora's Box theory, etc. "Maybe
that's why he did it," etc.

I say: "Bullshit, Lt., and on the contrary. This Schadenfreude is what keeps them going," etc.

What I cannot tell Lt.: If R.R. had been a good pornographer, he would not have suicided. His death was due, not
to lewdness, but to the failure of lewdness.

I say to Val: Re Sweden: increase in suicides in Sweden
due not to increase in lewdness but to decline of lewdness.
When Sweden was post-Christian but had not yet forgotten Cx (circa 1850–1914), Swedish lewdness intact and
suicides negligible. But when Swedes truly post-Christian
(not merely post-Christian but also post-memory of Cx),
lewdness declined and suicides rose in inverse relation.

Val to me: Don't sell Sweden short. (I notice that her language has taken on the deplorable and lapsed slanginess

found in many religious, priests and nuns, and in *Our Sunday Visitor*.) The next great saint must come from Sweden, etc. It is only from desolation of total transcendence of self and total descent of world of immanence that a man can come who can recover himself and world under God, etc. Give me suicidal Swede, says she, over Alabama Christian any day, etc.

I say: Very good, very good talk, but it is after all only that, that is the kind of talk we have between us.

The bar turned in his head, synapses gave way, and he slept ten hours dreamlessly and without spansules.

Still no sign of the Trav-L-Aire the next morning, but after a great steaming breakfast of brains and eggs and apple rings served in front of the Zenith. (Captain Kangaroo: Uncle Fannin and Merriam cackled like maniacs at the doings of Captain K. and Mr. Greenjeans, and the engineer wondered, how is it that uncle and servant, who were solid 3-D persons, true denizens of this misty Natchez Trace country, should be transported by these sad gags from Madison Avenue? But they were transported. They were merry as could be, and he, the engineer, guessed that was all right: more power to Captain K.)

After he had transacted his oil-lease business with his uncle, the telephone rang. It was the deputy sheriff in Shut Off. It seemed a little "trailer" had been stolen by a bunch of niggers and outside agitators and that papers and books in the name of Williston Bibb Barrett had been found therein. Did Mr. Fannin know anything about it? If he did and if it was his property or his kin's, he might reclaim the same by coming down to Shut Off and picking it up.

The uncle held the phone and told his nephew.

"What happened to the, ah, Negroes and the outside agitators?" asked the latter calmly.

Nothing, it seemed. They were there, at this moment, in Shut Off. It needed but a word from Mr. Fannin to give the lie to their crazy story that they had borrowed the trailer from his kinsman and the lot of them would be thrown in jail, if not into the dungeon at Fort Ste. Marie.

"The dungeon. So that's it," said the nephew, relieved despite himself. "And what if the story is confirmed?" he asked his uncle.

Then they'd be packed off in twenty minutes on the next bus to Memphis.

"Confirm the story," said the nephew. "And tell him I'll be there in an hour to pick up my camper." He wanted his friends free, clear of danger, but free and clear of him too, gone, by the time he reached Shut Off.

After bidding his uncle and Merriam farewell—who were only waiting for him to leave to set off with the dogs in the De Soto—he struck out for the old landing, where he retrieved his boat and drifted a mile or so to the meadows, which presently separated the river from Shut Off. So it came to be called Shut Off: many years ago one of the meanderings of the river had jumped the neck of a peninsula and shut the landing off from the river.

5.

The boy and the man ate breakfast in the dining car Savannah. The waiter braced his thigh against the table while he laid the pitted nickel-silver knives and forks. The water in the heavy glass carafe moved up and down without leaving a drop, as if water and glass were quits through usage.

A man came down the aisle and stood talking to his father, folding and unfolding his morning paper.

"It's a bitter thing, Ed. Bitter as gar broth."

"I know it is, Oscar. Son, I want you to meet Senator Oscar Underwood. Oscar, this is my son Bill."

He arose to shake hands and then did not know whether to stand or sit.

"Bill," the senator told him, "when you grow up, decide what you want to do according to your lights. Then do it. That's all there is to it."

"Yes sir," he said, feeling confident he could do that.

"Senator Underwood did just that, son, and at great cost to himself," said his father.

"Yes sir."

*

He awoke, remembering what Senator Underwood looked like, even the vein on his hand which jumped back and forth across a tendon when he folded and unfolded the fresh newspaper.

Dear God, he thought, pacing his five-foot aisle, I'm slipping again. I can't have met Senator Underwood, or could I? Was it I and my father or he and his father? How do I know what he looked like? What did he look like? I must find out.

Stooping, he caught sight of a forest of oil derricks. He dressed and went outside. The camper was parked in the gravel plaza of a truckers' stop. In the café he learned that he was in Longview, Texas. While he waited for his breakfast, he read from Sutter's notebook:

You're wrong about Rita, Val. She saved my life and she meant no harm to Kitty—though that does not answer your charge. I had left the old ruined South for the transcending Southwest. But there transcendence failed me and Rita picked me up for the bum I was and fed and clothed me.

The day before I left home I stood in a lewd wood by the golf links. My insurance had been canceled and I could not hospitalize patients or even treat them at home save at my own risk. The wood was the lewd wood of my youth where lovers used to come and leave Merry Widow tins and where I dreamed the lewd dreams of youth. Therefrom I spied Jackie Randolph towing her cart up number 7 fairway sans caddy and sans partner. Invited her into the woods and spoke into her ear. She looked at her watch and said she had 20 minutes before her bridge luncheon. She spread her golf towel on the pine needles, kept her spiked shoes on, and cursed in my ear.

The innocence of Mexican country women.

That evening my father gave me $100,000 for not smoking until I was 21.

Looked in J.A.M.A. classifieds, found job in Santa Fe clinic, telephoned them my credentials (which were ever good), was accepted on spot, packed my Edsel and was on my way. Clinic dreary—found my true vocation at Sangre de Cristo guest ranch.

Genius loci of Western desert did not materialize. Had hoped for free-floating sense of geographical transcendence, that special dislocatedness and purity of the Southwest which attracted Doc Holliday and Robert Oppenheimer, one a concrete Valdosta man who had had a bellyful of the concrete, the other the luckiest of all abstract men: who achieved the high watermark of the 20th century, which is to say: the device conceived in a locus of pure transcendence, which in turn worked the maximum effect upon the sphere of immanence, the world. (Both men, notice, developed weapons in the desert, the former a specially built sawed-off shotgun which he carried by a string around his neck.)

It didn't work. I found myself treating senior citizens for post-retirement anomie and lady dudes for sore rears and nameless longings. I took my money and bought a ranch, moved out and in a month's time was struck flat by an acute depression, laid out flat in the desert and assaulted by 10,000 devils, not the little black fellows of St. Anthony but wanton teenagers who swung from the bedpost and made gestures. I stopped eating. Rita found me (she was looking for volunteer MD's for her little Indians), toted me back to her cozy house in Tesuque, fed me, clothed me, bucked me up, and stood for no nonsense. She saved my life and I married her to stay alive. We had a good time. We ate the pure fruit of transcendence. She is not, like me, a pornographer. She believes in "love" like you, though a different kind. She "falls in love." She fell in love with me because I needed her, and then with Kitty because she thought I didn't need her because Kitty seemed to, with that Gretel-lost-in-the-woods look of hers. Now Kitty is "in love" with someone and Rita is up the creek. I told her to forget all that stuff, e.g., "love," and come on back with me to the Southwest, where we didn't have a bad time. But she is still angry with me. I forgive her sins but she doesn't mine. Hers: like all secular saints, she canonizes herself. Even her sins are meritorious. Her concern for Kitty gets put down as "broadening her horizons" or "saving her from the racists." And all she really wanted for Jamie was that he should get Barrett out of the way. She got extremely angry when I suggested it, though I told her it wasn't so bad, that she was no more guilty than everyone else. Eh, Val? You want to know the only thing I really held against her? A small thing but it got under my skin. It was an expression she used with her transcendent friends: she would tell them she and I were "good in bed." I am an old-fashioned Alabama pornographer and do not like forward expressions in a woman.

Feeling unusually elated—then I am Kitty's "someone"!— he stopped at the public library in Longview and looked up Senator Oscar W. Underwood in the *Columbia Encyclopedia*. The senator died in 1929, ten years before the engineer's birth. When he asked the librarian where he might find a picture of Senator Underwood, she looked at him twice and said she didn't know.

The same evening he called Kitty from a Dallas trailer park. To his vast relief, she sounded mainly solicitous for him. She had even supposed that he had been hurt and suffered another attack of "amnesia"—which he saw that she saw as a thing outside him, a magic medical entity, a dragon that might overtake him at any moment. Fortunately too, the events occurring that night on the campus were themselves so violent that his own lapse seemed minor.

"Oh, honey, I thought you'd been killed," cried Kitty.

"No."

"I couldn't have met you anyway. They herded us down into the basement and wouldn't let us leave till Sunday afternoon."

"Sunday afternoon," said the engineer vaguely.

"Are you all right?" asked Kitty anxiously when he fell silent.

"Yes. I'm going on now to find, ah, Jamie."

"I know. We're counting on you."

"I wish you were here with me."

"Me too."

All of a sudden he did. Love pangs entered his heart and melted his loin and his life seemed simple. The thing to do—why couldn't he remember it?—was to marry Kitty and get a job and live an ordinary life, play golf like other people.

"We will be married."

"Oh yes, darling. Just between you and I, Myra is going to take the Mickle house off the market till you get back."

"Between you and me," he said absently, "the Mickle house?" Oh my. He'd forgotten Cap'n Andy and his lookout over the doleful plain.

"You two big dopes come on back here where you belong."

"Who?"

"You and Jamie."

"Oh yes. We will."

"You shouldn't have done it."

"Done what?"

"Told Poppy to stop payment of my dowry."

"Somebody stole it."

"Then you'll still accept it?"

"Sure."

"He wrote me another one."

"Good."

But his foreboding returned as soon as he hung up. He lay abed stiff as a poker, feet sticking up, listening to patriotic programs. When at last he did fall asleep, he woke almost immediately and with a violent start. He peeped out of the window to see what might be amiss. Evil low-flying clouds reflected a red furnace-glow from the city. Lower still, from the very treetops, he fancied he could hear a ravening singing sound. Wasting no time, he uncoupled his umbilical connections with dread Dallas, roared out onto the freeways, and by sun-up was leveled out at eighty-five and straight for the Panhandle.

Past Amarillo the next day and up a black tundra-like country with snow fences and lonesome shacks to Raton Pass. He stopped for gas at an ancient Humble station, a hut set down in a moraine of oil cans and shredded fan belts and ruptured inner tubes. The wind came howling down from Colorado, roaring down the railroad cut like a freight train. There was a meniscus of snow on the black mountainside. The attendant wore an old sheepskin coat and was as slanty-eyed as a Chinaman. Later the engineer thought: why he is an Indian. He steered the

Trav-L-Aire out onto a level stretch of tundra, locked himself in, and slept for twenty hours.

When he woke, it was very cold. He lit the propane panel ray and, as he waited for the cabin to warm, caught sight of his own name in Sutter's casebook.

Barrett: His trouble is he wants to know what his trouble is. His "trouble," he thinks, is a disorder of such a character that if only he can locate the right expert with the right psychology, the disorder can be set right and he can go about his business.

That is to say: he wishes to cling to his transcendence and to locate a fellow transcender (e.g., me) who will tell him how to traffic with immanence (e.g., "environment," "groups," "experience," etc.) in such a way that he will be happy. Therefore I will tell him nothing. For even if I were "right," his posture is self-defeating.

(Southern transcenders are the worst of all—for they hate the old bloody immanence of the South. Southerners outdo their teachers, just as the Chinese Marxists outdo the Soviets. Did you ever talk to a female Freudian Georgia social worker? Freud would be horrified.)

Yes, Barrett has caught a whiff of the transcendent trap and has got the wind up. But what can one tell him? What can you tell him, Val?

Even if you were right. Let us say you were right: that man is a wayfarer (i.e., not transcending being nor immanent being but wayfarer) who therefore stands in the way of hearing a piece of news which is of the utmost importance to him (i.e., his salvation) and which he had better attend to. So you say to him: Look, Barrett, your trouble is due not to a disorder of your organism but to the human condition, that you do well to be afraid and you do well to forget everything which does not pertain to your salvation. That is to say, your amnesia is not a symptom. So you say: Here is the piece of news you have been waiting for, and you tell him. What does Barrett do? He attends in that eager flattering way of his and at the end of it he might even say *yes*! But he will receive the news from his high seat of transcendence as one more item of psychology, throw it into his immanent meat-grinder, and wait to see if he feels better. He told me he's in favor of the World's Great Religions. What are you going to do about that?

I am not in favor of any such thing. We are doomed to the transcendence of abstraction and I choose the only reentry into the world which remains to us. What is better then than the beauty and the exaltation of the practice of transcendence (science and art) and of the delectation of immanence, the beauty and the exaltation of lewd love? What is better than this: one works hard during the day in the front line and with the comradeship of science and at night one goes to La Fonda, where one encounters a stranger, a handsome woman. We drink, we two handsome thirty-five-year-olds, she dark-eyed, shadowy of cheek, wistful in her own transcendence. We dance. The guitar makes the heart soar. We eat hearty. Under the table a gentle pressure of the knee. One speaks into her ear at some length. "Let's go." "But we ordered dinner." "We can come back." "All right." The blood sings with voluptuousness and tenderness.

Rita says I do not love anyone. That is not true. I love all women. How lovable they are, all of them, our lovely lonely bemused American women. What darlings. Let any one of them enter a room and my heart melts. You say there is something better. *Ich warte.*

Where he probably goes wrong, mused the engineer sleepily, is in the extremity of his alternatives: God and not-God, getting under women's dresses and blowing your brains out. Whereas and in fact my problem is how to live from one ordinary minute to the next on a Wednesday afternoon.
Has not this been the case with all "religious" people?

6.

Down, down into the sunny yellow canyon of the Rio Grande, down through the piney slopes to the ocher cliffs and the red clay bottoms. He stopped to see the famous river. When he came out of a fugue, he was in some ways like a sailor, horny and simple-minded, and with an itch to wander and see the sights, the famous places, take them in, dig every detail. But what a piddling little creek it was! A far cry from the Big Muddy: the trickle of whitish alkali water looked like the run-off from a construction site. Beside him a gold aspen rattled like foil in the sunlight. But there was no wind. He moved closer. A single leaf danced on its pedicle, mysteriously dispensed from energy laws.

Another Indian at a Phillips 66 station in Santa Fe directed him to Rancho la Merced, which he, the Indian, knew by name but not by owner. It meant leaving the highway south of the city and bumping across the desert, through scrubby junipers and fragrant piñon, up and down arroyos. Four times he had to dismount to open cattle gates.

Rancho Merced was something more than he expected. The building was not large but its lowness made it look far-flung. One almost looked down upon it: you got down into it like a sports car and with the same expectation of the chthonic dividends of living close to the ground. The windows, set in foot-thick 'dobe walls, were open. He knocked. No one answered. There were tire tracks but no car. He walked around the house. Above the piñon arose an ugly galvanized cistern and a Sears windmill. Though its tail was not folded, it did not turn. It was three o'clock.

He sat down under the cistern and sniffed a handful of soil. The silence was disjunct. It ran concurrently with one and did not flow from the past. Each passing second was packaged in cottony silence. It had no antecedents. Here was three o'clock but it was not like three o'clock in Mississippi. In Mississippi it is always Wednesday afternoon, or perhaps Thursday. The country there is peopled, a handful of soil strikes a pang to the heart, *déjà vus* fly up like a shower of sparks. Even in the Southern wilderness there is ever the sense of someone close by, watching from the woods. Here one was not watched. There was no one. The silence hushed everything up, the small trees were separated by a geometry of silence. The sky was empty map space. Yonder at Albuquerque forty miles away a mountain reared up like your hand in front of your face.

This is the locus of pure possibility, he thought, his neck

prickling. What a man can be the next minute bears no relation to what he is or what he was the minute before.

The front door was unlocked. He stooped down into the house. For thirty seconds he stood blinking in the cool cellar-like darkness. The windows opened into the bright hush of the desert. He listened: the silence changed. It became a presiding and penultimate silence like the heavy orchestral tacet before a final chord. His heart began to pound. Presently it came to him: what is missing are the small hums and clicks of household motors. He went into the kitchen. The refrigerator was empty and the hot-water tank was cold but there were four cans of Chef Boy-ar-dee spaghetti on the shelf. In the bedroom the bedclothes were tied up and ready for the laundry, a pile on each bed. There was no sign of clothes or suitcases. A year-old *Life* magazine had been left on the bureau. He spotted Sutter's script running around all four edges of the Winston ad on the back cover. He held it eagerly to the light—could it be a message to him? a clue to Sutter's whereabouts?—peering intently and turning it slowly as he read. Sutter's hand was worse than usual.

> Kennedy. With all the hogwash, no one has said what he was. The reason he was a great man was that his derisiveness kept pace with his brilliance and his beauty and his love of country. He is the only public man I have ever believed. This is because no man now is believable unless he is derisive. In him I saw the old eagle beauty of the United States of America. I loved him. They, the ——— (unreadable: bourgeois? burghers? bastards?), wanted him dead. Very well, it will serve them right because now—

The script ran off into the brown stipple of a girl's thigh and he could make out no more.

He frowned, feeling suddenly put off and out of sorts. This was not what he was looking for and did him no good at all.

Under one bed he found a book of photographs of what appeared to him to be hindoo statuary in a jungle garden. The statues were of couples locked in erotic embraces. The lovers pressed together and their blind lozenge-eyes gazed past each other. The woman's neck arched gracefully. The man's hand sustained the globe of her breast; his pitted stone shaft pressed against the jungle ruin of her flank.

Outside he sat in the cab of the Trav-L-Aire and waited. The Sangre de Cristo range began to turn red. At five o'clock a breeze sprang up. The windmill creaked and presently little yellow flycatchers began to fly down from the mountain and line up on the rim of the cistern.

Dark fell suddenly and the stars came out. They drew in and in half an hour hung as large and low as yellow lamps at a garden party. Suddenly remembering his telescope, he fetched it from the cabin and clamped it to the door of the cab like a malt tray. Now spying the square of Pegasus, he focused on a smudge in the tail and there it was, the great cold fire of Andromeda, atilt, as big as a Catherine wheel, as slow and silent in its turning, stopped, as tumult seen from far away. He shivered. I'm through with telescopes, he thought, and the vasty galaxies. What do I need with Andromeda? What I need is my Bama bride and my cozy camper, a match struck and the butane lit and a friendly square of light cast upon the neighbor earth, and a hot cup of Luzianne between us against the desert cold, and a warm bed and there lie dreaming in one another's arms while old Andromeda leans through the night.

Returning to Santa Fe, he found a snug court in the Camino Real, in a poplar grove hard by the dry bed of the Santa Fe River, and went shopping for groceries. There was no grits to be had, and he had to buy Cream of Wheat. The next morning after breakfast he telephoned every hotel, motel, clinic, and hospital in town, but no one had heard of Dr. Sutter Vaught.

Two days later he was stamping about and hugging himself in the plaza, shivering and, for lack of anything better to do, reading the inscription on the Union monument.

To the heroes of the Federal Army who fell at the Battle of Valverde fought with Rebels   February 21, 1862

Strangely, there occurred no stirring within him, no body English toward the reversing of that evil day at Valverde where, but for so-and-so's mistake, they might have gotten through to California. Then if they could have reached the ocean— But he felt only the cold.

At ten o'clock the sun rose over the 'dobe shops and it grew warmer. Indians began to come into the plaza. They spread their jewelry and beaded belts on the hard clay and sat, with their legs stretched out, against the sunny wall. It seemed like a good idea. He found a vacant spot and stretched out his Macy's Dacrons among the velvet pantaloons. The red Indians, their faces flat as dishes, looked at him with no expression at all. He had only just begun to read from Sutter's casebook:

> You cite the remark Oppenheimer made about the great days of Los Alamos when the best minds of the Western world were assembled in secret and talked the night away about every subject under the sun. You say, yes they were speaking *sub specie aeternitatis* as men might speak anywhere and at any time, and that they did not notice that—

when he happened to look up and catch sight of a thin man in shirtsleeves coming out of a 'dobe Rexall. He carried a paper bag upright in the crook of his arm. His shirt ballooned out behind him like a spinnaker. Without a second's hesitation the engineer was up and on his way. But when he caught up, the thin man had already gotten into a dusty Edsel and the car was moving.

"Sir," said the courteous engineer, trotting along and leaning down to see the driver.

"What?" But the Edsel kept moving.

"Wait, sir."

"Are you Philip?" asked the driver.

"Eh?" said the engineer, cupping his good ear, and for a moment was not certain he was not.

"Are you Philip and is this the Gaza Desert?" The Edsel stopped. "Do you have something to tell me?"

"Sir? No sir. I am Williston Barrett," said the engineer somewhat formally.

"I knew that, Williston," said Sutter. "I was making a joke. Get in."

"Thank you."

The hood of the car was still stained with the hackberries and sparrow droppings of Alabama. Edsel or not, it ran with the hollow buckety sound of all old Fords.

"How did you find me?" Sutter asked him. Unlike most thin men, he sat in such a way as to emphasize his thinness, craned his neck and hugged his narrow chest.

"I found a map in your room with the route traced on it. I remembered the name of the ranch. An Indian told me where it was. There was no one at the ranch, so I waited in the plaza. There was also this in your room." He handed the casebook to Sutter. "I thought you might have forgotten it."

Sutter glanced at the casebook without taking it. "I didn't forget it."

"I have pondered it deeply."

"It is of no importance. Everything in it is either wrong or irrelevant. Throw it away."

"It seems to be intended for your sister Val."

"It isn't." After a moment Sutter looked at him. "Why did you come out here?"

The engineer passed a hand across his eyes. "I—think you asked me, didn't you? I also came out to see Jamie. The family want him to come home," he said, remembering it for the first time as he spoke. "Or at least to know where he is."

"They know where he is."

"They do? How?"

"I called them last night. I spoke to Kitty."

"What did she say?" asked the engineer uneasily, and unconsciously hugged himself across the chest as if he too were a thin man.

"For one thing, she said you were coming. I've been expecting you."

The engineer told Sutter about his fugue. "Even now I am not too clear about things," he said, rubbing his eyes. "But I knew that I had business here."

"What kind of business?"

He frowned. "As I told you: that I was to see you, as well as find Jamie." He waited, hoping the other would tell him something, but Sutter was silent. The engineer happened to look down and caught sight of the two bottles in the Rexall bag. It was a bourbon called Two Natural. The cork showed a pair of dice rolling a lucky seven. "How is Jamie? Where is he?"

"Jamie is very sick."

"Did you tell Kitty?"

"No."

"Why not?"

"Jamie doesn't want them to come out."

"How sick is he?"

"He got a sore throat driving out."

"That's not so bad, is it?"

"It wouldn't be if he had any leucocytes."

"I see."

"The strep also lit up an old rheumatic lesion."

"You mean in his heart?" asked the engineer, arming himself against the dread sweetness of bad news.

But Sutter merely grunted and went on driving the Edsel in his old-fashioned sporty style, forefinger curled around the spoke of the steering wheel, left elbow propped on the sill. Presently the Edsel stopped in a shady street of tall Victorian houses which flanked a rambling frame building.

"Is he in the hospital?" he asked Sutter.

"Yes," said Sutter, but made no move to get out. Instead he hung fire politely, inclined sooty-eyed and civil over the wheel as if he were waiting on the engineer.

The engineer blinked. "Is Jamie in there?"

Sutter nodded and sat back with a sigh. "I'm very glad you're here," he said tapping the wheel.

"Do you wish me—"

"Go on in and see him. I have to go to work. I'll be back in a couple of hours."

"Where do you work?"

"At a guest ranch," said Sutter absently. "It's something like being a ship's doctor. It's only temporary, until—" He shrugged. "Jamie and I ran out of groceries."

When he got out, Sutter called him back.

"I forgot to tell you about the purpura."

"Purpura?"

"Like bruises. It's a new development, not particularly serious in itself but somewhat disconcerting. I thought it might bother you if you didn't know."

"Thank you." Don't worry, thought the engineer confidently. It won't bother me.

7.

But the purpura upset him badly. Jamie's face was covered with splotches of horrid color like oil slicks. It was as if a deep fetor, a swamp decay, had come to the surface. Speaking to him meant straining a bit as if one had to peer this way and that to see him through an evil garden of flowers.

It was an odd, unfitting business anyhow, Jamie being here. Jamie was as sick as he could be, yet he lay in a room off the street, so to speak. Could one be truly sick without proper notice and an accounting? The door was wide open and anyone could walk in. Yet no one did. He was alone. Should not some official cognizance be taken of his illness, some authorized person interposed between visitor and patient? One had only to ask the room number downstairs and walk up. The engineer could not get over the feeling that Jamie was not properly sick.

The patient was asleep. For some minutes the visitor stood about uncertainly, smiling warily, then, becoming alarmed, leaned closer to the sickbed. A sour heat radiated from the hollow of the pillow. In the triangle of Jamie's neck, a large vein pulsed in a complex rhythm. Jamie was not noticeably thinner. In fact, a deposit of new tissue, or perhaps dropsical fluid, had occurred under his skin. His face, always puddingish and ill-defined, had gone even more out of focus.

But no sooner had the engineer sat down than the patient opened his eyes and spoke to him quite naturally.

"What are you doing in these parts?" Though he was fairly goggling with fever, Jamie kept his soldierly way of lying abed. He lounged like a wounded man, pushed down his thigh, made a grimace.

"Looking for you and Sutter."

"Well, you found me. What do you want?"

"Nothing," said the engineer as wryly as the other. He rose. "I'll be seeing you."

Jamie laughed and made him sit down. "What's the matter with your leg?" the engineer asked.

"Got the rheumatiz."

Jamie began to speak fondly of Sutter, catching his breath now and then in his new warrior style. "You ought to see that rascal," said Jamie, shaking his head.

The engineer listened smilingly as Jamie told of Sutter's guest ranch whose cottages had such names as O.K. Corral and Boot Hill. Sutter lived at Doc's. "Though it's called a guest ranch, it's really a way station for grass widows. Ol' Sutter is busy as a one-armed paperhanger."

"I imagine," said the engineer fondly and gloomily. Jamie, he saw, had just got onto the trick of tolerating adults in their foibles. "Where is this place?"

"On the road to Albuquerque. It's the biggest guest ranch in the world. Have you seen him?"

"Yes." The engineer told of coming upon Sutter just after he bought two fifths of Two Natural. "Does he still drink bad whiskey?"

"Oh Christ," whispered Jamie joyfully and began to thrash his legs as of old.

After a while the youth began to sweat and, quite as abruptly as he had waked up, collapsed and fell back in the hot hollow of his pillow. Dear God, I stayed too long, thought the engineer, but as he arose to leave, one hand detained him with a weak deprecatory wave.

"What," said the engineer, smiling.

But there was no reply, save the hand moving over the covers, as tentative as a Ouija. For a long ten seconds he stood so, stooped slightly and hearkening. The hand stopped. No doubt he is asleep, thought the engineer, sighing with relief. Then he noticed that the soft mound of a vein in Jamie's neck was going at it hammer and tongs.

Frankly alarmed now, he began turning on switches and pressing buttons, all the while keeping a wary eye on the sick youth. How easy was it to die? When no one came—damn, what is this place?—he rushed out into the corridor and went careening off the walls toward the nurses' station. There sat a hefty blonde with a bald forehead which curved up under a brassy cone of hair. She looked like Queen Bess. She was making notes in a chart.

"Excuse me, nurse," said the courteous engineer, when she did not look up.

She did not seem to hear, though he was not five feet away.

"Excuse me," he said loudly, but nodding and smiling to deprecate his boldness when she did look.

She did not look! She went on making notes in violet ink.

He caught sight of himself in a convex mirror, placed at a corner to show the hall, standing like a pupil at teacher's desk. He frowned and opened the gate of the station and walked in. She turned a baleful lizard eye upon him. Then her eye traveled down and came to rest upon—his hand! He was touching the metal cover of a chart. Despite himself he blushed and removed his hand: teacher had caught him doing a bad thing with his hand. She went back to her work.

"Nurse," he said in a strangled voice. "Kindly come at once to room three-two-two. The patient is having an attack."

Still she did not answer! He had clenched his fist—at least he could hit her, lay her out cold—when at last she screwed cap to pen and with every appearance of ignoring him still and going about her business got up and brushed past him. He followed, sweating with rage—if she doesn't go to Jamie I am going to strike her. And even when she did turn into Jamie's room, she managed to convey that her going had nothing to do with his summons. She was still on business of her own.

No matter! She was with him now, taking his pulse. As the visitor watched through the doorway, Jamie's head turned wearily in the hot socket of his pillow. Whew! The bolus of hatred subsided in his throat. He forgave her. And now, instead of fearing that Jamie might die, he made light of it. It was, after all, only a sore throat.

And in fact when he returned in the afternoon, Jamie felt better. The visitor brought a deck of cards and they played gin in the cheerful yellow sunlight. Death seemed out of the question. How can anyone play a six of clubs one minute and die the next? Sick as he was, Jamie asked to be cranked up straight and now sat like a very old man, weaving a bit as the artery socked away at his head.

For the next few days they played cards morning and afternoon. Sutter came at night. It was understood that the universe was contracted to enclose the two young men. If it can be kept so, Jamie as good as said and the visitor agreed, a small sunny corner where we can play a game and undertake small tasks, nothing very serious can go amiss. For the first time the engineer understood how men can spend a week playing poker,

women a lifetime at bridge. The game was the thing. One
became impatient with non-game happenings—a nurse coming
in to empty the urinal. Time disposed itself in short tolerable
stretches between the bright beads of the games. The score
itself, totted up and announced, had the cheerful workaday
effect of a small tidy business.

It came to be understood too that one was at the other's
service and that any service could be required. As it sometimes
happens between two young men, a kind of daredevil bargain
was struck in which the very outrageousness of a request is itself
grounds for obeying.

"Go out and buy me a quart of Monarch applesauce," said
Jamie at the end of a game.

"All right."

Sutter came later in the evening. He was both affable and
nervous and told them half jokingly of his two new patients,
"noble intelligent women who still read Lawrence and still
believed in the dark gods of the blood, why make a god of
it, that was the Methodist in him, anyhow can you imagine
anyone still reading Lawrence out here *now*," etc. How uneasy
and talkative Sutter had become! It suddenly dawned on the
engineer that Sutter, strange as it seemed, could not stand the
sickroom. A hospital, of all places, made him nervous. Jamie,
he noticed too, became irritable because Sutter's coming broke
the golden circle of the card games. They both wished Sutter
would leave. And when Jamie frowned and picked up the deck
of cards, Sutter took the hint and did leave. He made a sign to
the engineer, who followed him to the solarium.

"Again I can't tell you how glad I am you're here," he said,
placing his feet carefully inside the black and white tiles. The
hospital was old and well preserved. It looked like an army
hospital from the days of Walter Reed. "He doesn't want to see
me and there is no one else. Or was."

The engineer looked at him curiously. "I thought that was
what you and he wanted."

"I didn't want him to be—sunk. I thought he might do
better, though I was afraid of this all along—" Sutter trailed
off.

"Isn't he sunk?"

"Your showing up has meant a great deal," said Sutter hurriedly and looked at his watch.

"What's the matter with him? Why does he have those spells?"

"Heart block," said Sutter absently. "With some right-sided failure and pulmonary edema. And you see, he can't read for long. His retina is infiltrated. You can read to him."

"What do you mean, heart block? Is that serious?"

Sutter shrugged. "Do you mean will he die today or next week?" He eyed the other. "Can you take a pulse?"

"I suppose so."

"I can't get a private nurse. If you are here when he has a syncope, take his pulse. It will almost certainly start up in a few seconds. Now I've got—"

"Wait. Good God. What are you talking about?"

"If then his pulse is steady, O.K. If it is fibrillating, call the resident."

"Good God, what do you mean, fibrillating?"

"Try to nod your head in time with his pulse. If you can't, he's fibrillating."

"Wait."

"What?"

"Nothing."

Sutter eyed him and, shoving his hands in his pockets, began to step off the tiles in an absent-minded hopscotch. With his Curlee pants down around his hips and his long-waisted shirt, Sutter looked like Lucky Lindy in the 1930's, standing in a propeller wash.

"I tell you what you do," said Sutter.

"What," said the engineer gloomily.

"Call Val. Tell her how sick Jamie is. He likes Val and wants to see her but doesn't want to send for her himself."

"Why don't you—" began the engineer.

"No, I tell you what you do," said Sutter, drawing him close in an odd little bantering confidence. "Call Rita."

"Rita," repeated the puzzled engineer.

"Yes, call Rita and Val and tell them to keep it to themselves and come on out." He held the younger man by the arm in an awkward little burlesque of Lamar Thigpen's old-buddy style.

"Why don't you call them: after all, you're the brother of one and the—"

"Because I'm like Jamie. I don't want to be the one to call either."

"I'm sorry. Jamie asked me not to call them. He trusts me."

"Then you've got nothing to worry about," said Sutter, his eyes going vacant.

"But—"

But Sutter was already on his way.

8.

With Sutter gone, it was possible to restore the golden circle of games. Jamie was dizzy and short of breath but not uncomfortable. His illness was the sort which allows one to draw in closer to oneself. Already Jamie had discovered the small privileges and warmths of invalidism. It was not a bad thing to lie back and blink at the cards lined up on the bed table, heave up on one elbow to make a play, flop down again in simple weariness. He wrapped himself snugly in his fever like a scarf. The next afternoon the engineer sat beside the bed in the sunny corner, which smelled of old wax and honorable ether. Outside in the still air, yellow as butter, the flat mathematical leaves of the aspens danced a Brownian dance in the sunlight, blown by a still, molecular wind. Jamie would play a card and talk, gaze at a point just beside the engineer's head where, it seemed, some privileged and arcane perception might be hit upon between them. Presently he fell back in the socket of his pillow and closed his eyes.

"Do me a favor."

"All right."

"Go get me a copy of *Treasure Island* and a box of soda crackers."

"All right," said the engineer, rising.

The youth explained that he had been thinking about the scene where Jim steals the dinghy and drifts offshore, lying down so he won't be seen, all the while eating soda crackers and looking at the sky.

"Also go by the post office and see if there's any mail in general delivery."

"Right."

But when he returned with the crackers and a swollen fusty library copy of *Treasure Island* showing hairy Ben Gunn on the frontispiece, Jamie had forgotten about it.

"There was no mail?"

"No."

"I tell you what let's do."

"What?"

"Call old Val."

"All right."

"Tell her I've got a crow to pick with her."

"All right. Do you want to see any of your family?"

"No. And I don't want to see her either. Just give her a message."

"All right."

"Ask her what happened to the book about entropy."

"Entropy? Then you correspond?"

"Oh, sure. Give her a hard time about the book. She promised to send it to me. Tell her I think she lost heart in the argument. She claims there is a historical movement in the direction of negative entropy. But so what? You know."

"Yes."

The youth's eyes sought his and again drifted away to the point in the air where the two of them found delicate unspoken agreement and made common cause against Val's arguments.

"There's a phone booth downstairs, but let's finish the game."

They didn't finish the game. Jamie went out of his head with fever, though it was a minute before the engineer realized it.

"Get me a line," exclaimed the youth in an odd chipper voice.

"What? All right," said the other, rising again. He thought Jamie meant make a phone call: get a long-distance line.

"A line, a lion," Jamie called to him at the door.

"A lion?"

"Ly-in."

Then he perceived that the youth was out of his head and was hearing words according to some fashion of his own.

"I will."

He waited until Jamie closed his eyes and, returning to the

bed, pressed the buzzer. This time someone came quickly, a pleasant little brunette student nurse who took Jamie's temperature and went off, but not too anxiously he was pleased to observe, to get the resident. Jamie was not dying then.

Perhaps he'd better call somebody though. Beyond a doubt Jamie was sick as a dog and also beyond a doubt Sutter had, in his own fashion, decamped. It was the inconsequence and unprovidedness of Jamie's illness which distressed him most. For the first time he saw how it might be possible for large numbers of people to die, as they die in China or Bombay, without anybody paying much attention.

As he passed the nurses' station, slapping his pockets for change, he met the eyes of the disagreeable blonde. Her malevolent expression startled him. Her bulging eye was glossy with dislike. She hated his guts! Amazing.

Thoughtfully he stacked money on the metal shelf of the phone booth. As the wires went clicking away to the East, he gazed through the open door and out into the disjunct afternoon with its simple spectrum-yellow and its flattened distances. Was it possible to call Alabama from here?

No. The line was busy.

He tried for half an hour and gave up.

When he returned to the room the pleasant student was giving Jamie an alcohol rub. Afterward the patient sat up in his right mind and began to read *Treasure Island* and eat soda crackers.

"Don't you want me to read to you?" the engineer asked him.

"No, that's all right!"

Jamie was polite but the engineer could tell he wanted to be alone.

"I'll be back after supper."

"Fine." The patient smiled his best smile because he wanted the visitor to leave. The book was the safest sunniest most inviolate circle of all.

9.

The next morning Jamie was even better. His fever was gone, but he was tired and wanted to sleep. For the first time he spoke seriously of going home, no, not home but to the Gulf Coast, where they could lie in the sand dunes and get in shape for the next semester. "I have the strongest hunch that the combination of cold salt water and the warm sunny dunes would be great!"

The engineer nodded. Sure enough it might.

Would the engineer take him?

"Let's go," said the latter rising.

Jamie laughed and nodded to signify that he knew the other meant it. "But I'll leave tomorrow, no kidding," he said as the engineer cranked him flat for his nap.

"We can make it in three days," the engineer told him. "Your monk's pad is still on the upper berth."

Jamie said no more about calling Val.

But for the present it was the engineer who lay in the upper berth and read:

Christ should leave us. He is too much with us and I don't like his friends. We have no hope of recovering Christ until Christ leaves us. There is after all something worse than being God-forsaken. It is when God overstays his welcome and takes up with the wrong people.

You say don't worry about that, first stop fornicating. But I am depressed and transcendent. In such a condition, fornication is the sole channel to the real. Do you think I am making excuses?

You are wrong too about the sinfulness of suicide in this age, at least the nurtured possibility of suicide, for the certain availability of death is the very condition of recovering oneself. But death is as outlawed now as sin used to be. Only one's own suicide remains to one. My "suicide" followed the breakdown of the sexual as a mode of reentry from the posture of transcendence.

Here is what happened. I became depressed last summer when I first saw Jamie's blood smear, depressed not because he was going to die but because I knew he would not die well, would be eased out in an oxygen tent, tranquilized and with no sweat to anyone and not even know what he was doing. Don't misunderstand me: I wasn't thinking about baptism.

The depression made me concupiscent. On a house call to the Mesa Motel to examine a patient in diabetic coma (but really only to collect blood for chemistry—I was little more than a technician that summer). Afterwards spied a chunky blonde by the pool, appraised her eye, which was both lewd and merry. She 41, aviatrix, winner of Powder Puff Derby in 1940's, raced an old Lockheed P-38 from San Diego to Cleveland. We drank two glasses of straight whiskey. I spoke in her ear and invited her to her room. Afterwards very low. Went to ranch, shot myself, missed brain, carried away cheek.

Recovery in hospital. The purity of ordeal. The purity of death. The sweet purity of the little Mexican nurse. Did Americans become lewd when they banished death?

I saw something clearly while I had no cheek and grinned like a skeleton. But I got well and forgot what it was. I won't miss next time.

It was the last entry in Sutter's casebook. When he finished reading, the engineer left the Trav-L-Aire and threw the pad into the trashburner of Alamogordo Motor Park. As he watched it burn, glowering, his head sinking lower and lower, mouth slack and drying, he became aware that someone was speaking to him. It was a fellow Trav-L-Aire owner, a retired fire inspector from Muncie. He and his wife, the man had told him, were in the midst on their yearly swing from Victoria, B.C., to Key West. They kept just ahead of winter on the way down and just behind spring going north. It was a courtesy of the road that camper owners show their rigs to each other. The engineer invited him in. The Hoosier was polite enough—the engineer's was the most standard of all Trav-L-Aires—but it was obvious that the former had a surprise in store. After showing off his cabin, which had a tinted sun-liner roof, he pressed a button. A panel above the rear door flew open and a contraption of aluminum spars and green netting unhinged in six directions. With a final grunt of its hidden motor the thing snapped into a taut cube of a porch big enough for a bridge game. "You take off your screen door and put it here," the Hoosier told him. "It's the only thing for west Florida, where you're going to get your sand flies."

"Very good," said the engineer, nodding and thrusting his hand through his pocket, for his knee had begun to leap.

Returning to his own modest camper, he became at once agitated and lustful. His heart beat powerfully at the root of his neck. The coarsest possible images formed themselves before his eyes. But this time, instead of throwing a fit or lapsing into a fugue as he had done so often in the past, he became acutely conscious of the most insignificant sensations, the slight frying sound of the Servel refrigerator, the watery reflection on the Formica table, which seemed to float up the motes of dust. His memory, instead of failing, became perfect. He recalled everything, even a single perception years ago, one of a thousand billion, so trivial that it was not even remembered then, five minutes later: on a college field trip through the mangy Jersey woods looking for spirogyra, he had crossed a utility right-of-way. When he reached the farther woods, he had paused and looked over his shoulder. There was nothing to see: the terrain dipped, making a little swale which was overgrown by the special forlorn plants of rights-of-way, not small trees or bushes or even weeds exactly but just the unclassified plants which grow up in electric-light-and-power-places. That was all. He turned and went on.

Desolate places like Appomattox and cut-over woods were ever the occasion of storms of sexual passion. Yet now when he rushed out into the abstract afternoon to find a maid (but who?) he forgot again and instead found himself picking through the ashes of the trashburner. What was that last sentence? It had a bearing. But the notebook was destroyed.

Jumping into the cab of the G.M.C., he tore out of the poplar grove, forgetting his umbilical connections until he heard the snappings of cords and the shout of the Hoosier.

"What the—" yelled the latter like an astounded comic-strip character, Uncle Walt (so that's where the expression "What the—" comes from—Indiana).

"I'm going over to Albuquerque," shouted the engineer as if this were an explanation and as quickly changed his mind, stopped, and strode past the still-astounded Hoosier. "Pardon," he said, "I think I'll call Kitty—" and nodded by way of further explanation to a telephone hooked contingently to a telephone pole. Could he call Kitty from such a contingent telephone?

Perhaps if he could talk to a certain someone he would stop hankering for anyone and everyone, and tender feelings of love would take the place of this great butting billygoat surge which was coming over him again. He clung to the pole, buffeted by an abstract, lustful molecular wind, and might even have uttered a sound, brayed into the phone, for the Hoosier looked astounded again and rushed into his deluxe Sun-Liner.

10.

"I remember everything now, Dr. Vaught," he said calmly, no longer agitated. "You said I was to come and find you. Very well, here I am. What was it you wished to tell me?"

So distracted had been the engineer in his headlong race across the desert that he had noticed not a single thing on the way and could not have said how he found his way here. Only now as Sutter sighed and sank into himself could he spare time to take a breath and see where he was.

Sutter was sitting in a sheriff's chair on the front porch of Doc's cottage. Doc's was one of a hundred or more such cottages fronting on a vast quadrangle of rich blue-green winter grass bordered by palm trees, a rectangular oasis in a scrabbly desert of mesquite. The evening rides were over and it was almost suppertime. Doors slammed as the dudes, mostly women, began the slow promenade to the chuck wagon. The sun was already down behind Sandia Mountain but the sky was bright and pure and empty as map space. The dudes smiled and nodded at Doc as they passed but the latter sat slumped and unresponsive, his dried-up Thom McAn shoes propped on the rail and Curlee pants hitched halfway up his skinny legs.

Sutter didn't seem to hear him. He slumped further and gazed at the bare mountain. The material of his trousers bunched up between his legs like curtain drapes.

"Then you have nothing to tell me," the engineer asked him again.

"That is correct. Nothing."

"But, sir, you wrote many things in—"

"In the first place I didn't write them to you. In the second place I no longer believe a word of it. Did you ever read the great philosopher Wittgenstein?"

"No sir," said the other gloomily.

"After his last work he announced the dictum which summarized his philosophy. He said: Whereof one cannot speak, thereof one should keep silent. And he did. He stopped teaching and went to live in a hut and said no more."

"And you believe that?"

"No, I don't even believe that."

They watched the women for a while. Presently the engineer said, "But you told me to come out and find you."

"I did?"

"Therefore you at least owe me the explanation of what happened to make you change your mind."

"What has happened?" Sutter looked puzzled.

"What has happened to you?"

"Nothing has happened."

From the chair beside him, where he must have held it all along and out of the other's sight, Sutter raised the Colt Woodsman and sighted it at an airliner which sparkled like a diamond in the last of the sunlight.

"But Val told me that you—"

"Val." Sutter smiled as he tracked the airliner.

"Oh, I know you don't agree with Val."

"Oh, but I do agree with her."

"You do?"

"Oh yes, in every respect. About what has happened to the world, about what God should be and what man is, and even what the Church should be."

The engineer sighed. "Yes sir. That is very interesting, but I think you know why I am here."

"You see, Barrett, Val had a dream of what the Church should come to. (And I agree! Absolutely!) For example, she did not mind at all if Christendom should be done for, stove in, kaput, screwed up once and all. She did not mind that the Christers were like everybody else, if not worse. She did not even mind that God shall be gone, absent, not present, A.W.O.L., and that no one noticed or cared, not even the believers. Because she wanted us to go the route and be like Sweden, which is not necessarily bad, but to go the route, to leave God out of it and be happy or miserable, as the case might be. She believes that then, if we go the route and run out of Christendom, that the air would be cleared and even that God might give us a sign. That's how her own place makes sense, you see, her little foundation in the pines. She conceived herself as being there with her Delco and her butane tanks to start all over again. Did you notice how much it looked like one of those surviving enclaves after the Final War, and she's probably right: I mean, who in the hell would want to bomb South Alabama? But yes, I agree with her. Absolutely! It's just that nothing ever came of it."

"Dr. Vaught. Excuse me, but—"

"Don't you see? Nothing happened. She got all dressed up for the bridegroom and the bridegroom didn't come. There she sits in the woods as if the world had ended and she was one of the Elected Ones Left to keep the Thing going, but the world has not ended, in fact is more the same than usual. We are in the same fix, she and I, only I know it and she doesn't. Here I sit in Sweden—most of those women are Swedes, spiritual Swedes, if you will notice—but I do wait for a sign because there is no sign. I will even agree with her that when I first came to the desert I was waiting for a sign, but there was no sign and I am not waiting for one now."

"Yes sir. That is very interesting. But the reason I came, if you will recall, is that you told me—"

"But she changed, you see, and that was when we parted company. I could make some sense of her notion of being the surviving remnant of her Catholic Thing (which has to prevail, you see, in spite of all, yes, I don't mind that) set down back there in that God-forsaken place. That was fitting. But she changed, you see. *She became hopeful.* She goes to confraternity meetings in Mobile. She has dealings with the Methodist preacher, even the Baptists. She corresponds with scientists. She begs from the Seven-Up man and slips him a K.C. pamphlet ('How many churches did Christ found?'). She talks the Klonsul into giving her a gym. In short, she sold out. Hell, what she is is a Rotarian."

"Yes sir, very true, but what I want to—"

"Barrett."

"Sir?"

"Which is the best course for a man: to live like a Swede, vote for the candidate of your choice, be a good fellow, healthy and generous, do a bit of science as if the world made sense, enjoy a beer and a good piece (not a bad life!). Or: to live as a Christian among Christians in Alabama? Or to die like an honest man?"

"I couldn't say," said the engineer. He was bitterly disappointed by Sutter's refusal to take him seriously.

"How is Jamie?" asked Sutter.

"Better," said the other absently. "I am on my way there now. If you will answer my question, I'll leave."

"What question?"

"The last time I saw you you said you had something to tell me. What was it?"

"I don't remember."

The engineer, who had been pacing the tiny porch, which abutted Wells Fargo on one side and the O.K. Corral on the other, paused and fixed Sutter with a lively clairvoyant expression. Now at last he remembered everything, knew what he knew and what he didn't know and what he wished to know. He even remembered every sentence in Sutter's notebook.

"I want to know what it was you discovered while you were in the, ah, hospital out here last summer."

"*What?*" said Sutter, coming down hard on all four legs of the captain's chair.

The engineer was not disconcerted. "I've finished your casebook. I wish to know whether you meant only that when you're in a bad way things look better than they do ordinarily."

"Oh," said Sutter, replacing his feet. "That. I don't remember. That was a long time ago and, as I told you, I attach no importance to that stuff. It was written to be rid of it, excreta, crap, and so intended."

"I just finished speaking to Kitty." The engineer drew up another sheriff's chair. "We spoke for two hours. It cost twenty-four dollars. I had to reverse the charges."

"Good Lord. I can't imagine talking to Kitty for five minutes."

"We settled a great many things," said the engineer, frowning—who in hell was Sutter to patronize Kitty?

"Are you getting married?" asked Sutter politely, turning his chair a few degrees but keeping his pale eyes fixed on the brown schematic mountain.

"Yes. After—things are more settled. But that is not why I drove out here this afternoon. I want to know this," he said, leaning over and grabbing the rim of Sutter's chair so hard that his knuckles turned white. "I want to know why you brought Jamie out here."

Sutter tried to tear his eyes from the mountain. "You're right. It didn't work, did it?"

"Right? What do you mean? What didn't work?"

Sutter shrugged. "Jamie's little idea of a vacation."

"Jamie's? But according to what you wrote, it was your idea too. What did you expect him to do?"

"It's not what I expected."

"Then he expected something?"

"Yes."

"What?"

"He expected something to happen."

"What? Not get well?"

Sutter shrugged.

"But you brought him out. You must have hoped for something."

"Only that he might get a little better."

"Get better?" He watched the other like a hawk. "No, you mean die better, don't you?"

Sutter shrugged and said nothing.

"You didn't answer," said the engineer after a moment.

Again Sutter's feet hit the floor. "Goddamn it, Barrett, what do you mean by requiring answers from me? Why should I answer you? What are you to me? Christ, if you recall I never solicited your company in the first place."

"I am asking nevertheless," said the engineer cheerfully.

"Why me, for Christ's sake?"

"I don't know."

"What do you take me for, some pissant wise man, ole rebel Sutter whom the yokels back home can't stand and who therefore by your peculiar logic must be onto something just because they're not? You know something, Barrett? There's one thing I've never been able to get the straight of, and that is what it is you want of me. I suspect it is one of two things. You either want me to tell you to fornicate or not to fornicate, but for the life of me I can't tell which it is."

"Then tell me," said the engineer smiling.

"I will not tell you."

"Tell me to be chaste and I will do it. Yes! I will do it easily!" he said, striking the rail softly with his fist. "All you have to do is tell me."

"I will not tell you."

"Then tell me not to be chaste."

"I will not."

"Why not?"

"Barrett, since when is failure, my failure, a badge of wisdom?"

"I did not think of it that way," said the engineer, frowning. Suddenly he did see Sutter for the first time as the dismalest failure, a man who had thrown himself away. He marveled at his, the engineer's, being here.

"I know you don't," said Sutter, not unkindly. "But maybe you better start. For both our sakes. Be done with me. Go stay with Jamie."

"That's what I'm trying to do," said the other absently.

"What?"

"Be done with you."

"I fervently wish you success."

"Yes," said the engineer, cheering up. "Yes! You're right. There is no reason why I can't just get up and go about my business, is there?"

"No reason."

"To answer your earlier question: yes, Kitty and I are getting married."

"You mentioned it."

"We spoke of many things."

"Good."

"And settled a fair proportion of them."

"Good."

"It turns out we see eye to eye on most things."

"Excellent."

"It seems that Mr. Vaught has made Lamar a vice-president

and that he is going to offer me the position of personnel manager. I actually feel I might do well at it."

"I have no doubt of it."

"For the first time I feel fairly certain of what I want to do."

"I'm glad to hear it."

"We even have a house in mind. Cap'n Andy Mickle's place on South Ridge. Do you know it?"

"Very well indeed."

"You've been there?"

"A dozen times."

"Why? Oh. You mean to treat Cap'n Andy?"

"A colossal bore. He bored himself to death. But that's no reflection on the house. An ideal spot. The best view on the ridge."

The engineer frowned, thinking of the buzzards circling the doleful plain and Cap'n Andy striding the "bridge." But he quickly brightened. "We've even agreed on the same denomination."

"The same *what?*"

"Denomination. Church. Kitty has become quite religious. She is convinced of the wisdom of our having the same church home, to use her expression." The engineer laughed tolerantly, shaking his head at the ways of women, and wiped a merry tolerant little tear from his eye.

"Jesus," muttered Sutter.

"Eh?" The other cocked his good ear.

"Nothing."

"You don't fool me, Dr. Vaught. Don't forget that I've read your casebook. Though I do not pretend to understand everything, that part didn't escape me."

"What part?"

"Your awareness of the prime importance of the religious dimension of life."

"The religious dimension of life?" Sutter looked at him suspiciously. "Barrett, are you putting me on?"

"No sir."

"Then if you're not, you're doing something worse."

"Sir?" asked the engineer politely.

"Never mind."

"Dr. Vaught," said the engineer earnestly. "There is one more thing. Then I will leave."

"What is that?"

"Dr. Vaught, Kitty and I are getting married. I am going to take a good position with your father, settle down on the South Ridge, and, I hope, raise a family."

"Yes," said Sutter after a pause.

"I think I'm going to be a pretty fair member of the community. God knows the place could use even a small contribution of good will and understanding."

"Beyond a doubt. Good will and understanding. Yes. Very good."

"Well?"

"Well what?"

"What's wrong with that?"

"Nothing. I think you'll be very happy. In fact I'll go further than that. I don't think you'll have any more trouble with your fugues. And I take it back: I don't think you are kidding me."

"I see. Dr. Vaught."

"What?"

"I know you think there is something wrong with it."

"You do?"

"Yes. I know you think there is everything wrong with it."

"Nonsense." Sutter laughed. "Would you rather join me here?"

"No, but—"

"But what?"

"But nothing." The engineer rose. "There is nothing wrong with it. Truthfully I see now there is nothing wrong with such a life."

"Right!"

"It is better to do something than do nothing—no reflection, sir."

"No reflection."

"It is good to have a family."

"You are quite right."

"Better to love and be loved."

"Absolutely."

"To cultivate whatever talents one has."

"Correct."

"To make a contribution, however small."

"However small."

"To do one's best to promote tolerance and understanding between the races, surely the most pressing need before the country."

"Beyond question the most pressing need. Tolerance and understanding. Yes."

The engineer flushed. "Well, isn't it better?"

"Yes."

"Violence is bad."

"Violence is not good."

"It is better to make love to one's wife than to monkey around with a lot of women."

"A lot better."

"I am sure I am right."

"You are right."

The engineer gazed gloomily at the chuck wagon, a large red dining cottage across the quadrangle. Cookie, a Chinese with a black cap and a queue, came out and seizing the branding iron rang it around the iron triangle.

"You know, Dr. Vaught, I have lived a rather abnormal and solitary life and have tended to get things backwards. My father was a proud and solitary man. I had no other family. For a long time I have had a consuming desire for girls, for the coarsest possible relations with them, without knowing how to treat them as human beings. No doubt, as you suggested, a good part of my nervous condition stems from this abnormal relationship—or lack of relationship—"

"As I suggested? I never suggested any such goddamn thing."

"At any rate," the engineer went on hurriedly, looking down at the other, "I think I see for the first time the possibility of a happy, useful life."

"Good. So?"

"Dr. Vaught, why was that man screaming?"

"What man?"

"The man you told me about—the Deke from Vanderbilt—with the lovely wife and children—you know."

"Oh, Scotty. Christ, Barrett, for somebody with fugues, you've got quite a memory."

"Yes sir."

"Don't worry about Scotty. You won't scream. I can assure you, you will not scream."

"Then it is better not to?"

"Are you asking me?"

"Yes."

Sutter shrugged.

"You have nothing more to tell me?"

"No, Barrett, nothing." To his surprise, Sutter answered him quietly, without making a face or cursing.

The engineer laughed with relief. "For the first time I think I really might live like other men—rejoin the human race."

"I hope you'll all be happy. You and the race, I mean."

"Oh, I forgot something. It was something Kitty said to tell you. God, I'm selfish."

"But in the future you're going to be unselfish."

"What? Oh. Yes," said the engineer, smiling. He declined to conspire with Sutter's irony. "Kitty said to tell you Lamar was going to take a special course in management at the Harvard Business School."

"Good Lord, what do I care what Lamar does?"

The engineer kept a wary eye on him. "And that while he is in Boston, Myra is going to stay with Rita in New York."

"Myra Thigpen? I see. Do you want to know something? It figures."

"Rita is already gone. Myra is leaving after—afterwards."

"So Rita is gone." Sutter gazed into the empty sky, which instead of turning rosy with sunset was simply going out like a light.

As the other watched him, Sutter began idly picking off dudes, sighting the Colt at one after another of the passing women, idly yet with a regardlessness which was alarming. It was a very small thing, no more than that Sutter did not take pains to conceal the pistol from the women, but for some reason the engineer's heart began to pound against his ribs.

"On the other hand," Sutter was saying between shots, "it is also possible to die without significance and that is hardly an improvement of one's state of life. I knew a man once, not my own patient I am glad to say, who was sitting with his family one Sunday evening watching Lassie, who had befriended a crippled duck and was protecting him from varmints. During the commercial he got up and got out his old army forty-five. When his family asked him what he intended to do, he told them he was going outside to shoot a varmint. So he went outside to the garage and got into the family's second car, a Dodge Dart, and blew the top of his head off. Now that's a lot of damn foolishness, isn't it?"

"Yes sir," said the engineer, who was now more irritated than frightened by Sutter's antics with the pistol. Nor did he any longer believe Sutter's dire little case histories. "The other thing I want to tell you is that—" he said as Cookie rang second call with the branding iron. "Kitty said to tell you that the, ah, legal difficulties in your case have been cleared up and that—"

"You mean the coast is clear."

"Yes sir."

"Poppy has fixed things up and Doc Holliday can come back home to Valdosta."

"Sir, you have an enormous contribution to make—" began the engineer.

Sutter rose so suddenly that the younger man was afraid he'd made him angry again. But Sutter's attention was elsewhere.

Following his eye, the engineer alighted upon one of the guests who had left the O.K. Corral next door and was presently coming abreast of Doc's cottage. To judge from her Levis, which were stiff and blue, she was a new arrival. The old civil sorrowful air of the East still clung to her; she walked as if she still wore a dress. Though she had hooked her thumbs into her pockets, she had not yet got into the way of making herself free of herself and of swinging her legs like a man. She even wore a cowgirl hat, not at all the thing here, which had fallen down her back and was supported by a string at her throat. But she was abstracted and did not care, and instead of ambling along with the others, she went musing alone, tongue set against her teeth and hissing a solitary little tune. There was about her the wryness and ruefulness of a twenty-eight-year-old who has been staggered by a not quite mortal blow and has her own woman's way of getting over it and in fact has already done so. She knew how to muse along a path and hiss a little tune and keep herself to herself.

Sutter rose creakily but cheerfully and rubbed his dry reedy hands together. "I do believe it is time to eat. Will you join me?"

"No sir. I promised Jamie I'd be back by seven."

To his relief, Sutter left the Colt in his chair and had, apparently, forgotten about it.

"I'll be in by nine."

"Yes sir."

"Barrett, I think you'd better call the family."

"But I just—"

"Tell them they'd better get out here."

"Yes sir."

"Tell them I said so."

"All right."

"Somebody will have to be here to take care of things after Jamie's death."

"I'll be here."

"Some member of the family."

"You'll be here."

"No, Barrett, I'll not be here."

"Why not?" asked the other angrily—he had had enough of Sutter's defections.

"Barrett," said Sutter as cheerfully as ever, craning his neck to keep track of the new guest, "if you know anything at all—and, what with your peculiar gifts, you know a good deal more than that—you ought to know why not."

"I don't," said the engineer, at a total loss. He had lost his intuition!

"If I do outlive Jamie," said Sutter, putting on his Curlee jacket (double breasted!), "it will not be by more than two hours. What in Christ's name do you think I'm doing out here? Do you think I'm staying? Do you think I'm going back?"

The engineer opened his mouth but said nothing. For the first time in his life he was astonished.

"You won't join me, Barrett?"

"What? No. No, thanks."

Sutter nodded cheerfully, dropped the pistol in the side pocket of the jacket, and hurried down the path after the last of the dudes.

Perhaps this moment more than any other, the moment of his first astonishment, marked the beginning for the engineer of what is called a normal life. From that time forward it was possible to meet him and after a few minutes form a clear notion of what sort of fellow he was and how he would spend the rest of his life.

11.

The pleasant little brunette was coming out of Jamie's room when he turned the corner. He smiled at her and experienced a pang of pleasure when she veered and he saw she meant to stop him. But she was not smiling, and instead of speaking she held out a thermometer. He couldn't see for looking, save only that the red line came dizzyingly near the top.

"Is he conscious?" he asked her.

"If you want to call it that. He's delirious."

"Do you think you should—"

"I've already notified Dr. Bice."

"How is his pulse?"

"One-thirty, but regular."

"He's not, ah, fibrillating?"

"No."

"Would you come back later, that is, from time to time when you can—as often as you can, in fact, to take his pulse."

Now she did smile. "Why yes."

One look at Jamie and he went for the phone. The youth's face was turned to the window. His dusty dead friable hair lay on the pillow as if it had been discarded, a hank.

As he got change from the cashier—he wouldn't dare reverse the charges to Val—he began to grieve. It was the shame of it, the bare-faced embarrassment of getting worse and dying which took him by surprise and caught his breath in his throat. How is this matter to be set right? Were there no officials to deal with the shame of dying, to make suitable recompense? It was like getting badly beat in a fight. To *lose*. Oh, to lose so badly. Oh, you bastards living and well and me dying, and where is the right of that? Oh, for the bitter shame of it.

At last the circuits clicked open into the frying frazzling silence of Alabama. He fancied he could hear the creak of the cancerous pines.

"Hello," he cried after a wait. "Hello!"

"Hello," came a voice as faint and faraway as 1901.

"Who is this?"

"This here Axel." It sounded like a child standing a good two feet below a wall phone.

"Axel, let me speak to Sister Johnette Mary Vianney."

"Who?"

He repeated it.

"Who dat?"

"Sister—"

"Sister Viney?"

"Yes, Sister Viney."

"Yes suh, she here."

"Well, go get her, Axel."

"Yes suh."

The ancient Alabama silence fried away in his ear. His foot went to sleep. Twice he had to stoke the box with quarters. That black cretin Axel—

"Hello."

He gave a start. He had almost forgotten where he was. "Hello, is this Val? That is, Sister—"

"This is Val."

"Val, this is—" Christ, who? "—Will Barrett."

"Yes?" The same calculated buzzing non-surprise—he felt a familiar spasm of irritation.

"I, ah—Jamie asked me to call you."

"Yes?"

"It's about a book. A book about entropy. Actually, that is not the real reason I'm—"

"Entropy," she repeated.

"Jamie said you promised to send him a book."

"How is Jamie?"

"He asked me—"

"Never mind about the book. How is he?"

"He is very sick."

"Is he dying?"

"I think so."

"I'm leaving now. I'll get a plane in New Orleans."

"Good."

He slumped with the relief of it. She'd do, nutty as she was. It came over him suddenly: there is another use for women after all, especially Southern women. They knew how to minister to the dying! It was they all along who had set at nought the shame of it and had done it so well that he had not even known that it took doing. He'd rather have a proper Southern woman (even one of his aunts!) but he'd settle for this one. "Very good. And would you call the rest of the family. My change is gone and I have to get back to Jamie." All women come. The more women, the less shame.

"If anything happens before I get there, you'll have to attend to it."

"Yes, ma'am. Attend to what?"

"His baptism."

"Ma'am? Eh?"

"I said you'll have to see to his baptism if I don't get there in time."

"Excuse me," said the courteous but terrified engineer. "Much as I'd like to oblige you, I don't believe I can take the responsibility."

"Why not?"

"For one thing, I'm not a member of the family."

"You're his friend, aren't you?"

"Yes."

"Would you deny him penicillin if it would save his life?"

"No," he said, stiffening. None of your Catholic tricks, Sister, the little tricky triumphs of analogy. You learned more in Paterson, New Jersey, than you realize. But he said only: "Why don't you get Sutter?"

"I don't know where he is."

"As a matter of fact, he asked me to call you too."

"Good. Then you hold the fort till I get there."

"I don't believe in baptizing anybody against their will," said the sweating engineer, for lack of anything better to say.

"Then ask him if it's against his will."

"Ask him?"

"Barrett, I charge you to ask him." She sounded serious enough but he couldn't swear she wasn't laughing at him.

"It's really none of my business, Sister."

"It's my responsibility but I am giving it to you until I get there. You can call a priest, can't you?"

"I am not of your faith, Sister." Where did he get these solemn religious expressions?

"Then call a minister for God's sake. Or do it yourself. I charge you. All you have to do is—"

"But—"

"If you don't call someone, then you'll have to do it yourself."

Then God knows I'll call someone, thought the prudent engineer. But he was becoming angry. To the devil with this exotic pair, Sutter and Val, the absentee experts who would deputize him, one to practice medicine, the other to practice priestcraft. Charge him indeed. Who were they to charge anybody?

"Barrett, look. I know that you are a highly intelligent and an intuitive man, and that you have a gift for fathoming people. Isn't that true?"

"I don't know," he said glumly.

"I think you can tell when somebody is deadly serious about something, can't you?"

"I couldn't say."

"Then I am charging you with the responsibility. You will have to fathom that according to your own lights."

"You can't—" But the circuits had closed on unhappy old Alabama, frying away in its own juices.

The poor addled engineer took the steps four at a time, racing to do he knew not what. So that when he reached the sickroom and found Jamie both unconscious and unattended, he was of two minds about it: dismayed that the worst had happened, that Jamie was very likely dying here and now; yet relieved despite himself that Jamie was unconscious and so he didn't have to ask him any such question (for it was of course absolutely the last question to be tolerated by the comradely and stoic silence generated between the two of them). Here he stood, therefore, stooped over the machinery of Jamie's veins, hoist not only by the vast awkwardness of dying but now by religion too. He became angrier than ever. Where was the hospital staff? Where was the family? Where was the chaplain? Then he noticed, almost idly as if he had spied a fly on the pillow, that there was something amiss about the vein. Its machinery rhythm was out of kilter.

All along he had known it would come to this and that he couldn't do it. He couldn't take the pulse. The thread of artery stirred fitfully under his finger but there was no profit in it. Which stirrings to count?

Without knowing how he came there, he had fetched up again at the nurses' cage where reigned bald Queen Bess. Once again he made noises and motions and once again she annihilated him, rendered him invisible and of no account.

"Nurse," he said sternly, four feet away. He actually raised a forefinger.

She answered the telephone.

All at once time fell in, bent, and he was transported over the Dutch sort of door—it didn't seem to open—flew over it like a poltergeist and found himself inside the station. He seemed to be listening. "You hear me, goddamn it," thundered a voice terrible and strange. It was for the two of them to listen as the voice went on. "—or else I'm going to kick yo' ass down there." An oddly Southern voice, then not his surely. Yet her glossy eyes were on *him*, round as a dollar watch, the lids nictitating from below like a lizard's. Her smile, stretching open the rugae, the troughs of which he noticed were bare of lipstick, proffered a new ghastly friendship for *him*. Now as he watched, dreaming, she was using the phone again.

"Yes sir. But Mr. Barrett seems a little upset. Yes, good." She knew him! Perhaps she had known him all along. On the other hand, there seemed to have sprung up between them a brand-new friendship, a species of roguish fondness.

Again segments of time collapsed, fell away, and he was transported magically into the corridor, she at his side, squeezing his arm in a love-joke. Doors flew open. Elevators converged on the floor.

The next thing he knew he was speaking in a businesslike and considered manner to the resident and chaplain outside Jamie's closed door. He had survived the hiatus of his rage. There remained only the smell of it, strong as burnt meat; he hugged his arms close to his armpits.

The resident had just come out of Jamie's room. He spoke seriously but in a measured, relaxed way. That's what I wanted, thought the engineer, sighing—someone to give measure and form to time itself. Was that the worst of dying, dying without permission, license, so to speak?

The engineer nodded and turned to the chaplain. He explained the commission.

"Therefore it seemed proper to me," he concluded, "to pass along to you the request of his sister, who is a religious of your faith."

"I see," said the priest, who, however, instead of listening to what the engineer said, was eyeing this strange young man himself. Evidently he could not make out what kind of bird he was dealing with. Three times he asked the engineer where he came from, as if this might shed some light.

"Do you know Father Gillis from Conway, Arkansas?" the priest asked him. If only he could get a fix on him!

"No sir." Damnation, did they have to hit upon a mutual friend?

They were a curious pair, the resident and the priest. The resident was hollow-eyed and green-skinned and sunken of cheek. His hair grew down his neck in ringlets like a hyacinth. There was a rash on his throat under his loose collar. But unhealthy as he was he affected the easy nonchalance of an athlete and swung his fist softly. The priest was a neat chunky man whose thick auburn hair had been freshly cut and combed, exposing a white healthy scalp in the wide part. The gold stems of his bifocals pressed snugly against muscular temples. His hand, which he gave the engineer in a tentative interrogatory clasp (what sort of a bird are you, asked the hand), was thick through the palm and heavily freckled.

"He's fibrillating," said the haggard resident, first addressing the engineer. Then, not quite getting hold of him either, he turned to the priest, all the while making a few soft swings of fist to hand. "A heavy presystolic murmur. Temperature one-o-five point three, lungs filled up to the seventh interspace, spleen down to here."

"What does that mean?" asked the frowning engineer.

The resident shrugged, squared off with his fist for a combination punch but didn't throw it. "Pulmonary edema, for one thing. He's drowning in his own fluids."

"Will he regain consciousness?"

The resident frowned. There was a protocol here, a way of speaking-in-the-hall which the resident and priest were onto and he, the engineer, was not. The question did not pass muster, for the resident turned to the priest.

"Do you know what that joker told me last night?" (This is the way we speak.) "I always horse around with him. I wanted to take his temperature and I asked him what he wanted me to do, meaning which did he prefer, rectal or oral. So he says to me: Bice, you know what you can do with it. Oh, you can't make a nickel on him," he said, trying the engineer again (Now do you see? This is the way death itself can be gotten past).

The priest hung fire, vague and fond, until he saw the resident had finished. "Now, ah," he said, touching the engineer's elbow with just the hint of interrogatory pressure, as if he meant to ask the time. But the touch was skillful. The engineer found himself guided into the solarium.

"Let me see if I understand you," said the priest, putting his head down and taking hold of a water pipe in his thick freckled hand. He watched intently as his perfect thumbnail creased a blister of paint. "This young man you say has never been baptized, and though he is unconscious now and perhaps will not regain consciousness, you have reason to believe he desires baptism?"

"No sir. His sister desires the baptism."

"But he has a Catholic background?"

"If you mean Roman Catholic, no. I'm an Episcopalian," said the engineer stiffly. Where in the world did these ready-made polemics come from? Never in his entire lifetime had he given such matters a single thought and now all at once he was a stout Anglican, a defender of the faith.

"Of course, of course. And the young man in there, is he also from a Protestant, that is, an Episcopal background?"

"No sir. His background was originally Baptist, though his family later became Episcopalian—which accounts for the delay." The engineer, who could not quite remember the explanation, fell silent. "Delay in baptism, that is," he added after a moment.

The priest examined another blister on the water pipe. "I don't quite see why I have been summoned," he said softly. "Perhaps you'd better call the Protestant chaplain."

"Oh, no, sir," said the engineer hastily, breaking out in a sweat lest the priest leave and he, the engineer, should have to go careening around the walls again. "Jamie professed no faith, so it is all the same which of you ministers, ah, ministers to him." For some reason he laughed nervously. He didn't want this fellow to get away—for one thing, he liked it that the other didn't intone in a religious voice. He was more like a baseball umpire in his serviceable serge, which was swelled out by his muscular body. "As I told you, his sister, who is a nun, made me promise to send for you. She is on her way out here. She is a religious of a modern type. Her habit is short, to about here." Then, realizing that he was not helping his case, he added nervously: "I wouldn't be surprised if she didn't found her own order. She is doing wonderful work among the Negroes. Aren't foundresses quite often saints?" He groaned.

"I see," said the priest, and actually stole a glance at the other to see, as the engineer clearly perceived, whether he was quite mad. But the engineer was past minding, as long as the priest got on with it. Evidently this was an unusual case. The priest tried again.

"Now you. Are you a friend of the family?"

"Yes, a close friend and traveling companion of the patient."

"And the other gentleman—he is the patient's brother?"

"Sutter? Is he here?" For the second time in his life the engineer was astonished.

"There is a visitor with the patient who I gather, from his conversation with Dr. Bice, is a doctor."

"That must be Sutter."

"The only thing is, I don't yet quite understand why it is you and not he who is taking the initiative here."

"He was not here when Jamie had his attack. But he told me—he must have just come."

The priest took off his glasses, exposing naked eyes and a naked nosebridge, and carefully polished the lenses with a clean handkerchief. Making a bracket of his hand, he put the glasses back on, settling the stems onto his healthy temples.

"It would help if we had some indication from the patient or at least from the immediate family. Otherwise I don't want to intrude. In fact, I would say it is a 'must.'"

"Yes sir." Unhinged as he was, the engineer was still sentient. He perceived that the priest had a certain style of talking which he no doubt shared with other priests. It was a good bet that quite a few priests liked to say such things as "It is a 'must'" or perhaps "Now that is the sixty-four-dollar question."

"Sir, could we go in and speak to the patient's brother?"

"Well, let's see what we shall see."

The resident had left. Sutter was leaning against the window in Jamie's room, his foot propped on the radiator.

"Dr. Vaught," said the engineer, handing the priest along ahead of him—the goods to be delivered at last. "This is Father—"

"Boomer," said the priest.

"Father Boomer," said Sutter, shaking hands but not taking his foot from the radiator.

After a glance at Jamie—the youth's head had fallen to the side and his eyes were closed—the engineer told Sutter: "Val asked me to call Father Boomer."

"You spoke to Val just now?"

"Yes."

"What did she say?"

"She's flying out."

"You called because I asked you?"

"Jamie also asked me."

Sutter put both feet on the floor and gave him an odd look. "You say Jimmy asked you?"

"He asked me to call Val about a book she promised him. That was earlier."

Sutter sank into thought. There was time for another look at Jamie. The bed had been freshly made, the seersucker counterpane drawn tightly across the youth's bony chest. It seemed to the engineer that Jamie's nose had grown sharper and that his skin clove closer to his cheekbones.

"He's developed a spruelike diarrhea and lost some fluid." said Sutter from the radiator. Was this an explanation? Sutter turned to the priest. "I refused to allow intravenous fluid, Father," he said in what struck the engineer as a challenging tone. "Even though it might prolong his life a few days. What do you think of that?"

"No objection," said the priest, scratching his fist absently. "Unless he is unconscious and you want him conscious for some reason."

Sutter's eye gleamed and he lifted an eyebrow toward the engineer. *How about this fellow?* Sutter asked him. But the engineer frowned and turned away. He wanted no humbug with Sutter.

"Of course, whether he is unconscious or not, I'll be glad to baptize him conditionally," said the priest, settling the glasses with the bracket of his hand.

"Conditionally, Father," said Sutter with a lively expression.

The priest shrugged. "I have no way of knowing whether he's been baptized before."

"Is that what the canon prescribes, Father?" Sutter's eyes roamed the ceiling.

"I think, Father—" began the engineer sternly. He would have no part of Sutter's horsing around. At the same moment he glanced at Sutter's coat pocket: it still held the pistol.

"This young man asked me to come in here," said the priest.

"That's right," said the engineer sternly.

"Therefore I should like to ask you, sir," said the priest straight to Sutter, "whether you concur in your sister's desire that I administer the sacrament of baptism to the patient. If you do not, then I shall be going about my business."

"Yes," said the engineer, nodding vigorously. He thought the priest expressed it very well in his umpire's way, taking no guff from Sutter.

"By all means stay, Father," said Sutter somewhat elaborately.

"Well?" The priest waited.

"Why don't you ask him yourself, Father." Sutter nodded to the bed behind the other two.

They turned. Jamie was getting out of bed! One hand had folded back the covers quite cogently, and the left knee had started across the right leg, his eyes open and bulging slightly with seriousness of intent.

Later Sutter told the engineer that, contrary to popular notions, dying men often carry out complex actions in the last moments of life. One patient he recalled who was dying of tuberculosis had climbed out of bed, washed his pajamas in the sink, hung them out to dry, returned to the bed, pulled the covers up to his chin to hide his nakedness, and died.

"Hold it, son," Sutter stopped Jamie fondly and almost jokingly, as if Jamie were a drunk, and motioned the engineer to the cabinet. "Jamie here wants to move his bowels and doesn't like the bedpan. I don't blame him." The priest helped Sutter with Jamie. After a moment there arose to the engineer's nostrils first an intimation, like a new presence in the room, a somebody, then a foulness beyond the compass of smell. This could only be the dread ultimate rot of the molecules themselves, an abject surrender. It was the body's disgorgement of its most secret shame. Doesn't this ruin everything, wondered the engineer (if only the women were here, they wouldn't permit it, oh Jamie never should have left home). He stole a glance at the others. Sutter and the priest bent to their task as if it were nothing out of the ordinary. The priest supported Jamie's head on the frail stem of its neck. When a nurse came to service the cabinet, the engineer avoided her eye. The stench scandalized him. Shouldn't they all leave?

Sutter conducted Jamie back to bed fondly and even risibly. Suddenly the engineer remembered that this was the way Negro servants handle the dying, as if it were the oldest joke of all.

"Hold it now, son. Look out. There you go." Leaning over the bed, Sutter took hold of Jamie's chin, almost chucked it. "Listen, Jimmy. This is Father Boomer. He wants to ask you something."

But the youth goggled and closed his eyes, giving no sign of having heard. Sutter took his pulse, and stepped back.

"If you have any business with him, Father," he said dryly, "I think you'd better conduct it now."

The priest nodded and leaned on the bed, supporting himself on his heavy freckled fists. He looked not at Jamie but sideways at the wall.

"Son, can you hear me?"—addressing the wall. The engineer perceived that at last the priest had found familiar territory. He knew what he was doing.

But Jamie made no reply.

"Son, can you hear me?" the priest repeated without

embarrassment, examining a brown stain on the wall and not troubling to give his voice a different inflection.

Jamie nodded and appeared to say something. The engineer moved a step closer, cocking his good ear but keeping his arms folded as the sign of his discretion.

"Son, I am a Catholic priest," said Father Boomer, studying the yellow hairs on his fist. "Do you understand me?"

"Yes," said Jamie aloud. He nodded rapidly.

"I have been asked by your sister to administer to you the sacrament of baptism. Do you wish to receive it?"

The engineer frowned. Wasn't the priest putting it a bit formally?

"Val," whispered Jamie, goggling at the engineer.

"That's right," said the engineer, nodding. "I called her as you asked me to."

Jamie looked at the priest.

"Son," said the priest. "Do you accept the truths of religion?"

Jamie moved his lips.

"What?" asked the priest, bending lower.

"Excuse me, Father," said the sentient engineer. "He said 'what.'"

"Oh," said the priest and turned both fists out and opened the palms. "Do you accept the truth that God exists and that He made you and loves you and that He made the world so that you might enjoy its beauty and that He himself is your final end and happiness, that He loved you so much that He sent His only Son to die for you and to found His Holy Catholic Church so that you may enter heaven and there see God face to face and be happy with Him forever."

Without raising his eyes, the engineer could see the curled-up toe of Sutter's Thom McAn shoe turning to and fro on the radiator trademark.

"Is that true?" said Jamie clearly, opening his eyes and goggling. To the engineer's dismay, the youth turned to him.

The engineer cleared his throat and opened his mouth to say something when, fortunately for him, Jamie's bruised eyes went weaving around to the priest. He said something to the priest which the latter did not understand.

The priest looked up to the engineer.

"He wants to know, ah, why," said the engineer.

"Why what?"

"Why should he believe that."

The priest leaned hard on his fists. "It is true because God Himself revealed it as the truth."

Again the youth's lips moved and again the priest turned to the interpreter.

"He asked how, meaning how does he know that?"

The priest sighed. "If it were not true," he said to Jamie, "then I would not be here. That is why I am here, to tell you."

Jamie, who had looked across to the engineer (Christ, don't look at me!), pulled down the corners of his mouth in what the engineer perceived unerringly to be a sort of ironic acknowledgment.

"Do you understand me, son?" said the priest in the same voice.

There was no answer. Outside in the night the engineer saw a Holsum bread truck pass under the street light.

"Do you accept these truths?"

After a silence the priest, who was still propped on his fists and looking sideways like a storekeeper, said, "If you do not now believe these truths, it is for me to ask you whether you wish to believe them and whether you now ask for the faith to believe them."

Jamie's eyes were fixed on the engineer, but the irony was shot through with the first glint of delirium. He nodded to the engineer.

The engineer sighed and, feeling freer, looked up. Sutter hung fire, his chin on his knuckles, his eyes half-closed and gleaming like a Buddha's.

Jamie opened his mouth, it seemed, to say something bright and audible, but his tongue thickened and came out. He shuddered violently. Sutter came to the bedside. He held the youth's wrist and, unbuttoning the pajamas, laid an ear to the bony chest. He straightened and made a sign to the priest, who took from his pocket a folded purple ribbon which he slung around his neck in a gesture that struck the engineer as oddly graceless and perfunctory.

"What's his name?" the priest asked no one in particular.

"Jamison MacKenzie Vaught," said Sutter.

"Jamison MacKenzie Vaught," said the priest, his fists spread wide. "What do you ask of the Church of God? Say Faith."

Jamie said something.

"What does Faith bring you to? Say Life Everlasting."

Jamie's lips moved.

The priest took the bent sucking tube from Jamie's water glass. "Go fill that over there."

"Yes sir," said the engineer. But surely it was to be expected that the priest have a kit of some sort, at least a suitable vessel. He half filled the clouded plastic glass.

As he returned with the water, Jamie's bowels opened again with the spent schleppen sound of an old man's sphincter. The engineer went to get the bedpan. Jamie tried to lift his head.

"No no," said Sutter impatiently, and coming quickly across simply bound the dying youth to the bed by folding the counterpane into a strap and pressing it against his chest. "Get on with it, Father," he said angrily.

The priest took the plastic glass. "I baptize you in the name of the Father—" He poured a trickle of water into the peninsula of fried dusty hair. "And of the Son—" He poured a little more. "And of the Holy Ghost." He poured the rest.

The three men watched as the water ran down the youth's bruised forehead. It was dammed a moment by the thick Vaught eyebrows, flowed through and pooled around the little red caruncle in the corner of his eye.

The priest bent lower still, storekeeper over his counter, and took the narrow waxy hand between his big ruddy American League paws. "Son," he said in the same flat mercantile voice, looking first at the brown stain on the wall and then down at the dying youth. "Today I promise you that you will be with our Blessed Lord and Savior and that you will see him face to face and see his mother, Our Lady, see them as you are seeing me. Do you hear me?"

The four white vermiform fingers stirred against the big thumb, swollen with blood (did they, thumb and fingers, belong to the same species?).

"Then I ask you to pray to them for me and for your brother here and for your friend who loves you."

The fingers stirred again.

Presently the priest straightened and turned to the engineer as blank-eyed as if he had never laid eyes on him before.

"Did you hear him? He said something. What did he say?"

The engineer, who did not know how he knew, was not even sure he had heard Jamie or had tuned him in in some other fashion, cleared his throat.

"He said, 'Don't let me go.'" When the priest looked puzzled, the engineer nodded to the bed and added: "He means his hand, the hand there."

"I won't let you go," the priest said. As he waited he curled his lip absently against his teeth in a workaday five-o'clock-in-the-afternoon expression.

After several minutes Sutter let go the sheet which he still held as a strap across Jamie.

"All right, Father," said Sutter in an irritable voice when the priest didn't move. "On the way out, would you send in the nurse and the resident?"

"What?" said the priest, bracketing his glasses with his free hand. "Oh, yes. Certainly." He started for the washstand, thought better of it, turned and left the room. Pausing in the doorway, he turned again. "If you need me for anything else, I'd be glad to—"

"We won't," said Sutter curtly, managing to embarrass the engineer after all.

The engineer followed the priest out into the corridor and thanked him. He wondered if one was expected to "make an offering," but he had no notion of how to hand money over except to hand it over. He contented himself with wringing the priest's hand warmly and thanking him twice.

12.

It took him two blocks at top walking speed to overtake Sutter, who strode along with his hands in his pockets, bent forward as if he were bucking a strong wind.

"Where are you going?" the engineer asked in an unexpectedly loud voice.

"What?" said Sutter, giving a start. "Oh, to the ranch."

"The ranch," repeated the engineer absently. When Sutter started to leave, he held up his hand. "Wait."

"Wait for what?"

"What happened back there?"

"In the hospital room? You were there."

"I know, but what did you think? I could tell you were thinking something."

"Do you have to know what I think before you know what you think?"

"That does not mean that I would necessarily agree with you," said the engineer, trying to see Sutter's expression. Suddenly the engineer felt his face flush. "No, you're right. I don't need to know what you think. Wait. Did you say ranch?"

"Yes." Still he could not make out Sutter's face.

"Do you mean your ranch?"

"Yes."

"Why?"

"I have a date."

"A date?" His heart began to thud. "No, wait. Please don't go to the ranch!" Without realizing that he had done so, he had taken hold of Sutter's sleeve.

Sutter angrily shook himself free. "What in God's name do you want now?"

"Oh. I—what about the family?"

"What about them?"

"I mean, meeting them. Val should be here tonight and the rest tomorrow."

"Yes."

"They won't know. Shall I meet them? Perhaps I could even call the Vaughts and catch them before they leave."

"Good. Fine."

"Then I'll call the airport and see what the plane schedule is."

"Very good."

"What about the arrangements?"

"Arrangements? You make them. You do very well."

Sutter reached the Edsel and got into the driver's seat but made no sign that the engineer should follow.

"All right. Wait—" cried the engineer when the old buckety

Ford motor caught and roared (he wondered if Sutter had ever changed the oil or whether it had oil).

"What?"

He peered down into the dark car.

"Dr. Vaught—ah—"

"What?"

"What are you going to do now?"

"I'm going to have a drink."

"No. I mean, what are you going to do?"

There was no answer. All the engineer could see was that Sutter had put his hands on the wheel at six o'clock and nine o'clock, left elbow on the window sill, a style of driving which the engineer faintly recalled from the 1940's when Delta sports used to pick up their dates and drive to the Marion Parlor on Front Street.

"Are you going home, I mean."

"I told you, Barrett, I'm going to the ranch."

"Dr. Vaught, don't leave me."

"What did you say?"

"Dr. Vaught, listen to me. I'm going to do what I told you I planned to do."

"I know. You told me."

"Dr. Vaught, I want you to come back with me."

"Why? To make this contribution you speak of?"

"Dr. Vaught, I need you. I, Will Barrett—" and he actually pointed to himself lest there be a mistake, "—need you and want you to come back. I need you more than Jamie needed you. Jamie had Val too."

Sutter laughed. "You kill me, Barrett."

"Yes sir." He waited.

"I'll think about it. Here's some money for the arrangements, as you call them."

"Oh, no, sir." He backed away. "I have plenty."

"Anything else?"

"No sir."

But as the Edsel took off, spavined and sprung, sunk at one corner and flatulent in its muffler, spuriously elegant and unsound, like a Negro's car, a fake Ford, a final question did occur to him and he took off after it.

"Wait," he shouted in a dead run.

The Edsel paused, sighed, and stopped.

Strength flowed like oil into his muscles and he ran with great joyous ten-foot antelope bounds.

The Edsel waited for him.

LOVE IN THE RUINS

THE ADVENTURES OF A BAD CATHOLIC AT A TIME NEAR THE END OF THE WORLD

FOR SHELBY FOOTE

JULY FOURTH

In a Pine Grove on the Southwest Cusp of the Interstate Cloverleaf

5 P.M. / JULY 4

NOW IN these dread latter days of the old violent beloved U.S.A. and of the Christ-forgetting Christ-haunted death-dealing Western world I came to myself in a grove of young pines and the question came to me: has it happened at last?

Two more hours should tell the story. One way or the other. Either I am right and a catastrophe will occur, or it won't and I'm crazy. In either case the outlook is not so good.

Here I sit, in any case, against a young pine, broken out in hives and waiting for the end of the world. Safe here for the moment though, flanks protected by a rise of ground on the left and an approach ramp on the right. The carbine lies across my lap.

Just below the cloverleaf, in the ruined motel, the three girls are waiting for me.

Undoubtedly something is about to happen.

Or is it that something has stopped happening?

Is it that God has at last removed his blessing from the U.S.A. and what we feel now is just the clank of the old historical machinery, the sudden jerking ahead of the roller-coaster cars as the chain catches hold and carries us back into history with its ordinary catastrophes, carries us out and up toward the brink from that felicitous and privileged siding where even unbelievers admitted that if it was not God who blessed the U.S.A., then at least some great good luck had befallen us, and that now the blessing or the luck is over, the machinery clanks, the chain catches hold, and the cars jerk forward?

It is still hot as midafternoon. The sky is a clear rinsed cobalt after the rain. Wet pine growth reflects the sunlight like steel knitting needles. The grove steams and smells of turpentine. Far away the thunderhead, traveling fast, humps over on the horizon like a troll. Directly above, a hawk balances on a column of air rising from the concrete geometry of the cloverleaf. Not a breath stirs.

The young pine I am sitting against has a tumor and is bowed to fit my back. I am sweating and broken out in hives from drinking gin fizzes but otherwise quite comfortable. This spot, on the lower reaches of the southwest cusp, was chosen carefully. From it I command three directions of the interstates and by leaning over the lip of the culvert can look through to the fourth, eastern approach.

Traffic is light, an occasional milk tanker and produce trailer.

The hawk slants off in a long flat glide toward the swamp. From the angle of its wings one can tell it is a marsh hawk.

One of the roof tiles of the motel falls and breaks on the concrete.

The orange roof of the Howard Johnson motel reminds me of the three girls in rooms 203, 204, and 205. Thoughts of the girls and the coming catastrophe cause my scalp to tingle with a peculiar emotion. If the catastrophe occurs, I stand a good chance, knowing what I know about it, of surviving it. So do the girls. Surviving with one girl who likes you is not such a bad prospect. But surviving with three girls, all of whom like you and each of whom detests the other two, is both horrible and pleasant, certainly enough to make one's scalp tingle with a peculiar emotion.

Another reason for the prickling sensation is that the hives are worse. Fiery wheals bloom on my neck. My scalp feels airy and quilted and now and then pops a hair root like a dirigible popping its hawsers one by one.

These are bad times.

Principalities and powers are everywhere victorious. Wickedness flourishes in high places.

There is a clearer and more present danger, however. For I have reason to believe that within the next two hours an unprecedented fallout of noxious particles will settle hereabouts and perhaps in other places as well. It is a catastrophe whose cause and effects—and prevention—are known only to me. The effects of the evil particles are psychic rather than physical. They do not burn the skin and rot the marrow; rather do they inflame and worsen the secret ills of the spirit and rive the very self from itself. If a man is already prone to anger, he'll go mad with rage. If he lives affrighted, he will quake with terror. If he's already abstracted from himself, he'll be sundered from himself and roam the world like Ishmael.

Here in my pocket is the very means of inoculating persons against such an eventuality or of curing them should it overtake them.

Yet so far only four persons have been inoculated: myself and the three girls yonder in the motel.

Just below me, abutting the deserted shopping plaza, rises the yellow brick barn-and-silo of Saint Michael's. A surprisingly large parish it was, big enough to rate a monsignor. But the church is empty now, abandoned five years ago. The stained glass is broken out. Cliff swallows nest in the fenestrae of its concrete screen.

Our Catholic church here split into three pieces: (1) the American Catholic Church whose new Rome is Cicero, Illinois; (2) the Dutch schismatics who believe in relevance but not God; (3) the Roman Catholic remnant, a tiny scattered flock with no place to go.

The American Catholic Church, which emphasizes property rights and the integrity of neighborhoods, retained the Latin mass and plays *The Star-Spangled Banner* at the elevation.

The Dutch schismatics in this area comprise several priests and nuns who left Rome to get married. They threw in with the Dutch schismatic Catholics. Now several divorced priests and nuns are importuning the Dutch cardinal to allow them to remarry.

The Roman Catholics hereabouts are scattered and demoralized. The one priest, an obscure curate, who remained faithful to Rome, could not support himself and had to hire out as a fire-watcher. It is his job to climb the fire tower by night and watch for brushfires below and for signs and portents in the skies.

I, for example, am a Roman Catholic, albeit a bad one. I believe in the Holy Catholic Apostolic and Roman Church, in God the Father, in the election of the Jews, in Jesus Christ His Son our Lord, who founded the Church on Peter his first vicar, which will last until the end of the world. Some years ago, however, I stopped eating Christ in Communion, stopped going to mass, and have since fallen into a disorderly life. I believe in God and the whole business but I love women best, music and science next, whiskey next, God fourth, and my fellowman hardly at all. Generally I do as I please. A man, wrote John, who says he believes in God and does not keep his commandments is a liar. If John is right, then I am a liar. Nevertheless, I still believe.

A couple of buzzards circle the interchange a mile high. Do I imagine it, or does one cock his head and eye me for meat? Don't count on it, old fellow!

Thoughts about the coming catastrophe and the three girls cause my scalp to tingle with a peculiar emotion. Or perhaps it is the hives from drinking gin fizzes. A catastrophe, however, has both pleasant and unpleasant aspects familiar to everyone—though no one likes to admit the pleasantness. Just now the prospect is unpleasant, but not for the reasons you might imagine.

Let me confess that what worries me most is that the catastrophe will overtake us before my scientific article is published and so before my discovery can create a sensation in the scientific world.

The vanity of scientists! My article, it is true, is an extremely important one, perhaps even epochal in its significance. With it, my little invention, in hand, any doctor can probe the very secrets of the soul, diagnose the maladies that poison the wellsprings of man's hope. It could save the world or destroy it—and in the next two hours will very likely do one or the other—for as any doctor knows, the more effective a treatment is, the more dangerous it is in the wrong hands.

But the question remains: which prospect is more unpleasant, the destruction of the world, or that the destruction may come before my achievement is made known? The latter I must confess, because I keep imagining the scene in the Director's office the day the Nobel Prize is awarded. I enter. The secretaries blush. My colleagues horse around. The Director breaks out the champagne and paper cups (like Houston Control after the moon landing). "Hats off, gentlemen!" cries the Director in his best derisive style (from him the highest accolade). "A toast to our local Pasteur! No, rather the new Copernicus! The latter-day Archimedes who found the place to insert his lever and turn the world not upside down but right side up!"

If the truth be known, scientists are neither more nor less vain than other people. It is rather that their vanity is the more striking as it appears side by side with their well-known objectivity. The layman is scandalized, but the scandal is not so much the fault of the scientist as it is the layman's canonization of scientists, which the latter never asked for.

The prayer of the scientist if he prayed, which is not likely: Lord, grant that my discovery may increase knowledge and help other men. Failing that, Lord, grant that it will not lead to man's destruction. Failing that, Lord, grant that my article in *Brain* be published before the destruction takes place.

Room 202 in the motel is my room. Room 206 is stacked to the roof with canned food, mostly Vienna sausage and Campbell's soup, fifteen cases of Early Times bourbon whiskey, and the World's Great Books. In the rooms intervening, 203, 204, and 205, are to be found Ellen, Moira, and Lola respectively.

My spirits rise. My quilted scalp pops another hair root. The silky albumen from the gin fizzes coats my brain membranes. Even if worst comes to worst, is there any reason why the four of us cannot live happily together, sip toddies, eat Campbell's chicken-and-rice, and spend the long summer evenings listening to Lola play the cello and reading aloud from the World's Great Books stacked right alongside the cases of Early Times, beginning with Homer's first words: "Sing, O Goddess, the anger of Achilles," and ending with Freud's last words: "—but we cannot help them and cannot change our own way of thinking on their account"? Then we can read the Great Ideas, beginning with the first volume, Angel to Love. Then we can start over—until the Campbell's soup and Early Times run out.

The sun makes bursts and halos through the screen of pine needles. The marsh hawk ends his long glide into the line of cypresses, which are green as paint against the purple thunderhead.

At first glance all seems normal hereabouts. But a sharp eye might notice one or two things amiss. For one thing, the inner lanes of the interstate, the ones ordinarily used for passing, are in disrepair. The tar strips are broken. A lichen grows in the oil stain. Young mimosas sprout on the shoulders.

For another thing, there is something wrong with the motel. The roof tiles are broken. The swimming pool is an opaque jade green, a bad color for pools. A large turtle suns himself on the diving board, which is broken and slanted into the water. Two cars are parked in the near lot, a rusty Cadillac and an Impala convertible with vines sprouting through its rotting top.

The cars and the shopping center were burnt out during the Christmas riot five years ago. The motel, though not burned, was abandoned and its rooms inhabited first by lovers, then by bums, and finally by the native denizens of the swamp, dirt daubers, moccasins, screech owls, and raccoons.

In recent months the vines have begun to sprout in earnest. Possum grape festoons Rexall Drugs yonder in the plaza. Scuppernong all but conceals the A & P supermarket. Poison ivy has captured the speaker posts in the drive-in movie, making a perfect geometrical forest of short cylindrical trees.

Beyond the glass wall of the motel dining room still hangs the Rotary banner:

> *Is it the truth?*
> *Is it fair to all concerned?*
> *Will it build goodwill and better friendships?*

But the banner is rent, top to bottom, like the temple veil.

The vines began to sprout in earnest a couple of months ago. People do not like to talk about it. For some reason they'd much rather talk about the atrocities that have been occurring ever more often: entire families murdered in their beds for no good reason. "The work of a madman!" people exclaim.

Last Sunday as I was walking past the house of a neighbor, Barry Bocock, a Boeing engineer transplanted from Seattle, I spied him riding his tiny tractor-mower like a big gringo astride a burro. The next moment my eye was caught by many tiny vines sprouting through cracks in the concrete slab and beginning to cover the antique bricks that Barry had salvaged from an old sugar mill.

Barry got off his tractor simply by standing up and walking.

"It looks as though your slab is cracked, Barry," I told him.

Barry frowned and, seeming not to hear, began to show me how the tractor could cut grass right up to the bark of a tree without injuring the tree.

Barry Bocock is the sort of fellow who gives the most careful attention to details, especially to those smaller problems caused by germs. A very clean man, he walks around his yard in his shorts and if he should find a pustule or hickey on his clean hairy muscular legs, he takes infinite pains examining it, squeezing it, noting the character of the pus. One has the feeling that to Barry there is nothing wrong with the world that couldn't be set right by controlling germs and human wastes. One Sunday he invited me into his back yard and showed me the effluence from his new septic tank, letting it run into a drinking glass, where in fact it did look as clear as water.

But when I called his attention to the vines cracking his slab, he seemed not to hear and instead showed me his new mower.

"But, Barry, the vines are cracking your slab."

"That'll be the day," said Barry, flushing angrily. Then, drawing me close to his clean perfect West-Coast body, he asked me if I'd heard of the latest atrocity.

"Yes. What do you think?"

"The work of a madman!" he exclaimed and mounted his burro-size tractor.

Barry is a widower, his wife having died of alcoholism before he left Seattle. "Firing the sunset gun" he called her drinking. "Every day she'd be at it as early as one o'clock." "At what?" "Firing the sunset gun."

The buzzards are lower and more hopeful, rocking their wings this way and that and craning down for a look.

When I think of Barry, I can't help but wonder whether he, not I, should be the doctor, what with his keen interest in germs, boils, hickeys, bo-bos, pustules, scabs, and such. Moreover, I could tell from Barry's veiled expression when I mentioned the vines sprouting that he knew of my own troubles and that he was accordingly discounting my alarm. Physician, heal thyself. . . .

The truth is that, though I am a physician, my health, especially my mental health, has been very poor lately. I am subject to attacks of elation and depression, as well as occasional seizures of morning terror. A few years ago my wife left me, running off with an Englishman, and I've led an irregular life ever since.

But to admit my infirmities is not necessarily to discredit my discoveries, which stand or fall on scientific evidence. After all, van Gogh was depressed and Beethoven had a poor time of it. The prophet Hosea, if you will recall, had a bad home life.

Some of the best psychiatrists, it is hardly necessary to add, have a few problems of their own, little rancors and terrors and such.

Who am I? you well might wonder. Let me give a little dossier.

I am a physician, a not very successful psychiatrist; an alcoholic, a shaky middle-aged man subject to depressions and elations and morning terrors, but a genius nevertheless who sees into the hidden causes of things and erects simple hypotheses to account for the glut of everyday events; a bad Catholic; a widower and cuckold whose wife ran off with a heathen Englishman and died on the island of Cozumel, where she hoped to begin a new life and see things afresh.

My afflictions attract some patients, repel others. People are generally tolerant. Some patients, knowing my frailties, calculate I'll understand theirs. I am something like old Doc in Western movies: if you catch old Doc sober, he's all right, etcetera. In fact, he's some kind of genius, I heard he went to Harvard, etcetera etcetera.

Not that I make much money. Sensible folk, after all, don't have much use for a doctor who sips toddies during office hours. So I'm obliged to take all kinds of patients, not merely terrified and depressed people, but people suffering with bowel complaints, drugheads with beriberi and hepatitis, Bantus shot up by the cops, cops shot up by Bantus.

Lately, however, I've discouraged patients in order to work on my invention. I don't need the money. Fortunately for me, my wife, who left me and later died, either didn't or wouldn't change her will and so bequeathed me forty thousand shares of R. J. Reynolds stock she inherited from her father.

Loose bark from the pine is beginning to work through my shirt. My scalp is still quilted, my throat is whistling with hives—albumen molecules from the gin fizzes hum like bees in the ventricles of my brain—yet I feel quite well.

Where is the sniper? Shading my eyes, I examine every inch of the terrain.

A flag stirs fitfully on its pole beside the green rectangle dug into the slope of the near ridge like a step. It is the football field of the Valley Forge Academy, our private school, which was founded on religious and patriotic principles and to keep Negroes out. Earlier today—could it have been today?—the Christian Kaydettes, our champion baton-twirlers, practiced their twirling, little suspecting what dread misadventure would befall them.

Beyond the empty shopping plaza at my foot rise the low green hills of Paradise Estates. The fairways of the golf links make notches in the tree line. Pretty cubes and loaves of new houses are strewn among the pines like sugar lumps. It is even possible to pick out my own house, a spot of hot pink and a wink of glass under the old TV transmitter. By a trick of perspective the transmitter tower seems to rise from the dumpy silo of old Saint Michael's Church in the plaza.

Here in the old days I used to go to mass with my daughter, Samantha. My wife, an ex-Episcopal girl from Virginia, named our daughter Samantha in the expectation that this dark gracile pagan name would somehow inform the child, but alas for Doris, Samantha turned out to be chubby, fair, acned, and pious, the sort who likes to hang around after school and beat Sister's erasers.

The best of times were after mass on summer evenings when Samantha and I would walk home in the violet dusk, we having received Communion and I rejoicing afterwards, caring nought for my fellow Catholics but only for myself and Samantha and Christ swallowed, remembering what he promised me for eating him. that I would have life in me, and

I did, feeling so good that I'd sing and cut the fool all the way home like King David before the Ark. Once home, light up the charcoal briquets out under the TV transmitter, which lofted its red light next to Venus like a ruby and a diamond in the plum velvet sky. Snug down Samantha with the *Wonderful World of Color* in the den (the picture better than life, having traveled only one hundred feet straight down), back to the briquets, take four, five, six long pulls from the quart of Early Times, shout with joy for the beauty of the world, sing "Finch 'han dal vino" from *Don Giovanni* and "Holy God We Praise Thy Name," conceive a great heart-leaping desire for Doris, go fetch Doris, whose lip would curl at my proposal but who was nonetheless willing, who in fact now that she thought of it was as lusty as could be, her old self once again, a lusty Shenandoah Valley girl, Apple Queen of the Apple Blossom Festival in Winchester. Lead her by the hand beyond the azaleas where we'd fling ourselves upon each other and fall down on the zoysia grass, thick-napped here as a Kerman rug.

A flutter of white in the motel window. The sniper? I tighten my elbow against the carbine belt. No, it is one of the girls' rooms. Moira's. Moira washing her things out and hanging them out to dry as if it were any other Tuesday. A good omen, Moira washing her underwear. Her I always think of so, standing barefoot in her slip at the washstand, legs planted far apart and straight, even a bit past straight, so that the pad at the back of her knees stands out as firm as rubber; yellow eyes musing and unfocused as she puts her things to soak in Lux.

Lola, on the other hand, I always see playing the Dvořák concerto, hissing the melody with her tongue against her teeth, straddling the cello with her splendid knees.

Ellen Oglethorpe appears in my mind as in fact she is, a stern but voluptuous Presbyterian nurse, color high in her cheeks, eyes bright with disapproval. I think of her as having her fists planted on her hips, as they used to say, akimbo.

All quiet in front. Could he, the sniper, have gotten behind me? I turn around slowly, keeping under the low spreading limbs of the longleaf.

Beyond the hump of the interchange rise the monoliths of "Fedville," the federal complex including the hospital (where I've spent almost as much time as a patient as doctoring), the medical school, the NASA facility, the Behavioral Institute, the Geriatrics Center, and the Love Clinic.

In "Love," as it is called, volunteers perform sexual acts singly, in couples, and in groups, beyond viewing mirrors in order that man might learn more about the human sexual response.

Next door is Geriatrics Rehabilitation or "Gerry Rehab," a far-flung complex of pleasant low-lying white-roofed Daytona-type buildings. Here old folk from Tampa to Tucson are treated for the blues and boredoms of old age. These good folk, whose physical ailments are mostly cured nowadays, who at eighty-five, ninety, even a hundred, are as spry as can be, limber-jointed, smooth-faced, supple of artery, nevertheless often grow inexplicably sad. Though they may live in the pleasantest Senior Settlements where their every need is filled, every recreation provided, every sort of hobby encouraged, nevertheless many grow despondent in their happiness, sit slack and empty-eyed at shuffleboard and ceramic oven. Fishing poles fall from tanned and healthy hands. Golf clubs rust. *Reader's Digests* go unread. Many old folk pine away and even die from unknown causes like victims of a voodoo curse. Here in Gerry Rehab, these sad oldsters are encouraged to develop their "creative and altruistic potential." Yet mysterious deaths, and suicides too, continue to mount. The last Surgeon General's report named the nation's number-one killer as "Senior Citizens' anomie," known locally as the St. Petersburg blues.

To my left, white among the cypresses, are the old frame buildings of the Little Sisters of the Poor. During the week the Little Sisters run a school for poor children, black and white, feed and clothe them, and on weekends conduct religious retreats for Christian folk. The scientists help the sisters with the children during the week. On weekends Christians come to make retreats and pray for the conversion of Communists.

The scientists, who are mostly liberals and unbelievers, and the businessmen, who are mostly conservative and Christian, live side by side in Paradise Estates. Though the two make much of their differences—one speaking of "outworn dogmas and creeds," the other of "atheism and immorality," etcetera etcetera—to tell the truth, I do not notice a great deal of difference between the two. Both sorts are generally good fellows, good fathers and husbands who work hard all day, come home at five-thirty to their pretty homes, kiss their wives, toss their rosy babes in the air, light up their charcoal briquets, or perhaps mount their tiny tractor mowers. There are minor differences. When conservative Christian housewives drive to town to pick up their maids in the Hollow, the latter ride on the back seat in the old style. Liberal housewives make their maids ride on the front seat. On Sundays Christian businessmen dress up and take their families to church, whereas unbelieving scientists are apt to put on their worst clothes and go bird-watching. As one of my behaviorist friends put it, "my cathedral is the blue sky and my pilgrimage is for the ivory-billed woodpecker," the fabulous and lordly bird that some say still inhabits the fastness of the swamp.

Beyond the cypresses, stretching away to the horizon, as misty as a southern sea, lies the vast Honey Island Swamp. Smudges of hummocks dot its savanna-like islands. The north-south interstate, crossing it on a causeway, flies due south straight as two lines drawn with a ruler to converge at a point on the horizon.

From the hummocks arise one or two wisps of smoke. Yonder in the fastness of the swamp dwell the dropouts from and castoffs of and rebels against our society: ferocious black Bantus who use the wilderness both as a refuge and as a guerrilla base from which to mount forays against outlying subdivisions and shopping plazas; all manner of young white derelicts who live drowsy slothlike lives, sustaining themselves on wild melons and catfish and green turtles and smoking Choctaw cannabis the livelong day. The lonely hummocks, once the haunt of raccoon and alligator, are now rubbed bare as monkey islands at the zoo by all manner of disaffected folk: Bantu guerrillas, dropouts from Tulane and Vanderbilt, M.I.T. and Loyola; draft dodgers, deserters from the Swedish army, psychopaths and pederasts from Memphis and New Orleans whose practices were not even to be tolerated in New Orleans; antipapal Catholics, malcontented Methodists, ESPers, UFOers, Aquarians, ex-Ayn Randers, Choctaw Zionists who have returned to their ancestral hunting grounds, and even a few old graybeard Kerouac beats, wiry old sourdoughs of the spirit who carry pilgrim staffs, recite sutras, and leap from hummock to hummock as agile as mountain goats.

The town where I keep an office is north and to my right. By contrast with the swamp, the town has become a refuge for all manner of conservative folk, graduates of Bob Jones University, retired Air Force colonels, passed-over Navy commanders, ex-Washington, D.C., policemen, patriotic chiropractors, two officials of the National Rifle Association, and six conservative proctologists.

Paradise Estates, where I live now, is another matter. Directly opposite me, between swamp and town, its houses sparkle like jewelry in the sunlight. Emerald fairways run alongside sleepy bayous. Here everyone gets along well, heathen and Christian, Jew and Gentile, Northerner and Southerner, liberal and conservative. The Northerners, mostly businessmen and engineers from places like Kenosha and Sheboygan and Grosse Pointe, actually outnumber the Southerners. But they, the Northerners, have taken to Southern ways like ducks to water. They drink toddies and mint juleps and hold fish fries with hush puppies. Little black jockeys fish from mirrors in their front yards. Life-size mammy-dolls preside over their patios. Nearly everyone treats his servants well, picking them up in Happy Hollow and taking them home, allowing "totin' privileges" and giving them "Christmas gifs."

The Negroes around here are generally held to be a bad lot. The older Negroes are mostly trifling and no-account, while the young Negroes have turned mean as yard dogs. Nearly all the latter have left town, many to join the Bantus in the swamp. Here the conservatives and liberals of Paradise agree. The conservatives say that Negroes always have been trifling and no-account or else mean as yard dogs. The liberals, arguing with the conservatives at the country club, say yes, Negroes are trifling and no-account or else mean as yard dogs, but why shouldn't they be, etcetera etcetera. So it goes.

Our servants in Paradise are the exceptions, however: faithful black mammies who take care of our children as if they were their own, dignified gardeners who work and doff their caps in the old style.

Paradise Estates, where I live, is a paradise indeed, an oasis of concord in a troubled land. For our beloved old U.S.A. is in a bad way. Americans have turned against each other; race against race, right against left, believer against heathen, San Francisco against Los Angeles, Chicago against Cicero. Vines sprout in sections of New York where not even Negroes will live. Wolves have been seen in downtown Cleveland, like Rome during the Black Plague. Some Southern states have established diplomatic ties with Rhodesia. Minnesota and Oregon have their own consulates in Sweden (where so many deserters from these states dwell).

The old Republican Party has become the Knothead Party, so named during the last Republican convention in Montgomery when a change of name was proposed, the first suggestion being the Christian Conservative Constitutional Party, and campaign buttons were even printed with the letters CCCP before an Eastern-liberal commentator noted the similarity to the initials printed on the backs of the Soviet cosmonauts and called it the most knotheaded political bungle of the century—which the conservatives, in the best tradition, turned to their own advantage, printing a million more buttons reading "Knotheads for America" and banners proclaiming "No Man Can Be Too Knotheaded in the Service of His Country."

The old Democrats gave way to the new Left Party. They too were stuck with a nickname not of their own devising and the nickname stuck: in this case a derisive acronym that the Right made up and the Left accepted, accepted in that same curious American tradition by which we allow our enemies to name us, give currency to their curses, perhaps from the need to concede the headstart they want and still beat them, perhaps also from the secret inkling that our enemies know the worst of us best and it's best for them to say it. LEFT usually it is, often LEFTPAPA, sometimes LEFTPAPASAN (with a little Jap bow), hardly ever the original LEFTPAPASANE, which stood for what, according to the Right, the Left believed in: Liberty, Equality, Fraternity, The Pill, Atheism, Pot, Anti-Pollution, Sex, Abortion Now, Euthanasia.

*

The center did not hold.

However, the Gross National Product continues to rise.

There are Left states and Knothead states, Left towns and Knothead towns but no center towns (for example, my old hometown over yonder is Knothead, Fedville behind me is Left, and Paradise Estates where I live now does not belong to the center—there is no center—but is that rare thing, a pleasant place where Knothead and Left—but not black—dwell side by side in peace), Left networks and Knothead networks, Left movies and Knothead movies. The most popular Left films are dirty movies from Sweden. All-time Knothead favorites, on the other hand, include *The Sound of Music, Flubber,* and *Ice Capades of 1981,* clean movies all.

I've stopped going to movies. It is hard to say which is more unendurable, the sentimental blasphemy of Knothead movies like *The Sound of Music* or sitting in a theater with strangers watching other strangers engage in sexual intercourse and sodomy on the giant 3-D Pan-a-Vision screen.

American literature is not having its finest hour. The Southern gothic novel yielded to the Jewish masturbatory novel, which in turn gave way to the WASP homosexual novel, which has nearly run its course. The Catholic literary renascence, long awaited, failed to materialize. But old favorites endure, like venerable Harold Robbins and Jacqueline Susann, who continue to write the dirty clean books so beloved by the American housewife. Gore Vidal is the grand old man of American letters.

Both political parties have had their triumphs.

The Lefts succeeded in removing "In God We Trust" from pennies.

The Knotheads enacted a law requiring compulsory prayers in the black public schools and made funds available for birth control in Africa, Asia, and Alabama.

But here in Paradise, Knothead lives next to Leftist in peace. On Wednesday nights one goes to a meeting of Birchers, the other to the ACLU. Sunday one goes to church, the other in search of the lordly ivory-billed woodpecker, but both play golf, ski in the same bayou, and give "Christmas gifs" to the same waiters at the club.

*

The war in Ecuador has been going on for fifteen years and has divided the country further. Not exactly our best war. The U.S.A. sided with South Ecuador, which is largely Christian, believing in God and the sacredness of the individual, etcetera etcetera. The only trouble is that South Ecuador is owned by ninety-eight Catholic families with Swiss bank accounts, is governed by a general, and so is not what you would call an ideal democracy. North Ecuador, on the other hand, which many U.S. liberals support, is Maoist-Communist and has so far murdered two hundred thousand civilians, including liberals, who did not welcome Communism with open arms. Not exactly our best war, and now in its sixteenth year.

Even so, most Americans do well enough. In fact, until lately, nearly everyone tried and succeeded in being happy but me. My unhappiness is not the fault of Paradise. I was unlucky. My daughter died, my wife ran off with a heathen Englishman, and I fell prey to bouts of depression and morning terror, to say nothing of abstract furies and desultory lusts for strangers.

Here's the puzzle: what is an unhappy psychiatrist to do in a place where everyone else is happier than he is? Physician, heal thy . . .

Fortunately for me, many other people have become unhappy of late. Certain psychiatric disorders have cropped up in both Lefts and Knotheads.

Conservatives have begun to fall victim to unseasonable rages, delusions of conspiracies, high blood pressure, and large-bowel complaints.

Liberals are more apt to contract sexual impotence, morning terror, and a feeling of abstraction of the self from itself.

So it is that a small Knothead city like my hometown yonder can support half a dozen proctologists, while places like Berkeley or Beverly Hills have a psychiatrist in every block.

It is my misfortune—and blessing—that I suffer from both liberal and conservative complaints, e.g., both morning terror and large-bowel disorders, excessive abstraction and unseasonable rages, alternating impotence and satyriasis. So that at one and the same time I have great sympathy for my patients and lead a fairly miserable life.

But my invention has changed all this. Now I know how to

be happy and make others happy. With my little machine I can diagnose and treat with equal success the morning terror of liberals and the apoplexy of conservatives. In fact it could save the U.S.A. if we can get through the next hour or so.

What's wrong with my eyes? My field of vision is narrowing from top to bottom. The world looks as if it were seen through the slit of a gun turret. But of course! My eyes are swelling with hives! It could only come from the delicious gin fizzes prepared for me by Lola, my lovely cellist.

Still I feel very well. My brain, lubricated by egg white from the gin fizzes, hums like a top; pangs of love for the three girls—two anyhow—pierce my heart (how beautiful did God make woman!). Yet I am able to observe every detail of the terrain through my turret slit. A single rank weed, I notice, has sprouted overnight in the sand trap of number 12 fairway next to the interstate right-of-way—this despite the fact that the champs are to play here tonight "under the arcs."

Far away church steeples puncture the globy oaks. Ordinary fat grayish clouds sail over the town blown by map winds with pencil lines.

The sand trap and the clouds put me in mind of being ten years old and in love and full of longing. The first thing a man remembers is longing and the last thing he is conscious of before death is exactly the same longing. I have never seen a man die who did not die in longing. When I was ten years old I woke one summer morning to a sensation of longing. Besides the longing I was in love with a girl named Louise, and so the same morning I went out to this same sand trap where I hoped chance would bring us together. At the breakfast table, I took a look at my father with his round head, his iron-colored hair, his chipper red cheeks, and I wondered to myself: at what age does a man get over this longing?

The answer is, he doesn't. My father was so overwhelmed with longing that it unfitted him for anything but building martin houses.

My father, also a physician, had his office in town and I kept it, poor place though it was, even after I became a professor at the medical center.

We are not exactly a distinguished family. My father was a failed physician who also drank. In early middle age he got

himself elected coroner and more or less retired, sat alone in his
office between the infrequent autopsies and made spectacular
bird houses, martin hotels, and wren houses of cypress with
brass fittings.

My mother, a "realtor" and a whiz at getting buyer and seller
together, really supported us.

Our family's only claim to singularity, if not distinction, is
that we are one of that rare breed, Anglo-Saxon Catholics who
were Catholic from the beginning and stayed Catholic. My
forebears remained steadfast in the old faith both in Hertford-
shire, where Elizabeth got after them, and in Maryland, where
the Episcopalians finally kicked them out. Sir Thomas More, in
fact, is a collateral ancestor. Our name anyhow is More. But if
such antecedents seem illustrious, recent reality is less so. It is
as if the effort of clinging to the faith took such a toll that we
were not fit for much else. Evicted from Maryland, my ancestor removed to Bardstown, Kentucky, where he and his sons
founded a whiskey distillery—and failed at that.

My grandfather took dentistry at Loyola of the South and
upon graduation married a Creole heiress with timberlands
and never drilled a tooth.

All Mores, until I came along, were good Catholics and went
to mass—I too until a few years ago. Wanderers we became,
like the Jews in the wilderness. For we were Catholic English-
Americans and most other English-Americans were Protestant
and most Catholics were either Mediterranean or Irish. In the
end we settled for Louisiana, where religious and ethnic confusion is sufficiently widespread and good-natured that no one
keeps track of such matters—except the Baptists, who don't
like Catholics no matter what. My forefathers donned Knights
of Columbus robes, wore swords and plumed hats, attended
French shrimp boils and Irish wakes, made retreats with Germans, were pallbearers at Italian funerals. Like the French and
Germans here, we became easygoing Louisianians and didn't
think twice about our origins. We fought with Beauregard next
to old blue-light Presbyterian Stonewall Jackson and it seemed
natural enough. My father was only a third-degree Knight of
Columbus, but he too went regularly to Holy Name shrimp
boils and Lady of the Lake barbecues and was right content.
For twenty-five years he sat out the long afternoons in his dim

little coroner's office, sipping Early Times between autopsies and watching purple martins come skimming up to his splendid cypress-and-brass hotel.

The asphalt of the empty plaza still bubbles under the hot July sun. Through the shimmer of heat one can see the broken store fronts beyond the plaza. A green line wavers in midair above the pavement, like the hanging gardens of Babylon. It is not a mirage, however. I know what it is. A green growth has taken root on the flat roofs of the stores.

As for me, I was a smart boy and at the age of twenty-six bade fair to add luster to the family name for the first time since Sir Thomas More himself, that great soul, the dearest best noblest merriest of Englishmen. My contribution, I hasten to add, was in the realm of science not sanctity. Why can't I follow More's example, love myself less, God and my fellowman more, and leave whiskey and women alone? Sir Thomas More was merry in life and death and he loved and was loved by everyone, even his executioner, with whom he cracked jokes. By contrast, I am possessed by terror and desire and live a solitary life. My life is a longing, longings for women, for the Nobel Prize, for the hot bosky bite of bourbon whiskey, and other great heart-wrenching longings that have no name. Sir Thomas was right, of course, and I am wrong. But on the other hand these are peculiar times. . . .

When I was a young man, the question at the time was: where are the Catholic Einsteins, Salks, Oppenheimers? And the answer came, at least from my family: well, here comes one, namely me. The local Catholic paper and the K.C. magazine wrote me up, along with some well-known baseball players, bandleaders, and TV personalities. It was the end of the era of Lawrence Welk, Perry Como, Bing Crosby, Stan Musial, Ed McMahon, all good Catholics, good fellows, decent family men, etcetera etcetera, though not exactly the luminaries of the age—John Kennedy was the exception—and the question was, who was going to take their place, let alone measure up to Einstein.

One proof of the divine origin of the Catholic Church: that I found myself in the same Church as Lawrence Welk and Danny

Thomas and all those Irishmen and did not feel in the least peculiar.

What happened was that as a young physician in New Orleans I stumbled onto an extraordinary medical discovery, wrote an article for the *Journal of the American Medical Association* that was picked up by *Time*, *Newsweek*, and the papers. Caption under *Time* photo: "Psychic Fallout?" In *Newsweek*: "Doctor Treats Doctors in Switch." Headline in New York *Daily News*: "Beautiful Girl Interne Disrobes—Fallout Cause Says Doc."

I was the doc and a very promising doc at that. How many doctors achieve fame in their twenties?

Alas, the promise didn't pan out. On the contrary. There followed twenty years of silence and decline. My daughter, Samantha died; my wife ran off with a heathen Englishman— come to think of it, I haven't seen a Christian Englishman for years—and I left off research, left off eating Christ in Communion, and took to sipping Early Times instead and seeking the company of the fair sex, as they used to say.

My wife and I lived a good life. We used to get up in the morning in a beautiful house, sit down to breakfast in our "enclosed patio," watch Barbara Walters talk about sexual intercourse on the *Today* show. Nevertheless, I fell prey to morning terror, shook like a leaf at the breakfast table, and began to drink vodka with my grits. At the same time that I developed liberal anxiety, I also contracted conservative rage and large-bowel complaints.

But—and here is the point—the period of my decline was also a period of lying fallow and of the germination of some strange quirky ideas. Toynbee, I believe, speaks of the Return, of the man who fails and goes away, is exiled, takes counsel with himself, hits on something, sees daylight—and returns to triumph.

First, reader and especially my fellow physicians, let me set forth my credentials, recall to your mind my modest discovery twenty years ago, as well as give you an inkling of my recent breakthrough.

Do you recall the Heavy Sodium experiments that were conducted years ago in New Orleans under the stands of the Sugar Bowl stadium? and the mysterious accident that put an end to the same? There occurred an almost soundless explosion, a *whssssk* like tearing silk, a few people were killed, and a curious yellow lens-shaped cloud hung over the French Quarter for a day or two.

Here's what happened. At the time I was encephalographer-in-residence at Tulane University. Part of my job was to do encephalograms on students with the hope of eliminating those who were subject to the sundry fits and seizures that were plaguing universities at the time, conservative fits and radical seizures. Another duty was to assist the team of physicists assigned to the secret Vieux Carré project under the Sugar Bowl. I doubled as medical officer and radiation monitor. The physicists were tinkering with a Heavy Sodium pile by means of which they hoped to hit on a better source of anticancer radiation than the old cobalt treatment. The Heavy Sodium was obtained from the massive salt domes of southern Louisiana where it occurs (along with the Heavy Chloride ion) as a trace element. The experiment was promising for two reasons. One was that Heavy Sodium radiation was thought not to injure normal tissues—hence no X-ray burns. The other was evidence that it destroyed cancer cells in mice.

The long and short of it is that the reactor got loose, killed a brace of physicists, sent up an odd yellow cloud, and accordingly rated a headline on the second page of the New York *Daily News*, as might a similar accident at Oak Ridge or Los Alamos.

In the weeks that followed, however, I noticed something curious and so made my, to date, sole contribution to medical annals. You may still find it in the textbooks, where it usually rates a footnote as "More's Paradoxical Sodium Radiation Syndrome." Something peculiar happened in the Tulane Psychiatric Hospital, where I was based. Nobody thought to make a connection between these peculiar events and the yellow cloud. Was it not John Locke who said that the mark of genius is the ability to discern not this thing or that thing but rather the connection between the two?

At any rate I noticed a remarkable change in the hospital people. Some of the patients got better and some of the psychiatrists got worse. Indeed, many of our most disturbed patients, the suicidal, the manic, the naked, the catatonic, in short the mad, were found one morning sitting fully clothed and in their right minds. A number of residents and staff physicians, on the other hand, developed acute symptoms out of the blue. One doctor, for example, a noted authority on schizophrenia, uttered a hoarse cry on rounds, hurled himself through a window, ran over the levee, and disappeared into the waters of the mighty Mississippi. Another, a lady psychologist and by the way a very attractive person and something of a radio-TV personality, stripped off her clothing in staff conference and made gross sexual overtures to several male colleagues—hence the somewhat inaccurate headline in the New York *Daily News*.

A third case, a fellow resident and good friend of mine, a merry outgoing person both at work and play, underwent a marked personality change. In the hospital he became extremely cold in mien, abstracted and so absorbed with laboratory data that he treated his patients like guinea pigs in a cage, while in his off-duty hours he began to exhibit the lewdest sort of behavior, laying hands on strange women like a drunken sailor.

Shortly thereafter I awoke one morning and it occurred to me that there might be a connection between these peculiar events and the lens-shaped cloud. For though I attached no weight to the superstitions flying around—one good soul, a chambermaid in the hospital, said that the yellow cloud had driven the demons out of the mad patients and into the doctors—nevertheless, it did occur to me that the cloud might have contained, and turned loose, something besides demons. I ordered esoteric blood chemistry on both sane patients and mad doctors. Sure enough, both groups had significant levels of Heavy Sodium and Chloride in their blood.

What I didn't know at the time and what took me twenty years to figure out was why some got better and others got worse. I know now that the heavy ions have different effects on different brain centers. For example, Heavy Sodium radiation stimulates Brodmann Area 32, the center of abstractive activity or tendencies toward angelism, while Heavy Chloride stimulates the thalamus, which promotes adjustment to the environment, or, as I call it without prejudice, bestialism. The two conditions are not mutually exclusive. It is not uncommon nowadays to see patients suffering from angelism-bestialism. A man, for example, can feel at one and the same time extremely abstracted and inordinately lustful toward lovely young women who may be perfect strangers.

So ran my report in the *J.A.M.A.*, a bald observation of a connection, without theory. The explanation, now that I look back on it, seems so simple now. Then I was like Benjamin Franklin getting a jolt from his kite and having no notion what hit him. Now I know.

A second thunderhead, larger and more globular, is approaching from the north. A breeze springs up. There is no thunder but lightning flickers around inside the cloud like a defective light bulb.

While there is still time, let me tell you what my invention does, just in case worst comes to worst and my article in *Brain* can't be published. Since catastrophe may overtake us within the hour, I am dictating these words into a pocket recorder so that survivors poking around the ruins of Howard Johnson's a hundred years from now will have a chance of avoiding a repetition.

My discovery, like all great scientific breakthroughs, is simplicity itself. The notion came to me during my work with the encephalograph, with which instrument, as you know, one tapes electrodes to the skull and records brain waves, which in turn may reveal such abnormalities as tumors, strokes, fits, and so on.

It happened while I was ill.

One stormy night I lay in a hospital bed recovering from seizures of alternating terror and delight with intervening periods of immense longing. These attacks are followed in my case by periods of extraordinary tranquillity of mind, of heightened perception, clairvoyance, and increased inductive powers. The storm roared and crashed outside the acute ward; I lay on my back in bed, hands at my side, surrounded by thirty-nine other madmen moaning and whimpering like souls in the inner circle of hell. Yet I felt extraordinarily happy. Thoughts flew into my head like little birds. Then it was that my great idea came to me. So confident was I of its value that I leapt out of bed at the height of the storm and yelled at my fellow patients:

"Don't be afraid, brothers! Don't cry! Don't tremble! I have made a discovery that will cure you! Believe me, brothers!"

"We believe you, Doc!" the madmen cried in the crashing thunder, and they did. Madmen, like possessed souls in the Gospels, know when you are telling the truth.

It was my fellow physicians who gave me trouble.

My idea was simply this: if the encephalograph works, why not devise a gadget without wires that will measure the electrical activity of the separate centers of the brain? Hardly a radical idea. But here was the problem: given such a machine, given such readings, could the readings then be correlated with the manifold woes of the Western world, its terrors and rages and murderous impulses? And if so, could the latter be treated by treating the former?

A large order, yes, but so was Edward Jenner's dream of eradicating the great pox.

A bit of luck came my way. Once I got out of the acute wing, they put me to work as assistant to the resident encephalographer, one of those super-Negroes who speak five languages, quote the sutras, and are wizards in electronics as well. He, Colley Wilkes, got interested in my ideas and helped me rig up my first working model. Another break came my way from Kino Yamaiuchi, a classmate, presently with Osaka Instruments, who cut every piece of red tape and got the first five hundred production models turned out in record time—a little order that cost me $150,000 worth of my wife's R. J. Reynolds stock.

My invention unites two principles familiar to any sophomore in high school physics. One is the principle of electrical induction. Any electrical activity creates a magnetic field, which in turn will induce a current in a wire passed through the field. The other is the principle of location by triangulation. Using microcircuitry techniques, Colley and I rigged up two tiny electronic "listeners," something like the parabolic reflectors with which one can hear a whisper at two hundred feet. Using our double receiver, we could "hear" the electrical activity of a pinhead-sized area anywhere in the brain: in the cortex, the pineal body, the midbrain—anywhere.

So we "listened." Colley was interested in locating brain

tumors and such, but I was after bigger game. We listened and sure enough Colley found his brain tumors. What I found was a horse of a different color.

Colley, I will admit, has not gone along with my idea of measuring and treating the deep perturbations of the soul. Unfortunately, there still persists in the medical profession the quaint superstition that only that which is visible is real. Thus the soul is not real. Uncaused terror cannot exist. Then, friend, how come you are shaking?

No matter, though. Later I was made a professor and didn't need Colley's help.

I have called my machine More's Qualitative Quantitative Ontological Lapsometer.

A curtain moves in a window of the front wing of the motel, opposite the girls' rooms. Could it be that some Bantu S.O.B. is still trying to shoot me?

Allow me to cite, in simplified terms, a couple of my early case histories.

Patient #1

One hot summer afternoon as I sat at my father's old coroner's desk by the open back door sipping Early Times, watching the flight patterns of the martins, and pondering the singularity of being forty-four years old, my nurse, whom I mainly employ to keep patients away, brought in a patient.

Nothing changes in a man, I was thinking. I felt exactly as I felt when I was ten years old. Only accidentals change. Hair begins to sprout from your ears, your toes rotate, showing more skin.

My nurse first put away the bottle. She is a beautiful though dour Georgia Presbyterian of the strict observance named Ellen Oglethorpe. Her eyes, blue as Lake Geneva, glittered in triumph as she stowed the Early Times and closed the door behind the patient. For she had, to her way of thinking, killed two birds with one stone. She was striking a blow at my drinking and at the same time delivering one of the "better sort" of patients, the sort who have money. She approves of money on religious grounds.

The patient was P. T. Bledsoe, president of Brown-Betterbag Paper Company. The poor man had his usual blinding sick headache. I gave him a shot of corticaine and sat and looked at him.

P. T. Bledsoe is a sixty-year-old man, an upright citizen, a generous Knothead, good hunting companion, churchgoer, deacon, devoted husband and father, Lion, Kiwanian, 33rd-degree Mason who, however, is subject to seizures of rage and blinding headaches and is convinced of several conspiracies against him. The Negroes for one, he told me, were giving him a hard time at the plant, wanting to be promoted and all. He was certain that the Negroes and Communists were after him (as a matter of fact, the Negroes *were* after him, I happened to know) as well as a Jewish organization that he called the "Bildebergers" and that he had reason to believe had taken over the Federal Reserve system. Though he lived on the ninth hole squarely in the middle of Paradise Estates, which is protected by an electrified ten-foot fence, a guard house at every entrance, and a private patrol, he kept two fierce Rhodesian ridgebacks, one outside and one inside the house. His ambition was to move to Australia. He never tired of telling of the year in his youth he spent in the Outback.

"Look, P. T.," I said at last. "Why don't you move to Australia?"

"Yeah," said P. T. sourly, disappointed at what he took to be a conversational gambit.

"No, I mean it."

"I'm not ready to retire."

"Doesn't your company have a million acres in Queensland?"

"I'm not walking away from anything."

I sighed. Perhaps he was right. It's just that in recent months I've found it an effective rule of therapy to accept as more self-evident every day a certain state of affairs, namely, that most people nowadays are possessed, harboring as they do all manner of demonic hatred and terrors and lusts and envies, that principalities and powers are nearly everywhere victorious, and that therefore a doctor's first duty to his patient is to help him find breathing room and so keep him from going crazy. If P. T. can't stand blacks and Bildebergers, my experience is that there is not time enough to get him over it even if I could. Nor can I cast out his demon nor forgive his sin if that's what it is. Why not then move to the Outback, if that is what you like and especially if there is not a Jew or a black for a hundred miles around?

But we'd been over this ground before and P. T. now sat wearily in his chair.

Catching sight of the first crude model of my invention in an open drawer, I had an idea. Until that moment I had not tried it on anyone but myself—where I confess I had uncovered a regular museum of pathology, something like passing a metal detector over the battlefield of Iwo Jima.

Why not begin my clinical series with P. T. Bledsoe?

His blood pressure and other physical signs were normal. So, standing behind P. T., I passed the lapsometer over his skull, taking readings and feeling a bit like a phrenologist.

His cortical readings were normal, as was his pineal self-hood. Then, having a hunch, I focused upon the red nucleus in the floor of the fourth ventricle and asked him about the Bildebergers.

To my astonishment and even as I watched, the needle swung from a moderate 2.6 mmv to a great whacking rage level of 9.4 mmv.

"Your headache's coming back, isn't it?"

P. T. looked up in surprise, his eyes hazed with pain, and spied my machine, which at this stage looked for all the world like a Brownie box camera.

"Does that thing register headaches?"

"In a way."

"Can you cure them?"

Now it was his turn to be excited and mine to be depressed. "No, not yet." At the time I had not yet made my second breakthrough.

I could not cure his headache then. Now I can. But here's the curious thing. The very act of locating the site, touching the sore spot, so to speak, seemed to make him feel better. He refused a second shot and left quite cheerfully.

Patient #2

Later the same afternoon I saw Ted Tennis, a well-educated, somewhat abstracted graduate student who suffered from massive free-floating terror, identity crisis, and sexual impotence.

It didn't take my machine to size him up. Every psychiatrist knows the type: the well-spoken slender young man who recites his symptoms with precision and objectivity—so objective that they seem to be somebody else's symptoms—and above all with that eagerness, don't you know, as if nothing would please him more than that his symptom, his dream, should turn out to be interesting, a textbook case. *Allow me to have a proper disease, Doctor,* he all but tells me.

As we watched the sooty martins through the doorway come skimming up to the hotel—it helps with some patients if we can look at the martins and not at each other—he tells me his troubles with the usual precision, using medical words—he's read more medical books than I have—like a case history! The usual story: daytime terror and nighttime impotence, even though he feels "considerable warmth and tenderness" toward his wife, Tanya (why doesn't he just say he loves her?), and so forth. He is wondering again about the "etiology" of the impotence. Dear God, how could he be anything other than impotent? How can a man quaking with terror make love to his wife?

But today he's got a new idea. If I'd been as sharp-witted and alert to small clues as a good psychiatrist should be, I should have guessed from the way his eye kept straying to my big bottom drawer. Here I keep my samples. The untreatable maladies of any age, reader, may be ascertained from the free samples a doctor receives. My desk drawer contains hundreds of suppositories, thousands of pills for treating terror, and dozens of rayon "training" organs for relieving male impotence.

None of these things works very well.

In short, my patient asked—for the first time and in a halting, scarcely audible voice—to be fitted with a rayon organ. If he could not "achieve an adequate response" himself, he said—why doesn't he say "make love"—he could at least see that his wife did.

Again we cast an eye toward my bottom drawer, which did in

fact contain a regular arsenal of male organs, the best of which are for some reason manufactured in Bayonne, New Jersey.

"Very well, Ted," I said, opening the drawer and taking out not a Bayonne-rayon organ but my invention.

"What's that?"

"I'd like to do a personality profile using a new tele-encephalographic technique." This is the way you talk to Ted.

"Eh? How's that?" asked Ted, pricking up his ears. "You mean you can measure electrical activity with that?"

"Yes."

"Without electrodes?"

"Yes."

"And correlate the readings with personality traits?"

"Yes."

"Wow."

He was willing enough, of course. He sees something magic in it, scientific magic, like being touched by the king for the king's evil. But it is more than that. When I touched him—strange, but this happened earlier with P. T. Bledsoe—he already seemed better. Who of us now is not so strangely alone that it is the cool clinical touch of the stranger that serves best to treat his loneliness?

"Should be interesting," said Ted, bowing his head.

It was. He registered a dizzy 7.6 mmv over Brodmann 32, the area of abstractive activity. Since that time I have learned that a reading over 6 generally means that a person has so abstracted himself from himself and from the world around him, seeing things as theories and himself as a shadow, that he cannot, so to speak, reenter the lovely ordinary world. Instead he orbits the earth and himself. Such a person, and there are millions, is destined to haunt the human condition like the Flying Dutchman.

Ellen Oglethorpe peeped in and closed the door again as discreetly as if we were lovers. Her eyes sparkled. She was having a good day. Two rich patients in one day! Ted Tennis's wife, Tanya, is a Milwaukee beer heiress and their house in Paradise is bigger than mine.

Over his coeliac plexus, soothed though he was, he still clocked a thunderous anxiety of 8.7 mmv. His hand trembled slightly against mine. And all at once I could see how he lived his life: shuddering in orbit around the great globe, seeking some way to get back. Don't I know? We are two of a kind, winging it like Jupiter and spying comely maids below and having to take the forms of swans and bulls to approach them. Except that he, good heathen that he is, wished only to reenter his own wife. I, the Christian, am the fornicator.

"Well?" he asked anxiously when I finished.

So I told him my findings and he listened with the intensest interest, but I made the mistake of using such words as "angelism," "spiritual apogee," etcetera, all of which are just technical words to me but had the wrong connotations to him. He's a biologist. So he looked disappointed.

"Look, Tom," said Ted patiently. "All I want is a Bayonne-rayon training member. Would you—"

"O.K. You can take your pick—if." I open the drawer of members.

"If?"

"If you follow my prescription first."

"Oh, very well."

"First, take these. . . ." I write him a prescription. "Now, tomorrow, here's what you do."

"Yes?"

"Instead of taking the car pool home tomorrow, walk."

"Walk twenty-five miles on the interstate?"

"No, walk six miles through the swamp."

"Through the swamp." He nodded dolefully, worst fears realized.

"Yes. Unfortunately, until we make a therapeutic breakthrough comparable to this diagnostic breakthrough"—I wave my invention at him—"the only way to treat a disorder like this is by rough-and-ready empirical methods. Like putting an ice pack on a toothache. We don't know much about angelism."

"Angelism," repeated Ted sourly. "So to treat angelism, you walk through a swamp."

"Is that worse than the indignity of strapping on a Bayonne-rayon member?" I gave him a few technical details about Layer V of Brodmann Area 32. He brightened. If it's scientific, he'll do it.

"Well, it's worth a try. I'll do it for Tanya's sake. I'd do anything to restore our relationship along the entire spectrum."

"Very well. Get a compass and after work tomorrow on Monkey Island, strike out due north across the swamp."

Ted does his research on Monkey Island in the middle of the swamp. There dwells a colony of killer apes, *Gorilla gorilla malignans*, thought to be an unevolved descendant of one of man's ancestors. No other ape kills for pleasure.

The question is: how to account for man's wickedness? Biologists, for some reason, find it natural to look for a wicked monkey in the family tree. I find it more reasonable to suppose that monkeys are blameless and that something went wrong with man. Many people hereabouts, by the way, blame the recent wave of atrocities on escaped killer apes. Some Knothead whites, however, blame black guerrillas. Some liberals blame white Knotheads.

If you measure the pineal activity of a monkey—or any other subhuman animal—with my lapsometer, you will invariably record identical readings at Layers I and II. Its self, that is to say, coincides with itself. Only in man do you find a discrepancy: Layer I, the outer social self, ticking over, say, at a sprightly 5.4 mmv, while Layer II just lies there, barely alive at 0.7 mmv, or even zero!—a nought, a gap, an aching wound. Only in man does the self miss itself, *fall* from itself (hence *laps*ometer!). Suppose—! Suppose I could hit on the right dosage and weld the broken self whole! What if man could reenter paradise, so to speak, and live there both as man and spirit, whole and intact man-spirit, as solid flesh as a speckled trout, a dappled thing, yet aware of itself as a self!

But we were speaking of Ted. Yes, I prescribed for Ted, Ted promised to follow the prescription, and he did. The next afternoon, instead of leaving Monkey Island at five, climbing into a sealed refrigerated bubbletop and gliding home on the interstate, home where in his glass-walled "enclosed patio" he would surely sit quaking with terror, abstracting himself from himself and corrupting the here and now—instead he wore jeans and tennis shoes and, taking a compass reading bearing nor'-nor'east, struck out through Honey Island Swamp. The six miles took him five hours. At ten o'clock that night he staggered up his back yard past the barbecue grill, half dead of fatigue, having been devoured by mosquitoes, leeches, vampire bats, tsetse flies, snapped at by alligators, moccasins, copperheads, chased by Bantu guerrillas and once even set upon and cuffed about by a couple of Michigan State dropouts on a bummer who mistook him for a parent. It was every bit the ordeal I had hoped.

At that time the only treatment of angelism, that is, excessive abstraction of the self from itself, was recovery of the self through ordeal.

So it came to pass that half-dead and stinking like a catfish, he fell into the arms of his good wife, Tanya, and made lusty love to her the rest of the night.

The freshening wind smells of rain and trees.

Behind the motel a tumbleweed blows through the vineclad posts of the drive-in movie. Its sign has advertised the same film for the past five years:

HOMO HIJINKS
ZANY LAFF RIOT

It took a lot to get people out to movies in the last days of the old Auto Age. A gimmick was needed. In *Homo Hijinks* it was an act of fellatio performed by two skydivers in a free fall on 3-D Ektachrome on a two-hundred-foot screen.

Patient #3

Charley Parker, the Paradise golf pro, came to see me last year for a life insurance examination. In the physical, he checked out well in all categories, being indeed a superb physical specimen as well as a genial outgoing sort of fellow. A fifty-year-old blond stud pony of a man, he once made the winter tour with the champs and even placed at Augusta. But Charley is best known for having been the first pro to introduce night golf to a major course. Paradise Country Club, thanks to Charley Parker, inaugurated the famous Southern "Moonlight" summer tour of the champs, played "under the arcs" in the cool of the evening. It is a "new concept" in tournament golf. Making use of cheap electricity and cheap sodium vapor, Charley concealed hundreds of lamps in cypress trees, behind

Spanish moss. To Charley goes the credit for delighting the fans with the romance of golf and repelling insects as well.

I made routine readings with my lapsometer. Hm, what's this? Healthy as he was, and with every reason to be happy, Charley's deep pineal, the site of inner selfhood, was barely ticking over at a miserable 0.1 mmv.

I asked Charley if he was sure he felt all right, no insomnia? no nervousness? no depression? no feelings of disorientation or strangeness?

"Are you kidding, Doc?" Charley began, ticking off his assets: his lovely wife, Ramona; one boy at M.I.T.; the other boy at fourteen winner of the J.C. tournament; his success in bringing the champs to Paradise (this very weekend, by the way) for a Pro-Am tournament; boosting the prize money to a cool million; being voted Man of the Year by the Optimists, etcetera etcetera.

But he paused in his counting. "Nervousness? strangeness? It's funny that you should ask."

"Why?"

As I waited, I was thinking: surely my machine is wrong this time. Charley never looked better, tan skin crinkled in healthy crow's-feet, blond, almost albino, eyelashes thick and sand-sprinkled as so many athletes' are. He's a healthy bourbon-cured stud of a man with a charming little-kid openness about him: it does not occur to him not to say how he feels. Charley's the sort of fellow, you know, who always turns up in a pinch and does what needs doing. Maybe he's the best American type, the sergeant-yeoman out of the hills, the good cop. When the hurricane comes, he's the fellow with the truck: come on, we got to get those folks out of there.

Charley blinked his sandy lashes and passed a hand across his eyes.

"I mean like this morning I looked at myself in the mirror and I said, Charley, who in the hell are you? What does it all mean? It was strange, Doc. What does it all mean, is the thing."

"What does what all mean?"

"What about you, Doc?" asked Charley, with a glint in his eye, meaning: look who's asking about nervousness. But he forgave me as quickly. "Doc, you ought to stay in condition.

You got a good build. What you need is eighteen every night under the arcs, like the other docs."

I nodded, taking hope. He could be right.

A note for physicians: if you listen carefully to what patients say, they will often tell you not only what is wrong with them but also what is wrong with you.

Six months later I was called out to Charley's house by his wife, Ramona. Charley was in an acute depression. As a matter of fact, I was not feeling well myself. My feet moved in glue. It was March 2, the anniversary of Samantha's death and the date too of the return of the first martin scouts from the Amazon basin. I had been sitting at the back door of my office waiting for them and putting off going to see Charley.

It was four o'clock when I got there. Ramona and I sat there in the cathedral living room and watched Charley in his Naugahyde recliner set uncomfortably in the up position. Ramona had just got back from a garden club luncheon and still had her hat on, bright blue and fur-trimmed to match her suit. A thick white droning afternoon light filled the room. Through the open pantry door I could see Lou Ann, the cook, fixing to leave the kitchen with her plastic bag of scraps. The dishwasher had already shifted into the wash cycle *chug-chug-chug*.

Charley's appearance was shocking. He was dressed in sport clothes but wore them like an old man, aloha shirt, high-stomached shorts, but business shoes and socks. His elbows had grown tabs. His tan had an undertone of jaundice. The crow's-feet around his eyes were ironed out, showing white troughs.

"Did you want to see me, Charley?"

He cupped his hand to hear. Not that he was deaf, but it was hard to hear in that room. Voices sounded reedy. The vaulted ceiling crossed by simulated hand-hewn beams roared like a conch.

Charley looked at me.

"You look like hell, Doc."

"I know."

"You got a good build. You ought to stay in shape."

"You're right." I was feeling bad. Samantha was dead and the martins had not come back. It was a bad white winter day.

"What did you mean when you asked me if I felt strange?" Charley asked me, resuming our conversation of six months earlier.

"What? Oh. As I recall, it was a routine question."

"Why in hell should I feel strange?" Charley's reedy voice buzzed up into the vaulted ceiling like a cicada. He felt very low, but my own low spirits revived him sufficiently so that he pulled a lever and lay back in the recliner.

"He loves to talk to you," said Ramona in a loud drone as if Charley were not talking, were not even present. Discovering that she still had her hat on, she clucked and, feeling for hat-pins, stood up and went into the pantry. Her inner calves still had the tender straight undeveloped lines of pretty girls in the Lower Piedmont, the sort who sit drinking Cokes for twenty years. She is from Spartanburg, South Carolina.

It seemed permissible to slump as low as Charley. Charley and I could talk along the floor while Ramona went sailing through the roaring upper air as if it were her medium.

Charley was depressed but he didn't know why. Nothing much had changed in his life, except that his son had dropped out of M.I.T. and taken to the swamp, hardly an uncommon occurrence these days. But he and his son had never been close.

"So what?" said Charley. "My old man ran me off when I was fourteen."

So there seemed to be no external cause for Charley's distress. On the contrary. Just the week before, the champs had signed up again to play under the arcs on the Moonlight Summer Tour. The new Paradise 36 was finished. A new concept in golf courses, its initial cost of forty million was also its final cost. What with its fleet of carts, elimination of caddies, its automatic sprinkler system with each outlet regulated by a moisture sensor, its new Tifton 451 Bermuda, which required neither mowing nor fertilizing, labor costs were eliminated.

Then what was the trouble?

Charley shrugged. "I don't know, Doc. I mean, what's the use? You know what I mean?"

"Yes." Something occurred to me. "When did you see your son last?"

"What's that got to do with it?"

"When?"

"Last month. On his way to Honey Island Swamp."

"Did you quarrel with him?"

"Do you know what that sapsucker wanted to do?"

"No."

"Move the three of them into his old room while he looks for a new cave."

"The three of them?"

"Him and his little yehudi and their cute little bastard. Up they go to bed without a by-your-leave."

"Yehudi?"

"Introduces her as Ethel Ginsberg or Finklestein."

"Yes?"

"What do you mean, yes? I mean, don't you think he could at least have had enough consideration for his mother to pretend they were married?"

"What happened then?"

"What do you mean, what happened? I threw his ass out. Wouldn't you have?"

"I don't know."

I was thinking of my daughter, dead these seven years. Would I have thrown her ass out if she had gone up to bed with a Ginsberg? Yes. No. I don't know.

Rising unsteadily, I blew my nose and reached for my lapsometer. What I was curious about was whether his deep pineal reading stayed low during his excitement. Charley was so wound up that he didn't even notice that I was going over his head like a barber. He kept swinging around to tell me something. It was like giving a haircut to a three-year-old.

(The reading was up: getting mad helped him. Or was it the talking?)

"Be still, Charley."

Charley shut up. But he had to do something, so he started pressing buttons on his recliner. The stereo-V came booming on and stayed on.

In a minute Ramona came in and turned it down. Her hat was off and her hair was piled up in tiers like a garden-club arrangement.

"It's a goddamn lie," said Charley.

"What's a lie?" Was he talking about the news or his son?

"That's what he does all day," Ramona told me, as if Charley were absent. "Fusses about the news and can't wait till the next. He listens to the news every hour."

"Fusses" seemed to be the wrong word for Charley's anger.

Then it was that the idea first occurred to me: what would happen if one were able to apply electrical stimulation to the pineal region?

But the best I could do in those days was a kind of "historical therapy," as I called it then: a recapture of the past and one's self.

Only one thing worked with Charley. After his anger had subsided (something in the news—the Negroes, the Lefts, the love people, I didn't notice—made him mad), I picked up the glass paperweight and I gave it a shake to set the snow whirling. The scene was the Battle above the Clouds atop Lookout Mountain. "Remember when we got this, honey," Charley would usually say. "Yes. At Ruby Falls on our honeymoon."

But that day Charley was either too angry still or too low to notice the paperweight.

"Ain't nobody starving in no swamp," he muttered.

I nodded, thinking he meant his son.

Ramona, who is quick and intuitive, saw my mistake and corrected me (women are smarter than psychiatrists).

"He"—still the absent *he*—"was talking about the news. You know, niggers supposed to be starving around here like in Beauford."

"I see."

Ramona gave me another hint. "He thinks they're accusing him."

"They?"

"That's humbug," said Charley.

"Guess what he told him," said Ramona. "He told him it was his fault."

He? Him? His? Which *he* is Charley and which his son and whose fault is it?

"Well of course," I said somewhat vaguely, "everyone knows that Charley is a generous—"

"No! No!" They both turned on me. I hadn't got the

straight of it yet. I felt stupid, but on the other hand some married people, you know, carry on these mysterious six-layered conversations with all manner of secret signs.

Ramona set me straight. "Why should anyone blame Charley when all he did was build a golf course and invent the arcs? It wasn't his forty million dollars that filled in the swamp. He was just doing his job. Is it Charley's fault that Tifton 451 eliminates labor?"

"Yes. Hm," I said in the best psychiatric style, pretending I knew all along. "You mean he and Chuck quarreled?"

"Quarreled, hell," said Charley. "I kicked his ass out."

"You should have heard them," said Ramona. "Both of them acted ugly." Ramona tried to put it down to menfolk's ordinary foolishness. They had a fuss. But it was more than that. So serious was the quarrel that Charley was still worried about not winning it.

"I told him exactly like I'm telling you now: get your little yehudi and your little bastard and get your ass out."

"They used to go hunting together," said Ramona in her Spartanburg drone. But she was crying. "They never missed a dove season."

"You know what he accused me of?" Charley asked me.

"No."

"Starving niggers. You know what he called me?"

"No."

"A hypocritical son of a bitch."

"He didn't actually say—" began Ramona. "That was ugly, though."

"You too, Doc," said Charley.

"Me?"

"You were included. All of us here are hypocritical sons of bitches."

"I see."

"He told me he knew for a fact that niggers come up from the swamp at night and eat soybean meal off the greens. Now you know that's a lie."

"Well, I've never heard—"

"In the first place, we haven't used soybean meal since last summer. Tifton 451 doesn't need it. As a matter of fact, I've got a whole barnful left over I've got to get rid of."

"I see."

I shook the paperweight again and in the end succeeded in getting Charley to tell me about his first tour when he had to borrow a hundred dollars to qualify at Fort Worth because Ramona had spent their last money on Sears sport clothes for him so he wouldn't look like a caddy. But he was a caddy and wore sneakers instead of spiked shoes.

He told me about placing at Augusta. His deep pineal reading got up to 6 mmv.

"Doc, have you ever played thirty-six holes on three Baby Ruths?"

"No."

"Do you think I'm a hypocritical son of a bitch?"

"No."

"What do you think I am?"

What do I think? The mystery of evil is the mystery of limited goodness. Charley is a good man. Then how did things turn out so badly? What went wrong? I gave the paperweight a shake and sent snow swirling around Lookout Mountain.

Charley wanted to talk about whether the niggers were starving or not, etcetera, but what interested me and where my duty lay was with Charley. I saw how his life was and what he needed. Charley was a tinkerer, like GM's famous Charley Kettering, a fellow who has to have one idea to worry with twenty-four hours a day. Without it he's blown up. Charley's the sort of fellow who retires to Florida hale and hearty and perishes in six months.

Here's what happened.

Some months later I made my second breakthrough and added the ionizer to my lapsometer. I was able to treat an area as well as "listen" to it. It worked. Accordingly, a few days ago—when was it? a day? two days? dear Lord, how much has happened—I gave him a pineal massage and he came to himself, his old self, and began to have one idea after another. One idea: an electronic unlosable golf ball that sends signals from the deepest rough. Another: a "golfarama," a mystical idea of combining a week of golf on a Caribbean island with the Greatest Pro of Them All—a week of revivals conducted by a member of the old Billy Graham team, the same revivalist, incidentally, who is in Paradise this weekend.

*

The interstate swelters in the sun.

My eyes are almost swelled shut, breath whistles in my throat, but my heart is full of love. Love of what? Women. Which women? All women. The first night I ever spent on the acute ward, a madman looked at me and said, not knowing me from Adam: "You want to know your trouble? You don't love God, you love pussy."

It might be true. Madmen like possessed men usually tell the truth. At any rate, through a crack of daylight I catch sight of a face, a blurred oval in the window of room 203. Lola.

The question is: if worst comes to worst, what is the prospect of a new life in a new dead world with Lola Rhoades, to say nothing of Moira Schaffner and Ellen Oglethorpe? Late summer and fall lie ahead, but will they be full of ghosts? That was the trouble with long summer evenings and the sparkling days of fall, they were haunted. What broke the heart was the cicadas starting up in the sycamores in October. Everyone was happy but our hearts broke with happiness. The golf links canceled themselves. Happy children grew up with haunted expressions and ran away. No more of that. Vines sprout in the plaza now. Fletcher Christian began a new life with three wives on faraway Pitcairn, green as green and unhaunted by old Western ghosts. I shall be happy with my three girls. Only Ellen, a Presbyterian, may make trouble.

Patient #4

Late last night a love couple crept up out of the swamp and appeared in my "enclosed patio." This often happens. Even though I am a psychiatrist, denizens of the swamp appear at all hours suffering from malaria, dengue, flukes, bummers, hepatitis, and simple starvation. Nobody else will treat them.

I saw them from my bedroom window. It was three o'clock. I had been reading my usual late-night fare, Stedmann's *History of World War I*. For weeks now I've been on the Battle of Verdun, which killed half a million men, lasted a year, and left the battle lines unchanged. Here began the hemorrhage and death by suicide of the old Western world: white Christian

Caucasian Europeans, sentimental music-loving Germans and rational clear-minded Frenchmen, slaughtering each other without passion. "The men in the trenches did not hate each other," wrote Stedmann. "As for the generals, they respected or contemned each other precisely as colleagues in the same profession."

Comes a tap at the door. Is it guerrilla, drughead, Ku Kluxer, Choctaw, or love couple?

Love couple.

What seems to be the trouble? It seems their child, a love child, is very sick. I know you're not a pediatrician but the other doctors won't come, etcetera. Will I come? O.K.

Grab my bag, and down through the azaleas and into a pirogue, I squatting amidships, boy and girl paddling as expertly as Cajuns. A sinking yellow moon shatters in the ripples.

They speak freely of themselves. He's a tousled blond lad with a splendid fan-shaped beard like Jeb Stuart (I can tell he's from these parts by the way he says *fo'teen for fourteen, Bugaloosa for Bogalusa*), gold-haired, gray-jeaned, bare-chested and -footed. She's a dark little Pocahontas from Brooklyn (I judge, for she speaks of *hang-gups*). They've given up city, home, family, career, religion, to live a perfect life of love and peace with a dozen others on a hummock with nothing else for a shelter in the beginning than an abandoned Confederate salt mine. There they've revived a few of the pleasanter Choctaw customs such as building chickees and smoking rabbit cannab, a variety of *Cannabis indica* that grows wild in the swamp.

"You don't remember me, Dr. More." The boy speaks behind me.

"No."

"I'm Chuck."

"Chuck?"

"Chuck Parker."

"Yes of course. I know your father very well."

"My poor father."

How is it that children can be more beautiful than the sum of their parents' beauty? Ramona is a stork-legged, high-hipped, lacquer-headed garden-clubber from Spartanburg. Charley is a pocked-nosed, beat-up, mashed-down Gene Sarazen. And here is golden-haired golden-limbed Chuck looking like Phoebus Apollo or Sir Lancelot in hip-huggers.

When we reach the hummock, the sky in the east has turned sickly and tentative with dawn.

They're camping near the mouth of old Empire Number Two, the salt mine that supplied Dick Taylor during the Red River campaign. Except for an ember or two there is no sign of the others. In a swale springy with cypress needles Chuck has built a chickee of loblolly chinked with blue bayou clay.

As we enter the chickee, fragrant with bayberry smoke, a tall brown-haired girl rises and closes a book on her finger, for all the world like a baby-sitter in Paradise when the folks come home—except that her reading light is a candle made from wax myrtle and bayberries. Chuck stops her and introduces us. Her name is Hester. Instead of leaving, she squats cross-legged on the cypress needles.

Afterwards Chuck tells me in her hearing, "Hester has her own chickee."

"Is that so," I answer, scratching my head.

I take a look at Hester's book, still closed on her finger. A good way to size up people. It is not what you might think, Oriental or revolutionary. It is, of all things under the sun, Erle Stanley Gardner's first novel, *The Case of the Velvet Claws.*

The baby, as I had reason from experience to expect and had in fact prepared my bag for, suffers from dehydration. He's dried up like a prune. The treatment is simple and the results spectacular. Slip a needle in his scalp vein and hang a bottle of glucose from a loblolly twig.

Mama watched her baby get well before her eyes, reviving like a wilted hydrangea stuck in a bucket of water. I watched Mama. Ethel is a dark, quick little Pocahontas with hairbraids, blue Keds, jean shorts, and sharp soiled knees. She's not my type, being a certain kind of Smith girl, a thin moody Smithie who props cheek on knee, doesn't speak to freshmen, doesn't focus her eyes, and is prone to quick sullen decisions, leaping onto her little basketed bike and riding off without explanation.

(Hester is my type: post-Protestant, post-rebellion, post-ideology—reading Perry Mason here on a little ideological island!—reverted all the way she is, clear back to pagan innocence like a shepherd girl piping a tune on a Greek vase.)

When the sun clears the hummock, we sit on the bayou bank feeling the warmth on our backs, Ethel holding the baby, Chuck holding the infusion bottle. Hester sits cross-legged and stare-eyed, looking at nothing, smoothing her calves with her hands.

"How about that?" murmurs Chuck, as the baby's wrinkles disappear. What a lordly youth, with a smooth simple chest, simple large golden arms and legs, the large wrists and boxy knees of a tennis player.

Now the sun, breaking through the morning fog and live oaks, strikes shafts into the tea-colored water. Mullet jump. Two orange-colored warblers fly at each other in the sunlight, claws upraised like cockerels. A swarm of gnats hangs over the water motionless and furious, like a molecule. I eat a scuppernong. It is fat and tart.

"It wouldn't be bad to live here," I tell Chuck.

"Why don't you? Come and live with us." He turns to Ethel but she gives him her hooded Smithie look.

"Where would I live?"

"Here," says Hester. "There's my chickee."

Does she mean live with her or build my own chickee close by? She's from Massachusetts or Rhode Island. For car she says *că*.

"What have you got to lose, Doc?" asks Chuck.

"Well—"

The glucose bottle is empty. Ethel frowns and takes baby and bottle inside.

"Are you happy over there?"

"Happy?"

"We're happy here."

"Good."

"Everyone here lives a life of perfect freedom and peace."

"Good."

"We help each other. We love."

"Very good."

"That is, all except Hester. She hasn't found anyone she likes yet. Eh, Hester?"

"I'm not quite sure," says Hester, not blushing.

Oh those lovely hollowed-out Holyoke vowels. Her voice is a Congregational bell.

"We're basically religious here, Doc."

"Good."

"We have God every minute."

"Good."

"Don't you see that I am God, you are God, that prothonotary warbler is God?"

"No."

"We always tell the exact truth. Will you answer me honestly, Doc?"

"All right."

"What is your life like? Are you happy?"

"No."

"What's wrong?"

"It's hard to say." For some reason I blush under Hester's clear gaze.

"But you don't have a good life."

"No."

"Then why do you live it?"

"I don't know."

"We have a good life here."

"Good."

"There's nothing wrong with sex, Doc. You shouldn't put it down."

"I don't."

"It's not even the most important thing."

"It's not?"

"With us it's far down the list."

"Hm." I look at my watch. "You can take me back."

"O.K. if I pay you later? Or do you want some Choctaw cannab?"

"No thanks. Don't worry about it." Some time ago Chuck lit up a calumet of Choctaw or "rabbit" cannabis and has now begun to jump a bit, feet together, kangaroo style. He passes the calumet around. Hester smokes and passes it to me.

"No thanks."

Ethel, returning from her chickee, also refuses. "Pay the man," she tells Chuck. "Can't you tell he wants to be paid?"

"You're all right, Doc," says Chuck, jumping. "I've always liked you. I've always liked Catholics. We've got some liberated Catholics here."

"I'm not a liberated Catholic."

"What's this about your invention?"

"Did your father tell you?" I am surprised. Perhaps Chuck and his father have patched things up.

"No. My mother. She said you passed a miracle. Have a drag, Doc?"

"No thanks."

I tell them briefly about my lapsometer and about the new breakthrough, my ionizer that corrects electrical malfunctions. High though he's getting, Chuck, what with his three years at M.I.T. and 800 SAT score, is digging me utterly.

"Wow, Doc! Great! Wild!" cries Chuck, jumping straight up and down like a Choctaw at the jibiya dance. "You got to stay! We'll massage everybody on the mainland with your lapsometer and get rid of the old sad things!"

"Do you mean you can actually treat personality hang-gups?" asks little Brooklyn-Pocahontas Ethel.

"Well, yes."

"Do you have it with you?"

"As a matter of fact I do."

"Give us a reading, Doc!" says Chuck.

Even Hester shows a spark of interest.

"Treat Hester, Doc!" cries Chuck. "She's still Springfield bourgeois. Look at her! She likes you, Doc."

"This is the last place I'd treat anybody."

"Why?" asks Ethel, frowning.

"Too much heavy salt hereabouts." I pick up a chunk of dirty Confederate salt. "This stuff assays at about point oh-seven percent heavy salt. I wouldn't dare use my ionizer."

Chuck snaps his fingers. "You mean sub-chain reaction? Silent implosion? Whsssssk?"

"Yes."

"Wowee! Hot damn!" Now Chuck is jumping like a pogo.

"But you could do the diagnostic part?" asks Hester in her lovely hollow-throat voice.

"Yes."

"Do one on me," says Ethel.

"Doc, tell me the truth now," says Chuck, capering and jerking his elbows.

"All right."

"Are you telling me that with that thing you can actually register the knotheadedness of the Knotheads, the nutty objectivity of the scientists, and the mad spasms of the liberals?"

"That's an odd way of putting it, but yes."

"And you're also telling me that you can treat 'em, fry 'em with your ray and make 'em human?"

"With the same qualification, yes."

"And you're also telling me that something is afoot with all those nuts over yonder and that today on the glorious Fourth of July something is going to happen and they're all going to do each other in?"

"Well, not quite but—"

"And finally you're saying that some of your gadgets have fallen into the wrong hands and there's a chance the whole swamp might go up in a Heavy-Sodium reaction?"

"Yes."

"Wow! Whee! Hot damn!" Off he goes in his goat dance.

"Will you sit down, you idiot," says Ethel crossly. "What's got into you?"

"It's so *funny*. And Doc here. Doc, man you the wildest of all. Doc, you got to stay here with us. Who's going to believe all that great wild stuff over there?"

"You don't believe me?"

"Believe? Sure. Because you're putting down on all of them, including the scientists."

"I'm a scientist."

"You're better. You're a shaman. The scientists have blown it."

"Still and all, scientists are after the truth."

"I believe you," says Hester suddenly, clear post-Puritan Holyoke eyes full on me.

"I said, do one on me," says Ethel, handing my bag to me. "Why?"

"Because I don't believe you."

"That's all right."

"I think you're afraid to."

"No, I'm not afraid."

"I wish you would," Hester says, pulling her brown heels across her calves.

"I can do a diagnosis here but not a treatment."

"Do it!"

I shrug. "Very well."

It takes three minutes to run a standard profile. Ethel bows her head so that her Pocahontas braids fall along her cheeks.

"Hm."

"Doc, you kill me," says Chuck.

"Hm. She's got a contradictory reading."

"A what?"

"Look here. She's got a strong amplitude and high millivoltage over the temporal lobe, Brodmann 28, which correlates in my experience with singular concrete historical awareness, vivid childhood memories, you know, as well as a sense of the uniqueness of one's tradition. But see here: an even stronger reading over parietal lobe, Brodmann 18. That's the site of ahistoric perceptions that are both concrete and abstract. You should be an excellent artist, Ethel."

"You see there, Ethel! She is, Doc."

"Tch," says Ethel sourly. "I've got the same thing from fortune cookies."

"Are you Jewish, Ethel?"

"What? Yes. What do you mean by asking?"

"You exhibit here what I have termed contradictory Judaism."

"What in hell do you mean?" Ethel swings around on her knees and looks at me squarely for the first time.

"Because you believe at one and the same time that the Jews are unique and that they are not. Thus you would be offended if a Jew told you the Jews were chosen by God, but you would also be offended if a non-Jew told you they were not."

"You hear that, Ethel," yells Chuck, beginning to jump again. "Why only last week—"

Ethel has picked up my lapsometer. "You better take Dr. More home," she tells Chuck without taking her eyes from me.

"O.K., honey, but I mean, gee— Look, I'm sorry, Doc—"

"I'm not listening to some bastard tell me I have a Jewish brain."

"Well actually," I tell Ethel, "I show the same reading, believing as I do both that God—" I stop, mouth wide open. "*Look out!—don't throw it!*—Jesus!—"

But she threw it and in doing so must have flipped the adaptor switch because, before I can catch it, the lapsometer swings through a slow arc, adaptor down. The dirty salt on the bank spits and smokes.

"Good God, what is that?" asks Chuck, instantly sober.

"That was close." Turning off the switch, I pack the lapsometer with trembling hands.

"Yeah, but what was that stuff? Was it what I think it was?"

"Brimstone, no doubt," says Ethel drily.

"As a matter of fact, it was."

"What else?" says Ethel.

"It's the sulfur in the salt. Don't worry. No harm done. Now I've got to go."

"Right," says Chuck soberly. "I want to thank you for—"

"Never mind. Goodbye, Hester."

"Goodbye. Come back."

"All right."

How stands it with a forty-five-year-old man who can fall in love on the spot with a twenty-year-old stranger, a clear-eyed vacant simple Massachusetts girl, and desire nothing more in this life than to move into her chickee?

On the Interstate

IT IS GETTING DARK. Lightning flickers like a genie inside the bottle-shaped cloud.

Why am I so sleepy? It is almost impossible to keep my eyes open! Fireflies of albumen molecules spark in my brain. Yet I don't feel bad. Then concentrate! The next few minutes are critical.

At this moment the President is beginning to speak in New Orleans and the Vice-President is mounting the platform at NASA a few miles away. Both are making a plea for unity. The President, who is an integrationist Mormon married to a liberated Catholic, will appeal to Leftists to respect law and order. The Vice-President, a Southern Baptist Knothead married to a conservative Unitarian, is asking Knotheads for tolerance and understanding, etcetera.

The poor U.S.A.!

Even now, late as it is, nobody can really believe that it didn't work after all. The U.S.A. didn't work! Is it even possible that from the beginning it never did work? that the thing always had a flaw in it, a place where it would shear, and that all this time we were not really different from Ecuador and Bosnia-Herzegovina, just richer. Moon Mullins blames it on the niggers. Hm. Was it the nigger business from the beginning? What a bad joke: God saying, here it is, the new Eden, and it is yours because you're the apple of my eye; because you the lordly Westerners, the fierce Caucasian-Gentile-Visigoths, believed in me and in the outlandish Jewish Event even though you were nowhere near it and had to hear the news of it from strangers. But you believed and so I gave it all to you, gave you Israel and Greece and science and art and the lordship of the earth, and finally even gave you the new world that I blessed for you. And all you had to do was pass one little test, which was surely child's play for you because you had already passed the big one. One little test: here's a helpless man in Africa, all you have to do is not violate him. That's all.

One little test: you flunk!

God, was it always the nigger business, now, just as in 1883,

579

1783, 1683, and hasn't it always been that ever since the first tough God-believing Christ-haunted cunning violent rapacious Visigoth-Western-Gentile first set foot here with the first black man, the one willing to risk everything, take all or lose all, the other willing just to wait and outlast because once he was violated all he had to do was wait because sooner or later the first would wake up and know that he had flunked, been proved a liar where he lived, and no man can live with that. And sooner or later the lordly Visigoth-Western-Gentile-Christian-Americans would have to falter, fall out, turn upon themselves like scorpions in a bottle.

No! No fair! Foul! The test was too much! What do you expect of a man? Yet even so we almost passed. There was a time . . . You tested us because bad as we were there was no one else, and everybody knew it, even our enemies, and that is why they curse us. Who curses the Chinese? Who ever imagined the Chinese were blessed by God and asked to save the world? Who ever expected anything else from them than what they did? What a laugh. And as for Russia and the Russian Christ who was going to save Europe from itself: ha ha.

Flunked! Christendom down the drain. The dream over. Back to history and Bosnia-Herzegovina.

No! No fair!

But wait. It is still not too late. I can save you, America! I know something! I know what is wrong! I hit on something, made a breakthrough, came on a discovery! I can save the terrible God-blessed Americans from themselves! With my invention! Listen to me. Don't give up. It is not too late. You are still the last hope. There is no one else. Bad as we are, there is no one else.

I crack one eye. Through my turret slit, I notice that the sand trap is smoking. The champs, swinging sand wedges, are converging in the fiery bunker.

It has begun.

A yellow lens-shaped cloud hangs like a zeppelin over the horizon beyond the swamp. From the direction of NASA to the north comes a rattle of gunfire.

Then why don't I get up and go down to the motel and see to the girls?

Because I am so sleepy. One little catnap . . .

JULY FIRST

At Home

SOMEONE TOOK a shot at me at the breakfast table.

At this moment I am lying in a corner out of the line of fire and thinking to myself: why is it better down here?

The shots, three of them, came from the direction of the swamp. I was eating breakfast in my "enclosed patio." First there was the sound of the shot heard through the glass, not close, not alarming, not even noteworthy. Undoubtedly a gunshot, though it is too early for squirrel season. Then, more or less at the same time as the second shot, the glass panel shattered. I say more or less at the same time because I did not infer a connection between the two, the shot and the glass shattering.

The third shot was lower, closer, louder. It made a hole in the glass, and in my mind the shot bore a relation to the hole. Somebody is shooting at me, I thought as I drank a warm orange drink named Tang. As I was considering this at the top of my head, something at the heart of me knew better and I found myself diving for the corner even as I ruminated. Saved by a reflex learned with the First Air Cav in the fifteen-year war in Ecuador.

The corner is a good choice, flanked as it is by two low walls of brick that support the glass panels, high enough for protection and low enough to see over if I crane up. But I don't have to crane up. There is a fenestration in the bricks at eye level.

Here I used to tell Samantha the story of Rikki-Tikki-Tavi, how the cobra got into the house by crawling through a hole in the bricks. Samantha shivered with delight and stopped up the hole with newspapers.

A description of my wife: the sort of woman who would name our daughter Samantha though there was no one in our families with this name.

A plan takes shape. Wait a few minutes, get the Smith & Wesson, leave the house by the lower "woods" door, circle the yard under cover of the sumacs, and get behind the sniper.

Is someone after my invention? By craning my head I can catch a glimpse of the box in the hall, the lovely crafted crate from Osaka Instruments. It is the first shipment of the More Qualitative-Quantitative Ontological Lapsometer, the stethoscope of the spirit, one hundred compact pocket-sized machines of brushed chrome. I've come a long way since my Brownie model.

I am lying on the floor drinking warm Tang to which two duck eggs have been added plus two ounces of vodka plus a dash of Tabasco.

The reason the Tang is warm is that the refrigerator doesn't work. Nothing works. All my household motors are silent: air-conditioner, vacuum, dishwasher, dryer, automobile. Appliances and automobiles are more splendid than ever, but when they break down nobody will fix them. My car broke down at the A & P three weeks ago and nobody would come fix it so I abandoned it. Paradise is littered with the rusting hulks of splendid Pontiacs, Olds, and Chryslers that developed vapor locks and dead batteries and were abandoned. Nowadays people buy cars, drive them until they break down, abandon them and buy another. Most of my friends have switched to Toyotas, which have one moving part.

Don't tell me the U.S.A. went down the drain because of Leftism, Knotheadism, apostasy, pornography, polarization, etcetera etcetera. All these things may have happened, but what finally tore it was that things stopped working and nobody wanted to be a repairman.

The bricks smell of old wax. After all these years particles of Pledge wax still adhere to the cindery pits that pock the glaze. Doris used to wax the bricks once a week. "Annie Mae," she'd tell the maid, "Go Pledge the bricks."

I polish off the Tang-plus-vodka-plus-duck-eggs-plus-Tabasco. I feel better.

Another peep through the cobra hole: nothing moves in the swamp, but there is a flash of light. A telescopic sight?

By moving back a few inches I can see the curving loess slope on which my house stands. The house next door has been abandoned, its slab cracked and reclaimed by the swamp, by creeper and anise with its star-shaped funky-smelling flower. Wild grape festoons the carport.

Honeysuckle has invaded Doris's azaleas. A particularly

malignant vine with rank racemose leaves has laid hold of her Saint Francis, who appears to be lifting his birdbath above these evil serpents. Titmice and cardinals used to drink here. Saint Francis was Doris's favorite saint, not because he loved Christ but because he loved titmice.

The evil vine, I notice, has reached the house. A tendril pokes through the cobra hole and curls up looking for purchase.

Wait! Something moves.

But it is only a swamp bird, a gloomy purplish-green heron that flaps down out of a cypress and lights on Saint Francis's bird-limed head. There he perches, neck drawn into his shoulders, yellow bill pointed straight up. He looks as frowsty and ill-conceived as a bird drawn by a child.

Now I've got my revolver, by crawling to the closet and back. The carbine is downstairs.

No sign of the sniper. Has he gone?

Directly above my head on the glass-topped coffee table are Doris's favorite books just as she left them in the "enclosed patio." That was before I roofed it, and the books are swollen by old rains to fat wads of pulp, but still stacked so:

> *Siddhartha*
> *Atlas Shrugged*
> *ESP and the New Spirituality*

Books matter. My poor wife, Doris, was ruined by books, by books and a heathen Englishman, not by dirty books but by clean books, not by depraved books but by spiritual books. God, if you recall, did not warn his people against dirty books. He warned them against high places. My wife, who began life as a cheerful Episcopalian from Virginia, became a priestess of the high places. I loved her dearly and loved to lie with her and would and did whene'er she would allow it, but most especially in the morning, at breakfast, in the nine o'clock sunlight out here on the "enclosed patio." But books ruined her. Beware of Episcopal women who take up with Ayn Rand and the Buddha and Dr. Rhine formerly of Duke University. A certain type of Episcopal girl has a weakness that comes on them just past youth, just as sure as Italian girls get fat. They fall prey

to Gnostic pride, commence buying antiques, and develop a
yearning for esoteric doctrine.

Doris stood on these black pebbles, which we brought from
Mexico, and told me she was leaving me.

Samantha had been dead some months. Doris began talking
of going to the Isle of Jersey or New Zealand where she hoped
to recover herself, learn quiet breathing in a simple place, etcetera etcetera, perhaps in the bright shadow of a 'dobe wall or
perhaps in a stone cottage under a great green fell. She wanted
to leave the bad thing here and go away and make a fresh start.
That was all right with me. I was ready to go. I wanted out
from the bad thing too. What I didn't know at the time was
that I was for her part of the bad thing.

"I'm leaving, Tom."

"Where are you going?"

She did not reply.

The morning sun, just beginning to slant down into the
"enclosed patio," struck the top of her yellow hair, sending
off fiery aureoles like sunflares. I never got over the splendor
of her person in the morning, her royal green-linen-clad self,
fragrant and golden-fleshed. Her flesh was gold amorphous
stuff. Though it was possible to believe that her arm had the
usual layers of fat, muscle, artery, bone, these gross tissues were
in her somehow transformed by her girl-chemistry, bejeweled
by her double-X chromosome. Those were the days of short
skirts, and she looked like long-thighed Mercury, god of morning. Her heels had wings. Her legs were long and deep-fleshed,
bound laterally in the thigh by a strap of fascia that flattened
the triceps. Was it her slight maleness, long-leggedness—perhaps 10 percent tunic-clad Mercury was she—that set my heart
pounding over breakfast?

No, that's foolishness. I loved her, that's all.

"Where are you going?" I asked again, buttering the grits
and watching her hair flame like the sun's corolla.

"I'm going in search of myself."

My heart sank. This was not really her way of talking. It
was the one tactic against which I was defenseless, the portentous gravity of her new beliefs. When she was an ordinary
ex-Episcopalian, a good-humored Virginia girl with nothing
left of her religion but a fondness for old brick chapels, St.

John o' the Woods, and the superb English of the King James Version, we had common ground.

"Don't leave, Doris," I said, feeling my head grow heavy and sink toward the grits.

"I have to leave. It is the one thing I must do."

"Why do you have to leave?"

"We're so dead, Tom. Dead inside. I must go somewhere and recover myself. To the lake isle of Innisfree."

"Jesus, let's go to the lake isle together."

"We don't relate any more, Tom."

"I'd like to relate now."

"I know, I know. That's how you see it."

"How?"

"As physical."

"What's wrong with physical?"

Doris sighed, her eyes full of sunlight. "Who was it who said the physical is the lowest common denominator of love?"

"I don't know. Probably a Hindoo. Would you sit here?"

"What a travesty of love, the assertion of one's conjugal rights."

"I wasn't thinking of my conjugal rights. I was thinking of you."

"Love should be a joyous encounter."

"I'm joyous."

She was right. Lately her mournful spirituality had provoked in me the most primitive impulses. In ten seconds' time my spirits had revived. My heart's desire was that she sit on my lap in the yellow muscadine sunlight.

I took her about the hips. No Mercury she, here.

She neither came nor left.

"But we don't relate," said Doris absently, still not leaving though, eyes fixed on Saint Francis who was swarming with titmice. "There are no overtones in our relationship, no nuances, no upper mansions. Build thee more stately mansions, O my soul."

"All right."

"It's not your fault or my fault. People grow away from each other. Spiritual growth is the law of life. Our obligation is to be true to ourselves and to relate to this law of life."

"Isn't marriage a relation?"

"Our marriage is a collapsed morality, like a burnt-out star which collapses into itself, gives no light and is heavy heavy heavy."

Collapsed morality. Law of life. More stately mansions. Here are unmistakable echoes of her friend Alistair Fuchs-Forbes. A few years ago Doris, who joined the Unity church, got in the habit of putting up English lecturers of various Oriental persuasions, Brahmin, Buddhist, Sikh, Zoroastrian. Two things Doris loved, the English people and Eastern religion. Put the two together, Alistair Fuchs-Forbes reciting *I Ching* in a B.B.C. accent, and poor Episcopal Doris, Apple Queen, from Winchester, Virginia, was a goner.

Alistair Fuchs-Forbes, who came once to lecture at Doris's Unity church, took to coming back and staying longer. He and his boy friend Raymond. Here they would sit, in my "enclosed patio," on their broad potato-fed English asses, and speak of the higher things, of the law of life—and of the financial needs of their handicraft retreat in Mexico. There in Cozumel, it seemed, was the last hope of the Western world. Transcendental religion could rescue Western materialism. How? by making-and-meditation, meditating and making things with one's hands, simple good earthbound things like clay pots. Not a bad idea really—I'd have gone with her to Cozumel and made pots—but here they sat on my patio, these two fake English gurus, speaking of the law of spiritual growth, all the while swilling my scotch and eating three-dollar rib-eye steaks that I barbecued on my patio grill. They spoke of Hindoo reverence for life, including cattle, and fell upon my steaks like jackals.

It didn't take Alistair long to discover that it was Doris, not I, who was rich.

"A collapsed morality?"

"I am truly sorry, Tom."

"I'm not sure I know what a collapsed morality means."

"That's it. It's meaning we've lost. What is meaningful between us? We simply follow rules and habit like poor beasts on a treadmill."

"There is something in that. Especially since Samantha died. But why don't we work at it together. I love you."

"I love you too, Tom. I'm extremely devoted to you and I

always will be. But don't you see that people grow away from each other. A part of one dies, but the rest grows and encysts the old part. Like the chambered nautilus. We're dead."

"I love you dead. At this moment."

My arms are calipers measuring the noble breadth of her hips. She doesn't yield, but she doesn't leave.

"Dead, dead," she whispered above me in the sunlight.

"Love," I whispered.

We were speaking in calm matutinal voices like a pair of wood thrushes fluting in the swamp.

"My God, how can you speak of love?"

"Come here, I'll show you."

"Here?" she said crossly. "I'm here."

"Here."

We had not made love since Samantha's death. I had wanted to, but Doris had a way of ducking her head and sighing and looking elegaic that put me off and made me feel guilty besides. There is this damnable female talent for making a man ashamed, not merely turning him down but putting the guilt of it on him. She made me feel like a high school boy with impure thoughts. Worse than that: a husband with "conjugal rights," and that's enough to chill the warmest heart.

But not mine this morning. I pick up the napkin from my lap.

"Come here."

"What for?" A tiny spark of old Virginny, the Shenandoah Valley, rekindling in her: her saying "what for" and not "why."

"Come and see."

What she did was the nicest compromise between her far-away stare, her sun worship, and lovemaking. She came closer, yet kept her eye on the titmice.

"But you don't love *me*," she said to Saint Francis.

"Yes I do."

She gave me a friendly jostle, the first, and looked down.

"Tch. For pity's sake!" Again, a revival of her old Shenandoah good humor. "Annie Mae is coming, you idiot."

"Close the curtains then."

"I'm leaving," she said but stood closer, again a nicely calculated ambiguity: is she standing close to be close or to get between me and the window so Annie Mae can't see?

"Don't leave," I say with soaring hopes.

"I have to leave."

Then I made a mistake and asked her where she was going. Again her eyes went away.

"East of the sun and west of the moon."

"What crap."

She shrugged. "I'm packed."

Knowing I was wrong, I argued.

"Are you going to meet Alistair and that gang of fags?"

Doris was rich and there was much talk of her financing the Cozumel retreat and even of her coming down and making herself whole.

"Don't call him that: He's searching like me. And he's almost found peace. Underneath all that charm he's—"

"What charm?"

"A very tragic person. But he's a searcher like me, a pilgrim."

"Pilgrim my ass."

"Did you know that for two years he took up a begging bowl and wandered the byways with a disciple of Ramakrishna, the greatest fakir of our time?"

"He's a fakir all right. What he is is a fake Hindoo English fag son of a bitch." Why did I say the very thing that would send her away?

Here was where I had set a record: that of all cuckolds in history, I am the first American to be cuckolded by two English fruits.

"Is that what he is?" said Doris gravely.

"Yes."

"What are you, Tom?"

"I couldn't say."

She nodded absently, but now (!) her hand is on my head, ruffling my hair and strumming just as she used to strum her fingers on the Formica in the kitchen.

"Who was it who said: if I were offered the choice between having the truth and searching for it, I'd take the search?"

"I don't know. Probably Hermann Hesse."

"Hadn't we better close the curtains?"

"Yes. You do it. I can't get up."

She laughed for the first time in six months. "Boy, you are a mess."

We're back in Virginia, at school, under the apple blossoms. She looked down at me. "Annie Mae's going to see you."

"She'd be proud of me."

"Don't be vulgar."

Annie Mae is a big hefty black girl whom Doris dressed up like a French maid with a tiny white cap and a big butterfly bow on her tail.

"Sit in my lap."

"How?"

"This way."

"O.K."

"Easy!"

"Oh boy," she said, nodding and tucking her lip in her old style. Her hand rested as lightly on my shoulder as it did at the Washington and Lee Black-and-White formal. What a lovely funny Valley girl she was before the goddamn heathen Oriental English got her.

"You know the trouble with you, Tom?" She was always telling me the trouble with me.

"What?"

"You're not a seeker after the truth. You think you have the truth, and what good does it do you?"

"Here's the truth." Nobody can blaspheme like a bad Catholic.

"Say what you like about Alistair," she said—and settled herself! "He's a seeker and so am I."

"I know what he seeks."

"What?"

"Your money."

"That's how you would see it."

"That's how I see it."

"Even if it were true, would it be worse than wanting just my body?"

"Yes. But I don't want just your body."

"What do you want?"

"You."

"But not the real me."

"Jesus."

But she was jostling me, bumping me carelessly like a fraternity brother in a stagline.

"You know the trouble with you, Tom?"

"What?"

"You don't understand a purely spiritual relationship."

"That's true."

Somewhere Doris had got the idea that love is spiritual. So lately she'd had no use for my carrying on, as she called it, or messing about, putting her down in the zoysia grass, etcetera, with friendly whacks on the thick parts and shouts of joy for the beauty of the morning, hola! I do truly believe that she came to look upon her solemn spiritual adultery with that fag Alistair as somehow more elevating than ordinary morning love with her husband.

"You never grasped that," said Doris, but leaning closer and giving me a hug.

"Then grasp this."

We sat in the chair, the chair not being an ordinary chair, which would have been fine, but a Danish sling, since in those days ordinary chairs had canceled out and could not be sat on. Married as we were and what with marriage tending to cancel itself and beds having come not to be places for making love in or chairs for sitting on, we had no place to lie or sit. We were like forlorn lovers in the street with no place to go.

But love conquers all, even a Danish sling.

"Darling," said Doris, forgetting for once all the foolishness.

"Let's lie down," I said.

"Fine, but how?"

"Just hold still. I'll pick you up."

Have you ever tried to get up out of a Danish sling with a hundred-and-forty-pound Apple Queen in your lap?

But I got up.

We lay on the bricks, here in this spot. Perhaps that is why I feel better lying here now. Here, at any rate, we lay and made love for the last time. We thought no more of Hermann Hesse that day.

In two weeks she was gone. Why? I think it was because she never forgave me or God for Samantha's death.

"That's a loving God you have there," she told me toward the end, when the neuroblastoma had pushed one eye out and around the nosebridge so that Samantha looked like a two-eyed Picasso profile. After that, Doris went spiritual and

I became coarse and disorderly. She took the high road and I
took the low. She said I was like a Polack miner coming up out
of the earth every night with no thought but to fill his belly
and hump his wife. The expression "hump" shocked me and
was unlike her. She may have lost her faith but she'd always
kept her Virginia-Episcopal decorum. But she'd been reading
current novels, which at the time spoke of "humping" a great
deal, though to tell the truth I had not heard the expression.
Was this a word invented by New York novelists?

2

At last, getting up and keeping clear of the windows, I fetch
my medical bag, which is packed this morning not merely with
medicines but with other articles that I shall presently describe,
and stick the revolver in my belt and slip out the lower "woods"
door at the back of the house where it is impossible to be seen
by an assailant lurking in the swamp.

The door, unused since Doris left, is jammed by vines. I
squeeze through into the hot muscadine sunlight. Here the
undergrowth has almost reached the house. Wistaria has taken
the stereo-V antenna.

Two strides and I'm swallowed up in a plantation of sumac.
It is easy to keep cover and circle around to the swamp edge
and have a long look. Nothing stirring. Egrets sail peacefully
over the prairie. A wisp of smoke rises from a hummock. There
some drughead from Michigan State lies around smoking
Choctaw cannab while his girl fries catfish.

I rub my eyes. Did I imagine the sniper's shots? Was it part
and parcel of the long night's dream of Verdun, of the terrible
assault of the French infantry on Fort Douaumont? No. There
is the shattered window of the "enclosed patio."

What to do? The best course: walk to town by a route known
only to me in order to avoid ambush. Call the police at the first
telephone.

But in the thick chablis sunlight humming with bees, it is
hard to credit assassination. A stray guerrilla perhaps, using my
plate glass for target practice.

Anyhow, I have other fish to fry. First to the Center, where
I hope to have a word with Max Gottlieb, ask a favor of him;

then perhaps catch a glimpse of Moira in Love Clinic; thence
to Howard Johnson's to arrange a trysting place, a lover's rendezvous with Moira my love from Love.

Afterwards there should be time for a long Saturday afternoon in my office—no patients, no nurse today—where I
shall sip Early Times and listen to my father's old tape of *Don
Giovanni* with commentary by Milton Cross.

Using my bag to fend off blackberries, I angle off to a curve
of Paradise Drive where the woods notch in close.

Standing in the schoolbus shelter, now a cave of creeper and
muscadine, I get my bearings. Across the road and fifty feet of
open space, a forest of longleaf begins. A hundred yards into it
and I should pick up the old caddy path that leads from town
to country club.

Wait five minutes to be sure. No sound but the droning of
bees in honeysuckle.

Step out and—bad luck! In the split second of starting
across, a car rounds the curve. There's no not seeing him or he
me. It's like turning the corner of a building and walking into
someone's arms.

He stops. It is no stranger. But do I want to see friends now?
I get along with everybody except people. Psychiatrist, heal—

It is Dr. George "Dusty" Rhoades in his new electric Toyota
bubbletop, a great black saucer of a car and silent as a hearse.

He's waving me in. Hm, not exactly my choice for a companion. Why? Because he's Lola's father and he may believe I
have injured him, though I have not. Shall I accept the lift?
The question does not arise. The fierce usages of friendship
take command. Dusty leans out waving and grinning. Before
I know what I'm doing I'm grinning too and hopping around
to the door with every appearance of delight.

"There you go!" cries Dusty in an eccentric greeting that has
evolved between us over the years. Renewed friendship sweeps
all before it. We are like lovers after a quarrel.

Dusty is a big surgeon with heavy freckled hands that like
to feel your bones and a red rooster shock of hair gone straw-
colored in middle age. It is his manner to pay terrific attention
to the controls of his car, the dials of the dashboard, while
shouting eccentric offhand remarks. So does he also shout, I

know, at his operating nurse, not to be answered or even to be heard but to make an occupational sound, so to speak.

"Fine, fine," I say, settling myself. He nods and keeps on nodding.

Dusty Rhoades is a conservative proctologist, though he does other surgery as well, from Tyler, Texas. He played tackle for Texas A & M, is a reserve Air Force colonel. An excellent surgeon, he works fourteen hours a day, caring nought for his own comfort, and owns a chain of Chicken Delight stands. The money rolls in faster than he can spend it even though he bought Tara, the showplace of Paradise, and an $80,000 Guarnerius cello for his daughter Lola.

Like saints of old, Dusty spends himself tirelessly for other men, not for love, he would surely say, or even for money, for he has no use for it, but because people need him and call him and what else would he do with himself? His waking hours are spent in a dream of work, nodding, smiling, groping for you, not really listening. Instead, his big freckled hands feel your bones like a blind man's. He's conservative and patriotic too, but in the same buzzing, tune-humming way. His office is stacked with pamphlets of the Liberty Lobby. In you come with a large-bowel complaint, over you go upside down on the rack, in goes the scope, ech! and Dusty humming away somewhere above. "Hm, a diverticulum opening here. The real enemy is within, don't you think?" Within me or the U.S.A., you are wondering, gazing at the floor three inches from your nose, and in goes the long scope. "You know as well as I do who's really causing the trouble, don't you?" "Do you mean—?" "I mean the Lefts and Commonists, right?" "Yes, but on the other hand—" In goes the scope the full twenty-six inches up to your spleen. "Oof, yessir!"

"Am I glad to see you, you rascal!" cries Dusty, coming out of his trance and looking over at me. His hand, going its own way, explores the crevices of my knee.

I blink back the beginning of a tear. He's forgiven me! Why do I forget there is such a thing as friends?

He's forgiven what he could only have understood as my misconduct with his daughter Lola, and misconduct it was, though in another sense it was not. Lola and I were discovered by him lying in one another's arms in the deep canyon-size bunker of the eighteenth hole. Though Lola is twenty-six, single, and presumably had the right to embrace whomever she chose, I fancied nevertheless that Dusty took offense. Though he was careful not to let me know it and I was careful not to find out. Certainly no offense was intended. Lola is a big, beautiful, talented girl who teaches cello at Texas A & M. We fell in love for a few hours last Christmas Eve, literally fell, came upon each other like strangers in a forest and fell to the ground in one another's arms, and the next day went our separate ways, she back to Texas and I to the nuthouse broken out with giant hives and quaking with morning terror and night exaltations.

The consequences of this misbehavior in Paradise, where everyone else behaves very well, were muted by my self-commitment to the mental hospital. Thus, it is possible that I have been expelled from the local medical society: no notices have come in the mail—but on the other hand, perhaps notices were suspended because of my illness. I dare not inquire. One consequence was certain: an anonymous communication did come in the mail, a copy of the Hippocratic oath with that passage underlined which admonishes physicians about their relations with female patients. But Lola was not, at the time, my patient.

"You making house calls, Doctor!" Dusty shouts.

I jump. "No no. I was . . . I felt like walking to town." For some reason I do not wish to speak of the sniper.

Dusty nods vigorously, as if my stepping out of the woods with my medical bag was no more or less than he expected. But even as he speaks, his eyes caress the mahogany dashboard and brass knobs and dials. These days it is the fashion to do car interiors in wood and brass like Jules Verne vehicles.

When we shake hands, he opens his meaty hand to me in his old tentative way like a porter taking a tip.

"I wish I could work like you!" he shouts at the rushing pines. "It must take discipline to cut down hack work and make time for research and writing."

How graceful and kind of him. Though Dusty knows all there is to know about me, my family troubles, my cuckoldry, my irregular life, my alcoholism—he connives at the best available myth about me, that I am "smart" but unlucky. People are kind. They find it easy to forgive you in the name of tragedy or insanity and most of all if you are smart. Certain mythic sayings come easily to the lips of my doctor friends when they wish to speak well of me, and lately they do since they know I've had a bad time of it. They'll speak of a mythic, storied diagnosis I made ten years ago. . . .

"No, I'm not working today," I tell Dusty. "I have a few errands to run, then I'm going down to my office and fix myself a little drink and listen to the opera."

"Yes! Right! Absolutely!" cries Dusty joyfully and strikes himself eccentrically in several places.

He fiddles with the controls. All of a sudden a hundred-piece orchestra is blasting away on the back seat, playing Viennese Waltz Favorites. The hot glistening pines fall away as the road climbs along the ridge. The dry refrigerated air evaporates my sweat. Strains of *Wienerblut* lilt us over the pines. We might be drifting along in a Jules Verne gondola over happy old Austria.

I feel better. There are no ruins here. We are beginning to pass sparkling new houses with well-kept lawns. What a lovely silent car. What lovely things money can buy. I have money. Why not spend it? Until this moment it has never occurred to me to spend a penny of Doris's two million on myself. I look down at my frayed cuffs, grubby fingernails. Why not dress well, groom myself, buy a good car, meet friends for lunch, good fellows like Dusty, chaff with them, take up golf? Money is splendid!

But today I have other fish to fry.

"Would you mind dropping me off at the plaza?"

"What in hell for?" asks Dusty, frowning. But his freckled hand continues to browse among the knobs and dials.

"I have a date."

When I left the hospital, I resolved not to lie. Lying cuts one off. Lying to someone is like blindfolding him: you cannot see the other's eyes to see how he sees you and so you do not know how it stands with yourself.

"Like the fellow says, that's a hell of a place to take a woman. All those tramps, outlaws . . ."

"Yes, well . . . I think it's safe."

"Is that why you're wearing your handgun?"

"What?" I had forgotten my pistol and didn't see Dusty look at it. The gun had worked its way around to my belt buckle where it sticks out like Billy the Kid's sixshooter. "The fact is somebody took a shot at me this morning."

"That a fact?" says Dusty with routine astonishment expressing both incredulity and affection. "I tell you the truth, nothing would surprise me nowadays."

"It was probably a wild shot from some nut in the swamp," I say, shoving the pistol out of sight. Indeed, is anything less likely than a *sniper* on this lovely old-fashioned Viennese morning?

"I happened to notice it is all. You're not going to the club?"

"The club?"

"For the Pro-Am."

"Oh, of course!" I laugh heartily. How could I have forgotten the most important event of the year, the Paradise Moonlight Pro-Am tournament played every Fourth of July weekend under the arcs? "But the champs don't tee off till tonight, do they?"

"Right. I thought you might be going to the Bible Brunch."

"No. No, I have to go to the Center."

"O.K. I'll take you over to the plaza."

"No no! Go on to the club. I'll walk from there. I need to walk."

"O.K.," says Dusty, frowning thoughtfully. The freckled hand browses like a small animal patrolling its burrow. "You know, it's something my running into you like this. It's really something."

"It is?"

"I've been looking for you."

"You have?" I look at him with interest. "Did you read my paper?"

"Paper? Well, I haven't finished it."

I sent Dusty a copy of my breakthrough article. He is president-elect of the American Christian Proctological Society and could be useful when I apply for N.I.M.H. funds. Dusty is highly regarded, both in Knothead and Left circles.

"As a matter of fact, I have one of the new models here," I say, taking out a lapsometer and putting it on the seat between us.

Dusty moves away an inch.

"Tom," says Dusty as we go lilting along to *Wine, Women, and Song.* "I want you to take my clinic for me."

Dusty holds a fat clinic on Tuesdays and Thursdays, dispensing thousands of pills to women and encouraging them in their dieting.

We've stopped at a gate and sentry box where a red-faced colonel of Security gives us the once-over before admitting us to the inner circle of Paradise. He's dressed like General Patton, in helmet, jacket, and pearl-handle revolvers.

"O.K., Doc," says Colonel Ringo, stooping down to the window. "Two docs! Ha ha." He waves us on.

Now we've stopped again, this time in front of Tara, Dusty's house. Thinking he's dropping me off, I open the door to go my way. But Dusty's browsing hand finds my knee and holds me fast.

"You know, life is funny, Tom."

"Yes, it is."

"You a brilliant professor and you losing your wife and all."

"Yes."

"And Lola coming home."

"Coming home?"

"Coming here, that is."

"I see."

"She's come to stay."

Tara is on the right, and to see it, Dusty leans over me. He makes himself surprisingly free of my person, coming much closer than men, American men, usually do. His strong breath, smelling of breakfast, breathes on me. An artery socks away at his huge lion-head causing it to make tiny rhythmic nods as if he were affirming this view of his beautiful house, Tara.

"Tom," says Dusty, taking his hand off my knee and fingering the tape deck. A Victor Herbert medley comes on.

"Yes?"

"I'm going home."

"O.K., I'll get out."

But the knuckle of his hand turns hard into my knee, detaining me.

"No, I mean I'm going back to Texas."

"I see."

"No, my old daddy died and I'm going back to the ranch outside of Tyler."

"You mean you're retiring?"

"Oh I reckon I'll work some—"

"I reckon you'll have to."

"Right!" Dusty laughs. "But I'm slacking off before I kill myself."

"I'm glad to hear it." But I'm also concerned about the knuckle turning hard into my knee.

"Lola is not leaving. She's staying here. This is what she wants. So I'm giving her Tara," muses Dusty, gazing past me. The huge head is in my lap, so to speak, nodding as the artery socks away.

"Is that right? You mean she's going to live here by herself?"

"Yep. She's home for good."

"Is that so?"

"You know, this is home to her. And she's got her Eastern gaited horses here, why I don't know."

"Yes."

"And to tell you the damn truth," Dusty goes on in exactly the same voice, lidded eyes peering past me at the white columns of Tara, breathing his breakfast breath on me, "that girl is ever more crazy about you, Tom."

"She is? Well, she is a wonderful girl and I am extremely—"

"In fact, your mother was only saying yesterday," Dusty breaks in, and his head swivels a few degrees, nodding now at the hipped roof of my mother's cozy saltbox next door. "She said: you know Tom and Lola are a match if ever I saw one. You know your mother."

"Yes." I know my mother and I can hear her say it in her trite exclamatory style: they're a match if ever I saw one!

For some reason I am nodding too, in time with Dusty. From the point where Dusty's knuckle is turning into my knee, waves of prickling spread out in all directions.

Now the hand lets go my knee and settles in a soft fist on my shoulder.

"I'm giving Tara to Lola, Tom."

"You are?"

"You want to know the reason she's staying?"

"No. That is, yes."

"You."

"Me?"

"She thinks the world of you."

"And I of her."

"She can't live here by herself."

"No?"

"No way. Tom, you see this place?"

"Yes?"

"I'm putting it and my little girl in your hands."

"You are?"

"Ha ha, that will give you something to think about, won't it?"

"Yes."

"You know, neither one a y'all got good sense."

"No?"

"You laying up in the bed with a bottle, shooting rats, out in the woods by yourself, talking about snipers and all. Lola taking long rides by herself in the backcountry where some crazy nigger's going to knock her in the head. I'm counting on you to take care her." Dusty gazes attentively at the kingbird sitting on the white Kentucky fence.

"All right."

"Both a y'all can damn well straighten up and fly right! That's what I told your mama I was going to tell you and now I done told you." For some reason Dusty begins to talk in a broad Texas accent. He gives a final joky-serious nod with his big head. "You reading me, Doctor?"

"Yes."

"That's settled then." Dusty settles back with a sigh. "I told your mama you would."

"Would what?"

"Do the right thing."

I sigh, relieved at least to have Dusty's great lion-head off my chest.

Again the car drifts along, a silent gondola. With a sudden inspiration, Dusty presses a button and a thousand violins play *Hills of Home*, the Tara theme.

"That's my favorite music," muses Dusty.

"Very nice."

"I'll tell Lola."

"Tell her what?"

"About our understanding."

"What understanding?"

"Ha ha, you're a card, Tom. I always thought you had the most wonderful sense of humor."

As we approach the clubhouse, more people are abroad. The Christian Kaydettes are practicing in the schoolyard. Suntanned golfers ply the fairways in quaint surrey-like carts, householders bestride tiny tractors, children splash in pools, their brown bodies flashing like minnows.

"Will you also take my Tuesday clinic?"

Also? Does that mean that I've agreed to take Tara and Lola?

"Thanks, Dusty. But I'm using all my spare time developing my lapsometer. I'm applying for an N.I.M.H. grant. You could help."

"Use it in the clinic!" cries Dusty, socking himself eccentrically in several places. He's in the best of humors. "Read their frontal lobes with your gadget and they'll believe you! They'll believe you anyhow! You know, Tom, you're the best diagnostician around here. If you wanted to, you could be—" Dusty shrugs and falls silent.

Then he did read my paper! Dusty's nobody's fool. Though he pretends to be a country boy, his mind can devour a scientific article with one snap of its jaws.

"Since you've read my paper, you know that my lapsometer has more important uses than treating fat women."

"Sho now. But is there anything wrong with treating fat women?"

"In fact," I tell Dusty earnestly, "with this device in hand any physician can make early diagnoses of potential suicides, paranoiacs, impotence, stroke, anxiety, and angelism/bestialism. Think of the significance of it!"

"Chk." Dusty winks and clucks tongue against teeth, signifying both a marveling and an unseriousness.

"This country is in deep trouble, Dusty."

"You don't have to tell me that."

"This device could be decisive."

"Well, I'm just a country doctor."

"Did you read about the atrocity last night?"

"Yeah."

"What do you think?"

"The work of a madman."

"Yeah, but there's a reason."

"Reason? You mean you're going to cure all the crazy niggers?"

"And crazy whites, crazy Lefts, and crazy Knotheads."

"I don't know about you, but me I see very few Lefts and no niggers at all."

We've reached the clubhouse. Pennants stream from the twin copper peaks of the roof, like a castle at tournament time. Gaily colored pavilions are scattered through the pines. A few pros and ams, early arrivals, enter the clubhouse for the Bible Brunch. A banner strung the length of the eaves announces: Jesus Christ, the Greatest Pro of Them All.

"Come on in with me," says Dusty impulsively.

"Thank you, but I've got to be going."

"Many devout Catholics are coming."

"I'm not a devout Catholic."

"Cliff Barrow Junior is preaching."

"Good."

"Lola and I will be looking for you at the fish fry tonight."

As he talks, Dusty picks up the new lapsometer on the seat between us. He hefts it.

"Very compact."

"Yes."

It *is* a lovely device, all brushed chrome, pointer and dial, and a jade oscilloscope screen the size of a half-dollar, the whole as solid as a good camera. Just the thing, I see now, to take Dusty's fancy.

"You take readings?" says Dusty, turning it every which way. He's all business now, buzzing away while his big fleshy hand hefts, balances, knows.

"That's right."

"What do you take readings of?"

I shrug. "You know. Local electrical activity in cortical and subcortical centers. It's nothing but an EEG without wires, with a stereotactic device for triangulating."

"Yeah, I see. Here you measure your micromillivolts." The

lizard scales have fallen from his blue eyes, which bear down like gimlets. His thumb rubs the jade screen as if it were a lucky piece. "And this here—"

"That's your oscilloscope to display your wave patterns, with this, see?—a hold-and-stack device. You can stack ten patterns and flip back at will."

"You take your readings, then what?"

"Like the article says, you correlate the readings with various personality traits, attitudes."

"You mean, like emotions?" asks Dusty, frowning.

"Well, yes, among other things."

"Isn't that all rather . . . subjective?"

"Is a pointer reading subjective?"

"But there's a lot of room for interpretation."

"Isn't there also in an electroencephalogram?" I turn it over. "Here on the back you've got your normal readings at key centers."

"Yeah. Like a light meter." He takes it back. The freckled hand can't leave it alone. Again the thumb tests the grain of the brushed chrome, strokes the jade screen.

"How long does it take to do a, uh what? An examination?"

"A reading. I can do a standard profile in less than three minutes." I look at my watch and open the door. "Thanks for the ride."

"Do one on me."

"What?"

"Couldn't you do a reading right here and now?"

"Sure, but—"

"But what?"

"It's not a play toy."

"Well, damn it, does it work or doesn't it?"

"It works."

"Show me."

"I've learned that it's not to be used lightly."

Dusty nods ironically. We're both thinking of the same thing. It was using my first Brownie model on Lola that got me into trouble. That Christmas Eve six months ago I'd made my breakthrough and had the first inkling what I'd got hold of. I was abstracted, victorious, lonely, drunk, and full of love, and lo, there was Lola, also victorious (she'd had a triumphant

concert in Tyler, Texas) and also lonely and full of love. My
lapsometer revealed these things. But it was not the cause of
our falling in love. Rather the occasion.

"You need controls for your series, don't you?" Dusty asks
shrewdly.

"Yes."

"Then use me as a control."

"You wouldn't stick a proctoscope up me here in the car,
would you?"

Dusty laughs, but his knuckle turns into my knee. "If you
want my endorsement, I'd like to see how it works."

"I see." Why do I feel uneasy? "Oh very well. Take off
your coat and lean over the steering wheel, like a sleepy truck
driver."

"O.K., Doctor." Dusty says "Doctor" with exactly the same
irony priests use in calling each other "Father."

It takes two and a half minutes to clock seven readings.

There is one surprise. He registers good pineal selfhood,
which I expected; an all but absent coeliac anxiety—he is, after
all, an ex-fullback and hardworking surgeon, a man at home
with himself and too busy to worry about it. That is to say: he
may fear one thing or another but he's not afraid of no-thing,
which is the worst of fears. His abstractive index is not excessive—he lets his hands do the knowing and working. His red
nucleus shows no vagal rage.

But—

His love-sex ratio is reversed.

That is to say: the reading from Brodmann Area 24, the
locus of "higher" or interpersonal relations, is a tiny 0.5 mmv
while the hypothalamus, seat of organic sexual activity, registers a whacking stud-level 7.9 mmv. The display wave of the
latter is well developed. It is the wave of a powerful, frequently
satisfied, but indiscriminate sexual appetite. Dusty is divorced.

"Well?" asks Dusty, buttoning his collar.

"No real pathology," I say, pocketing the lapsometer and
adjusting my six-gun. I seize the door handle.

"Hold it, son!" cries Dusty, laughing. "Don't pull that!"

"What?"

"Tell me, you rascal!" Joyfully he socks me with a few eccentric blows.

"Very well," I say doubtfully, remembering my vow to tell the truth.

I show him, clicking back over the wave-displays stacked in the oscilloscope circuit, and tell him, glossing over as best I can the love-sex reversal. But I have not reckoned with Dusty's acuteness.

"I see," he says at last, looking straight ahead, lizard scales lowering over his eyes. "What you're saying is I'm messing around with my nurses."

"I said no such thing. You asked for the readings. I gave them to you. Make your own interpretation."

"Is that thing nonpartisan?" he asks in the same voice, yet somehow more ominously.

"How do you mean?"

"Does it also measure alcoholism, treachery, laziness, and white-trash morals?"

"If you like," I reply in a low voice, but relieved to have him strike at me so hard.

The freckled hand browses. A switch clicks, locking the doors. It clicks again, unlocking, locking. Is Dusty thinking of beating me up?

"There's the door, Doctor." Click, unlock.

"Very well. Thanks for the ride."

"Don't mention it. One piece of advice."

"Yes?"

Dusty begins his rhythmic nodding again as the artery pounds away.

"Lola has a lot more use for you than I do, though I used to. I know you been through a bad time. But let us understand each other." He still looks straight ahead.

"All right."

"You going to do right by Lola or, Doctor, I'm going to have your ass. Is that clear?"

"Yes."

"Goodbye, Doctor."

"Goodbye."

3

Leaving Dusty's car, I skirt the festive booths of the Bible Brunch.

The heat of the concrete pool apron strikes up like the Sahara sands. The sun strikes down into the top of my head. Chunks of Styrofoam water-toys are scattered in the weeds like dirty wedding cake. The pool is empty and drifted with leaves.

Why has the pool been abandoned?

A breath of cool air stirs in the doorway of the old pro shop bearing the smell of leather and of splintered pine flooring. The shop too is empty save for a life-size cutout of Gene Sarazen dipping toward the floor. Gene is dressed in knickerbockers and a British cap. A trumpet vine sprouts through the floor and twines around a rusty mashie.

Why is the pro shop empty? Is there a new pro shop in another part of the building?

It was not empty when I stood here and kissed Lola.

I went to the catfish fry and fell in love with Lola and performed with her the act of love in the grassy kidney-shaped bunker of number 18 green (par 4, 275 yards).

I was standing in the Paradise Country Club bar shaking the worn leather cup of poker dice and gazing at the rows of bottles lined up against the brand-new antiqued wormholed cypress, when I noticed something. The vines had begun to sprout. It was the first time I had noticed it. A whitish tendril of vine, perhaps ivy, had sprouted through a wormhole and twined about a bottle of Southern Comfort.

"Give me a drink of Southern Comfort," I told Ruby, the bartender, and watched to see if he would notice anything amiss.

Ruby, a thin sly Chinese-type Negro, took the bottle without noticing the tendril, which broke off in his hand.

"How long has that vine been here?"

"What vine?"

"In your hand."

He shrugged.

"How long has it been since anybody asked for Southern Comfort?"

"It been a while," said Ruby with a sly smile. "Christmas gif, Doc."

Absently I gave him a bill, a dollar.

Ruby's face went inscrutable like an Oriental's. He expected, rightly, a higher tip at Christmas. The dollar was received as an insult. We dislike each other. He sucked his teeth. Leaving him and my drink, I went out among the catfish crowd and found myself hemmed up with Lola Rhoades against a stretch of artificially wormholed cypress.

The pro shop seems to darken in the morning light. Gene Sarazen straightens. I sit on a pedestal holding a display of irons arranged in a fan. There is a chill in the room. The summer spins back to chilly azalea crucifixion spring, back further to Christmas with its month of cheerful commercial jingling shopping nights and drinking parties.

I see Lola clearly, holding her gin fizz.

"I am glad to see you," says Lola, who is five feet nine and in her high heels looks me straight in the eye and says what she thinks.

"So am I," I say, feeling a wonder that there should be such a thing as a beautiful six-foot woman who is glad to see me. Women are mythical creatures. They have no more connection with the ordinary run of things than do centaurs. I see her clearly, gin fizz in one hand, the other held against her sacrum, palm out, pushing herself rhythmically off the wall. Women! Music! Love! Life! Joy! Gin fizzes!

She is home for Christmas from Texas A & M. She looks like her father but the resemblance is a lovely joke, a droll commentary on him. His colorlessness, straw hair, straw skin, becomes in her a healthy pallor, milkiness over rose, lymph over blood. Her hair is a black-auburn with not enough red to ruin her skin, which has none of the green chloral undertones of some redheads. Her glance is mild and unguarded. It is the same to her whether she drinks or does not drink, talks or does not talk, looks one in the eye or does not look.

She drinks and hisses a cello tune in her teeth and pushes herself off the wall.

The gin fizzes come and go. We find we can look into each

other's eyes without the usual fearfulness and shamefulness of eye meeting eye. I am in love.

A Negro band, dressed in unpressed Santa suits, is blasting out Christmas carols. Bridge-playing ladies surround us, not playing bridge but honking their Wednesday bridge-playing honks and uttering Jewish-guttural *yuchs* which are fashionable this season.

Lola asks me something. I cannot hear and, stooping, put my ear to her mouth, registering as I go past a jeweled reflection of red and green Christmas lights in a web of saliva spinning between parted rows of perfect teeth.

"Don't you want to ask about your patient?"

"You look well. How are you?" I had treated her last summer for a mild depression and a sensation of strangeness, quite common these days, upon waking in the morning.

"Well enough," she says, nodding in order to lever her sacrum off the wall. "But you seem—odd."

"Odd?" I speak into her ear, which crimsons in the canal like a white orchid.

"You look both happy and—sad."

It is true. Women are so smart. In truth I am suffering from simultaneous depression and exaltation. So I tell her about it: that this very day I perfected my invention and finished my article, which will undoubtedly be recognized as one of the three great scientific breakthroughs of the Christian era, the others being Newton hitting on his principles and Einstein on his field theory, perhaps even the greatest of all because my discovery alone gives promise of bridging the dread chasm between body and mind that has sundered the soul of Western man for five hundred years.

She believes me. "Then why do you feel bad?"

I explain my symptoms in terms of my discovery: that when one records the thalamic radiation, a good index of one's emotional state, it can register either as a soaring up, a sine curve, or a dipping down, a cosine curve. "Mine registers both at the same time, sine and cosine, mountain on a valley."

She laughs, thinking I am joking.

"Why should that be?"

Since I am in love, I can feel with her, feel my sacrum tingle when hers hits the wall.

"Well, I've won, you see. Won the big one. But it's Christmas Eve and I'm alone. My family is dead. There's nobody to tell."

"Tell me."

"Do you know what I planned to do tonight?"

"No."

"Go home and watch Perry Como's Christmas show on stereo-V." Perry Como is seventy and still going strong.

Lola nods sympathetically, ducks her head, drinks, and hisses a tune in her teeth. I bend to listen. It is the Dvořák cello concerto.

Trays pass. I begin to drink Ramos gin fizzes with one swallow. At one time. I was allergic to egg white but that was long ago. These drinks feel silky and benign. The waiters too are dressed as Santa. They grin sideways from their skewed Santa hoods and shout "Christmas gif!" I give them money, a dollar, ten dollars, whatever.

"Listen to this," I tell Lola and hum the *Don Quixote* theme in her ear.

"Very good. You have absolute pitch. And you look better! Your face is fuller."

I feel my face. It is fuller.

"I feel fine. I am never happier than when I am in love."

"Are you in love?"

"Yes."

"Who with?"

"You."

"Ah huh," says Lola, nodding, but I can't tell whether the nodding is just to get her sacrum off the wall.

"Christmas gif!"

Another black Santa passes and I take three gin fizzes. The tingling sacrum should have been a warning, but love made me happy, love and the sight of tiny jewels strung along the glittering web of saliva. Her membranes are clear as light, the body fluids like jeweler's oil under a watch crystal. A lovely inorganic girl.

Her company stabilizes me. Abstracted still, my orbit becomes lower. Bending close to her, close to the upper reaches of her breast, is like skimming in silence, power off, over the snowy slopes of Kilimanjaro. I close my eyes.

"When I close my eyes, I can see you teaching cello in the

Texas A & M cello class, a drafty gym-like room, the cello between your knees. It is during a break and you're wearing a sweatshirt and resting your arm on the cello."

"Ah huh." She nods. "It gets cold in there." She believes everything I say, knowing it is true.

Handing Lola her gin fizz, I touch her. A hive, a tiny red wheal, leaps out at the point of touch, as if to keep touch. The touch of her is, as they say, a thrill.

"Why did you bring your physician's bag here?" Lola asks me.

"I haven't been home yet. The first working model of my lapsometer is inside, can't afford to lose it."

"Can you really measure a person's innermost self?"

"In a manner of speaking."

"Can you measure mine?"

"Sure."

"Do it."

"Where? Right here?"

"Yes."

"Well—over here." Taking her by the hand, I lead her through the bridge women to the pro shop. We stand behind Gene Sarazen while I take a few snapshots of her with my Brownie.

She registers zero anxiety—music saves her! she goes dreaming through the world as safe and sure as Schubert's trout—but her interpersonal wave is notable in two respects: it is both powerful and truncated, lopped off at the peak like Popocatepetl.

"Well?"

"You see?" I show her the snail tracks on jade, a faint cratered Fuji in a green dawn.

"What does that mean?"

"It means you have a heart full of love and no one to give it to, but that is not so bad because you have your music, which means a great deal to you."

"Yes. I don't. It does. Yes!"

Now it is she who does the hemming up and I who am backed up against the cypress, sacrum fiery and quilted. My head is turning against the wormholes. Hairs catch and pop.

"Why is that?" she asks, brown eyes level with mine.

"Why is what?"

"Why is there—no one?"

"Well you're a bit much, you know. You scare most men. Also, your music is hard to compete with. You always hear singing." I show her the lilting curve of her aesthetic radiation.

"Yes! I understand! It is true! Can love be like that?"

She takes my hand urgently, her cello calluses whispering in my palm.

"Yes, it can, if the love is like that, singing."

"Do you love me like that?"

"Yes."

"How do I know?"

I kiss her hand. My lip leaps out to keep touch, ridges with a wheal.

She feels it. "Good heavens!"

We are laughing and touching.

"Christmas gif!"

A waiter comes up. We take four gin fizzes. Under the monk-like Santa hood, I recognize a Negro named Willard Amadie. Long ago he used to be a caddy, before the electric surreys came along. A very strong short black man, he would stand down the fairway for the drive and with the heavy bag still on his shoulder take a full swing at the clover with an iron. It is a surprise to see him. Years ago he went off to the Ecuadorian wars and became, I heard, a career soldier. Somber even as a youth, he'd stand waiting at the lie, club selected and proffered handle first, face bitter-black, bee-stung, welted laterally like an Indian's.

Now he's dressed like Santa and grinning a ghastly grin.

"Christmas gif, Doc!"

I look at him.

"What's wrong, Willard?"

"Nothing, Doc! Christmas gif to you and missee."

"Missee?" The outer corners of my eyes are filling up with hives, forming a prism. Willard and Lola are edged in rainbows. "What in hell are you talking about?"

Willard doesn't leave but stands watching. His sclerae are yellow as egg yolk. At last I give Willard ten dollars, blushing, as I do so, with rage or shame, I'm not sure which.

"Thankee, Doc!" says Willard in the same goofy Gullah accent. "May you and missee have many a more!"

I refuse to look at Willard, watching instead sections of a road map, pieces of highway, dots of towns, drifting across my retina.

But Lola is pleased. She sees Willard's courtliness (what is wrong with him?) as a sanction. Christmas is sanctioned. Our love is sanctioned. Willard's nutty good manners (something is up, I know that, like the vines sprouting, but what?) are part of the singing, life made to lilt.

"Let's go outside," I say, to go outside but mainly to get away from Willard, and take her again by the hand, her left hand, her fingering hand, calluses whispering in my palm.

Out into the gloaming we go.

It is a warm Christmas Eve. A south wind blows fat little calypso clouds over a new moon.

We kiss in the grassy bunker. She kisses oddly, stooping to it, developing a torque and twisting down and away, seeming to grow shorter. Her breath catches. What she puts me in mind of is not a Texas girl at all but a smart Northern girl, a prodigy who has always played the cello ten hours a day, then one day finds herself at a summer festival and twenty-one and decides it is time to be kissed. So she stoops to it with an odd, shy yet practiced movement, what I fancy to be the Juilliard summer-festival style of kissing.

Now her hands are clasped in the small of my back. My hands are clasped in the small of her back. She hisses Dvořák. My hot chicken blood sings with albumen molecules. Her hand is warm and whispery as a horn.

We lie in the grassy bunker, she gazing at the winter constellations wheeling in their courses, I singing like a cello between her knees. Fiery Betelgeuse hangs like a topaz in the south. We kiss hungrily, I going around after her.

"Doris," I whisper, forgetting she is Lola. Fortunately my breath whistles in my throat and she doesn't hear me.

She is like Doris, except for her Juilliard torque and her odd going-away persimmon-tasting kisses. A big lovely girl, big and white and cool-warm, a marble Venus with a warm horned hand.

Her callused fingertips strew stars along my flanks. Hot wheals of love leap forth at her touch.

"What's the matter with you?" Lola asks, leaning out of the moon's shadow to inspect my bumps.

"I've got hives."

"You've got bobos on your shoulder," she says, minding my bobos attentively and curiously like a child.

When I look sideways, the wedge of sky is narrower.

"Hold still, hon," she whispers, from Tyler Texas now, Juilliard forgotten. "You'll be all right. Lola'll hold you tight."

"I have to go."

"Where you going?"

"For a walk. Stay here, I'll be right back."

I can't hold still. Why? The longing is back. Longing for what? I don't know. For Doris? For the Valley of Virginia and sycamore trees and cicadas unwinding in October? I don't know. God knows.

Now running down 18 fairway, knowing it in the black dark (for the "old" 18 is the terrain of my youth), to the tee and back, eyes squeezed shut like a Chinaman's. Back to the bunker to lie at Lola's breast, a blind babe. My scalp quilts and pops. Lymph engorges me. Love returns. Again I sing between Lola's knees, blind as a bat.

Go now, I try to tell her, you better leave, but my larynx squeaked shut.

So it was that Lola, noble cellist, saved my life at the cost of her reputation. She could have gone, left me to die in the bunker, swell up and die and be found stiff as a poker in the foggy dew. But she fetched her brother, who fetched Willard Amadie, and they both fetched me home, finding me in some disarray, I think, for Lola, putting first things first, had thought only to save my life.

Did I dream it or do I have a recollection of Willard Amadie bending over me, his Santa hood pushed back on his shoulders like a Carmelite's, his face no longer farcical but serious and tender but also risible in his old style. "—If you ain't something now," did he not say; bending over to pick me up and seeming in the same motion to adjust my clothes before Dusty came up.

So it was not even a great scandal but just enough to allow the possibility that Dusty could have been offended, though perhaps not, and the possibility that my name was dropped by the medical society, though perhaps it wasn't. I did receive the

anonymous Hippocratic oath, however. But I was in love and
Lola was not my patient at the time.

Dusty saved my life, finding me without breath, shot me
full of epinephrine, helped Willard carry me home, where he,
Dusty, put a tube in my nose and stayed with me until I came
to myself.

All this, if you can believe it, in less than an hour's time
from the moment I hoisted the first gin fizz until I opened my
Chinaman's eyes in my own bed.

Christmas Eve fell out thereafter as planned. With the last
of my strength I pressed the button on the headboard and saw
Perry Como's Christmas show after all.

There came Perry, seventy years young and snowy-thatched
but hale as old Saint Nick himself, still wearing his open cardi-
gan, color off a bit, face orange, lips violet, but all in good 3-D.

He sang *Silent Night* sitting on his stool.

It was during the following week, between Christmas and New
Year, that I became ill, suffering simultaneous depressions and
exaltations, assaulted at night by longings, succubi, and the
hideous shellfire of Verdun, and in the morning by terror of
unknown origin. One morning—was it Christmas morning
after listening to Perry Como?—my wrists were cut and bleeding. Seeing the blood, I came to myself, saw myself as itself
and the world for what it is, and began to love life. Hm, better
stop the bleeding in that case. After all, why not live? Bad
as things are still when all is said and done, one can sit on a
doorstep in the winter sunlight and watch sparrows kick leaves.
So, hugging myself, I stuck a wrist in each armpit like a hobo,
squeezed the arteries shut, and walked to Max's house. Max
mostly sewed me up without making much over it, fetched a
surgeon to suture a tendon, and at my request allowed me to
commit myself to the federal hospital.

4

Going to see Max. Is the sniper following?

As I walk across the pool apron, powdered by chlorine
dust and littered by dirty cakes of Styrofoam, I try to collect

my wits, badly scattered by memories of Lola and by Dusty
Rhoades's plans for me. Lola did not come to see me in the
hospital. But perhaps she returned to Texas A & M without
knowing I was ill.

Two things to do today—no, three things: (1) see Max Gottlieb, who knows the value of my discovery, and ask him to
speak to the Director about sponsoring my article in *Brain*
and my application for funding from N.I.M.H.; (2) complete
arrangements for a trysting place at the ruined Howard Johnson motel for my date with Moira on the Fourth; (3) go to my
office where, undisturbed by patients or my shrewish nurse (it
is Saturday), I can put the finishing touches on my article, sip a
toddy or two, listen to music, and watch the martins fly home
in the evening.

Shortest and safest route is by foot. Across the fairways of the
old 18 waist-high in Johnson grass, past the old Bledsoe house,
a streaked Spanish stucco from the thirties, in the dogleg of
number 5. Here for fifty years lived the Bledsoes, locked in,
while golf balls caromed around the patio, ricocheted off Spanish balconies and window grills.

Clink clink. Clink clink.

A great thunderhead hides the sun, but it is dry on the fairways. The anthills are abandoned, worn away to a comb of
cells.

Clink clink. Clink clink.

Stop and listen.

Someone is following me. But there is no sound but the whir
and snap of grasshoppers.

Clink clink.

There it is again: a sound very much like—yes, the very sound
my caddy Willard Amadie used to make when he'd hump it for
the angle of the dogleg to watch the drive, running level and
flat out and holding the clubheads in the crook of his arm so
they wouldn't rattle and disturb the drivers already poised over
their balls, but even so the faces of the irons would slap *clink
clink.*

There is no one. I stop on a high bald green dotted with
palmetto. The flagpole flies a pennant of wistaria.

Now into a dry wash out of bounds and among the flared
bladed trunks of tupelo gums. *Clink clink*, it's ahead of me.

Stop and calculate: really it seems unlikely that anyone is trying to shoot you here or even following you or, if he is, that he would be carrying a golf bag.

Nevertheless, suppose that he is. Suppose he has seen me and, knowing me, knows where I am going and is going ahead to wait. Where would he go?

One place: the "island" of number 11, a sporty hole where the drive has to carry a neck of the swamp, which the golfers cross by two Chinese footbridges connecting a little loess lump in the swamp. Here I'd cross if I were going to the Center and here on the island stands a pagoda shelter that commands both bridges.

Instead of using the bridge, drop down the soft cliff, using a boy's trick of walking along the face dropping two steps for every step forward.

Now behind the "Quarters," a long rowhouse, a ruin of soft warm brick which housed sugar-plantation slaves and which, set just above water level of the bayou, was thought of by the Paradise developers as a kind of Natchez-under-the-hill and so restored and reroofed for domestic servants, even a chapel added so that strains of good old spirituals would come floating up to our patios in the evening, but the domestic preferred their Hollow, dank and fetid though it was. So back to the jungle went the Quarters, new tin roof and all.

A crashing in the vines ahead of me. My heart stops: if it is a sniper, there's an army of them. Wait. Yes, whew. I spot Colley's pith helmet and Gottlieb's fishing cap. It is the Audubon Society, on the trail of the lordly ivorybill.

Moving swiftly in deep shade and without sound on the moss bank of the bayou, I reach the hogback of the island, high and dry now, and climb its gentlest slope, angling for the path and keeping an eye peeled for the roof of the pagoda.

There it is, directly above, but the loess loam, soft as meal, has eroded badly under the near quadrant of the pagoda so that one may no longer walk into it but has to climb up through the vines. Thunder rumbles. A big sour drop spatters on my hand. The wind smells of trees. It is a simple matter to climb into the quadrant, put bag on seat, hold pistol, stand on seat to see over the partition.

Is anyone there?

The two adjacent quadrants are empty. The opposite quadrant? It is difficult to see because the angle between partitions is choked with potato vine and dirt-dauber nests. The space between the eaves and the intersecting rafters allows a view of a stretch of the coast with a church steeple and parade ground. There the Kaydettes are drilling, the sun is shining. By a trick of light and distance, the field seems to be tilted like an Andes farm. Tiny figures march up and down. The twirling batons make silver coins in the sunlight.

Safe in the thunder and wrapped in potato vine, I wait. The wind is sour with raindrops but the storm is veering off.

In a brief quiet between thunder rolls, close as close, a man clears his throat. So close that I feel my head incline politely as if he were addressing me. In a panic I grip the center post and hollow my throat to keep breathing quiet.

"That's a pretty sight now." The voice is so close that the dry wood of the partition vibrates like a sounding board.

"They fixing to parade." A second voice, the sentence uttered civilly, an observation.

"They'll parade all right." A third voice, even closer, grim, rich in ironies.

Thunder rolls, covering the voices. Dropping slowly, I sit in the angle, feeling behind me the press and creak of wood as bodies shift weight.

"What do we need with him?" asks the third voice.

"Victor's all right now. He know how to get along with people. Victor what you call our contract man." First voice: a familiar two-layered voice, one layer speaking to meaning, the other risible, soliciting routine funniness: we might as well be funny as not.

"Contract? Do you mean contact?"

"Contract, contact."

I recognize two voices but not the third.

The rolling thunder becomes more discrete, coming after lightning cracks. I count the intervals. Two seconds, three. The storm is going away. At the next crack I count four and stand up in the thunder.

Use the potato vine as screen, crane up and over into it, far enough to see through the leaves but not be seen.

The man sitting at the end of the seat, facing the path toward the club, is, I know already, Willard Amadie. Bent forward, forearms on knees, he can look up and see the others, see the path, only by wrinkling his low wide welted forehead. He wears a Marine camouflaged coverall. Beside him, propped against the bench, butts grounded, are a rifle and shotgun fitted with straps. Then it was they, not golf irons, that clinked.

Stretched out on the bench, only its forequarters visible, head lolling to the ground, tongue smeared with dust, is a young buck deer.

"No reason why people can't get along," says the first voice in the style of uttering platitudes agreeably.

"People?" Voice number three. "What people? I'll tell the truth, I never know what he's talking about."

I know what he's talking about. *People* uttered so, in a slight flatting of tone, means white people. Uttered another way, it means black. A third way means people in general.

"I'll tell you this!" exclaims the first voice, shouting a platitude. "I'm not going have anything to do with people"— second meaning—"who looking to hurt other people." First meaning. "That's not what the good Lord intend."

"The good Lord," says the third voice. "What is it with this dude? Jesus."

"Victor is all right. He's with us. In fact, we couldn't do without him," says Willard, looking up from his black welted brow. "He's for the plan, he's for the school, don't worry. Aren't you, Brother?" The *brother* too I recognize, though I doubt if number three does. This is Baptist brother: Victor is a deacon in Starlight Baptist Church.

"Sure I'm for it! Education is good for everybody and everybody is entitled to it!"

"I'll tell you this, Uru," says Willard. "We need Victor more than he needs us. Where do you think we get our medicine? People respect him." All kind of people.

"I don't understand anybody down here. This dude sounds like some old uncle from Memphis."

"Those old uncles in Memphis are tougher than you think," says Willard, grinning.

Victor Charles sits opposite Willard, feet planted flat on the ground, hands prone on his knees. A strong, grave, heavy-thighed man, he is purple-black and of an uncertain age. He could be forty and looking older for his dignity. Or he could be sixty and flat-bellied from his life as a laborer. Dressed like a hospital attendant in white duck trousers, white shirt, white interne shoes, he does in fact work in the animal shelter as caretaker. A black belt circles his wide, flat hips, buckle worn to the side and I recall why: so the buckle won't scrape against the high metal table when he holds the big dogs.

"Look like he not coming," says Willard after a pause, squeezing his fist in his hand.

Who's not coming? Me? A corkscrew tightens in my sacrum.

"Where are they going now?" asks the third man.

The other two look toward the coast.

"They marching over to the club for a show this evening," says Willard. Willard has a slight stammer. Once in a while the words hang in his throat, he touches his eye and out they come, hooting.

"All right. Now you know the route Tuesday."

"Sure I know the route," hoots Willard.

"How about the brother here?"

Willard and Victor look at each other and laugh.

"I know," says Victor gravely.

"Here," says Willard, bending over. Something scrapes in the dirt. He's drawing a map. "Intercept the bus here. Brother, we counting on you to watch them."

"I'm going to be watching more than them," says Victor, spreading his fingers over his knees.

"What does he mean?" asks the third man.

"He means you, Brother Uru," says Willard, laughing.

"Ain't nobody going to hurt anybody long as I got anything to do with it!" cries Victor. "I mean nobody!"

"I don't know. I just don't know," mutters number three to himself. "What kind of damn country is this?"

"Victor's going to lead them to Honey Island."

"That's right and I'm staying there."

"What you worrying about, old man?"

"You."

"Me?"

"Ain't nobody bothering those little ladies."

"What in the hell—"

Willard opens his mouth, touches his eye: "Listen!"

There is a crackling in the swamp, a sound that becomes louder and more measured. It is the little safari of bird-watchers.

"See. I told you," says Willard softly. "They pass here every Saturday this time of day, and on Tuesday the Fourth they'll do the same."

"Well well well," says the third man, pleased for the first time. "Here come our teachers."

"Teachers?" says Victor Charles. "What you talking about. They the doctors from the Center out for a walk. With their spyglasses."

"They going too," says Willard quietly. "We need teachers at the school."

"You mean they going out to Honey Island too!" cries Victor.

"That's right, Brother. Some of them, anyhow."

"Lord to God. Now I done heard it all."

"Why not, Uncle," says the third man. "I think it proper and fitting that our children be taught by Ph.D.'s."

"I think ever'body entitled to an education!" exclaims Victor in his singsong.

The crashing grows louder as the safari works around the hogback. Presently, by standing at the end of the bench, I can see them: Colley and Gottlieb still in the lead, Colley in pith helmet, bermuda shorts, and bush jacket; Gottlieb in his long-billed meshtop hat, the sort retirees wear in Fort Lauderdale. There follow a dozen or so behaviorists, physicians, Love counselors, plus a NASA engineer or two.

Returning to the corner, I discover I can hear by putting an ear to the partition, which acts as a sounding board.

"And I'll tell you something else," says the voice at the center pole, a voice without antecedents, black yes, Midwestern perhaps, but mainly stereo-V, an announcer's voice, a Detroit disc jockey's voice. "This is war and don't you forget it. All this talk about some people being nice, listen. They're nice all right. They're so nice and polite that you mothers been castrated without knowing it."

"What you talking about, my mother being—" begins Victor, outraged.

"No, what he means, Victor," says Willard, touching his eye and hooting, "is—"

"Never mind," says the third man in disgust. "Jesus."

"I hear you say Jesus!" cries Victor.

"I said, never mind."

"I say bless Jesus!"

"O.K., O.K."

Guns clink together. Wood, lightened of its load, creaks. The deer carcass slides over the rough wood of the bench. A man grunts as the load is hefted.

"Well, they going to eat today," says a voice, Willard's, going away.

Wait five minutes to make sure.

5

Shortcut into rear of hospital and through the day room of my old ward. The attendant peering through the screened glass lets me in, though he is not clear about my position. Am I professor, patient, doctor, what? But he knows me from somewhere, sees my bag, lets me through. Did I remember to put pistol in bag? Yes.

Though the building is new, the day room already has the worn look of all day rooms. Its scuffed tile and hard-used blocky wooden furniture is for all the world like a child's playhouse. The picture on stereo-V rolls slowly. The room smells of idle man-flesh, pajamas stiffened by body dandruff and dried urine. Great sky-high windows let in the out-of-doors through heavy security screens that render the world gauzy green and pointillist.

Here dwell my old friends and fellow madmen. I recognize them. They gaze at me, knowing me and knowing me not. I am like a dream they have dreamed before. A man standing at the window twitters his fingers, sending out radar beams to the vague, gauzy world, and cocks his ear, listening for returning blips. *Who are you out there?* Another man carries his head under his arm. A blond youth, a pale handsome exchange student from Holland, remembers that he owes me a debt of some sort and pays me off with feces money, a small dry turd, which I accept in good part, folding it into my handkerchief and pocketing same.

Here I spent the best months of my life. In a few days my high-lows leveled out, my depression-exaltation melded into a serene skimming watchfulness. My terror-rage—cowardly lionheartedness and lionhearted cowardice—fused into a mild steady resolve. Here in the day room and in the ward we patients came to understand each other as only fellow prisoners and exiles can. Sane outside, I can't make head or tail of people. Mad inside, we signaled each other like auctioneers, a wink here, a wag of finger there. I listened and watched. Outside there is not time to listen. Sitting here in the day room the day after Christmas next to a mangy pine tree decorated with varicolored Kleenex (no glass!), the stereo-V showing the Blue-Gray game and rolling flip flip flip, my hands on my knees and wrists bandaged, I felt so bad that I groaned aloud an Old Testament lamentation AAAAIEOOOOOW! to which responded a great silent black man sitting next to me on the blocky couch: "Ain't it the truth though."

After that I felt better.

We love those who know the worst of us and don't turn their faces away. I loved my fellow patients and hearkened to them and they to me. I loved Max Gottlieb. He sewed up my wrists in his living room without making a fuss about it. How did I get to his house? By walking, I think. The last thing I remember clearly is Perry Como, hale as Saint Nick but orange of face and livid of lip.

As Max worked, he was holding my wrist pressed with pleasant pressure against his stomach, and I remember thinking he was like a trainer lacing up his fighter's gloves.

He clucked in mild irritation.

"What's the matter, Max?"

"Tch. I can't fix the tendon here. You'll have to wait. Sorry."

"That's all right, Max."

Here's an oddity. Max the unbeliever, a lapsed Jew, believes in the orderliness of creation, acts on it with energy and charity. I the believer, having swallowed the whole Thing, God Jews Christ Church, find the world a madhouse and a madhouse home. Max the atheist sees things like Saint Thomas Aquinas, ranged, orderly, connected up.

Here it was in this very day room that I, watchful and prescient, tuned into the palpable radiations of my fellow patients and my colleagues as well, the tired hollow-eyed abstracted doctors, and hatched my great principle, as simple and elegant and obvious as all great principles are. It is easy to understand how men do their best work in prison or exile, men like Dostoevsky, Cervantes, Bonhoeffer, Sir Thomas More, Genet, and I, Dr. Thomas More. Pascal wrote as if he were in prison for life and so he was free. In prison or exile or a mental hospital one has time to watch and listen. My question was: how is it with you, fellow patient? how is it with you, fellow physician? and I saw how it was. Many men have done that, seen visions, dreamed dreams. But it is of no use in science unless you can measure it. My good luck came when I stumbled onto a way of measuring the length and breadth and motions of the very self. My little machine is the first caliper of the soul.

Then one day in May I had had enough of the ward and wanted out. I had made my breakthrough. I had done my job. Though I was still on the ward, I was working on the staff as well, even presenting cases to students in The Pit. But I still had to get out. What was it like out there in the gauzy pointillist world? Would my great discovery work out there?

So I went AWOL, walked out and haven't been back since. I walked to town along the interstate. Wham! there it was, the world, solid as a rock, dense as a doorknob. A beer can glinted malignantly on the shoulder. The grains of concrete were like rocks on the moon. Here came old friend, morning terror, corkscrewing up my spine. Dear God, let me out of here, back to the nuthouse where I can stay sane. Things are too naked out here. People look and talk and smile and are nice and the abyss yawns. The niceness is terrifying.

But I went on to town, to the Little Napoleon tavern where I greeted Leroy Ledbetter, the owner, and other old friends, sipped a few toddies and soon felt better. From the Little Napoleon I telephoned an acquaintance, Dr. Yamaiuchi of Osaka Instruments, with whom I had been in correspondence and who had my specifications, and placed an order for one hundred lapsometers, certified check to follow upon his estimate. The pay phone in the Little Napoleon cost me $47.65 in quarters and nickels.

Leroy and my pals did not find the call remarkable and fed

me coins: old Doc is making a call to Japan, scientific medical business, etcetera, keep the money coming, fix him a drink.

Max and Colley, just back from birding, are sitting in the chief resident's office. Max has donned his white clinical coat but hasn't changed his boots. Colley, still wearing bush jacket and bermuda shorts, lounges in a tattered aluminum chaise, puffing a briar that sends out wreaths of maple-sugar smoke.

Max is glad to see me, Colley is not. Colley is a super-Negro, a regular black Leonardo. He is chief encephalographer, electronic wizard, ornithologist, holds the Black Belt in karate, does the crossword in the Sunday *Times*. A native of Dothan, Alabama, he is a graduate of Amherst and N.Y.U. medical school. So he lounges around like an Amherst man, cocking a quizzical eyebrow and sending out wreaths of maple-sugar smoke, or else he humps off down the hall like a Brooklyn interne, eyes rolled up in his eyebrows, shoes pigeoning in and going *squee-gee* on the asphalt tile. Yet if he gets excited enough or angry enough, the old Alabama hambone shows through. His voice will hit up into falsetto and he might even say *aksed* instead of *asked*.

When I was in the open ward and working on staff, he was very good to me. He immediately saw what I was getting at and helped me wire up my first lapsometer, read my article and refused to take credit as coauthor. "Too metaphysical for me," he said politely, knocking out his briar. "I'll stick to old-fashioned tumors and hemorrhages"—and off he went humping it down the hall *squee-gee*.

But we were always wary of each other. Our eyes never quite met. It was as if there was something between us, a shared secret, an unmentionable common past, an unacknowledged kinship. We were somehow onto each other. He recognized my Southern trick of using manners and even madness guilefully and for one's own ends. I was onto his trick of covering up Alabama hambone with brave old Amherst and humping it like a Brooklyn interne. What is more, he knew that I knew and I knew that he knew. We were like two Jews who have changed their names.

Max sits behind his desk in his perfectly fitted white coat, erect as a young prince, light glancing from the planes of his forehead. But when he rises, like Toulouse-Lautrec he doesn't rise much.

Colley drums his fingers on his pith helmet in his lap, Jungle Jim after the safari.

"Well well," says Max with pure affection, an affection without irony. He loves me because he saved my life. "The prodigal has returned."

"Prodigal or prodigy?" asks Colley quizzically-Amherstly.

We're all three prodigies. Max is a prodigy. His performance on grand rounds is famous. There he stands at the foot of my bed in the ward, the small erect young prince, flanked by a semicircle of professors, psychiatrists, behaviorists, love counselors, reminding me of the young Jesus confounding his elders.

He saved me twice. Once the night before by suturing my arteries. The next morning by naming my terror, giving it habitation, standing at the foot of my bed, knowing the worst of me, then naming it with ordinary words, English common nouns, smiling and moving on.

A bad night it had been, my wrists bandaged and lashed to the rails, crucified, I by turns exalted, depressed, terrified, lustful. Miss Oglethorpe, a handsome strapping nurse (she's now my nurse) came on at eleven and asked me what I wanted. "I want you, Miss Oglethorpe. You are so beautiful and I need you and love you: Will you lie here with me?" Since she was and I did, was beautiful and I did love and need her, and she being a woman knew the truth when she heard it, she almost did. She almost did! But of course she didn't and instead made a horrid nurse-joke about how I couldn't be so bad off what with chasing the nurses etcetera, but what a good nurse!

Later, lust gave way to sorrow and I prayed, arms stretched out like a Mexican, tears streaming down my face. Dear God, I can see it now, why can't I see it other times, that it is you I love in the beauty of the world and in all the lovely girls and dear good friends, and it is pilgrims we are, wayfarers on a journey, and not pigs, nor angels. Why can I not be merry and loving like my ancestor, a gentle pure-hearted knight for our Lady and our blessed Lord and Savior? Pray for me, Sir Thomas More.

Etcetera etcetera. A regular Walpurgis night of witches, devils, pitchforks, thorns in the flesh, upkneed girl-thighs.

Followed by contrition and clear sight. Followed, of course, by old friend morning terror.

There stood Max at the foot of my bed flanked by my former colleagues, the ten o'clock sunlight glancing from the planes of his forehead and striking sparks from the silver of his reflex hammer and tuning fork in his breast pocket, Max smiling and spreading the skirts of his immaculate white coat and saying only, "Dr. More is having some troublesome mood swings—don't we all—but he's got excellent insight, so we hope we can enlist his services as soon as he'll let us, right, Tom?" And all at once it, the terror, had a habitation and name—I was having "mood swings," right, that's what they were—and the doctors nodded and smiled and moved to the next bed. And suddenly the morning sunlight became just what it was, the fresh lovely light of morning. The terror was gone.

That, sirs, is love.

In a week, I got up cheerfully and went about my business. Another week and, lying in my bed, I became prescient and clairvoyant, orbiting the earth like an angel and inducing instant angelic hypotheses. Another week and I had made my breakthrough.

"The prodigal returns," says Max, smiling his candid unironic smile (Max, who is from Pittsburgh, doesn't know all the dark things Colley and I know, so is not ironic). "This time to stay, I hope."

"No," I say quickly, taking a tiny shaft of fright. For I've just remembered that legally I'm still committed and that they could, if they wished, detain me.

"Yeah, very nice," says Colley, shaking hands without enthusiasm. He appears to knock out two pipes at the same time. The smoke has leveled out in a layer like leaf smoke in Vermont.

"What can we do for you, Tom?" asks Max, his princely head shedding light.

"I've a favor to ask."

"Ask it."

For some reason I frown and fall silent.

"I thought you'd come by to prepare for The Pit," says Max. "The Pit?"

"Sure, Tom," says Colley, cheering up at my confusion.

"You're down for Monday. This is the last go-round of the year for the students, you know, the annual Donnybrook."

Max hastens to reassure me. "You've got quite a following among the students, Tom. You're the new matador, Manolete taking on Belmonte."

Buddy Brown, my enemy, must be Belmonte. O God, I had forgotten. The Pit is a seriocomic clinic, an end-of-year hijinks put on by the doctors for the students. Doctors, you may know, have a somewhat retarded sense of humor. In medical school we dropped fingers and ears from cadavers on pedestrians. Older doctors write doggerel and satirical verse. When I was a young man, every conservative proctologist in town had a cartoon in his office showing a jackass kicking up his heels and farting a smoke ring: "LBJ has spoken!"

"God, I had forgotten. No, Max, I came to ask you a favor."

"Ask it."

"You know what it is. I want you to speak to the Director about my article and my lapsometer before my appointment with him Monday."

Colley straddles the chaise and rises.

"Wait, Colley. I want to tell you something too."

He shrugs, settles slowly, unfolds a silver pipe tool.

"Well, Max?"

"Sure sure." Max swivels around to the gold-green gauze. "If—"

"If what?"

"If you'll come back."

"You mean as patient?"

"Patient-staff. As you were."

"Why?"

"You're not well."

"I'm well enough. I can't come back."

"Why not?"

"Something is afoot."

"What?"

I sit down slowly and close my eyes. "You were both out birding this morning, weren't you? Down by the Quarters."

"Yeah!" says Max, lighting up. Rummaging in his desk for something, he hands it to me, a piece of bark. "Take a look at those cuttings."

"O.K."

"What do you think?"

"I don't know."

"That's from an overcup oak and it's not a pileated."

"You mean you think—"

"Ask Colley. He's the ornithologist."

"No question about it," says Colley, rubbing his briar on his nose. "It's the ivorybill. He's out there. Just think of it, Max."

"Yes."

"No one's seen him since nineteen-three and he's out there. Think of it. I think he's on Honey Island."

"Yes." Max's eyes are shining. For him the ivorybill, which the Negroes used to call the Lord-to-God, is the magic bird, the firebird, the sweet bird of youth. For the ivorybill to return after all these years means—

Colley is different. The search for the bird is for him not a bona fide search. It is something he has got the knack of. How happy he is to have got the knack of searching for the ivorybill!

(No idle speculation this: once, before Colley and I fell out, I measured his pineal region. He had good readings at layer I, little or nothing at layer II. Diagnosis: a self successfully playing at being a self that is not itself. I told him this—he asked me!—and he took offense, rolled his eyes up in his eyebrows, and went humping off down the hall *squee-gee*.)

Max is looking at me sharply. "Why do you ask? Did you see us? Why didn't you join us? It would be good—"

"I couldn't. I was trapped."

"Trapped?"

Colley, I see, is wondering whether he should risk an exchange of glances with Max. His eyes stray. He doesn't.

"Yes," I say and relate to them the events of the morning, beginning with the sniper and ending with my eavesdropping on the three conspirators in the pagoda. I don't tell it badly, using, in fact, Max's own low-keyed clinical style of reciting case histories on grand rounds.

Silence falls. Colley, who has lit up again, screws up an eye against the maple-sugar smoke. Max's expression does not change. He listens attentively, unironically. Daylight glances interestingly from his forehead.

"Let me be sure I understand you," says Max at last, swinging to and fro. "You are saying first that somebody tried to shoot you this morning; second, that there is a conspiracy planned for the Fourth of July, a conspiracy to kidnap the Paradise baton-twirlers as well as staff members here who participate in the Audubon outings?"

"Not exactly. The shooting is a fact. The other is what I heard."

"And they're planning to run a school on Honey Island for the Bantus and Choctaws," says Colley, drumming his fingers on his helmet.

"They said it."

Silence.

I rise. "Look. I felt obliged to pass it on to you. Make of it what you will. Perhaps it is foolishness. It is not even necessary that you believe me. I simply—"

"I didn't say I didn't believe you, Tom," says Max affectionately. "Belief. Truth values. These are relative things. What interests me is—"

"Yeah, don't give me that either. Skip it. Look, will you speak to the Director?"

"Of course. Will you come back?"

Colley beats me to the door. "I'm off. Max. Tom. You know your job is still open?"

"Thanks," I say sourly.

Colley gone, Max nods toward the lounge. "You look tired, Tom. Did you have a bad night?"

"Yes."

"How are you feeling?"

"Fine fine."

"No depression?"

"Not much."

"No highs?"

"They come together, sine-cosine."

"What?"

"Nothing. Max, you read my paper and you've seen my lapsometer."

"Yes."

"Do you think they're of value?"

"Yes. I think you've hit on something extremely intriguing.

You've got a gift for correlation, but there's too much subjectivity here and your series is too short. You need to come back in the hospital and spend about a year at it."

"At what?" I ask him suspiciously.

"At this." He picks up my paper. "And at treatment."

"Whose treatment?"

"Your treatment of other patients and our treatment of you."

"I know my mental health is bad, but there's not much time."

"Let's talk about this sense of impending disaster."

"Bullshit, Max. Are you going to help me with the Director or aren't you?"

"I am. And you take the job back."

"What job?"

"Your same job. As a matter of fact, Kenneth Stryker over in Love just read your earlier paper and I told him something about this. He's quite excited and thinks you can help him out over there."

"Max, I don't seem to be getting across. You're talking about doing business at the same stand here. I'm talking about a crash program involving N.I.M.H. and twenty-five million dollars."

"A crash program? You mean on a national scale? You think there is a national emergency?"

"More even than that, Max! It's not even the U.S.A., it's the soul of Western man that is in the very act of flying apart HERE and Now. Christ, Max, you read the paper. I can measure it, Max! Number one, I've got to get this thing mass-produced and in the hands of G.P.'s; number two, I've got to hit on a therapeutic equivalent of my diagnostic breakthrough. Don't you agree?"

"Well now. The soul of Western man, that's a large order, Tom. Besides being rather uh metaphysical—"

"Metaphysical is a word, Max. There is nothing metaphysical about the tenfold increase in atrocities in this area. There's nothing metaphysical about the vines sprouting. There's nothing metaphysical about the Bantu guerrillas and this country falling apart between the Knotheads and the Leftpapas. Did you know the President and Vice-President will both be in this area on the Fourth—"

"What was that about the vines?" asks Max, cocking an ear.

"Never mind," I say, blushing. I shouldn't have mentioned the vines.

Max is shifting about in his chair.

"I get uh uncomfortable when politics gets mixed with medicine, to say nothing of angels."

"Very well."

"Wait. What are your immediate plans?"

"For today? I'm headed for my office in town, stopping off on the way at old Howard Johnson's. I want to make sure it's safe. Moira and I have a date there on the Fourth."

"Moira? Isn't she the little popsy over in Love?"

"Yes. She's a secretary at the Love Clinic."

"Yes indeed. I saw her at the square dance with Buddy."

"Buddy?" I frown.

"She's a charmer."

Max calls all attractive young women "popsies." Though he is a neobehaviorist, he is old-fashioned, even courtly in sexual matters. Like Freud himself, he is both Victorian and anatomical, speaking one moment delicately of "paying court to the ladies" or "having an affair of the heart," and the next of genitalia and ejaculations and such. Whenever he mentions women, I picture heavy black feather-boa'd dresses clothing naked bodies and secret parts.

"Then will you come back, Tom?"

"Come back?"

"To the hospital. I'll work like a dog with you."

"I know you will."

"We were just getting the cards on the table when you left."

"What cards?"

"We found out what the hangup was and we were getting ready to condition you out of it."

"What hangup?"

"Your guilt feelings."

"I never did see that."

"You did see that your depression and suicide attempt were related to sexual guilt?"

"What sexual guilt?"

"Didn't you tell me that your depression followed *une affaire* of the heart with a popsy at the country club?"

"Lola is no popsy. She's a concert cellist."

"Oh." Max has a great respect for stringed instruments. "Nevertheless your guilt did follow *une affaire* of the heart."

"Are you speaking of my fornication with Lola in number 18 bunker?"

"Fornication," repeats Max, nodding. "You see?"

"See what?"

"That you are saying that lovemaking is not a natural activity, like eating and drinking."

"No, I didn't say it wasn't natural."

"But sinful and guilt-laden."

"Not guilt-laden."

"Then sinful?"

"Only between persons not married to each other."

"I am trying to see it as you see it."

"I know you are."

"If it is sinful, why do you do it?"

"It is a great pleasure."

"I understand. Then, since it is 'sinful,' guilt feelings follow, even though it is a pleasure."

"No, they don't follow."

"Then what worries you, if you don't feel guilty?"

"That's what worries me: not feeling guilty."

"Why does that worry you?"

"Because if I felt guilty, I could get rid of it."

"How?"

"By the sacrament of penance."

"I'm trying to see it as you see it."

"I know you are."

"What I don't see is that if there is no guilt after *une affaire*, what is the problem?"

"The problem is that if there is no guilt, contrition, and a purpose of amendment, the sin cannot be forgiven."

"What does that mean, operationally speaking?"

"It means that you don't have life in you."

"Life?"

"Yes."

"But you didn't seem much interested in life that night. On the contrary."

"I know."

"In any case, your depression and suicide attempt did follow your uh 'sin.'"

"That wasn't why I was depressed."

"Why were you depressed?"

"It was Christmas Eve and there I was watching Perry Como."

"You're blocking me."

"Yes."

"What does 'purpose of amendment' mean?"

"Promising to try not to do it again and meaning it."

"And you don't intend to do that?"

"No."

"Why not, if you believe it is sinful?"

"Because it is a great pleasure."

"I don't follow."

"I know."

"At least, in the matter of belief and action, you are half right."

"That's right."

"But there remains the tug of war between the two."

"There does."

"If you would come back and get in the Skinner box, we could straighten it out."

"The Skinner box wouldn't help."

"We could condition away the contradiction. You'd never feel guilt."

"Then I'd really be up the creek."

"I'm trying to see it."

"I know you are."

"I notice that in speaking of your date with the little popsy from Love, you choose a setting that emphasizes the anonymous, transient, and sordid character of the relationship as you see it."

"How's that?"

"Not merely a motel, but an abandoned motel, a ruin, a secret hole-in-corner place, an assignation."

"Yes, that's the beauty of it, isn't it?" I say, cheering up.

"No. No no. You misunderstand me. It's a question of maturity—"

"You're right, Max," I say, wringing his hand affectionately and rushing off. "You're a good friend!" I call back from the hall.

Poor Max did his best for me. Once he devised a psychological test, tailored to my peculiar complaint.

"You see those two doors," he said to me one day, sitting behind the same desk.

"Yes." I could tell from the sparkle in his eye and from the way light glanced interestingly from his forehead that he had cooked up something for me.

"Behind those two doors are not the lady and the tiger but two ladies."

"O.K.," I say, perking up. Max, I saw, had gone to some trouble devising a test that would reveal to me the nature of my problem.

"Behind that door," said Max, wheeling in his chair, "is a lovely person, a mature, well-educated person who is quite fond of you."

"Yes?"

"You have much in common. She can converse on a variety of topics, is psychiatrically-oriented, empathetic toward you, and is quite creative in the arts. She is equally at home discussing the World Bank or a novel by Mazo de la Roche."

"Mazo de la Roche? Jesus, Max. Look, do you have someone in mind?"

"And she is dressed in the most seductive garb"—Max would say garb—"and you find her reclining on a couch in a room furnished with the costliest, most tasteful fabrics. Exotic perfumes are wafted toward you"—Max says *wäfted*—"You talk. She responds warmly at all levels of the interpersonal spectrum. The most seductive music is playing—"

"What music in particular, Max?"

"What difference does it make? *Scheherazade.*"

"God, Max, it all sounds so Oriental." What makes Max's attempt to find me a girl both odd and endearing is that he is so old-fashioned. He and his wife, Sylvia, are like Darwin and Mrs. Darwin at their fireside in Kent. "Who's behind the other door, Max?"

"Oh, a popsy in a motel room."

"What is she like?"

"Oh, ordinary. Say a stewardess. You've spoken to her once on a flight from Houston."

"She fancies me?"

"Yes."

"You want to know which I prefer?"

"Yes."

"The stewardess."

"Exactly!" cried Max triumphantly. "You prefer 'fornication,' as you call it, to a meaningful relation with another person qua person."

"Right, and you're saying the other case is not fornication."

"Yes."

Thus Max devised a specific test to reveal me to myself, I flunked the test, was in fact revealed to myself. But nothing came of it.

After saving my life, he tried to make it a good life. He invited me along on Audubon bird walks and to Center square dances and even introduced me to an attractive lady behaviorist named Grace Gould. Was this the lady behind the first door, I wondered. He even invited me to his home. Grace and I would sit in Max's living room while Max barbecued kebabs outside and his wife, Sylvia, a tall stooped one-shoulder-hitched-up ruddy-faced girl from Pittsburgh, passed around a dip. We spoke of politics, deplored Knotheads, listened to Rimski-Korsakov, played Scrabble, watched educational stereo-V. Max himself had many interests besides medicine and looking for the ivory bill: tropical fish, square dancing, gem-polishing, tree-dwarfing—which he tried to interest me in, without success. Grace Gould was his last and best effort. Grace, who came from Pasadena, was indeed attractive, was nimble as a cat at square dancing, could spot a Louisiana waterthrush at one hundred feet, and could converse on a variety of topics. Max and Sylvia would retire early, leaving us to our devices downstairs. Upstairs the Gottliebs lay, quiet as mice, hoping something was cooking downstairs (for Max loved me and wanted for me what he had). Nothing was cooking, however, though Grace and I liked each other. But there seemed to be nothing to do but drink and look at the walls which, though the house was a new one in Paradise, nevertheless gave the effect of being dark and varnished inside like an old duplex in Queens. The bookshelves contained medical, psychiatric, and psychological texts, a whole shelf of *Reader's Digest* four-in-one novels, and the complete works of Mazo de la Roche. The night Max sewed up my wrists at his house, found a cut tendon, went out to beat the bushes for a surgeon, I read *Whiteoaks of Jalna* at one sitting. There we sat, Grace and I, agreeing on everything, until I developed a tic, commenced to wink, and so took her home, keeping one side of my face averted.

6

Passing through the geriatric cottages on the way to Love. Here in cold glassed porches sit despondent oldsters, exiled from Tampa and Tucson for crankiness, misanthropy, malcontent, solitariness, destructiveness, misery—in short, the St. Petersburg Blues.

Each has two electrodes in his head, like a Martian with antennae. They're being reconditioned, put in Skinner boxes, which are pleasant enough chambers furnished with that "recreational or avocational environment" which the patient shows highest aptitude for—pottery wheel, putting green, ceramic oven, square-dance therapist—and conditioned. Positively conditioned when he responds positively: spins wheel, hops to music—by a mild electric current flowing through electrode A inducing a pleasant sensation, an unlocated euphoria, hypothalamic joy. Negatively conditioned when he responds negatively: breaks wheel, kicks therapist, sits in corner—by a nasty shock through electrode B inducing a distinct but not overpowering malaise.

Those who respond? Back home to Senior Citizen compounds in Tampa and Tucson with other happy seniors.

Those who don't respond? Off they're packed to the Happy Isles of Georgia, the federal Good Time Garden where reconditioning is no longer attempted but rather the opposite: whenever they behave antisocially they're shocked into bliss, soon learning to press the button themselves, off and dreaming so blissful that they pass up meals—

Here's the hottest political issue of the day: euthanasia. Say the euthanasists not unreasonably: let's be honest, why should people suffer and cause suffering to other people? It is the quality of life that counts, not longevity, etcetera. Every man is entitled to live his life with freedom and to end it with dignity, etcetera etcetera. It came down to one curious squabble (like the biggest theology fight coming down to whether to add the *que* to the *filio*): the button *vs.* the switch. Should a man have the right merely to self-stimulation, pressing the button that delivers bliss precisely until the blissful thumb relaxes and lets go the button? Or does he not also have the right to throw a switch that stays on, inducing a permanent joy—no meals, no sleep, and a happy death in a week or so? The button *vs.* the switch.

And if he has such a right and is judged legally incompetent to throw the switch, cannot a relative throw it for him?

The debate rages. The qualitarians, as the euthanasists call themselves, have won in Maryland and New York and Hawaii where legislatures have passed laws that allow sane oldsters to choose a "joyful exitus" as it is called in Maryland, or a *kawaneeolaua* as it is called in Hawaii, and throw the on-switch on. In the case of the insane, the consent of both physician and spouse is necessary.

Whup. Up ahead I spy my enemy, Dr. Buddy Brown, sailing his coattails, and duck into Love Clinic just in time.

I don't want to talk to him about our coming shoot-out in The Pit. Am I afraid of him?

7

The small observation room in Love is not crowded. Moira is perched on a stool at the viewing mirror, steno pad open on her knees. My heart melts with love. Does not a faint color spread along her throat? She blushes! I nod merely—or do I blush?—and go on talking to Stryker. But her presence is like sunlight. No matter which way I turn I feel a ray of warmth, now on my cheek, now between my shoulder blades. There is a sextant in me that keeps her position.

Father Kev Kevin sits reading *Commonweal* at his console of vaginal indicators. Only the regular staff is present today— though there may be students in the amphitheater above—Dr. Kenneth Stryker, chief of staff of Love; Dr. Helga Heine, his assistant, a West German interpersonal gynecologist; Father Kev Kevin, an ex-priest now a Love counselor; and Moira Schaffner, my own true love.

Stryker and Moira are glad to see me. Father Kev Kevin and Helga are not, though they are civil enough. Helga thinks I don't like Germans. I suspect, too, she believes I am Jewish because I was always with Gottlieb and I look somewhat Jewish, like my illustrious ancestor, Sir Thomas More.

Father Kev Kevin was a curate at Saint Michael's, my old parish church. So he is skittish toward me, behaving now too brightly, now too sullenly. I think he fears I might call him Father. A handsome Irishman, he is not merely chaplain of the clinic but jack of all trades: counsels persons in Love who cannot love—love or die! he tells them—takes clinical notes, operates the vaginal console. Imagine a young genial anticlerical Pat O'Brien who reads *Commonweal*.

The behavior room beyond the viewing mirror is presently unoccupied. It has an examining table with stirrups, a hospital bed, a tray of instruments, a tube of K-Y jelly, and a rack for the sensor wires with leads to the recording devices in the observation room.

A subject comes in, a solitary lover. I gaze at her, feeling somewhat big-nosed.

I recognize her. She is Lillian, Stryker's first subject. No doubt she will go down in history like Freud's first patient, Anna O. For it was she, Lonesome Lil as the students called her, who exhibited in classic form the "cruciform rash" of love that won for Stryker the Nobel Prize.

Lillian wears a sensible gray suit and sturdy brown low-heeled shoes. Her outfit, with shoulder bag and matching hat, a kind of beret with up-arching hoop inside, puts me in mind of Lois Lane of the old *Superman* comics of my childhood. Lillian is a good deal sturdier, however. As she opens her shoulder bag and begins to remove small fitted devices of clear Lucite, lining them up neatly on the surgical tray, she is for all the world like a visiting nurse come to minister to a complex ailment.

But, unlike a visiting nurse, she undresses. As briskly as a housewife getting ready for her evening bath and paying no more attention to the viewing mirror than if it were her vanity, she sheds jacket, skirt, underwear—the lower article a kind of stretch step-in garment, the upper a brassiere with a bodice-like extension—and finally her up-arched beret, holding a bobby pin in her teeth and giving her short dark hair a shake as any woman would. Not fat, she is heavy-legged and heavy-breasted, her olive skin running to pigment. Though there is glass between us, there is the sense, almost palpable, of the broad, low, barefooted heft of her, of a clothed-in cottoned-off body heat and of the keratin-rasp of her bare feet on the cork floor.

Now, clipping Lucite fittings to sensor wires—and again with the impression of holding a bobby pin in her teeth—she inserts one after another into the body orifices, as handily and thriftily as a teenager popping in a contact lens.

Cameras whir, tapes jerk around, needles quiver, computers wink, and Lillian begins her autostimulation.

My eyes meet Moira's. She blushes and glances down. Here we meet, at Lillian's recording session, as shyly as two office workers at the water cooler, touch fingers and—! Yes, my hand strays along the vaginal computer, our fingers touch. A thrill pierces my heart like an arrow, as they say in old novels. I am in love.

Stryker tells me his problem, I listen attentively, and sure enough he offers me a job. It disconcerts me that he speaks in a loud voice, in the hearing of others, and pays no attention to Lillian, who is doing her usual yeoman-like job. Isn't it impolite not to watch her? Stryker is a tall, willowy doctor who feels obliged by the nature of his work to emphasize the propriety, even the solemnity of his own person. So he dresses somewhat like a funeral director in a dark suit, perfectly laundered shirt, and sober tie. Yet there persists about him the faint air of the dude: his collar has a tricky pin that lofts the knot of his tie. Overly long cuffs show their jeweled links and cover part of his hand, whose fingers are still withered from his years as a chemist before he went into behavior. He is a wonderful dancer, hopping nimbly through the complicated figures of the Center's square dances. Even now, in the observation room, there is about him a lightness of foot, a discreet bounciness, as if he were keeping time to an inner hoedown. His foot swings out. Yet there pervades the observation room a strong tone, at once solemn and brisk. Embarrassment is not to be thought of.

Nor, on the other hand, would it be thinkable to crack vulgar jokes as surgeons do in the scrub room.

Dr. Helga Heine has caught the same note of brisk solemnity. She is a jolly matronly Bavarian gynecologist, neither young nor old, a regular hausfrau, hair done up in a bun, breast conformed to a single motherly outcurve. Moira tells me that Helga takes pains to remember the birthdays of staff members and veteran performers, brings a cake and plays *Zwei Herzen* on her little Bavarian guitar. I gaze big-nosed at her plump pink fingertips.

"Thanks to you," says Stryker solemnly, balancing lightly on the balls of his feet, "we've made a breakthrough in the whole area of sexual behavior."

"Oh, I wouldn't say—" I begin, sweeping out a foot like Stryker. So he's read my paper! In the corner of my eye Moira listens and registers pride. To Moira, who believes in Science without knowing much about it, my triumph has all the grace and warrant of a matador's.

"Your article in the *J.A.M.A.* delineated a new concept."

"Oh. I wouldn't say that."

And I wouldn't. The "article" he speaks of is not the epochal paper I just finished, but a minor clinical note, small potatoes indeed. It noted nothing more than a certain anomaly in the alpha wave of solitary lovers (as Colley's assistant, I read the EEG's of all the lovemakers in Love). Stryker's praise is something like congratulating Einstein for patenting a Swiss watch. I accept it for Moira's sake.

Moira's eyes are shining.

Lillian is going about her task at a fair clip. Drums revolve, heartbeats spike on a monitor, her skin conductivity ascends a gentle slope. Stryker keeps a casual eye on the dials, now and then dictates a clinical note to Moira. Helga and Father Kev Kevin, hearing my praises, look glum.

Moira perches on her stool, heels cocked on a rung, and manages both to take notes and keep her short skirt tucked under her knees. What lovely legs. Her kneecaps are smooth and tan as a beaten biscuit. To plant kisses on those perfect little biscuits, I'm thinking, as Stryker dances a step. Moira and I do not quite look at each other but my cheek is aware of hers.

> *She never told her love*
> *But let concealment, like a worm i' the bud*
> *Feed on her damask cheek.*

Lillian is going at a good clip now.

"There's the old methodology," says Stryker, waving a hand at Lillian without bothering to look. "Thanks to you, we're onto something new."

"I'm not sure I understand," I murmur out of Moira's hearing.

"Not that the old wasn't useful in its way—"

"Useful!" chime in Helga and Father Kev Kevin. "Useful enough to take the Nobel!"

But Stryker waves them off. "Useful, yes, to a point. But without your note on the alpha wave, we'd never have struck out on a new path."

"A new path?" I ask, puzzled. But my Moira-wards cheek glows.

> *Her cheek like the rose is, but fresher, I ween,*
> *She's the loveliest lassie that trips on the green.*

I ween she is.

Stryker sways closer, balancing lightly on his toes. "I think you might be interested to learn, Tom, that since June we've been using not one subject at a time"—he touches my arm with a withered finger—"but two."

"Two?"

"Yes. A man and a woman. Here's the breakthrough."

"Breakthrough?"

"Yes. And guess what?"

"What?"

"We've got rid of your alpha wave anomaly. You were right."

"Very good. But actually I was only reading EEG's and not making recommendations about future techniques, you understand—"

"Moral scruples, Doctor?" asks Father Kev Kevin, eyes alight. He clears the orgasm circuit.

"Perhaps."

"Oh, that's neither here nor there!" cries Stryker cheerfully.

"All I'm saying is that using couples instead of singles we've got rid of your alpha wave anomaly and kept the cruciform rash. I thought you'd want to know."

"Yes," I say gloomily, watching Lillian. My nose is getting bigger. I try to think. "Then if that's the case, what's your problem?"

"Yeah, here's the thing." Stryker glances at Lillian like a good cook watching a pot of beans. I notice that as Lillian progresses, Stryker becomes ever more light-footed. His black pumps swing out. His watching Lillian is like a poet reading his best poem. "Our problem is that our couples do not perform regularly."

"Ted 'n Tanya do!" Helga objects.

"Not lately. Only one out of four couples interact successfully," says Stryker drily. "Hardly an adequate base for observation."

"Ted 'n Tanya?" I ask, scratching my head. There could only be one Ted 'n Tanya. It must mean that my prescription for Ted didn't, in the end, work, and that they've come here. "But what do you think I can do about it?"

Lillian seems to be looking at me. But I know she can only see mirror. It is herself she is watching. Her eyes are unfocused and faraway. Her eyebrows are unplucked, the heavy black sort one used to see in daguerreotypes of frontier women.

"Do some studies on our noninteracting couples!" cries Stryker. "I hear you've developed a special sort of EEG."

"Not exactly."

"Join our team! We're even funded for a full-time consultant."

"Well, thank you, Ken, but . . ." On the other hand, I could see Moira all day if I did.

"Twenty thousand a year, full professorship, and do as you please."

"Well . . ."

"We've hit a snag in the interpersonal area and both Max and I feel you could iron it out."

"The fact is . . ." What does Moira's cheek say, my cheek wonders.

"*Here-we-are*," says Stryker in a routine rush, glancing at Lillian. All the quiet pride of a scientist demonstrating his best trick.

The Love team springs into action, each to his station.

Lillian turns to show her famous cruciform rash. She embraces herself. Her pale loins bloom. Stryker presses buttons with a routine skill, a practiced climactic.

"Beautiful!" murmurs Helga.

"Pathognomonic!" cries Father Kev Kevin.

Moira bends to her note-taking, scribbles furiously as Stryker dictates.

Helga speaks by microphone to Lillian.

"Turn around slowly, dear."

She addresses the unseen students, perched in their roost above us.

"You will notice please the cruciform morbilliform eruption extending bilaterally from the sacral area—"

Moira breaks her pencil and goes to sharpen it. The others are busy with Lillian and I see my chance. I follow her into a small closet-sized room, which houses a computer and a cot littered with dusty scientific journals. A metal label on the door reads Observer Stimulation Overflow Area. Standard equipment in all Love clinics. Known more familiarly to the students as the "chicken room," it is provided to accommodate those observers who are stimulated despite themselves by the behavior they observe. For although, as Stryker explained, the observer hopes to retain his scientific objectivity, it must be remembered that after all the observers belong to the same species as the observed and are subject to the same "environmental stimuli." Hither to the closet, alone or in pairs or severally, observers may discreetly repair, each to relieve himself or herself according to his needs. "It iss the same as a doctor having hiss own toilet, *nicht*?" Helga told me somewhat vulgarly. "*Nicht*," I said but did not argue. I have other fish to fry.

While moral considerations are not supposed to enter into scientific investigation, "observer stimulation overflow" is nevertheless discouraged. It is Stryker's quiet boast, moreover, that whatever may happen in Palo Alto or Berkeley or Copenhagen, scientific objectivity has been scrupulously preserved in the Paradise Love Clinic. No observer has ever used the chicken room. The closet houses not lovers but dusty journals and a computer.

Moira, in fact, tells me she feels safer in Love than when she worked as secretary to the chief psychologist.

"Can I see you after work today?" I whisper and take her hand. It is cold. *Che gelida manina.* Thy tiny hand is frozen.

"Can't today!" she whispers back. "But I can't wait till the Fourth! Where are we going?" Her lovely gold eyes look at me over her steno pad like a Moslem woman's.

I frown. An ugly pang pierces my heart. Why can't she see me today? Does she have a date with Buddy? Here's the misery of love: I don't really want to see her today, was not prepared to, have other plans, yet despite myself hear myself insist on it.

"But—"

She shushes me, seals my lips with her finger, and, glancing through the open door at Lillian who is unwiring herself, brushes her lips with her fingers, brushes mine.

"You better go."

"Yes." Ah.

Returning to the observation room, I sink into a chair and dreamily watch Lillian dress. Here's my trouble with Moira. She's a romanticist and I'm not. She lives for what she considers rare perfect moments. What I long to share with her are ordinary summer evenings, cicadas in the sycamores.

She whispers behind me. "Where are we going this time? To Dry Tortugas again? Chichén Itzá? Tombstone?"

I shrug and smile. She likes to visit ghost towns and jungle ruins, so I'll show her the one in our back yard, the ruined Howard Johnson motel. She'll savor the closeness of it. One weekend we flew to Silver City, Arizona, and stood in the deserted saloon and watched tumbleweeds blow past the door. "Can't you just hear the old rinky-dink piano?" she cried and hugged me tight. "Yeah," I said, taking delight in the very commonplaceness of her romanticism. "How about a glass of red-eye, Moira?" "Oh yes! Yes indeed!"

Lillian dresses quickly, pins on her Lois Lane hat, using the viewing mirror as her vanity, shoulders her bag, trudges out.

In comes the next subject. No, subjects. A couple. I recognize one, a medical student who is doubtlessly making money as a volunteer. He is J. T. Thigpen, a slightly built, acned youth who wears a blue shirt with cuffs turned up one turn.

He carries a stack of inky books in the crook of his wrist. His partner, whom the chart identifies only as Gloria, is a largish blonde, a lab worker, to judge from her stained smock, with wiry bronze hair that springs out from her head. Volunteers in Love get paid fifty dollars a crack, which beats giving blood.

"These kids are our pioneers," Stryker tells me, speaking softly now for some reason. "And a case in point. Something has gone wrong. Yet they were our first and best interaction subjects. Our problem, of course, with using two subjects was one of visualization. Colley, who is a wizard, solved that for us with his Lucite devices. We can see around curves, you see, between bodies. So we figured if Colley could help us out in mechanics, you could help us out with interpersonal break-downs. How about it?"

"Well . . ."

Gloria and J. T. are undressing. J. T. takes off his shirt, reveal-ing an old-fashioned undershirt with shoulder straps. He's a country boy from hereabouts. The spots of acne strewn across his shoulders turn livid in the fluorescent light. Removing his wristwatch with expansion band, he hesitates for a moment, then hangs it on the crank handle of the hospital bed.

Gloria wears a half-slip, which comes just short of her plump white knees, and a half-brassiere whose upper cups are missing.

"Okay, keeds!" cries Helga, clapping her hands into the microphone. "*Mach schnell!* Let's get the show on the road!"

"We have found," Stryker explains to me, "that you can inspire false modesty and that by the same token a brisk no-nonsense approach works wonders. Helga is great at it!"

I clear my throat and stretch up my heavy-lidded eyes. My nose is a snout.

"I've got to be going."

J. T. and Gloria, half-undressed, are standing around like strangers at a bus stop. J. T. sends his fingers browsing over his acned shoulder. Gloria stands foursquare, arms angled out past her hips as if she were carrying milkpails.

Father Kev Kevin clears the orgasm circuit. He won't look at me.

"I've got to be going, Stryker."

"Wait. How can you spot the hangup if you don't watch them?"

"Yeah. Well, later. Thank you very much, all of you. Hm. I'm already late—" I look at my watch and start for the door.

"Wait! Ted 'n Tanya are next. They're our best. Or were. Don't you want to—"

"No."

"What about the job?"

"I'll let you know."

"We're funded, man! The money is here!"

"Very good."

Leaving, I catch a final glimpse of J. T. Thigpen, bare-chested and goose-pimpled, gazing around the porcelain walls with the ruminant rapt expression of a naked draftee.

"*Mach schnell!* Keeds—" cries Helga, clapping her hands.

Whew! Escape! Escape, but just in time to run squarely into Buddy Brown, my enemy, in the corridor.

He smiles and nods and grips my arms as if we shared a lover's secret. What secret? Who is he waiting for?

I brush past and do not wait to find out. Am I afraid to find out?

8

To the motel to fix a room for a tryst with Moira on the Fourth.

No sign of sniper or anyone else for that matter. But I take no chances, slip into Howard Johnson's through the banquet room where the rent Rotary banner still flies from Tuesday's meeting five years ago:

> *Is it the truth?*
> *Is it fair to all concerned?*
> *Will it build goodwill and better friendships?*

and straight up the inside stairs without exposing myself to the patio.

Room 203, the most nearly intact, was nevertheless a mess when we first saw it: graffiti, illuminations of hairy pudendae, suspicious scraps of newspaper littering the floor. The beds moldy, the toilet fouled. I've been working on the room for a month, installed a generator for air-conditioner and TV and coffee-maker and lights and bed vibrators; brought in hose water from Esso station next door; laid in supplies for a day or so.

And I haven't finished. This weekend, knowing what I know, I'll lay in supplies for six months, plus clothes for Moira, books, games. All hell will break loose on the Fourth and Moira and I may need a place to stay. What safer place than a motel in no man's land, between the lines so to speak?

This is the place. Moira, in fact, picked it. She and I came here for a few minutes last month. She likes the byways. That weekend we hadn't time to fly to Mérida or Tombstone. So we took a walk. A proper ruin this, and what is more, it has a bad reputation and people don't come here. But I think it is safe. The whites think the black guerrillas have it. The blacks think the white drugheads have it. Neither wants any part of the other, so both stay away. I think.

Moira was delighted with the motel. There was a soupçon of danger, just enough. She clutched my arm and shrank against me. We stood by the scummy pool. Spanish moss trailed from the balcony. Alligator grass choked the wading pool. A scarlet watersnake coiled under the lifeguard's perch. Moira found a pair of old 1960 harlequin glasses and an ancient vial of Coppertone.

"It's like Pompey!" she cried.

"Like what? Yes, right."

We kissed. Ruins make her passionate. Ghosts make her want to be touched. She is lovely, her quick upturned heart-shaped face and gold-brown eyes bright with a not quite genuine delight, a willingness rather to be delighted. Are you going to delight me? isn't this the time? aren't things falling out just right? Pleasing her is fathoming and fulfilling this expectation. Her face. Her cropped wheat-colored hair with a strong nap that aches my hand to brush against, her rather short tanned perfect legs drawn with strong simple strokes like the Draw Me girl in magazine contests. She's poor, having left her West Virginia parents early and supported herself in civil service, worked in Bethesda for N.I.M.H. before transferring here. I can see her in Washington in the evening washing out her things in the washstand, keeping her budget, minding herself.

. . . But she has her own views and likes. She opposes the war in Ecuador, subscribes to *Playgirl*, a mildly liberated, mildly Left magazine, and carries in her purse a pocket edition of Rod McKuen, a minor poet of the old Auto Age, which she likes to read aloud to me: "Don't you just love that?" "Yes." But what I love is her loving it, her faintly spurious love of loving things that seem lovable.

A turtle plopped into the pool.

"Can't you just see them!" she whispered, swaying against me.

"Who?"

"All the salesmen and flappers."

"Yes."

"Aah!" said Moira, stretching out on a convex lounge which pushed her up in the middle. I perched somewhat precariously beside her.

Moira, who is twenty-two and not strong on history, thinks that the great motels of the Auto Age were the haunt of salesmen and flappers of the Roaring Twenties. Whereas, of course, it was far more likely that it was the salesman and his wife and kids and station wagon who put up here in the sixties and seventies.

A green lizard did push-ups on Moira's lounge, blew out a red bladder. Moira screamed and hopped into my lap. We kissed. I kissed her smooth biscuit-shaped kneecaps. Her eyes went fond and faraway. "Just think," she said.

"What?"

"It's all gone. Gone with the wind."

"Yes."

"The lion and the lizard keep The courts where Samson gloried and drank deep."

"Right." I held her close, melting with love, and whispered in her ear: "The wild ass Stamps o'er his head, but cannot break his sleep."

"Don't be nasty!" cried Moira, laughing and tossing her head like Miss Clairol of olden time.

"Sorry."

Taking my hand like a child, she led me exploring. In a rusted-out Coke machine in the arcade we found warm, five-year-old Cokes. I opened two, poured out half and filled the bottles with Early Times.

"This is how the salesmen and flappers used to drink."

"Wonderful!" She took a big swig.

The hot sun blazed in the patio. We could not swim in the foul pool. So we sweated and drank Coke and bourbon like a salesman and a flapper. The Spanish moss stirred on the balcony. We went up to get the breeze. Then we explored the rooms, sat on the moldering bed in 203 and drank some more.

"A penny for your thoughts," said Moira thoughtfully.

"I fancy you. Do you fancy me?"

"Yes."

"Let's lie down."

"On this? Ugh."

"Then let's sit in the chair."

"Not today, Josephine."

"Why not?"

"I didn't bring my Cupid's Quiver."

"Your what?"

"My sachet, silly."

"I'm not sure I understand. In any case, I don't mind."

"I do."

"Then let's have a drink."

Again she took a mighty pull. Again we kissed. Her gold eyes gleamed.

"Ugh," she said again, noticing the graffiti and pudendae on the walls. Damn, why didn't I clean the walls? But she refused to be shocked by dirty pictures. To prove it, we had to make a museum tour. Love, where is love now? We gazed at the poor penciled organs, same and different, same and different, like a figure in the wallpaper, and outside the swifts twittered down the sky and up sang the old skyey sounds of June and where was love?

So we walked hand in hand and read the graffiti. Moira had taken a course in semantics and knew there was nothing in dirty words.

Above the Gideon Bible: *For a free suck call room 208.*

Moira shook her head sadly. "What an unhappy person must have written that."

"Yea. That is, yes." Desire for her had blown my speech center. "Love, I, you," I said.

"Love I you too," she said, kissing me, mouth open, gold eyes open.

Holding hands, we read the graffito under *The Laughing Cavalier: Room 204 has a cutout on her pussy.*

"The poor man."

"Yes."

"What is a cutout?"

"It is a device salesmen used to attach to their auto mufflers."

"But how—? Never mind. Ummm, what a good place for a picnic!"

"Yes."

"Far from the maddening crowd."

"That's true."

It was then that the notion occurred to me to fix the room up properly and spend a weekend here.

"Tom, do you remember the quaint little hotel in Mérida?"

"Yes, I do."

"There's a small hotel With a wishing well."

"Right."

"Remember the coins we threw in the fountain after our love and the wish we made?"

"Yes."

She is right. I must remember that women like to think of the act of love as a thing, "our love." There are three of us, like a family, Moira and I and our love.

"I wish you'd worn your Mexican pleated shirt."

"Why?"

"You look just like Rod McKuen, if you had more hair."

"He's an old man."

"No, he's not. Look." She showed me his picture on the back of her book, Rod hoofing it along a California beach, arms open to the sea gulls.

"That was twenty years ago."

"Let's have a picnic here."

"We will."

"A jug of wine, a loaf of bread, and thou."

"Yes, thou."

9

That was last month. I've been working on this room ever since. Today I finish the job. No bowerbird ever prepared a bower for his love more carefully.

The hard work was done last week, Delco generator installed downstairs, hose run two hundred feet from the Esso station faucet up through the bathroom window.

Room 203 still has suspicious smells. Pull back curtains, open front panels and bathroom window to get a breeze. Unpack from doctor's bag and line up on dresser: one sani-flush, one wick deodorizer, one tube of cold solder, one roll of toilet paper, one boxed gift copy of *Stanyan Street*, one brass shower head, one jar of instant coffee.

Half an hour and my work is done, floors mopped, fungoid mattresses and horrid foam-rubber pillows slung over balcony rail to sun, coffee-maker restocked, graffiti wiped from wall revealing original hunt-and-hound design, *Laughing Cavalier* straightened, ancient color TV and bed vibrator plugged into Delco lead, shower head screwed onto hose from Esso station and tested (hot bitter hose water), *Stanyan Street* lined up with the Gideon.

Test vibrator: sit on bed and drop in quarter. Z-Z-Z-Z-Z goes the vibrator and suddenly I am thinking not of Moira but of Samantha, my dead daughter, and the times she and I and Doris used to travel in the Auto Age all over the U.S.A. and Samantha would explore the motel and drop coins in every slot. First off she'd have found the Slepe-Eze and fed it a quarter.

Tears spurt from my eyes. Removing a pint of Early Times from my bag, I sit on the humming bed and sip a few drinks.

Why does desire turn to grief and memory strike at the heart?

10

Off to town. Past empty Saint Michael's Church and school, a yellow brick dairy-barn-with-silo.

Here I went to mass with Samantha, happy as a man could be, ate Christ and held him to his word, if you eat me you'll have life in you, so I had life in me. After mass we'd walk home to Paradise through the violet evening, the evening star hard by the red light of the TV tower like a ruby and diamond in the plush velvet sky, and I'd skip with happiness, cut the fool like David while Samantha told elephant jokes, go home, light the briquets, drink six toddies, sing *Tantum Ergo*, and "Deh vieni alla finestra" from *Don Giovanni* and, while Samantha watched *Gentle Ben*, invite Doris out under the Mobile pinks, Doris as lusty and merry a wife then as a man could have, a fine ex-Episcopal ex-Apple Queen from the Shenandoah Valley. Oh Shenandoah, I long to see you.

Cliff swallows are nesting in the fenestrated concrete screen in front of Saint Michael's.

In this Catholic church, the center did not hold. It split in three, Monsignor Schleifkopf cutting out to the right, Father Kev Kevin to the left, leaving Father Smith. There is little to be said about Father Smith since he is in no way remarkable, having been a good and faithful if undistinguished priest for twenty-five years, having baptized the newborn into a new life, married lovers, shriven sinners, comforted the sick, visited the poor and imprisoned, anointed the dying, buried the dead. He had his faults. He was a gray stiff man. Like me, he was thought to drink and on occasion was packed off, looking only a bit grayer and stiffer than usual, to a Gulf Coast home for addled priests. Now he and his little flock are looking for a new home, I hear, having used for a while a Pentecostal church and later Paradise Lanes, my bowling alley here in the plaza, until it became too dangerous.

The plaza is empty now save for the rusting hulks of cars abandoned or burned in the time of troubles.

Five and a half years ago, on Christmas Eve, Paradise Plaza was sacked by Bantu guerrillas foraying up out of the swamp. Store windows were smashed, the new Sears looted, some stores burned, cops shot up by Bantus, Bantus shot up by cops. Noncombatants fled, Christmas shoppers, storekeepers, motel occupants, drive-in movie patrons watching *Homo Hijinks*. Monsignor Schleifkopf left by the front door of the church, abandoning his burning Buick and golf clubs in the garage, where they are to this day. Nobody came back these five and a half years save lovers and bums and drugheads and in the end only the original denizens of the swamp, owls, alligators, and moccasins.

I should have known trouble was brewing. The night before, Leroy Ledbetter had kicked out a black couple from Tougaloo who wanted to bowl at Paradise Lanes. That very morning, walking to town, I met Nellie Bledsoe, who told me her cook had quit and she was ready "to shoot some niggers."

"Eh? What? What's that? My God," I said, "you don't mean you want to shoot some niggers because your cook quit."

"Oh yes I do!" she cried, laughing and winking and kneading her arm. "Don't you know what they do?"

"What?"

"They go on welfare and have little illegitimate nigger babies and get paid for it, paid more than they make working."

"Yes, but you're not saying that you're going out and—"

"Oh yes I am!" says Nellie, winking and laughing. "Ho ho ho!"

Earlier the same morning, at six, a young jaundiced Bantu came up out of the swamp and appeared at my "enclosed patio" to be treated for liver flukes.

After I gave him his shot, he too winked at me with his yellow eye.

"I can't pay you now, Doc, but since you're so nice, we won't shoot you when the shooting starts."

"Who are you planning to shoot?"

"Anybody who gets in our way."

"In the way of what?"

"In the way of our taking over this goddamn parish, Doc," he said, pulling out a copy of Fanon with one hand and patting a bulge under his coat with the other.

"My God, you're not really going to shoot anybody, are you?"

"We're taking over, Doc."

"Why don't you take over by the vote? You got the vote and there are more of you than of us."

"Shit on voting, Doc."

There was something in the air all right.

II

On McArthur Boulevard now: a defunct parkway that dead-ends in a weedy lot and an ancient putt-putt course. Follow it as far as the L & N overpass and take the short cut to town through Happy Hollow.

A bit shaky now, faintified but not hungry. The Early Times is not sitting well.

The thunderhead fills the whole eastern sky. A hot wind blows me toward it over the asphalt playground of the school. A chain rings against a flagpole.

The short cut turns out to be a mistake. Happy Hollow is a hot airless hole. The sun slants down like a laser. My stomach churns acid. When did I eat last?

The bare ground between the shacks and under the chinaberry trees never dries out. Where the sun does strike, the earth steams and gives off a smell of dishwater and chicken fat. Duck eggs rise in my throat.

But people seem happy here. Happy pot-bellied picaninnies play in the alley. Old folk rock on the porches. The unhappy young men are gone. The kindly old folk doff their caps politely. Yellow yarddogs lie chained to the chinaberry trees. They lift an eyebrow and snarl as I pass.

It is collection day. Up one side of the alley goes Moon Mullins collecting rent for his shacks. Down the other side goes old Mr. Jack Bourgeois collecting burial-insurance premiums. Both are cheerful and good-humored with their clients, exchanging jokes and pleasantries at each shack before moving on. Both collect in exactly the same way. If the householder is sitting on his porch, he will pass the time of day and hand down the money to the collector, who stands on the ground. If the porch is vacant, the collector will put his foot on the second step, rest an elbow on his knee and rap the porch floor with his knuckles, all the while looking down at the ground with a musing expression. Old Mr. Jack bangs the porch with his fat premium book.

The collectors greet me cordially.

"Hot enough for you, Doc!" cries Moon.

"How you doing, Doc!" cries old Mr. Jack.

"Yes, it is. All right," I reply, weaving a bit.

The Negroes greet me uneasily. Why do the yarddogs snarl at me and not at Moon and old Mr. Jack? I am unwell.

How will I get up the hill to town? The sun laser bores into the top of my head, but my feet are blocks of ice. If only I could make it to the Little Napoleon, where I could sit in a dark nook and drink a little toddy to settle my stomach.

Halfway up the hill it becomes clear I won't make it. Flowers of darkness are blooming in the weeds. Rank vines sprout in the path. In times of ordeal one's prayers become simple. I pray only that I will faint in a private place where no one will disturb me and where especially Moon and old Mr. Jack won't see me.

I have drawn abreast of the new animal shelter, a glass-and-concrete air-conditioned block of a building cantilevered from the hillside like a Swiss sanitorium.

My knees knock.

But here's a good spot.

I sit down in a dry ditch under a chinaberry whose dense branches come down and make a private place. It is next to the dog-runs that slope down the hill under the pines. Where are the dogs?

Something in the ditch catches my eye. It is a Garrett snuff can. I lean forward to pick it up and faint. Not keel over but settle down comfortably propping my head on my bag. The weeds smell like iron.

Where are the dogs?

12

Here are the dogs. Inside where it is cool.

When I come to, I am lying on the large-dog table in the treatment room of the animal shelter. I feel well but so weak I cannot lift my head. Delicious cool air bathes my forehead. A great blue surgical lamp shines straight down. When my eyes get used to the glare, I notice the dogs, several dozen glossy-coated curs, seated behind grills and watching with interested expressions. This is why the outside runs are empty: the dogs have come inside to enjoy the cool breezes.

Gazing down at me, hands shoved deep in his pockets and fingering coins, stands Victor Charles. I know him without seeing his face. His flat abdomen engages the edge of the table. His belt buckle is to the side. The white duck is soiled by a horizontal streak I've seen before. Now I know where the streak comes from. It coincides with the metal edge of the table.

I try to get up.

"Hold it, Doc." Victor places skilled large-dog hands on my shoulders.

I close my eyes. There is a pleasant sense of being attended, of skills being practiced, strong hands laid on, of another's clothes rustling nearby.

I open my eyes. The lamp is reflected in one coppery highlight from Victor's forehead. The rest of his face is blue-black. I notice that his sclerae are lumpy and brown.

"How long have I been here?"

"No more than fifteen minutes, Doc."

"How did you find me?"

"I saw you sit down out yonder."

"Were you watching me?"

"Watching you?"

"And you carried me in?"

Victor nods.

I am thinking: it is true. All day I have had the sense of being watched.

"Where's my bag?"

"Right here, Doc."

"O.K., Victor. Thank you. I think I'll sit up."

He helps me. I am well but weak.

"Eat this, Doc."

Victor gives me a piece of corn bread and a cold glass of buttermilk. Though the bread is hard and unbuttered, it is very good. I don't remember anything ever tasting better. The buttermilk slides under the acid.

"Thank you again."

"You're welcome." Victor presses against the table and fingers his coins.

"I've got to go."

"You ought to take better care yourself, Doc. And be more careful where you takes a nap."

"Why?"

"Crazy folks everywhere now, Doc."

"Folks? What folks?"

"Folks. You know."

"You ought to be more careful too, Victor."

"How's that, Doc?" Victor, who has been pushing himself off the table with his stomach, stays off.

"I mean who you meet and where you meet, though it's none of my business."

"What you talking 'bout, Doc?"

For some reason all three tiers of dogs start barking.

Presently Victor shouts, "You'll be all right, Doc. Just rest here a while. You know what you need? Somebody to take care you. Why don't you move in with your mama, Miss Marva? She be glad to do for you."

I wait for the dogs to subside.

"You were there at number 11 on the old 18. This morning."

"What you talking 'bout, Doc?"

"I was there, Victor. On the island. In the pagoda."

"Oh, you talking about—!" Victor begins to shake a loose hand toward the east as if he just remembered.

"What the hell is going on, Victor?"

"Like I told you, Doc—"

"Like you told me! You haven't told me anything. I saw you, I saw Willard Amadie. Who was the third man?"

"Willard bringing meat for the swamp. Folks going hungry out there, Doc."

"I saw the deer. Was that all?"

"All? How you say, all?"

"Victor, I heard you. I was sitting in the pagoda."

"Oh, you talking about—" Again Victor salutes the east.

"Yes. Who was the third man?"

"Him? Doc, they say he *mean*," says Victor, laughing.

"They?"

"Everybody. You talk about mean and lowdown!"

"Then what are you laughing about?"

"You, Doc. You something else."

"Victor, is Willard trying to shoot me?"

"Shoot you! Willard!" Victor falls back.

"You mean somebody else is trying to shoot me?"

"Doc, why in the world anybody want to shoot you? You help folks. Like I tell people, you set up with my auntee when other doctors wouldn't even come out."

"You mean somebody is trying to shoot me and you tried to talk them out of it?"

"Doc, look. How long me and you known each other?"

"All our lives."

"How long did I work for y'all, first for Big Doc, then for Miss Marva clearing land?"

"I don't know. Twenty years."

"And didn't you set up with my auntee many a night before she died?"

"Yes."

"You think I wouldn't do the same for you?"

"I think you would. But—"

"Wasn't I working as a orderly in the hospital last year when they brought you in and didn't I take care you?"

"Yes, you did."

"When you said to me, Victor, there's something crawling on the wall, get it out of here, didn't I make out like I was throwing it out?"

"Yes."

Victor is laughing in such a way that I have to smile.

"I couldn't see but I threw it out anyhow."

"Yes, you did."

"You think I wouldn't tell you right?"

"I think you would."

"Then, Doc, listen." Victor comes close again, presses stomach against metal table. "Move in with Miss Marva. She'll do for you. Miss Marva, she'd love nothing better. I help you move over there, Doc."

"How come you want me out of my house?"

"I'm worried about you, Doc. Look at you. Fainting and falling out in a ditch."

"Victor, who were you waiting for in the pagoda?"

"Waiting?"

"I heard Willard say: Looks like he's not coming."

"Oh yeah. Willard."

"Was he waiting for me?"

Victor is silent.

"Did he or the third man intend to shoot me?"

"Shoot you! Lord, Doc. We just want to talk to you."

"Well, here I am."

"That's what I'm telling you. Move in with your mama."

"What's she got to do with it?"

Silence.

"What about that other stuff?"

"What other stuff?"

"All that stuff about the Kaydettes, the doctors, and the school."

"Doc, all in the world I want to do is help you. You say to me, do this, that, or the other, and I'll do it."

Victor's his old self, good-natured, reserved, with just the faintest risibility agleam in his muddy eyes.

"How you feeling, Doc?"

"I think I can make it."

But when I stand up, one knee jumps out.

"Whoa, look out now. Why don't you stay here till you are stronger? Ain't nobody going to bother you here."

"I got to get on up the hill."

"I was going up there too. I'll carry your bag—no wonder, Lord, what you got in here? Just hang on to Victor."

We are near the top. Victor wants me to hang on to him, but I don't feel like it.

"You never did like anybody to help you, did you, Doc?"

I stop, irritated with Victor and because the faintness is coming back. Flowers of darkness begin to bloom on the sidewalk.

We sit on the wooden steps of an abandoned Chinese grocery angled into the hill. Again I invite Victor to go back—I know he's along just to help me. He refuses.

"You've been away, haven't you, Victor?" I say to hide my irritation.

"I been back for two years, Doc."

"Where did you go?"

"I lived in Boston and worked in the shipyard. I made seven fifty an hour."

"Why did you come back?"

"You know something, Doc? You don't trust anybody, do you?"

I look at Victor with astonishment.

"What do you mean?"

"Nothing, Doc. I know that when you ask me a question like that, you really want to know."

I blink. "You're humbugging me, aren't you, Victor?"

"No, Doc. You know what I remember? You asked me why I

came back. I don't know. But I remember something. I remembered in Boston and when I did, you were in it. You remember the shrimp jubilees?"

"Yes."

"The word would come that the shrimp were running and everybody would go to the coast at night and as far as you could see up and down the coast there were gas lamps of people catching shrimp, setting up all night with their chirren running around and their picnics, you remember? And long before that me and you learned to throw a cast-net holding it in your teeth."

"Yes. Those were the days."

"Not for you, Doc."

I, who am seldom astonished, am astonished twice in a minute. "What do you mean?"

"You never did like—you didn't even like the jubilees. You were always . . . to yourself."

I shrug. "Are you telling me you came back because of the jubilees?"

"I don't know. I just wanted to come back. You know, I been a deacon at Starlight Baptist for twenty years."

"I know."

"Mr. Leroy, though, he used to love the jubilees."

"So you and Leroy Ledbetter like the jubilees and that's why you came back?"

"Not exactly. But I remember when everybody used to come to the jubilees. I mean everybody. You and Mr. Leroy came one night, you and your family on one side of me and he on the other."

"In the first place the shrimp don't run any more. In the second place, even if they did, Leroy Ledbetter wouldn't be next to you now."

"That's right, but you know something, Doc?"

"What?"

"You ought to trust people more. You ought to trust in the good Lord, pick yourself out a nice lady like Miss Doris, have chirren and a fireside bright and take up with your old friends and enjoy yourself in the summertime."

"For Christ's sake."

"What say, Doc?" Victor, who is slightly deaf, cups an ear.

"You kill me."

"How's that?"

"Here're you complaining about me and acting like you and Leroy Ledbetter are sharing the good life. Hell, Leroy Ledbetter, your fellow Baptist, wants no part of you. And one reason you're living in this pigpen is that Leroy is on the council and has turned down housing five times."

"That's the truth!" says Victor, laughing. "And it's pitiful."

"You think it's funny?"

My only firm conclusion after twenty years of psychiatry: nothing is crazier than life. Here is a Baptist deacon telling me, a Catholic, to relax and enjoy festivals. Here's a black Southerner making common cause—against me!—with a white Southerner who wouldn't give him the time of day.

That's nothing. Once I was commiserating with a patient, an old man, a Jewish refugee from the Nazis—he'd got out with his skin but lost his family to Auschwitz—so I said something conventional against the Germans. The old fellow bristled like a Prussian and put me down hard and spoke of the superiority of German universities, German science, German music, German philosophy. My God, do you suppose the German Jews would have gone along with Hitler if he had let them? Nothing is quite like it's cracked up to be. And nobody is crazier than people.

"It would be funny if it wasn't so pitiful," says Victor. He looks at me from the corner of his eye. Something has occurred to him. "Do you think you could speak to Mr. Leroy?"

"About what?"

"About— Never mind. It's too late."

"Victor, what in the hell is going on?"

He is shaking his head. "It's so pitiful. You would think people with that much in common would want to save what they have."

"Are you talking about you and Leroy?"

"Now everything's got to go and everybody loses."

I rise unsteadily. "Everybody?"

Victor jumps up, takes my arm. "Not you, Doc. All you got to do is move in with your mama. She'll do for you."

13

Victor takes me as far as the Little Napoleon. There I make a mistake, a small one with small consequences but a mistake nevertheless, which I'd ordinarily not have made. But it has been a strange day. Hanging on to Victor, I did not let him go until we were inside. I should have either dismissed him outside or held on to him longer. As it was, letting go Victor when the bar was within reach, I let go a second too early, so that Leroy Ledbetter, turning toward me in the same second, did not see me let go but saw Victor just beside me and so registered a violation. Not even that: a borderline violation because Victor was not even at the bar but still a step away. What with his white attendant's clothes and if he had been a step closer to me, it would have been clear that he was attending me in some capacity or other. A step or two in the other direction and he'd have been past the end of the bar and in the loading traffic where Negroes often pass carrying sacks of oysters, Cokes, and such. As it was, he seemed to be standing, if not at the bar, then one step too close and Leroy, turning, saw him in the split second before Victor started to leave, Victor in the act of backing up when Leroy said as his eyes went past him, said not even quite to Victor, "The window's there," nodding toward the service window opening into the alley; even then giving Victor the benefit of the doubt and not even allowing the possibility that Victor was coming to the bar for a drink, but the possibility only that he had come to buy his flat pint of muscatel and for some reason had not known or had forgotten about the service window. In the same second that he speaks, Leroy knows better, for in that second Victor steps back and turns toward me and I can see that Leroy sees that Victor is with me, sees it even before I can say, too late, "Thank you, Victor, for helping me up the hill," and signifies his error by a pass of his rag across the bar, a ritual glance past Victor at the storm cloud above the saloon door, a swinging back of his eyes past Victor and a saying in Victor's direction, "Looks like we going to get it yet," said almost to Victor but not quite because it had not been quite a violation so did not quite warrant a correction thereof. Victor nods, not quite acknowledging because total acknowledgment is not called for, withholding perhaps 20 percent acknowledgment (2 percent too much?). He leaves by the side door.

A near breach, an insignificant incident. A stranger observing the incident would not have been aware that anything had happened at all, much less that in the space of two seconds there had occurred a three-cornered transaction entailing an assignment of zones, a near infraction of zoning, a calling attention to the infraction, a triple simultaneous perception of the mistake, a correction thereof, and an acknowledgment of that—a minor breach with no consequences other than these: an artery beats for a second in Leroy's temple, there is a stiffness about Victor's back as he leaves, and there comes in my throat a metallic taste.

It is not even worth mentioning even though Victor withholds perhaps 2 percent of the acknowledgment that was due and his back is 2 percent stiffer than it might be.

"What's wrong with you, Tom?"

"I'm all right now. It was hot in the Hollow. I got dizzy."

He gives me my toddy. I peel an egg.

"Is that your lunch? No wonder you fainted. And you a doctor."

I look at the mirror. Behind the bar towers a mahogany piece, a miniature cathedral, an altarpiece, an intricate business of shelves for bottles, cupboards, stained-glass windows, and a huge mirror whose silvering is blighted with an advancing pox, clusters of vacuoles, expanding naughts. Most of the customers of the Little Napoleon have long since removed to the lounges of the suburbs, the nifty refrigerated windowless sealed-up Muzaked hideaways, leaving stranded here a small band of regulars and old-timers, some of whom have sat here in the same peaceable gloom open to the same twilight over the same swinging doors that swung their way straight through Prohibition and saw Kingfish Huey P. Long promise to make every man a king on the courthouse lawn across the street. Next door *Gone with the Wind* had its final run at the old Majestic Theater.

The vines are sprouting here in earnest. A huge wistaria with a tree-size trunk holds the Little Napoleon like a rock in a root. The building strains and creaks in its grip.

The storm is closer, the sun gone, and it is darker than dusk. The martins are skimming in from the swamp, sliding down the dark glassy sky like flecks of soot. Soon the bullbats will be thrumming.

Leroy Ledbetter stands by companionably. Like me he is seventh-generation Anglo-Saxon American, but unlike me he is Protestant, countrified, sweet-natured. He's the sort of fellow, don't you know, who if you run in a ditch or have a flat tire shows up to help you.

We were partners and owners of the old Paradise Bowling Lanes until the riot five years ago. In fact, the riot started when Leroy wouldn't let a bushy-haired Bantu couple from Tougaloo College have an alley. I wasn't there at the time. When Leroy told me about it later, an artery beat at his temple and the same metallic taste came in my throat. If I had been there. . . . But on the other hand, was I glad that I had not been there?

"Lucky I had my learner ready," Leroy told me.

"Your learner?" Then I saw his forearm flex and his big fist clench. "You mean you—"

"The only way to learn them is upside the head."

"You mean you—?" The taste in my mouth was like brass.

Where did the terror come from? Not from the violence; violence gives release from terror. Not from Leroy's wrongness, for if he were altogether wrong, an evil man, the matter would be simple and no cause for terror. No, it came from Leroy's goodness, that he is a decent, sweet-natured man who would help you if you needed help, go out of his way and bind up a stranger's wounds. No, the terror comes from the goodness and what lies beneath, some fault in the soul's terrain so deep that all is well on top, evil grins like good, but something shears and tears deep down and the very ground stirs beneath one's feet.

"Ellen was looking for you," Leroy is saying, leaning close but not too close, a good drinking friend. He's fixed himself a toddy. "She's got some patients."

"That's impossible. I don't see patients Saturday afternoon."

"You're a doctor, aren't you?"

Leroy, like Ellen, believes that right is right and in doing right. You're a doctor, so you do what a doctor is supposed to do. Doctors cure sick people.

The terror comes from the piteousness, from good gone wrong and not knowing it, from Southern sweetness and cruelty, God why do I stay here? In Louisiana people still stop and help strangers. Better to live in New York where life is simple, every man's your enemy, and you walk with your eyes straight ahead.

Leroy believes that doctors do wonders, transplant hearts, that's the way of it, right? Isn't that what doctors are supposed to do? He knows about my lapsometer, believes it will do what I say it will do—fathom the deep abscess in the soul of Western man—yes, that's what doctors do, so what? Then do it. Doctors see patients. Then see patients.

"Looks like it's going to freshen up," says Leroy. We drink toddies, eat eggs, and watch the martins come skimming home, sliding down the glassy sky.

In the dark mirror there is a dim hollow-eyed Spanish Christ. The pox is spreading on his face. Vacuoles are opening in his chest. It is the new Christ, the spotted Christ, the maculate Christ, the sinful Christ. The old Christ died for our sins and it didn't work, we were not reconciled. The new Christ shall reconcile man with his sins. The new Christ lies drunk in a ditch. Victor Charles and Leroy Ledbetter pass by and see him. "Victor, do you love me?" "Sho, Doc." "Leroy, do you love me?" "Cut it out, Tom, you know better than to ask that." "Then y'all help me." "O.K., Doc." They laugh and pick up the new Christ, making a fireman's carry, joining four hands. They love the new Christ and so they love each other.

"You all right now?" Leroy asks, watching me eat eggs and drink my toddy.

"I'm fine."

"You better get on over there."

"Yes."

I leave cheerfully, knowing full well that Ellen must be gone, that I shall be free to sit in my doorway, listen to *Don Giovanni*, sip Early Times, and watch the martins come home.

14

The back doors of the Little Napoleon and my father's old office let on to the ox-lot in the center of the block. It is getting dark. The thunderhead is upon us. A sour raindrop splashes on my nose. It smells of trees. The piles of brickbats scattered in the weeds are still warm. A dusty trumpet vine has taken the loading ramp of Sears and the fire escape of the old Majestic Theater. In the center of the ox-lot atop a fifteen-foot pole sits my father's only enduring creation: a brass-and-cedar martin hotel with rooms for a hundred couples. Overhead the martins wheel and utter their musical burr and rattle. They are summer residents. Already they are flocking with their young, preparing for their flight to the Amazon basin.

I sit at my desk and listen to *Don Giovanni* and watch the martins through the open door. From the lower desk drawer, where I also keep the free samples of Bayonne-rayon Skintone organs, I fetch a fresh bottle of Early Times.

My office is exactly as my father left it twenty years ago: three rooms, one behind the other like a shotgun cottage, but with a hall alongside, my office at the rear, treatment room in the middle, and at the front the waiting room furnished with the same sprung green wicker and even the same magazines: the *Ford Times, National Geographic*, the Knights of Columbus magazine, and the *S A E Record* (my father was an S A E).

The offices are dark. No sign of Ellen, my nurse, and no patient in the waiting room. A sigh of relief and a long happy evening.

No such luck.

A half hour of happiness, the fresh sour evening, the gathering storm, a warm toddy, and the singing god-like devilish music of *Don Giovanni* and—*bang*.

Bang up front, the door slams, and here comes Ellen clop-clopping down the hall.

It seems I've got not one but three patients. They went away all right, but they've come back. Ellen told them: don't worry, she'd find me.

I sigh and console myself: I should be able to polish them off in thirty minutes—and do right by them, Ellen! Leroy! Hippocrates!—and get back to my researches. I've the strongest feeling that the second breakthrough is imminent, that if I wait and be still and listen, it will come to me, the final refinement of my invention that will make it the perfect medicine. I've the strongest feeling that the solution is under my nose, one

LOVE IN THE RUINS

of those huge simple ideas that are so big you can't see them for being too close.

"Good heavens, Chief, where've you been? I've been looking for you all day."

"Why?"

"Why what?"

"Why have you been looking for me? Today is Saturday."

I lean back in my chair and watch Ellen sadly as she picks up the fifth of Early Times and puts it back in the drawer of organs. Then she rinses out my toddy glass, closes the back door, turns off Mozart, pops a chlorophyll tablet in my mouth, wets her thumb with her tongue and smooths my eyebrows with firm smoothings like a mother. My eyebrows feel wet and cool.

Ellen Oglethorpe is a beautiful but tyrannical Georgia Presbyterian. A ripe Georgia persimmon not a peach, she fairly pops the buttons of her nurse's uniform with her tart ripeness. She burgeons with marriageable Presbyterianism. It somehow happens that the strict observance of her religion gives her leave to be free with her own person. Her principles allow her a kind of chaste wantonness. She touches me, leans against me, puts spit on me. I shudder with horrible pleasure and pleasurable horror. Caught up by her strong female urgings, one to mother, one to marry, one to be a girl-child and lean against you, she muses and watches and is prodigal with herself—like an eleven-year-old who stands between your legs, eyes watching your eyes, elbows and knees engaging you in the lap, anywhere, each touch setting off in you horrid girl-child tingles. She doesn't know how close is close.

Now she stands in front of me even closer than usual, hands behind her. I have to look up. Her face is tilted back, the bones under her cheeks winged and wide as if the sculptor had spread out the alar ridges with two sure thumb thrusts. The short downy upper lip is lifted clear of the lower by its tendon. Her face, foreshortened, is simple and clear and scrubbed and peach-mottled, its beauty fortuitous like that of a Puritan woman leaning over her washtub and the blood going despite her to her face.

"Look, Ellen, it's Saturday. What are you doing here?"

"Not an ordinary Saturday."

"No?"

"It's your birthday."

And what she's hiding behind her is a present. She hands it to me. I feel a prickle of irritation. My birthday is but one more occasion for her tending to me, soliciting me, enlisting me. Yes, it is my birthday. I am forty-five. As I unwrap it, she comes round and leans on my chair arm and breathes on me.

It is the sort of present only a woman would buy. A gift set of Hell-for-Leather pre-shave and after-shave lotion. Through the chair arm comes the push of her heedless body weight. Her sweet breath comes through her parted lips. There is nothing to do but open a bottle. It smells like cloves.

"We've got customers, Chief."

Though she is an excellent nurse, I wish she would not call me Chief and herself my girl Friday.

Forty-five. It is strange how little one changes. The psychologists are all wrong about puberty. Puberty changes nothing. This morning I woke with exactly the same cosmic sexual-religious longing I woke with when I was ten years old. Nothing changes but accidentals: your toes rotate, showing more skin. Every molecule in your body has been replaced but you are exactly the same.

The scientists are wrong: man is not his own juices but a vortex, a traveling suck in his juices.

Ellen pats some Hell-for-Leather on me.

"How do you like it, Chief?"

"Very much," I say, eyes watering with cloves.

Ellen, though she is a strict churchgoer and a moral girl, does not believe in God. Rather does she believe in the Golden Rule and in doing right. On the whole she is embarrassed by the God business. But she does right. She doesn't need God. What does God have to do with being honest, hard-working, chaste, upright, unselfish, etcetera. I on the other hand believe in God, the Jews, Christ, the whole business. Yet I don't do right. I am a Renaissance pope, an immoral believer. Between the two of us we might have saved Christianity. Instead we lost it.

"Are you ready now, Chief?"

"Ready for what?"

"You've got two patients. Or rather three. But two are together."

"Who?"

"There's Mr. Ives and Mr. and Mrs. Tennis."

"Good God. Who is Mr. Ives?"

"You know. He's an old patient of yours."

"Wait a minute. Isn't he from Gerry Rehab over in Fedville?"

"Yes."

"Then what's he doing here?"

"He wanted to see you."

"He's the patient who's up for The Pit Monday, isn't he?"

"Yes."

"I still don't understand how he got here."

"He wanted to see you. I brought him."

"You?"

"Don't forget, Chief, I used to work over there."

She did. She even took care of me in the acute ward when I was strung out, bound by the wrists, yet in the end free and happy as a bird, by turns lustful and exalted, winging it like a martin, inducing scientific theories, remembering everything, quoting whole pages of Gerard Manley Hopkins:

> *Glory be to God for dappled things—*
> *For skies of couple-color as a brinded cow;*
> *For rose moles all in stipple upon trout that swim;*
> *Fresh-firecoal chestnut-falls;*

and inviting her into my bed, *her* of all people.

Nevertheless, when I left the hospital, she came with me and set up as my nurse. Toward me she feels strong Presbyterian mother-smoothings.

"Did Mr. Ives want to come or was it your idea?"

"My idea?"

"Did you think I needed a little briefing before appearing in The Pit?"

"Tch. What do you mean?"

"Are you afraid Dr. Brown is going to beat me?"

"He can't hold a candle to you as a doctor."

"But you were afraid?"

"Afraid? Oh yes, I'm afraid for Mr. Ives. Oh, Chief, do you think he'll be sent to the Happy Isles?"

"I don't know."

"Do they really throw the Switch there?"

"Yes."

"No!"

"You don't think they ought to?"

"Oh no, Chief!"

"Why not?" I ask her curiously.

"It's not right."

"I see."

"I think Mr. Ives is putting on."

"But if he were not?"

"Oh, Chief, why do you have anything to do with those people?"

"What people?"

"Those foul-mouthed students and that nasty Dr. Brown."

"It's all in good fun. End-of-year thing."

"You're much too fine to associate with them."

"Hm. Well, don't worry. I have other fish to fry."

"You mean you're not going to The Pit?"

I shrug. "What difference does it make? By the way, what's Brown's diagnosis of Mr. Ives?"

She reads: "Senile psychopathy and mutism."

"And his recommendation?"

"The Permanent Separation Center at Jekyll, Georgia. Doesn't that mean the Happy Isles?"

I nod.

"And the Euphoric On-Switch?"

"Yes. But you think the diagnosis is wrong?"

"Because you did."

"I did? Well, let's see him."

She wheels him in. Mr. Ives sits slumped in a folding chair, a little bald-headed monkey of a man, bright monkey eyes snapping at me. His scalp is a smooth cap of skin, heavily freckled, fitted over his low wrinkled brow. The backs of his hands are covered with liver spots and sun scabs. His eyes fairly hop with—what? rage or risibility? Is he angry or amused or just plain crazy? I leaf through his chart. He was born in Sherwood, Tennessee, worked for forty years as controller in a Hartford insurance company, lost his wife, retired to Louisiana, lived in the woods in a camper, dug up potsherds in a Choctaw burial mound, got sick, was transferred to a Tampa Senior Citizens' compound, where he misbehaved and was referred to Gerry Rehab here. I remember him from the old days. He used to call me for one complaint and another and we'd sit in his camper and play checkers and through the open door watch the wild turkeys come up and feed. He was lonely and liked to talk. Now he's mute.

I get up and open the back door. Ellen frowns.

"What's the trouble, Mr. Ives?"

He doesn't reply but he's already looking past me at the martins scudding past and turning upwind for a landing. Gusts of warm air sour with rain blow in the open doorway.

"Ecccc," says Mr. Ives.

The old man can't or won't speak but he lets me examine him. Physically he's in good order, chest clear, abdomen soft, blood pressure normal, eyegrounds nominal. His prostate is as round and elastic as a handball. Neurological signs normal.

I look at his chart. ". . . Did on August 5 last, expose himself and defecate on Flirtation Walk." Hm. He could still suffer from senile dementia.

I look at him. The little monkey eyes snap.

"Do you remember playing checkers out at the mound?"

The eyes snap.

"You never beat me, Mr. Ives." I never beat him.

No rise out of him. His eyes slide past me to the martins rolling and rattling around the hotel.

"He doesn't look senile to me," I tell Ellen. I take out my lapsometer and do a complete profile from cortex to coeliac plexus. Ellen jots down the readings as I call them out.

"No wonder he won't talk," I say, flipping back through his stack of wave patterns.

"Won't or can't?" Ellen asks me.

"Oh, he can. No organic lesion at all. Look at his cortical activity: humming away like a house afire. He's as sharp as you or I."

"Then why—?"

"And he's reading me right now, aren't you, Mr. Ives?"

"Ecccc," says Mr. Ives.

"You asked me why he won't talk," I tell her loudly. "He's too damn mad to talk. His red nucleus is red indeed. Look at that."

"You mean—"

"I mean he doesn't trust you or me or anybody."

"Who's he mad at?"

"Who are you mad at?" I ask Mr. Ives.

His eyes snap. I focus the lapsometer at his red nucleus.

"At me?" No change.

"At Communists?" No change.

"At Negroes?" No change.

"At Jews?" No change.

"At students?" No change.

"Hm. It's not ordinary Knothead anger," I tell Ellen.

"How do you know he understands you at all?" asks Ellen.

"Watch this." I aim in at the medio-temporal region, near Brodmann 28, the locus of concrete memory. "Do you remember our playing checkers in your camper ten years ago on summer evenings like this?"

The needle swings. The eyes snap, but merrily now.

"Chief!" cries Ellen. "You've done it!"

"Done what?"

"You've proved your point!"

"I haven't proved anything. He still won't talk or can't, won't walk or can't. All I've done is make a needle move."

"But, Chief—! You're a hundred years ahead of EEG."

"I can't prove it. I can't treat him. This thing is purely diagnostic and I can't even prove that." Mr. Ives and I watch the last of the martins come home. "I feel like a one-eyed man in the valley of the blind."

"You'll prove it, Chief," says Ellen confidently. She tells me a story about a famous Presbyterian (she said) named Robert the Bruce who sat discouraged in a cave and watched a spider try seven times to span the cave with its web before it succeeded. "Remember Robert the Bruce!"

"O.K. Who's the next patient?"

"Mr. and Mrs. Ted Tennis."

"Are you going to take Mr. Ives back to the hospital?"

"No. They'll send for him."

"Very well. Goodbye, Mr. Ives. Don't worry. You're going to be all right."

He takes my hand with his old wiry grip. I can't understand why he won't talk. His prefrontal gyrus is as normal as mine.

Ted 'n Tanya are next. They must have come directly from Love. It is a bit of a surprise that they've come here, since his former complaint of impotence had been pretty well cleared up by my prescription of an occasional tramp through the swamp, so successfully in fact that only today I've learned that Ted 'n Tanya have become star performers in Love.

They come in together and sit opposite me across the desk. Ellen closes the door and turns on the lights and leaves discreetly. Hm. Have they come to gloat, to tell me of the superiority of Love Clinic to the swamp? But no. They look glum.

But Ted is more than ever the alert young crop-headed narrow-necked Oppenheimer. Tanya is an angular brunette who has smoldering violet eyes, one of which is cocked, and wears a ringlet of hair at each temple like a gypsy. They love each other, do Ted 'n Tanya, and, though heathen, are irrevocably monogamous and faithful.

That much I know. Ted brings me up to date. The swamp treatment of impotence did indeed work for a while but wore off after a few months, as I had told Ted it might. Whereupon they applied for treatment at Love, where they were put in a Skinner box and conditioned so successfully that they became one of the first volunteer couples in the new program of "multiple-subject interaction." A breakthrough. Here too, encouraged by Stryker, Dr. Helga Heine, and Father Kev Kevin, they succeeded admirably.

"I understand that. The only thing that puzzles me is why you're here at all." Making sure Ellen is up front, I open the drawer of organs and recover my Early Times. Ted 'n Tanya don't mind my drinking.

"I know," says Ted glumly.

"Weren't you over at Love today?" I ask them, pouring a little toddy.

"Yes," whispers Tanya, one lovely violet eye fixed on me, the other drifting out a bit as if it were keeping track of my second self, my pneuma.

"Well?" They're sitting side by side on a bench, like children in the principal's office. "How did it go today in Love?"

Ted 'n Tanya look at each other. "It didn't," says Ted.

"It hasn't for weeks," whispers Tanya.

"Hm. I expect the effect of the conditioning is wearing off too, though to tell you the truth I've always suspected that the good results came more from the sympathetic third party, the observer, rather than—"

"Exactly!" cries Ted.

Puzzled, I wait.

Again Ted 'n Tanya exchange glances. "Shall we tell him, Tanya?" She nods.

"Tell me what?"

Ted leans forward, big Oppenheimer head bobbing on its slender neck. "That we never did succeed at home."

"You mean—"

"I mean even at the peak of our performances at Love, we were never able to achieve orgasm at home, except after floundering around the swamp, but even that wore off."

"Pity. Would you care for a drink?"

"No thanks, Tom."

We fall silent. The storm is closer. Thunder rumbles.

I sigh and open the drawer. "Well, I suppose you're here for a Bayonne-rayon member."

But Ted is shaking his head. "That's not the idea, Tom."

"You don't want a member?"

"No."

"Then what can I do for you?" I am genuinely puzzled.

Ted leans forward. "Tom, you were right in thinking that it was the presence of the sympathetic observer that was crucial."

"Yes?"

"The trouble with the observers in Love Clinic is precisely that, that they are too clinical."

"Yes?"

"We thought perhaps if we could enlist the services of an observer-therapist team who were more sympathetic and in surroundings less clinical."

LOVE IN THE RUINS

"Hm."

"When we put the two ingredients together, friend plus professional, naturally our thoughts turned in this direction."

"What direction?"

"To you and Miss Oglethorpe."

"You want me and Miss Oglethorpe . . ."

"We thought we could use your waiting room with that wonderful campy old couch, and you and Miss Oglethorpe could stay in the examining room with the door cracked and spy a bit, to add piquancy to the observer factor."

"Miss Oglethorpe is a Presbyterian."

"So what? Don't Presbyterian nurses treat patients?"

"I expect she's gone home."

"No, she said she'd wait."

I spill my drink. "You mean you asked her?"

"She said anything you wanted to do was all right with her." Ted turns to Tanya. "Do you know what that couch reminds me of?"

"I know, I know."

"The porch at the old dorm in Lansing."

"I know, I know," says Tanya, looking at Ted, but her out eye strays toward me.

"I'm feeling like a kid, wow," says Ted, rising. "I'll go get Miss Oglethorpe."

"Wait," I say.

"Yes?"

"Why Miss Oglethorpe? Why the two of us? Why not me?"

Ted frowns impatiently. "Studies in Palo Alto have shown that when observers are of both sexes, successful reconditioning increases by sixty-two percent."

"Yes. Hm. But I fear today is out of the question. I'm tied up." The prospect of watching Ted 'n Tanya make love is lugubrious enough, but it is the enlisting of Ellen Oglethorpe that makes me nervous. In fact, I've broken out in a cold sweat.

"You couldn't give us half an hour, Tom?" asks Tanya, patting a gypsy ringlet.

"I'm afraid not."

"What about Wednesday?" asks Ted.

"Yes!" I say, seizing at the straw. By Wednesday anything

could happen. The world could end. "Check with Ellen for a new appointment."

"Dear?" Ted stretches out both hands to Tanya, lifts her up. Ted is smiling. Two spots of color glow in Tanya's cheeks. They exit, arms about each other like Rudolfo and Mimi.

15

I sit in the dark wondering where Ellen is. The storm breaks at last. My lapsometer gleams in the lightning flashes. If only . . . If only my lapsometer could treat as well as diagnose, I wouldn't be caught up in these farces.

The back door is open. The tape rolls. Don Giovanni begins his descent into hell. A bolt of lightning strikes a transformer with a great crack. Sparks fly. The ox-lot is filled with a rinsing blue-white light. Trees jump backward. The lights go out.

Ellen comes in to tell me she is leaving and that someone else wants to see me.

"I'm not seeing any more patients."

"I think he's a detail man. He said he wouldn't keep you long."

"But—"

"Don't forget, Chief, your mother expects you tomorrow."

"What? Wait—"

But she's gone. In the lightning flashes a man seems to come forward by jumps. He carries an outsize attaché case like a drug salesman.

"Look, I see detail men on weekdays."

But he's not a detail man.

"Art Immelmann is the name," he says, sticking his hand across the desk. "Funding is my game."

"Very good, Art, but—" I notice gloomily that he's sat down. Did he say Immerman, or Immelmann like the German ace and inventor of the Immelmann turn?

"It's a new concept in funding, Doctor." Art is shouting over the storm as he takes papers out of his attaché case. He frowns at the open door but I don't feel like closing it.

I try to turn on the lights to see him better, but the current is off. The lightning flashes, however, are almost continuous.

He's an odd-looking fellow, curiously old-fashioned. Indeed, with his old-style flat-top haircut, white shirt with short sleeves, which even have vestigial cuff buttons, and neat dark trousers, he looks like a small-town businessman in the old Auto Age, one of those wiry old-young fifty-year-olds, perhaps a Southern Bell manager, who used to go to Howard Johnson's every Tuesday for Rotary luncheon. His face is both youthful and lined. The flat-top makes a tangent with the crown of his skull, giving the effect of a tonsure. Is it an early bald spot or a too-close flat-top?

When he leans across the desk to shake hands, air pushes ahead of him bearing to my nostrils a heavy complex odor, the intricate canceled smell of sweat neutralized by a strong deodorant.

"A lovely little lady, Doc," says the stranger, nodding at the closed door.

"Who? What's that?" I say sharply, frowning with irritation. Did he wink at me or is it the effect of the lightning?

"Very high-principled and efficient, yet most attractive. Most. I'd like to beat you out of her."

"How—! What in hell do you mean?" At a loss for words—I almost said, How dare you?—I jump up from the chair.

"No offense! Take it easy, Doc! Ha ha, made you come up for air, didn't I?"

"What do you want?"

"I only meant that I admire your nurse and wish I had someone as good to assist me in my own researches. What is the saying: All is fair in love and war and hiring cooks?"

"Are you selling something?" My hair prickles with an odd, almost pleasurable dislike.

"Not selling today, Doc. We're giving it away." With that, Art hands over what appear to be application forms. "Don't worry!" He laughs heartily. "They're already filled in."

I haven't been listening carefully. The papers seem to jump back and forth in the lightning. "What are these for?" (Why don't I throw him out?)

"For the money you need."

"Money? Who are you representing, Art?"

"I'm one of those liaison fellows from Washington."

"Liaison? Between whom?"

"Between the public and private sectors."

"What does that mean?"

"Ha ha, you might well ask." His young-old face, I notice, goes instantly serious between laughs. "In this case it is between the National Institute of Mental Health in the public sector and the Ford, Carnegie, and Rockefeller foundations in the private sector."

"Good."

"It does sound impressive, doesn't it?"

"I didn't say that."

"Actually, I'm a glorified errand boy."

"Is that so," I say gloomily, trying to read my watch.

"We of N.I.M.H. and"—for a moment his words are lost in a clap of thunder—"you may have come up with the most important integrative technique of our time."

"What's that?" I say. The wind shifts and a fine mist blows in the doorway. There is a smell of wet warm brick.

"You've done it, Dr. More!"

"Done what?"

"You've come up with a technique that maximizes and unites hardware and software capabilities."

"How's that?" I ask inattentively. What to make of this fellow who talks like a bureaucrat but looks—and smells—like a hard-working detail man? "What technique are you talking about?"

"The More Qualitative-Quantitative Ontological Lapsometer," says Art Immelmann, laughing. "What a mouthful. Everybody at the office calls it the MOQUOL. Sounds like a hole in the ground, doesn't it?"

I set down my toddy. My hand, feeling light and tremulous, levitates. I put it in my pocket.

"Surprised, eh, Doc?"

After a moment I decide to fix a drink. Though my hand feels normal, I decide to hold the glass in both hands.

"What I don't understand is how you knew about it."

"Think about it a moment, Doc, and you'll see."

I see in the next lightning flash. Either the Director has approved my article, or *Brain* has accepted it, or both, and either or both have leaked the news to N.I.M.H.

"You've won, Doctor," says Art gravely. Again the hand comes across the desk. We shake hands. Again comes the intricate canceled sweat-and-deodorant smell.

I've won.

Now I know how Einstein felt when the English astronomers flashed the news from Venezuela that sure enough, Arcturus's light had taken a little bend as it swept past the sun.

Victory.

I sit back and listen to the steady rain and the peepers tuning up in the ox-lot. What to do now? I recall my uncle's advice: guard against the sadness of hubris. How to do that? By going to the Little Napoleon and having a drink with Leroy Ledbetter.

"We're interested in funding truly innovative techniques. Yours is truly innovative."

"Yes."

"You've got your own built-in logistical factor. The results, moreover, are incremental."

"Yes." What in hell is he talking about? It doesn't matter. I've won.

"You are aware of the national implications?"

"Yes, I am."

"For the first time the behavioral sciences have a tool for dealing with the heretofore immeasurable and intangible stresses that are rending the national fabric."

"Yes."

"Dr. More." Again Art stands up, not to shake hands again I hope, no, but again there is the heavy mollified protein smell.

"Yes?"

"We're prepared to fund an interdisciplinary task force and implement a crash program that will put a MOQUOL in the hands of every physician and social scientist in the U.S. within one year's time."

"You are?" Why don't I feel excited? My eyes don't blink.

"As you know better than I, your MOQUOL has a multilevel capacity. It is operative at behavioral, political, and philosophical levels. I would even go so far as to say this, Doc—" Art pauses to hawk phlegm and adjust his crotch with an expert complicated pat.

"What's that, Art?"

"If the old U. S. of A. doesn't go down the drain in the next year, it will be thanks to your MOQUOL."

"Well, I wouldn't say that, but—"

In the last flash of lightning, a legal-size blue-jacketed document appears under my nose and a pen is pointed at my breastbone.

"What's this, Art?"

"A detail. A bureaucratic first step, ha ha." Art laughs his instant laugh and goes as sober as a mortician.

"Hey, this is a transfer of patent rights!"

"Boilerplate, Doc. Standard procedure for any contract with the private sector. And look at your return!" Expertly he flips pages. "Seventy-five percent!"

"Yeah, but I mean, goddamn, Art—!" I begin, but Art Immelmann turns white and falls back a step.

"Pardon. I only meant to say that the money doesn't interest me." Art must be a Holy Name man or a hard-shell Baptist.

"I told them you'd say that. But let's don't worry about it. The important thing is to get the MOQUOL distributed in time."

"Well, I've already got a hundred production models."

"*Where?*" Art nearly comes across the desk.

I sit back in surprise. "In a safe place. Don't worry."

"You don't want to leave something like MOQUOL lying around, Doc."

"I know." I tell him of my plans, my appointment with the Director Monday, the submission of my article to *Brain*. "I just don't see the necessity of signing over my patent rights."

"You know, you could be disappointed, Doc," says Art thoughtfully but beginning, I see with relief, to put the application forms back in his case.

"Well, I'm hopeful."

"You know how people resist a really radical innovation."

"Yes, but this thing works, Art."

"I know. Tell you what, Doc," says Art cheerfully, snapping up his attaché case. "I'll drop in next week."

"Can't the funding be arranged without signing over control of the MOQUOL?"

"No doubt. But I'll be seeing you in a day or two. Just in case."

"In case of what?"

"In case you hit a snag. You never know about people, Doc," says Art mysteriously.

"Very true," I say, anxious only to get rid of him and get over to the Little Napoleon, a snug and friendly haven in any storm.

Some seconds pass before I realize that Art left by the back door, striking out across the dark ox-lot. I shrug. Perhaps he's taking the short cut to the old Southern Hotel, where a few drummers and detail men still put up.

But how would he know about the short cut?

JULY SECOND

My Mother's House

SUNDAYS I eat breakfast with my mother. But today is special. Yesterday was my birthday. Today is Property Rights Sunday. My mother, who is president of the altar society and also of the Business & Professional Women, is leading an ecumenical delegation to Saint Pius XII Church (A.C.C.). (A.C.C. = American Catholic Church.)

The Summer Moonlight Tour of the Champs is in full swing. The fish fry will be held this afternoon. Later this morning the Kaydettes corps of Christian baton-twirlers will give a performance. Tuesday they leave for the nationals at Oxford, Mississippi.

It seems I promised to go to church with Mother—because it is my birthday, because it is Property Rights Sunday, and because she wants me to "come back to the Church."

We are sitting on a terrace overlooking the golf links where we are served a hearty breakfast by Eukie, Mother's little black houseboy. His white jacket is too dazzling to be looked at. The pile of steaming grits is also white and glittering in the morning sunlight. I've already had my warm Tang plus duck eggs plus vodka, and my pulse races along at a merry clip. I am both alert and shaky.

Everything is lovely and peaceful here. Towhees whistle in the azaleas. Golfers hum up and down the fairways in their quaint surrey-like carts. Householders mow their lawns, bestriding tiny burro-size tractors. Why am I so jumpy?

On the other hand, the vines are encroaching. Mother's yard is noticeably smaller.

My chair is placed so that I am facing Tara next door, Dusty Rhoades's plantation house, which he purchased from Vince Marsaglia, a gangster from New Orleans who runs Louisiana.

Mother, I see, has all sorts of schemes afoot for me. She is saying:

"I can just see you and Lola walking up and down by moonlight while from the inside come the strains of lovely old-world music."

"Lola Rhoades?"

"Ho ho, you can't fool your mother! I know what's going on between you two."

"You do? What is going on?"

"I couldn't be more pleased. She's wild about you, Tom! What a wonderful girl!"

I am scratching my head: this is odd. Until now Mother hasn't had much use for Lola, considering her Texas-raw and Texas-horsy. Lola's cello-straddling always struck Mother as somehow unladylike. She's been talking to Dusty, I reckon.

"You're a Cancer and she's a Taurus. It couldn't be better!"

"That may be, Mother, but the fact is I don't really—"

"Beware of Aries and Libra."

"O.K., Mother, but—"

"Isn't that little nurse of yours an Aries?"

"Who? Ellen? Good Lord, I have no idea, Mother. In any case, Ellen and I have no—"

"And isn't that little Left snippet of yours a Libra?"

"Who? Moira? My Lord, Mother, how in the world do you know? And in any case why do you say 'of mine'?"

"She's not for you, son."

"Are you speaking of marriage? Moira has no intention of marrying me."

"Then all the more reason for breaking it off. But I'm not really worried about that. Here's what's been on my mind."

"Yes?"

"Being a Cancer means that you are deeply sensitive and that family strife tends to cause you much suffering. God knows this is true in your case."

"That it is."

"Ginger Rogers and Red Skelton were Cancers."

"I didn't know that."

"You are also under Moon rule, which means that you are emotionally unstable and tend to form will-o'-the-wisp relationships with more than one sweetheart.'

"That's true."

"What I wanted to tell you is that in this, the first week of July, I believe that certain things are going to become clear to you and that you will make some important decisions, but—"

"I believe that too."

"But—! Do not make any real estate transfers until later in the month. I've told Dusty and Lola the same thing."

"Real estate transfers," I say, scratching my head.

"I've told Dusty and Lola and I'm telling you: whatever plans you all might have, don't sell anything now or buy anything now." She nods meaningfully at Tara.

"Sell anything? Mother, Lola and I have no plans. What did Dusty tell you?"

"Ho ho *ho*. I know a thing or two. And I know that Lola is a wonderful girl."

It is true. Lola, a big beautiful cellist, is a wonderful girl. Last Christmas Eve we lay in one another's arms in the grassy bunker of number 18 and watched the summer constellations wheel in their courses—I, smashed out of my mind with love, with scientific triumph, and brain hives, she full of love and music, hissing cello tunes in my ear. A brave girl, she saved my life at the expense of her reputation, went to fetch her father as I lay dying of love and hives in the bunker.

What Mother doesn't understand is that we loved each other for one night and that was the end of it. One night I sang between her knees like an antique cello while she watched the wheeling constellations. A perfect encounter, but it is not to be thought that we could repeat it.

And yet—here's the wonder of love—even as I bend shivering over the glittering mound of grits, love revives! Love is always possible, even here in the ashes of my forty-five-year-old life. Something stirs, a phoenix. Bad as things are, perhaps just because they are so bad, why not go to the fish fry this afternoon, see Lola again, drink a gin fizz or two?

"Doris was not for you, Tom," Mother is saying. "God knows she was a wonderful person, but she was never for you. A Capricorn, your exact opposite. I told you!"

No, she didn't. The truth is she was all for Doris at the beginning, embracing her as a Virginia aristocrat, which she was not, being no more than a good-looking Shenandoah Valley girl.

"Doris was not for you, Tom!" says Mother, swishing her leg angrily.

"Evidently she wasn't."

Look at Mother! Look at the difference between us! I, a
shaky decrepit forty-five, she in her sixties as pert as a sparrow and on good terms with the world. She sits bolt upright,
handsome legs crossed, nylon swishing against nylon, one hand
pressed deep into her waist to emphasize her good figure. This
morning she's been up for hours, rooting around in her garden,
ordering the help around, calling prospects—she's a "realtor,"
makes forty thousand a year, is more successful now than my
father in his prime.

She sparkles with good health and is at one with herself. I?
I am six feet ahead of myself, ricocheting between terror and
elation. My toes are rotating. The out-of-doors doesn't suit
me. I feel like Henry Miller, seedy and stove up, sitting in a
park in Jacksonville, Florida. Her plate is clean. She eats like a
longshoreman, yet is trim as can be, has a good skin and a clear
eye. What a bowel she has! Unfortunately I have my father's
bowel, which is subject to conservative rages and liberal terror.

"Tom," says Mother, lowering her voice and rolling her eyes.
"I feel that something is about to happen. *They* are going to
do something."

"I have the same feeling," I say, watching her curiously. "But
what's your reason for thinking so?" Whenever Mother lowers
her voice and rolls her eyes, it means she's going to talk about
them, Negroes.

"I've seen them," Mother whispers, "riding around,
looking."

"Who, the Bantus or the locals?"

"Both. But that's not the main thing."

"What's the main thing?"

"Last Sunday I saw a black cloud with something coiling in
it hovering over the Infant Jesus of Prague."

"You took that to be a sign something is going to happen
here soon?"

"Haven't I always been proved right in the past?"

"What was the 'something coiling'?"

"Entrails. Which is a sign of the Bantus. They divine and
foretell by examining entrails. You think I'm ridiculous."

"I think you're right about something happening."

Mother has a reputation hereabouts as a seer and prophetess.
What she is is a Catholic gnostic. Though she believes in God,

she also relies on her crystal ball—she actually has a crystal ball, which she looks into—and her gift for seeing signs and divining hidden meanings. But she is quite brisk about it, puts on no psychic airs, has no truck with séances and such. Her clairvoyant powers have rather to do with business and politics. She will not close a deal with a Leo in May. Most of her visions and dreams are about plots of the Lefts against the Knotheads. She predicted four out of the last five assassinations.

"Don't ask me how it happens!" she chides her admirers. "All I know is it does. Why, I would no more sell a Capricorn to a Cancer than fly to the moon. Because I know what happens when I do. I not only lose the sale but also the deposit." She is referring to the astrology of the vendor and vendee. "And I also know, without knowing how it happens, that when I'm saying the third decade of the rosary on the third day of a novena and when I come to the third bead, I'm going to see something. Don't ask me why!" she cries, laughing at herself.

When she says see, she means it. Last year she saw a vision of a dragon fighting a bear over the statue of the Infant Jesus of Prague, to be specific: over the little globe the Infant Jesus held. War between Russia and China broke out the next week.

Her fame is spreading. "Marva, it's a gift from God," her friends tell her. "Why don't you share it with the world?" But she laughs it off.

She doesn't even interpret her visions, leaving that to others. But the meanings are clear to her friends and they usually have political overtones, auguring ill for conservatives and good for liberals. On the eve of the last national election, for example, she came to the third bead of the third decade of her rosary and saw Old Glory, the Stars and Stripes, slowly sinking into the waters of the Great Salt Lake. Her friends understood. The new President is an integrationist Mormon from Salt Lake City.

It is only after breakfast that Mother gets around to telling me that I received a telephone call earlier. She makes a face. She disapproves of the caller.

"He said for you to come see him. He said it was urgent. I deliver the message without comment."

"Who, Mother?"

"Your friend, the Roman priest."

"Roman?"

"*Father* Smith," she says, accenting *Father* sarcastically.

"What did he want?"

"He wouldn't tell me. Only that you were to come to see him."

"Where?"

"You'd never imagine."

"Well?"

"He said he'd be down in the Slave Quarters. Now wouldn't you know it?"

"Know what?"

"That that's where he'd end up."

"What do you mean?"

"You know," says my mother, pushing her hand deep into her waist and arching her back. "I think he's in with them."

"Who?" I ask. "You mean the guerrillas?"

"So I told him in my sweetest voice that you were coming over here and going to church with me. I just dared him to say there was anything wrong with our mass."

"You used to like him." She did. He was a favorite with the ladies. He had a courtly manner, used to look like Ricardo Montalban playing a lithe priest and saying things like "Do not worry about the bell, my children. God will provide the bell, you will see," etcetera. "What have you got against him now?" I ask Mother.

"He who is not with you is against you," says Mother darkly. Her eyes glitter. She's a bad enemy.

"Yes. Well—hm." I shiver in the sunlight. I notice that the vines are encroaching. A tendril has twined about Mother's antique wrought-iron Singer table.

Before we go to church, Dr. Dusty Rhoades hops the hedge. Eukie pours him a cup of coffee.

Dusty and Mother hit it off very well, I notice. Dusty winks at me and feels my bones. Then he's got nothing against me. They both kid me.

"Marva," says Dusty to Mother, but at the same time exploring my shoulder with his big freckled hand. "Do you think Tom's going to invite us white trash up to the big house?" Now he's gazing at Tara with his fond filmed-over eyes.

"Eh? What's that?" I ask.

"He better, the scamp!" cries Mother.

"What big house?" I ask them. They both laugh merrily. I find that I am grinning too.

But Dusty goes suddenly serious. He shakes his big lion head slowly.

"You know I'm leaving for Texas in a week. And I feel bad about leaving Lola over there alone. Do you know we haven't had a servant for a week? You don't know how lucky you are to have your little nigger."

Mother rolls her eyes and raises her finger to her lips. "Eukie is a treasure."

Eukie is worthless, but that is not what bothers me.

"Guess who is going to look after my little Lola when I leave," says Dusty past me. He and Mother are exchanging all manner of glances over my head.

"I wish the child would move in with me." Again a regular semaphore of eye messages.

"She's not about to leave Tara," muses Dusty. "She says her roots are there."

"You should have seen her over there this morning, feeding her horses, planting greens—"

"Where is Lola now?" I ask them.

"You'll see her this afternoon at the fish fry, it's all settled," says Mother. "But you should have seen her, standing there in that old garden, her hands potty black, her face glowing. She never looked prettier or more determined."

"I still don't like to leave her there alone," says Dusty, wagging his head.

"Do you remember what Scarlett said about the land?" asks Mother. "Or was it in *The Good Earth*?"

"Yes," says Dusty, popping his great jaw muscles.

Mother squeezes my hand. "We're making a foursome this evening, Tommy," she says in a strange soft voice, a rushing low-pitched thrilling voice, the sort women use on solemn occasions, funerals and weddings. "You and I and Dusty and Lola."

Hm. Is something cooking between Mother and Dusty? And are they cooking up something between me and Lola? Warning signals flash in my brain. Look out! They're making a match. And yet. And yet, despite all, love kindles. Lola is a lovely girl after all. And a brave girl. And what lovely sounds the Guarnerius makes clasped between her lovely knees. There are worse lives, after all, than sitting on the gallery of Tara and . . . I look at Tara, a preposterous fake house on a fake hill: even the hill is fake, dredged up from the swamp by the state of Louisiana for Vince Marsaglia. The very preposterousness of life in Tara with Lola inflames me with love. —Yes, sitting on the gallery sipping Early Times while Lola plants greens or plays *Don Quixote* or we hold hands, her cello-callused fingers whispering in my palm. Lovely Lola.

The question is: how can I bear not to marry Lola? Why did God make woman so beautiful and man with such a loving heart?

"Time for mass," says Mother, rising briskly. "Won't you come with us, Dusty?"

But Dusty, who is a Baptist, makes his excuses, socks himself in his joyful-eccentric style, and hops the hedge.

2

We walk over to Saint Pius XII's. Pius XII, the last Pope recognized by the American Catholic Church, was canonized by the Sacred College of Cicero, Illinois. The present "Pope" of the A.C.C., a native of Anaheim and Bishop of San Diego, took the name Pius XIII.

Property Rights Sunday is a major feast day in the A.C.C. A blue banner beside the crucifix shows Christ holding the American home, which has a picket fence, in his two hands.

Mother sits up front with the other Business & Professional Women. I skulk at the rear with the ushers, one foot in church, one foot in the vestibule. It is possible to leave at any time, since I told Mother I had to keep my appointment and might not see her after church.

I can leave any time I please, but it is deliciously cool in here. The superb air-conditioning always puts me in mind of the words of the old Latin mass (to which the A.C.C. has returned as a patriotic gesture): "Grant us we beseech Thee a *locum refrigerii.* . . ."

Monsignor Schleifkopf reads the Gospel from Matthew that relates how Joseph of Arimathea, a rich man, believed in Christ and gave him his tomb. He preaches on the resurrection of Lazarus, who was also well off.

"Dearly Beloved: we are reminded by the best commentators that Lazarus was not a poor man, that he lived comfortably with sisters in a home that he owned. Our Lord himself, remember, was not a social reformer, said nothing about freeing the slaves, nor are we obliged to."

After the sermon Monsignor Schleifkopf announced triumphantly that this week the congregation had paid off the debt on the new church, the air-conditioning, the electronic carillon that can be heard for five miles, and the new parochial school.

Moon Mullins, who is an usher, greets me in the vestibule. He stands around in true usher style, hawking phlegm and swinging his fist into his hand.

Monsignor Schleifkopf prays for victory over North Ecuador and for the welfare of our brothers in Christ and fellow property owners throughout Latin America and for the success of the Moonlight Tour of the Champs in the name of "the greatest pro of them all."

I begin to think impure thoughts. My heart, which was thumping for no good reason, begins to thump for love of Lola Rhoades and at the prospect of seeing her this very afternoon and later inviting her out into the gloaming.

When the congregation rises for the creed, I see my chance and slip out.

Christ have mercy on me. Sir Thomas More, pray for me. God bless Moon Mullins, a good fellow, a better man than I. Lord have mercy on your poor church.

Goodbye, Pius XII. Hello, Lola baby, big lovely cellist. Let us go out into the gloaming and lie in one another's arms and watch the constellations wheel in their courses.

3

Father Rinaldo Smith is sitting on the tin-roofed porch of the tiny slave-quarter chapel. In his rolled-up shirt sleeves he looks more than ever like Ricardo Montalban. He is waiting, I suppose, for his tiny flock. The Roman Catholics are a remnant of a remnant.

We sit on the steps.

"You know what we need, Tom?" he asks me with a sigh.

"What's that, Father?"

"A bell."

"Right, Father. And I have an idea where I might lay my hands on one."

"Splendid," says Father Smith, kicking a cottonmouth off the steps.

Though Father Smith is a good priest, a chaste and humble man who for twenty-five years had baptized the newborn into a new life, shriven sinners, married lovers, anointed the sick, buried the dead—he has had his troubles.

Once he turned up in the bed next to mine in the acute wing. It seemed he had behaved oddly at the ten o'clock mass and created consternation among the faithful. This happened before the schism, when hundreds of the faithful packed old Saint Michael's. When he mounted the pulpit to make the announcements and deliver his sermon, he had instead—fallen silent. The silence lasted perhaps thirty seconds. Thirty seconds is a very long silence. Nothing is more uncomfortable than silence when speech is expected. People began to cough and shift around in the pews. There was a kind of foreboding. Silence prolonged can induce terror. "Excuse me," he said at last, "but the channels are jammed and the word is not getting through." When he absently blew on and thumped the microphone, as priests do, the faithful thought he was talking about the loudspeaker and breathed a sigh of relief. But Father Smith did not continue the mass. Instead he walked to the rectory in his chasuble, sat down in the Monsignor's chair in a gray funk and, according to the housekeeper, began to mutter something about "the news being jammed"—whereupon the housekeeper, thinking he meant the TV, turned it on (strange: no matter what one says, no matter how monstrous, garbled, unfittable, whoever hears it will somehow make it fit). Monsignor Schleifkopf later said to Father Kev Kevin, the other curate, "Beware of priests who don't play golf or enjoy a friendly card game or listen to *The Lawrence Welk Show*—sooner or later they'll turn their collar around and wear a necktie." This was before Father Kev Kevin married Sister Magdalene and took charge of the vaginal computer in Love.

So there was Father Rinaldo Smith in the next bed, stiff as a board, hands cloven to his side, eyes looking neither right nor left.

"What seems to be the trouble, Father?" asked Max, pens and flashlight and reflex hammer glittering like diamonds in his vest pocket.

"They're jamming the air waves," says Father Smith, looking straight ahead.

"Causing a breakdown in communication, eh, Father?" says Max immediately. He is quick to identify with the patient.

"They've put a gremlin in the circuit," says Father Smith.

"Ah, you mean a kind of spirit or gremlin is causing the breakdown in communication?"

"No no, Max!" I call out from the next bed. "That's not what he means." What Max doesn't understand is that Father Smith is one of those priests, and there are a good many, who like to fool with ham radios, talk with their fellow hams, and so fall into the rather peculiar and dispirited jargon hams use. "When he said there was a gremlin in the circuit, he meant only that there is something wrong, not that there is a, um, spirit or gremlin causing it." Priests have a weakness for ham radio and seismology. Leading solitary lives and stranded in places like Pierre, South Dakota, or the Bronx or Waycross, Georgia, they hearken to other solitaries around the world or else bend an ear to the earth itself.

"Yes, they're jamming," says Father Smith.

When I spoke, Max and the other doctors looked at me disapprovingly. They had finished with me, passed my bed. I am like a dancing partner who's been cut in on and doesn't go away.

"They?" asks Max. "Who are they?"

"They've won and we've lost," says Father Smith.

"Who are they, Father?"

"The principalities and powers."

"Principalities and powers, hm," says Max, cocking his head attentively. Light glances from the planes of his temple. "You are speaking of two of the hierarchies of devils, are you not?"

The eyes of the psychiatrists and behaviorists sparkle with sympathetic interest.

"Yes," says Father Smith. "Their tactic has prevailed."

"You are speaking of devils now, Father?" asks Max.

"That is correct."

"Now what tactic, as you call it, has prevailed?"

"Death."

"Death?"

"Yes. Death is winning, life is losing."

"Ah, you mean the wars and the crime and violence and so on?"

"Not only that. I mean the living too."

"The living? Do you mean the living are dead?"

"Yes."

"How can that be, Father? How can the living be dead?"

"I mean their souls, of course."

"You mean their souls are dead," says Max with the liveliest sympathy.

"Yes," says Father Smith tonelessly. "I am surrounded by the corpses of souls. We live in a city of the dead."

"Are the devils here too, Father?" asks Max.

"Yes. But you fellows are safer than most."

"How is that, Father?"

"Because you don't know any better," says the priest, cheering up all of a sudden. He laughs. "Do you want to know the truth?"

"We always want to know the truth, Father," says Max gravely.

"I think it is you doctors who are doing the will of God, even though you do not believe in him. You stand for life. You are trying to help us in here, you are good fellows, God bless you all. Life is what—" begins the priest and, as suddenly as he laughed, now covers his face with his hands and bursts into tears.

The doctors nod silently, pat the foot of the bed, and move on.

But today at Natchez-under-the-Hill the priest is his old self, sits fully clothed and in his right mind, a gray-faced gray-haired gray man with flat hairy forearms like Ricardo Montalban. He looks at his wristwatch and, explaining that it is time for him to go into the confessional, makes as if to rise.

"Don't go on my account, Father," I say, noticing no other penitents.

"No?" Sighing, he sits down again.

"I'm sorry, Father, but you could not give me the sacrament of penance. One of the elements is missing."

"Which element?"

"Contrition. To say nothing of a firm purpose of amendment."

"I understand. I'll pray for you."

"Good."

"Um, pray for me."

"I haven't prayed much lately. But excuse me, Father."

"Yes?"

"I thought you wanted to see me about something."

"See you? Oh yes. Right. It occurred to me the other day," says the priest, working his expansion band around his wide hairy wrist (a Spanish athlete's futbol wrist), "that it would be a good idea for you to move out of your house."

I look at him curiously. "Why should I do that?"

"I am not at liberty to tell you why."

"You mean someone told you something under the seal of the confessional?"

"I am just telling you that it would be better for you to leave. Now. Today."

"Is something going to happen, Father?"

The priest shrugs.

"Father, if my life is in danger, I think you're obliged to tell me."

"You should move. Say, why don't you move down here with me? You know, it's quite cool down here." He nods toward the restored slave quarters, a long brick row house already engulfed by creeper and swamp cyrilla.

"But, Father—"

He rises. His parishioners are arriving. They're an odd lot, a remnant of a remnant, bits and pieces, leftovers, like the strays and stragglers after a battle. I know most of them. They recognize me and so signify by noncommittal nods. Am I one of them?

They are:

Three old-style Roman Catholics, the sort who are going to stick with the Roman Pope no matter what—let's hear it for the Pope!—Knights-of-Columbus types, Seven-Up Holy-Name Prudential Western-Auto types, and their wives, good solid chicken-gumbo and altar-society ladies.

A scoffing Irish behaviorist, the sort in whom irony is so piled up on irony, jokes so encrusted on jokes, winks and nudges and in-jokes so convoluted, that anticlericism has become anti-anticlerical, gone so far out that it has come back in as clericism and comes down on the side of Rome where he started.

An old scold, a seventy-year-old lady sacristan, the sort who's been lurking in the shadows of the tabernacle since the prophetess Anna.

A love couple from the swamp, dressed in rags and seashells, who, having lived a free life, chanted mantras, smoked Choctaw cannab, lain together dreaming in the gold-green world, conceived and bore children, dwelled in a salt mine—chanced one day upon a Confederate Bible, read it as if it had never been read before, the wildest unlikeliest doctrine imaginable, believed it, decided to be married and baptize their children.

An ordinary Knothead couple recently transferred from Jackson, he the new manager of Friendly Finance, they having inquired after the whereabouts of the local Catholic church and being directed here, perhaps as a joke, and now standing around, eyes rolled up in their eyebrows, wondering: could this be the right church, a tin-roofed hut in a briar patch? They're in the wrong place.

Two freejacks, light-skinned sloe-eyed men of color, also called "Creoles" by other Negroes but generally called freejacks ever since their ancestors were freed by Andy Jackson for services rendered in the Battle of New Orleans.

Two nuns who refused either to get married, quit, or teach in all-white Knothead schools and so have no place to go.

Three seminarians, two lusty white fellows, lusty Notre Dame types, the sort who run up and down basketball courts swinging sweaty Our Lady medals, and one graceful black youth, face set in a conventional piety, who reminds me of Saint Aloysius Gonzaga, the Jesuit boy-saint who was reputed never to have entertained an impure thought.

Two secretaries from the Center, you know the sort, good Catholic girls thirty-one or -two and not exactly gorgeous, one dumpy and pudding-faced, the other an Olive Oyl.

Everyone stands around at sixes and sevens, eyeing each other and wondering if he's in the right place. The love couple look at the K.C. types swinging their fists into their hands. The Friendly Finance couple look at the freejacks and wonder if they are black or white.

Father Rinaldo Smith sighs and mounts the steps. The others follow silently.

"You coming, Tom?" he asks.

"Not today."

"Wouldn't it be wonderful to have a good old bell to summon the faithful and ring the angelus?"

"Yes. I believe I know where a good old plantation bell might be found."

"Grand."

4

In my "enclosed patio."

I decide to skip the fish fry and spend the afternoon sipping toddies and reading Stedmann's account of Verdun.

At six o'clock on the morning of May 23, 1916, the French Thirty-fourth Infantry attacked the fort at Douaumont. The Germans had 2,200 artillery pieces, of which 1,730 were heavy. The French division advanced to the fort, losing four out of five men. The survivors reached the roof of the fort but could not get in. They were soon killed by artillery.

The slaughter at Verdun was an improvement over the nineteenth century, in which, for example, Grant lost 8,000 men, mostly white Anglo-Saxon Protestants named Smith, Jones, and Robinson, in forty minutes at Cold Harbor to Lee's army, also mainly Anglo-Saxon, white, and Protestant, named Smith, Jones, Robinson, and Armstrong.

Here's the riddle. Father Smith speaks of life. Life is better than death. Frenchmen and Germans now choose life. Frenchmen and Germans at Verdun in 1916 chose death, 500,000 of them. The question is, who has life, the Frenchman now who chooses life and will die for nothing or the Frenchman then who chose to die, for what? I forget.

Or a Pennsylvanian. This afternoon during the assault on Fort Douaumont, I heard a sportscaster listing the football powers of the coming season. Number one on his list were the Nittany Lions of Penn State. I do not care to hear about the Nittany Lions. But what would it be like to live in Pennsylvania and every day of your life hear sportscasters speak of the prospects of the Nittany Lions?

With my lapsometer I can measure the index of life, life in death and death in life. It is possible, I suspect, to be dying and alive at Verdun and alive and dying as a booster of the Nittany Lions.

An example of life in death: for fifty years following the Battle of Verdun, French and German veterans used to return every summer to seek out the trench where they spent the summer of 1916. Why did they choose the very domicile of death? Was there life here? Afterwards they would sit for hours in a café on the Sacred Way.

But I must prove my case. I must be present with my lapsometer in circumstances where the dying are alive and the living are dead. Observe, measure, verify: here's the business of the scientist.

Outside my "enclosed patio" the weeds are sprouting through the black pebbles Doris brought back from Mexico. Virginia creeper has taken the $500 lead statue of Saint Francis she ordered from Hammacher-Schlemmer. The birdbath and feeder Saint Francis holds are empty. Tough titty for the titmice.

Sunday night: awake till 5 A.M. Reading Stedmann on Verdun, listening to a screech owl crying like a baby in the swamp, assaulted by succubi, night exaltations, morning terror, and nameless longings; sipped twelve toddies.

But why should I be afraid? Tomorrow—today—I meet with the Director and hear the triumphant news about my lapsometer, the first caliper of the soul and the first hope of bridging the dread chasm that has rent the soul of Western man ever since the famous philosopher Descartes ripped body loose from mind and turned the very soul into a ghost that haunts its own house.

JULY THIRD

At the Director's Office to Hear the Good News About My Article and Invention

11:00 A.M. / MONDAY, JULY 3

THIRTY MINUTES early for my appointment. Quite nervous. But why? My article speaks for itself. The evidence is there. My invention works.

There is time to go the roundabout way through Love Clinic in hopes of catching a glimpse of Moira, my love.

No one is in but Father Kev Kevin, who is sitting at the vaginal computer reading a book, *Christianity Without God*.

"Is it good?"

"What? Oh. Yes, this is where it's at."

He jumps up and greets me with suspicious cordiality, flashing his handsome Pat O'Brien grin and shaking my hand with both of his just as he used to when he was chaplain for the Knights of Columbus. He must have bad news. He does.

"Are you looking for Miss Schaffner?"

"Yes."

"I'm afraid she's no longer with us," says Father Kev Kevin, rocking back on his heels in his old clerical style.

"Where is she?"

"She's working over in Geriatrics with Dr. Brown."

"Very good," I say, but my heart gives an ugly leap sideways. But really, why should I be jealous? Buddy Brown is a licentious man, but Moira knows this. Undoubtedly it is the hapless old folk who interest her and whom she wants to help.

"Thank you. Goodbye, Father," I say absently.

Father Kev Kevin frowns and returns to the vaginal computer. At the same moment Lonesome Lil enters the clinic, lines up her Lucite fittings on the table, and begins taking off her good gray suit.

It does not help matters when I run into Buddy Brown in the hall. He greets me even more effusively.

"See you in The Pit this afternoon," he says, coming close and pinching my flank in a loving kind of hate.

"The Pit?"

"At two o'clock. Me and you. Let's give them a real show, what do you say?"

"Yes. But just now I have an appointment with the Director."

"It's a good case. You saw him first, then I saw him. We both know him backwards and forwards."

"Which case? Oh, Mr. Ives."

"Which case! Ho ho." Buddy twists my flank a bit too hard for comfort. "Son, this time I got you by the short hairs."

"Perhaps. What do you think is wrong with him?"

"I know what's wrong with him."

"And you've got him down for the Happy Isles."

"What would you do with him?"

"I don't know." I am gazing down at Buddy's tanned bald head and lustrous spaniel eyes. His jaw muscles spread up like a fan under the healthy skin. Could Moira like him? There is to commend him his health, strength, brains, and cleanliness. He is very clean. His fingernails are like watch crystals. His soft white shirt and starched clinical coat sparkle like snow against his clear mahogany skin. Burnished hairs sprout through the heavy gold links of his expansion band.

Buddy is winking at me. "I understand that you diagnosed uh no pathology in Mr. Ives."

"Yes."

"You mean you think there's nothing wrong with him?"

"Yes."

"Then how come he can't walk or talk?"

"I don't know."

"Me and you going to have it."

"All right."

"This time you're wide open."

"How do you figure?"

"Because you have allowed nonscientific considerations to affect your judgment."

"Nonscientific considerations?"

"Religious considerations."

"I? Religious? How's that?"

"Tell the truth. You oppose in principle Happy Isles and the Euphoric Switch."

"Yes."

"And you don't want Mr. Ives to be sent there."

"That's true."

"Why?"

"Why what?"

"Why do you disapprove?"

I fall silent.

"Tom, you and I don't disagree," says Buddy in an earnest friendly voice.

"We don't?"

"It's the quality of life that counts."

"Yes."

"And the right of the individual to control his own body."

"Well—"

"And above all a man's sacred right to choose his own destiny and realize his own potential."

"Well—"

"Would you let your own mother suffer?"

"Yes."

"I don't believe you. I know you too well and know that you place a supreme value on human values."

"Yes."

"We believe in the same things, differing only in the best way to achieve them."

"We do?"

"See you in The Pit!"

One last squeeze—we are good friends now—and off he goes, white skirts sailing.

The Pit is a curious institution, a relic of medieval disputations and of doctors' hankering for horseplay, satiric verse, heavy-handed clinical jokes, and such. Once a month a clinical-pathological conference is held in the student amphitheater, before four hundred odd students, professors, nurses, and staff members. Local physicians are invited and sometimes come, if only to see what the Leftpapasan psychiatrists and behaviorists are up to. Today's Pit is the grand finale of the arduous ten-month school year. The seats of The Pit slope steeply to a small sunken arena, a miniature of the bullring at Pamplona. The Pit is popular with students because it is the one occasion when the Herr Professors try publicly to make fools of each other and the students can take sides (perhaps it is an Anglo-Saxon institution: no German Herr Professor would put up with it). They can clap, cheer, boo, point thumbs down, scrape their feet on the concrete. Contending physicians present and defend their diagnoses. Opponents are free to ridicule, even abuse each other. One doctor, none other than Buddy Brown in fact, routed an opponent who had diagnosed the "typical red butterfly rash of Lupus" by demonstrating that he, the opposing doctor, was color-blind.

Buddy exaggerates when he says I have my "following." My one small success in The Pit might be compared to a single well-executed *estocada* by an obscure matador. I was able to demonstrate that a lady suffering from frigidity and morning terror and said to have been malconditioned by her overly rigid Methodist parents was in truth terrified by her well-nigh perfect life, really death in life, in Paradise, where all her needs were satisfied and all she had to do was play golf and bridge and sit around the clubhouse watching swim-meets and the Christian baton-twirlers. She woke every morning to a perfect husband, perfect children, a perfect life—and shook like a leaf with morning terror. All efforts to recondition her in a Skinner box failed. I thought they had got it backward, that the frigidity followed from the terror, not vice versa. How can a lady quaking with terror make love to her husband? For the first time I produced my lapsometer in The Pit—yes, the students know about my invention but are not sure whether it is a serious diagnostic tool or a theatrical prop. It registered normal readings in both the erogenous and interpersonal zones. The lady had a loving heart. Ah, but what to do about it? How to demonstrate it in The Pit? An idea came to me. Sizing her up, noting her suggestibility—she was one of those quick slim ash-blondes whose gray eyes are onto you and onto what you want before you know it yourself and are willing to follow your lead: a superb dancing partner—I gambled on a quick hypnosis, put her under and implanted the posthypnotic suggestion that she had nothing to worry about, that as soon as possible she should make an excuse and leave in search of her husband. Whereupon she did, waking up, rising with parted lips and a high color, patting the back of her hair and looking at her watch: "Good heavens, I'm late. I've got to meet Harry. This is his day off and if I hurry, I'll be home before he finishes his nap." Exit, blushing. The students cheered and sang "I'm Just Wild about Harry."

My little triumph, of course, was more theatrical than medical. As you well know, medical colleagues, and as Freud proved long ago, hypnosis is without lasting benefit.

2

Five minutes to eleven. Time for a last visit to the men's room. Why am I so nervous? The Director has to be on my side. Else how would Art Immelmann have found out about my invention?

Speak of the devil. A man takes the urinal next to me though there are six urinals and mine is at the end. I frown. Here is a minor breach of the unspoken rules between men for the use of urinals. If there are six urinals and one uses the first, the second man properly takes the sixth or perhaps the fifth, maybe the fourth, tolerably the third, but not the second.

This fellow, however, hawks and spits in the standard fashion, zips and pats himself and moves to the washstand, again the next washstand. In the mirror I notice it is Art Immelmann, the man from the Rockefeller-Ford-Carnegie foundations who looks like a drug salesman.

"Well well, Doc."

When I turn to speak, I notice another minor oddity. In the mirror, which reverses things, there was nothing amiss. But as Art adjusts his trousers, I notice that he "dresses" on the wrong side. He dresses, as tailors say, on the right, which not one American male in a thousand, ask any tailor, does. In fact, American pants are made for left-dressing. A small oddity, true, but slightly discommoding to the observer, like talking to a cross-eyed man.

"Well, Doc," says Art, turning on the hot water, "have you thought about our little proposition?"

"It's out of the question."

"May I ask why?"

"I wouldn't want my invention to fall into the wrong hands. It could be quite dangerous."

"Don't you trust the National Institute of Mental Health and the Ford, Carnegie, and Rockefeller foundations?"

"No. Besides, my invention is not perfected yet. I haven't finished with it."

"What's not perfected?" Art bends his knees, mambo style, and combs his hair like a sailor with quick alternating strokes of comb and hand.

"My sensors won't penetrate melanin pigment in the skin."

"Hm." Art wets his comb. "You mean your MOQUOL doesn't work on darkies?"

"No, it doesn't." I look at him with surprise. Darkies?!

"Anything else wrong?"

"Yes. I don't yet have a therapeutic component. As it stands, my device is a diagnostic tool, no more."

"I know." Art goes on riffling his flat-top with a wet comb. Is he trying to make it lie down? Some hairs stick up like a wet airedale's. "What would you say, Doc, if I told you your invention has the capacities and is incremental for both components?"

"Eh?"

"That the solution to both the melanin problem and the therapeutic problem is under your nose."

"Where?"

Art laughs. "You know all I'm good for, Doc? I'm a coordinator. You've got the big ideas. I'm a tinkerer. In fact, I've got a little gadget right here that would fit your device—"

"Excuse me. I'm late. I've got to—"

"We'd make a team, Doc! All you've got to do is sign the funding application!"

"No."

But we say goodbye and shake hands agreeably enough. His is curiously inert, as if all he knew about shaking hands he had learned from watching others shake hands. A heavy smell of sweat neutralized by deodorant pushes to my nostrils.

Art holds my hand a second too long. "Doc. Just in case anything should go wrong, I'll be around."

"What could go wrong?"

"Just in case!"

As I leave him, he opens his attaché case on the windowsill. He looks like a traveling salesman doing business in the post office.

My hour of triumph is at hand.

3

In the outer office of the Director the typists do not look up, but the secretary is pleasant. She nods toward a bench. There are no staff members present. A row of patients, dressed in the familiar string robes of the wards, sit on the bench, hands on their knees. They look at me without expression. There is no place to sit but the bench.

Quite correct of the Director not to make a fuss! Yet it is an annoyance when one of the patients is called before me. I do not mind. The encounter with Art Immelmann has left me thoughtful. Was he trying to tell me something?

When my turn does come, the Director greets me warmly, if somewhat vaguely, at the door. The first thing I catch sight of over his shoulder is—yes!—my *Brain* article and my lapsometer lined up side by side on his desk.

"You are very imaginative!" cries the Director, waving me to a chair opposite him.

"Thank you." What does he mean?

The Director is a tough old party, a lean leathery emeritus behaviorist with a white thatch and a single caliper crease in his withered brown cheek. Though he is reputed to have a cancer in his lung that is getting the better of him, one can easily believe that the growth is feeding on his nonvital parts, fats and body liquors, leaving the man himself worn fine and dusty and durable as Don Quixote. The only sign of his illness is a fruity cough and his handkerchiefs, which he uses expertly, folding them flat as a napkin over his sputum and popping them up his sleeve or into the slits of his white coat.

Though he is a behaviorist and accordingly not well disposed to such new ideas as an "ontological lapsometer," I take heart from two circumstances: one, that he is an honorable man of science and as such knows evidence when he sees it; two, that he is dying. A dying king, said Sir Thomas More, is apt to be wiser than a healthy king. A dying behaviorist may be a good behaviorist.

The Director coughs his fruity cough. His eyes bulge. Handkerchiefs pop in and out of his pockets.

"With your permission, Tom, we're going to do a feature about your project in the *Rehab Weekly*."

"The *Rehab Weekly*?"

"Yes. We think you've shown a great deal of imagination."

"Sir, the *Rehab Weekly* is the patients' mimeographed magazine."

"I know," says the Director, his eyes bulging amiably.

The unease that has been flickering up and down my spine turns into a pool of heat in the hollow of my neck. Strange, but I feel only a mild embarrassment for him.

"Sir," I say presently. "Perhaps you have misunderstood me. You say there are plans to do a feature on my work in the *Rehab Weekly*. Very good. But the reason I submitted my article to you was to obtain your approval and support before submitting it to *Brain*."

"Yes, I know," says the Director, coughing.

"It is also necessary to obtain your sanction of my application to N.I.M.H. for funding."

"Yes. In the amount of—" The Director is leafing through—not my proposal but my medical chart!

"Twenty-five million," I say, blushing furiously. Why am I so embarrassed? What is shameful about twenty-five million?

"I see." The Director lays his head over, eyes bulging thoughtfully. "You are on patient-staff status."

"Technically, but—"

"Doctor, don't you think that before launching such a ah major undertaking, it might be well to wait until you are discharged?"

"Discharged?"

He slides the chart across the desk. "According to our records you are still a patient on A-4, which means that though you perform staff duties, you have not yet reached an open ward."

I find myself nodding respectfully, hands on my knees—like a patient! I blink at my trousers. Where is my string robe?

"Sir, I left the hospital five months ago."

"Left?" The glossy eyes bulge, the pages flip past. He's lost me somewhere in the chart. "Here. You're still on A-4."

"No sir."

"You're still on patient-staff status."

"Yes sir, technically."

"I remember that. It is the first time in my experience that a doctor-patient on A-4 has ever been put on patient-staff. Remarkable. We have great respect for your abilities, Doctor. Let's see, you're in encephalography with Dr. Wilkes. How is it going?"

"I was with Colley Wilkes. Five months ago."

"I noticed today you're down for The Pit, heh heh heh. I saw you once before, Doctor. Great, heh heh heh. What'll it be today, high medicine or hijinks or both? You know, Doctor, if you could ever get on top of your mood swings, you have a real contribution to make. Hm"—again poking through the chart—"too bad the Skinner box didn't do more for the anxiety and elation-depression. I wonder if we hadn't better get on with implanting electrodes—"

"Sir, excuse me. I believe I understand. Rather, there is a misunderstanding. You are under the impression that I am here as a patient, together with the other patients outside, for my monthly visit with you. Right, I'd forgotten, Monday is patient day."

"That reminds me." He consults his watch. "I fear we're running a bit over. But don't worry about it. Always glad to see you. I predict you'll soon make A-3 and permanent staff. For the time being, hang in right where you are."

"With Colley Wilkes."

"Tremendous fellow! A renaissance man."

We rise. There lying on the desk between us like a dog turd is my lapsometer. I can't bear to look at it. Neither can the Director.

"But, sir—"

"Dr. More, tell me the truth."

"Yes sir."

"Do you think you are well?"

"No sir, I'm not well."

"Well—?" He spreads his hands.

My God, he's right. $25,000,000. An ontological lapsometer. I'm mad as a hatter.

But the Director suddenly feels so much better that in an excess of goodwill he does look at my machine and even gives it a poke with his pencil.

"Amazing! What workmanship. Say, why don't you use it in The Pit today, heh heh heh. Where did you get it machined?"

"In Japan," I say absently. "You remember Dr. Yamaiuchi."

"The Japanese are amazing, aren't they?"

We reflect on the recent excellence of Japanese workmanship.

"What do you call this thing, Doctor?" the Director asks, exploring the device with his pencil.

"Lapsometer." I am unable to tear my eyes from his strong brown farmer's hands.

"The name interests me."

"Yes sir?"

"It implies, I take it, a lapse or fall."

"Yes," I say tonelessly.

"A fall perhaps from a state of innocence?"

"Perhaps." My foot begins to wag briskly. I stop it.

"Does this measure the uh depth of the fall?"

I stand up.

"Sir?"

"Yes, Doctor?"

"Am I to understand then that you do not intend either to approve my article for *Brain* or my application for funding from N.I.M.H.?"

"We'll cross that bridge at our next month's meeting. Right now I'm more interested in the hijinks in The Pit, heh heh. And don't worry about being on A-4 much longer. I believe you're ready for A-3. Glad to have you aboard. You've no idea how hard it is to keep staff these days. Now back at the old hospital in Boston—"

"Sir?"

"Yes?"

"There is one thing I don't understand."

"What's that?" I've gone past my ten minutes. His glossy eyes bulge at his watch.

"Why did you tell Art Immelmann you had approved my application?"

"Who?"

"Art Immelmann."

"I never heard of him."

"He's a liaison man between N.I.M.H. and the funds."

"Oh my, one of those fellows. They're bad news. They all say the same things: the war in Ecuador has dried up the money."

"He says Ford, Carnegie, and Rockefeller are willing to fund me."

"Good!" He doesn't believe me.

"But you don't know him?"

"I steer clear of those fellows!" For some reason the Director laughs immoderately, which in turn sets him off into a fit of coughing.

"Then you've told no one about my invention or article?"

Handkerchiefs pop in and out. The Director, still red-faced, shakes his head and gazes past me. He has other patients!

The next patient passes me in the doorway, a sorrowful angry man in a string robe who stares at me furiously, tapping his watch with trembling forefinger. His cheek quivers with rage. I've encroached upon his time. Rage shakes him like a terrier. I recall being possessed by this demon. Once, after brooding two days over a remark made by a fellow patient, I walked up to him with clenched fists. "I resent that remark you made two days ago. In fact, I can't stand it any longer. Take it back!" "O.K.," said the startled man and took it back.

4

My feet shuffle past the elevators, my hands groping for the pockets of my string robe.

Where am I going? Back to the wards?

The center is not holding.

Where am I going? Back to my narrow bed on A-4 with its hard mattress and seersucker spread stretched tight as a drum, a magic carpet where I can lie and wing it like a martin.

Why is it I feel better, see more clearly, can help more people when I am crazy? Not being crazy, being sane in a sane world, is the craziest business of all.

What I really want to do is practice medicine from my bed in

A-4, lie happy and stiff on my bed, like a Hindoo on his bed of nails, and treat sane folk and sane doctors from the sane world, which is the maddest world of all.

Where am I? Going past Love. On the bench in the hall sit volunteers J. T. Thigpen and Gloria and Ted 'n Tanya. J. T. strokes his acne with his fingernails. Gloria reads a textbook open on her plump thighs. Through the diamond-shaped window I catch a glimpse of Father Kev Kevin reading *Commonweal* at the vaginal console.

"See you Wednesday!" whispers Ted.

"What's that? Oh."

On the lower level Buddy Brown and Moira are standing next to Mr. Ives in a wheelchair. Moira hangs her head. Buddy greets me with the cordiality of a good enemy.

"You're just in time, Tom!"

"In time for what?"

"To give Mr. Ives the once-over. Be my guest."

"No thanks."

"Look at this." Taking a reflex hammer from his pocket, he taps Mr. Ives's knee tendon with quick deft taps.

Mr. Ives dances a regular jig in his chair, all the while watching me with his mild blue gaze.

"Isn't that upper-motor-neurone damage, Doctor?" Buddy asks me.

"I don't think so."

"Try it yourself." He hands me his hammer, a splendid affair with a glittering shaft and a tomahawk head of red rubber.

"No fanks."

"What? Oh. Then I'll see you shortly."

"Fime."

I do not speak well. I've lost. I'm a patient. But Buddy doesn't notice. Like all enemies, he puts the best construction on his opponent. But Moira knows something is wrong. She hangs her head.

"Is something wrong?" she asks in a low voice.

"I'm fime." I notice that they are waiting outside the tunnel that leads into The Pit from the lower level.

"Don't forget Howard," says Moira.

"Who? Oh." Howard Johnson. "Nopes."

"Who is Howard?" Buddy asks.

"We can go now," whispers Moira. She sees the abyss and is willing to save me.

"When will you come in?" asks Buddy.

"Eins upon a oncy," I reply.

"O.K. *Eins zwei drei*," says Buddy, willing to give me the benefit of the doubt. "He's going to the men's room," he tells Moira, trying to make sense of me.

"Rike," I say.

"Rotsa ruck."

5

So I go back to the men's room.

At the washstand there is a step behind me. A familiar smell of sebum-sweat overlaid by unguents.

"Hello, Art." Where did he come from? He must live in a cubicle. Now he's wearing a tie and jacket, as if he were dressed for an occasion. But where did he get the tie and jacket? I take a closer look in the mirror. It is a tight gabardine "bi-swing" jacket, a style popular many years ago, with little plackets under each shoulder.

"How does it go, Doc?"

"Not so good."

"Win a few, lose a few, eh?"

"What? Yes."

I am gazing at my face in the mirror intently, like the man in Saint James's epistle. The image reverses on the retina and a hole opens. Removing the bottle of Early Times from my bag, I take two long pulls.

"Where to now, Doc?"

"I don't know. Back to A-4."

"As a patient."

"I suppose."

"Do you give up so easily?"

I shrug.

"What about our little proposition?"

"What proposition?"

"Let me see your MOQUOL."

"Gladly." Taking the device from my bag, I loft it toward the used-towel bin.

Art intercepts it, rubs it on his shirt front like a street urchin finding a dime.

"You got to have faith, Doc."

"Faith?"

"Listen to me for a minute."

"Why?"

"Sit here." Taking my arm, he leads me to the shoeshine chair. I sit on the platform. Art hops up to the throne and fits his shoes to the treadles. The whiskey catches hold in my stomach like a gear. I feel better, engaged.

"And to make matters worse," says Art cheerfully, "somebody's beating your time with your girl." Beating my time. I haven't heard that expression since childhood.

"What do you want?" I ask him, slumping around the pleasant engaged gear in my stomach.

"To show you something." He hops over me, fumbles in his attaché case, which still lies open on the windowsill. It is a short barrel, like a telephoto lens, fitted with an adapter ring. He screws it onto my lapsometer.

"Life is funny, Doc."

"It is."

"There is such a thing as being too close to the woods to see the trees."

"What is that thing?"

"It's really your discovery. The principle is yours. This is just a bit of tinkering. If you want to give me credit in a footnote, ha ha—"

"What's it for?"

"Doc, the trouble with your invention has always been that you could diagnose but not treat, right?"

"That's right."

"Now you can treat." He tosses me the lapsometer.

"How's that?"

"Don't you know? You discovered it twenty years ago."

"What—"

A behaviorist comes in to take a leak. Art begins combing his hair again, wetting his comb and bending his knees mambostyle. The behaviorist washes his hands, nods at me, and leaves. Art hops nimbly up into the shoeshine chair.

"Doc, you recall that you discovered the effects of Heavy Sodium fallout?"

"Yes." I am wondering: if two drinks of Early Times makes me feel good, wouldn't three drinks make me feel better?

"You had the answer. Don't you see?"

"See what?"

"The possibility of treating personality disorders with Heavy Sodium and Chloride."

"That would be like exploding a cobalt bomb over New Orleans to treat cancer."

"That's the point. How do you treat cancer with cobalt radiation?"

"I've thought of that. But you know, of course, that sodium radiation is a two-edged sword. In the same moment that you assuage frontal terror you might increase red-nucleus rage."

"Exactly!" Art's feet fairly dance on the treadles above my head. "And you of all people should know how to avoid that."

"How?"

"With this."

"What is that?"

"A differential stereotactic emission ionizer. Beams in either your Heavy Sodium or Chloride ion. Using your principle."

"How?"

"Don't you see? You don't even move your MOQUOL. Say you take a reading at the red nucleus and find a plus-five milli-volt pathology. All you do is swing your dial to a minus-five Chloride charge and ionize."

"And what will that do?"

"Tranquilize red-nucleus rage."

"Sure."

"You don't believe me? Where are you going?"

"To get a drink."

"That's the point, Doc. Drink this drink and you'll never want a drink. Let me show you something."

"What?"

"Sit down here."

As I sit on the lower platform, Art holds the machine to my head. It feels like barber's clippers.

"Now. Using your diagnostic circuit, I observe that you

are registering a plus-three on the anxiety scale. A little high but not unusual considering the pace of modern living. Now suppose I keep the MOQUOL in place and switch over to a plus-two ion emission. You should feel a bit worse."

The machine hums like a tuning fork against my head.

I begin to shiver. My shoulders are rounded and I am gazing at my hands clenched in my lap. At last I raise my eyes. A horrid white light streams through the frosted window and falls into the glittering porcelain basins of the urinals. It is the Terror, but tolerable. The urinals, which are the wall variety, are shaped like skulls. The dripping water sounds hollow like water at the bottom of a well.

"Now. We'll reverse and give you a minus-seven Chloride dose, which should throw you over into minus-two anti-anxiety."

My head is leaning against the metal support of the treadle. Again the machine hums.

When I open my eyes, I am conscious first of breathing. Something in my diaphragm lets go. I realize I've been breathing at the top of my lungs for forty-five years. Now my diaphragm moves like a piston into my viscera, pulling great drafts of air into the base of my lungs.

Next I become aware of the cool metal of the support against my neck.

Then I notice my hand clenched into a fist on my knee. I open it slowly, turning it this way and that, inspecting every pore and crease. What a beautiful strong hand! The tendons! The bones! But the hand of a stranger! I have never seen it before.

How can a man spend forty-five years as a stranger to himself? No other creature would do such a thing. No animal would, for he is pure organism. No angel would, for he is pure spirit.

"Feeling better, Doc?"

"Yes."

"It's quite a device, isn't it?"

"Yes."

"And the Director doesn't appreciate it, does he?"

"No."

"Now." Art is at my head again, fiddling about, pressing bony protuberances, measuring salients of my skull with a cold metal centimeter scale. It feels good to be measured. "I'm going to show you something I think will interest you. I'm going to stimulate Brodmann 11 mildly. You know what that is?"

"Yes, but I'd like to hear what you think it is."

"It lies in the frontal-temporal sulcus of course, betwixt and between the abstractive areas of the frontal and the concrete auditory radiation of the frontal. It is the area of the musical-erotic."

"Hm, that's not my terminology."

"But you know what I mean. Here the abstract is experienced concretely and the concrete abstractly. Take women, for example. Here one neither loves a woman individually, for herself and no other, faithfully; nor does one love a woman organically as a dog loves a bitch. No, one loves a woman both in herself and insofar as she is a woman, a member of the class women. Conversely, one loves women not in the abstract but in a particular example, this woman. Loves her truly, moreover. One loves faithlessly but truly."

"Truly?"

"Loves her as one loves music. A woman is the concrete experienced abstractly, as women. Music is the abstract experienced as the concrete, namely sound."

"So?"

"Ha! Old stuff to you, eh, Doc? Well, that's not the end of it. Don't you see? Stimulate this area and you stimulate both the scientist and the lover but neither at the expense of the other. You stimulate the scientist-lover."

"I see."

But it is Art himself who interests me. How does Art, who looks like the sort of fellow who used to service condom vendors in the old Auto Age, know this?

"So that in the same moment one becomes victorious in science one also becomes victorious in love. And all for the good of mankind! Science to help all men and a happy joyous love to help women. We are speaking here of happiness, joy, music, spontaneity, you understand. Fortunately we have put behind us such unhappy things as pure versus impure love, sin versus virtue, and so forth. This love has its counterpart in scientific knowledge: it is neutral morally, abstractive and godlike—"

"Godlike?"

"In the sense of being like a god in one's freedom and omniscience."

"You surprise me, Art."

"Hold still, Doc."

Again the cold steel hums like a tuning fork against my skull.

The tone of the tuning fork turns into music: first, a plaintive little piping, the dance of happy spirits in a high meadow; the flute trips along, hesitates, picks up again, and here's the beauty of it, in the catch, the stutter, and starting up again. Now comes the love music of man in particular for women in general: happy, faithless, seductive music: the race and rip of violins dancing, whipping, tricking, fizzing in a froth of May wine, sunshine sunshine, and cotton dresses in summertime.

Who am I?

I am he who loves. I am in love. I love.

Who do you love?

You.

Who is "you"?

A girl.

What girl?

Any girl you please. You.

How can that be?

Because all girls are lovable and I love them all. I love you. I can make you happy and you me.

Only one thing can make you happy and it is not that.

Love makes me happy. Knowing makes me happy.

Love is God, because God is love. Knowing God is knowing all things.

Love is not God. Love is music.

"Who are you talking to, Doc?"

"What?"

"Why don't you sit down?"

"What was I doing?"

"It doesn't matter, as long as you feel good."

Art pushes up the frosted window. We gaze out into the

gold-green. Fat white clouds are blown by map winds. Swallows dip. Cicadas go *zreeeee*.

"You look good, Doc. Look at yourself. You're not a bad-looking guy. You're still young, you got a good build if you took care of yourself. Here, wash your face in cold water and comb your hair." He hands me his pocket comb. "Now, no need to look like a hairy elf." In a flash he produces a pocket klipette, clips the hair in my nose, ears, and eyebrows. "Tch, your fingernails!"—and gives me a manicure on the spot. In two minutes my nails become glossy watchglasses like Buddy Brown's. Art comes close and sniffs: "Pardon, Doc, but you're a little high, you know. Here's a man's deodorant. Now!"

Art gazes at me. I gaze at the gold-green summer.

"How do you feel, Doc?"

"Fine."

"Isn't it better to feel good rather than bad?"

"Yes."

"Isn't it better to be happy than unhappy?"

"Yes."

"How can you take care of unhappy patients if you are unhappier than they are? Physician, heal thyself."

"Yes."

"Your terror is gone, you're breathing well, your large bowel should be slack as a string, clear as a bell. How is it?"

"Slack as a string, clear as a bell."

"O.K., Doc, now what?"

"I don't know. What?"

"Well, what is the purpose of life in a democratic society?"

"A democratic society?" I ask him, smiling.

"Sure. Isn't it for each man to develop his potential to the fullest?"

"I suppose so."

"What is your potential?"

"I don't know, what?"

"Doc, you have two great potentials: a first-class mind and a heart full of love."

"Yes."

"So what do you do with them?"

"I don't know, what?"

"Know and love, what else?"

"Yes."

"And win at both."

"Win?"

"Is there anything wrong with being victorious and happy? With curing patients, advancing science, loving women and making them happy?"

"No."

"Use your talents, Doc. What do you know how to do?"

"I know how to use this." I pick up the lapsometer.

"What can you do with that?"

"Make people happy."

"Who do you love, Doc?"

"Women, knowing, music, and Early Times."

"You're all set, Doc. One last thing—"

"Yes?"

"Where is your crate of MOQUOLs?"

"In a safe place."

"Let me have them. The situation is critical and I think we ought to get them in the right hands as soon as possible."

"No. I'd better not. That is not part of our contract."

"Why not?"

"There are dangers. I can't be too careful."

"What dangers?"

"Physical and political dangers."

"What do you mean?"

"I think you know what I mean. If one of these falls into the wrong hands, it could produce a chain reaction in the Heavy Sodium deposits hereabouts or a political explosion between the Knotheads and the Lefts. Do you realize that the President and Vice-President will be here tomorrow?"

"Realize it! Why do you think I want your MOQUOLs?" Coming close, he opens and closes his wallet, giving me a glimpse of a metal shield.

"F.B.I.?"

"A bit more exalted. Let's just say I make security reports from time to time. That's why we're interested in making sure your invention stays in the right hands."

"This seems a bit far afield from your work with mental health and the foundations."

"Everything is interdisciplinary now, Doc. As well as being third-generational. You understand."

"No. But don't worry about my invention."

"O.K., Doc. Now. Sign here." He nods to the contract on the windowsill. A ballpoint pen leaps to his hand, clicks, and backs toward my chest.

"Very well." Standing at the windowsill, which seems to be his place of business, I sign the blue-jacketed contract.

"You won't be sorry, Doc." All in one motion he takes pen and contract, clicks pen, stuffs both into his inside breast pocket. As usual, he stands too close and when he buttons his coat it exhales a heavy breath. "Now you can use your talents for the good of mankind and the increase of knowledge. All you have to do is never look back and never be sorry, as per agreement."

"As per what agreement?" I ask vaguely, frowning. But my colon is at peace and my heart beats in time to Mozart.

"We're in business, Doc."

"Yeah. Let's have a drink."

"What? Oh. Well—"

The bottle of Early Times passes between us. The whiskey catches hold in my stomach, gear engaging gear. Art chokes, his eyes water.

"That's good stuff," says Art, blinking. I could swear it was his first drink.

"Yes," I say, laughing.

It's like being back in Charlottesville, in the spring, in the men's room, at a dance, at old Saint Anthony Hall.

6

The Pit is in an uproar. Students roost like chickens along the steep slopes of the amphitheater, cackling and fluttering their white jackets as they argue about the day's case. Bets are placed, doctors attacked and defended. The rightwing Knothead Christian students occupy the right benches, the Lefts the left.

The lower reaches are reserved for professors, residents, consultants, and visiting physicians. The Director, for example, sits in the front row, elbows propped on the high retaining wall, next to his fellow Nobel laureate Dr. Kenneth Stryker, who first described the branny cruciform rash of love. Gottlieb is directly behind them, erect as a young prince, light glancing from his forehead. His eyes search mine with a questing puzzled glance, seeking to convey a meaning, but I do not take the meaning. In the same row sit Dr. Helga Heine, the West German interpersonal gynecologist; Colley Wilkes, the super-Negro encephalographer and his wife, Fran, a light-colored behaviorist and bird-watcher; Ted 'n Tanya and two visiting proctologists from Paradise: my old friend Dr. Dusty Rhoades and Dr. Walter Bung, an extremely conservative albeit skillful proctologist recently removed from Birmingham.

The pit itself, a sunken area half the size of a handball court and enclosed by a high curving wall, is empty save for Dr. Buddy Brown, the patient, Mr. Ives, in a wheelchair, and behind him a strapping blond nurse named Winnie Gunn, whose stockings are rolled beneath her knees. Where is Moira? Ah, I see: sitting almost out of sight in the approach tunnel with no more of her visible than her beautiful gunmetal legs. Is she avoiding me?

I enter not through the tunnel but from the top, walking down the steep aisle like a relief pitcher beginning the long trek from the left-field bullpen. As I come abreast of successive rows of students, there occurs on the left a cutting away of eyes and the ironic expression of the fan confronted by the unfavorite. These are by and large Buddy's fans and mostly qualitarians (= euthanasists).

From here and there on the right comes a muted cheer, a vigorous nodding and lively corroborative look from some student who remembers my small triumph and imagines that he and I share the same convictions.

I don't pay much attention to left or right.

Students are, if the truth be known, a bad lot. En masse they're as fickle as a mob, manipulable by any professor who'll stoop to it. They have, moreover, an infinite capacity for repeating dull truths and old lies with all the insistence of self-discovery. Nothing is drearier than the ideology of students, left or right. Half the students here revere Dr. Spiro T. Agnew, elder statesman and honorary president of the American Christian Proctological Society; the other half admire Hermann Hesse, Dr. B. F. Skinner, inventor of the Skinner conditioning box, and the late Justice William O. Douglas, a famous qualitarian who improved the quality of life in India by serving as adviser in a successful program of 100,000,000 abortions and an equal number of painless "terminations" of miserable and unproductive old folk.

People talk a lot about how great "the kids" are, compared to kids in the past. The only difference in my opinion is that kids now don't have sense enough to know what they don't know.

On the other hand, my generation is an even bigger pain.

It seems today in The Pit I am favored by the Christian Knothead antieuthanasic faction, but I'm not sure I like them any better than the Hesse-Skinner-Douglas qualitarians.

But I do not, on the whole, feel bad. My large bowel is clear as a bell, my coeliac plexus is full of blood. Anxiety flickers over my sacrum but it is not the Terror, rather a useful and commensurate edginess. What I fear is not nothing, which is the Terror, but something, namely, getting beat by Buddy Brown in front of Moira. Otherwise I feel fine: my heart is full of love, my mind is like a meat grinder ready to receive the raw stuff of experience and turn out neat pattycake principles.

The thing to do, it occurs to me halfway down into the pit, is to concern myself with the patient and what ails him, and forget the rest.

In the pit itself a casual air is cultivated. Mr. Ives's bright monkey eyes snap at me. Buddy Brown leans against the high wall talking to the Director, who hangs over, cupping an ear. Nurse Winnie Gunn, who stands behind the wheelchair, gives me a big smile and shifts her weight, canting her pelvis six degrees starboard. Moira? Her face swims in the darkness of the tunnel. Are her eyes open or closed?

The uproar resumes. The doctors are free to unhorse each other by any means fair or foul. The students are free to boo or cheer. Last month one poor fellow, a psychiatrist who had diagnosed a case as paranoia, was routed and damned out of his own mouth, like Captain Queeg, by Buddy Brown, who led the man to the point of admitting that yes, he was convinced that all the students and the faculty as well had it in for him and were out to get him. Jeers from the students, right and left, who have no use for weakness in their elders.

The door opens at the top and in strolls Art Immelmann

and perches in the back row. In the same row but not close sit two women. The two women are—good Lord!—*my* two women, Lola Rhoades and Ellen Oglethorpe. What are they doing together?

There is no time to speculate. The uproar subsides and Buddy Brown begins, flipping through the chart held above Mr. Ives, who sits slumped in his string robe, head jogging peacefully, monkey eyes gone blank for once and fixed on the wall in front of him.

Buddy presents the medical history, physical examination, and laboratory findings. He stands at his ease, looking fondly at Mr. Ives.

"My differential diagnosis: advanced atherosclerosis, senile psychosis, psychopathic and antisocial behavior, hemiplegia and aphasia following a cerebrovascular accident."

Murmurs and nods from the students.

"Doctor." With a flourish Buddy hands me the chart.

The Early Times is turning like a gear in my stomach. I am looking at my hand again. What a hand.

"Doctor?"

"Yes. Oh. By the way, Dr. Brown. You made no therapeutic recommendations."

Buddy spreads his fingers wide, shrugs an exaggerated Gallic shrug (he is part Cajun and comes from Thibodeaux).

"You have no recommendations?"

"Do you, Dr. More?"

"Then you plan to transfer him?"

"Yes."

"Where?"

"To the Happy Isles Separation Center."

This is what the students have been waiting for.

"Euphoric Switch! Euphoric Switch!" cry the euthanasists.

"Button! Button!" cry the right-benchers. "Not to Georgia!"

"Where would you send him, Doctor?" asks Buddy sarcastically.

The heavy warm gear is turning in my stomach. My hand is the hand of a stranger. Music is still playing. I must have swayed to the music because Winnie Gunn has seized my forearm with both hands.

"Are you all right, Doctor?" she whispers.

"Fine."

"We are still waiting for your diagnosis, Dr. More," says Buddy with the gentleness of victory.

"I found no significant pathology."

"Louder!" from the back benches. The Director cups his ear.

"I said I found no significant pathology."

"No significant pathology," says Buddy as gently as Perry Mason beating Hamilton Burger for the thousandth time. "And what is your recommendation, Doctor?"

"Discharge him."

"Discharge him," repeats Buddy. "He can't walk or talk, and if he could, he would presumably return to his former atrocious behavior. And yet you want to discharge him. As cured, Doctor?"

"If indeed there was anything wrong with him."

"You think there was nothing wrong with him?"

"No. That is, yes."

"Then what's he doing here in a wheelchair?"

Titters.

I shrug.

"Dr. More, what do you think his chances are of recovering from his stroke?"

"You mean, assuming he's had one."

"Very well. Assuming he's had one."

"Very small."

"And if he did recover, what are the chances he'd return to his former mode of behavior?"

"Very large."

"Do you recall his former behavior?"

I am silent.

"Allow me to refresh your memory, Doctor." Again Buddy flips through the chart. "These," he explains to the amphitheater, "are progress reports during the last year of the patient's residence at the Golden Years Senior Citizen Settlement in Tampa. I quote:

"'The subject has not only refused to participate in the various recreational, educational, creative, and group activities but has on occasion engaged in antisocial and disruptive behavior. He refused: shuffleboard tournament, senior softball, Golden Years gymkhana, papa putt-putt, donkey baseball, Guys and

Gals a go-go, the redfish rodeo, and granddaddy golf. He refused: free trip to Los Angeles to participate in Art Linkletter II's "the young-olds," even though chosen for this trip by his own community.

"'Did on two occasions defecate on Flirtation Walk during the Merry Widow's promenade.

"'Did on the occasion of the Ohio Day breakfast during the period of well-wishing and when the microphone was passed to him utter gross insults and obscenities to Ohioans, among the mildest of which was the expression, repeated many times: piss on all Ohioans!

"'Did in fact urinate on Ohio in the Garden of the Fifty States.

"'Was observed by his neighbors on Bide-a-wee Bayou to be digging furiously with a spade on the patio putt-putt, defacing same. When asked what he was digging for, he replied: the fountain of youth.'"

More titters from the student roosts.

Buddy goes on:

"'Despite extensive reconditioning in the Skinner box, the patient continued to exhibit antisocial behavior. This behavior,'" Buddy hastens to add, "'occurred before his stroke last month.'"

"If he had a stroke," I say.

"If he had a stroke," Buddy allows gravely. "Well, Doctor?"

"Well what?"

"What would you do with him?"

"Discharge him."

"To suffer another thirty years?" asks Buddy, smiling. "To cause other people suffering?"

"At least he'd have a sporting chance."

"A sporting chance to do what?"

"To avoid your packing him off to Georgia, where they'd sink electrodes in his head, plant him like a carrot in that hothouse which is nothing more than an anteroom to the funeral parlor. Then throw the Euphoric Switch—"

"Doctor!" interrupts the Director sternly.

"Aaah!" The students blush at the word *funeral*. Girls try to pull their dresses down over their knees.

Buddy flushes angrily.

The Director is angrier still.

"Doctor!" He levels a quivering finger at me, then crooks it, summoning me. Craning down, he croaks into my ear. "You know very well that the patient is present and that there is no guarantee that he cannot understand you."

"Excuse me, sir, but I hope—indeed I have reason to believe—that he does understand me."

The Director goes off into a fit of coughing. His eyes bulge glassily. Handkerchiefs fly in and out of plackets in his coat. The students are in an uproar. Cheers from the Knotheads, boos from the Lefts.

"This is too much!" The Director throws up both hands. Now he's grabbed me, hooked me with his claws like the ancient mariner. "It's my mistake, Doctor," he croaks. "My putting you on patient-staff status. I beg your pardon. It is only too clear that your illness does not yet permit you to function."

"I can function, sir," I tell him, speaking into his great hairy convoluted ear. "You'll see."

"Be careful, Doctor!" The powerful old hands squeeze my arm by way of warning. "Proceed!"

Mr. Ives's bright monkey eyes have begun to snap again.

"I repeat," I say to the back rows. "If Mr. Ives is going to be referred to the Happy Isles of Georgia, which is nothing but a euthanasia facility, he has the right to know it and to prepare himself accordingly. And he has the right to know who his executioner is."

"I warned you, Doctor!" The Director is on his feet and shouting. "Perhaps you'd better go back to the ward, to A-4."

"Yes sir," I say. Perhaps he is right.

The students, struck dumb, gaze at me, gaze at each other.

"Sir!"

It is Buddy, advancing toward me, hands clasped behind his back. He holds one hand up to quiet the uproar. The other hand is still behind him. "Sir!"—to the Director, in a loud voice. "I submit to you, sir, that you are mistaken!"

"Eh?" The Director cups his ear.

"Sir, you do an injustice both to Dr. More as well as to your own clinical judgment!"

"Eh? How's that?"

"Your first decision about Dr. More was quite correct. Your

confidence in him is not misplaced. His illness does not in the least interfere with his functioning. In short, sir, I submit to you that his odd behavior today cannot be laid to his illness at all. The truth is—" Buddy, quick as a cat, steps behind me, embraces me with one arm, with the other hidden hand claps a mask over my face. His grip is like iron. There is nothing to do but squirm and, at length, gasp for breath. Three, four, five seconds and Buddy flings one arm up like a cowboy bulldogging a steer. He holds the dial aloft for all to see, presents it to the Director like the bull's ears. "Point three percent ethyl alcohol. The truth is Dr. More is drunk as a lord!"

Relieved laughter from the students—along with the gasps. At least they recognize a familiar note of buffoonery.

Even the Director looks relieved despite himself.

"Fun is fun," he announces to no one in particular. "But The Pit may be getting out of hand."

Moira has shrunk even farther into the tunnel.

Unbuckling my physician's bag, I take out my modified lapsometer. Buddy makes way for me, giving my arm a friendly squeeze, handing me on to the patient with a reassuring smile. *You see*, his smile tells the students, *it's all in the spirit of The Pit. Dr. More and I are not mad at each other.*

"Your patient, Doctor." Your witness, Mr. Burger. Twenty years and Ham Burger never won a case.

"Thank you, Doctor, but I don't want the patient. I want you."

A beehive murmur. Buddy holds up both hands.

"It's all right!" he cries, smiling. "Turnabout is fair play. Dr. More is going to diagnose me. Why not? He is going to measure, not my blood alcohol, but my metaphysical status. The device he holds there—correct me if I'm wrong, Doctor—is the More Quantitative-Qualitative Ontological Lapsometer."

Laughter from the left.

"Qualitative-Quantitative," I correct him.

More laughter from the left. Consternation from the right benches. Stony stares from my colleagues. But the Director's glossy eyes bulge amiably—at least he is relieved to see the tone change to the acceptable medical-farcical.

Moira is all but invisible. Have I lost her?

"Be my guest, Doctor," says Buddy, presenting his bald brown crown to me.

With Buddy standing at ironic attention, arms folded, I do a quick diagnostic pass from cortex to brain stem. Over the top of his head I catch a glimpse of Dr. Helga Heine's bare thighs crossed on the aisle, and far above in the shadows, Art Immelmann, who is standing like a bailiff in front of the swinging doors. Working up Buddy's brain stem now, I focus moderate inhibitory dosages over the frontal cerebrum and, letting it go at that, step back. It is enough, I calculate, to inhibit the inhibitory centers and let Buddy be what he is.

Buddy does not move. "Is that all, Doctor?" he asks in his broad stage voice. "How is my metaphysical ontology? Or is it my ontological metaphysics?"

Giggles. I wait. Silence. Throats are cleared. Could I be mistaken?

Again the Director stirs restlessly. Our crude theatrics don't bother him as much as my silence.

"Doctor," he begins patiently and coughs his fruity cough. "Please get on with it."

Helga uncrosses her thighs.

"Doctor, I really think that unless—" says the Director, eyes bulging with alarm.

"I see Christmas," says Buddy, peering up Helga's dress.

"What's that?" asks the Director, leaning forward.

"I see Christmas."

"What did he say?" the Director asks Max, cupping an ear. Max shrugs.

"Nurse!" cries the Director sternly. "This is too much. Remove the patient. What's wrong with that woman?" he asks Max, for now Winnie Gunn is standing transfixed at the tunnel entrance. Try as she might, she can't tear her eyes from Buddy Brown, who has swung around to face her.

"Nothing wrong with Winnie," Buddy tells me, winking and giving me an elbow in the ribs. "You know what they say about the great white whale: thar she blows, but not the first night out."

"Eh?" says the Director.

"Not so loud," I tell Buddy uneasily. It is not clear how

much the students, who are gaping and shushing each other, can hear.

But Buddy pays no attention. He flexes his elbow in a vulgar Cajun gesture, forearm straight up. "*Voilà!* Eh, Winnie?"

Uproar among the students. The doctors blink at each other. Only Art Immelmann sees nothing amiss. Somehow, even though I don't watch him, his every movement makes itself known to me. He hawks and swallows and adjusts his uncomfortable right-dressed pants leg. Now he steps through the swinging doors and drags in a carton. My lapsometers! How did he get hold of them?

"Look at the leg of that woman," says Buddy and makes another crude Cajun gesture, common on the bayous. "*Ça va!* What say, old coonass?"

"It's all right, Buddy," I tell him.

"I think," says the Director, rising and looking at his watch, "that we will call it a day—"

"Sir—" I say, either so loudly or so urgently that everyone falls silent. "May I proceed with the case?"

"If only you would, Doctor!" cries the Director fervently, snatching handkerchiefs from several pockets.

The students laugh and settle back. They are telling themselves they must have heard wrong.

"Let 'em have it, little brother!" Buddy nods encouragement to me and takes a stool. "Go!"

Winnie Gunn stands stolidly behind the wheelchair, eyes rolled up.

Mr. Ives sits still as still, yet somehow twittering in his stillness. His monkey eyes snap. There is something boyish and quick about his narrow face. He is like one of those young-old engineers at Boeing who at seventy wear bow ties and tinker in their workshops.

"It is quite true that Mr. Ives has not walked or talked for a month," I say loudly enough to be heard by Art Immelmann in the back row. "It is also true that he is afflicted by some of the pathologies listed by Dr. Brown. Dr. Brown is quite right about the atherosclerosis."

"You old fucker," says Buddy affectionately, giving me the Cajun arm. "Give 'em hell."

"I deny, however, that he is paralyzed or aphasic. His pineal selfhood, as well as other cerebral centers, is intact."

"Spare us the metaphysics, Doctor," says the Director bluntly. "The best proof that a man can talk is hearing him talk. And walk."

"Yes sir," I say, nodding in admiration of the Director's toughness. A tough old party he is, wasted by disease to his essential fiber, a coat upon a stick. "Sir, I can assure you that speech and locomotion are no problem here. What is interesting is the structure of his selfhood as it relates both to his fellow seniors in the Tampa settlement and to the scientists here."

"No metaphysics!" says the Director, coughing. "I'm a simple man. Show me."

"Speech! Speech!" cry the students.

I shrug. Mr. Ives could, if he wanted, have spoken without further ado. But, to make sure, I administer a light Chloride dampening to his red nucleus (whence his rage) and a moderate Sodium massage to his speech area in the prefrontal gyrus.

Mr. Ives blinks, takes out a toothpick, and begins to suck it.

"Mr. Ives, what was your occupation before you retired?"

"You know that as well as I do, Dr. More," says Mr. Ives, cocking his lively monkey's head. He's got a deep drawling voice!

"I know, but tell them."

"I was controller at Hartford Travelers Insurance. We lived in Connecticut forty years until my wife, Myrtle, God rest her soul, died. I got restless."

"Mr. Ives, what were you digging for down there at the Golden Years Center in Tampa?"

"You know what I was digging for."

"The fountain of youth?"

"That's right."

"Did you find it?"

"I did."

"You see!" cries Buddy, whose ionization is wearing off. He blinks and shakes himself like a spaniel.

"The fountain of youth," says the Director in his old sour-civil style. "Why didn't you drink some? Or, better still, bring some back with you?"

The students, spiritual pimps that they are, reassured that things are back on the track and that laughing is in order, laugh.

"Mr. Ives," I say when the laughing subsides, "what was your avocation while you lived in Hartford?"

"Linguistics."

"And what were you especially interested in?"

Mr. Ives blows out his cheeks. "I've had the hunch for the last twenty years that I could decipher the Ocala frieze."

"What is the Ocala frieze?"

"A ceramic, an artifact discovered in the Yale dig and belonging to the proto-Creek culture. It has a row of glyphs so far undecipherable."

"Go on."

"I found a proto-Creek dictionary compiled by a Fray Bartolomeo who was with the original Narvaez expedition."

"How did you happen to find it?"

"Browsing through the Franciscan files in Salamanca."

"What were you doing there?"

"Looking for the dictionary."

"Did that decipher the glyphs?"

"No, but it gave me the Spanish for certain key proto-Creek words."

"But that wasn't enough."

"No."

"What else did you need?"

"One or two direct pairings of glyphs and Spanish words might break the cipher."

"Did you find such a pairing?"

"Yes."

"In the fountain of youth?"

Mr. Ives cackles and stomps his feet on the treadles of the wheelchair. "Sure!"

"There is such a fountain?"

"Oh sure. Not the fountain of youth and not de León, but there was a fountain, or at least a big spring, where Narvaez parleyed with Osceononta. It was known to be in the general area of the Oneco limestone springs near Tampa. Why else would I hang around that nuthouse?"

"So you had a hunch?"

"I knew there had been a spring there, and a mound that had been bulldozed. I was poking around. It wasn't the first time. I've been digging around there off and on for years."

"Did you find anything?"

"Enough."

"Enough for what?"

"To crack the cipher."

"You deciphered the frieze?"

"Oh sure. Look in next month's Annals."

"What did you find?"

"This." Mr. Ives hunches over and sticks his hand in his pocket.

"Could you bring it here?"

Lurching out of his chair, he comes weaving across The Pit like a jake-legged sailor and drops it in my hand, a crude coin that looks like a ten-dollar gold piece melted past its circumference.

"What is it?" I offer to help him back to his chair but he waves me off and goes weaving back. The students cheer.

"It's a do-it-yourself medal the Spaniards struck on the spot for the occasion of the Narvaez-Osceononta parley. What they did was take one of their own medals showing a salamander on one side and scratch a proto-Creek glyph on the reverse. My hypothesis was that the glyph meant fish. It worked."

I hand it to the Director, who holds it up. The students cheer again.

Mr. Ives watches nervously. "Be careful. There ain't but one of them."

The Director examines the medal intently.

"I'd just as soon have it back," says Mr. Ives, who is afraid the Director is going to pass it around.

The latter hands it back to me. I give it to Mr. Ives.

"Mr. Ives," says the Director. "Would you answer one question?"

"Sure."

"Why did you behave so badly toward the other retirees, hurling imprecations at folk who surely meant you no harm and"—coughing, snatching handkerchiefs—"defecating on, what was it? Flirtation Walk?"

"Doctor," says Mr. Ives, hunkering down in his chair,

monkey eyes glittering, "how would you like it if during the most critical time of your experiments with the Skinner box that won you the Nobel Prize, you had been pestered without letup by a bunch of chickenshit Ohioans? Let's play shuffleboard, let's play granddaddy golf, Guys and Gals à go-go. Let's jump in our Airstream trailers and drive two hundred miles to Key West to meet more Ohioans and once we get there talk about—our Airstream trailers? Those fellows wouldn't let me alone."

"Is it fair to compare the work of science to the well-deserved recreational activities of retired people?"

"Sir, are you implying that what retired people do must necessarily be something less than the work of scientists? I mean is there any reason why a retired person should not go his own way and refuse to be importuned by a bunch of chickenshit Ohioans?"

"Excuse me." It is Stryker, rising slowly behind the Director. "I am not a chauvinistic man. But as a graduate of Western Reserve University and a native of Toledo, I must protest the repeated references to natives of the Buck-eye state as a 'bunch of chickenshit Ohioans.'"

"No offense, sir," says Mr. Ives, waving him off. "I've known some splendid Ohioans. But you get a bunch of retired Ohioans together in Florida—you know, they get together on the west coast to get away from the Jews in Miami. But I'll tell you the damn truth, to me it's six of one and half a dozen of the other."

"Just a minute," says Max, rising to a stoop. "I see no reason for the ethnic—"

"Where are you from?" Stryker asks Mr. Ives.

"Originally? Tennessee."

Stryker turns to Max. "I mean Jesus Christ, Tennessee."

"Yeah, but that's not the point, Ken," says Max, still aggrieved. "I still see no reason for the ethnic reference."

"But you have no objection to his referring to us as a bunch of chickenshit Ohioans?"

"You're missing my point."

"Let me quote you a figure!" cries Mr. Ives to Stryker, warming to it. "Did you know that there are three thousand and fifty-one TV and radio announcers in the South, of which twenty-two hundred are from Ohio, and that every last one of these twenty-two hundred says 'the difference between he and I'? In twenty years we'll all be talking like that."

But Max and Stryker, still arguing, pay no attention.

The students are both engrossed and discomfited. They chew their lips, pick their noses, fiddle with pencils, glance now at me, now at Mr. Ives. Who can tell them who's right? Students are a shaky dogmatic lot. And the "freer" they are, the more dogmatic. At heart they're totalitarians: they want either total dogmatic freedom or total dogmatic unfreedom, and the one thing that makes them unhappy is something in between.

Art Immelmann looks restive too. He fidgets around on the top step, hands in pockets hiking the skirts of his "bi-swing" jacket, and won't meet my eye. Now what the devil is he doing? He has removed one of the new lapsometers from the carton and is showing it to a student.

The doctors are unhappy too. The behaviorists, I know, don't like Mr. Ives dabbling in science. The visiting proctologists don't like anything they see. Colley Wilkes reverts to an old Alabama posture, hunched forward, hands clasped across wide-apart knees, pants hitched up black fuzzy shins. He clucks and shakes his head. "Man, what is all this?" I imagine him saying.

Moira has emerged from the shadows and taken charge of Mr. Ives's chair from Winnie Gunn, who is out of sight in the tunnel. Moira smiles at me!

Buddy Brown is trying to pick up the pieces of his anger but he's still out of it. He can't make out what happened to him.

Ellen Oglethorpe is torn between her disapproval of The Pit and what seems to be my triumph. But is it a triumph? She sits disgruntled, fingers shoved up into her cheek, shooting warm mothering glances at me, stern Calvinistic glances at the rowdy students.

Lola Rhoades is not paying strict attention. She moves to her own music, lips parted, hissing Brahms. Brahms, old Brahms! We'll sing with you yet of a summer night.

Lola fills every inch of her seat with her splendid self, her arms use both arm rests, her noble knees press against the seat in front.

"Mr. Ives, a final question."

The Director is speaking.

"Why have you neither walked a step nor uttered a word during the past month?"

Mr. Ives scratches his head and squints up the slope. "Well sir, I'll tell you." He lays on the cracker style a bit much to suit me. "There is only one kind of response to those who would control your responses by throwing you in a Skinner box."

"And what would that be?" asks the Director sourly, knowing the answer.

"To refuse to respond at all."

"I see." The Director turns wearily to me. "Doctor, be good enough to give us your therapeutic recommendations and we'll wind this up."

"Yes sir. May I have a word with the patient?"

"By all means."

"Mr. Ives, what are your plans? I mean, if you were free to make plans."

"I intend to go home if I ever get out of this nuthouse."

"Where is home?"

"Sherwood, Tennessee. It's a village in a cove of the Cumberland Plateau. My farm is called Lost Cove."

"What are you going to do there?"

"Write a book, look at the hills, live till I die."

The students avert their eyes.

The Director looks at his watch. "Dr. More?"

"I recommend that Mr. Ives, instead of being sent to the Separation Center in Georgia, be released immediately and furnished with transportation to Sherwood, Tennessee."

"To Tennessee!" cries a student.

"To Tennessee! To Tennessee!" chime in both right-benchers and left-benchers.

Applause breaks out. I take some comfort in it, even though students are a bad lot, fickle as whores, and no professor should take pleasure in their approval.

"Hold it!" cries Buddy Brown, who has pulled himself together. He strides back and forth, sailing his white coat. "This may be good show-boating, but it's sorry damn science. Dr. More has proved he's a good hypnotist, but as for his metaphysical machine—"

"To Tennessee!" cry the students.

Art is busy as a bee.

Some of the students, I notice, have acquired lapsometers from Art, which they wear about their necks like cameras and aim and focus at each other. Now Art Immelmann bounds up the aisle for a fresh supply. Feverishly he hands them out, squatting beside a student to explain the settings and point out skull topography. A dark circle of sweat spreads under his armpit.

A student near the top turns to the girl next to him, lifts her ponytail and places the MOQUOL muzzle on her occiput.

"Wait! No!" I yell at the top of my lungs and go bounding up the steps past the startled Director. "No, Art!"

But Art can't or won't hear. Lapsometers are stacked up his arm like a black marketeer wearing a dozen wristwatches.

Dr. Helga Heine aims a lapsometer at Stryker's midfrontal region.

"Wait, Helga!" I cry. "That thing is not a toy! It is not a prop for The Pit! It's for real! No, Helga!"

"But, *liebchen*, all we're doing is what you yourself suggested," says Helga as Stryker points his lapsometer at the region of her interpersonal sulcus.

"Yes, but my God, what's the setting? Let me see. Oh Lord, he's set the ionization at plus ten!"

Everywhere lapsometers are buzzing like a swarm of bees. Students and doctors and nurses either duck their heads or buzz away at their neighbors' heads with their new hair-dryers.

"STOP I BEG OF YOU!" I yell at the top of my voice.

But nobody pays attention except the Director, who plucks at my sleeve.

"Isn't this all part of the hijinks, Doctor, heh heh. Just what is it you fear?" he asks and cups his ear to hear me in the uproar.

"Goddamn sir," I yell into the hairy old ear. "As I told you earlier, this device is not a toy. It could produce the most serious psychic disturbances."

"Such as?"

"If it were focused over certain frontal areas or the region of the pineal body, which is the seat of selfhood, it could lead to severe angelism, abstraction of the self from itself, and what I call the Lucifer syndrome: that is, envy of the incarnate condition and a resulting caricature of the bodily appetites."

"Eh? What's that? Angelism? Pineal body? Seat of the self? Lucifer? Oh, I get it. Heh heh heh. Very good. Good show, Doctor. But really, I'm afraid The Pit is getting away from us."

"Sir, you don't understand. What I meant—" But Helga jostles me.

She has unwound her hair and let it down like Brunhilde. Placing her hand on her breast, she tells Stryker: "Everything is spirit. *Alles ist Geist.*"

"Right." Stryker nods and puts his hand on her other breast.

"Hold it," I tell Stryker and turn to the Director. "Sir, this is not what it appears."

A powerful grip, catching my arm, yanks me erect. I find myself standing between the two proctologists, Dusty Rhoades and Dr. Walter Bung. Have they—? Yes, Dr. Bung carries a lapsometer slung from his shoulder.

Yet they seem in the best of humors. They nod and wink at each other, claim me as an ally, and give every appearance of approval.

"Did you ever in your life," says Dr. Walter Bung, holding us close, "see this many commonists, atheists, hebes, and fags under one roof?"

"Excuse me, Dr. Bung," I say, unlimbering my lapsometer, "but the fact is that neither they nor you are quite yourselves."

"How's that, son?"

"I'll warrant you your red nucleus is at this moment abnormally active. May I take a reading?"

"What the hell you talking about, boy, my *red*—"

"The reason you're both so upset is this," I tell them both, but at that moment someone, perhaps one of them, pushes me violently and I stumble backward into the pit, nearly cracking my skull.

Moira is standing transfixed behind Mr. Ives's chair.

"Let's go to Howard Johnson's," she whispers, leaning over me as I struggle to get up.

"Get the patient out of here," I tell her.

Moira hesitates, opens and closes her mouth. Mr. Ives rises and takes her arm.

"I'll take care of her, Doctor."

"Thank you."

"Where shall I take her?"

"Are we going to Howard Johnson's?" Moira asks, coming close.

"Yes."

"Then I'll go to my room first."

"I'll take her to her room," Mr. Ives assures me.

"Thank you."

They disappear into the tunnel, Mr. Ives escorting Moira like the Tennessee gentleman that he is.

Colley Wilkes is trying to reach his wife, Fran, by detouring through the pit. But Buddy Brown stands in his way.

"Who you shoving?" asks Buddy.

"Out of my way."

"If there is anything I can't stand, it's a smart-mouth coon."

Buddy picked the wrong man. For Colley is no ordinary Negro, smart-mouthed or not, but a super-Negro who besides speaking five languages and being an electronic wizard, also holds the Black Belt in karate.

Colley pokes his hand, fingers held stiff as a plank, straight into Buddy's throat. Buddy sits down in Mr. Ives's wheelchair and tries to breathe.

I must see to Ellen and Lola.

Halfway up the aisle two students are fighting over a girl. I recognize J. T. Thigpen. The girl is Gloria, by no means a beauty, still dressed in her soiled lab coat, her brass-colored hair sprung out in a circle like a monstrance. The second student is a Knothead named Trasker Gluck. Seeing Trasker and Gloria together, I suddenly realize they are brother and sister.

Trasker and J. T. have each other elbow around neck, grunting and cursing, the way boys fight.

"Hold it, fellows." I try to stop them.

"You stay away from my sister, you son of a bitch," says Trasker, who is a clean-living athletic Baptist type like pole vaulter Bob Richards.

"It's a meaningless relationship and nothing for you to take exception to," grunts J. T. "We get fifty bucks for a successful performance. Let me go, I need the money. Let me go! I feel if we can get over to Love right away we can make it for sure. Let me go! There is nothing between us. Ask your sister."

"Why you son of a bitch, that makes it worse," says Trasker, slamming J.T. squarely on the nose with his big fist.

"Do something, Dr. More!" pleads Gloria. "I love him!"

"Who?"

"J. T.!"

"Excuse me," I say, spying Ellen and Art Immelmann in the next aisle.

Ted 'n Tanya are lying under the seats. I almost step on Ted's back.

"Tom, you were wonderful," says Tanya over Ted's shoulder.

"Thank you."

"Your invention works! We can love. We are loving!"

"Good. Pardon." I step over them.

"All we feared was fear itself."

"I know."

"Stay with us! Share our joy!"

"I can't just now. Pardon."

Warm arms encircle my waist. I find myself sitting in Lola's lap.

"Hi, Sugah!"

"Hi, Lola."

"My, you're a big fine boy!" She gives me a hug.

Reaching back, I give her a hug. She warms my entire back from shoulders to calves.

"Do you love Lola?"

"Yes, I do." I do.

"Lola's got you."

"She sure has."

"When are you coming to see Lola?"

"Tomorrow. No, this evening."

"Lola will make you some gin fizzes and we'll go walking out in the moonlight."

"Absolutely. But you better go home now. I don't want you to get hurt."

"O.K., Sugah," says Lola, giving me a final tremendous squeeze.

*

Dusty seizes my shoulder in his huge hand, working the bones around like dice.

His face looms close, his breath reeks like a lion's.

"You listen here, Doctor."

"Yes, Dusty?"

"You mess with my daughter one more time without wedding bells and you done messed for the last time. You read me?"

"Yes."

"You all right, boy," says Dusty and, taking Dr. Walter Bung in one arm and me in the other, draws the three of us close.

Ellen is shouting angrily at Art Immelmann, who surveys the pit, swinging his arms idly and whistling loudly and accurately *Nola*, the piano theme of Vincent Lopez, a band leader in the Middle Auto Age.

I snatch Ellen away.

"Stay away from him."

"Chief, he got your lapsometers!" Ellen is sobbing with rage.

"I know."

"What are we going to do?" asks Ellen, wringing her hands.

"Just look."

Below us the pit writhes like a den of vipers. Now and then an arm is raised, fist clenched, to fall in a blow. Bare legs are upended.

"Listen." I whisper in Ellen's ear. "While I am talking to Art, take the rest of the lapsometers in the carton and put them in your car. I'll call you tomorrow."

"O.K., Chief. But are you leaving?"

"I have to collect all the loose ones."

"I'm not leaving without you!"

"You son of a bitch," I tell Art. "What did you pull this stunt for?"

"I am not a son of a bitch," says Art, looking puzzled. "Take it easy, Doc." As usual he has no sense of distance, comes too close, and blows Sen-Sen in my face.

"I told you specifically to leave my lapsometers alone."

"How are we going to run a pilot on your hardware without using your hardware?"

"Pilot! Is this what you call a pilot?"

"Doc, we can't go national until we test the interactions in a pilot. That's boilerplate, Doc."

"Boilerplate my ass. Goddamn it, don't you know the dangers of what you're doing? We're sitting on a dome of Heavy Salt, the President is coming tomorrow, and what do you do? Turn loose my lapsometers cranked up to ten plus."

"Doc, does this look political to you?" He nods at the lovers and fist-fighters. "This is not political. It is a test of your hypotheses about vagal rage and abstract lust, as you of all people should know. And as for the dangers of a chain reaction, there's no Heavy Salt within three miles of here."

"We're through, Art. I'm canceling the contract."

"You'll be right as rain tomorrow, Doc. Just remember: music, love, and the dream of summer."

Max Gottlieb and Ellen hold me tight, one at each elbow.

"Let's go home, fella," says Max. "You've been great."

"Wait a minute. I'm needed here, Max."

"He's right, Chief. You're worn out."

"I'm not leaving until I collect all the lapsometers."

"I'll get them for you," says Max. "You go home and get a good night's sleep. Or better still, go back to A-4."

"Damn it, Max, don't you realize what's happening?"

"I'm afraid I do. Your device has triggered a mass hysteria. Like the St. Vitus's dance in the Middle Ages. These are strange times."

"Listen to me, Max. Number one, my lapsometer works. You saw it. Number two, it has fallen into the wrong hands. Number three, the effect here is mainly erotic but it could just as easily have been political. Number four, the President and Vice-President will be in this area tomorrow. Number five, there are plans to kidnap you and hold you prisoner in the Honey Island wilderness. Number six, we're sitting on the biggest Heavy Salt dome in North America."

"Oh boy," says Max to Ellen.

Ellen frowns. She is loyal to me.

"I believe you, Chief. But if what you say is true, you're going to need all your strength tomorrow."

"That's true. But I feel fine right now." How lovely you are, Ellen. Perspiration glitters like diamonds in the down of her short upper lip.

"What's that, Chief?" asks Ellen quickly. Did I say it aloud? She blushes and tugs at my arm. "Come on now!" At the same time I feel a pinprick in my other arm. Max has given me a shot through my coat sleeve.

"You're going to get a good night's sleep. Ellen will take you home. I'll drop in on you tomorrow morning." He holds my hand affectionately. I see him look at the scars on my wrist. "Take care of yourself now."

"I feel fine, Max." I do. I can still hear music.

"Let's go out through the tunnel, Chief. My car is in the back."

I say goodbye to the Director, but he is engrossed with a young medical student. It is Carruthers Calhoun, scion of an old-line Southern family, a handsome peach-faced lad.

"Wasn't it Socrates," the Director is saying, a friendly arm flung across the boy's shoulders, "who said: A fair woman is a lovely thing, truth lovelier still, but a fair youth is the fairest of all?"

"No sir," replies Carruthers, who graduated from Sewanee with a classical education. "That was Juvenal and he didn't quite say that."

JULY FOURTH

On the Way to Meet Moira
at Howard Johnson's
8:30 A.M. / JULY 4

ONLY THREE hours' sleep after my night call to the love couple with the diarrheic infant in the swamp.

A cold shower and a breakfast of warm Tang-vodka-duck-eggs-Tabasco and I'm back to normal, which is to say tolerably depressed and terrified.

At the first flicker of morning terror I remember the modified lapsometer and fetching it from my bag, an odd-looking thing with its snout-like attachment, give myself a light brain massage.

Terror gone! Instantly exhilarated! The rip and race of violins. By no means drunk, clairvoyant rather, prescient, musical, at once abstracted, seeing things according to their essences, and at the same time poised for the day's adventure in the wide world, I achieve a noble evacuation and go forth, large bowel clear as a bell. Clay lies still but blood's a rover.

A hot still gold-green Fourth of July. Not a breath stirs. No squirrels scrabble in the dogwoods, no jaybirds fret in the sycamores.

Cutting now through the "new" 18, which is really the old since the construction of the Cypress Garden 36. Hm. Something is amiss. The Fourth of July and not a soul on the links. What with the Pro-Am using Cypress Garden, the "new" 18 ought to be jammed!

Weeds sprout in the fairways. Blackberries flourish in the rough. Rain shelters are green leafy caves.

Someone is following me. *Clink-clink.* I stop and listen. Not a sound. Start and there it is again: *clink-clink, clink-clink*, the sound a caddy makes when he's humping it off the tee to get down to the dogleg in time for the drive, hand held over the clubs to keep them quiet but one or two blades slap together *clink-clink*.

But there's no one in sight.

Now comes the sound of—firecrackers? Coming from the direction of the school.

There is a roaring and crackling in the dogleg of number 5. Rounding the salient of woods and all of a sudden knowing what it is before I see it, I see it: the Bledsoe Spanish-mission house burning from the inside. The fire is a cheerful uproarious blaze going like sixty at every window, twenty windows and twenty roaring hearths, fat pine joists popping sociably and not a soul in sight. No fire department, no spectators, nothing but the bustling commerce of flames in the still sunlight.

I watch from the green cave of a shelter. Yonder in the streaked stucco house dwelled the childless Bledsoes for thirty years while golf balls caromed off the walls, broke the windows and rooftiles, ricocheted around the patio.

The house roars and crackles busily in the silence. Flames lick out the iron grills and up the blackened stucco.

Into these very woods came I as a boy while the house was a-building, picked up triangles of new copper flashing, scraps of aluminum, freshly sawn blocks of two-by-fours—man's excellent geometries wrought from God's somewhat lumpish handiwork. Here amid the interesting carpenter's litter, I caressed the glossy copper, smelled the heart pine, thought impure thoughts and defiled myself in the skeletal bathroom above the stuffed stumps of plumbing, a thirteen-year-old's lonesome leaping love on a still summer afternoon.

My chest is buzzing. Ach, a heart attack for sure! Clutching at my shirt, I shrink into the corner. For sure it is calcium dislodged and rattling like dice in my heart's pitiful artery. Poor Thomas! Dead at forty-five of a coronary! Not at all unusual either, especially in Knothead circles here in Paradise: many a good Christian and loving father, family man, and churchgoer has kicked off in his thirties. A vice clamps under my sternum and with it comes belated contrition. God, don't let me die. I haven't lived, and there's the summer ahead and music and science and girls— No. No girls! No more lewd thoughts! No more lusting after my neighbors' wives and daughters! No hankering after strange women! No more humbug! No more great vaulting lewd daytime longings, no whispering into pretty ears, no more assignations in closets, no more friendly bumping of nurses from behind, no more night adventures in bunkers and sand traps, no more inviting Texas girls out into the gloaming: "I am Thomas More. You are lovely and I love you. I have a heart full of love. Could we go out into the gloaming?" No more.

My chest buzzes away.

Clutching at my shirt in a great greasy cold sweat, I encounter it, the buzzing box. Whew. Well. It is not my heart after all but my Anser-Phone calling me, clipped to my shirt pocket and devised just for the purpose of reaching docs out on the golf links.

Whew. Lying back and closing my eyes, I let it buzz. If it wasn't a heart attack, it's enough to give you one.

It is Ellen Oglethorpe. Switch off the buzzer and move around to a shady quarter of the green cave to escape the heat of the fire.

Now resting in the corner and listening to Ellen and giving myself another brain massage. I could use an Early Times too.

"What is it, Ellen?"

"Oh, Chief, where have you been? I've been out of my mind! You just don't know. Where've you been all night?" Comes the tiny insectile voice, an angry cricket in my pocket.

"What's the trouble?"

"You've got to get down here right away, Chief."

"Where are you?"

"At the office."

"It's the Fourth of July and I have an engagement."

"Engagement my foot. You mean a date. You're not fooling me."

"O.K., I'm not fooling you."

"I know who you have a date with and where, don't worry about that."

"All right, I won't."

"Chief—"

"Ellen, listen to me, I want you to call the fire department and send them out to Paradise. The Bledsoe house is on fire."

"Are you kidding?"

"Eh? I can hardly hear you." I incline an ear to my bosom.

"They're not taking calls out there, not the police or anybody. That's why I was so worried about you."

"What are you talking about?"

"There's some sort of disturbance out there. Riffraff from the swamp, I believe."

"Nonsense. There's not a soul here."

"Everybody out there has moved into town. It's an armed camp here, Chief. You wouldn't believe it."

"What happened?"

"It started with the atrocity last night—right where you are. At the Bledsoes'."

"Atrocity?"

"Mrs. Bledsoe was killed with that barbecue thing. Mr. Bledsoe has disappeared. No doubt he's dead too. The work of madmen."

Mrs. Bledsoe. Skewered with P. T.'s kebab skewer.

"Chief, you better get out of there!"

"There's no one here," I say absently.

"Oh, and we've got a roomful of patients."

"On the Fourth of July?"

"Your new assistant is treating them."

"Who? Speak up, Ellen, I can't hear you."

"I can't talk any louder, Chief. I'm hiding in the EEG room. I said Dr. Immelmann has a roomful of patients and some very strange patients, I must say."

"Dr. Immelmann! What the hell is he doing there?"

"Treating patients with your lapsometer. He said you would understand, that it was part of your partnership agreement. But, Chief, there's something wrong here."

"What?"

"They're fighting. In your waiting room and in the street."

"Who's fighting?"

"Mr. Ledbetter and Mr. Tennis got in a fight, and—"

"Let me speak to Art Immelmann."

"He just left. I can see him going down the street."

"All right. Ellen, here's what you do. Are the lapsometers still there?"

"Well, only half of them. And only because I hid them."

"Where did you hide them?"

"In a crate of Bayonne-rayon training members."

"Good girl. Now here's what you do. Take the crate to your car. Lock it in the trunk. Go home. I'll get back to you later."

"When?"

"Shortly. I have something to attend to first."

"Don't think I don't know what it is."

"All right, I won't."

Ellen begins to scold. I unclip the Anser-Phone and hang it in the rafters among the dirt-daubers. While Ellen buzzes away, I take a small knock of Early Times and administer a plus-four Sodium jolt to Brodmann 11, the zone of the musical-erotic.

Waltzing now to *Wine, Women and Song* while Ellen Oglethorpe chirrups away in the rafters, a tiny angry Presbyterian cricket.

"Chief," says the insectile voice. "You're not living up to the best that's in you."

"The best? Isn't happiness better than misery?"

"Because the best that's in you is so fine."

"Thank you." From the edge of the woods comes a winey smell where the fire's heat strikes the scuppernongs.

"People like that, Chief, are not worthy of you."

"People like what?" *People* pronounced by Ellen in that tone has a feminine gender. Female people.

"You know who I mean."

"I'm not sure. Who?"

"People like that Miss Schaffner and Miss Rhoades."

"Are you jealous?"

"Don't flatter yourself, Doctor."

"Very well." I'm waltzing.

Wien Wien, du du allein

"Oh, Chief. Are you drinking?"

I must be singing out loud.

"Goodbye, Ellen. Go home and sit tight until you hear from me."

I turn off the cricket in the rafters and snap the Anser-Phone in a side pocket, away from my heart.

Again the popping of firecrackers. The sound comes from the south. Taking cover in the gloom of the pines, I look between the trunks down number 5 fairway, 475 yards, par five. Beyond the green are the flat buildings of the private school. The firecrackers come from there. The grounds are deserted, but a spark of fire appears at a window, then a *crack*. Is somebody shooting? Two yellow school buses are parked in front. Now comes a regular fusillade, sparkings at every window, then a sputtering like a string of Chinese crackers. People run for the buses, majorettes and pom-pom girls for the first bus, their silver uniforms glittering in the sun. The moms bring up the rear, hustling along, one hand clamped to their hats, the other swinging big tote bags. A police car pulls ahead, the buses follow, a motorcycle brings up the rear. As soon as the little cavalcade disappears, the firing stops.

Was it fireworks or were people inside the building directing covering fire at an unseen enemy?

2

At Howard Johnson's.

Moira gives me a passionate kiss tasting of Coppertone. She is sunbathing beside the scummy pool. Her perfect little body, clad in an old-fashioned two-piece bikini, lies prone on a plastic recliner. Though her shoulder straps have been slipped down, she makes much of her modesty, clutching bra to breast as, I perceive, she imagines girls used to in the old days.

"A kiss for the champ," she says.

"For who?"

"You beat Buddy."

"Oh."

"Poor Buddy. Wow, what a bombshell you dropped. Total chaos. Did you plan it that way?"

"Chaos?"

"In The Pit, stupid."

"Yes, The Pit. Yes. No, I didn't plan it exactly that way." I notice that she has a dimple at each corner of her sacrum, each whorled by down.

"I heard the Director tell Dr. Stryker to sign you up and keep you here at any cost."

"What do you think that meant?"

"Before Harvard or M.I.T. grab you, silly."

"I'm not so sure. What was going on over there when you left this morning?"

"Quiet as a tomb. Everyone's gone to the beaches."

The golden down on her forearm is surprisingly thick. I turn her arm over and kiss the sweet salty fossa where the blood beats like a thrush's throat.

Spying two snakes beside the pool, I pick up a section of vacuum hose and run around the apron and chase them off, and sing *Louisiana Lou* to hear the echoes from the quadrangle.

"Are you going to take the job, Tom?" asks Moira, sitting up. The lounge leaves a pattern of diamonds on the front of her thighs.

"What job? Oh. Well, I'm afraid there's going to be some trouble around here. You're sure you didn't notice anything unusual this morning?"

"Unusual? No. I did meet that funny little man who was helping you yesterday."

"Helping me?"

"Helping you pass out your props. Wow, how did you do it?"

"He wasn't helping me. He was—never mind. What was he doing this morning?"

"Nothing. He passed me carrying a box."

"How big?"

"Yay big."

I frown. Ordinarily I don't like girls who say *yay big*.

The box. Oh my. Terror flickers. I take a drink.

"He was very polite, knew my name and all. In fact, he sent his regards to you. How did he know I was going to see you? Did you tell him?"

"Certainly not."

"Rub some of this on me, Tommy." She hands me the ancient Pompeian phial of Coppertone.

"O.K. But you realize you can't go in the pool."

"Ugh," she says, looking at the pool. "I can't. What'll I do?"

"I'll show you. But let me rub you first."

Foreseeing everything, I had earlier made an excuse and hopped up to the room, cranked up the generator and turned on the air-conditioner.

Now, when Moira's had enough of the sweat and the grease and the heat, I lead her by the hand to the balcony. From the blistering white heat of the concrete we come into a dim cool grotto. Fogs of cold air blow from the shuddering tin-lizzy of an air-conditioner. The yellow bed lamp shines down on fresh sheets. A recorder plays ancient Mantovani music—not exactly my favorite, but Moira considers Mantovani "classical."

Moira claps her hands and hugs me.

"Oh lovely lovely lovely! How perfect! Whose room?"

"Ours," I say, humming *There's a Small Hotel with a Wishing Well.*

"You mean you fixed it up like this?"

"Sure. Remember the way it was?"

"My heavens. Sheets even. Air-conditioner. Why did you do it?"

"For love. All for love. Let me show you this."

I show her the "shower": a pistol-grip nozzle screwed onto two hundred feet of garden hose hooked at the other end to the spigot in the Esso station grease-rack next door.

"And soap! And towels! Go away, I'm taking my shower now."

"O.K. But let me do this." I turn on the nozzle to get rid of two hundred feet of hot water.

While Moira showers, I lie on the bed and look at *The Laughing Cavalier* and the Maryland hunt scene in the wallpaper. Mantovani plays, the shower runs, Moira sings. I mix a toddy and let it stand on my chest and think of Doris, my dead wife who ran off to Cozumel with a heathen Englishman.

Doris and I used to travel the highways in the old Auto Age before Samantha was born, roar seven hundred miles a day along the great interstates to some glittering lost motel twinkling away in the twilight set down in the green hills of Tennessee or out in haunted New Mexico, swim in the pool, take steaming baths, mix many toddies, eat huge steaks, run back to the room, fall upon each other laughing and hollering, and afterwards lie dreaming in one another's arms watching late-show Japanese science-fiction movies way out yonder in the lost yucca flats of Nevada.

Sunday mornings I'd leave her and go to mass. Now here was the strangest exercise of all! Leaving the coordinate of the motel at the intersection of the interstates, leaving the motel with standard doors and carpets and plumbing, leaving the interstates extending infinitely in all directions, abscissa and ordinate, descending through a moonscape countryside

to a—town! Where people had been living all these years, and
to some forlorn little Catholic church up a side street just in
time for the ten-thirty mass, stepping up on the porch as if I
had been doing it every Sunday for the past twenty years, and
here comes the stove-up bemused priest with his cup (what am
I doing out here? says his dazed expression) upon whose head
hands had been laid and upon this other head other hands and
so on, for here off I-51 I touched the thread in the labyrinth,
and the priest announced the turkey raffle and Wednesday
bingo and preached the Gospel and fed me Christ—

—Back to the motel then, exhilarated by—what? by eating
Christ or by the secret discovery of the singular thread in this
the unlikeliest of places, this geometry of Holiday Inns and
interstates? back to lie with Doris all rosy-fleshed and creased
of cheek and slack and heavy-limbed with sleep, cracking one
eye and opening her arms and smiling.

"My God, what is it you do in church?"

What she didn't understand, she being spiritual and seeing
religion as spirit, was that it took religion to save me from
the spirit world, from orbiting the earth like Lucifer and the
angels, that it took nothing less than touching the thread off
the misty interstates and eating Christ himself to make me
mortal man again and let me inhabit my own flesh and love
her in the morning.

Moira comes out wound up in a towel, rubbing her short
blond hair with another towel.

"Feel me."

The flesh of her arm is cold-warm, the blood warmth just
palpable through her cold smooth skin.

"Let me get up to take a shower." Moira is sitting in my lap.
She won't get up so I get up with her and walk around holding
her in my arms like a child.

"Don't," says Moira.

"Don't what?"

"Don't take a shower."

"Why not?"

"I like the way you smell. You smell like Uncle Bud."

"Who is Uncle Bud?"

"He has a chicken farm out from Parkersburg. I used to go
see him Sunday mornings and sit in his lap while he read me

the funnies. He always smelled like whiskey and sweat and seersucker."

"Do I look like Uncle Bud?"

"No, you look like Rod McKuen."

"He's rather old."

"But you both look poetic."

"I brought along his poems for you."

"Which ones?"

"The ones about sea gulls."

"You've thought of everything."

"You're a lovely girl," I say, holding and patting her just as I used to pat Samantha when she had growing pains.

"Do you love me?"

"Oh yes."

"How much?"

"Enough to eat you," I say and begin to eat her kneecap.

"Enough to marry me?"

"What?"

"Do you love me enough to marry me?"

"Oh yes."

"Do you know what I've always wanted?"

"No."

"To keep some chickens."

"All right."

"Golden banties. You know what?"

"What?"

"That work at the clinic is a lot of bull. I'd love to stay home raising golden banties while you are doing your famous researches."

"All right." I suck the cold-warm flesh of her forearm covered by long whorled down. The fine hair rises to my mouth and makes a skein like the tiny ropes that bound Gulliver.

"Could we live in Paradise?"

"Certainly."

Eating her, I have visions of golden cockerels glittering like topazes in the morning sun in my "enclosed patio."

"When?"

"When what?"

"When will we do that?"

"Whenever you like," I say, marveling at her big littleness. My arms gauge a secret amplitude in her. She is small and heavy.

"No really. When?"

"When we leave here."

"When will that be?"

"A week, a month. Perhaps longer."

"My Lord," says Moira, straightening in my arms like a child wanting to be put down. "What do you mean?"

"I'm afraid something is going to happen today, in fact is happening now, which will make it impossible for us to leave here for a while. At least until I make sure it's safe for us either in Paradise or the Center."

"What do you *mean*? When I left there this morning, the place was dead as a doornail."

"For one thing a revolution may have occurred. There is a report that guerrillas from Honey Island are in Paradise. I fear too that there may be disorders today at the political rally near Fedville."

"You don't have to go to this much trouble to keep me here, you know."

"Let me show you something."

I carry her to the window, where she pulls back the curtain. Five columns of smoke come from the green ridge above the orange tiles of the ice-cream restaurant.

"There was only one fire when I was there earlier."

"What does that mean?"

"They're burning the houses on the old 18."

"O my Lord."

"But that's not the worst. I'm afraid my invention has fallen into the wrong hands."

"What does that mean?"

"Two things. Civil war and a chain reaction in the Heavy Sodium deposits."

"But I can't stay here." Moira straightens in my arms again. "Why not?"

"I don't have anything to wear! All I have is the clothes on my back—the clothes in there, that is."

"Let me show you something else. Open the top drawer."

She opens it. "What in the world?" The top drawer has underclothes, blouses, slips. The other drawers have skirts, dresses, shorts, etcetera.

"Whose are they?" asks Moira, frowning.

"Yours."

"Were they your wife's?"

"No. She'd make two of you."

"Gollee." Moira gets down, opens the bottom drawer, sits drumming her fingers on the Gideon. "And what are we going to live on? Love?"

"Let me show you."

I take her to the closet. She gazes at the crates and cartons stacked to the ceiling, cartons of Campbell's chicken-and-rice, Underwood ham, Sunmaid raisins, cases of Early Times and Swiss Colony sherry (which Moira likes). And the Great Books stacked alongside.

"That's enough for a small army."

"Or for two people for a long time."

"Who's going to read all those books?"

"We'll read them aloud to each other."

Think of it: reading Aeschylus, in the early fall, in old Howard Johnson's, off old I-11, with Moira.

"What about Rod McKuen?"

"He's over there. Under the Gideon."

"There's no pots and pans," says Moira suddenly.

"The kitchenette's next door."

"Good night, nurse."

"Let me show you something else." We sit on the bed. "Put this quarter in the slot there."

The Slepe-Eze starts up and sets the springs gently vibrating.

"Oh no!" Moira's eyes round. "I guess they had to have this."

"They?"

"The salesmen."

"Yes."

"Those poor lonely men. Think of it."

"Yes."

"Making love and dying in a place like this, far from home."

"Dying?"

"The Death of a Salesman."

"Right. Come sit in Uncle Bud's lap."

"All right. Honey?"

"Yes."

"Let's have children."

"All right." How odd. The idea of Moira and me having a child is the oddest thing in the world. But why? "First, let's fix us a drink."

"All right."

She sits in my lap and we drink. She insists on whiskey rather than her sherry since that was what the flappers and salesmen drank.

"This beats Knott's Berry Farm," she whispers.

"Yes."

One difference between Moira and my wife, Doris, is that Doris liked motels that were in the middle of nowhere, at the intersection of I-89 and I-23 in the Montana badlands. While Moira likes a motel near a point of interest such as Seven Flags over Texas.

Now we lie in one another's arms on the humming bed. She is as trim and quick as one of her banty hens. She's a West Virginia tomboy brown as a berry and strong-armed and -legged from climbing trees.

Cold fogs of air blow over us, Mantovani plays Jerome Kern. "I love classical music," whispers Moira. *The Laughing Cavalier* smiles down on us, hundreds of Maryland hunters leap the same fence around the walls.

Locked about one another we go spinning down old Louisiana misty green, slowly revolving and sailing down the summer wind. How prodigal is she with and how little store she sets by her perfectly formed Draw-Me arms and legs.

Now she lies in the crook of my arm, eyes open, tapping her hard little fingernail on her tooth. Her little mind ranges far and wide. She casts ahead, making plans, no doubt, doing my living room over. I took her there once and it was an unhappy business, she keeping her head down and looking up through her eyebrows at Doris's great abstract enamels that went leaping around the walls like the seven souls of Shiva.

"Do you like my hair long?"

"Do you call it long now?"

"Yes."

"Yes."

When my daughter, Samantha, was a freshman in high school, she had her first date, a blind one for the Introductory Prom, the boys from Saint Aloysius drawing the Saint Mary's girls from a hat. Samantha and I sat waiting for the date, I with my instructions not to open the front door until she had a chance to leave the room so that she could then be a little late, she with her blue pinafore skirt tucked under her fat knees. We watched *Gunsmoke* as we waited. The boy didn't come. *Gunsmoke* gave way to the Miss America pageant. Bert Parks went nimbly backstepping around snaking the mike cord out of his way. Samantha's acne began to itch.

"I wouldn't have missed this, Poppa," said Samantha as we watched Miss Nebraska recite "If" in the talent contest. But she was clawing at herself.

"Me neither."

I began to itch too and needed only a potsherd and dung-heap. Curse God, curse the nuns for arranging the dance, goddamn the little Celt-Catholic bastards, little Mediterranean lowbrow Frenchy-dago jerks. Anglo-Saxon Presbyterians would have better manners even if they didn't believe in God.

"Why are you crying?" Moira asks me, rubbing my back briskly. She wants to get up.

"I'm not crying."

"Your eyes are wet."

"Tears of joy."

But Moira, paying no attention, raises herself on one elbow to see herself in the mirror.

"Nothing is wrong with two people in love loving each other," says Moira, turning her head to see her hair. "Buddy says that joy not guilt—"

"Buddy says!" Angrily I pull back from her. "What the hell does Buddy have to do with it?"

"All I meant was—"

"And just when did the son of a bitch say it? On just such an occasion as this?"

"At a lecture," says Moira quickly. "Anyhow"—she levels her eyes with mine—"what makes you so different?"

"Different? What do you mean? Do you mean that you—that he—? Don't tell me."

"I won't. Because it's not true."

But I can't hear her for my own groaning. Why am I so jealous? It's not that, though. It's just that I can't understand how Moira can hold herself so cheaply. Why doesn't she attach the same infinite values to her favors that I do? With her I feel like a man watching a child run around with a forty-carat diamond. Her casualness with herself makes me sweat.

"It's just that—" I begin when the knock comes at the door.

For a long moment Moira and I search each other's eyes as if the knock came from there.

"The Bantus," whispers Moira.

"No," I say, but get up in some panic and disarray. Getting killed is not so bad. What is to be feared is getting killed in a bathtub like Marat.

Moira breaks for the bathroom. I finish off my toddy and brush my hair.

Comes the knock again, light knuckles on the hollow door. Somehow I know who it is the second my hand touches the doorknob.

It is Ellen, of course, in uniform, with the wind up, color high in her cheeks, head reared a little so that the curve of her cheek narrows her eyes, which are icy-Lake-Geneva blue. It is hotter than ever, but a purple thunderhead towers behind her. Her uniform is crisp. The only sign of the heat is the sparkle of perspiration in the dark down of her lip.

"Come in come in come in."

She's all business and a-bustle, starch whistling as if she were paying a house call. When she sets down her bag, I notice her hands are trembling.

"What's the matter?"

"Somebody shot at me," she says, leafing nervously through the Gideon, unseeing.

"Where?"

"Coming past the church."

"Maybe it was firecrackers."

She slams the Bible shut. "Why didn't you answer the Anser-Phone?"

"I guess I turned it off."

Ellen, still blinded by the sunlight, gazes uncertainly at the dim fogbanks rolling around the room. I guide her to the foot of the bed. I sit on the opposite bed.

"Chief, I think you better come back to the office."

"Why?"

"Dr. Immelmann found the box of lapsometers."

"I know."

"You know? How?"

"Moira told me she saw him."

"Oh. Chief, he's been handing them out to people."

"What sort of people?"

"Some very strange people."

"Yes, hm." I am eyeing the dressing room nervously. Moira is stirring about but Ellen pays no attention.

"I heard him send one man to NASA, another to Boeing."

"It sounds serious."

"When the fight started, I left."

"What fight?"

"Between Mr. Tennis and Mr. Ledbetter."

"Is that Ted Tennis, Chico?" cries Moira, bursting out of the dressing room. "Oh hello there!" She smiles brilliantly at Ellen and strides about the room, hands thrust deep in the pockets of the blue linen long-shorts I bought for her. They fit. "These really fit, Chico," she says, wheeling about.

Chico? Where did she get that? Then I remember. When we stayed in the small hotel with the wishing well in Mérida, she called me Chico a couple of times.

"Yes. Ah, do you girls know each other?"

"Oh yes!"

"Yes indeed!"

Ellen then goes on talking to me as if Moira had not come in.

"And that's not the worst, Chief."

"It isn't?"

Ellen and I are still sitting at the foot of separate beds. Moira stretches out behind *me*. Both girls are making me nervous.

"I heard him tell the same two men that five o'clock was the deadline."

"Deadline?"

"I didn't know what he meant either. When I asked him, he

said that was the time when we'd know which way your great experiment would go. What did he mean by that?"

"I'm not sure."

"He said you'd know. He said if worst came to worst, you had the means of protecting us and that you would know what he meant."

"I see."

"What do you suppose that means, Chico?" asks Moira, giving me a nudge in the back with her toe. I wish she wouldn't do that. "Is that why we have to stay here?"

"Ahem, it may have something to do with that."

"Give me a quarter."

"O.K.," I say absently.

Moira puts the quarter into the slot. The Slepe-Eze begins to vibrate under me. I jump up.

Ellen manages to ignore the vibrating bed.

"Chief, he said you would know what to look for at five o'clock."

"Right," I say eagerly. The prospect of a catastrophe is welcome. "Three things are possible: a guerrilla attack, a chain reaction, and a political disturbance at the speech-making."

"Pshaw," says Moira, gazing at the ceiling. "I don't think anything is going to happen. Idle rumors."

My eyes roll up. Never in her life has Moira said *pshaw* before—pronounced with a *p*. She read it somewhere.

"That was no rumor that took a shot at me," says Ellen, looking at me blinkered as if I had said it. She hasn't yet looked at Moira.

"I imagine not," I say, frowning. I wish the mattress would stop vibrating. I find myself headed for the door. "I better take a look around. I'll bring y'all a Dr. Pepper."

"Wait, Chico." Moira takes my hand. "I'll go with you. Don't forget you promised me a tour of the ruins, the ice-cream parlor, the convention room where all the salesmen used to glad-hand each other." She swings around. "It's been nice seeing you again, Miss Ah—"

"I'll be running on," says Ellen, reaching the door ahead of us.

"No, Ellen." I take her arm. "I'm afraid you can't leave."

"Why not?"

"I want to make sure the coast is clear."

"Very well, Chief."

To my surprise, Ellen shrugs and perches herself—on the still-humming bed!

"You want to come with us?"

"No no. You kids run along. I'll hold the fort. I see you have food. I'll fix some sandwiches while you're gone."

"Let me show you where everything is, honey," says Moira. The two huddle over the picnic basket.

Oh, they're grand girls though. Whew. What a relief to see them get along! There's no sight more reassuring than two women working over food. Women needn't be catty! Perhaps we three could be happy here.

"We'll be back, Ellen!" cries Moira, yanking me after her. "If things get slow, there's always the Gideon."

Now why did she have to say that?

"You mean you didn't bring your manual from Love?" laughs Ellen, waving us on our way.

"Ha ha, very good, girls," I say, laughing immoderately. They are great girls, though. Whew. A relief nevertheless to close the door between the two of them and be on our way.

3

Moira was never more loving or lovable. By turns playful, affectionate, mournful, prattling, hushed, she darts ahead like a honeybee tasting the modest delights of this modest ruin.

"Do you think there's any danger, Chico?" she calls back.

"I doubt if there's anyone around."

"What about Ellen's sniper?"

"Well—"

"She spooks easy, huh?"

"No. On the contrary."

"Do you like her?"

"She's a fine nurse."

"But do you like her?"

"Like?"

"Or as you say, fancy."

"No. I fancy you."

We're behind the registration desk reading the names of long-departed guests, not salesmen, I notice, but families, mom and pop and the kids bound for the Gulf Coast or the Smokies or Seven Flags.

Now we're under the moldering Rotary banner in the dark banquet room arm in arm and as silent as we were last summer at Ghost Town, U.S.A. Moira reads the banner.

> *Is it the Truth?*
> *Is it fair to all concerned?*

I squeeze her pliant belted rough-linened waist. The linen reminds me of Doris. Was that why I got it?

"Let's stay here a while." I draw her behind the banner. What an odd thing to be forty-five and in love and with exactly the same pang of longing in the heart as at age sixteen.

Moira laughs. "Let's go get a Dr. Pepper."

In the arcade, dim and cool as a catacomb, she skips along the bank of vending machines pulling Baby Ruth levers. Pausing in her ballet, she stoops and mock-drinks at a rusted-out watercooler.

I stoop over her, covering her, wondering why God gave man such an ache in his heart.

"You're a lovely girl," I say.

CooooorangEEEEEEEE. The cinderblock at my ear explodes and goes singing off down the arcade. It seems I am blinking and looking at the gouge in the block and feeling my cheek, which has been stung by twenty mosquitoes.

CoooooRUNK. The block doesn't sing. But I notice that a hole has appeared in the lip of the basin where the metal is bent double in a flange. I fall down on Moira, jamming her into the space between cooler and ice machine.

"You crazy fool! Get off me! You're killing me!"

"Shut up. Somebody is trying to kill us."

Moira becomes quiet and small and hot, like a small boy at the bottom of pile-on. Craning up, I can see the hole in the lip of the cooler basin but not through to the top hole. The second shot did not ricochet. It is possible to calculate that the shot came into the arcade at an angle and from a higher place. No doubt from a balcony room across the pool. Perhaps directly opposite the room where Ellen is.

My feet feel exposed, as if they were sticking off the end of a bed. My arms tremble from the effort of keeping my weight off Moira.

The third shot does not come.

"Here's what we're going to do," I tell her, still covering her. "I think we can squeeze around behind the ice-maker and come out beyond the line of fire. You go first."

Moira nods, dumb, and begins to tremble. She has just realized what has happened.

"Now!"

I follow her. We wait between Coke machine and ice-maker.

"Now!"

We break for the far end of the arcade and the rear of the motel.

Out to the weedy easement where my water hose runs from the Esso station. The elderberry is shoulder high. We keep low and follow the hose. It turns up the wall to the bathroom window.

It is an easy climb up the panel of simulated wrought-iron and fairly safe behind the huge Esso oval.

"I'll go up first," I tell Moira, "take a look around and signal you."

I climb in the window and run for my revolver in the closet without even looking at Ellen, who is shouting something from the bed.

"Bolt the door, Ellen."

Back to the bathroom to cover Moira, who is looking straight up from the elderberries, mouth open. I beckon her up.

Turn off the air-conditioner.

We three sit on the floor of the dressing room. No sound outside. Moira begins to whisper to Ellen, telling her what happened. I am thinking. Already it is hotter.

"He's going to kill us all," says Ellen presently. She sits cross-legged like a campfire girl, tugs her skirt over her knees. "It must be a madman."

"A very very sick person," says Moira, frowning.

They're wrong. It's worse, I'm thinking. It's probably a

Bantu from the swamp, out to kill me and take the girls. It comes over me: why, the son of a bitch is out to kill me and take the girls!

Presently the girls relax. I stand at the front window and watch the opposite balcony.

Does the curtain move?

But there is nothing to be seen, no rifle barrel.

Ellen is leafing through a directory of nationwide Howard Johnson motels. Moira is clicking her steely thumbnail against a fingernail.

Whup! Something about the revolver looks wrong. I spin the cylinder. Something is wrong. It's not loaded. Heart sinks. What to do? Fetch my carbine. But that means leaving the girls. Then I'll have to take the sniper with me.

I think of something.

"Where is your car parked, Ellen?"

"Beyond the restaurant."

"Next to the fence?"

"Yes."

"All right. Listen, girls. We can't stay here like this—with him out there. Not for days or weeks."

"Weeks!" cries Ellen. "What do you mean?"

"Here's what we're going to do. Who can shoot a pistol?"

"Not me," says Moira.

Ellen takes the empty revolver. It'll make them feel better.

"It's cocked and off safety. Shoot anybody who tries to get in. If it's me, I'll whistle like a towhee. Like this. Now lock the bathroom window behind me. I'll have to undo the hose."

"What do you have in mind, Chief?" asks Ellen, all business. She's my girl Friday again. She's also one up on Moira.

"I'm going to get my carbine. I also have to check on my mother. Truthfully I don't think anybody's going to bother you here. I'm going to make a lot of noise just in case somebody's still hanging around, and I think he'll follow me. He's been following me for days. Ellen, let's check the Anser-Phones. We'll stay in touch. See what you can find out about what's going on. Sorry about the air-conditioner, but I think it's going to rain."

The girls look solemn. I take a drink of Early Times and fill my flask.

4

A simple matter to follow the weedy easement past the ice-cream restaurant to Ellen's neat little Toyota electric parked between a rusted hulk of a Cadillac and a broken-back vineclad Pontiac. No bullet holes in the windows.

Head out straight across the plaza making as big a show as possible, stomping the carriage bell and zigzagging the tiller—you sit sideways and work a tiller and scud along like a catboat. Ellen's car is both Japanese and Presbyterian, thrifty, tidy, efficient, chaste. As a matter of fact, Ellen was born in Japan of Georgia Presbyterian missionaries.

No one follows. Then double back, circle old Saint Michael's, bang the Bermuda bell—and head out for the pines.

Someone should follow me.

Now wait at the fork behind the bicycle shed where the kids parked their bikes and caught the school bus. One road winds up the ridge, the other along the links to the clubhouse. It is beginning to rain a little. Big dusty drops splash on the windshield.

Here he comes.

Here comes something anyhow. Rubber treads hum on the wet asphalt. He pauses at the fork. A pang: did I leave tracks? No. He goes past slowly, taking the country-club road, a big Cushman golf cart clumsily armored with scraps of sheet-iron wired to the body and tied under the surrey fringe. The driver can't be seen. It noses along the links like a beetle and disappears in the pines.

There is no one in sight except a picaninny scraping up soybean meal on number 8 green.

Why not take the ridge road and drive straight to my house?

I do it, meeting nobody, enter at the service gate and dive out of sight under a great clump of azaleas. Then up through the plantation of sumac that used to be the lawn, to the lower "woods" door. It is the rear lower-level door to the new wing Doris added after ten years of married life had canceled the old.

It occurs to me that I have not entered the house through this door since Doris left. I squeeze past the door jammed by wistaria. It is like entering a strange house.

The green gloom inside smells of old hammocks and

ping-pong nets. Here is the "hunt" room, Doris's idea, fitted out with gun cabinet, copper sink, bar, freezer, billiard table, life-size stereo-V, easy chairs, Audubon prints. Doris envisioned me coming here after epic hunts with hale hunting companions, eviscerating the bloody little carcasses of birds in the sink, pouring sixteen-year-old bourbon in the heavy Abercrombie field-and-stream glasses and settling down with my pipe and friends and my pointer bitch for a long winter evening of man talk and football-watching. Of course I never came here, never owned a pointer bitch, had no use for friends, and instead of hunting took to hanging around Paradise Bowling Lanes and drinking Dixie beer with my partner, Leroy Ledbetter.

The carbine is still in the cabinet. But before leaving I'd better go topside and check the terrain. At the top of a spiral stair is Doris's room, a kind of gazebo attached to the house at one of its eight sides. An airy confection of spidery white iron, a fretwork of ice cream, it floats like a tree house in the whispering crowns of the longleaf pines. A sun-ray breaks through a rift of cloud and sheds a queer gold light that catches the raindrops on the screen.

Here sat Doris with Alistair and his friend Martyn whom, I confess, I liked to hear Alistair address not as we did, with the swallowed *n*, *Mart'n*, but with the decent British aspirate *Martyn*. Even liked hearing him address me with his tidy rounded *o*, not as we would say, Täm, but Tōm: "I say, Tōm, what about mixing me one of your absolutely smashing gin fizzes? There's a good chap?" Where's a good chap? I would ask but liked his English nevertheless, mine having got loosed, broadened, slurred over, somewhere along the banks of the Ohio or back in the bourbon hills of Kentucky, and so would fix gin fizzes for him and Martyn.

Alistair: half-lying in the rattan settee, tawny-skinned, tawny-eyes, mandala-and-chain half-hidden in his Cozumel homespuns, his silver and turquoise bracelet (the real article with links as heavy and greasy as engine gears) slid down his wrist onto his gold hand, which he knows how to flex as gracefully as Michelangelo's Adam touching God's hand.

Mar-tyn: a wizened Liverpool youth, not quite clean, whose low furrowed brow went up in a great shock of dry wiry hair; Mar-tyn, who gave himself leave not to speak because it was understood he was "with" Alistair; who mystified Doris with his unattractiveness and who when I gave him his gin fizz in a heavy Abercrombie field-and-stream glass, always shot me the same ironic look: "Thanks, mite."

Doris happy though, despite Mar-tyn. Here in her airy gazebo in the treetops it seemed to her that things had fallen out right at last. This surely was the way life was lived: Alistair sharing with her the English hankering for the Orient and speaking in the authentic mother tongue of reverence for life and of the need of making homely things with one's own hands; of a true community life stripped of its technological dross, of simple meetings and greetings, spiritual communions, the touch of a hand, etcetera etcetera.

"We're afraid of touching each other in our modern culture," said Alistair, extending his golden Adam's hand and touching me.

"You're damn right we are," I said, shrinking away.

He would discuss his coming lecture with Doris, asking her advice about the best means of penetrating the "suburban armor of indifference."

Doris listened and advised breathlessly. To her the very air of the summerhouse seemed freighted with meanings. Possibilities floated like motes in the golden light. Breathlessly she sat and mostly listened, long-limbed and lovely in her green linen, while Alistair quoted the sutras. English poets she had memorized at Winchester High School sounded as fresh as the new green growth of the pines.

> *The world is too much with us; late and soon,*
> *Getting and spending, we lay waste our powers,*

said Alistair, swishing his gin fizz.

"How true!" breathed Doris.

"Holiness is wholeness," said Alistair, holding in his cupped hand a hooded warbler who had knocked himself out against the screen.

"That is so true!" said Doris.

Not that I wasn't included, even after Alistair found out that it was Doris, not I, who had the money. Alistair was good-natured and wanted to be friends. Under any other circumstances we might have been: he was a rogue but a likable one. Mar-tyn was a Liverpool guttersnipe, but Alistair was a likable rogue. We got along well enough. Sunday mornings he'd give his lecture at the Unity church on reverence for life or mind-force, and Samantha and I'd go to mass and we'd meet afterwards in the summerhouse.

They were a pair of rascals. What a surprise. No one ever expects the English to be rascals (compare Greeks, Turks, Lebanese, Chinese). No, the English, who have no use for God, are the most decent people on earth. Why? Because they got rid of God. They got rid of God two hundred years ago and became extraordinarily decent to prove they didn't need him. Compare Merrie England of the fifteenth and sixteenth centuries. A nation of rowdies.

"I greatly admire the Catholic mass," Alistair would say.

"Good."

"I accept the validity of all religions."

"I don't."

"Pity."

"Yes."

"I say, Tōm."

"Yes?"

"We could be of incalculable service to each other, you know."

"How's that?"

"You could help our work on mind-force with your scientific expertise in psychiatry. We're on the same side in the struggle against materialism. Together we could help break the laws of materialism that straitjacket modern science."

"I believe in such laws."

"We could oppose the cult of objectivity that science breeds."

"I favor such objectivity."

"I have unending admiration for your Church."

"I wish I could say the same for yours."

"You know, Origen, one of the greatest doctors of your Church, was one of us. He believed in reincarnation, you know."

"As I recall, we kicked his ass out."

"Yes. And the poor man was so burdened with guilt, he cut off his own member."

"I might do the same for you."

"You're a rum one, Tōm."

Mar-tyn laughed his one and only laugh: "Arr arr arr. Cut off 'is ruddy whacker, did he?"

Doris would have none of this, either Catholic vulgarity or Liverpool vulgarity, and she and Alistair would get back on reverence for life while I grilled rib-eye steaks on the hibachi, my specialty and Alistair's favorite despite his reverence for steers.

What happened was not even his fault. What happened was that Samantha died and I started drinking and stayed drunk for a year—and not even for sorrow's sake. Samantha's death was as good an excuse as any to drink. I could have been just as sorry without drinking. What happened was that Doris and I chose not to forgive each other. It was as casual a decision as my drinking. Alistair happened to come along at the right time.

Poor fellow, he didn't even get the money he wanted. He got Doris, whom he didn't want. Doris died. God knows what Doris wanted. A delicate sort of Deep-South Oriental life lived with Anglican style. Instead, she died.

Alistair was right, as it turned out, to disapprove my religious intolerance. I, as defender of the faith, was as big a phony as he and less attractive. Perhaps I'd have done worse than follow Origen's example, poor chap.

Feeling somewhat faint from hunger, I return to my apartment in the old wing and fix myself a duck-egg flip with Worcestershire and vodka. Check the phone. Dead. Call into Ellen on the Anser-Phone. The line is already plugged in. The Anser-Phone operator got frightened about something, Ellen said, and left. But all quiet at the motel. She and Moira are playing gin rummy.

Two lovely girls they are, as different as can be, one Christian, one heathen, one virtuous, one not, but each lovely in her own way. And some Bantu devil is trying to take them from me. He must be dealt with.

Back in the hunt room, I take the 30.06 from the cabinet. It is still greased and loaded. I pocket an extra clip. Get 38's for the revolver!

5

Take the Toyota onto the links, use cart paths next to the woods, cross the fairway to my mother's back yard, run under her mountainous Formosa azaleas and out of sight.

The back door is unlocked. All seems normal hereabouts. Eukie, Mother's little servant, is sitting in the kitchen polishing silver and watching Art Linkletter III interview some school children from Glendale.

"Eukie, where is Mrs. More?"

"She up in the bathroom."

"What's been going on around here?"

Eukie is a no-account sassy little black who is good for nothing but getting dressed up in his white coat and serving cocktails to Mother's bridge ladies.

Check the phone. Dead.

For a fact Mother is in the bathroom, all dressed up, blue-white Hadassah hair curled, down on her hands and knees in her nylons, scrubbing the tile floor. Whenever things went wrong, I remember, a sale fallen through, my father down on his luck sunk in his chair watching daytime reruns of *I Love Lucy*, my mother would hike up her skirt and scrub the bathroom floor.

"What's wrong, Mama?"

"Look at that workmanship!" She points the scrub brush to a crack between tile and tub. "No wonder I've got roaches. Hand me that caulk!"

"Mother, I want to talk to you." I pull her up. I sit on the rim of the tub. She closes the lid and sits on the john. "Now. What's going on around here?"

"Humbug, that's what's going on."

"Has anybody bothered you?"

"Who's going to bother me?"

"Then why are you scrubbing the bathroom floor in your best clothes?"

"My car won't start and I can't call a taxi. My phone's dead."

"Is that all?"

"What else?" She is sitting straight up, smoothing her waist down into her hip, wagging her splendid calf against her knee.

"I mean, have you noticed anything unusual?"

"People running around like chickens with their heads cut off. You'd think a hurricane was on the way."

"What people?"

"The Bococks down the street. He and the children threw their clothes in the boat and drove away."

"Boat? Oh, you mean on the trailer. Is that all?"

"What else? Then this trash backs up a truck to the Bocock house."

"Trash? What trash?"

"White trash. Black trash. Black men in yellow robes and guns."

"You mean they moved in?"

"Don't ask me!"

"Or did they take things and leave?"

"I didn't notice."

I sit on the tub thinking. Mother dips brush into Clorox.

"Mother, you're leaving."

"Leave! Why should I leave?"

"I'm afraid you're in some danger here."

"There's not a soul in the neighborhood. Anyhow Euclid is here."

"Eukie ain't worth a damn."

"I can't leave. My car won't start." I see she's frightened and wants to leave.

"Take my car. Or rather Ellen's. Take Eukie with you and go to Aunt Minnie's in town and stay there till you hear from me. Go the back way by my house."

"All right," says Mother distractedly, looking at her wrinkled Cloroxed fingertips. "But first I have to pass by the Paradise office and pass an act of sale."

"Act of sale! What are you talking about?"

"Then I'm coming back and stay with Lola. Lola's not leaving."

Dusty Rhoades, Mother tells me, had come by earlier, argued with the two women, had an emergency call, and left.

"You mean Lola's over there now?"

"She won't leave! She's a lovely girl, Tommy."

"I know."

"And she comes from lovely people."

"She does?"

"She's the girl for you. She's a Taurus."

"I know."

"Ellen is not for you."

"Ellen! Who said anything about Ellen? Last time you were worried about Moira."

"She doesn't come from the aristocratic Oglethorpes. I inquired. Her father was a mailman."

"My God, Mother, what are you talking about? There were no aristocratic Oglethorpes. Please go get your things."

My mother, who sets no store at all by our connection with Sir Thomas More, speaks often of her ancestor Sieur de Marigny, who was a rascal but also, she says, an aristocrat.

I give Eukie my father's twelve-gauge pump gun loaded with a single twenty-five-year-old shell.

"Eukie, you ride shotgun."

"Yes suh!" Eukie is delighted with the game.

"If anybody tries to stop Miss Marva, shoot them."

Eukie looks at me. "Shoot them? Who I'm going to shoot?"

"I don't know." Euclid is sitting opposite Mother, holding the shotgun over his shoulder like a soldier. "Never mind."

Off they go in the Toyota, facing each other across the tiller.

6

Lola, in jeans and gingham shirt, is hoeing her garden at Tara. A straight chair at the end of a row holds a .45 automatic and a cedar bucket of ice water with a dipper. Her shirttails are tied around in front leaving her waist bare. The deep channel of her spine glistens.

I lean my carbine against the chair.

"What are you planting?"

"Mustard." Lola jumps up and gives me a big hug. "You're so smart!"

"Smart?"

"Yesterday. I didn't know you were a genius."

"Genius?"

"In The Pit. Lola's so proud of you." She gives me another hug.

"Do you think you ought to be here by yourself? Where's Dusty?"

"Nobody's going to mess with Lola."

"I see." I fall silent.

"Did you come to see me?"

"Yes."

"Well? State your business."

"Yes. Well, I don't think you ought to stay here." It's where she should stay that gives me pause. Lola sees this.

"And just where do you propose that I go?"

"Into town."

She commences hoeing again. "Nobody's running Lola off her own place. Besides, I doubt there is any danger. All I've seen are a few witch doctors and a couple of drugheads."

"There was another atrocity last night."

"Nellie Bledsoe? I think P. T. got drunk and let her have it with the shish kebab."

"I've been shot at twice in the last hour."

"Tommy!" cries Lola, dropping the hoe. She takes my hand in her warm, cello-callused fingers. "Are you hurt?" she asks, feeling me all over for holes.

"No. He missed me."

"Who in the world—?"

"I don't know. I think it's a Bantu."

Lola slaps her thigh angrily. Eyes blazing, she places her fists on her hips, arms akimbo. She nods grimly. "That does it."

"Does what?"

"You stay here with Lola."

"I can't do that."

"Why not?"

"I have, ah, other responsibilities." Such as two girls in a motel room, but I can't tell her that.

"Such as?"

"My mother."

"Very well." She waits, searching my eyes. She's waiting for me to ask her to stay with me. When I don't, she shrugs and picks up the hoe. "Don't worry about Lola. Lola can take care of herself."

"Why won't you leave?"

"I can't leave my babies." She nods toward the stables.

"You mean the horses? Turn them loose. They'll be all right."

"Besides that, I've just laid in one thousand New Hampshire chicks."

"Chickens, mustard greens. What are you planning for?"

"I think we're in for a long winter and I'm planning to stick it out here."

"Why do you say that?"

She shrugs and mentions the possibility of civil disturbances between Knothead and Leftpapas, between black and white, etcetera. "So I think the safest place in the world is right here at Tara minding my own business."

I nod and tell her about my fears for the immediate future, about the mishap that befell my lapsometers and the consequent dangers of a real disaster.

Lola listens intently. It is beginning to drizzle. Suddenly taking my hand in hers, warm as a horn, and picking up her gun, she leads me impulsively to the great gallery of the house, where we sit in a wooden swing hung by chains from the ceiling.

"Tommy," she says excitedly, "isn't it great here? Look at the rain."

"Yes."

"Dusty's leaving. Let's me and you stay here and see it through, whatever it is."

"I'd certainly like to."

"You know what I truly believe?"

"What?"

"When all is said and done, the only thing we can be sure of is the land. The land never lets you down."

"That's true," I say, though I never did know what that meant. We look out at six acres of Saint Augustine grass through the silver rain.

The great plastered columns, artificially flaked to show patches of brickwork, remind me of Vince Marsaglia, boss of the rackets. He built Tara from what he called the "original plans," meaning the drawings of David O. Selznick's set designer, whose son Vince had known in Las Vegas. Once, shortly after I began to practice medicine, I was called to Tara to treat Vince for carbuncles. Feeling much better after the lancings, he and his boys sat right here on the gallery shying playing cards into a hat from at least thirty feet, which they did with extraordinary skill. I watched with unconcealed admiration, having tried unsuccessfully to perfect the same technique during four years of fraternity life. I also admired the thoroughbreds grazing in the meadow.

"You like that horse, Doc? Take him," said Vince with uncomplicated generosity.

Now the swing moves to and fro in an almost flat arc on its long chains. We sit holding hands and watch the curtains of silvery rain. Lola smells of the fresh earth under her fingernails and of the faint ether-like vapors of woman's sweat.

Her cello calluses whisper in my hand. At the end of each arc I can feel her strong back thrust against the slats of the swing.

"Now here's what we're going to do, Tom Tom," says Lola, ducking her head to make the swing go. "Lola's going to fix you a big drink. Then you're going to sit right there and Lola will play for you."

"For how long?"

"Until the trouble is over."

"That might take weeks—if it's over then."

"O.K. Lola will do for you. We'll work in the garden, and in the evenings we'll sit here and drink and play music and watch the mad world go by. How does that sound?"

"Fine," I say, pleased despite myself at the prospect of spending the evenings so, sipping toddies here in the swing while Lola plays Dvořák, clasping the cello between her noble knees.

"Tom Tom singing to Lola?" she asks and I become aware I am humming "Là ci darem" from *Don Giovanni*. My musical-erotic area, Brodmann 11, is still singing like a bird.

I pick up the 30.06. "There's something I have to take care of first."

Lola shoves her .45 into her jeans. "Lola will go with you."

"No, Lola won't."

"I can shoot."

Before I know what has happened, she takes out the .45 and, aiming like a man, arm extended laterally, shoots a green lizard off the column. I nearly jump out of the swing. In the bare gallery the shot is like a crack of lightning in a small valley. Thunder roars back and forth. Brick dust settles.

My ears are ringing when I stand up to leave.

"Darling Tom Tom," whispers Lola, putting away the gun

and giving me a hug, eye to eye, shoulder to shoulder, hip to hip. "Come back to Tara. Lola will be waiting. Come back and put down roots with Lola."

"All right. Now listen. If anything happens—if there is an invasion by the Bantus or if you see a peculiar yellow cloud—I want you to do exactly what I tell you."

"Tell Lola!"

"Come to the old plaza. To Howard Johnson's. I'll be there. You understand?"

"O.K.," says Lola, hugging me and giving me some hard pats on the hip. "But don't be surprised if you see Lola sooner than you think." She winks.

I frown. "Don't you follow me, Lola. I forbid it, goddamn it."

"Tom Tom act masterful with Lola? Lola like that. Howard Johnson's. Wow." She hands me my carbine. "Come back to Tara!"

7

Colonel Ringo's distinguished head is outlined in the window of the guardhouse at the gates of Paradise. A reassuring sight. Hm, things cannot be too bad. The Colonel's armored Datsun is parked behind the guardhouse.

"Halt! Who goes there!" yells the Colonel from a crouch in the doorway, his revolver pointed at me.

"It's me, Colonel!" I hold the carbine over my head.

"What's the password? Oh, it's you, Dr. More." The Colonel holsters his revolver and yanks me inside. "You're in the line of fire."

"What is the password?"

"Lurline, but get on in here, boy."

"What's up, Colonel?"

Now that I take a second look, I perceive that all is not well with him. His silvery eyebrows are awry and one eye, which has been subject for years to a lateral squint, has turned out ninety degrees. His scarlet and cream uniform is streaked with sweat.

"Rounds have been coming in for the past thirty minutes." He nods toward the shattered glass of the far window.

"Rounds? From where, Colonel?"

"From the pro shop as best as I can determine," he says, scanning the distant clubhouse through a pair of binoculars.

"Did you notice a golf cart pass here a while ago?"

"No, but I've only been here half an hour. That's why I'm here, though."

"Why?"

"To mount a rearguard action until they could get the golf carts and swim trophies out. I'm also worried about the molasses cakes and soybean meal in the barn yonder." He looks at his watch. "The patrol is supposed to pick me up in fifteen minutes. You better get out too."

"Colonel, what's going on?"

"Son, the Bantu boogers have occupied Paradise Country Club."

"But, Colonel, I haven't seen any Bantus."

"Then who in hell is shooting at me, the tennis committee?" The Colonel slumps against the wall. "What's more, they got Rudy and Al."

Noticing that the Colonel's hands are shaking, I offer him a drink from my flask.

"I thank you, son," says the Colonel gratefully. "Reach me a Seven-Up behind you. They cut the wires but the box is still cold."

The Colonel knocks back a fair portion of my pint, chases it with Seven-Up, sighs. Presently he takes my arm, cheek gone dusky with emotion. One eye drifts out.

"Doc, what is the one thing you treasure above all else?"

"Well—" I begin, taking time off to fix my own drink.

"I'll tell you what I cherish, Doc."

"All right," I say, taking a drink and feeling the good hot bosky bite of the bourbon.

"The Southern womanhood right here in Paradise! Right?"

"Yes," I reply, even though 90 percent of the women in Paradise are from the Midwest.

"And I'll tell you something else!"

"All right."

"We may be talking about two gentlemen who may have laid down their lives for just that."

"Who's that?"

"Rudy and Al!"

"What happened to them?"

"Damnedest thing you ever saw," says the Colonel, settling down in his canvas chair and putting his good eye to a crack that commands a view of the clubhouse.

I look at my watch impatiently and then study the shattered window. Could a bullet have done it? Perhaps, but the Colonel is a bit nutty today. Taking no chances, I sit in the doorway and keep the heavy jamb between me and the clubhouse, even though the latter is a good four hundred yards distant.

The Colonel takes another drink. "I've never seen anything like it, son, since I was with the Alabama National Guard in Ecuador." The Colonel is from Montgomery.

As best I can piece out the Colonel's rambling, almost incoherent account, the following events took place earlier this morning. There is no reason to doubt their accuracy. For one thing, I witnessed the beginning of the incident on the golf links this morning.

The Colonel was in charge of the security and the transportation of the corps of Christian Kaydettes to Oxford, Mississippi, for the national baton-twirling contest. The Kaydettes had put on an early show for the Pro-Am Bible breakfast, immediately thereafter embarking for Mississippi in two school buses, the first transporting the girls, the second their moms, a formidable crew of ladies who had already fallen out with each other over the merits of their daughters and had boarded the bus carrying their heavy purses in silence. (It was this boarding that I had witnessed earlier in the day.) Firecrackers (not rifles, as I had thought) had been discharged. Banners on the buses read BEAT DAYTON, Dayton, Ohio, being the incumbent champs. Colonel Ringo rode point in his armored Datsun followed by the bus carrying the Kaydettes, followed by Rudy on his Farhad Grotto motorcycle, followed by the busload of moms, each a graduate of the Paradise karate school. The rear was brought up by Al Pulaski, formerly of the Washington, D.C., police and now president of PASHA (Paradise Anglo-Saxon Heritage Association), in his police special, an armored van fitted out with a complete communications system.

Mindful of rumors, however preposterous, of a conspiracy to kidnap the entire Kaydette corps and spirit them off to the fastness of Honey Island Swamp, Colonel Ringo was careful in plotting his route to the Mississippi state line, where the little convoy was to be turned over to the Mississippi Highway Police. Ruling out the interstate as the obvious site of ambush, he selected old state highway 22. All went well until they reached the wooden bridge crossing a finger of Honey Island Swamp formed by Bootlegger Bayou. The Colonel, riding point, felt a premonition ("I learned to smell an ambush in Ecuador," he told me). Approaching the bridge, however, he saw nothing amiss. It was not until he was halfway across and coming abreast of the draw that he saw what was wrong, saw two things simultaneously and it was hard to say which was worse: one, the cubicle of the drawbridge was occupied by a bridge-tender in an orange robe—Bantu!—two, the draw was beginning to lift. In the space of two seconds he did three things, hit the accelerator, hit the siren to warn the buses, and began to fire his turret gun ("You got to shoot by reflex, son, and I can fire that turret gun like shooting from the hip").

He made the draw, felt the slight jolt as he dropped an inch or so, shot up the cubicle with the turret gun and, he felt sure, got the Bantu. The girls made it too, though they were badly shaken up by the two-foot drop.

"I got ever last one of those girls to Mississippi, son," says the Colonel, taking another drink. I watch my flask worriedly. "You talk about some scared girls—did you ever see a school bus make eighty miles an hour on a winding road? But we made it."

"But, Colonel, what happened to the others?"

The Colonel clucks and tilts his head. "That's the only bad part."

Once across the bridge, he didn't have much time to look back. But he saw enough. The Bantu bridge-tender was out of commission, dead or winged, but the draw went on lifting. Rudy, on his Farhad Grotto Harley-Davidson, saw he couldn't make the draw and tried to stop short, braking and turning. The Colonel's last sight of him ("a sight engraved on my memory till my dying day") was of the orange and green bike flying through the air, Rudy still astride, and plummeting into the alligator-infested waters of Bootlegger Bayou.

The moms? The second bus stopped short of the draw, Al Pulaski in his van behind them.

"You mean the Bantus have captured the mothers?" I ask.

The Colonel looks grave. "All we can do is hope." On the plus side, the Colonel went on to say, were two factors. Al was there with his van. And the mothers themselves, besides carrying in their heavy purses the usual pistols, Mace guns, and alarms, were mostly graduates of karate and holders of the Green Belt.

"Many a Bantu will bite the dust before they take those gals," says the Colonel darkly.

"Well, I mean, were there any Bantus attacking? Did you see any? Maybe the bus had time to turn around and get back."

"I didn't see any, but we must assume the worst."

We sit drinking in companionable silence, reflecting upon the extraordinary events of the day.

Presently the Colonel leans close and gives me a poke in the ribs. "I'll tell you the damn truth, son."

"What's that, Colonel?"

"I wouldn't take on those ladies in a month of Sundays. Whoo-ee," says the Colonel and knocks back another inch of my Early Times. He laughs.

"Ha ha, neither would I, Colonel," I say, laughing. "I feel sure they will be all right."

Suddenly the Colonel catches sight of something through the crack. He leaps up, staggering to the doorway.

"Stop thief!" he cries hoarsely.

"What's wrong, Colonel?"

"They're back, the little boogers!" he cries scarlet-faced, lunging about and picking up helmet and revolver and riding crop. "I'll fix the burrheads!"

"Wait, Colonel! The sniper!"

But he's already past me. Looking out the window, I catch sight of a dozen or so picaninnies and a few bigger boys running from the stables with armfuls of molasses cakes. One big boy totes a sack of feed. It's too late to stop the Colonel. He's after them, lumbering up a bunker. With his steel helmet and revolver, he looks like a big-assed General Patton. The culprits, catching sight of the furious red-faced Colonel thundering down on them, drop their ill-gotten goods and flee for the woods—all but one, the boy with the feed sack. The Colonel collars him, gives him a few licks with the crop and, dragging him to the shack, hurls him past me into the corner. "You watch this one. I'm going after the others."

"Wait, Colonel—!" I grab him. "You've forgotten the sniper."

"No, by God! I have my orders and I'm carrying them out."

"Orders? What orders?"

"To guard the molasses cakes and soybean meal."

"Yes, but, Colonel—"

He wrenches loose. "Here I come, you commonist Bantu burrheads!" cries the Colonel, charging the bunker and firing his revolver. "Alabama has your ass." Up he goes and— "Oof!"—as quickly comes reeling back. He stumbles and sits down hard on the doorsill. At the same moment there comes a slamming concussion, a rifle shot, very loud, from the direction of the clubhouse. The youth shrinks into his corner.

Gazing down at the Colonel, I try to figure out what hit him. He looks all in one piece.

"What happened, Colonel?" I ask, pulling him out of the line of fire.

"They got me in the privates," groans the Colonel. "What am I going to do?"

"Let me see."

"What am I going to tell Pearline?" he asks, swaying to and fro.

"Who is Pearline?" I ask in a standard medical tone to distract him while I examine him, and from curiosity because his wife is named Georgene.

"Oh, Lordy."

At last I succeed in stretching him out on the floor. There is a bloodstain on his cream-colored trousers. I borrow the youth's pocketknife and cut out a codpiece.

The Colonel is a lucky man. The bullet pierced a fold of scrotum, passed between his legs and went its way. I take out a clean handkerchief.

"You're O.K., Colonel. A scratch. Son, hand me a cold Seven-Up."

"Yes suh, Doc."

"Colonel, hold this bottle here and close your legs on it tight as you can. You'll be right as rain."

There is time now to examine the black youth, who has been very helpful, uttering sympathetic noises and an exclamation of amazement at the nature of the Colonel's wound: "Unon*unh*!"

"Aren't you Elzee Acree?"

"Yes suh!"

I recognize him now, a slender brindle-brown youth with a cast in his eye, the son of Ellilou Acree, a midwife and a worthy woman.

We make the Colonel as comfortable as possible, propping his head on his helmet. He lies stretched out the length of the tiny hut, the king-size Seven-Up in place between his legs.

"Elzee, what in hell are you doing here?"

"Nothing, Doc!"

"Nothing! What do you mean, nothing?"

"I heard they needed help unloading the barn."

"So you were unloading a few sacks to help them out?"

"That's right, Doc. I was stacking them under that tree so the truck could pick them up."

"Never mind. Listen Elzee. I want you to do something." I give him five dollars. "You stay here and tend to the Colonel until the patrol picks him up."

"I'll be right here! Don't you worry, Doc. But what I'm gon' tell the patrol?"

"The patrol won't bother you. The Colonel here will tell them you helped him, won't you, Colonel?"

"Sho. I been knowing Elzee, he's a good boy. Bring me a Seven-Up, Elzee."

"Yes suh!"

"Now pour out the neck and fill it up from Doc's bottle there."

Collecting the carbine—the flask is empty—I stand in the doorway a minute, gathering my wits when: *thunk* ka-POW! Splinters fly from the jamb three inches from my nose. I sit down beside the Colonel.

"Why, that son of a bitch is trying to kill us all!" I say.

"Like I told you!" cries the Colonel.

"Unh unh tch," says Elzee, not unhappily. "Those some turrible folks over there."

"That fellow's been after me for three days," I mutter.

"It sho look like it, Doc," murmurs Elzee sympathetically and hands the Colonel the spiked Seven-Up.

"What do you know about them, Elzee?" I ask, looking at him sharply. "Who all's down there?"

"I don't know, Doc, but they some mean niggers, don't you worry about that," says Elzee proudly.

"You mean there's more than one?"

"Bound to be."

"Or is there just one?"

"I just seen one pass by and I didn't know him."

I look at him in disgust. "Elzee, you don't know what in the hell you're talking about."

"That Elzee's a good boy, though," says the Colonel, who feels a lot better after taking a drink. "Aren't you, boy?"

"Yes suh! I been knowing the Colonel here!"

"Oh shut up," I say disgustedly to both. Between the two of them they've struck up an ancient spurious friendship and I've had enough of both. Let me out of here. I look at the clubhouse through the crack. The sun is out. The fairways sparkle with raindrops. Pennants fly from the pavilions set up for the Pro-Am tournament, but not a soul is in sight. The legend of the banner, Jesus Christ Greatest Pro of Them All, can't quite be read from this distance.

There must be a way of getting behind the sniper.

A drainage ditch runs from the higher ground behind the stable toward the clubhouse road and angles off across two fairways before it enters the strip of woods along the bayou.

"Elzee, how deep is that dredge ditch over by the tree there?"

"That grudge ditch at least ten feet deep, Doc!" cries Elzee.

Shouldering my carbine, I bid farewell to the drunk Colonel and the obliging Elzee.

8

The ditch crosses the road under a cattle guard directly in front of the guardhouse. The danger here is thirty feet of open ground between the door and the ditch. There's a better way. The north window of the guardhouse lets into a grove of live oaks whose thick foliage droops at the margins, the heavy limbs propped like elbows on the ground. The ditch skirts the far perimeter of the grove. Though the distance is a good hundred feet, at least ninety feet of it is covered by the grove.

Drop from the window, three long steps and dive for the grove. No shot. Once inside the oak, the going is good. The ground is still dry. It is like walking across a circus tent, the dusty twilight space sparkling with chinks of sunlight in the shifting canopy.

Elzee lied as usual. The ditch is no more than five feet deep, but it is dry and unchoked and walkable at a stoop. The worst part is near the cattle guard, where it rises to within two feet of the bars. Through the briars on hands and knees, cradling the carbine in my elbows Ecuador-style.

It takes ten minutes to reach the woods.

Once again in deep shade and walking is possible, through little bare swales and hollows studded with cypress knees, all the while angling gradually toward the water and diverging from the raised shell road. My objective is the marina some two hundred feet upstream from the clubhouse. My face, elbows, and knees are scratched, but I don't feel bad.

Aiming for a point on the bayou where, as I recall, the bank curves out and anchors the downstream end of the docks.

A piece of luck: a gleam of white directly ahead. It is fresh white sand deposited under willows that run out in a towhead. Here is both cover and footing where I expected muck.

My knees make musical rubs in the sharp cool shearing sand, which is wet only on top. Not bad: I missed the end of the marina by no more than a few yards, hitting the lower docks at the fourth slip. This end of the dock is unroofed and low-lying, designed for skiffs and canoes. A reef of alligator grass runs in front of the slips. Mullet jump. Gold dust drifts on the black water. The bayou is brimming from a south wind. Upstream, yachts and power boats drift in their moorings. Sunlight shatters like quicksilver against their square sterns.

I lie at the edge of the willows and watch. Three hundred yards upstream, at a point, two men are pole-fishing in the outside curve. A peaceful sight—but here's an oddity. Their caps are the long-billed mesh-crowned kind Midwesterners wear, pulled low, shadowing their faces; but they fish Negro-style

from the bank out, poles flat. Something wrong here: Michi-
ganders don't fish like that and Negroes don't wear caps like
that.

From their spot on the outer curve I calculate that they command two reaches of the bayou.

The next-but-last slip has a child's pirogue of warped plywood. It is unlocked and dry. Next to it floats a locked canoe
with a paddle.

Reach the pirogue, keeping lower than the alligator grass,
and slip downstream lying on my back and paddling with both
hands. Now past the reef of grass but under cover of the cyrilla
and birch, which, caving and undermined, slant toward the
water. A smell of roots and fresh-sloughed earth.

Once round the bend and out of sight of the fishermen, it is
safe enough to sit up and paddle straight to the water entrance
at the rear of the clubhouse—but no! Downstream now, at the
next point, sit another brace of fishermen, faces shaded, poles
flat out!

Did they see me? Hardly, because I'm already behind the
Humble yacht tied the length of the club dock and standing
off just enough, two feet, to let me slip between. I can't see
the fantail above me where white-coated waiters would ordinarily be serving up frozen drinks to Humble bigshots. But
today there is no sound but the slap of water. The yacht, I
reason, must be empty because the ports are closed and the air-
conditioning is silent. The cabins must be like ovens. Turning
now into the dark boathouse that runs under the ground-level
floor of the clubhouse.

Wedging the pirogue between the dock and the high water,
I climb up, keeping an eye peeled for the fishermen. But the
yacht blocks the entire boathouse. Anyhow, it is too dark to be
seen under here.

Up the concrete service stairs, little used at best, but which
ascend, I know, into a kind of pantry between the kitchen and
the men's bar. (I was on the Building Committee.) If the sniper
is still in the pro shop and the rest of the building is empty,
it should be possible to slide open the panel at the rear of the
bar where golfers in the pro shop are served, so saving the
floors from their spikes (my sole contribution to the Building
Committee).

Silence, the keeping of it, is the problem. The door at the top of the stairs is open a crack. I stand on the landing listening. The kitchen sounds empty. It roars with silence and ticks away like any kitchen in the morning. No motors run. A bird hops on the roof.

Will the door creak? Yes. But it can be opened silently, I discover, by warping it open, pushing high with one hand and pulling low with the other. The pantry is dark, darker than the Bayou Bar because the window in the swinging door makes a faint gray diamond. I look through, first from one side then the other, using the obliquest possible angle without touching the door. The bar is empty, but the far door into the main hall is open. The Portuguese fishnet droops from the ceiling, its glass floats gleaming like soap bubbles in the dim light.

Test the swinging door for creaking. No creaks up to ten inches. Ten inches is enough.

Slip along pecky cypress wall to hinged section of bar. Don't lift, go under—damn! I trip and almost fall. Forgot the raised slatting on the floor to save the barman's feet. Will the slatting creak? Yes. Try the nailed joints. No creak. The quality of the silence is different here. A more thronging, peopled silence—as thick as last Christmas Eve's party. Perhaps it is the acoustic effect of the bottles.

The panel opening into the pro shop is closed. Take a full minute to unsling carbine and prop it against the cushioned edge of the bar. Wait and blink and get used to the light.

Listen.

The leather dice cup is in place, worn and darkened by sweat and palm oil. The bottles are visible now, the front row fitted with measuring spouts. Whitish tendrils of vine have sprouted through the simulated wormholes and twined around the necks of the bottles. I blink. Something is wrong. What? Then I see. What is wrong is that nothing is wrong. The bottles are intact and undrunk.

Someone clears his throat, so close that my breath catches. I open my throat and let my breath out carefully.

The sound comes from behind me, behind the panel.

Again the hawking: I breathe easier. It is a careless habituated sound, deep-throated and resonant with blow-out cheeks, the sound of a man who has been alone for some time.

A chair creaks. Something—its front legs?—hits the floor.

I listen—for a second man and to place the first. If you know a man, you can recognize his voice in his throat-clearings.

French windows, I remember, open from the pro shop onto a putting green. Beyond, the shell drive winds through the links and joins the main road. A hundred yards farther is the gate and the guardhouse.

How does the panel fit in its frame? Does it run on channel bearings? Test its hang by putting a finger into the finger recess. The panel sits, simply, in a wooden slot. Test lateral motion: a faint grate. Lubricate it. With what? spit? No, Benedictine. The liqueur pours like 40-weight oil. Test again. The panel moves an eighth-inch with a slight mucous squeak.

More hawking and throat-clearing. I do not recognize the voice. Wait for a long hawk and slide the panel a quarter-inch. But the panel clears the frame by no more than a crack: a bright line of light but not wide enough to see anything.

Another hawk, another quarter-inch.

I can see him but it's the wrong man: Gene Sarazen in plus fours and slanted forty-five degrees to the floor. To my nostrils comes the smell of the spike-splintered pine floor and of sweated leather. The sunlight is bright. I can hear the open window.

The hawking again but now I can also hear the liquid sound of throat muscles swallowing—and even a light click of the uvula popping clear of the tongue.

Ahem.

I reflect: better get the carbine in position now rather than later. The problem now is balance and position, clearing shelf space for my elbows. I calculate he is sitting ten or fifteen feet to the left of my line of sight and that the panel must be opened two or three inches to take the carbine at this angle.

Open it then: with right hand, forefinger in recess, holding carbine stock in left elbow. Open it till I can see him. It takes five minutes.

There he is. Up he comes swimming into view like a diver from the ocean depths.

I don't know him.

He sits at the window, back turned, but I see him at an angle. One cheek is visible, and the notch of one eye. His feet are propped on the low sill—it is not a French window, as I had remembered—the front legs of the director's chair clear of the floor. The feet flex slightly, moving the chair. The rifle lies on the floor under his right hand. It is an M-32, the army's long-barrel sniper rifle with scope. How did he miss me with that? He must be a poor shot.

He is dressed as an *inyanga*, a herbalist, in a *monkhuб*, a striped orange and gray tunic of coarse cotton. From his belt hangs an *izinkhonkwani*, a leather bag originally worn to carry herbs and green sticks but now no doubt filled with .380 mm shells. The foot propped on the sill wears a dirty low-quarter Ked, the kind pro ballplayers wear for scrimmage. His head, shaved, ducks slightly in time with the rocking. His right wrist, dangling above the rifle, wears a large gold watch with a metal expansion band.

I judge he was or is a pro. The lateral columns of neck muscles flare out in a pyramid from jaw to the deep girdle of his shoulders. The bare leg below the tunic is rawboned and sharp-shinned, as strong and stringy as an ostrich's. The skin is, on his neck, carbon-black. It blots light. Light hitting it drains out, it is a hole. The skin at the heel of the loosely flexed hand shades from black to terra cotta to salmon in the palm.

The front sight of my carbine is on his occipital protuberance. The sweetish smell of the Benedictine fills my nostrils. I must shoot him. He will experience light, a blaze of color, and nothing else.

Then shoot him.

He tried to shoot you three times and he would shoot you now. Worse, he wants to take your woman, women.

Saint Thomas Aquinas on killing in self-defense: Q.21, Obj. 4, Part I, *Sum. Theol.* But did he say anything about shooting in the back?

My grandfather on sportsmanship (my grandfather: short on Saint Thomas, long on Zane Grey): Don't ever shoot a quail on the ground or a duck on the water.

Then what do I do now for Christ's sake, stomp my foot to flush him and shoot him on the fly?

Or in Stereo-V-Western style: Reach, stranger?

No. Just shoot him. The son of a bitch didn't call you out. Shoot him then.

Wound him?

No, kill him.

The trouble is my elbow is not comfortable.

Get it comfortable then.

Now.

Consider this though: would Richard Coeur de Lion have let Saladin have it in the back, heathen though he was?

The trouble is that my grandfather set more store by Sir Walter Scott than he did by Thomas More.

What would Thomas More have done? Undoubtedly he would have—

"Hold it, Doc."

The voice, which is both conversational and tremulous, comes from close behind me.

"All right."

"Just set the gun down real easy."

"I will."

"You wasn't going to do it anyway, was you, Doc?"

"I don't know."

"You wasn't. I been watching you. Now turn around."

"All right."

It is Victor Charles. He sighs and shakes his head. "Doc, you shouldn't ought to of done this."

"Well, I didn't."

Victor stands against one flap of the saloon doors, single-barrel shotgun held in one hand like a pistol. The weak light from the hall gleams on his white ducks and white interne shoes.

The gun was aimed at my middle but now strays off. Victor, I know, will shoot me if he has to. But I perceive that an old etiquette requires that he not point his gun at me.

"Doc Doc Doc. You sho done gone and done it this time?"

"Yes."

"Doc, how come you didn't do like I told you and move in with your mama and tend to your business?"

"You didn't tell me why."

"How come you had to come over here?"

"That fellow in there has been trying to kill me."

"O.K., Doc. Now let's us just move on out of here and up in the front."

It is odd: the main emotion between us is embarrassment.

Each is embarrassed for the other. We cannot quite look at each other.

As he waits for me to get in front, Victor picks up the carbine and shoves it under the slatting!

We walk around to the pro shop. At the door I hesitate, wondering if the *inyanga* will shoot me. Victor fathoms this and calls out: "It's all right, Uru. It's just me and Doc."

Uru has swung his chair around to face us. His rifle is still on the floor, his hands clasped behind his head. I notice with surprise that he is very youthful. His pleasant broad face has a sullen expression. A keloid, or welted scar, runs off one eyebrow, pulling the eyebrow down and giving him a Chinese look.

"Well well well. The hunted walks in on the hunter."

"Then I was the hunted." I look at him curiously, shifting my head a bit to get a fix on him. What sort of fellow is he?

"Where did you find him, Victor?"

"He was in there." Victor nods toward the panel. "Fixing hisself a drink. Can't you smell it?"

I take some hope in Victor not mentioning my carbine and in Uru not picking his up. Perhaps they are not going to shoot me.

"What were you doing in there, Doctor?" asks Uru, straining his clasped hands against his head.

"Doc was picking up a couple of bottles," says Victor, shaking his head. "Doc he like his little toddy."

"I didn't ask you. I asked him."

Uru diphthongs his *I*'s broadly and curls his tongue in his *R*'s. I judge he is from Michigan. He sprawls in his chair exactly like a black athlete at Michigan State sprawling in the classroom and shooting insolent glances at his English instructor.

"So Chuck here was going to have himself a party," says Uru lazily. He turns to me. "Chuck, your party days are over."

"Is that right?"

"All right, Victor. You found him. You take care of him."

"D-D-Doc's all right!" cries Victor. Victor's stammering worries me more than Uru's malevolence. "When Doc give you his word, he keep it. Doc, tell Uru you leaving and not coming back."

"Leaving your house?" Uru asks.

"As a matter of fact, I have left. Moved out."

"So we're taking Doc's word now," says Uru broadly, imitating Victor. He frowns. The chair legs hit the floor. "Victor, who are you taking orders from?"

"You, but I'm going to tell you about Doc here," says Victor, rushing his speech, a frightening thing. He is afraid for me. "Doc here the onliest one come to your house when you're sick. He set up all one night with my auntee."

Uru is smiling broadly—a very pleasant face, really. "So Chuck here set up all night with your auntee." He rolls his eyes up, past Gene Sarazen, to the ceiling. "I don't know. I just don't know."

"Do you mind if I ask you something?" I ask Uru.

"Make it quick, Chuck."

"Just what is it you all have in mind to do around here?"

"Doc," says Victor, sorrowful again. "You know we can't tell you that."

"Why can't we tell him? Chuck's not going to tell anybody, are you, Chuck?"

"Are you all taking over Paradise Estates?"

"No, we all not," says Uru, like any other Yankee.

"Not in the beginning, Doc," says Victor patiently. "All we wanted was the ridge houses since they were empty anyhow, all but yours and you wouldn't leave. We had to have your house."

"Why?"

"The TV tower, Doc."

"What?" I screw up an eye.

"We had to have the transmitter, Chuck," says Uru almost patiently.

"And there you setting under it, Doc." The pity of it comes over Victor. "How come you didn't move in with Miss Marva?"

"Then the shootings were to frighten me away?"

Uru looks at Victor.

"What about the kidnappings?" I ask.

Victor shrugs. "That was just insurance. We just going to keep the little ladies out in Honey Island till y'all sign the papers with us. Ain't nobody going to harm those little ladies, Doc! In fact, my other auntee out there looking after them right now. She raised half of them, like Miss Ruthie and Miss Ella Stone."

"I don't know," says Uru to Gene Sarazen. "I just don't

know. They told me about coming down here." He shakes himself and looks at me with an effort. "Victor is right, Chuck. That's all we wanted in the beginning. But now it looks like all the chucks and dudes have moved out. So: we can use the houses."

"It won't work. How long do you think you can hold the place?"

"Just as long as you value your womenfolk."

I am wondering: does he mean the moms and does he know that the Kaydettes were not taken?

The chair legs hit the floor again. Uru looks straight at me.

"I'm going to tell you exactly how it is, Doctor. You chucks had your turn and you didn't do right. You did bad, Doc, and now you're through. It's our turn now and we are going to show you. As Victor say, we sho going to move your ass out."

"I didn't say no such of a thing," says Victor. "I don't talk nasty."

"It won't work," I say.

"Doc, you don't know who all we got out there," says Victor. "And we holding enough folks so nobody's going to give us any trouble."

"That's not what he means," says Uru grimly. "Is it, Doctor?"

I am silent.

"What he means, Victor, is that even if we win, it won't work. Isn't that right, Doctor?" Uru has a light in his eye.

I keep silent.

"He means we don't have what it takes, Victor. Oh, he likes you and your auntee. You're good and faithful and he'll he'p you. Right, Doctor? You don't really think we got what it takes, do you?" Uru taps his temple.

"I don't know."

"Come on, Doctor, tell us the truth."

"Doc always tell the truth!"

"Shut up, Victor. Doctor?"

"I'm not sure what you mean."

"Do you always tell the truth?"

"Yes."

"Then tell it now."

"All right."

"You don't really think we're any good, do you?"

"How do you mean, good?"

"I'm talking about greatness, Doctor. Or what you call greatness. I'm talking about the Fifth Symphony, the *Principia Mathematica*, the Uranus guidance system. You know very well what I'm talking about."

"Yes."

"Well?"

"Well, you—"

"And don't tell me about music and rhythm and all."

"All right." I fall silent.

"Let me put it this way, Doctor. You know what we're going to do. We're going to build a new society right here. Right? Only you don't think we can do it, do you?"

I shrug.

"What does that mean?"

"Well—you haven't."

"Haven't what, Doctor?"

"You haven't done very well so far."

"Go on. Let's hear what you mean."

"I think you know what I mean."

"You're not talking to Victor now. You're talking to a Ph.D. in political science. Only I didn't choose to be a black-ass pipe-smoking professor."

"Didn't you used to play split-end for Detroit?"

"Don't change the subject."

"Aren't you Elijah Washington?"

"We have no Jew-Christian names, least of all Washington. I'm Uru. You didn't answer my question."

"What question?"

"About us not doing very well."

"You've had Liberia a long time."

"So?"

"Look at Liberia. You've had Haiti even longer."

"So?"

"Look at Haiti."

"You know something, Chuck. You got a smart mouth. We're liable to do to you what you did to the Indians."

"Do you mind if I have a drink?"

"We don't use it."

"I'll fix you a drink, Doc," says Victor.

"No you won't," says Uru, showing anger for the first time. "You're not his goddamn houseboy."

"You know, my name's Washington too," Victor tells Uru. "After George Washington Carver."

"Jesus Christ," says Uru to Gene Sarazen.

"Blessed be Jesus," says Victor.

"Look what you done to him," Uru says to me.

"What he done to me!" cries Victor.

"You did a good job, Doctor. It took you four hundred years but you really did a good job. Let me ask you something."

"All right."

"What would you do about it if you were me? I mean what with the four hundred years and Victor here."

"What's wrong with Victor?"

"You know what I mean. What would you do about the four hundred years?"

"I'd stop worrying about it and get on with it. To tell you the truth, I'm tired of hearing about the four hundred years."

"You are."

"Yes."

"And if it were up to you?"

"If it were up to me, I'd get on with it. I could do better than Haiti."

"That's what we're going to do, Doctor," says Uru in a changed voice. He picks up his rifle and rises.

Victor grabs my arm. "I'll take care of him, Uru. Like you asked." He gives me a yank, pulls me close. "Goddamn, Doc, ain't you got any sense?"

Uru seems to keep on getting up. He is at least six feet nine. "All right, Chuck. Let's go."

"Very well, but please let me tell you one thing."

Quickly I tell them about my invention, about its falling into the wrong hands and the likelihood of a catastrophe. I describe the danger signs. "So even though your pigment may protect you to a degree, I'd advise you to take cover if you should sight such a cloud."

Uru laughs for the first time. "Doctor, Victor's right. You something all right. What you telling us is the atom bomb is going to fall and we better get our black asses back to the swamp?"

"Doc is not humbugging," says Victor.

Uru takes a step forward. "Take him, Victor. If you don't, I will."

"Let's go, Doc."

"Where're we going?"

"To headquarters."

"Man, don't answer his questions," says Uru furiously. "When did he answer your questions? He knows what he going to get."

Again Victor pulls me close. "Don't worry, Doc. We holding you for ransom. Ain't that right, Elij—, I mean Uru?"

The two look at each other a long moment. "Doc's worth a lot to us, Uru."

Uru nods ironically. "Very well. But I'm coming with you. I wouldn't put it past you to turn him loose—after fixing him a toddy."

"I ain't fixing Doc nothing, but I might pick me up a bottle," says Victor, disappearing into the hall. I look after him in surprise. Victor doesn't drink.

Uru waves me ahead of him with his rifle.

Victor is waiting for us at the armored Cushman cart. He's got a bottle under his arm. In the golf bag behind him, among the irons, are two gun barrels, his—and mine! Victor doesn't look at me. Uru pays no attention.

9

They take me to "headquarters," which is located in, of all places, the abandoned rectory of old Saint Michael's in the plaza. A good choice: its construction is sturdy and there are no windows to defend.

We drive through Paradise in the armored golf cart, I squatting behind Uru and Victor in the bag well. Victor drives. Uru keeps an eye on me.

Uru is feeling good. "Chuck, you have to admit that Victor here is a remarkable man. He still thinks he can get along with you chucks, sit down and talk things over."

"That's right!" says Victor sententiously. "You can talk to folks! Most folks want to do what's right!"

"Uh huh," says Uru. "They really did right by you, Victor.

Here you are fifty years old and still shoveling dog shit. And Willard. Ten years with the U.S. Army in Ecuador and they're nice enough to put him on as busboy at the club. I'll tell you where right comes from—they know it, Chuck knows it, only you don't." Uru swings the muzzle of the M-32 into Victor's neck.

"Ain't nobody going to hold no gun on me," says Victor, frowning and knocking down the barrel.

"That's where they're smarter than you, Victor. They don't need a gun. They made you do what they want without a gun and even made you like it. Like Doc here, being so nice, sitting with your auntee. That's where they beat you, Victor, with sweet Jesus."

"What you talking about?"

"These chucks been fooling you for years with Jehovah God and sweet Jesus."

"Nobody's fooling me."

"And what's so damn funny is that you out-Jesused them."

"What you mean?"

Uru winks at me. "Doc here knows what I mean, don't you, Doc?"

"No."

"He knows the joke all right and the joke's on you, Victor. All these years you either been in trouble or else got nothing to your name, they been telling you about sweet Jesus. Now damned if you don't holler sweet Jesus louder than they do. What's so funny is they don't even believe it any more. Ask Doc. You out-Jesused them, Victor, that's what's so funny. And Doc knows it."

"Now Doc here is a Catholic," says Victor. "But that don't matter to me. I never had anything against Catholics like some folks."

"I'm sure glad to hear that you and Doc have composed your religious differences," says Uru, grinning.

"I don't see how a man can say he doesn't believe in God," says Victor. "The fool says in his heart there is no God. Myself, I been a deacon at Starlight Baptist for twenty years."

"Christ, what a revolution," mutters Uru, eyeing a burning house.

While he and Victor argue religion, I notice something: a

horse and rider, glimpsed now and then through the side yards of houses. The horse must be on the bridle path that runs along the margin of the links behind the houses. His easy trot just keeps pace with the cart. It is—!

—Lola! on her sorrel mare Yellow Rose. She could be out for her morning ride, erect in her saddle, hand on her thigh, face hidden in her auburn hair. Foolish impetuous gallant girl! Beyond a doubt she's trailing me, out to rescue me and apt to get herself caught or killed or worse. Something else to worry about, yet worry or not and despite my sorry predicament I can't but experience a pang of love for this splendid Texas girl.

As we leave the pines and head straight out across the deserted plaza, I sigh with relief. Lola is nowhere in sight. At least she has sense enough not to show herself. But what is she up to?

The Anser-Phone buzzes on my chest. Feigning a fit of coughing, I switch it off. Uru doesn't seem to notice. Ellen is calling! Somehow I must reach her. At least she is well. And Moira, my love! Pray to God the Bantus don't search me and take my Anser-Phone. My heart melts with love and my brain sings in the musical-erotic sulcus when I think of Lola and Moira. How lovely are the daughters of men! If I live and love Moira, who's to love Lola and how can I tolerate it? Same with Lola-Moira. And will Ellen stand for it in either case? Only one solution: I must live with all three.

Victor parks at the cloistered walk between church and rectory. Up the steps past the Bantu guard in a dirty white belted *kwunghali* stationed behind the concrete openwork (has he been here for weeks?) who salutes Uru with respect. He carries a Sten gun propped in his waist.

Time for one quick glance toward Howard Johnson's: all quiet. The balcony is deserted.

Down the front hall of the rectory and through the parlor with its ancient horsehair nose-itching furniture. From his *izinkhonkwani* Uru takes out a key chain, unlocks the door to Monsignor Schleifkopf's office and without further ado bumps me inside—with a basketball player's hip-bump.

"Sweat it, Chuck," says Uru, closing the door.

"Sorry, Doc," says Victor as the latch clicks.

*

Try the switch. No lights, of course. No windows either, but a row of glass bricks under the ceiling mutes the July sun to a weak watery light like a cellar window.

The trouble is the room is as hot and breathless as an attic.

While my eyes are getting used to the gloom, I call in to Ellen. She and Moira are still in the motel, safe and sound but nervous.

"Chief," says Ellen in a controlled voice. "The news is bad. We watched on TV. There is fighting on the highway."

"You mean the guerrillas have gotten that far?"

"No, Chief. It's the town people fighting the federal people. Not two miles from here. And Chief," says Ellen, lowering her voice. "You better do something about your so-called friend."

"Friend? Who's that?"

"Miss S. She's getting a little hysterical."

"Where is she?" I ask in alarm.

"In the bathroom. I never saw anybody go to the bathroom so much."

"Hm. Have you seen anybody around there?"

"Not a soul. But, Chief, I think you better get over here. Things are coming unstuck."

"I'm tied up just now. Perhaps later. I was wondering—"

"Yes?"

"Perhaps the best thing for you to do would be to get back to town."

"Chief, you've got my car!"

"So I have." What did I do with it? Oh yes, gave it to Mother.

"Anyhow, there's fighting between here and town."

"Well, sit tight."

"All right. But it's so *hot* here."

"Here too. But don't make any noise."

"Very well, Chief."

"Over."

"Over and out."

My eyes have accommodated to the gloom. Rocking back in Monsignor Schleifkopf's executive chair, I survey the room. Evidently it has been used by the Bantus. A couple of ceremonial garlic necklaces hang from the hatrack. A Coleman gas stove sits on the coin counter. Baby Ruth wrappers and used TV dinners litter the wall-to-wall carpet; shreds of collard greens bestrew the desk.

Behind me the door of the walk-in vault swings open. In one corner stands a stack of boxes full of Sunday envelopes exactly as they stood years ago when I used to attend Holy Name meetings here. Good rough fellows they were, the Holy Name men. We'd meet once a month and mumble gruff embarrassed prayers for the intentions of the Holy Father and so that we might leave off swearing and using the name of our dear Lord in vain and uttering foulness in general.

The four walls are hung with huge Kodacolor murals of Monsignor Schleifkopf's native Alps. Tiny villages are strung out along narrow green valleys. Great snowy peaks indent a perfect cobalt sky. In the foreground rises a rude roadside crucifix.

I am sweating profusely and breathing through my mouth. I am losing water and there is no water here. They had better turn me loose soon. Or I had better get out.

The room swims in a watery heat. A thin tatter of cloud flies from one alp. Ice crystals. Hot as it is, though, and bad as I feel, my eye wanders around the room appraising its construction. The rectory was built, I remember, early in the Ecuadorian wars, when there were bomb scares and a lot of talk about shelters. The rectory was to serve as a bomb shelter in case of attack. It is windowless and double-walled and equipped with back-up electrical systems. Yes, I recall some restiveness in the congregation about the cost of the generator, which was the latest type and heaviest duty—the sort that could run indefinitely without a human soul to service it. Samantha liked to imagine it humming away for thirty years after everyone was dead. Yes, I remember the sight of Monsignor Schleifkopf presiding over the control panel with that special proprietorship priests develop for things they don't own. Here was an oddity: that in the latter days when laymen owned everything they didn't care much for anything, yet some priests who owned little or nothing developed ferocious attachments for ordinary objects—I once knew a monk who owned nothing, had given it all away for Christ, yet coveted the monastery typewriter with a jealous love, flew into rages when another monk touched it.

The Alps swim in the heat. My tongue swells and cleaves to my palate. Stale hot bourbon breath whistles in my nose.

Monsignor Schleifkopf used to hover over the panel, one hand caressing the metal, the other snapping switches like a bomber pilot. . . .

The control panel. Wait. I close my eyes and try to think. Sweat begins to drip through my eyebrows. I remember. It is in the walk-in vault behind me. Here Monsignor Schleifkopf kept the valuables, gold chalices, patens, the Sunday collection, bingo money, and yes, even the daily gleanings of the poor box after the drugheads from the swamp began to break into it.

I feel my way inside. The vault door is open but it opens toward the glass bricks and it is dark inside. The panel was in the tiny foyer, wasn't it? I stumble over a bingo squirrel-cage. Feel the walls. Yes, here it is: rows of switches in a console of satiny metal, switches for lights, air-conditioning, electronic carillon. Some are up, some are down. Is up on? I close my eyes and try to remember (I was on the Building Committee). What time of day was the rectory evacuated? The Christmas Eve riots started in the afternoon and the Monsignor barely got away with his skin—that night.

Panting and sweating in the dark. Somewhere in my head two ideas grope for each other but it is too hot to . . . I return to the chair and look at the alp and the banner of ice crystals. The panorama of the high alpine valley is spoiled by a large metal grill set in the wall beside the roadside crucifix. It is the main intake vent of the air-conditioner.

I look at it, sweat, pant, and sock my forehead, trying to think what it is I already know.

Well but of course.

At least it is a chance. And the chance must be taken. I've got to get out of here.

Think.

The compressor is in the garage. The return duct therefore must run along the wall past the vault, past the kitchen whose inside wall is, must be, continuous with the back wall of the garage. Yes. I was on the Building Committee.

Sitting on the floor. A bit cooler here. I feel the metal frame of the grill. Phillips screws. Hm, a dime is no good. Look around. Yonder is Saint Michael on a pedestal, a somewhat prissy bronze archangel dressed to the nines, berobed like Queen Victoria but holding a proper bronze sword. Which I know is loose in his hand because I used to fiddle with it during the Holy Name meetings.

Slide it out of the bronze hand, a foot-long papercutter and, as I had recalled, dull. Dull enough to turn a Phillips screw.

The grill out and set down carefully on the rug, I stick my head in the duct. Plenty of room to crawl. Close my eyes and try to remember whether the compressor stands against the back wall of the garage or a ways out. It better be the latter. Also: does the jut of the garage from the side of the rectory clear the corner so that it is visible from the front of the church, where, behind the concrete screen, a guard is almost certain to be stationed? I can't remember.

Back to the console in the vestibule of the vault. The problem is to create a diversion, sufficient noise to cover my exit in the garage, where I'll have to kick out a panel and make a racket. The trouble is I don't know how many Bantu guards are here or where they're stationed. Is there only the one in front?

Feel the switches again. Some are up, some down, but which position is on? Here's the emergency starter button. Monsignor Schleifkopf—God bless him for his love of manufactured things, their gear and tackle and trim, good Buicks, Arnold Palmer irons—bought the best nickel-cadmium battery money could buy, a $500 job with a self-charging feature guaranteed for ten years.

The four speaker electronic carillon sits atop the silo tower a good two hundred yards from here and even farther from the garage. If I could start the carillon, it would create a commotion and the guards would, surely, look for the trouble where the sound was and not here. But which is the carillon switch? No telling. The only thing to do is take a chance and throw all switches up—surely up is on—and turn all knobs to the right.

Flip all switches up.

Hit the starter button for a second just for the feel of it. *Urr*, it goes, the very sound of an old Dodge starting up of a winter morning.

Get ready then. Resisting an impulse to cross myself, I press the button.

Urr-urr-urr and then BRRRRRROOM.

On goes the twelve-cylinder motor, God bless General Motors.

On goes the light.

On goes the air-conditioner compressor and blower.

On goes the carillon—

—a shriek of sound. The carillon resumes in the middle of the phrase of *O Little Town of Bethlehem* it left off five years ago on Christmas Eve:

> *. . . how still I see thee lie.*

I find myself running around the office with Saint Michael's sword, heart thumping wildly. The sound and the lights are panicking. The sound is an alarm, up go the lights and here's the burglar, me, caught in the act. The thing to do is get out of here, I tell myself, loping around the Alps. The hot air is moving out.

Thinking now: do this, pocket the screws, hop into the intake vent and pull the grill into place after me. If they see no screws, they won't notice.

It's tight in here, but a few feet along and I'm in a cloaca of ducts converging from the church. The air, thundering toward the 100-ton Frigiking (I was on the Building Commtitee), is already cooler.

Suddenly it comes over me that I am, for the moment, completely safe. Why not lie down in this dark cool place, an alpine pass howling with mountain gales, and take a little nap? *Indulgeas locum refrigerii*: refrigeration must be one of the attributes of heaven.

Now forty or fifty feet along and able to stand up. A cave of winds, black as the womb, but I'm against the unit, a great purring beast encased in metal filter mesh.

Press the panel to my right. Here I calculate is the garage. Metal bends and a chink of light opens. Daylight, moreover. At least the garage door is open. Try to see something. Cannot. Try to hear something. Nothing but the roar of the blower and compressor and soaring above, the piercing obligato of *White Christmas*:

> *May your days be merry and bright . . .*

Feel along the edge of the panel. It is fastened by sheet-metal screws, one every three or four inches and screwed in from the outside. Discard Saint Michael's sword. Try pushing one corner loose. No good.

Nothing for it then but to lie down, shoulders braced against the opposite panel (this panel against concrete), wait for the final major chord of *White Christmas*, and kick with both feet.

Out she goes with a heart-stopping clatter, metal against concrete, metal against car metal—now I know they'll find me—and out I come feet-first, born again, ejected into the hot bright perilous world—tumbling somehow forward until I am wedged between the inner wall and the bumper of Monsignor Schleifkopf's burnt-out Buick, a hulk of rusted metal and moldering upholstery. Mushrooms flourish in the channel between bumper and grill. A fern sprouts upside down from the crankcase.

The music, I tell myself, comes from the silo at the other end of the church and nobody will come here.

Wait and watch a minute. I have a cockroach's view under the Buick.

The broad three-car garage opens onto the plaza. Still not a soul in sight! How can this be with such a racket? A very loud noise needs tending to. Someone should do something about it and no doubt will. An unattended din is a fearsome thing.

The July sun blazes, the tar in the plaza bubbles, the green growth atop the storefronts shimmers and there is sky under it like the Hanging Gardens of Babylon.

The Drummer Boy,

rumpa-pum-pum,

thunders its artillery and echoes from the giant screen of Joy Drive-In.

The questions are: Is there a guard posted at the rear of the rectory? If so, did he and the guard at the front of the rectory head for the silo when the sound commenced? My hope is that the Bantus do not know where the control panel is and will assume that the source of the mischief is in the church.

Creeping now past the Buick, to the far wall and along it to the slight jut that frames the door now levered up along the ceiling. Slowly work around jut—still no one in the entire plaza—and around the outside corner of the garage: yes, here is the concrete screen ending flush with the garage door and—

—Jerk back almost before I see him, shutting my eyes against him in a magic gesture to make *me* invisible to him, jerking back around the corner and clear around the jut into the garage, and there in the dark corner I consult my retina's image of him: the same Bantu guard in the same dirty *kwung-hali*—then he must have heard the clatter of my exit—six feet away and back turned, face in profile and Sten gun pointed at the four speakers: they're the villains!

It is strange but, belatedly, indeed only now as I consult the image of him, I recognize him. It is Ely, who was bagboy at the A & P for forty years. What a transformation! He's turned into a tough hombre. Forty years a favorite at the A & P, toting bags to cars for housewives, saluting the tips, now he looks as if he'd just as soon stitch me with Sten gun as not.

I need his gun, I need him out of the way, so I need a weapon of my own. The Buick's trunk is open, lock prized, tire swiped. I crane over the tail fin looking for a lug wrench. No lug wrench, nothing but Monsignor Schleifkopf's moldering golf bag grown up in fennel and bladderwort, pockets ripped, clubs all gone, no, all but one, an ancient putter passed over perhaps five years ago for its age and decrepitude even then.

It is possible to reach the club without exposing myself past the jut.

Round yon virgin mother and child . . .

The putter has a lead blade and a hickory handle. Test it for heft.

Inch around ell.

He's closer, within range. He's still looking back toward the silo. It is a simple matter, surely, to take one step and hit him, with the heel of the putter taking care not to kill him. Then step.

Sorry, Ely—and aim for the occiput, the hardest skull plate, a glancing blow at that. But I take too much care and he's moved suddenly, closer, and it's a bad blow and the shaft shudders like shanking a ball. Staggering less from hurt than from surprise

and outrage, he's already swinging around toward me and I
see the Sten muzzle swinging as slowly as a ship's boom and
I'm shrinking into the inner corner of the jut and touching the
steel of the door mechanism as if we were playing a game and
it were base: safe! You can't shoot me now! But he is going to
shoot me, I can see. It's a matter of getting the gun around.

We are looking at each other. I notice that he is going bald
the way some Negroes go bald, his high studious umber forehead shading off into hair of the same color, and that he has a
mustache like Duke Ellington of old with a carefully tended
gap in the middle. We are looking at each other, I knowing
him and he me and he even signifying as much but his only
care is getting the Sten around, his face all screwed up with
the effort, and I see all of a sudden that all he's thinking about
is whether he's going to do it right, that he's exactly like a
middle-aged British home guard who patrols Brighton beach
against a possible Nazi and sure enough here comes a Nazi.
My God, he's thinking, IT has happened! Here's the real thing!
Here's a Nazi in the flesh! Will I do right? Why is everything
moving in slow motion?

He is shooting, too soon!—and I am flinching and touching
base, no fair! The steel is ringing like a hammer on boilerplate.
He's got me. But as I open my eyes, he's swinging away. How
did he miss me or did he or, better still, how did bullets hit the
outside of the steel I-beam at my elbow?

Who is shooting? He's not.

"Wait!" I'm yelling, having caught no more than one glimpse
of the sorrel rump prancing sideways. "Don't shoot him! It's
Ely!"—swinging the putter sideways and backhanded and not
having time to aim and so of course catching Ely properly on
the parietal skull, the Sten swinging away now and down and
Ely going down and around with it.

I drag him into the garage and test his pulse and pupils. He's
all right. I still haven't had time to look at Lola, who comes
in leading the sorrel and holstering her automatic in her jeans.

"You almost killed Ely," I tell her.

"Why, you damn fool, he was trying to kill you!"

"I know. Thank you. How did you know I was here?"

"Yellow Rose and I were watching from over there." She

nods toward the Joy Drive-In. "We saw you come crashing through the wall. Crazy Tom Tom! What would you do without Lola?"

"I don't know. Let's get out of here." We have to yell to be heard above the racket of the carillon with its guaranteed five-mile radius at top volume.

We three kings of Orient are . . .

"What is all that?" asks Lola, making a face.

"Christmas carols."

"Oh," says Lola, accepting it, July or not. "Where're we going?"

"Back over there. Where's the horse?"

Yellow Rose has wandered off. Lola gives an ear-splitting whistle through her fingers and here comes the mare, stirrups flying. I hop up.

Lola jumps up behind me and gives me a big hug. "Oh Tommy, I was so worried about you!"

"Keep worrying."

The nearest cover is the Drive-In with its tower of a screen and its speaker-posts gone to jungle, but a good two hundred yards of open plaza intervene, most of it clearly visible from the front of the church. How many Bantus are left?

We light out, my legs swinging free, for the stirrups are too short, past the concrete screen enclosing the cloister. Swallows nesting in the fenestrae take alarm and flutter up by the hundreds.

Many swallows but no shots, no outcries and no Bantus. Are they all in church trying to figure out what started the carillon?

The first Noel
The angels did sing . . .

Breathlessly we fetch up behind lianas of possum grape, which festoon the giant Pan-a-Vision screen.

"You like to fell off," says Lola, reverting to Tyler Texas talk.

Half off, I slide down. The noble girl faces me, arms as they say akimbo, breast heaving, color high in her cheek.

"What now?"

I explain that we'd best make our way to the motel, that indeed there is nowhere else to go.

"Wow!" says Lola, but as quickly frowns. "What about Rose?"

I shrug. "We can't take Rose any farther."

"Don't worry!" She loosens the girth and gives the mare a slap across the rump. "Back to Tara! She'll go home. We'll follow shortly, won't we, Tom?"

"Possibly."

Sure enough, the mare takes out for the pines, straight across the plaza, head tossing around as if she meant to keep an eye on us.

The firing begins when the mare reaches the drive-up window of the branch bank. Little geysers of tar erupt around her flying hoofs. Lola moans and claps her cheeks. "She's made it," I reassure her. Parting the grape leaves, I catch sight of the two Bantus, one kneeling and both firing, on the porch of the church. "Keep down."

But she's whipped out her automatic again. "What—" I begin turning to see what she sees behind me.

It's Victor!—standing in the doorway of the Pan-a-Vision screen structure. The screen is a slab thick enough to house offices.

"Don't shoot!" I jump in front of Lola.

"Why not?"

"It's Victor."

"Why not shoot Victor? He's got a gun." But she lowers her automatic.

"Here, Doc," says Victor and tosses me my carbine. "This is so you can protect your mama. I know you not going to shoot people."

I catch the carbine like old Duke Wayne up yonder on the giant screen.

"Thanks, Victor."

"Now you all get on out of here. Some people headed this way. Go to town. You take care this little lady too."

"O.K."

Lola can't tell the difference between the real Victor and the fake Willard. She claps her hands with delight. "Isn't Victor wonderful! Tom, let's go to Tara!"

"No." I grab her hand.

We run at a crouch through the geometrical forest of flowering speaker posts, past burnt-out Thunderbirds, spavined Cougars, broken-back Jaguars parked these five long years, ever since that fateful Christmas Eve, in front of the blank and silent screen. The lovers must have found the exit road blocked by guerrillas and had to abandon their cars and leave the drive-in by foot. In some cases speakers are still hooked to windowsills and we must take care not to run into the wires.

No more shots are fired, and when we reach the shelter of the weeds at the rear of the Howard Johnson restaurant, I feel fairly certain we've made our escape unobserved. But why take chances? Accordingly, we follow the easement between the motel and the fence. Directly below the bathroom window I take Lola's arm and explain to her the circumstances that prompted me to fit out the motel room and stock it with provisions for months—all the circumstances, that is, except Moira. "There is some danger," I tell her, "of a real disaster."

"Darling Tom!" cries Lola, throwing her arms around my neck. "Don't worry! I don't think we'll be here that long but we can have a lovely time! Lola will do for you. We'll make music and let the world crash about our ears. Twilight of the gods! Could I go get my cello?"

"I've told you we can't go back to Tara."

"No, I mean over at the Center. I could be back in fifteen minutes."

"Where?"

"At the Center. Don't you remember? I played a recital yesterday before the students rioted. There was so much commotion I thought the best thing to do was leave it in a safe place over there."

"Yesterday?" I close my eyes and try to remember. "Where is it now?"

"Ken told me he'd lock it up in his clinic."

"Ken?"

"Ken Stryker, idiot. Think of it, Tommy. We'll hole up for the duration and Lola will cook you West Texas chili marguerita and play Brahms every night."

"Very good. I'll get the cello for you but not just now. Now I think we'd better go up and join the ah, others."

"Others?"

"Yes. Other people have sought refuge here. I couldn't turn them away." Thank goodness there are two girls up yonder and not one.

"Of course you couldn't. Who are they?"

"My nurse, Miss Oglethorpe, and a colleague, a Miss Schaffner."

"Ken's research assistant?"

"She was."

"Should be cozy."

"There are plenty of rooms."

"I should imagine."

"Are you ready to go up?"

"Can't wait."

I give the sign, a low towhee whistle. Above us the window opens.

10

The girls are badly out of sorts, from fright but even more, I expect, from the heat. After the rainstorm they did not dare turn on the air-conditioner, the sniper might be hanging around. The room is an oven.

Moira is hot, damp, petulant, a nagging child.

"Where have you *been*, Chico?" She tugs at my shirt. There are beads of dirt in the creases of her neck.

Ellen sits straight up in the straight chair, drumming her fingers on the desk. Her eyes are as cool as Lake Geneva. The only sign of heat is the perspiration in the dark down of her lip.

"I thought you were going to get your mother," she says drily, not looking at Lola.

"Yes. Mother. Right. But Mother, you know, has her own ideas ha ha. No, Mother is in town and safe. Lola was at Tara and alone. I made her come." I jump up and turn on the air-conditioner. "With all the racket at the church, I doubt if anyone could hear this." Sinking down on the foot of the bed. "I could use a drink. I've been shot at, locked up, pushed around."

Ellen comes around instantly, sits behind me, begins probing my scalp with her rough mothering fingers. "Are you hurt, Chief?"

"I'm all right," I say, noticing that Lola is eyeing me ironically, thumbs hooked in her jean pockets.

"Quite a place you have here, Tommy," she says.

"Yes. Well. Now here's where we stand, girls," I say, rising and pacing the floor wearily. I am in fact weary but there are also uses of weariness. "I'm afraid we're in trouble," I tell them seriously because it is true but also because there are uses of seriousness. The three girls make me nervous. "As I believe all of you know, there is a good chance of a catastrophe this afternoon, of national, perhaps even world proportions. You asked about my mother, Ellen. Here's what has happened."

Everyone is feeling serious and better. The air-conditioner blows cold fogs into the room. Hands deep in pockets, I pace the floor, eyes on the carpet, and give them the bad news, reciting the events of the day in sentences as grave, articulate, apocalyptic, comforting as a CBS commentator. Now swinging a chair around, I sit on it backward and give the girls a long level-eyed look. "And that is by no means the worst of it. No," I repeat as somberly as Arnold Toynbee taking the long view. "As I also believe each of you also know, the Bantu revolt may be the least of our troubles."

"You're speaking, Chief," says Ellen, "of the danger of your lapsometer falling into the wrong hands."

"Yes."

"I'm afraid it's already happened, Chief," she says as gravely as I.

"I'm afraid it has."

"And what you fear is both a physical reaction and a psychical reaction, physical from the Heavy Salt domes in the area and psychical from its effect on political extremists."

"That is correct, Ellen."

The room is silent save for the rattling of the air-conditioner. Outside, like distant artillery, I can hear *The Drummer Boy* again.

Rumpa-pum-pum ...

Lola is sitting on the end of the other bed, cleaning her automatic. Moira lies behind her, flat, knees propped up, gazing at the ceiling.

"I'll fix you a drink, Tom. Where's the fixings?" says Lola.

"In there." I nod toward the dressing room.

"I'm afraid I've got bad news too, Chief."

"What's that?"

"It's the last message I got from Dr. Immelmann. Just before you came. On the Anser-Phone. Chief, how could he use the Anser-Phone? He didn't have a transmitter and he had no way of knowing our frequency."

"Never mind," I say hurriedly. "What did he want?"

"He said to tell you—now let me get this straight." Ellen consults her notebook. "To tell you that the program was third-generational and functional on both fronts; that he's already gotten gratifying overt interactions between the two extremes of the political spectrum, and that you would soon have sufficient data for a convincing pilot. Does that make sense?"

"I'm afraid so," I say gloomily. "Is that all?"

"I saved the good news, Chief," says Ellen, frowning at Lola, who is at the bar fixing drinks. "He also said to tell you—and this I wrote down word for word—that he's been in touch with the Nobel Prize committee in Stockholm, each member of which he knows personally, apprising them of the nature of your work, and that they're extremely excited about it. Chief, isn't the Peace Prize the big one? Anyhow, he's cabling them a summary of the present pilot and he closed with the cryptic remark that you should prepare yourself for some interesting news when the prize is announced in October. Does any of this make sense, Chief?"

"Yes," I say, frowning. "But October! What makes him think there'll be anything left in October? The damn fool is going to destroy everything." Then why is it, I wonder, that a pleasant tingling sensation spreads down the backs of my thighs?

"Here's your favorite, Tom Tom." Lola hands me a drink.

"Did she say 'Tom Tom'?" Moira asks Ellen.

I've tossed off the whole drink somewhat nervously before it comes over me that it is a gin fizz. Oh well, I've got anti-allergy pills with me. The drink is deliciously cool and silky with albumen.

"What are we going to do?" wails Moira, opening and closing her thighs on her hands, like a little girl holding wee-wee.

"Why don't you go to the bathroom?" suggests Ellen.

"I will," says Moira, jumping up. "No, I've just been. I have
to go to the Center to get my things."

"Right," Lola agrees instantly. "And I have to get my cello."

"No no," I say hastily. "You can't. Moira, you have everything here you need. I mean everyone has. I'll get your cello
for you, Lola."

"But my Cupid's Qui—" says Moira, coming close.

"Yes!" I exclaim, laughing, talking, hawking phlegm all at
once.

"Her Cupid's what?" asks Lola.

"Moira, like the rest of us," I tell Lola, "didn't know we'd
be stuck here."

"And besides, I can't wear the things you brought!" Moira
is in tears and is apt to say anything.

"What things?" asks Lola.

"I, ah, laid in some supplies as soon as I had reason to suspect the worst."

"In a motel?" Lola's fist disappears into her flank.

"It's a logical shelter for an emergency," says Ellen, "because
it's convenient to town, Center, and Paradise." Ellen is defend-
ing me!

"Right," I say, hawking and, for some reason, dancing like
Ken Stryker. I hand my empty glass to Lola.

"If I may make a suggestion, Chief," says Ellen briskly, "I
think we ought to find out exactly what is going on before we
do anything."

"Absolutely right!" Ellen is a jewel.

Ellen turns on the old Philco. "It's a bad color and 2-D but
it gets the local channel—the one over your house, Chief. In a
minute they'll have the news."

Lola takes my glass to the bar.

No one ever had a better nurse than Ellen.

II

On comes the picture, flickering and herringboned, of green
people in a green field under a green sky. There is a platform

and bunting and a speaker. The speaker has a ghost. The crowd mills about restlessly. "Hm, a Fourth of July celebration," I tell the girls—until all at once I recognize the place. It is the high school football field on the outskirts of town, not three miles from here!

The camera pans among the crowd. I recognize faces here and there: a conservative proctologist, a chiropractor, a retired Air Force colonel, a disgruntled Boeing executive, a Texaco dealer, a knot of PTA mothers from the private school, an occasional Knothead Catholic, and a Baptist preacher sitting on the platform. The speaker is the governor, a well-known Knothead.

Nearly everyone waves a little flag. The crowd is restive.

A reporter is interviewing a deputy sheriff, a good old boy named Junior Trosclair.

"We cain't hold these folks much longer," Junior is telling the reporter.

"Hold them from doing what?"

"They talking about marching on the federal complex."

"Why are they doing that, Deputy?" asks the reporter, already thinking of his next question.

"I don't know," says Junior, shaking his head dolefully. "All I know is we cain't hold them much longer."

"Sir," says the reporter, stopping a passerby, a pleasant-looking green-faced man who is wearing two hats and carrying an old M-1 rifle. "Sir, can you tell me what the plans are here?"

"What's that?" calls out the man, cupping an ear to hear over the uproar. His face has the amiable but bemused expression of a convention delegate.

The reporter repeats the question.

"Oh yes. Well, we're going to take a stand is the thing," says the man somewhat absently and, catching sight of a friend, waves at him.

"How is that, sir?" asks the reporter, holding the microphone over and grimacing at the engineer.

"What? Oh, we're going over there and clean them out."

"Over where?"

"Over to Fedville." The man gesticulates to the unseen friend and drifts off, nodding and smiling.

The reporter grabs his arm.

"Clean out who, sir? Sir!"

"What? Yes. Well, all of them."

"All of who?"

"You know, commonists, atheistic scientists, Jews, perverts, dope fiends, coonasses—"

The reporter drops the man's arm as if it had turned into a snake. "Thank you for your comment," he says, coming toward the camera. "Now I'll return you to—"

"And I'll tell you something else," says the man, who has warmed to the subject for the first time. He catches up with the fast-stepping reporter. "The niggers may be holed up over yonder in Paradise but you know where they're getting their orders from?"

"No sir. Now we'll have a message from—"

"From the White House, otherwise known as the Tel-a-Viv Hilton on Pennsylvania Avenue."

"Yes sir! Take it, David!"

During the exchange I've been watching another reporter with transmitter and back-pack passing with his ghost among the crowd. But no. It is—Art Immelmann, a green Art plus a green ghost of Art. No doubt about it. There's the old-fashioned crewcut and widow's peak. And he's carrying not a microphone but my lapsometer. And he's only pretending to do interviews: holding the device to people's mouths only when they are looking at him, otherwise passing it over their heads or pressing it into the nape of their necks.

"That's Dr. Immelmann!" cries Ellen, jumping up and pointing to the flickering screen, but at that moment the newscast ends and the afternoon movie resumes, a rerun of a very clean film, which I recognize as *The Ice Capades of 1981.*

"Did you see him, Chief?"

"It did look like him."

"And he had your invention."

"It did appear so."

Moira comes out of the bathroom, face scrubbed.

"I'm leaving," she announces and strides for the door.

"Wait!" I jump against the door, blocking her. "You can't go out there!"

"I'm going to get my Cupid's Quiver and my own clothes.
That is, if I come back."

"Get her what?" asks Lola.

"You can't leave just now. It's too dangerous."

"I must get my own clothes."

"What does she mean, her own clothes?" asks Lola, frowning.

"We may be here quite a while, Lola," I explain earnestly.

"Yes," says Moira. "Chico and I had plans to stay only for
the weekend."

"Weekend? Chico?" Lola has risen slowly and stands, one
fist on her hip, pelvis tilted menacingly. "Who is this Chico?"

"Ha ha," I laugh nervously. I'm sure everybody's plans for
the Fourth were spoiled. "I'll tell you what," I say quickly to
Moira. "Give me your key and I'll go for you."

Now it's Lola who heads for the door. "Out of my way,
Chico. I'm going too. I have to get my cello and look after my
horses. A horse you can trust."

"I'll get your cello too, Lola. It's in Love, didn't you tell
me?"

Both girls confront me.

"Well? Are you moving out of the way, Tom?" Lola asks.

I shrug and step aside.

Out they go—"I may not be back," says Moira over her
shoulder—and back they come, reeling back as if blown in by
a gale. They slam the door and stand, palms against the wood,
eyes rolling up. Two girls they truly seem and very young.

Lola swallows. "He's there."

"Who?"

"A Bantu."

I peep through the curtains. It is Ely in his *kwunghali* standing with his Sten gun in the shadow of the opposite balcony.
I recognize the classy Duke Ellington forehead. He is looking
right and left but not up.

"I'll go, O.K.?" I say wearily, holding out a hand for Moira's
key. "Lola, take out your automatic and sit here. Ellen, take my
revolver and sit there."

Moira has collapsed on the bed, where she lies opening and
closing her knees.

"Why don't you go to the bathroom, dear," says Ellen.

Moira obeys. She gives me her key without a word.

When she comes out, I open the bathroom window. Lola follows me.

"How are you going to get my cello through that window?"

"I'll put it in a safe place downstairs."

"What about the Bantu?"

"If he comes up on the balcony, shoot him."

"Very well, Chico," says Lola sarcastically. "Just you be careful with my cello—Chico."

I switch off the air-conditioner. "Sorry, girls."

"Be careful, Chief," whispers Ellen, helping me through the window. Absently wetting her fingertips with her tongue, she smooths out my eyebrows with strong mother-smoothings.

Before leaving, I give each girl a light Chloride massage over Brodmann 32 and pineal Layer I—to inoculate them against a Heavy Sodium fallout, an unlikely event in the next few hours, but who knows? After treatment, each girl looks so serene, both alert and dreamy-eyed, as sleepy and watchful as a waking child, that I do the same for myself.

12

A gaggle of unruly Left students mill about the main gate of the Behavioral Institute. Some drive nails into golf balls. Others fill Coke bottles with gasoline. They frown when they see me. I recognize several members of Buddy Brown's faction.

Professor Coffin Cabot, a famous scholar on loan from Harvard, is in their midst, a pair of wire-cutters in one hand and the flag of North Ecuador in the other, counseling, exhorting, and showing students how to clip the heads off nails after they are driven into a golf ball.

"What are *you* doing here, More?" he asks, his face darkening.

"What's wrong with my being here?"

"Haven't you done enough dirty work for the military-industrial-academic complex?"

"What do you mean?"

"You know very well what I mean. I suppose you didn't know that your cute little toy has been added to the Maryland arsenal along with its cache of plague bacilli and lethal gases."

"No, I didn't. By whom?"

"By your fascist friend, Immelmann."

"He's not a friend. But may I ask what you are doing?"

"We are organizing a nonviolent demonstration for peace and freedom in Ecuador."

"Nonviolent?" I ask, looking at the pile of spiked golf balls.

"We practice creative nonviolent violence, that is, violence in the service of nonviolence. It is a matter of intention."

Professor Cabot is a semanticist.

"When is this coming off?"

"This afternoon. We're marching against the so-called Fourth of July movement in town."

"So-called?"

"Yes. We recognize only the Fifth of July movement named in honor of the day Jorge Rojas parachuted into the mountains of South Ecuador."

"Jorge Rojas?"

"Of course. He's the George Washington of Ecuador, the only man beloved north and south and the only man capable of uniting the country."

"But didn't he kill several hundred thousand Ecuadorians who didn't love him?"

"Yes, but they were either fascists or running dogs or lackeys of the American imperialists. Anyhow, the question has become academic."

"How is that?"

"Because those who are left do love him."

I scratch my head. "Why are you carrying that flag?"

"Because North Ecuador stands for peace and freedom."

"But aren't you an American?"

"Yes, but America is a cancer in the community of democratic nations. Incidentally, More, my lecture on this subject last month in Stockholm received an even greater ovation than it got at Harvard."

"If that is the case, why don't you live in Sweden or North Ecuador?"

Professor Cabot looks at me incredulously as he adjusts a wick in a Coke bottle.

"You've got to be kidding, More."

"No."

He stands up, looks right and left, and says in a low voice, "Do you know what I'm pulling at Cambridge?"

"No."

"A hundred thousand a year plus two hundred thousand for my own institute. And Berkeley offered me more. What do you think of that?"

"Very good," I reply sympathetically, setting as I do as high a value on money as the next man.

"Say, why don't you join us, More?" asks Coffin Cabot impulsively.

"No thanks. I've got to pick up a ah cello." For some reason I blush.

Cabot grins. "That figures. Fiddling while Rome burns, eh?"

"No. The fact is there are three girls over there in the motel—"

"What?"

"Never mind." I was on the point of telling him about the dangers of the misuse of my invention when I catch sight of—! It can't be but it is. There over Coffin Cabot's shoulder, moving about among the students with my lapsometer, is Art Immelmann!

"Excuse me," I murmur, but Cabot is already preoccupied with the next batch of golf balls and does not notice Art.

I watch him.

Art Immelmann, it soon becomes clear, is demonstrating my device to the students as the famous fake prop of The Pit, laughing and shaking his head at the preposterousness of it, like a doctor unmasking the latest quackery. The students laugh. Yet, as he does so, he makes passes over the students' heads.

In the instant he catches sight of me I lay hands on my invention and snatch it away from him.

"Oh, Doc!" he cries with every sign of delight. "Just the man I'm looking for!"

I gaze at him in astonishment. "How did you get here?"

"What do you mean, Doc?"

"I saw you on TV not ten minutes ago and you were in town."

Art shrugs. "Perhaps it was a tape."

"It was no tape." I am examining the lapsometer. "Do you realize you've got this thing set for plus ten dosage at the level of the prefrontal abstractive centers?"

"It's only for purposes of demonstration."

"Do you realize what this would do to a man, especially a student?"

"I know," says Art, smiling good-naturedly. "But I like to hear you say it."

"It would render him totally abstracted from himself, totally alienated from the concrete world, and in such a state of angelism that he will fall prey to the first abstract notion proposed to him and will kill anybody who gets in his way, torture, execute, wipe out entire populations, all with the best possible motives and the best possible intentions, in fact in the name of peace and freedom etcetera."

"Yeah, Doc!" cries Art delighted. "Your MOQUOL surpasses my most sanguine expectations. I've already elicited positive interactions from both ends of the spectrum—"

"Goddamn, man, do you realize what you're saying?"

Art winces and turns pale. I swing him round to face me.

"I authorized you to use my invention to diminish, not increase tensions. It says so in the contract."

"Yeah, but Doc, this is the pilot. In the pilot you have to get the problem out on the table. Then when the pilot's complete—"

"Screw the pilot," I am yelling, beside myself with anger.

"How do you mean, Doc?" asks Art, mystified. "How is that possible?"

"Never mind. It's no use trying to tell you. I'm taking this lapsometer and I want the rest that you stole. Where are they?"

Art looks mournful. "I'm very sorry, Doc, but they're all in the hands of the interdisciplinary task force—"

"Listen, you son of a bitch, our agreement is canceled as of this moment."

"Excuse me, Doc." Art shakes his head regretfully. "In the first place, I don't understand your imputation about my mother when the fact of the matter is I don't—but that's neither here nor there. In the second place, I'm afraid the contract cannot be voided unilaterally."

"Get out of my way," I say, suddenly remembering the three girls in room 203.

"Don't worry about a thing, Doc!" Art waves cheerily. "Don't worry about the Nobel Prize either. You're in."

Though I fling away in a rage, a pleasant tingle spreads across my sacrum. Is it the prospect of the Nobel or the effect of the gin fizz?

13

I am surprised and dismayed to find Love Clinic humming with activity. Stryker explains that it was the volunteers themselves who, excited by a "new concept in therapy," had forgone the holiday in order to complete the research.

But how to retrieve the cello without awkward explanations?

Father Kev Kevin sits at the vaginal console reading *Commonweal*.

But I am blinking at the scene in the behavior room. What a transformation! Nothing is the same. The stark white clinical cube has been decorated in Early American and furnished with a bull's-eye mirror, cobbler's bench, rag rugs, and two bundling beds.

"What's going on?" I ask Stryker, who comes gliding up, one foot swinging wide in a tango step.

"You of all people should know!"

"Why me?"

"It's thanks to you we made the breakthrough."

"What breakthrough?"

"The use of substitute partners."

"The use of what?"

"Ha ha, don't be modest, Doctor! Your associate told me otherwise."

"My associate?" I ask with sinking heart.

"Dr. Immelmann."

"What did he say?"

"He showed us your paper in which you demonstrate that marital love often founders on boredom and the struggle to attain a theoretical orgasmic perfection."

"But I didn't suggest—"

"You didn't have to. We simply implemented your insight."

"With?"

"Substitute partners! A fresh start!" Like an impresario Stryker waves a graceful hand toward the viewing mirror.

Instead of the usual solitary subject, or at the most two subjects, there are four, two in each bed, J. T. Thigpen, Gloria, and Ted 'n Tanya. But Gloria is in one bed with Ted and J. T. in the other with Tanya. The couples are, for the most part, dressed: the women in Mistress Goody gowns, the men in Cotton Mather knee-britches.

"As you see, Tom, we also make use of your warnings about an abstract and depersonalized environment. We place our lovers in a particular concrete historical setting."

"But I didn't suggest—"

Dr. Helga Heine suddenly turns up the music, which is not Early American, however, but Viennese waltzes.

"Okay, keeds!" She speaks into a microphone, keeping time with her free hand. Though she is hefty, she balances lightly on the balls of her feet.

"*Zwei Herzen!* Now—bundling partitions up!"

"Hold it!" cries the chaplain from the vaginal console. "They haven't inserted the sensors! Rats!" He grabs Helga's microphone. "Hold it, kids! Bundling partitions down! Insert sensors!"

But it is too late. The couples are too engrossed with each other to pay attention. Nor do Stryker and Helga object.

"The important thing is the breakthrough," Stryker tells me. "The quantifying can come later."

"Go go go, keeds!" cries Helga, recovering the microphone and waltzing about in one place.

"Don't fret, Kev." Stryker tries to soothe the distraught chaplain. "We'll have the film and there'll be more sessions to collect data."

"Tch!" The chaplain stamps his foot and rends his *Commonweal*. "I wish somebody would tell me why we're paying these people!"

But Stryker is standing beside Helga, the two of them suddenly quiet as they watch the lovers.

"Wow," says Stryker, lips parted.

"And how," says Helga.

They look at each other.

"Are you thinking what I'm thinking?" asks Stryker, touching Helga's elbow.

"The chicken room?" asks Helga softly, her eyes radiant. She pronounces it *zhicken*.

Linking arms, they disappear through the doorway of the Observer Stimulation Overflow Area.

But wait! That's where the cello is!

It's too late. The door closes. Father Kev Kevin and I watch in dismay.

"I have to get a cello out of there," I tell the chaplain for lack of anything better to say.

"What are we going to do?" asks the chaplain frantically, wringing his hands, starting now for his console, now for the chicken room. He is sweating profusely.

"I don't know about you, but I've got to get that cello."

"Oh dear!" cries Father Kev Kevin. "If there was ever an existential decision—! Kenneth, how could you!" He groans aloud and, thrusting me aside, disappears into the cubicle.

After a moment of indecision, I rush after him.

Despite the urgency, I find myself knocking politely at the door. No response. Try the knob. It is unlocked. Hm, nothing for it but to slip in, find the cello, and slip out with as little fuss as possible.

I do so, trying as best I can to pretend nothing is out of the way, but the cello is propped in the far corner and I have to bend over the cot to reach it.

"Pardon," I murmur, eyes rolled up into eyebrows.

But there is no not seeing a large rosy buttock. Stryker is at Helga, Father Kev Kevin is at Stryker, but Helga is also patting the chaplain as if to reassure him lest he feel unwanted. The three embrace like lost children trying to keep warm.

The encased cello is as bulky as a sarcophagus. There is no purchase on it and there is the devil's own time getting it over and across the populous cot without knocking the occupants.

"Pardon."

Puffing and straining, I make it at last. Whew!

I rush through the observation room without bothering to look at the volunteer lovers. Wheels whir, pointers quiver, unattended.

Now to find Moira's room, her Cupid's Quiver and underwear, and I'm on my way!

14

It's raining again when I return to the motel. No sign of Ely, the Bantu home guard. I store the cello in the Rotary dining room and go up through the bathroom window.

In my absence Moira has taken a shower and looks lovely, but she and Lola have fallen out. In their quarrel they hardly take notice of my return. Lola hardly acknowledges the news that her cello is safe and sound.

Ellen brings me a Spam sandwich and a glass of bitter hose water. Noticing her, Lola fixes me a gin fizz. I decide to drink the gin fizz before eating.

"Don't think I don't know what goes on in that so-called Love Clinic," Lola is saying with an ironic smile.

"And what might that be?" asks Moira.

Both women are smiling and speaking to Ellen but really through Ellen to each other. They have reached that stage of a quarrel where both still smile but neither can stand the sight of the other.

"Everybody knows about the atheistic psychologists who encourage immorality under the guise of research," Lola tells Moira through Ellen.

Moira is sitting cross-legged on the bed, doing her nails. She looks like a sorority girl. "At least there is no hypocrisy, which is more than I can say about the goings on in the so-called country-club set."

"Such as?"

Now they're looking at me!

"Well well, girls," I tell them. "You'll be glad to hear I brought everything you sent me for."

"Such as what goes on at night on the golfing greens and the skinny-dipping in the pool," Moira tells me with a wink.

"Sounds like someone's been reading girlie magazines, Tom," says Lola, to me.

"Yes. Well, to tell the truth"—I sip the gin fizz and close my eyes with every appearance of exhaustion—"you must excuse me. I can't concentrate on such matters. I'm afraid the situation outside has deteriorated badly." I relate the events of my excursion to the Center, omitting only some of the occurrences in Love. Disaster has its uses. "We may be here longer than you think. I'm afraid we're in for a long evening."

"How's that, Chief?" asks Ellen seriously. She pulls up a chair and absently plucks beggar's lice from my pants leg.

"If there is going to be a major outbreak of violence, it will occur, I calculate, sometime this evening. I suggest that we all take a nap and prepare for what might be a bad night."

The grave news only partly mollifies Lola and Moira. Lola cants her pelvis and smolders, color high in her cheeks. Moira lies back on the bed, tucks her lip secretly, and holds up one pretty leg with both hands.

Ellen clears her throat and beckons me into the dressing room. "Chief, eat your sandwich!" she scolds and, as soon as we're inside, whispers: "You better do something about that pair."

"Yes," I say, noticing that Ellen is enjoying herself for the first time.

"Do you know what they did while you were gone?" she asks, scraping more beggar's lice from my sleeve. "They almost started scratching each other. I actually had to stand between them. They refused to stay in the same room, so what I did was fix up two other rooms. I had to! One's in 204 and the other in 205. I found some sheets and some Gulf spray, so we sprayed the mattresses and made them up."

"Then why are they back here?"

"Getting pillow cases!" Ellen nudges me. Her tone is the same she uses when she describes the antics of patients.

After a careful reconnoiter of the balcony, I tell the girls: "The coast is clear. Here's what we'll do. It's cool now, so everyone can go to his or her room and take a nap. I'll stand guard. Ellen, you keep this room."

"And where might *his* room be?" Lola asks *The Laughing Cavalier*.

"Don't worry, there are plenty of vacancies!" I say heartily.

"Then would you mind getting my cello?" asks Lola without looking at me.

"And I'll take my sachet," says Moira, stretching and yawning.

"Of course!" I say, laughing. Why am I laughing?

15

I take Moira and Lola to their rooms. The coast is clear. Ellen
is agitated when I return. She paces the carpet.

"I didn't tell you that I talked to Aunt Ellie—the last message before the Anser-Phone broke down and the operator left
for Mississippi."

"A fine woman, Miss Ellie."

Miss Ellie Oglethorpe, who raised Ellen, is a fine woman.
She looks like a buxom President Wilson with her horse face,
pince-nez, and large bosom. A virtuous and hard-working
woman, she supported herself as town librarian, raised and
educated Ellen, and still sends money to the African mission
where Ellen's parents were killed by Nigerian tribesmen.

"She doesn't want me to stay out here alone, Chief."

"You're not alone."

"If I don't come back tonight, she wants to come out here."

"Good Lord, she can't do that."

"She's worried about my safety."

"We're perfectly safe here. Besides, I wouldn't let anything
happen to you."

"It's not exactly that. She doesn't think it proper for me to
stay here without a chaperone."

"Good Lord, of all things to worry about now."

"You know Aunt Ellie."

"Yes."

I am wondering whether to mix another gin fizz, eat, nap,
or take a shower. Absently I mix a gin fizz.

"Aunt Ellie is something, isn't she?"

"Yes, she is."

"Do you know what she's been telling me for as long as I
can remember?"

"No."

"You wouldn't believe it."

"No?"

"Here I am, twenty-four, and she still takes me aside and
says: Ellen, think of yourself as a treasure trove that you're
guarding for your future husband. Can you imagine such a
thing?"

"No. Yes."

"For years I thought she was talking about Mama's silver service locked in the linen closet."

"Is that right?" Feeling a slight quilting of the scalp, I take an anti-hives pill. "Well, she's right, Ellen. And I envy the lucky man."

"Thanks, Chief."

"This is your room, by the way."

"What will your two girl friends say?"

I shrug. "Don't worry about them. Now. You take your nap. If you don't mind, I'm going to take a shower, put on some clean clothes, and eat your sandwiches. Then I think I'll feel better."

"I can't stand those on you," says Ellen, buttoning my unbuttoned collar tabs.

She lies on the bed, throwing the tufted chenille spread over her crossed ankles. How ill the chenille suits her! I blush at my summer's effort of fitting out this room as a trysting place. How shabby Ellen makes it all seem!

Take a shower. The water is hot at first from the sun, two hundred feet of bitter hot hose water between the motel and the Esso station, then suddenly goes cold.

A harsh toweling. Switch to an Early Times today. Eat Ellen's sandwiches? No, drink two gin fizzes.

Go fetch lapsometer, tiptoeing past Ellen, who sleeps, lips parted.

Now at mirror, set lapsometer for a fairly stiff massage of Brodmann 11, the frontal location of the musical-erotic.

The machine sings like a tuning fork. My head sings with it, the neurones of Layer IV dancing in tune.

The albumen molecules hum.

> *Everybody's talking at me,*
> *I can't hear a word they saying,*
> *Only the echoes of my mind.*

What does a man live for but to have a girl, use his mind, practice his trade, drink a drink, read a book, and watch the martins wing it for the Amazon and the three-fingered sassafras turn red in October?

Art Immelmann is right. Man is not made for suffering, night sweats, and morning terrors.

Doctor, heal thyself, I say, and give Brodmann 11 one last little buzz.

I feel much better, full of musical-erotic tenderness and gin fizzes and bourbon but fresh and clean and ravenous as well. I eat more of Ellen's sandwiches.

Time to fetch Lola's cello from the Rotary dining room.

The motel seems deserted. No activity at the church except for the carols still booming across the empty plaza:

A partridge in a pear tree . . .

July or not, it all comes back, the old pleasant month-long Santy-Claus-store-window Christmas. It wasn't so bad really, the commercial Christmas, a month of Christmas Eves, stores open every night, everyone feeling good and generous and spending money freely, handsome happy Americans making the cash registers jingle, the nice commercial carols, Holy Night, and soft-eyed pretty girls everywhere—

The carol stops in mid-phrase. Someone has finally found the control panel.

16

The rain slams in sheets against the windows of Lola's room. It is a small tropical storm. Lola plays a Dvořák Slavonic dance and ducks her head to its little lilt and halt and stutter and start again.

The only clean place in the room is the mattress, which has been Gulf-sprayed and spread with a fitted sheet snapped over the corners and stretched tight as a drumhead.

I lie on the drumhead sheet in my stocking feet, toddy balanced on my sternum.

Goodbye morning terror and afternoon sadness. Hello love and Anton Dvořák.

Above the racket of the storm and in the reek of warm bourbon and Gulf spray, old Dvořák sings of the sunny fields and twilit forests of Bohemia.

Lola closes her eyes as she plays. Her strong bare knees clasp

the cello's waist, her fingertips creak against the resin, her deltoid swells, the vibrato flutter of her fingering hand beats like
the wings of a hawk.

> *Three French hens, two turtle doves*
> *And a partridge in a pear tree,*

shrieks the carillon like a wind in the storm. Some damn fool
has started it up again. Lola laughs and puts the cello away.

We lie entwined on the tight sheet, kissing persimmon kisses,
Lola twisting down and around in her old Juilliard torque style
of kissing. When she loves, even lying down, there is a sense of
her stooping to it. The cello is still but music plays on. When
we're not kissing, her tongue cleaves to the back of her teeth
and she hisses cello themes in a boy's way of whistling, a paper-
boy hiss-whistling through his teeth on his route.

Her warm callused fingertips strew stars along my flank. My
scalp quilts a bit, popping a hair root or two. But I can see well
enough. Where are my pills?

She is both heavy and frail.

Now the idiot is fooling with the carillon controls, spinning
the tape backward into fall football music. The storm roars but
above it I recognize the Tarheel alma mater,

> *Hark the sound of Tarheel voices*
> *Ringing clear and true,*

played five years ago when Tulane played the Carolina Tarheels.

We close our eyes and go spinning back to those old haunted
falls, the happy-sad bittersweet drunk Octobers. What needs
to be discharged is the intolerable tenderness of the past, the
past gone and grieved over and never made sense of. Music
ransoms us from the past, declares an amnesty, brackets and
sets aside the old puzzles. Sing a new song. Start a new life,
get a girl, look into her shadowy eyes, smile. Fix me a toddy,
Lola, and we'll sit on the gallery of Tara and you play a tune
and we'll watch evening fall and lightning bugs wink in the
purple meadow.

Our heads lie in each other's arms. My hand explores the

tender juncture of her frailty and strength, a piece of nature's drollery, the flare of ribs from the massive secret paraspinal muscle columns.

"We'll live at Tara," says Lola past my arm in the prosaic casting-ahead voice of a woman planning tomorrow's meals. "While I'm showing horses and playing concerts, you can do your researches. You can have the garçonnière for your laboratory."

Lying cheek against the warm slump of her biceps, I am perceiving myself as she sees me, an agreeable H. G. Wells nineteenth-century scientist type, "doing my researches" in the handsome outhouse of Tara, maybe working on a time machine and forgetting time the way great inventors do so she has to remind me to eat, bringing a tray of collard greens and corn bread to the lab. "Darling, you haven't eaten all day!" So I take time off to eat, time off from my second breakthrough and my second Nobel.

Afterwards we sit on the gallery and Lola brings me toddies and plays happy old Haydn, whose music does not brook one single shadow of sadness.

Then we'll go to bed, not in the bunker to watch the constellations spin in their courses but upstairs to the great four-poster, the same used by Rhett Butler and Scarlett and purchased by Vince Marsaglia at the M-G-M prop sale in 1970.

Perhaps I'll even work at night. Happy is the man who can do science at midnight, of a Tuesday, in the fall, free of ghosts, exorcised by love and music of all past Octobers. Clasp Lola on Halloween and howl down the yellow moon and go to the lab and induce great simple hypotheses.

The rain slackens but still drums steadily on the orange tile roof of Howard Johnson's.

"You're so *smart*," says Lola, giving me a hug.

"And you're a fine girl." I speak into the sweet heavy slump of her biceps. "What a lovely strong back you have. It's good being here, isn't it?"

"Lovely."

"You're such a good girl and you play such good music."

"Do you really think I'm good?" She lifts her head.

"Yes," I say, frowning, realizing I've stirred up her Texas competitiveness. She's told me before about winning regional cello contests in West Texas.

"How good?"

"At music? The best," I say, hoping to make her forget about it and locking my fingers in the small of her back, a deep wondrous swale.

But her horned fingertips absently play a passacaglia on my spine as her mind casts ahead.

"You know what I think I'll do?"

"What?"

"Enter Yellow Rose in the Dallas show."

"Good." At least she's off music contests.

"Then take up Billy Sol on his idea of a winter tour."

"You have a truly splendid back. What a back. It's extremely strong."

"That's nothing, feel this."

So saying, she locks her legs around my waist in a nonerotic schoolboy's wrestling hold and bears down.

"Good Lord," I say, blinking to clear the fog from my eyes.

"What do you think of that?"

"Amazing."

"Nobody ever beat Lola at anything."

"I believe you." Sometimes I think that men are the only single-minded lovers, loving for love, that women love with the idea of winning, winning either at love or cello-playing or what. "Billy Sol? Winter tour?"

"Yes, darl. You want Lola to keep up her music, don't you?"

"Sure."

"This is Lola's big chance." Up and down goes the fingering hand warm as a horn on my backbone.

"Chance to do what?"

Billy Sol, it turns out, is Billy Sol Simpson of the music department at Texas A & M, who has offered her the "junior swing" for starters. It's a tour of the junior colleges of Texas, of which there are forty or fifty—with himself, Billy Sol, as her accompanist. After that, who knows? Maybe the senior circuit: Baylor, T.C.U., S.M.U., and suchlike.

"Well, I don't know," I say, thinking of this guy Billy Sol

squiring her around Beaumont Baptist College and West Texas
Junior College at Pecos. Should I trust her to a Texas A & M
piano player?

"Shoot, you ought to see Billy Sol. Just a big old prisspot,
but a real good boy. He's been wonderful to me."

"I'm glad."

"Don't you be like that—you want me to squeeze you again?"

"No."

"Anyhow, you're coming with us. You'll need a break from
your researches."

"Yes!" All of a sudden I feel happy again.

For a fact, it doesn't sound bad at all, swinging out through
all those lost lonesome Texas towns, setting up in Alamo Plaza
motels bejeweled in the dusk under those great empty heart-
stopping skies. A few toddies and I'll sit in the back row of the
LBJ Memorial auditorium behind rows of fresh-eyed, clean-
necked, short-haired God-believing Protestant boys and girls,
many dumb but many also smart, smart the way Van Cliburn
was smart, who came from Texas too, making straight A's at
everything and taking the prize in Moscow, while big prissy
Billy Sol tinkles away on the Steinway and Lola clasps her cello
between her knees and sends old Brahms singing out into the
great God-haunted Texas night.

. . . And afterwards eat a big steak and drink more toddies and
make love and watch Japanese 3-D science-fiction late movies.
(Dear God, I hope Lola won't develop an obsession about winning, winning horse shows and music contests, the way Doris
got hooked on antiques, Englishmen, and Hindoo religion.)

I must have been shaking my head, for she raises hers and
looks at me. "What?"

But I don't tell her. Instead I remind her that if worst comes
to worst this afternoon, there may not be any horse shows or
junior swings through Texas.

"Oh. You're right," she says, feigning gravity. She doesn't
really believe that anything could go wrong with the U.S.A.
or at least with Texas.

Her fingering fingers drift off my back. She's asleep. Her
breath comes strong and sweet in my neck, as hay-sweet as her
sorrel mare's.

Carefully I ease myself free of her slack heavy-frail body.

What a strong fine girl. If worst came to worst, she and I could rebuild Tara with our bare hands.

17

"Chief, the news is worse." Ellen watches me as I fix two gin fizzes. "Don't you think you're firing the sunset gun a little too early and too often?"

"What has happened now?"

"There are riots in New Orleans, and riots over here. The students are fighting the National Guard, the Lefts are fighting the Knotheads, the blacks are fighting the whites. The Jews are being persecuted."

"What are the Christians doing?"

"Nothing."

"Turn on the TV."

"It's on. The station went off the air."

"Then they've taken the transmitter," I say half to myself.

"What's that, Chief?"

"Nothing."

"Did you enjoy the concert?"

"What concert? Oh yes."

"I heard from Dr. Immelmann again."

"How did you hear from him?"

"On the Anser-Phone."

"I thought you said it was dead."

"It was. I don't understand it."

"What did he say?"

"He said to tell you 'it' was going to happen this afternoon."

"It?"

"He said you would know what I meant."

The gin fizz is good. Already the little albumen molecules are singing in my brain. My neck is swelling. I take a pill to prevent hives.

"What else did he say?"

"That if anything happens, we're to stay here. That we're safe with you because you can protect us with your lapsometer. He said you should watch and wait."

"Watch for what?"

"He said you would know. Signs and portents, he said. He told me, don't go back and get your coat."

"Hm. Did he say how long we should wait here?"

"He said it might be months."

"Did you ask him about your aunt and my mother?"

"He said they would be fine. Chief, do you know what is going to happen?"

"No. At least I am not sure."

"What are you going to do?"

"Right now I have to see how Moira is."

"Well, excuse me!"

"What's the matter?"

"Frankly I don't see what you see in either one of them."

"They're both fine girls. I'm very fond of them. I may as well tell you that I'm thinking of marrying again."

"Congratulations. But don't you have one girl too many?"

"Things are going to be very unsettled for the next few weeks," I say vaguely.

"What does that mean?"

I shrug.

Ellen uncrosses her legs and leans forward. "Well, what do you mean? Do you mean you want to—marry both of them?"

"Right now, I'm responsible for all three of you."

My scalp is beginning to quilt.

Ellen blinks. "I'm not sure I understand you."

"It's a question of honor."

"Honor?"

"I don't believe a man should trifle with a girl."

"Well yes, but—!"

"However, if a man's intentions are honorable—"

"But—"

"I mean if a man intends to marry a girl—"

"But, Chief, there are two of them."

"It is still a matter of intentions," I say, feeling scalp-hawsers pop.

"You mean you're going to marry both of them?"

"These are peculiar times. Abraham had several wives."

"Abraham? Abraham who? My God, you couldn't handle one wife."

"Never mind," I say stiffly. "The fact is I am responsible for all three of you."

"Ho ho. Include me out!"

"Nevertheless—!"

"With those two"—she nods toward the wall—"you need me?"

"That's right."

"You need something. Chief, I don't understand what is happening to you. You have so much to offer the world. There is so much that is fine in you. You're a fine doctor. And God knows, if the world ever needed you, it needs you now. Yet all you want to do is live here in this motel with three women for months on end."

"Yes!" I laugh. "You and I will spend the summer reading Calvin and Thomas Aquinas and let those two women squabble."

"Not me, big boy! I'm leaving this afternoon."

"You can't. You heard what Art said."

"It's Art who's picking me up."

"What?"

"Dr. Immelmann offered me a job."

"Doing what?"

"As his traveling secretary."

"What in hell does that mean?"

"He's going to Sweden to coordinate your MOQUOL program."

"You and Art Immelmann in Sweden!"

"What's wrong with that?"

"That's the goddamnest thing I ever heard."

"Your cursing doesn't help the situation."

"You don't want to go with him."

"No, I don't, Chief," says Ellen quietly. She sits bolt upright at the desk, starchy as a head nurse on the morning shift, eyes blue as Lake Geneva.

"Stay with me, Ellen. Things will settle down. We'll go back to work. Somebody will have to pick up the pieces."

Ellen is silent.

"Well?"

"There would have to be some fundamental changes before I would stay," she says at last.

"Changes? What changes?"

"You figure it out, Chief."

What does she mean, I wonder as I give myself a light lapsometer massage, firming up the musical-erotic as well as pineal selfhood.

A better question: why do I want all three women? For I do. I can't stand the thought of losing a single one! How dare anyone take one of my girls?

Stepping out into the silvery rain, I notice a Bantu squatting cross-legged atop the Joy screen, looking toward the Center with a pair of binoculars.

The carillon has jumped back to Christmas.

Silent night,
Holy night.

18

Moira sits on the bed reading *Cosmopolitan*. Damn, I wish she wouldn't! I brought Rod McKuen and some house and home magazines for our weekend at Howard Johnson's, but no, she has to bring *Cosmopolitan*. Why? Because of Helen Gurley Brown, her favorite author. She's reading an article of Helen's now, "Adultery for Adults." Damn! For years now Helen has been telling girls it's all right to screw anybody you like.

But what if she likes Buddy Brown?

I hand her *House and Garden*. "You shouldn't read that stuff."

"Why not?"

"It's immoral."

She shrugs but takes *House and Garden*. "You didn't mind my reading it before."

"That was before."

"What's wrong with my reading it now?"

"Everything."

"What's the difference?"

"It's a matter of intention," I begin, but she's not listening. Something in *House and Garden* has caught her eye.

"I can't decide which I like better, the now look or the Vermeer look."

"What is the Vermeer look?"

"You know—Dutch doors with the top open, everything light and airy, tile."

"Very good."

"Myself I've always been partial to the outdoor-indoor look, green leaves in the kitchen, a bedroom opening to the treetops."

"We had that." I sit on the foot of the bed.

"Don't you love this kitchen?"

"Yes."

Moira must have had a nap. At any rate she's rosy and composed, her old thrifty self. Cross-legged she sits, lower lip curled like a thick petal. Above her perfect oval face, a face unwounded, unscarred, unlined, unmarked by sadness or joy, the nap of her cropped wheat-colored hair invites the hand against its grain. My hand brushes it. My heart lifts. I am in love.

She's the girl of our dreams, Americans! the very one we held in our hearts as we toiled in the jungles of Ecuador. She is! Sitting scrunched over and humpbacked, she is beautiful despite herself, calf yoga-swelled over heel, one elbow propped, the other winged out like a buzzard for all she cares. Prodigal she is with her own perfection, lip tucked, pencil scratching her head. She holds herself too cheap, leaves her gold lying around like bobby pins.

My throat is engorged with tenderness.

Planning a house she is, marking the margins of *House Beautiful*. She's beautiful too. A bit short in the limbs, I'll admit—I can stretch a hand's span from her elbow to her acromium—but perfected as it were in the shortening. Her golden deltoid curves in in a single strong arc, a whorl of down marking its insertion. Now she turns a page and supinates her forearm to hold the spine of the magazine: down plunges the tendon into the fossa at her elbow. Sweet fossa. I kiss it.

"See how the prints of the casual pillows pick up the daisies in the wall tile."

"Yes. I have any number of casual pillows at home."

"I like casual living."

"Me too."

"Could we do the whole house over?"

"What house."

"Your house."

"Sure."

"I think I'll collect Shaker tableware. Look at these."

"Very good. But I thought you were going to raise banties."

"I am. But my great-grandfather was a backsliding Shaker who got married."

"Is that so?"

"Here is something else I love: simple handcrafts."

"I do too."

She puts down her magazine, rises to stretch, sits in my lap.

"You are good enough to eat," I say and begin to eat her kneecaps, which are like beaten biscuits. My fiery scalp begins to pop hawsers.

"You're just like my Uncle Bud," says Moira, burying her face in my neck.

"I know."

"Only I like you better."

"You're a lovely girl."

"What do you think of my taking up tennis at the club?"

"You'd look lovely in a tennis outfit."

"I want to join a book club too."

"There is a poetry club in Paradise."

"I love poetry," she says and recites a poem.

> *There was a girl in Portland*
> *Before the winter chill*
> *We used to go a'courting*
> *Along October hill.*

"Very nice."

"It's always had a special meaning to me."

"Why?"

"Because we used to live in Portland, West Virginia."

"I'd like to take you down October hill."

"You look just like Rod McKuen, only stronger."

"Younger too."

"Wait a sec, Chico."

"Where're you going?"

"Next door. To get my sachet."

"Ah. Hm. Actually I don't . . . I didn't mean . . . I . . ."

"Don't worry. I'll fool the battle-ax."

"Battle-ax?" I say wonderingly.

She turns at the door, dimpling.

"Aunngh," I say faintly. Segments of a road map drift across my retina, crossroads, bits of highway, county seats.

Sitting slouched and poetic, as gracefully as Rod, I wait for Moira before the winter chill.

What I need is a nap, I tell myself, and fall asleep immediately. Do I hear Moira come and go while I am dozing?

19

"I quit, Dr. More," says Ellen. "Now. As of this moment. I no longer work for you."

"I wish you wouldn't." I fix a toddy, lie on the bed, slip a quarter in the Slepe-Eze, and close my eyes.

"Of all the shameless performances."

"Whose?"

"Not yours. I don't blame you nearly as much as them."

"You don't?" Taking heart, I open one eye.

"Chief," says Ellen, concerned, "what's the matter with your eye?"

"I don't know. What?"

"It's almost closed."

"Probably hives."

"My goodness! It's awful."

"My throat is closing too."

"Wait, Chief! I've got a shot of epinephrine in my bag."

"Good."

I watch with one eye while she gives me the shot.

"At least, Chief, I give you credit for honorable intentions."

"You do?"

"I think you're confused and exhausted."

"That's true."

"Anyhow, I don't blame men as much as women."

"I'm glad to hear it."

"Are you feeling better?"

"Yes."

"Your eye is opening. Now, Chief."

"Yes."

"We have to be clear on one or two things."

"Right," I say, cheering up. I've always taken delight in her orderly mind.

"First. Do you intend to marry?"

"Yes."

"Who?"

"I don't know."

"You really don't know?"

"I really don't."

"Do you want me to stay with you?"

"Yes."

Why do I take such delight in answering her question? I remind me of Samantha, who used to come home from school letter-perfect in her catechism and ask me to hear her nevertheless.

"Why did God make you?" And she'd answer, faking a hesitation, slewing her eyes around to me to gauge the suspense. She liked for me to ask and for her to answer. Saying is different from knowing.

"Are we going to go back to work?" asks Ellen.

"Yes."

I look at my watch.

Ellen takes a damp washrag and scrubs my mouth with hard mother-scrubs.

"Tch, of all the shameless hussies." She scrubs mother-hard with no mercy for my lip. "My word!" She grabs my shirt.

"What now?"

"They even pulled your shirttail out." Hard tucks all around.

"Thank you." The sugar in the toddy is reviving me.

"Now. What are the plans?"

"Here are the plans. In five minutes, as soon as I finish my drink, I'm going over to the high ground of the interchange. I'm taking the carbine and I'll be within sight and range of this balcony and these windows. From that point I can also see the swamp, the Center, the town, and Paradise. I know what to look for. It should happen by seven o'clock. If you need me here, wave this handkerchief in the window. And shoot anybody else who tries to come in."

"Right, Chief."

"After I leave, you can collect the others and bring them in here."

"Don't worry. I'll blow their noses and tuck them in. We've handled worse, haven't we?"

"Yes." I look at her. "And, Ellen."

"Yes?"

"You won't leave without telling me?"

"No. But wait."

"What for?"

"I'm going to fix you a sandwich to take with you to keep your strength up."

"Where are they?"

"Who?"

"The girls."

"Next door—in Miss ah Rhoades's room. All of a sudden they're thick as thieves."

"Hm," I say uneasily. What are they cooking up between them?

In a Pine Grove on the Southwest
Cusp of the Interstate Cloverleaf

7:15 P.M. / JULY 4

A WAKE AND feeling myself again, which is to say, alert, depressed-elated, and moderately terrified.

My leg has gone to sleep. One eye is closed either by sleep or by hives. Albumen molecules dance in my brain.

It is almost dark, but the sky is still light. The dark crowns of the cypresses flatten out against the sky like African veldt trees. A pall of smoke hangs over the horizon, marring the glimmering violet line that joins dark earth to light bowl of sky. The evening star glitters like a diamond next to the ruby light of the transmitter.

No sign of a sniper.

Three windows are lit at Howard Johnson's. The girls then are safe and sound and waiting for me.

Closer at hand a smaller column of smoke is rising. It is coming from a bunker off number 12 fairway which runs along the fence bordering the interstate right-of-way. The links lights are on, sodium-vapor arcs concealed in cypresses and Spanish moss, which cast a spectral light on the fairway and big creeping shadows in the rough.

Two police cars are parked on the shoulder. A small crowd stands around the bunker, gazing down.

Forgetting about my leg, I shoulder the carbine, stand up to start down the slope, and fall down. The exposed leg between shoved-up pants and fallen-down socks is ghostly and moon-pocked. I touch it. It feels like meat in the refrigerator.

I wait until the tingling comes and goes.

The smoke is coming from the sand trap under the bunker. Charley Parker, the golf pro, stands watering the sand with a hose.

P.G.A. officials run back and forth between Charley and his official tower, which also holds camera crews and floodlights. Players watch from their carts. One player, swinging his sand wedge, stands beside the bunker.

There are people from the Center and town. I recognize Max Gottlieb, Stryker, a Baptist chiropractor named Dr. Billy Matthews; Mercer Jones, a state trooper; Dr. Mark Habeeb, a Center psychiatrist; Elroy McPhee, a Humble geologist and a moderate Episcopal Knothead; Moon Mullins, a Catholic slumlord and Pontiac dealer.

"What do you say, Doc," says Charley as if we were teeing off on an ordinary Sunday morning. But I notice that his hand is trembling and his jaw muscles pop.

"All right, Charley. What are you doing?"

"Do you hear what that goddamn P.G.A. official said to me?"

"No."

"He said there was no rule in the book to cover this so I have to put the fire out."

"No rule to cover what?"

"A ball in a burning sand trap."

"Is that what's holding up the game?"

"I got to put the son of a bitch out!"

"I don't believe I'd do that."

"Do what?"

"Put water on it. It will only make it worse."

"I got to put it out. The sand is on fire."

"How could the sand be on fire? It's a Heavy Sodium reaction, Charley."

"What would you do about it?"

"Clear the area. The smoke contains Heavy Sodium vapor and could be extremely dangerous, especially if a wind should spring up."

Charley makes a sound. With the thumb and forefinger of his free hand he flings something—tears?—from his eyes.

"What's wrong, Charley?"

"What's wrong," repeats Charley. He gazes sorrowfully at the sand trap into which he directs the stream from the hose in an idle ruminative way, like a man pissing into a toilet. "The greatest event that ever happened to this town, to this state, the Pro-Am, gets to the finals, forty million people are watching on stereo-V, nine out of the top ten all-time money-winners and crowd-pleasers are on hand, half a million in prize money has been raised, the evangelistic team has arrived, the President himself plans to play a round tomorrow—and what happens? The goddamn bunkers catch on fire."

"You mean more than one?"

"All of them, man!"

"That figures," I say absently. "Charley, it's not the sand that's burning and the water will only—"

"Don't tell me the sand is not burning!" cries Charley, dashing tears from his eyes with thumb and forefinger. "Look!"

Fortunately a brisk breeze from the north is blowing the smoke straight out to the swamp.

"Mercer, do you have a bullhorn in your car?" I ask the state trooper.

"What do you want with a bullhorn, Doc," asks Mercer in the easy yet wary tone of an experienced policeman who is both at his ease in an emergency and prepared for any foolishness from spectators.

"I've got to warn these people about the smoke. Will you help me clear the area?"

"Why do you want to do that?" asks Mercer, inclining his head toward me carefully.

"Because it contains noxious sodium particles, and if the wind should shift, we could have a disaster on our hands."

"We have oxygen in case of smoke inhalation, Doc." Mercer looks at me sideways. He is wondering if I am drunk.

Stifling an impulse to recite the symptoms of Heavy Sodium fallout, I adopt the acceptable attitude of friend-of-policeman encountering policeman on duty and accordingly line up alongside him.

"Things pretty quiet this evening, Mercer?"

"More or less."

"Any other ah emergencies?"

The trooper shrugs. "An incident at the Center. A little civil disorder at the club."

"Haven't the Bantus taken over Paradise?"

Mercer clears his throat and cocks his head in disapproval. There: I've done it again.

"I wouldn't say that."

"What would you say?"

"There have been reports of vandalism at the old clubhouse,

some shots fired, and a house or two burned on the old 18 and out on the bluff." Mercer's cheek is set against me. Only our long acquaintanceship draws an answer from him. Do we really have to talk, Doc?

I sigh. "One more question, Mercer, and I'll let you alone. Is there any news about the President and Vice-President?"

"News?" asks Mercer, cheek stiff.

"I mean, have there been any attempts on their— Have any incidents occurred?"

Mercer's eyes slide around to me, past me, to the carbine, which I had forgotten. It is crossing his mind: what is nutty Doc doing with a gun and do you suppose he's a big enough fool to—no. But didn't Dr. Carl Weiss, another brilliant unstable doctor, shoot Huey Long?

"Not that I've heard? Been hunting rabbits, Doc?"

"Yes."

"With a thirty ought six?"

"As a matter of fact, a sniper has been shooting at me the last couple of days."

"Is that right!" says Mercer in a sociable singsong and swings his arms. "I'm telling you the truth unh unh unh!"—as if snipers were but one more trial of these troubled times.

Max Gottlieb, Ken Stryker, Colley Wilkes, and Mark Habeeb, all but Habeeb still wearing their white coats, stand leaning over the fence, their hands in their pockets. They have the holiday air of hard-working scientists who have been distracted from their researches and lean on windowsills to watch a street accident.

They gaze down at Charley Parker, who is still watering the bunker. Charley is conferring with a member of Cliff Barrow's evangelistic team on one side and an Amvet on the other. The former wears a Jesus-Christ-Greatest-Pro armband, the latter an American flag stuck in his overseas cap.

The scientists greet me affably and go on with their talk. Not far behind them Moon Mullins and Dr. Billy Matthews stand silently. The sight of them makes me uneasy.

"The cross and the flag," Ken Stryker is saying.

Colley nods. "A nice example of core values and symbol systems coming to the aid of economics."

"The most potent appraisive signs in our semiotic," says Dr. Mark Habeeb.

Colley asks him: "Do you know Ted's work in sign reversal in *Gorilla gorilla malignans*? You take a killer ape who responds aggressively to the purple rump patch of a baboon. He can be reconditioned by using lysergin-B to respond to the same sign without aggression, with affection, in fact."

"Peace!" says Habeeb, laughing. "Maybe we could use electrodes here, Max." He nods toward the trio in the bunker.

But Max only shrugs. His mind is elsewhere.

"Right, Tom?" Habeeb turns to me.

"I couldn't say."

"Come on, Tom." Habeeb persists, nodding to the crowd. "You're perceptive."

"Perceptive? I perceive you are suffering from angelism," I say absently.

"Cut it out, ha ha. I was talking about the behavior over there."

"I was talking about you."

"Me?"

"You're abstracting and withholding judgment."

"I'm a scientist. We don't judge behavior, we observe it."

"That's not enough." I stagger a bit. "Blow hold or cot."

"Eh? How's that?"

"I mean blow hot or cold but not—" The road map, I notice, is breaking up again. Stretches of highway come loose, float across the sky.

"Are you all right?" asks Mark, taking my arm.

"Tom?" Max comes close on the other side, puts his arm around me.

What good fellows.

"I'm all right, Max. But it's happened."

"What's happened?"

"You know damn well."

"I'm not quite sure—"

"This." I point to the smoking sand.

"Colley thinks it's a fire in the sulfur dome."

"It's a slow sodium reaction and you know it."

"Oh." Max drops his arm.

"And you know the danger, Max."

"What danger?"

"My God, after what happened in The Pit, how can you ask?"

At the mention of The Pit, the other three smile at me with the greatest good humor and affection.

Ken laughs out loud. "That was something—the best of the year! Did you see the Old Man carrying on, ha ha!" They all laugh at the recollection, all but Gottlieb. Colley pays me a rare, for him, compliment. "You something else, Tom."

"What are you talking about?"

"What you did in The Pit, to old Buddy, to everybody!"

"And just what do you think I did?" I ask the four of them. "Max?"

Max's face is in shadow.

"Well, Max?"

"You always did have a gift for hypnotherapy, Tom."

"For Christ's sake, do you think I hypnotized them?"

"You take four hundred overworked dexed-up strung-out students at the end of the year—" Max breaks off.

"And what about my invention?"

"I thought it was an extremely effective objective correlative," says Ken warmly.

"Objective correlative my ass." I turn to Max. "Max, I'm putting it to you. If you don't help me clear this area immediately, I am holding you responsible."

"Tell me first, Tom. Have you reached a decision about coming back to A-4?"

"As a patient?"

"Patient-therapist."

"We'll talk about it, Max. But don't you see what is happening right here?"

"I see what is happening to you." Max is looking at my carbine, at my clothes gummed with pine resin, smeared with lipstick.

"Charley, listen to me. There is something dreadfully wrong."

"You're damn right there's something wrong. The Pro-Am is screwed up and we'll probably lose the Camellia Open next year. And the goddamn sand is still on fire."

"Moon, maybe you and Dr. Billy Matthews could help me.

Unless we act now, the consequences could be nationwide and it will be too late."

"The consequences are already nationwide and it is already too late," says Dr. Matthews, shouldering between us. He is a tall heavy bald youngish man with shoulders and arms grown powerful from manipulating spinal columns in his chiropractic. His thick glasses are fitted with flip-up sun lenses, which are flipped up.

"What do you mean?" I ask fearfully. Has my lapsometer caused mischief in other places?

"The country has been taken over by our enemies and there is no respect for God or country," says Dr. Matthews menacingly. "Last Sunday some niggers tried to come into our church. And now this."

"Now what?"

"Those fellows," says the chiropractor in a loud voice and directly at the four scientists. "They're teaching disrespect for both the cross and Old Glory."

"Actually they were speaking of an experiment with primates."

"That's what I'm talking about! Monkeys! And that fellow there is a known Communist," he says in a lower voice, nodding toward Dr. Habeeb.

"I seriously doubt that," I say, remembering that Dr. Habeeb recently testified in a trial in which Dr. Billy Matthews had been sued by a woman whose husband had been treated for cancer of the liver by manipulating his spine.

"Where do you stand in this, Doctor?" asks Dr. Matthews, eyeing me suspiciously.

Moon shifts around uncomfortably. "Don't worry about Doc here. He's a hundred percent with us. Aren't you, Doc?"

"With you on what?"

"On God and country."

I am silent.

"You do believe in God and country, don't you, Doc?"

"Yes."

"I remember when Doc and I were in high school," Moon tells the chiropractor. "Doc wrote a prize-winning essay for the Knights of Columbus on how there was no real conflict between science and religion. You remember what you said about transubstantiation, Doc?"

"Yes."

"Transubstantiation is an invention of the Roman popes," says Dr. Billy Matthews, flipping his flip-ups down for some reason. "It's a piece of magic to fool the ignorant and has no basis in the Bible."

"Whoa, hold on, Billy!" cries Moon. "You don't know what you're talking about. Christ said 'This is my body.' Didn't he, Doc?"

"Yes," I say and utter a groan.

"That's the Eyetalian translation," says Dr. Billy Matthews. With his flip-ups down he looks blind as a bat.

"No, it isn't, is it, Doc? Tell him."

"Later. Oh Lord. What am I going to do?" I ask them, rending my shirt. "What if the wind springs up?"

My eyes are swelling again. The world is seen through the slit on a gun turret.

"Max, something is dreadfully wrong."

"You're damn right there is. We've lost our N.I.M.H. funding for next year, thanks to our Ecuadorian venture."

"No, I mean something a great deal wronger than that."

"You look ill, Tom."

"I'm very tired and my eyes are swelling but I feel fine deep down. In fact, I've got a heartful of love, Max."

"Love?"

"Max, I'm a lucky man. I've got three wonderful girls waiting for me."

"Three girls. Look, sit down here on the grass and let me check you out. Just as I thought. You're going into anaphylaxis again. What have you been eating this time?"

"Gin fizzes."

"Oh no. Not again. *Why?*"

"I don't know. Lola fixed one for me. She's a lovely girl." Feeling very tired, I lie down on the velvety Tifton 451 Bermuda at the bunker's lip. "But that's not what bothers me."

"What bothers you?"

"You. And them. That is, you four and those two." I nod

toward Moon and Dr. Billy Matthews, who are still arguing about transubstantiation.

"What about us and them?"

"You're both right and wrong."

"What does that mean?"

"I mean that it's almost hopeless now. One whiff of the vapor and you'll kill each other."

"What do you want me to do about it?" Max asks dryly.

I open my mouth to say something but can't utter a word. Max leans over and peers at me through the blue smoke and, suddenly seeing what is wrong, jumps up. "I'll be right back."

"Don't worry about—" I begin, lifting a feeble hand, and pass out.

There comes a familiar smell of sweat intricated by deodorant.

I open my eyes.

The smell comes from a push of air as Art Immelmann, who is sitting on the lip of the sand trap, leans over me and his bi-swing jacket flaps.

"I won't say I told you so, Doc."

"Told me what?"

"That nobody would believe you even if you showed them. Only two people in this world believe in you."

"Who?" Did Max give me a shot? My eyes open easily.

"I and your excellent nurse."

"Leave her out of it. She's no concern of yours."

"Then you'd better take care of her."

"What do you mean?"

"Get back to the motel, Doc."

"Why?"

"Because there is nothing you can do here and a great deal you can do there."

"But these people don't realize what is happening."

"And you can't tell them."

"They'll get hurt."

"Therefore you'd better save yourself for the long pull."

"I think you are somehow responsible, you and your god-damn foundations."

Art winces and shakes his head. "Doc, we operate on a cardinal principle, which we never violate. We never never

'do' anything to anybody. We only help people do what they
want to do. We facilitate social interaction in order to isolate
factors. If people show a tendency to interact in a certain way,
we facilitate the interaction in order to accumulate reliable
data."

"And if people cut each other's throats meanwhile, it's not
your fault."

"Doc, we're dedicated to the freedom of the individual to
choose his own destiny and develop his own potential."

"What crap," I mutter.

"Crap? Crap." Art searches his memory. "I'm not sure I
understand—but never mind. Aren't you feeling well enough
to go now?"

"Go where?"

"Back to the motel and look after the three ladies. Your
lapsometer is still there. You can protect the three of them and
yourself from any unfortunate little side effects from this." He
glances at the column of smoke, which is thicker than ever.
"Stay there three months."

"Three months?"

"It's your duty. By saving them and youself, you can save
millions later."

"What will we do for three months?"

"You have books, food, drink, music. But most of all you
have your obligation."

"To whom?"

"To the three ladies."

"And what do you suggest that I do with three women for
three months?"

Again the coat flaps as Art leans close. I'm enveloped by the
smell of sebum and Ban.

"Love them, Doc! Believe me, it lies within your power to
make all three of them happy and yourself too. Didn't God put
us here to be happy? Isn't happiness better than unhappiness?
Love them! Work on your invention. Stimulate your musical-
erotic! Develop your genius. Aren't we all obliged to develop
our potential? Work! Love! Music! That's what makes a man
happy."

"True."

"Then you better get going."

"In a minute. One little nap," I say, closing my eyes with a smile as I think of the future.

Somewhat confused. I examine the contents of my pockets to get a line on the significance of the past and the hope of the future. Contents: 12 Phillips screws and one small dry turd folded in a clean handkerchief. I recall the latter but not the former. 12 Phillips screws . . .

A light hand touches my shoulder. It is Ellen. She squats on her heels, tucking her uniform under her knee.

"You all right, Chief?"

"Fine. Just taking a nap."

"You'll be all right. Dr. Gottlieb gave you a shot."

"What are you doing here?"

"There was no reason for me to stay over there."

"Where are Moira and Ellen?"

"Your two little popsies have flown the coop."

Popsies. She's been talking to Max, all right.

"What happened?"

"Miss Rhoades went hiking off to Tara with the pistol stuck in her jeans and the cello slung over her shoulder. The last time I saw Miss Schaffner, she was getting in Dr. Brown's car in the plaza."

"Buddy Brown? How did that happen?"

"The Anser-Phone is working. She had me call him."

"I see."

"Now, come on. We're going home."

"Home?"

"Back to your house."

"What happened to the Bantus?"

"They've faded away."

"I think I'd better stay here a while."

"Come on. You're going to pick up your life where you left it. Dr. Gottlieb is wrong. You don't need to go to the hospital. All you need is good hard work and a—" She pauses.

"No. I can't go now."

"Why not?"

"The danger here is too great. I must do what I can. Did you bring my lapsometer?"

"Yes, Chief. But the important thing is to get you back in harness."

"Do you understand the danger?"

"Yes. I believe in you completely. That's why I want you to get out of here."

"And do what?"

"Go home and get some sleep. I'll meet you at the office tomorrow. We'll have our work cut out for us."

"I'm not going back to that."

"Back to what?"

"Back to my old life."

"It's your duty, Chief," says Ellen and means it.

"I still can't do it."

"Why can't you? You can. I'll help you. We'll do it."

I am thinking of my old life: waking up Monday Tuesday Wednesday as not myself, breakfast on Tang and terror in the "enclosed patio," Thursday Friday afternoons a mystery of longing. My old life was a useless longing on weekdays, World War I at night, and drunk every weekend.

"You wait here, Chief. I'll get my car. Your mother had Eukie bring it to the plaza. She's safe. The Bantus are under control. There was no real trouble. All the trouble was caused by a few outsiders and some hopped-up swamp rats. Most people here, white and black, like things the way they are."

"I don't."

"You will. Wait here. I'm going to get the car."

Three pairs of legs dangle over the lip of the bunker, two on one side of me, one on the other. They belong to Chuck Parker with his golden curls, his Jeb Stuart fan of a beard and his clamshell necklace, and Ethel, his little dark Smithie Pocahontas, Hester on my other side.

"Are you all right?" asks Hester in her lovely peculiar flatted New England vowels and laterals.

"I'm fine." With a bit of effort I hike up on my elbows and sit beside her. I look into her clear hazel eyes in which there is no secret or concealment such as causes one to look away. There is only clarity here and no shadow of the past. It's all gone, not only the old Priscilla-Puritan beginnings but what came later and opposed it: no Priscilla, no anti-Priscilla; no Puritanism, no transcendentalism, no -ism at all, not even an anti-ism, not even a going back like Ethel to Pocahontasism, no left no right. It's all gone, she's wiped the slate clean and now she sits in the wilderness and reads and rereads *The Case of the Velvet Claws*. She's waiting for something.

"What a sight, eh, Doc?" says Chuck, leaning out to see me. "I'm glad to be here, glad to have seen it."

"Seen what?"

"Seen the end. You're looking at it, Doc. The game is up." Chuck sweeps his arm past the smoking bunker, his father with the hose, the pros, the ams, the golf carts, the officials, the scientists, the stereo-V tower with its cameras, the sodium arcs. "A fitting end, wouldn't you say, Doc?"

"End to what?"

"Everything! Look at my poor father. His mind is blown, and you know why? Because of a game with a little ball and money. Money, Doc!"

"Actually it's not money at all."

"Look at him! It's too much for him. He thinks the sand is burning. But you and I know better, eh, Doc? We know why it's smoking and what is going to happen, wow! Doc, you are something else, you and your doomsday machine. What a way for them to go, in a golf game with the bunkers on fire, hee hee hee. You set it, didn't you, Doc? You fixed 'em all, not only Pop but the others."

"What others?"

"All of them. Look at them, the scientists, the manipulators, the killers of subjectivity, the jig is up with them too and they don't even know it; and them too, the Christian flag-wavers and hypocrites, and it's all thanks to you—you may be forty-five but you're one of us."

"Yeah, well—"

"So we're leaving now and you're coming with us."

"With you?"

"With Hester."

"Hester?"

"Hester wants you to live with her in her chickee."

I look at Hester. She looks back. There is no secrecy in the clear depths, no modesty or boldness. She smiles and nods. She neither blushes nor not blushes. I look at her bare brown legs, unscarred, not fat, not thin, thighs simple and deep in youth. I look at my ghostly moonpocked shins. It is just possible that—

"Will you come, Doc?" asks Chuck.

"I have my profession."

"Practice it. We need you. We'll start a new life in a new world. We'll hole up in Confederate number 2 until the fallout settles—your doomsday machine will protect us, wow, whee, you're our shaman, Doc, then we'll live on Bayou Pontchata-lawa, which means peace, and love one another and watch the seasons come and smoke a little cannab in the evening, hee hee hee, and live on catfish and Indian maize and wild grape and raise good sweet innocent children."

"Well—"

"Tell me the truth, Doc."

"All right."

"Have you ever lived your life?"

"Lived?"

"Lived completely and in the moment the way a prothono-tary warbler lives flashing holy fire?"

"Not often."

Chuck laughs. "Hoowee! You know what I mean, don't you, Doc?"

"Yes."

"Hester, don't you want Doc to come live with you in your chickee?"

For her answer, Hester, who is hugging her legs and has laid her cheek on her knees, facing me, sways to and fro and lightly against me.

"All right. Here's the deal, Doc," says Chuck. "I have to see Uru and get some maize seeds and ammunition to shoot rabbits this winter. You go get your gear, medicine and all, and one book—we each have one book—and meet us in an hour at the landing near the slave quarters. What book will you bring?"

"Stedmann's *World War I*," I say absently.

"Oh yeah! Wow! We'll all read it, all about those bad old days, and lead our new life!"

A light breeze springs up, swirling the smoke column. A whiff of brimstone comes to my nostrils.

Now a tuning fork sings against my skull. Art whispers behind me. "Just a little vaccination, Doc. You understand."

"Did you vaccinate the others?"

"Positively."

"Ellen says you lie."

"I don't believe you. She's a lovely person. If you go to Honey Island, I should like to employ her."

"You keep away from her, you bastard."

"I am not illegitimate."

"If you vaccinated the others, how come they're acting like that?"

"They act like that normally."

Dr. Billy Matthews, perhaps because he can't stand it any longer, perhaps because the vapors have irritated his vagal nucleus, comes charging up the grassy hillock, where he confronts the scientists.

"I heard you rascals!" he cries.

"Heard us say what?" asks Stryker easily.

"You insulted the United States, Old Glory, and Jesus Christ!"

"When did we do that?" asks Colley, also smiling, but his voice is shaky. The scientists are astonished at the sight of the burly chiropractor, fists clenched, bald head gleaming malignantly in the sodium light, sunshades flipped in place like black eye-patches.

"Don't think I don't know what you people are," says the furious chiropractor, gazing into one face after another.

"What are we?" asks Max.

"I know!"

Dr. Habeeb adjusts his glasses and peers closely at Dr. Billy Matthews. "A perfect example of *Homo Americanensis politicus paranoicus*, would you say, Max?"

"Don't fight!" I cry from the bunker. "Billy is a good fellow. Once when he and I were in Ecuador—"

"Say that again," says the chiropractor to Mark Habeeb.

"Or would it be more accurate to classify him as coonass or redneck?" Mark asks Max.

It is difficult to say which is the greater insult to Billy Matthews, to be called a coonass, a derogatory term for a Cajun, or a redneck, equally unflattering for a North Louisianian.

"Kike!"

"As a matter of fact, I'm Syrian."

"Atheist!"

"Coonass!"

"Communist!"

"Holy Roller!"

"That's not true. I am a Southern Baptist."

"Christ, that's worse."

"Un-American!"

"Kluxer!"

"One Worlder!"

"Racist!"

"Nigger lover."

"Knothead!"

"Liberal!"

For some reason, these last two epithets, the mildest of the list, proved the last straw. In a rage, yet almost happily, the two fall upon one another, fists flying. They grapple for each other, fall to the earth with a thud and roll into the sand trap.

"No!" I cry, getting up and staggering around. "Don't fight!"

"Don't jump in there," says Max, grabbing my arm.

The brimstone smell is stronger. Smoke swirls between us. Stryker, I see, is most strongly affected by the noxious vapors. His eyes go vacant and lose focus. The Heavy Sodium ions hit his pineal body, seat of self, like a guillotine, sundering self from self forever, that ordinary self, the restless aching everyday self, from the secret self one happens on in dreams, in poetry, during ordeals, on happy trips—"Ah, this is my real self!" Forever after he'll live like a ghost inhabiting himself. He'll orbit the earth forever, reading dials and recording data and spinning theories by day, and at night seek to reenter the world of creatures by taking the form of beasts and performing unnatural practices.

I even fancy that I see his soul depart, exiting his body through the top of his head in a little corkscrew curl of vapor, as the soul is depicted in ancient woodcuts. Or was it no more than a wisp of smoke blown from the bunker?

*

"Over here, Doc."

"What? Who's that?"

I open my eyes. A fog must have rolled in from the swamp. The sodium lights have turned into soft mazy balls. Voices come from the highway, but the bunker is deserted.

"Come over here, Doc."

It is Victor's voice. I follow it into the woods, staggering into a pocket of ground fog that has settled into a saucer-shaped glade.

"Is that you, Victor?" I say to a shadow tall as a cypress.

"No," says a different voice, muffled and flat. "Victor's gone. I sent him for you. Sit down."

It is Uru. He points to a stump. I sit down in a pool of fog, which is as thick and white as a CO_2 Transylvania fog.

"What do you want, Uru?"

"I want your machine."

"Why?"

"I don't know what's going on here but Victor and Willard say you know something and that your machine works. Let's have it."

"I don't have one."

"Well, I'll find one in your house."

"It wouldn't do you any good. You wouldn't know how to use it."

"We'll be the judge of that." Uru takes another stump. Hunched over in his *monkhu6*, he looks like a benched pro in a poncho. His face is in darkness.

"If we live through this, I'll bring the lapsometer wherever you like, test your people, and treat them if they need it."

"We can take care of our own."

"Very well. I'll be going."

"All we want from you is you off our backs."

"Very well. You got it."

Uru picks up his *izinkhonkwani*, which hangs between his legs like a Scotsman's sporran, and slings it to one side.

"We're taking what we want and destroying what we don't and we don't need you."

"Is that what Victor says?"

"Victor's got nothing to say about it. Let me tell you something." Uru hunches forward on his stump. We sit knee to knee like commuters but I still can't make out his face. "We got two hundred Bantus just from this town and not one of them, not one, got any use for Victor or sweet Jesus."

"So?"

"So we don't need any help from you or Victor in what we're going to do."

"Then why did you send for me?"

"You want to know what's funny, Doc?"

"No."

"The way you chucks sold Victor on sweet Jesus and he out-Jesused you. You beat him with Jesus but you beat him so bad that in the end he out-Jesused you and made liars out of you and that was the one thing you couldn't stand. So Victor won after all."

"Victor wouldn't think that was funny."

"No, he wouldn't but Victor doesn't matter now, not you or Victor. What matters is what we're going to do."

"What's that?"

"Like I said. Take what we need, destroy what we don't, and live in peace and brotherhood."

"Peace and brotherhood." The map has come back, crooked capillary county roads and straight stretches of interstate arteries. "Well, you're right about one thing. I couldn't help you now even if you'd let me. We're not talking about the same thing. We're talking about different kinds of trouble. First you got to get to where you're going or where you think you're going—although I hope you do better than that, because after all nothing comes easier than that, being against one thing and tearing down another thing and talking about peace and brotherhood—I never saw peace and brotherhood come from such talk and I hope you do better than that because there are better things and harder things to do. But, either way, you got to get to where you're going before I can help you."

"Help us do what?"

"There is no use my even telling you because, Ph.D. or not, you wouldn't know what I was talking about. You got to get to where we are or where you think we are and I'm not even sure you can do that."

"Like I told you, Doc, we can do it and without your help."

"Good luck, then." I rise.

"We don't need that either."

"Yes, you do."

"You better go back, Doc, while you can."

"Papa, have you lost your faith?"

"No."

Samantha asked me the question as I stood by her bed. The neuroblastoma had pushed one eye out and around the nose-bridge so she looked like a Picasso profile.

"Then why don't you go to mass any more?"

"I don't know. Maybe because you don't go with me."

"Papa, you're in greater danger than Mama."

"How is that?"

"Because she is protected by Invincible Ignorance."

"That's true," I said, laughing.

"She doesn't know any better."

"She doesn't."

"You do."

"Yes."

"Just promise me one thing, Papa."

"What's that?"

"Don't commit the one sin for which there is no forgiveness."

"Which one is that?"

"The sin against grace. If God gives you the grace to believe in him and love him and you refuse, the sin will not be forgiven you."

"I know." I took her hand, which even then still looked soiled and chalk-dusted like a schoolgirl's.

I wonder: did it break my heart when Samantha died? Yes. There was even the knowledge and foreknowledge of it while she still lived, knowledge that while she lived, life still had its same peculiar tentativeness, people living as usual by fits and starts, aiming and missing, while present time went humming, and foreknowledge that the second she died, remorse would come and give past time its bitter specious wholeness. If only— If only we hadn't been defeated by humdrum humming present time and missed it, missed ourselves, missed everything. I had the foreknowledge while she lived. Still, present time went humming. Then she died and here came the sweet remorse like a blade between the ribs.

But is there not also a compensation, a secret satisfaction to be taken in her death, a delectation of tragedy, a license for drink, a taste of both for taste's sake?

It may be true. At least Doris said it was. Doris was a dumbbell but she could read my faults! She said that when I refused to take Samantha to Lourdes. Doris wanted to! Because of the writings of Alexis Carrel and certain experiments by the London Psychical Society, etcetera etcetera. The truth was that Samantha didn't want to go to Lourdes and I didn't want to take her. Why not? I don't know Samantha's reasons, but I was afraid she might be cured. What then? Suppose you ask God for a miracle and God says yes, very well. How do you live the rest of your life?

Samantha, forgive me. I am sorry you suffered and died, my heart broke, but there have been times when I was not above enjoying it.

Is it possible to live without feasting on death?

Art and Ellen help me to my feet.

"Ready, Chief?"

"Where are we going?"

"My car is over there."

"Dr. More is going to Honey Island," says Art.

"I haven't decided," I say, frowning.

"Then you and I can go to Denmark," says Art.

"Denmark!" I repeat with astonishment. "Why?"

"Our work here is finished." Art gazes down at the bunker, which is smoking more than ever. Charley Parker's hose is still running but Charley is gone.

"Why Denmark?"

"Number one, it is my home base. Number two, it is close to the Nobel Prize committee. Number three, it is the vanguard of civilization. Number four, I can get you a job there."

"What kind of a job?"

"Of course after the Nobel you can write your own ticket. Meanwhile you've been offered the position of chief encephalographer at the Royal University."

Art advances with his lapsometer. I can't seem to move.

"He's not going off with you!" cries Ellen.

"I think he wants to," says Art quietly. For a second the tuning fork hums on my skull. I knock it away.

"Keep away from him!" warns Ellen.

"One little massage of his musical-erotic and he'll be right as rain," says Art.

He stoops over me. I watch him dreamily.

"Just a minute." Ellen touches his shirt. I frown but cannot rouse myself. "Step over here."

Ellen returns arm in arm with Art. She hands me her car keys. "You can go now, Chief."

I am peering at Art through the smoke. He nods reassuringly. "She's right. You can go on home, Doc."

"Where do you think you're going?" I ask Ellen.

"With Dr. Immelmann."

"What do you mean?"

She shrugs. "I need a job and you evidently don't need me. It's nothing new. Dr. Immelmann offered me a position the first day he came to see you."

"Doing what?"

"As his traveling secretary."

"You're not traveling anywhere with this bastard." I grab her hand and yank her away from Art. "Why you evil-minded son of a bitch," I tell Art.

"I can't understand why he calls me those extraordinary names," says Art to no one in particular.

"Get away from here," I say uneasily, for now Art is advancing upon us with his, with *my*, lapsometer.

Slinging the device from his shoulder, he holds out both hands. "The two of you will come with me."

"We have to go," whispers Ellen, shrinking against me.

"No we don't."

"If we both go, Chief, maybe it will be all right."

"No, it won't," I say, not taking my eyes from Art, whose arms are outstretched like the Christ at Sacre Coeur in New Orleans.

"We'll all be happy in Copenhagen," murmurs Art.

Beautiful beautiful Copenhagen.

"Let's sing, Doc!"

What is frightening is his smiling assurance. He doesn't even need the lapsometer!

"Let's go, kids," says Art. One hand touches Ellen.

"Don't touch her!" I cry, but I can't seem to move. I close my eyes. *Sir Thomas More, kinsman, saint, best dearest merriest of Englishmen, pray for us and drive this son of a bitch hence.*

I open my eyes. Art is turning slowly away, wheeling in slow motion, a dazed hurt look through the eyes as if he had been struck across the face.

"I think you hurt his feelings," whispers Ellen, trembling.

"How?"

"By what you called him."

"What did I call him?"

"S.O.B."

"Really?" I was sure I had not prayed aloud.

"What else were you mumbling? Something about a saint?"

"Nothing."

"Do you think you're a saint?"

"No." Then Ellen never heard of the other Thomas More.

"Look, he's leaving."

"So he is."

"Shouldn't we—"

"No." I hold her tight.

Art disappears into the smoke swirling beyond the bunker.

"Now what?" asks Ellen.

"I think I'll have a drink."

"No, you won't. Let's go home," she says, spitting on me and smoothing my eyebrows.

FIVE YEARS LATER

In the Slave Quarters

HOEING COLLARDS in my kitchen garden.

A fine December day. It is cold but the winter sun pours into the walled garden and fills it up.

After hoeing a row: sit in the sunny corner, stretch out my legs and look at my boots. A splendid pair of new boots of soft oiled leather, good for hunting and fishing and walking to town. For the first time I understand what the Confederate soldier was always saying: a good pair of boots is the best thing a man can have.

A poor man sets store by good boots. Ellen and I are poor. We live with our children in the old Quarters. Constructed of slave brick worn porous and rounded at the corners like sponges, the apartments are surprisingly warm in winter, cool in summer. They are built like an English charterhouse, a hundred apartments in a row along the bayou, each with a porch, living room or (in my case) library, two bedrooms, kitchen, garden, one behind the other.

Waiting and listening and looking at my boots.

Here's one difference between this age and the last. Now while you work, you also watch and listen and wait. In the last age we planned projects and cast ahead of ourselves. We set out to "reach goals." We listened to the minutes of the previous meeting. Between times we took vacations.

Through the open doorway I can see Ellen standing at the stove in a swatch of sunlight. She stirs grits. Light and air flow around her arm like the arm of Velázquez's weaver girl. Her half apron is lashed just above the slight swell of her abdomen.

She socks spoon down on pot and cocks her head to listen for the children, slanting her dark straight eyebrows. A kingfisher goes ringing down the bayou.

Meg and Thomas More, Jr., are still asleep.

Chinaberries bounce off the tin roof.

The bricks are growing warm at my back. In the corner of the wall a garden spider pumps its web back and forth like a child on a swing.

My practice is small. But my health is better. Fewer shakes

and depressions and unnatural exaltations. Rise at six every morning and run my trotline across the bayou. Water is the difference! Water is the mystical element! At dawn the black bayou breathes a white vapor. The oars knock, cypress against cypress, but the sound is muffled, wrapped in cotton. As the trotline is handed along, the bank quickly disappears and the skiff seems to lift and be suspended in a new element globy and white. Silence presses in and up from the vaporish depths come floating great green turtles, blue catfish, lordly gaspergous.

Strange: I am older, yet there seems to be more time, time for watching and waiting and thinking and working. All any man needs is time and desire and the sense of his own sovereignty. As Kingfish Huey Long used to say: every man a king. I am a poor man but a kingly one. If you want and wait and work, you can have.

Despite the setbacks of the past, particularly the fiasco five years ago, I still believe my lapsometer can save the world—if I can get it right. For the world is broken, sundered, busted down the middle, self ripped from self and man pasted back together as mythical monster, half angel, half beast, but no man. Even now I can diagnose and shall one day cure: cure the new plague, the modern Black Death, the current hermaphroditism of the spirit, namely: More's syndrome, or: chronic angelism-bestialism that rives soul from body and sets it orbiting the great world as the spirit of abstraction whence it takes the form of beasts, swans and bulls, werewolves, bloodsuckers, Mr. Hydes, or just poor lonesome ghost locked in its own machinery.

If you want and work and wait, you can have. Every man a king. What I want is no longer the Nobel, screw prizes, but just to figure out what I've hit on. Some day a man will walk into my office as ghost or beast or ghost-beast and walk out as a man, which is to say sovereign wanderer, lordly exile, worker and waiter and watcher.

Knowing, not women, said Sir Thomas, is man's happiness.

Learning and wisdom are receding nowadays. The young, who already know everything, hate science, bomb laboratories, kill professors, burn libraries.

Already the monks are beginning to collect books again. . . .

Poor as I am, I feel like God's spoiled child. I am Robinson

Crusoe set down on the best possible island with a library, a laboratory, a lusty Presbyterian wife, a cozy tree house, an idea, and all the time in the world.

Ellen calls from the doorway. Breakfast is ready. She sets a plate of steaming grits and bacon for me on a plain pine table. Like most good cooks, she hasn't a taste for her own cooking. Instead she pours honey on an old biscuit.

We sit on kitchen chairs in the sunlight. With one hand she absently sweeps crumbs into the other. Her hand's rough heel whispers over the ribs of pine. She keeps her apron on. When she sits down, she exactly fills the heart-shaped scoop of the chair. Her uptied hair leaves her neck bare save for a few strands.

In my second wife I am luckier than my kinsman Thomas More. For once I have the better of him. His second wife was dour and old and ugly. Mine is dour and young and beautiful. Both made good wives. Sir Thomas's wife was a bad Catholic like me, who believed in God but saw no reason why one should disturb one's life, certainly not lose one's head. Ellen is a Presbyterian who doesn't have much use for God but believes in doing right and does it.

Sunlight creeps along the tabletop, casting into relief the shiny scoured ridges of pine. Steam rising from the grits sets motes stirring in the golden bar of light. I shiver slightly. Morning is still not the best of times. As far as morning is concerned, I can't say things have changed much. What has changed is my way of dealing with it. No longer do I crawl around on hands and knees drinking Tang and vodka and duck eggs.

My stomach leaps with hunger. I eat grits and bacon and corn sticks.

After breakfast my heart leaps with love.

"Come sit in my lap, Ellen."

"Well—"

"Now then. Here."

"Oh for pity's sake."

"Yes. There now."

"Not now."

"Give me a kiss."

"My stars."

Her mouth tastes of honey.

"Tch. Not now," she whispers.

"Why not?"

"The children are coming."

"The children can—"

"Here's Meg."

"So I see. Kiss me."

"Kiss Meg."

2

Walk up the cliff to catch the bus in Paradise.

Up and down the fairways go carts canopied in orange-and-white Bantu stripes. Golfers dismount for their shots, their black faces inscrutable under the bills of their caps.

Recently Bantu golfers rediscovered knickerbockers and the English golf cap, which they wear pulled down to their eyebrows and exactly level. They shout "Fore!" but they haven't got it quite right, shouting it not as a warning but as a kind of ritual cry, a karate shout, before teeing off.

English golf pros are in fashion now, the way Austrian ski instructors used to be. Charley Parker moved to Australia.

"Fore!" shouts a driver, though no one is in sight, and whales into it.

"Good shot!"

"Bully, old man!"

"Give me my cleek."

Paradise has gone 99 percent Bantu. How did the Bantus win? Not by revolution. No, their revolution was a flop; they got beat in the Troubles five years ago and pulled back to the swamp. So how did they win? By exercising their property rights!

Why not? Squatting out in the swamp for twenty years, they came by squatter's rights to own it. Whereupon oil was struck through the old salt domes. Texaco and Esso and Good Gulf thrust money into black hands. Good old Bantu uncles burned $100 bills like Oklahoma Indians of old.

So they moved out of the swamp and bought the houses in Paradise. Why not? I sold mine for $70,000 and sank the money in my invention like many another nutty doctor.

Willard Amadie bought Tara and was elected mayor.

Uru, baffled by Southern ways, left in disgust, returned to Ann Arbor, and rejoined the Black Studies department of the U. of M., where life is simpler.

Others left. Many Knotheads, beside themselves with rage, driven mad by the rain of noxious particles, departed for safe Knothead havens in San Diego, Cicero, Hattiesburg, and New Rochelle. Many Lefts, quaking with terror and abstracted out of their minds, took out for Berkeley, Cambridge, Madison, and Fairfax County, Virginia, where D.C. liberals live.

Some stayed, mostly eccentrics who don't fit in anywhere else. I stayed because it's home and I like its easygoing ways, its religious confusion, racial hodgepodge, misty green woods, and sleepy bayous. People still stop and help strangers lying in ditches having been set upon by thieves or just plain drunk. Good nature usually prevails, even between enemies. As the saying goes in Louisiana: you may be a son of a bitch but you're my son of a bitch.

Only one woman to my name now, a lusty tart Presbyterian, but one is enough. Moira married Buddy Brown and removed to Phoenix, where he is director of the Big Corral, the Southwest Senior Citizens Termination Center. Lola, lovely strong-backed splendid-kneed cellist, married Barry Bocock, the clean West-Coast engineer, and removed to Marietta, Georgia, where Barry works for Lockheed and Lola is President of Colonial Dames, shows three-gaited horses, and plays cello for the Atlanta Symphony Orchestra.

I say Paradise is 99 percent Bantu. My mother is the remaining 1 percent. She stayed and made a second fortune selling astrological real estate to the Bantus, who are as superstitious as whites. Most of the younger and smarter Bantus are, to tell the truth, only nominally Bantu, having lost their faith at the Ivy League universities they habitually attend.

3

Borrow a newspaper from a tube near the bus stop. ATROCITIES SOLVED says the headline.

Read the story in the sunny quarter of a golf shelter. Hm. It seems the murderers who have terrorized this district for the past ten years turned out to be neither black guerrillas nor white Knotheads but rather a love community in the swamp. The leader is quoted as saying his family believes in love, the environment, and freedom of the individual.

4

Before the bus comes, a new orange Toyota stops to give me a lift. It is Colley Wilkes, super-Bantu. He and his light-colored wife, Fran, are on their way to Honey Island for the Christmas bird count. A pair of binoculars and a camera with massive telephoto lens lie on the Sunday *Times* between them. A tape plays Rudolf Friml. The Wilkeses are dressed in sports togs. Fran sits around catercornered, leg tucked under her, to see me.

"You catch us on the crest of the wave," she tells me. "We are ten feet high. Our minds are blown."

"How's that?"

"Tell him, Colley."

"We found him, Tom," says Colley portentously. "By George, we found him."

"Who?"

"He's alive! He's come back! After all these years!"

"Who?"

This morning, hauling up a great unclassified beast of a fish, I thought of Christ coming again at the end of the world and how it is that in every age there is the temptation to see signs of the end and that, even knowing this, there is nevertheless some reason, what with the spirit of the new age being the spirit of watching and waiting, to believe that—

Colley's right hand strays over the tape deck. The smooth shark skin at the back of his neck is pocked with pits that are as perfectly circular as if they had been punched out with a tiny biscuit cutter.

"Last Sunday at 6:55 A.M.," says Colley calmly, "exactly four miles west of Honey Island I—saw—an—ivory-billed—woodpecker."

"Is that so?"

"No question about it."

"That is remarkable."

"Do you realize what this means?" Fran asks me.

"No. Yes."

"There has not been a verified sighting of an ivorybill since nineteen-three. Think of it."

"All right."

"Wouldn't that be something now," muses Fran, breathing on her binoculars, "to turn in a regular Christmas list, you know, six chickadees, twenty pine warblers, two thousand myrtle warblers, and at the end, with photo attached: one ivory-billed woodpecker? Can't you see the Audubon brass as they read it?"

"Yes."

"Of course we have to find him again. Wish us luck."

"Yes. I do."

Colley asks politely after my family, my practice. I tell him my family is well but my practice is poor, so poor I have to moonlight with a fat clinic. At noon today, in fact, I meet with my fat ladies at the Bantu Country Club.

Fran shakes her head with an outrage tempered by her binocular-polishing. Colley pushes a button. The tape plays a Treasury of the World's Great Music, which has the good parts of a hundred famous symphonies, ballets, and operas. Colley knows the music and, as he drives, keeps time, anticipating phrases with a duck of head, lilt of chin.

"I don't get it, Tom," says Fran, breathing now on the telephoto lens, which is the size of a butter plate. "Everyone knows you're a marvelous diagnostician."

"It's very simple," I reply, nodding along with the good part of Tchaikovsky's *Romeo and Juliet*. "The local Bantu medical society won't let me in, so I can't use the hospital."

An awkward silence follows, but fortunately the love theme soars.

"Well," says Colley presently. "Rome wasn't built in a day."

"That's true."

"These things take time, Tom," says Fran.

"I know."

"Rest assured, however, that some of us are working on it."

"All right."

The *Anvil Chorus* starts up. Colley beats time with soft blows of his fist on the steering wheel.

"You've got to remember one thing," says Colley, socking

away. "You can sometimes accomplish more by not rocking the boat."

"I wasn't rocking the boat. You asked me a question."

"You're among friends, Tom," says Fran. "Who do you think led the fight to integrate the Bantu Audubon Society?"

"Colley."

"Right!"

Colley lifts his chin toward me. "And who do you think fixed a hundred Christmas baskets for peckerwood children?"

"Fran."

"Longhu6 baskets, dear," Fran corrects him. Longhu6 is the Bantu god of the winter solstice.

"Tell me something, Tom," says Colley quizzically-Amherstly, swaying in time to the good part of "Waltz of the Flowers" from *Nutcracker*. "Still working on your, ah—"

"Lapsometer? Yes indeed. Now that there is no danger of diabolical abuse, the future is bright."

"Diab—!" He frowns, missing the beat of *Nutcracker*. He's sorry he asked.

But he's full of Christmas cheer—or triumph over the ivory-bill—and presently comes back to it, as if to prove his goodwill. "Some day you're going to put it all together," he says, directing *Barcarole* with one gloved finger.

"Put all what together?"

"Your device. I'm convinced you're on the right track in your stereotactic exploration of the motor and sensory areas of the cortex. This is where it's at."

"That's not it at all," I say, hunching forward between them. "I'm not interested in motor and sensory areas. What concerns me is angelism, bestialism, and other perturbations of the soul."

"The soul. Hm, yes, well—"

"Just what do you think happened here five years ago?" I ask his smooth punchcarded neck.

"Five years ago?"

"In the Troubles. What do you think caused people to go out of their minds with terror and rage and attack each other?"

Fran looks at Colley.

"The usual reasons, I suppose," says Colley mournfully.

"People resorting to violence instead of using democratic processes to resolve their differences."

"Bullshit, Colley—beg your pardon, Fran—what about the yellow cloud?"

"Right. Well, here we are!" Colley pulls over to the curb and reaches around the headrest to open my door, which takes some doing.

"Merry Christmas," I say absently and thank them for the ride.

"Merry Longhu6!" says Fran, smiling but firm-eyed.

5

The office is lonesome without Ellen. Usually she comes with me, but Saturday is my fat-clinic day and I only spend a couple of hours here. Ellen is taking the kids to see Santy. It is Christmas Eve and I need a bit of cash. Ten dollars wouldn't hurt.

The solitude is pleasant, however. I open the back door opening onto the ox-lot. English sparrows have taken the martin hotel.

When I prop my foot on the drawer of Bayonne-rayon members, it reminds me of taking a drink. I close the drawer. No drink for six months. One reason is willpower. The other is that Ellen would kill me.

Across the ox-lot Mrs. Prouty comes out on the loading ramp of Sears. She smiles at me and leans against the polished steel pipe-rail.

I smile back. Most Saturdays we exchange pleasantries.

She wrote up my order for the new boots and Ellen's Christmas present, a brass bed, king-size (60") with nonallergenic Posture-mate mattress and serofoam polyurethane foundation, Sears Best. The whole works: $603.95.

A year's savings went into it, mainly from my fat clinic. No Christmas present ever took more thinking about or planning for. Even the delivery required scheming. How to get a bed past a housewife? Ask housewife to take children to plaza to see Santy (Santy is as big with the Bantus as with the Christians).

Did the bed make it? I lift my head in question to Mrs.

Prouty. She nods and holds up thumb to forefinger. The bed is on the way.

We've slept till now, Ellen and I, on single beds from my old house. A conceit of Doris's and much prized then, they are "convent" beds, which is to say, not even proper singles, narrower and shorter rather. For thirteen years my feet have stuck out, five with Doris, three alone, five with Ellen. Nuns must have been short. White-iron, chaste, curious, half-canopied the beds were, redolent of a far-off time and therefore serviceable in Doris's war on the ordinary, because at the time it was impossible to sleep in ORDINARY BEDS.

Did Mrs. Prouty wink at me? Across the weeds we gaze at each other, smiling. Her olive arms hug herself. A nyloned hip polishes a pipe-fitting. Mrs. Prouty is a good-looking good-humored lady. Whenever she used to see me buying a bottle next door at the Little Napoleon, she'd say: "Somebody's going to have a party. Can I come?" Her lickerish look comes, I think, from her merry eye and her skin, which is as clear and smooth as an olive.

When I ordered the brass bed, she swung the catalogue round on its lectern, leaned on it, and tapped her pencil on the counter.

"I know where I'd spend Christmas, huh, Docky?"

"What? Oh," I say, laughing before I take her meaning. Did she say Docky or ducky?

After I ordered the boots, she leaned on the catalogue again.

"These can go under mine any day," she says, merry eye roving past me carelessly.

"Ma'am? Eh? Right! Har har!"

These = my boots?

Mine = her bed?

Nowadays when a good-looking woman flirts with me, however idly, I guffaw like some ruddy English lord, haw haw, har har, harrr harrr.

Three patients come. Two Bantu businessmen, one with ulcers, the other with hypertension. Their own docs did 'em no good, so they want me to make magic passes with my machine. I oblige them, do so, take readings, hoard up data. They leave, feeling better.

The third is old P. T. Bledsoe. Even though he lost every-thing, including his wife, when the Bantus took Paradise and Betterbag Paper Company, he didn't leave and go to the Out-back after all. Instead, he moved out to his fishing camp and took to drinking Gallo muscatel and fishing for speckles. All he comes to me for is to get his pan-vitamin shot to keep his liver going. Out he goes rubbing his shiny butt and rattling off in his broken-down Plymouth.

Hm. Eleven dollars. Not a bad haul. My patients fork over cash, knowing I need it, five from each Bantu and one dollar from P. T., who also brings me a sack of mirlations and a fifth of Early Times. Not good. But he didn't know I had stopped drinking.

Mrs. Prouty is still on the ramp.

Now she points to her wristwatch.

Does she mean it is almost noon and she'll be off and why not have a little Christmas drink?

For she's spotted the Early Times. Rising, I unshuck gift box from bottle.

Comes again the longing, the desire that has no name. Is it for Mrs. Prouty, for a drink, for both: for a party, for youth, for the good times, for dear good drinking and fighting comrades, for football-game girls in the fall with faces like flowers? Comes the longing and it has to do with being fifteen and fifty and with the winter sun striking down into a brickyard and on clapboard walls rounded off with old hard blistered paint and across a doorsill onto linoleum. Desire has a smell: of cold lino-leum and gas heat and the sour piebald bark of crepe myrtle. A good-humored thirty-five-year-old lady takes the air in a back lot in a small town.

Insert thumbnail into plastic seal between glass rim and stopper. The slight pop is like a violation.

Comes a knock. Patient number four.

Put away the Early Times in the drawer of Bayonne-rayons.

It is a new patient, a young coffee-colored graduate student with intense eyes and a high bossed forehead like the late Harry Belafonte. Seems he has a private complaint. Nothing for it but to close the back door. He leans forward in a pleasant anxious way. I know what is wrong with him before he opens his mouth, but he tells me anyway.

Chief complaint: a feeling of strangeness, of not feeling himself, of eeriness, dislocation, etcetera etcetera.

Past history: native of Nassau, graduate of U. of Conn. and Syracuse. He tells me it is his plan to "unite in his own life the objective truths of science with the universal spiritual insights of Eastern religion."

Ah me. Another Orientalized heathen Englishman.

"Well, let's see," I say, and take out my lapsometer.

When he's gone, I open the back door.

The Sears ramp is empty.

Ah well. To my fat ladies, to the A & P for a turkey, to the toy store and home.

6

"Fore!"

"Good mashie, old man!"

In a bunker I noticed that, December or not, weeds are beginning to sprout.

A tractor pulling a gang mower stops beside me. The driver is greenskeeper Moon Mullins, a fellow Knight of Columbus, Holy Name man, ex-Pontiac salesman. Moon stayed because he owns half the shacks in Happy Hollow, now inhabited by peckerwoods, and can't sell them.

"How goes it, Moon?"

The greenskeeper shakes his head dolefully. Really, though, he's fit as can be. What he doesn't remember is his life as a Pontiac salesman in a Toyota town, standing around the showroom grinning and popping his knuckles while his colon tightened and whitened, went hard and straight as a lead pipe.

"You want to know where it all began to go wrong?" Moon asks me, nodding toward a foursome of sepia golfers.

"Where?"

"It started when we abandoned the Latin mass."

"You think?"

"Sure. You think about it."

"All right."

Off he roars, whistling a carol and showering me in a drizzle of grass cuttings.

"See you tonight!" he hollers back.

He comes down to the chapel now. Most A.C.C. (Cicero) Catholics have moved away. Monsignor Schleifkopf was transferred to Brooklyn. Moon and others who stayed have drifted back to Father Smith.

7

After holding fat clinic at the club, I am served lunch in the hall. The placing of my table in the hall between the men's bar crowded with golfers and the dining room overflowing with Mah-Jongg ladies is nicely calculated not to offend me.

I eat with the English pro.

From one side comes the click of Mah-Jongg tiles, from the other the rattle of poker dice in cup. My Bantu ladies, the weight watchers, are a hefty crew. They are all dressed in the fashion of the day, in velveteen, mostly green and wine-colored with hats to match, hats with tall stove-in crowns and large cloche-shaped brims.

The food is good—it comes straight from the rib room and is the same roast beef and Yorkshire pudding everyone is served. I eat heartily. Better still, I don't have to listen to "Christmas gif, Doc!" and I don't have to worry about tipping. Instead I get tipped. Beside my plate I find an envelope with check for $25 and poem attached. From my fat ladies.

> *Merry Longhu6 for our Doc*
> *Who tries to keep us slim.*
> *Don't get discouraged, Doc, we'll try harder*
> *More power to him.*

Reading poem and nodding and chewing roast beef.

8

The bell rings for midnight mass. Ellen decides to come with me.

"Thanks again for the bell, my son," says Father Smith on the tiny porch of the chapel. With his deep tan from fire-watching and his hairy Spanish futbol wrists he looks more than ever like Ricardo Montalban.

The bell is the plantation bell from Tara. It is the original bell provided by David O. Selznick for the original Tara. Lola hid it in the well before the Bantus came.

There is some confusion in the chapel. The Jews are leaving—it is their Sabbath. The Protestants are singing. Catholics are lined up for confession. We have no ecumenical movement. No minutes of the previous meeting are read. The services overlap, Jews wait for the Lord, Protestants sing hymns to him, Catholics say mass and eat him.

Bessie Charles is singing a spiritual:

> *He's got the little bitty baby in his hands,*
> *He's got the whole world in his hands.*

Catholics join in self-consciously and off-key.

Father Smith looks at his watch as usual and as usual says: "Time to get locked in the box. Coming?"

"Very well."

Blinking with surprise, he lets out a groan and looks at his watch again. Must he hear my confession in the few minutes he allots to polishing off the week's sins of his practicing Catholics? Well, he will if he must.

"Don't worry, Father. It won't take a minute."

He nods, relieved. Perhaps I've been slipping off to confess elsewhere.

My turn comes at last. I kneel in the sour darkness of the box, which smells of sweat and Pullman curtain.

The little door slides back. There is Father Smith, close as close, cheek propped on three fingers, trying to keep awake. He's cross-eyed from twelve hours of fire-watching. A hundred brushfires flicker across his retina. These days people, convinced of world-conspiracies against them, go out and set the woods afire to get even.

"Bless me, Father, for I have sinned," I say and fall silent, forgetting everything.

"When was your last confession?" asks the priest patiently.

"Eleven years ago."

Another groan escapes the priest. Again he peeps at his

watch. Must he listen to an eleven-year catalogue of dreary fornications and such? Well, he'll do it.

"Father, I can make my confession in one sentence."

"Good," says the priest, cheering up.

"I do not recall the number of occasions, Father, but I accuse myself of drunkenness, lusts, envies, fornication, delight in the misfortunes of others, and loving myself better than God and other men."

"I see," says the priest, who surprises me by not looking surprised. Perhaps he's just sleepy. "Do you have contrition and a firm purpose of amendment?"

"I don't know."

"You don't know? You don't feel sorry for your sins?"

"I don't feel much of anything."

"Let me understand you."

"All right."

"You have not lost your faith?"

"No."

"You believe in the Catholic faith as the Church proposes it?"

"Yes."

"And you believe that your sins will be forgiven here and now if you confess them, are sorry for them, and resolve to sin no more?"

"Yes."

"Yet you say you do not feel sorry."

"That is correct."

"You are aware of your sins, you confess them, but you are not sorry for them?"

"That is correct."

"Why?"

"I couldn't say."

"Pity."

"I'm sorry."

"You are?"

"Yes."

"For what?"

"For not being sorry."

The priest sighs. "Will you pray that God will give you a true knowledge of your sins and a true contrition?"

"Yes, I'll do that."

"You are a doctor and it is your business to help people, not harm them."

"That is true."

"You are also a husband and father and it is your duty to love and cherish your family."

"Yes, but that does not prevent me from desiring other women and even contriving plans to commit fornication and adultery."

"Yes," says the priest absently. "That's the nature of the beast."

Damn, why doesn't he wake up and pay attention?

"But you haven't recently," says the priest.

"Haven't what?"

"Actually committed adultery and fornication."

"No," I say irritably. "But—"

"Hm. You know, Tom, maybe it's not so much a question at our age of committing in the imagination these horrendous sins of the flesh as of worrying whether one still can. In the firetower on such occasions I find it useful to imagine the brushfires as the outer circle of hell, not too hot really, where these sad sins are punished, and my toes toasting in the flames. Along comes Our Lady who spies me and says: 'Oh, for heaven's sake, you here? This is ridiculous.'"

Damn, where does he come off patronizing me with his stock priestly tricks—I can tell they're his usual tricks because he reels 'em off without even listening. I can smell the seminary and whole libraries of books "for the layman" with little priest jokes. How can he lump the two of us together, him a gray ghost of a cleric and me the spirit of the musical-erotic?

More tricks:

"For your drinking you might find it helpful, at least it is in my case, to cast your lot with other drunks. Then, knowing how much trouble you're going to put your friends to if you take a drink, you're less apt to—though it doesn't always work."

"Thank you," I say coldly.

"Now let's see." He's nodding again, drifting off into smoke and brushfires. "Very well. You're sorry for your sins."

"No."

"That's too bad. Ah me. Well—" He steals a glance at his watch. "In any case, continue to pray for knowledge of your sins. God is good. He will give you what you ask. Ask for sorrow. Pray for me."

"All right."

"Meanwhile, forgive me but there are other things we must think about: like doing our jobs, you being a better doctor, I being a better priest, showing a bit of ordinary kindness to people, particularly our own families—unkindness to those close to us is such a pitiful thing—doing what we can for our poor unhappy country—things which, please forgive me, sometimes seem more important than dwelling on a few middle-aged daydreams."

"You're right. I'm sorry," I say instantly, scalded.

"You're sorry for your sins?"

"Yes. Ashamed rather."

"That will do. Now say the act of contrition and for your penance I'm going to give you this."

Through the little window he hands me two articles, an envelope containing ashes and a sackcloth, which is a kind of sleeveless sweater made of black burlap. John XXIV recently revived public penance, a practice of the early Church.

While he absolves me, I say an act of contrition and pull the sackcloth over my sports coat.

"Go in peace. I'll offer my mass for you tonight."

"Thank you," I say, dumping the ashes in my hair.

After hearing confessions, the priest gets ready to say mass. The pious black seminarian, who looks like Saint Aloysius Gonzaga, who never entertained a dirty thought, assists him.

Some of the Protestants stay, including Leroy Ledbettter and Victor Charles and his wife.

There is a flick of eyes as people notice my sackcloth. Ellen's cheek radiates complex rays of approval-disapproval. Approval that I will now "do right," be a better husband, cultivate respectable patients, remain abstemious, etcetera. What she disapproves is not that I am doing public penance. No, what bothers her is an ancient Presbyterian mistrust of *things*, things getting mixed up in religion. The black sweater and the ashes scandalize her. Her eyelid lowers—she almost winks. What have these *things*, articles, to do with doing right? For she mistrusts the Old Church's traffic in things, sacraments, articles, bread, wine, salt, oil, water, ashes. Watch out! You know what happened before when you Catholics mucked it up with all your things, medals, scapulars, candles, bloody statues! when it came finally to crossing palms for indulgences. Watch out!

I will. We will.

Father Smith says mass. I eat Christ, drink his blood.

At the end the people say aloud a prayer confessing the sins of the Church and asking for the reunion of Christians and of the United States.

Outside the children of some love couples and my own little Thomas More, a rowdy but likable lot, shoot off firecrackers.

"Hurrah for Jesus Christ!" they cry. "Hurrah for the United States!"

9

After mass, Victor Charles wishes me merry Christmas and tells me he's running for Congress.

"The U.S. Congress?"

"Why not?"

He wants me to be his campaign manager.

"Why me?"

"I got the Bantu vote. They've fallen out with each other and are willing to go with me. Chuck Parker's helping me with the swamp people. Max is working on the liberals. Leroy Ledbetter's got the peckerwoods. You could swing the Catholics."

"I doubt that. Anyhow, I'm not much of a politician." I have to laugh. He sounds exactly like a politician from the old Auto Age.

"You organized the SOUP chapter here, didn't you?"

SOUP is Southerners and Others United to Preserve the Union in Repayment of an old Debt to the Yankees Who Saved It Once Before and Are Destroying It Now.

For, in fact, much of the North is pulling out. The new Hanseatic League of Black City-States—Detroit, New York, Chicago, Boston, Los Angeles, Washington—refused last year to admit federal election commissioners. D.C. had to remove to Virginia, home of Jefferson.

"You're a good doctor, Doc. People respect you."

"What's that got to do with politics?"

"Everything, man!"

"You running as Knothead or Left?"

"Doc, I'm running under the old rooster." In Louisiana the rooster stood for the old Democratic Party.

I laugh. Victor laughs and claps his hands. It's the same old funny fouled-up coalition. Kennedy, Evers, Goldberg, Stevenson, L. Q. C. Lamar.

"All right."

"All right, what?"

"I will."

We laugh. Why are we laughing?

"Merry Christmas, Doc."

"Merry Christmas."

10

Barbecuing in my sackcloth.

The turkey is smoking well. The children have gone to bed, but they'll be up at dawn to open their presents.

The night is clear and cold. There is no moon. The light of the transmitter lies hard by Jupiter, ruby and diamond in the plush velvet sky. Ellen is busy in the kitchen fixing stuffing and sweet potatoes. Somewhere in the swamp a screech owl cries.

I'm dancing around to keep warm, hands in pockets. It is Christmas Day and the Lord is here, a holy night and surely that is all one needs.

On the other hand I want a drink. Fetching the Early Times from a clump of palmetto, I take six drinks in six minutes. Now I'm dancing and singing old Sinatra songs and the *Salve Regina*, cutting the fool like David before the ark or like Walter Huston doing a jig when he struck it rich in the Sierra Madre.

The turkey is ready. I take it into the kitchen and grab Ellen from behind. She smells of flour and stuffing and like a Georgia girl.

"Oh, for pity's sake," says Ellen, picking up a spoon.

"You're lovely here."

"You've been drinking."

"Yes."

"Put my dress down."

"All right."

"What are you doing?"

"Picking you up."

"Put me down."

I'm staggering with her, a noble, surprisingly heavy, Presbyterian armful.

"You're drunk."

"Yes."

"Where do you think you're going?"

"In here. Put the spoon down."

She puts the spoon down and I put her down on her new $600 bed.

To bed we go for a long winter's nap, twined about each other as the ivy twineth, not under a bush or in a car or on the floor or any such humbug as marked the past peculiar years of Christendom, but at home in bed where all good folk belong.

RELATED WRITINGS

Accepting the National Book Award for The Moviegoer

YOU, THE judges, have made it difficult for me. You must know that the main source of creative energy of a Southern writer is a well-nourished rancor against Yankees. His natural writing posture is that of a man drawing a bead on Yankee culture. Then something like this happens and spoils everything. It takes all the heart out of a Southerner to be treated so well. Why, a fellow is liable to go back home and not write another word for the next ten years. It has happened, you know.

Nevertheless, I wish to thank—and thank from the bottom of my heart—the judges, Miss Jean Stafford, Mr. Herbert Gold, and Mr. Lewis Gannett; the sponsors, the American Book Publishers Council, the American Booksellers Association, and the Book Manufacturers Institute. And, by your leave, I cannot let this opportunity pass without thanking two other people and two other institutions: my agent, Miss Elizabeth Otis, and my editor, Mr. Stanley Kauffmann, who contributed far beyond the call of duty and ten percent—in fact, I'd just as soon not say how much they did help me—the house of Knopf for their usual beautiful job of bookmaking, and finally my wife, for reasons known to her.

Somewhere in the novel the main character, Jack Bolling, talks about his aunt, who has diagnosed his difficulties as the symptoms of a previous incarnation. I have something of the same feeling now. Because the last time I was in New York (not counting one weekend) was twenty years ago and the occasion was so different that it is hard to believe it belongs to the same lifetime. I was employed as an intern at Bellevue Hospital, assigned to the morgue to do autopsies. The medical staff would assemble and go over a case and make their best guess as to the cause of death. Then it was my job to stand up with a trayful of organs, lungs, liver, spleen, and such, taken from the poor fellow, and give them the answers.

Yet, though these two occasions seem to belong to different incarnations, perhaps they are not unrelated. Providence works in strange ways.

Now, I'm not recommending that novelists of the future serve their apprenticeships in the Bellevue morgue, and I'm not saying that our culture is dying and all that remains is to cut out the organs and see at last what was wrong. And certainly I'm not saying that I have the answers in the way a Bellevue pathologist has the answers on a tray before him.

Nor do I claim any such pretensions for *The Moviegoer*, for when all is said and done, a novel is only a story, and, unlike pathology, a story is supposed first, last, and always to give pleasure to the reader. If it fails of this, it fails of everything.

But since it seems appropriate to say a word about *The Moviegoer*, it is perhaps not too farfetched to compare it in one respect with the science of pathology. Its posture is the posture of the pathologist with his suspicion that something is wrong. There is time for me to say only this: that the pathology in this case has to do with the loss of individuality and the loss of identity at the very time when words like the "dignity of the individual" and "self-realization" are being heard more frequently than ever. Yet the patient is not mortally ill. On the contrary, it speaks well for the national health that pathologists of one sort and another are tolerated and even encouraged.

In short, the book attempts a modest restatement of the Judeo-Christian notion that man is more than an organism in an environment, more than an integrated personality, more even than a mature and creative individual, as the phrase goes. He is a wayfarer and a pilgrim.

I doubt that I succeeded, but I thank you for what you have done.

"Special Message" to Readers of the Franklin Library's Signed First Edition Society Printing of The Moviegoer

THE WRITING of *The Moviegoer* came about as a consequence of the happy conjunction of several unhappy circumstances. These circumstances included exhaustion, disgust,
failure, surrender, boredom with writing in general, mine in
particular, and the first inklings of an important discovery.
The discovery was that no law of God or man required me to
write otherwise than it pleased me to write. It did not matter
what Faulkner had done. It did not matter what Dostoevski
had done. It did not matter what critics said. It did not matter
what rules of composition had been laid down. Not even good
advice mattered—and I had gotten some very good advice
from some very generous and competent writers: do this, do
that, for God's sake don't do the other. The best thing to do
with advice, even good advice, is to listen as hard as you can,
take it to heart, then forget it.

I had written two novels. One was a sort of Southern *bil-
dungsroman*, Thomas Wolfe transplanted from Carolina to
Mississippi and not traveling well, a good deal of soul-searching, a good many passages of beautiful lyrical prose. It ran
about eleven hundred pages. The other novel was a small *Magic
Mountain*, a hillock. Hans Castorp was magically reincarnated
on an unmagic alp in the Adirondacks. Sickness and sex were
rendered. Autopsies were performed. The nature of evil was
explored. The secrets of life and death were gotten at.

Neither novel was very bad, though not good enough that
I could ever bring myself to read either. Both followed established novelistic practice and were consciously freighted with
the tradition of Wolfe and Mann and other, better writers.
Fortunately they were not published.

Failure is not a bad thing, as long as it is recognized as such.
The good thing about failure recognized as such is that thereafter there is nothing to lose. The failed person is free to please
himself. He is his own man.

Why then not set out from zero, stranded, which was where

I found myself and which was where I put Binx Bolling in this novel? Why not strike out as if no novel had ever been written before, as if it were a new world? In fact it was a new world. Binx is stranded in a sense between traditions, between worlds, between the old modern world and the world to come. Everyone else in the novel is stranded too. The difference is that Binx knows it and they don't. Since he knows he is stranded and is not afraid to know it, his world becomes as fresh and unexplored and inviting as if it were newly made. He sets forth like Crusoe.

I sat on the back porch of a shotgun cottage in New Orleans, overlooking a rank overgrown patio. I wrote the first sentence of *The Moviegoer*. It had a sly, flat—yet cheerful—tone which pleased me.

W. P.

Covington, Louisiana,
1980

Concerning Love in the Ruins

I WANT TO THANK the Publishers' Publicity Association for inviting me to talk. I am happy to be here, although, to tell you the truth, I don't feel much like talking about this novel, which is to be published this spring by Farrar, Straus and Giroux. This is the case probably because of a writer's natural reluctance to say something about a book which presumably has already said what the writer wants to say, no more nor less. But this leaves me in the peculiar situation of talking about a book which you haven't read and which I don't feel like talking about.

One trouble is, no matter what I say about the novel, it will be misleading. For example, if I describe it as a futuristic satire set in the United States somewhere around 1983, the statement would be accurate. Yet it would be misleading. Because, inevitably, you would connect it with Orwell's *1984* or perhaps with Huxley's *Brave New World*. Whereas the fact is, it is not in the least like either.

Orwell and Huxley were writing political satire. They were concerned with certain totalitarian trends in society, Orwell with Big Brother Stalinism, Huxley with a scientifically manipulated anthill state. Their arguments were well taken, so much so that they rank as truisms now, and are accepted by everybody, even by some Soviet writers.

What I was concerned with in this novel is something else altogether. What interested me is what can happen in a free society in which Orwell and Huxley have carried the day. Everybody agrees with Orwell and Huxley, yet something has gone wrong. For this novel deals, not with the takeover of a society by tyrants or computers or whatever, but rather with the increasing malaise and finally the falling apart of a society which remains, on the surface at least, democratic and pluralistic.

One thing that happens is that words change their meanings. The good old words remain the same, but the meanings begin to slip. In 1983, you see, we will still be using words like "freedom," the "dignity of the individual," the "quality of life," and so on. But the meanings will have slipped. Right now, in 1971, the meanings have already begun to slip, in my opinion. It is the job of the satirist, as I see it, to detect slips and then to exaggerate them so that they become noticeable.

Let me hasten to say that I am not setting up as a prophet. A prophet aims to be right. A novelist prophesizes in order to be wrong. A novelist likes to think he can issue warnings and influence people. This is probably not the case.

I thought of using as a motto for the novel Yeats's line about the center not holding. For indeed, in the novel, the center does not hold. But even to say this is misleading. It suggests a political satire which attacks right and left and comes down on the side of moderate Republicans and Democrats. I had a different center in mind.

Actually, the novel is only incidentally about politics. It is really about the pursuit of happiness. The locale is a subdivision called Paradise Estates. Everyone there has pursued happiness and generally succeeded in being happy. Yet something is wrong. As one character says, we were all happy but our hearts broke with happiness. Liberals begin to develop anxiety. Conservatives begin to contract high blood pressure and large bowel complaints.

It is true that an almost total polarization does occur: between left and right, white and black, young and old; between Los Angeles and San Francisco, between Chicago and Cicero. But there is also a split within the person, a split between the person's self, a ghostly self which abstracts from the world and has identity crises, and the person's body, which has needs, in this case mostly sexual.

So the novel is satirical, but I wish to assure you that in its satire it does not discriminate on grounds of race, creed, or national origin. What I mean is, there is a little something here to offend everybody: liberal, conservative; white, black; hawk, dove; Catholic, Protestant, Jew, heathen; the English, the Irish, Swedes, Ohioans, to mention only a few. Yet I trust it is not ill-humored, and that only those will be offended who deserve to be.

Really, though, I was not concerned primarily with ideological polarization. What seemed more important to me are certain elements of self-hatred and self-destructiveness which have surfaced in American life, elements common to both left and right. This accounts for the apocalyptic themes of the book: love in the ruins, end of the world, a few people surviving, vines sprouting in the masonry, etc. For I sense a curious ambivalence in people's attitude toward such things. The prospect of catastrophe has its attractions. I have the same ambivalence myself. For example, there is something attractive about the idea of Forty-second Street falling into ruins and being covered by Virginia creeper.

So, when people talk about the greening of America, you have to remember that the greening can take place only where the masonry crumbles. I only wanted to call things by their right names. I mean to say, it is all very well for some young people and a few aging gurus to attack science and technology and to go live in the ruins, in love and peace, and to touch each other. On the other hand, it is not a small thing, either, to turn your back on two thousand years of rational thinking and hard work and science and art and the Judeo-Christian tradition. I am not arguing. Very well, one turns one's back. I only wanted to explore some of the consequences. What happens in the novel is that the hero finds himself living in a ruined greening Howard Johnson motel with three girls. One of the girls is a Presbyterian.

What I really wanted to do, I guess, was call a bluff. For it has often seemed to me that much of the violence and alienation of today can be traced to a secret and paradoxical conviction that America is immovable and indestructible. Hence the acts of desperation. Blowing up a building is, after all, a nutty thing to do. The fact is that America is not immovable and indestructible.

Just now, of course, the violence has abated. We are experiencing what has been described as a period of eerie tranquillity. People seem to be thinking things over. In fact, if I had to describe this novel, I would call it an entertainment for Americans who are thinking things over in a period of eerie tranquillity.

But the novel is not saying: Don't rock the boat, cool it, be moderate, vote moderate Republican or Democrat. No, it rocks the boat. In fact, it swamps the boat. What I wanted to investigate was how the boat might actually go under at the very time everybody is talking about the dignity of the individual and the quality of life. I wanted also to investigate the best hope of the survivors.

But rather than talk about the novel and mislead you, I prefer to close these remarks by mentioning two features of my own background which may account for the peculiarities, if not the virtues, of this novel.

One is that my original vocation was medicine and that for this reason my literary concerns are perhaps more diagnostic and therapeutic than they otherwise would be. The fact is, I can't resist the impulse to thump the patient and try to figure out what's wrong with him. This medical habit has its literary dangers. It could make for moralizing, telling people what to do, and for heavy-handed satire. I hope it doesn't.

The other thing is the circumstance that I come from the Deep South. I mention this only to call your attention to a remarkable event that has occurred in the last year or two, which has the most far-reaching consequences, and which has gone all but unnoticed. It is the fact that for the first time in a hundred and fifty years the South is off the hook and once again free to help save the Union. It's not that the South has got rid of its ancient stigma and is out of trouble. It's rather that the rest of the country is now also stigmatized and is in even deeper trouble.

So, if the novel has any messages, one might be this: Don't give up, New York, California, Chicago, Philadelphia! Louisiana is with you. Georgia is on your side.

CHRONOLOGY

NOTE ON THE TEXTS

NOTES

Chronology

1916   Born Walker Percy on May 28 at St. Vincent's Hospi-
          tal, in Birmingham, Alabama, the first of three sons of
          LeRoy Pratt "Puss" Percy and Martha Susan "Mattie
          Sue" Phinizy Percy. Named for paternal grandfather,
          an attorney. Father, educated at Lawrenceville School,
          Princeton University, and Harvard Law School, is an
          attorney in Birmingham family firm, and an Episcopa-
          lian. Mother, educated at Miss Finch's School, in New
          York, is from Presbyterian family in Athens, Georgia,
          prosperous through cotton and insurance. Grand-
          uncle, LeRoy, is former U.S. senator from Mississippi.
          Another ancestor, LeRoy Pope Walker, was Confeder-
          ate secretary of war.

1917–24   Preparing for a hunting trip, paternal grandfather
          shoots himself fatally with shotgun in his Birmingham
          mansion, located at 2127 Arlington Avenue in the Five
          Points district, on February 8, 1917; coroner rules the
          death a suicide. Afterward, father moves family from
          small house on Caldwell Terrace into the Arlington
          Avenue mansion, a dark "spooky" place, Percy will later
          recall, "like the Munsters' house on TV." Father joins
          Army Air Corps after the U.S. enters World War I on
          April 6, 1917, but remains stateside, seeing no action;
          father's first cousin, William Alexander Percy, of Green-
          ville, Mississippi, serves in Flanders. Brother LeRoy
          born on August 23, 1917. Brother Billups Phinizy born
          on January 3, 1922. Granduncle's article objecting to
          the Ku Klux Klan (written with his son Will's help)
          appears in July 1922 issue of *The Atlantic Monthly.*
          Percy's early childhood memories include watching
          "the first movie I ever saw, a Krazy Kat cartoon at a
          theater in Five Points," and catching the streetcar on
          Highland with his "black nurse and riding the 'loop'—
          for a nickel—a cheap way of babysitting." In 1924,
          family moves into new house in wooded suburb—the
          Shades Valley, "over the mountain" from town—and
          attends Independent Presbyterian Church, which holds
          services in Temple Emanu-El; father teaches Sunday
          school. With brother Roy, Walker attends private new

boys' academy, Birmingham University School; joins Boy Scouts, builds models, reads, rides bicycle, listens to music on Victrola.

1925   Father travels to Johns Hopkins University in Baltimore, seeking treatment for depression.

1926   Ten-year-old Walker sends story to *Liberty* magazine.

1927   Family meets Charles Lindbergh in Birmingham in May during aviator's publicity tour after solo Atlantic crossing. In Greenville, Mississippi, father's cousin William Alexander Percy organizes relief effort after catastrophic flooding of lower Mississippi River valley, which peaked in April and subsided only in August.

1928   Father's depression worsens, and in spring he attempts suicide by cutting his wrists.

1929   Walker and brother Roy travel with friends to summer camp at Camp Winnipee in Eagle River, Wisconsin. On July 9, with mother shopping in town, father kills himself, shooting himself in head with shotgun; mother learns of the death through newsboys' shouts on the sidewalk. Family moves from Birmingham to maternal grandmother's house, on 324 Milledge Avenue, in Athens, Georgia. Percy and brothers are enrolled in local public school.

1930   In spring, William Alexander Percy, a Harvard-educated lawyer and published poet, visits from Greenville, where he runs family plantation (settled in the 1840s) and takes a role in civic affairs; makes strong impression on Percy boys, who call their father's first cousin "Uncle Will." At his invitation, family spends summer in Greenville, then stays on in the house, with boys taking roles in the decision. Uncle Will shares Walker's enthusiasm for classical music, Shakespeare, Romantic poetry and fiction, Stoic philosophy, and European Catholic art and architecture. House at Main and Percy streets is stopover for writers, scholars, and artists traveling in the South, including novelist William Faulkner and psychiatrist Harry Stack Sullivan; Shelby Foote, a local boy Walker's age, whose father is also deceased, spends time there. Family attends Presbyterian church. In first year at Greenville High School, Percy receives straight C's; grades then improve.

1931   At prompting of older classmate Camille Sarasson, on whom Walker has a secret crush, writes gossip column for school paper, *The Pica*; also contributes articles, poems, and book reviews. Wins high school poetry contest (judge is Uncle Will). Reads three-volume *The Science of Life* by H. G. Wells and Julian Huxley and is drawn to science as a vocation.

1932   On April 2, Mother loses control of Buick when left wheels go over side of wooden bridge, northeast of Greenville, and car plunges twenty feet into Deer Creek, where she is drowned; brother Phin, also in the car, escapes. Uncle Will adopts the three boys. Walker and Roy are sent on summer trip west; Walker is taken with San Francisco, and eventually writes about city's Chinatown for school paper. Argues against Uncle Will's support for presidential candidate Franklin Delano Roosevelt and optimism about social reform. Begins courtly romance with popular classmate Margaret Kirk.

1933   Graduates from Greenville High School, with plans to enroll at the University of North Carolina. Spends three weeks at cottage acquired by Uncle Will near Lost Cove, not far from Sewanee, Tennessee, home to Uncle Will's alma mater, the University of the South. Reads Santayana's *The Last Puritan*, Lewis's *Arrowsmith*, Faulkner's *The Sound and the Fury*, and Dostoevsky's *The Brothers Karamazov*, discussing each with Foote. During summer, takes trip to Mexico with Roy via New Orleans. In September, arrives at Chapel Hill campus, settling into dormitory room in Manly Hall. For writing diagnostic test, submits single-paragraph, unpunctuated monologue, written in the manner of *The Sound and the Fury*; is diagnosed "language-deficient" and placed in remedial writing class.

1934   Pledges Sigma Alpha Epsilon fraternity. Earns a C in botany, only science course in 1933–34 freshman year. Yearbook includes photograph of Percy waiting in line outside local movie house. Travels to Germany during summer vacation with student group, following *Wanderjahr* precedent of forebears, visiting Bonn, Cologne, and Berlin and hiking in the Black Forest. Brief trip to Vienna following assassination of Austrian chancellor

Engelbert Dollfuss; in Bonn, engages in deep conversation with a member of Hitler Youth; in Berlin, by his own account, is bullied into giving Nazi salute as a parade including Adolf Hitler goes past. Back home in Greenville, vividly describes for Foote young Germans' sense of history and duty. Returns to Chapel Hill, accompanied by brother Roy, who will become an SAE fraternity brother. Spends long hours on the front porch of the SAE house, "drinking and observing the scene." Reads Shakespeare, Goethe, southern history, and modernist writing. Contributes articles and book reviews to college literary magazine, including "The Movie Magazine: A Low 'Slick,'" lambasting the clichéd formulas of movie magazines. Attends dances and formals with Margaret Kirk, now a student at Sweet Briar College in Virginia.

1935   Shelby Foote enrolls in University of North Carolina; however, is turned down by SAE due to partial Jewish ancestry. In SAE fraternity house, Walker's roommates include Harry Stovall, a Catholic. Reads Thomas Mann's *The Magic Mountain* in summer.

1936   With Foote, travels to New York City on spring break. Is elected vice president of pre-med fraternity Alpha Epsilon Delta, and is elected to Phi Beta Kappa. During summer vacation after junior year, reads *Gone With the Wind* when it is foisted on him by Uncle Will, sharing the latter's enthusiasm. That same summer, befriends David Scott, a young Black man and a Catholic, who works in Percy household and flies small planes as an avocation.

1937   Is rejected by Harvard Medical School but is accepted by Columbia University's College of Physicians and Surgeons, in upper Manhattan. Graduates from University of North Carolina with a degree in chemistry. Before matriculating at Columbia, lodges for several weeks at YMCA on Upper West Side, near Central Park. At Columbia, takes courses in anatomy and physiology. Is entered into Miss Cutting's Social Register and receives invitations to debutante parties. Dates several women while at Columbia, meeting them under the clock in Grand Central Station. Beginning in fall, undergoes daily psychoanalysis in midtown with Dr.

Janet Rioch and will continue to do so through end of medical school years; classmates think he is going to the movies.

1938   Writes short story, "Young Nuclear Physicist," about a student, alone in New York and haunted by suicides in his family, who feels "a certain permanent sense of strangeness." Upon returning to Greenville in summer after first year of medical school, learns that Uncle Will is ill. With Uncle Will and brothers, spends busy, eventful summer at Brinkwood, Uncle Will's "mountain cottage" in Sewanee, Tennessee. Has dinner with Allen Tate, poet, critic, and exponent of a southern literary point of view, and Tate's wife, novelist Caroline Gordon, who live nearby. Erects simple stone house with Shelby Foote on Uncle Will's property. Takes trip with Foote to Rowan Oak, Faulkner's house in Oxford, Mississippi, but refuses to get out of car while Foote goes inside to chat with novelist ("I don't know that man and he doesn't know me and I'm not going to bother him," he tells Foote). In second year of medical school, takes two courses in pathology.

1939   Serves as usher at brother Roy's wedding on January 3. Summer is spent in Greenville and at Brinkwood. In September, returns to New York by car, sharing driving with David Scott, who takes room at YMCA and seeks out aviation classes. With Scott and others, attends World's Fair in Flushing, Queens. In third year of medical school, commits to the field of pathology, working both in laboratories and on "rotations" with patients. Earns C in psychiatry. Reads Freud. Late in year, Foote informs him he has completed a draft of a novel.

1940   Travels to Princeton for a meal with Tate and Gordon. Continues to read Freud, marking up his copies of *General Introduction to Psychoanalysis* and *The Basic Works of Sigmund Freud*. Following year, will engage a new analyst, Dr. Goddard, a Freudian.

1941   During spring term, applies for internship in pathology at Manhattan's Bellevue Hospital. In March, Uncle Will's memoir, *Lanterns on the Levee*, is published by Alfred A. Knopf. Percy and brothers are its dedicatees;

book is praised in *The New York Times* for "the candor and completeness of the revelation of the Southern aristocrat's point of view." Graduates from Columbia's College of Physicians and Surgeons; is jailed briefly after raucous graduation party. Receives draft notices, which he defers, on the grounds that he will begin residency at Bellevue in 1942. In July, accompanied by a medical-school friend, takes road trip to Yellowstone Park, Jackson Hole, South Dakota, and elsewhere—and is exhilarated by perceived freedom of the West. Returns to Greenville, where he assists a local doctor in a medical clinic. Meets Mary Bernice "Bunt" Townsend, a nurse who assists in the clinic. Cares for Uncle Will, who has suffered a stroke.

1942   Uncle Will dies January 21, after another in a series of strokes. Percy, having just started his internship residency at Bellevue earlier in the month, travels back to Greenville for the burial rites, presided over by a Catholic priest. Returns to New York and performs numerous autopsies as an intern, transfixed by "the beautiful theater of disease." In June, is diagnosed with tuberculosis, contracted either while working on cadavers or with patients. In August, travels to the aggregation of "cure cottages" at Saranac Lake, in the Adirondack Mountains, five hours' drive north of New York City. Follows regimen of walks, meals, rest, and sleeping outdoors, even in freezing temperatures. Listens to classical music and radio reports of World War II. Reads Dostoevsky, Sartre, and Mann, and sees these novelists as pathologists, diagnosing "the problem of man himself." In fall, is visited by Shelby Foote, to whom he later reports, in a letter, that he is "resigned to the life of a hermit."

1943   At Saranac Lake, as tuberculosis recedes, moves from "cure cottage" to large sanatorium, and then to a cottage inhabited by doctors, whose love of medicine points up his own lack of passion for the discipline. Considers pursuing career as a novelist.

1944   In August, discharged from sanatorium at Saranac Lake. Travels in the Northeast before returning to Manhattan to teach pathology at Columbia; instead of living in campus housing, rooms with Huger Jervey, a close friend of Uncle Will. In October, stands as best man at Shelby Foote's wedding.

1945   In May, after learning of recurrence of tuberculosis, checks into Gaylord Farm Sanatorium in Wallingford, Connecticut. Reads Kierkegaard, whose critique of Hegel, in Percy's analysis, amounts to a critique of the scientific worldview, and gains respect for religious faith as a way of knowing. Has a desire to become a committed Christian. After discharge from Gaylord at end of year, returns to Greenville.

1946   Back in Greenville, lives in a garage apartment behind brother Roy's house. During spring and summer, dates several women. Embarks with Shelby Foote, newly divorced, for adventure in Santa Fe, New Mexico, setting of Willa Cather's novel *Death Comes for the Archbishop*, about Catholic missionaries. Speaks of plan to become a Catholic to Foote, who is disconcerted, seeing religion as a threat to a writer's freedom. After Foote returns east, remains in Santa Fe, where the air is salubrious for those with tuberculosis. Writes to Bunt Townsend, and then phones her, suggesting that she join him in Santa Fe; she declines. In October, returns east by plane, settling in rented apartment in New Orleans, where in summer Townsend had found work in a laboratory. Resumes his courtship of Townsend. Proposes marriage; she accepts. The couple are married on November 7 at First Baptist Church in New Orleans, with Shelby Foote standing as best man. They honeymoon at Brinkwood, in Sewanee, and stay on at family cottage through winter into the following summer. An X-ray taken before their arrival at Sewanee reveals a flare-up of disease. While at Brinkwood, Percy starts writing a novel, "The Charterhouse," influenced by Mann's *The Magic Mountain*, about a young man with tuberculosis.

1947   At Brinkwood, hosts family, friends, and Caroline Gordon and Allen Tate, who are teaching at Sewanee, and who have become Catholics. In September, returns with Bunt to New Orleans, settling in rented house at 1450 Calhoun Street, in the Garden District, going to Mass at the Church of the Holy Name, and seeking instruction in the Catholic faith at Loyola University.

Asks priest who gives instruction to explain Catholic
position on evolution; is disconcerted by the priest's
disdain for the theory. On December 13, he and Bunt
are baptized conditionally ("conditional baptism"
being a common practice in the Church when there are
questions about the fact or validity of earlier baptism).

1948   After efforts to conceive a child, without success, Percy
and Bunt adopt a baby girl in May, naming her Mary
Pratt Percy and having her baptized a Catholic. Using
inheritance from Will Percy, buys a house in Covington, Louisiana. New family moves into house in early
June. Percy works intensively on "The Charterhouse."

1949   Continues to work on "The Charterhouse," soliciting
feedback from Shelby Foote. Conducts intense correspondence with Foote that will continue until Percy's
death. In September, Foote's first novel, *Tournament*,
is published; Percy sends Foote money after funds from
modest advance are exhausted.

1950   Makes three-day retreat with Jesuits at Manresa retreat
center in Convent, Louisiana, early May; will return
often.

1951   In September, sends typescript of "The Charterhouse"
to Caroline Gordon for criticism; Gordon reports on
its arrival in letter to Flannery O'Connor, who had
arranged to send her own first novel, *Wise Blood*, to
Gordon in typescript ("I imagine that you'd find it
interesting to know each other"). For a fee of $100,
to be applied to "Catholic projects," Gordon reads
typescript. In letter to writer Brainard Cheney, Gordon
declares it "the best first novel I have ever read." Sends
Percy congratulatory telegram, then thirty-page letter
of analysis and critique. Percy sends Gordon two hundred dollars at end of December and begins revision in
response.

1952   Receives a novel from Gordon—likely proofs of
O'Connor's *Wise Blood*; compares "The Charterhouse"
with it, unfavorably. In November, sends fresh draft of
"The Charterhouse" to Gordon, who praises it, telling him that he is an "agent" of the Holy Ghost, and
setting out her wish to convene Catholic writers for a
workshop or seminar under the Holy Ghost's auspices.

Gordon sends Percy's 942-page typescript to Jack Wheelock, an editor at Scribner's.

1953   In February, Scribner's declines to make an offer for "The Charterhouse." Following month, it is rejected by Harcourt, Brace & World and soon thereafter by Viking. Regnery expresses interest in "The Charterhouse," but Percy sets it aside to work on a new novel, "The Gramercy Winner," influenced by Thomas Wolfe's novels of male coming-of-age in the South, and whose protagonist is a young man afflicted with tuberculosis.

1954   Sends typescript of "The Gramercy Winner" to Gordon, who, through a friend, puts Percy in touch with literary agent Elizabeth Otis. Otis submits novel to publishers; none take it. Reads German American philosopher Susanne K. Langer's books *Philosophy in a New Key* and *Feeling and Form*, philosophical explorations of semantics and meaning-making; thrills to implied synthesis of science and humanism, but wonders why humans "need" symbols. Publishes essay "Symbol as Need," proposing that human need for symbols is first step toward knowledge of truth, in September issue of *Thought*, journal of neo-Thomist philosophy published at Fordham, a Jesuit university. Daughter Ann born on July 11, and is baptized. By year's end, the Percys' suspicions are confirmed that Ann is deaf.

1955   Seeking care and schooling for Ann, learns history and literature of deafness, and deepens roots in language theory and emerging field of semiotics. In February, the Percys travel to St. Louis and Chicago to visit schools for the deaf but return determined, with the help of a specialist, to tutor Ann at home. Tuberculosis recurs in fall.

1956   Prompted by civil rights movement—and by memory of Will Percy, a segregationist—writes essay "Stoicism and the South," published in July 6 issue of Catholic lay journal *Commonweal* ("What the Stoic sees as the insolence of his former charge—and this is precisely what he can't tolerate, the Negro's demanding his rights instead of being thankful for the squire's generosity—is in the Christian scheme the sacred right which must be accorded to the individual"). Publishes essay "The Man on the Train: Three Existential Modes" in fall issue of *Partisan Review*.

1957   Publishes "The Coming Crisis in Psychiatry" in January 12 issue of the Jesuit magazine *America*. In July, sends letter about civil rights to *America*. Publishes "The Southern Moderate," about white southerners' response to civil rights movement, in December 13 issue of *Commonweal*. Buys a "Louisiana cottage" at 1820 Milan Street in Uptown district of New Orleans, where Ann works with speech-and-language tutor; will spend weekdays and weeknights there.

1958   At house on Milan Street, begins writing *The Moviegoer*, then titled "Confessions of a Movie-goer." Publishes "Metaphor as Mistake" in winter issue of *Sewanee Review*. Writes essay "The Loss of the Creature," published in fall issue of *Forum*. Works on essay "The Message in the Bottle," to be published the following fall in *Thought*.

1959   In spring, completes draft of "Confessions of a Movie-goer." Agent Elizabeth Otis submits novel to Stanley Kauffmann, editor at Alfred A. Knopf who is also film critic for *The New Republic*, in June, after Percy completes revisions that she urged on him. Kauffmann declines novel, feeling it falls apart after "the first 150 pages or so"; however, he encourages Percy to undertake further revisions. Percy resubmits revised typescript in fall; Kauffmann, while pleased by revisions, feels the novel still needs work. On the promise of these revisions, however, Kauffmann persuades Alfred Knopf to offer Percy a contract.

1960   In January, delivers revised manuscript of "Confessions of a Movie-goer" to his publisher; Kauffmann informs him that novel "is not yet . . . in publishable form." Percy revises again, clarifying the theme of "search" and strengthening plot elements. A section of the novel is published in the summer *Forum* as "Carnival in Gentilly: A Story." At Kauffmann's suggestion, shortens title of novel, now "Carnival in Gentilly, the Confessions of a Moviegoer," to *The Moviegoer*, adds Kierkegaard epigraph, and makes other, final adjustments. Kauffmann is fired by Alfred Knopf, Angus Cameron replacing him as Percy's editor.

1961   "The Symbolic Structure of Interpersonal Processes"
             appears in February issue of *Psychiatry: A Journal for
             the Study of Interpersonal Processes*. *The Moviegoer* is
             published by Knopf on May 15, receiving mostly favor-
             able coverage; however, sales are modest. His curiosity
             piqued by a review, *New Yorker* press columnist A. J.
             Liebling reads *The Moviegoer* during reporting trip in
             Louisiana and passes on his copy to his wife, novelist
             Jean Stafford, a fiction judge for the National Book
             Awards. In summer, the Percys move into new house
             off Jahnke Avenue, closer to the center of Covington.
             Publishes "Red, White, and Blue-Gray" in December
             22 issue of *Commonweal*. *Time* magazine names *The
             Moviegoer* one of ten best novels of 1961.

1962   Corresponds in January with Angus Cameron at
             Knopf about second novel—tentatively called "The
             Fall Out"—and book of essays. *The Moviegoer* wins the
             National Book Award in Fiction, prevailing over ten
             other nominees, among them Joseph Heller's *Catch-22*,
             William Maxwell's *The Château*, and J. D. Salinger's
             Franny and Zooey. Percy travels to New York alone by
             airplane for March 13 ceremony; New York stay will
             absorb much of $1,000 prize money. Shelby Foote
             and wife, Gwyn, surprise Percy at reception following
             awards ceremony. Learns that Alfred Knopf had hoped
             Maxwell's novel *The Château*, also published by Knopf,
             would win. Later that evening is snubbed by Blanche
             Knopf at her apartment. The following morning Percy
             is interviewed by Hugh Downs on NBC's *The Today
             Show*, finding the whole experience unpleasant. When
             asked why the South produced such good writers, Percy
             responds, "Because we lost the War." Back in Coving-
             ton, receives brief congratulatory letter from Flannery
             O'Connor ("I'm glad we lost the War and you won
             the National Book Award"). Writing in *The New York
             Times*, Gay Talese reports that Stafford "convinced the
             other two fiction judges of the merits of the novel."
             Stafford and other two judges deny undue influence.
             In May, Popular Library publishes *The Moviegoer* in
             paperback; by fall, 300,000 copies of the paperback
             are in print. Percy travels to Los Angeles with family
             to acquire hearing aid for Ann. Resumes work on
             new novel, now titled "Ground Zero"; by June, has

completed 148 pages. Takes family on summer trip out west to Jackson Hole, Wyoming, driving Rambler through Texas and Utah and camping outdoors. In September, film rights to *The Moviegoer* are sold to Ransdell Cox, New York architect, though the film will never be made. Hosts Cox in Covington, along with Kauffmann, consultant to film, in November. Attends reading by Flannery O'Connor at Loyola University of New Orleans in November; meets author briefly at party afterward.

1963   Named one of "21 Great Writers on the U.S.A." by Elizabeth Hardwick in February 1 issue of *Vogue*. Spends three weeks in Key West in March to alleviate hay fever; reads Henry James's *The Golden Bowl*. Publishes "Do Fictional Manners Require Sex, Horror?" in September 12 edition of *The Clarion Herald*, comparing *Gone With the Wind*, "engaging soap opera," with Flannery O'Connor's stories, "creations of the highest order." In November, makes retreat at Manresa monastery in Convent and reads theologians whose thought informs Second Vatican Council; while on retreat, learns that President Kennedy has been shot.

1964   Sends *The Moviegoer* to Thomas Merton, Trappist monk and best-selling author, via mutual friend at Abbey of Gethsemani in Kentucky, in January, and receives prompt laudatory letter in response. Putting to use his knowledge of semiotics, serves as a consultant in a study of schizophrenics at National Institutes for Health. Drives north to attend Institute Program for Teachers of the Deaf in Northampton, Massachusetts, in June; stops en route at Arlington National Cemetery, in Virginia, to visit President Kennedy's grave. Uses sign language to tutor Ann daily. In July, sends draft of novel, now titled *The Last Gentleman*, to Elizabeth Otis and then meets with her the following month in New York; agency associate Patricia Schartle recommends cuts. Considers move from Knopf to Farrar, Straus and Giroux, hopeful of working with editor-in-chief Robert Giroux and editor Henry Robbins.

1965   Visits Shelby Foote in Memphis in early March, and proposes they join civil rights march from Selma to Montgomery, Alabama, led by Rev. Dr. Martin Luther

King Jr; Foote demurs. Later that month, travels to Chapel Hill to hear Gabriel Marcel, French Christian existentialist, lecture on "The Myth of the Death of God in Contemporary Thought," and meets philosopher briefly. "Mississippi: The Fallen Paradise" is published in April issue of *Harper's*, devoted to "The South Today." Agrees to terms with Farrar, Straus and Giroux in May to publish *The Last Gentleman*, still in revision. To mark daughter Mary Pratt's high-school graduation, Percy family takes *Queen Mary* to England and Scotland (family's ancestral land), adding pilgrimage to Marian shrine at Lourdes, France. At end of October, sends promotional copy for *The Last Gentleman* to publicity staff at Farrar, Straus and Giroux, calling novel "an exploration . . . of life in the post-modern age." Publishes "The Failure and the Hope," on race in the South, in winter issue of *Katallagete*, journal of the Committee of Southern Churchmen, and joins journal's advisory board. Before Christmas, completes revision of *The Last Gentleman* and sends final typescript to publisher.

1966   Travels to Atlanta in March to meet with Caroline Gordon, who is teaching at Emory University; together they drive to the Trappist abbey Holy Ghost Monastery in Conyers, Georgia, for a weekend retreat. Editor-in-chief Robert Giroux sends galleys of novel to Gordon, who deems novel "undramatic," and to Trappist author Thomas Merton, who declares it "one of the sanest books I have read in a long time." *The Last Gentleman* is published on June 15 to strong reviews; Farrar, Straus and Giroux goes back to press twice, bringing total hardcover copies in print to 18,500. Spends July and part of August with family on Pawley's Island, South Carolina. Considers writing nonfiction book about semiotics. In fall, begins work on novel that will become *Love in the Ruins*. Travels to New York in December to take part in Rockefeller Foundation seminar about schizophrenia. Publishes "From Facts to Fiction," about his coming-of-age as a novelist, in December 25 *Washington Post Book Week*.

1967   Writes to Shelby Foote in January: "I have in mind a futuristic novel dealing with the decline and fall of the U.S., the country rent almost hopelessly between the rural knothead right and the godless alienated left, worse than the Civil War." *The Last Gentleman* is one of six finalists for National Book Award for Fiction, but Bernard Malamud's *The Fixer* is named the winner. With Bunt, takes train to New York for May 24 National Institute of Arts and Letters ceremony to accept a stipend in recognition of his literary achievements. Publishes commentary on Ralph Ellison in "Letters to the Editor" in May issue of *Harper's* (Ellison, he says, marks the "coming of age" of the American intellectual). Percy's review of Robert Coles's *Children of Crisis*, about effects of desegregation and the civil rights movement, appears on June 25 in *New York Times Book Review*. In July, travels to Abbey of Gethsemani for meeting of *Katallagete* board, hosted by Thomas Merton. Is surprised to find famous monk dressed in dungarees and carrying a camera and a bottle of bourbon. After board meeting, Percy and Merton find themselves in a halting conversation. Merton, in response to thank-you note sent from Covington, concurs that that day the "ecumenical sparks . . . did not spark." Percy and Merton will carry on brief, intense, jocular correspondence, comparing notes on books about Bantu philosophy and Zulu religion. Percy will draw on encounter and correspondence for emerging third novel, *Love in the Ruins*. Teaches fall literature seminar involving point of view in modern fiction at Loyola University, New Orleans. With film option on *The Moviegoer* due to expire on January 1, 1968, entertains fresh offer for film adaptation from Ben C. Toledano and Noel Parmentel, southern men of letters. Publishes "Notes for a Novel About the End of the World" in winter issue of *Katallagete*.

1968   Signs fresh agreement for film option on *The Moviegoer*; Stanley Kubrick is approached to direct, but he declines. Reviews William Gass's *In the Heart of the Heart of the Country* in March 29 issue of *Life* magazine. Joins Covington Community Relations Council, local pro-civil-rights group. Expresses strong commitment to Black civil rights in interview published in spring issue of *The Southern Review*. In May, after group of Catholic radicals sets fire to draft files outside

Selective Service Office in Catonsville, Maryland, sends letter to editor of *Commonweal*, approving activists' concern over Vietnam War but comparing their use of fire to that of the Ku Klux Klan. Publishes "New Orleans, Mon Amour," personal essay about the city, in September issue of *Harper's*.

1969   Contributes essay to spring issue of *Shenandoah*, devoted to Eudora Welty. Robert Giroux writes to Percy, providing an account of death of Thomas Merton in Bangkok the previous December. In spring, writes to local school board president in support of Black students protesting against display of Confederate flag in the school they attend; testifies on May 11 before federal judge in New Orleans that meaning of Confederate flag has changed over time, becoming a "symbol of segregation, white supremacy, and racism." Threatened by Ku Klux Klan, Percy family sleeps nights in attic. Resigns from Boston Club, social club in New Orleans with race-restrictive admissions policy. Accuses local Catholic school of "getting rid of the niggers, running a seg school with holy water thrown on it." Film version of *The Moviegoer* progresses; Sam Waterston agrees to play Bolling, Bruce Dern to play Walter, and Sam Hale to direct; several scenes are shot in New Orleans but project will founder. Works with Project Head Start, meant to aid poor people in Covington, and in fall helps families displaced by Hurricane Camille in Biloxi, Mississippi. By late autumn, finishes draft of third novel, "How to Make Love in the Ruins: The Adventures of a Bad Catholic at a Time Near the End of the World." In a letter of December 18 to Ben C. Toledano, chastises him for negative review of *Harper's* editor Willie Morris's memoir, *North Toward Home* ("you should not be attacking liberals like Willie Morris who, after all and whatever their faults, are on the right side on the big issue: race").

1970   First grandson, John Walker Lobdell, born to Mary Pratt on March 18. Through nephew Tom Cowan, meets Walter Isaacson, student at Newman School in New Orleans and an aspiring writer, whom he will mentor in years to follow. Revises novel into summer; on August 4, mails the typescript to his agent for submission to Farrar, Straus and Giroux, again with Henry

Robbins acting as editor. Robbins informs him the novel is in good shape except for epilogue. In November, critic Alfred Kazin visits Percy in Covington as preparation for piece in *Harper's*.

1971   Plans book about American pragmatist Charles Sanders Peirce's theories of language. Negotiates with Farrar, Straus and Giroux on title of new novel, settling on *Love in the Ruins* as main title and insisting on retaining subtitle, *The Adventures of a Bad Catholic at a Time Near the End of the World* ("After all, a *bad* Catholic ought to be attractive"). Dedicates the book to his friend Shelby Foote. In February, tells Foote of wish to write "proper planned-out Footean architectonic novel" about a man who has killed his wife and infant son but has "made himself forget"; this will be *Lancelot*, extensively outlined and written from notes. Travels to New York the following month to take part in dinner in his honor, hosted by Roger Straus at Four Seasons, and to address the Publishers' Publicity Association of the National Book Awards, choosing to speak about his forthcoming novel (see page 893 in this volume). Reviews Walter M. Miller's postapocalyptic novel *A Canticle for Leibowitz* for spring issue of *The Southern Review*. *Love in the Ruins*, an alternate selection of the Book-of-the-Month Club, is published on May 17 to wide review coverage, climbing briefly onto *The New York Times* Best Sellers list. Farrar, Straus and Giroux goes back to print twice, bringing the number of hardcover copies in print to 45,000. Percy tells editor Henry Robbins he is "disappointed" with performance of book. Turns down two different offers for film rights to *Love in the Ruins*. Second grandson, Robert Livingston Lobdell, born to Mary Pratt on August 3. In August, the Percys vacation on Hilton Head, South Carolina. Sits for interview about Kierkegaard and Sartre for winter issue of *Georgia Review*. Reads Madison Jones's novel *A Cry of Absence* ("a successful novel about RACE . . . without falling victim either to ideology . . . or to Gothic clichés").

1972   Is photographed in Covington by author-photographer Jill Krementz. Reads Mann's *Joseph and His Brothers* and Dickens's *Bleak House*. Publishes "Toward a Triadic

Theory of Meaning" in February issue of *Psychiatry*. In April, receives a letter from child psychiatrist Robert Coles, proposing a *New Yorker* profile. Is awarded honorary degrees by his alma mater, the University of North Carolina, Loyola University of New Orleans, and Saint Scholastica, in Duluth, Minnesota. Is elected to American Academy of Arts and Letters and National Institute of Arts and Letters; traveling to New York for ceremony in May, meets Eudora Welty on train; meets Truman Capote and Norman Mailer at ceremony. Is visited by Coles in June, and again in the fall; Coles is affable company but conducts no formal interview and takes no notes. Joins a book group, devoted to classics, then to short stories; members include a Benedictine monk and Episcopal priest. Writes searching letter to Foote about coming to "the damndest watershed in my life": "My life breaks exactly in half: 1st half = growing up Southern and medical; 2nd half = imposing art on 1st half. 3rd half?" Is drinking more alcohol, bourbon in particular. In October, with Bunt, visits Brinkwood for the first time in decades. In December, appears with Welty on *Firing Line*, TV opinion show hosted by William F. Buckley, taped in Jackson, Mississippi, and responds to the questions "What exactly is the Southern imagination? What does it come from and why? Does it have anything distinctive to say? What are its particular attributes?" Calls Welty "about the best we've got."

1973   Serving as a fiction judge for the National Book Awards, travels to New York twice, in February and again in April, for awards ceremony; after ceremony, joins informal drinks party of "Sothron Writers"—Willie Morris, James Jones, William Styron—at Blackstone Hotel. Struggles with structure of fourth novel, *Lancelot*. In June, vacations with extended family and Foote family on Gulf Shore cottage colony. In summer, writes an introduction to a new edition of Will Percy's memoir, *Lanterns on the Levee*. Works on long essay "Theory of Language," accepted for publication the following year by *The Southern Review*. Joins weekly discussion group made up of scholars at Louisiana State University in Baton Rouge.

1974   Prompted by Foote, envisions a book of his essays on
        language and philosophy. In summer, fearing recur-
        rence of tuberculosis, checks into Ochsner Hospital in
        New Orleans for tests; diagnosis is hepatitis. Begins
        teaching fall course in "the novel of alienation" at
        Louisiana State University; will teach spring course in
        fiction writing. Writes "The Delta Factor" and submits
        it to *The Southern Review*, which publishes it rather
        than the highly technical "A Theory of Language."
        Reads Austrian writer Peter Handke's work, sent to him
        by Farrar, Straus and Giroux; Handke will translate
        The Moviegoer and *The Last Gentleman* into German.
        Through Bunt's volunteer work with the St. Tammany
        Art Association, meets painter Lyn Hill.

1975   Rents studio in Victorian house in town, owned by art
        association, in order to finish novel; Hill's studio is next
        door. *The Message in the Bottle*, a collection of Percy's
        essays, is published by Farrar, Straus and Giroux on
        June 16; reviews are mixed, sales modest. In August,
        overcome by depression, abruptly takes long weekend
        trip to Las Vegas. Daughter Ann is married on Novem-
        ber 29 in church of St. Joseph's, Benedictine abbey in
        Covington. Publishes "Bourbon, Neat," about the
        aesthetics of drinking bourbon, in December issue of
        Esquire.

1976   Percy's creative energy finds outlet, unusually, in a
        poem: the sentimental "Community." By early Feb-
        ruary, completes draft of *Lancelot* and three months
        later submits it to Robert Giroux at Farrar, Straus and
        Giroux. In April, travels to Washington (D.C.) School
        of Psychiatry and gives talk, "The State of the Novel:
        Dying Art or New Science?" Spends Holy Week on
        Yucatán Peninsula with Bunt and friends. Receives
        honorary degree from the University of the South. Asks
        a friend to obtain some marijuana for him. Teaches fall
        course in creative writing at Loyola of New Orleans
        (declining teaching invitations from Vanderbilt, Yale,
        and Johns Hopkins); receives 150 novel manuscripts
        for admission into class limited to twelve students. At
        Loyola, is sought out in November by Thelma Toole,
        who foists on him unpublished novel by her son, John
        Kennedy Toole, who has committed suicide. Skeptical,

Percy reads it—*A Confederacy of Dunces*—and judges it "astonishingly original."

1977   At end of January, meets with publisher Roger Straus in New York, then travels to Cornell University to deliver a lecture on Chekhov entitled "Diagnosing the Modern Malaise." Commissions Lyn Hill to paint his portrait. A Book-of-the-Month Club main selection, *Lancelot* is published on March 1 to critical reviews. Flies to New York to promote the novel; while there, joins Robert Fitzgerald, Sally Fitzgerald, and Richard Gilman in PEN panel discussion of Flannery O'Connor's work. Back in Covington, lunch meetings with Lyn Hill and friends turn into a larger regular weekly lunch group at Bechac's restaurant on Lake Pontchartrain—the Sons and Daughters of the Apocalypse. Karen Black exercises movie option on *The Moviegoer*; in spring, she travels to New Orleans with collaborators Kit Carson and James McBride, but once again the film collapses. In May, Percy receives honorary degree from Tulane University. Speaks warmly to friends about new U.S. president Jimmy Carter. Shares *A Confederacy of Dunces* with Robert Giroux, who declines to publish it; then seeks publication with Louisiana State University Press. In summer, travels in France and Italy with Bunt. Buys vacation cottage in Mandeville, on Lake Pontchartrain. Disappointed by reception of *Lancelot* (which "fizzled saleswise"), begins new novel, *The Second Coming*, with Will Barrett, the protagonist of *The Last Gentleman*, now in midlife. Self-interview, "Questions They Never Asked Me," published in December issue of *Esquire*.

1978   On February 17, delivers lecture "Going Back to Georgia," in Athens, Georgia, an ancestral seat of the Percy clan. In October, Robert Coles's two-part profile of Percy is finally published in *The New Yorker*, and soon thereafter as a book, *Walker Percy: An American Search*. Percy writes new novel steadily, in contrast to the fits and starts on *Lancelot*.

1979   Completes draft of *The Second Coming* in mid-January. Daughter Ann, mother of two sons, David and Jack, operates local bookstore, The Kumquat; amid rumors of an affair with Lyn Hill, Percy moves studio to a room over the store at its new location. Revises novel in spring and summer. In fall, submits *The Second Coming* to Robert Giroux, who suggests minor changes.

1980   *The Second Coming* is published on July 7; reviews are largely favorable. Toole's *A Confederacy of Dunces*, with Percy's foreword, is published in May. Begins new nonfiction work, about humans and language, with working title "Novum Organum." *The Second Coming* is awarded the *Los Angeles Times* Book Prize in fiction. In winter, works steadily on new nonfiction book, now called "The Last Self-help Book."

1981   *A Confederacy of Dunces* is awarded the Pulitzer Prize for Fiction, an award that will elude Percy. Percy's letter, "A View of Abortion, with Something to Offend Everybody," appears in *The New York Times* on June 8. In summer, the Percys move to a newly built Cajun cottage next to the house they have lived in since the forties. By fall, completes draft of nonfiction book, now called *Lost in the Cosmos*—a playful reference to the popular Carl Sagan PBS series *Cosmos*—but tells a friend he has "put it out of sight and mind and hope after a couple of months to come back and see it afresh." Arranges sale of manuscripts and papers to the University of North Carolina, Chapel Hill, his alma mater.

1982   On March 15, delivers address "Novel-Writing in an Apocalyptic Time," inaugurating Eudora Welty Chair in Southern Studies at Millsaps College in Jackson, Mississippi. Before traveling to Charlottesville to receive PEN citation in April, makes annual retreat at Manresa in Convent, Louisiana. Later that month, delivers lecture "How to Be a Novelist in Spite of Being Southern and Catholic" at the University of Southwestern Louisiana. In summer, visits St. Francisville, Louisiana, home of several generations of Percy ancestors and relatives. Submits substantially revised typescript of *Lost in the Cosmos* to Robert Giroux in summer but continues to tinker well into fall, sending emendations to his editor. With Shelby Foote and their wives, takes late summer trip to West Coast. In December, participates in Farrar, Straus and Giroux sales conference in New York, to talk about *Lost in the Cosmos*.

1983   By end of February, returns corrected galleys of *Lost in the Cosmos* to Farrar, Straus and Giroux. Gives talk on Herman Melville as part of May 17 Frank Nelson Doubleday Lectures in Washington, D.C. (Eudora Welty and C. Vann Woodward are the two other featured speakers). *Lost in the Cosmos* is published on June 1, an excerpt running the prior month in *Vanity Fair*, auguring strong sales. Gives commencement address "A 'Cranky Novelist' Reflects on the Church" to graduates of Saint Joseph Seminary College in Covington. Plans new novel, incorporating scholar Jo Gulledge's suggestion that he revisit Dr. Tom More, protagonist in *Love in the Ruins*; in early September, makes another visit to St. Francisville, this time envisioning a setting for emerging novel (*The Thanatos Syndrome*). In fall, teaches English at Saint Joseph College, refusing payment. On mountain vacation in Highlands, North Carolina, reads fiction submissions for National Endowment of the Arts. In November, goes to Los Angeles with Bunt and the Footes to receive *Los Angeles Times* Book Prize in current interest for *Lost in the Cosmos*; on return trip, the couples rent a car in Albuquerque and drive to Santa Fe, reprising Percy and Foote's trip of nearly forty years earlier in 1946.

1984   On February 28, receives humanities award from Loyola University of Chicago. Continues to work on "troublesome" novel-in-progress, putting great strain on him. In summer, travels to Martinique with Bunt, and brother Phin and his wife; Bunt is concerned when several months later Percy seems unable to recall trip. In December, finishes introduction to forthcoming edition of Uncle Will's letters, *William Alexander Percy and the Fugitives*, edited by Jo Gulledge.

1985   Closes studio in town; will write in library at home. In an interview in January, indicates he is halfway through new novel. Goes to Vail, Colorado, with extended family for two weeks of vacation in February; leery of skiing, works on novel instead. Attends May 17 talk by Cleanth Brooks at Tulane in New Orleans. Following month, travels to New York to receive Compostela Award at St. James Cathedral in Brooklyn; jazz pianist Dave Brubeck is another recipient at the June 7 awards ceremony. In July, finishes draft of new novel, now called *The Thanatos Syndrome*. At fiftieth-anniversary event for *The Southern Review* in October, reads passages from *The Thanatos Syndrome*.

1986   In New Orleans, on February 2, receives Catholic Book Club's Campion Prize, presented by Patrick Samway, S. J., and agrees to Samway's proposal for a biography; will also later give backing to Jay Tolson, associate editor of *Wilson Quarterly*, for his biography of Percy. Finishes another draft of *The Thanatos Syndrome* in March and spends next month revising it. Submits novel to Robert Giroux at Farrar, Straus and Giroux in mid-May before turning seventy May 28; considers birthday a real milestone in a male lineage prone to suicide. Shares revised draft of novel with Shelby Foote and Robert Coles; the latter, a doctor like its protagonist, will be the novel's dedicatee. With Bunt, brothers Phin and Roy, and their wives vacations in Maine in October.

1987   *The Thanatos Syndrome* is published on April 1. Percy promotes book in various events in New York and Washington, D.C., including bookstore signings; however, several other events, as part of book tour, are canceled, as Percy, suffering internal bleeding, returns to Covington. In April, makes twenty-third and final retreat at Manresa. On June 5, enters hospital for endoscopy and dilation of esophageal stricture. Feels well enough the following month to go to Brinkwood, and visits cabin he and Foote built there in 1938. On September 9, is guest at Reagan White House for dinner in honor of Swedish prime minister Ingvar Carlsson. While on vacation in Tenants Harbor, Maine, in October, considers new nonfiction book about semiotics, particularly his theory of "the Delta Factor." Declines offer, from Professor William Alfred, to give Emerson Lecture at Harvard (and honorary degree associated with it).

1988   Travels to Rome, with Bunt, in January, and takes part in meetings of Pontifical Council for Culture, giving talk on "The Church, Culture, and Evangelization." Among small group, has a brief audience with Pope John Paul II. Feels ill on return to Covington; doctor diagnoses prostate cancer. On March 10, has surgery but is told that the cancer has spread. Undergoes hormonal treatment for cancer. Is invited by Lynn Cheney, head of the National Endowment for the Humanities, to give 1989 Jefferson Lecture in Washington, D.C.; plans to set out his ideas about semiotics. Takes summer vacation in Highlands, North Carolina, feeling well enough to climb Mount Satulah. On November 3, goes to Chicago to accept T.S. Eliot Award from the Ingersoll Foundation, gives talk, "Physician as Novelist." Completes draft of Jefferson Lecture. Joins lay confraternity of St. Joseph's Abbey with an eye to eventual burial in abbey cemetery.

1989   Revises Jefferson Lecture in New Year, shifting emphasis to tension between science and the humanities, indicated in the title, "The Fateful Rift: The San Andreas Fault in the Modern Mind." Having read article in Jesuit magazine *America* about "the Catholic Imagination of Bruce Springsteen"—Percy's nephew Will is a fan—sends handwritten letter to Springsteen in February. On May 3, delivers Jefferson Lecture to full house in Department of Commerce auditorium. Returns to Covington in pain (abdomen) and goes to hospital, suspecting cancer has spread further. At end of July, travels to Mayo Clinic in Minnesota for new experimental treatment. Plans short nonfiction book, "Contra Gentiles," named after work of disputation by St. Thomas Aquinas. Contributes essay, "Why Are You a Catholic?," to anthology of reflections by eminent men and women.

1990   Ceases treatments at Mayo Clinic in January; soon afterward stops radiation treatments; is prepared to die. On April 27, receives last rites from a Benedictine monk of St. Joseph's Abbey. Has final phone conversation with Foote. Ceases to eat solid food. Dies May 10, with family members and Foote present. Is buried two days later in cemetery of St. Joseph's Abbey, after Mass attended by present and emeritus archbishops of New Orleans. Memorial service is held in New York, on October 24, at Jesuit church of St. Ignatius Loyola; Welty, Foote, Giroux, Stanley Kaufmann, and Mary Lee Settle give reminiscences.

Note on the Texts

This volume contains Walker Percy's first three published novels—*The Moviegoer* (1961), *The Last Gentleman* (1966), and *Love in the Ruins: The Adventures of a Bad Catholic at a Time Near the End of the World* (1971)—as well as a selection of the author's related writings, comprising Percy's remarks upon accepting the National Book Award for *The Moviegoer*, his "Special Message" to readers of the Franklin Library's Signed First Edition Society printing of *The Moviegoer* (1980), and his address to the Publishers' Publicity Association of the National Book Awards concerning *Love in the Ruins*.

Percy began to write *The Moviegoer* in the spring of 1958 while living in the house on Milan Street in New Orleans that he and his wife, Bunt, had purchased the prior year. The following spring Percy's agent, Elizabeth Otis, submitted a draft of the novel, then titled "Confessions of a Movie-goer," to Stanley Kauffmann at Alfred A. Knopf. It was a lucky break for Percy, whose two earlier novels had failed to find a publisher. Though Kauffmann initially declined to make an offer for a novel that, in his opinion, unraveled "after the first 150 pages or so," he provided encouragement and—crucially—written feedback. Percy set about revising the novel through the summer of 1959, and Kauffmann offered terms that fall. Over the next year, the relationship between editor and author was at times strained as Percy struggled to bring a wealth of materials under control. On September 1, 1960, Otis telephoned Percy to say that his third, revised draft had been formally accepted. Kauffmann requested further, minor adjustments, including shortening the title—now "Carnival in Gentilly: Confessions of a Moviegoer"—to *The Moviegoer* and adding an epigraph by Kierkegaard. While preparing a final typescript in October, Percy learned that Kauffmann had been dismissed from Knopf. In a letter of October 28, 1960, to Kauffmann, Percy acknowledged his editor's crucial role. "I have no idea this book will go," he wrote, "but I know very well how little I could have dispensed with your help."

Published on May 15, 1961, by Knopf, *The Moviegoer* was reviewed favorably but not widely. It was not immediately a commercial success. *The Moviegoer*'s fortunes changed considerably in March 1962, however, when it won the National Book Award in Fiction. The award—and the gossip surrounding it—boosted sales and visibility. (It was a poorly kept secret that Alfred Knopf had wanted not *The Moviegoer* but another of his books, William Maxwell's *The Château*, to win, while Gay Talese, acting on a rumor perhaps started by Knopf himself, suggested in *The New York Times* that NBA judge Jean Stafford had strong-armed the other judges into selecting Percy's novel.) Published in May of that year, a Popular Library mass-market paperback edition advanced strongly—by the end of the year 300,000 copies of the paperback were in print. *The Moviegoer* was reissued in paperback in Percy's lifetime by several other American publishers, including Noonday Press in 1967 and Avon in 1980. Two years following its American publication by Knopf, Eyre and Spottiswoode published a hardcover in London using the Knopf plates. In 1980 the Franklin Library published a signed limited hardcover edition. Percy did not revise the novel after its initial publication. This volume prints the text of the 1961 Knopf edition of *The Moviegoer*.

After the publication of *The Moviegoer*, Percy began to plan a broader, more ambitious novel, told not in the first person (like *The Moviegoer*) but in the third person. In the spring of 1962, he turned again to Stanley Kauffmann for feedback, sending his former editor the first 148 pages of his novel-in-progress, then titled "Ground Zero." Kauffmann offered praise but urged Percy to keep in mind "the thematic action, the rationale, the purpose of the book." In early July 1964, Percy sent to Otis a completed draft of the novel, now called "Centennial," and undertook extensive revision based on criticism from Otis and another agent at McIntosh and Otis. As revisions progressed, Percy began to think about finding a new publisher. "All I know is that Mr. Knopf," Percy confided to Kauffmann in a letter of February 11, 1965, "is not going to extend himself in selling something I write." Percy had been courted the prior year by Henry Robbins, an editor at Farrar, Straus and Giroux, who wrote to Percy to inquire about the new novel, but Percy was not then ready to break his ties with Knopf. Before departing for a family summer trip to Europe in 1965, however, he instructed Otis to negotiate a contract with Farrar, Straus and Giroux (his publisher for the remainder of his career). By November he had completed final revisions. *The Last Gentleman* was published by Farrar, Straus and Giroux on June 15, 1966, in an initial printing of 10,000 copies. It was a selection of the Literary Guild, and reviews were generally positive. By the end of June, a third printing of the novel had been ordered. Signet published a mass-market paperback in February 1968 and a Noonday trade paperback followed in 1971. The year following its initial American publication by Knopf, Eyre and Spottiswoode published a hardcover in London using the Knopf plates.

In a letter of July 7, 1966, to his editor Henry Robbins, Percy identified a dozen corrections to be made in any subsequent printings, which appear in this volume as follows: at 213.15, a comma follows "decided"; at 240.14, ""Bavarian Illuminati,"" replaces ""Bavarian Illuminate,""; at 268.20–21, "suspiring vapors" replaces "surprising vapors"; at 289.7 and 289.15, "Val-pak" replaces "Val-pack"; at 301.33, "from Fiesole" replaces "for Fiesole"; at 343.26–27, "first tee" replaces "last tee"; at 351.22, "cosines" replaces "cosigns"; at 426.24, line is indented, as part of Sutter's notebook; at 468.11, "Merriam" replaces "Merrian"; and at 489.5, "totted" replaces "toted." The present volume prints the text of the 1966 Farrar, Straus and Giroux edition of *The Last Gentleman*, emended to account for these alterations authorized by Percy (the author's correspondence with his publisher is part of the records of Farrar, Straus and Giroux, housed in the Manuscripts and Archives Division at the New York Public Library).

The first mention by Percy of *Love in the Ruins* occurs in a letter of January 1967 to his friend Shelby Foote, though he likely began work on his apocalyptic novel the prior year amidst antiwar protests and the growing schism between the nonviolence of Martin Luther King and the "Black Power" advocacy of Stokely Carmichael. By the end of 1969 Percy had completed a draft of the novel, then titled "How to Make Love in the Ruins: The Journal of a Bad Catholic at a Time Near the End of the World." In August of the following year, he sent to Otis a revised draft of the novel, now titled "How to Make Love in the Ruins: The Adventures of a Bad Catholic at a Time Near the End of the World." He was still uncertain about the title, however, and in a letter of October 2, 1970, to Henry Robbins he offered three possibilities: "Love in the Ruins, "Last Days," and "The Last Days." By February 1971 he had completed final revisions and had settled on *Love in the Ruins* as the main title, insisting over the objections of the Farrar, Straus and Giroux sales department on keeping his subtitle, *The Adventures of a Bad Catholic at a Time Near the End of the World*. The novel was published by Farrar, Straus and Giroux on May 17, 1971, in an initial print run of 25,000 copies, and was chosen as an alternate selection for the Book-of-the Month Club. It was reviewed favorably and climbed briefly onto *The New York Times* Best Sellers list but did not stick. "I thought it had a chance of taking off," Percy wrote to Henry Robbins. "If *Herzog* could take off, why not *Love in the Ruins*?" In the same year as its debut American publication, Eyre and Spottiswoode published a hardcover in London using the Farrar, Straus and Giroux plates.

In a letter of November 1, 1971, to Henry Robbins, Percy supplied a list of "goofs" that he wished to see "cleared up in paperback" as follows: at 540.33, "fists" replaces "fist"; at 543.1, "returned to" replaces "returned from"; at 555.26, "accidentals" replaces "accidental"; at 559.35, "Ted" replaces "Ten"; at 698.36 and 887.28–29, "Saint Aloysius

Gonzaga" replaces "Saint Francis Borgia"; and at 881.11, "mirlations" replaces "melations." The present volume prints the text of the 1971 Farrar, Straus and Giroux edition of *The Last Gentleman*, emended to account for these subsequent alterations authorized by Percy.

The section of this volume titled "Related Writings" begins with Percy's acceptance speech for the National Book Award for *The Moviegoer*, delivered on March 13, 1962, at the Astor Hotel in New York City. It was published posthumously in *Signposts in a Strange Land*, edited by Patrick Samway (New York: Farrar, Straus and Giroux, 1991), and this volume prints that text. The next item, the text of Percy's "Special Message" to readers of the Franklin Library Signed First Edition Society printing of *The Moviegoer* (Wawa, PA: Franklin Mint Corporation, 1980), is taken from its original publication. The third selection is Percy's address to the Publishers' Publicity Association of the National Book Awards concerning *Love in the Ruins*, delivered on March 3, 1971, in New York City. It was published posthumously in *Signposts in a Strange Land*, edited by Patrick Samway (New York: Farrar, Straus and Giroux, 1991), and this volume prints that text.

This volume presents the texts of the original printings chosen for inclusion here, but it does not attempt to reproduce nontextual features of their typographic design. The texts are presented without change, except for the correction of typographical errors and the incorporation of Percy's requested changes that are enumerated above. Spelling, punctuation, and capitalization are often expressive features and are not altered, even when inconsistent or irregular. The following is a list of typographical errors corrected, cited by page and line number: 11.24, Nieman; 22.39, Gipsy; 26.35, Rosenkranz; 45.31, ninteen; 57.33, Jose; 76.8, mosying; 133.32, space in untenanted; 149.34, soul Now; 266.3, her. As; 295.28, ambigious; 307.22, its; 316.27, dryly. "that; 386.33, for this; 399.1, flouridation; 401.37, Garbaldi; 413.5, cetrain; 416.15, had un; 422.2, jo John; 428.9, unbottoned.; 431.36, name. And; 435.13, collecter; 437.1, Supersix; 466.24, agrieved; 468.15, reclinder; 470.23, wund; 470.24–25, 28 diam; 475.39, meritorius; 477.24, at least; 490.1, "You're; 518.35, across right; 554.26, Reynold's; 564.15–16, Naugehyde; 575.17, Brooklyn-Pochahontas; 626.24, Oglethrope; 645.24, Chichen Itza; 646.23, cusps; 648.11 (and *passim*), Merida; 655.1, shortcut; 658.26, *mean*, says; 680.33, time.; 694.10, annointed; 708.19, airdale's; 712.4, access; 715.29, pulls."; 720.17, cottton; 723.27–28, Anthony's; 724.9, proctoloigsts; 734.35, Leon; 798.28, question.; 820.12, "I'm; 821.16, girls; 829.4, pants'; 854.2, transubstantiation."; 855.6, others'; 860.2, understand"; 871.28, Velasquez's; 876.10, Wilkes; 884.4, Selznik; 898.6, prophesizes.

Notes

In the notes below, the reference numbers denote page and line of this volume (the line count includes chapter headings). Biblical quotations are keyed to the King James Version. Quotations from Shakespeare are keyed to *The Riverside Shakespeare*, ed. G. Blakemore Evans (Boston: Houghton Mifflin, 1974). For more detailed notes, references to other studies, and further biographical information than is contained in the Chronology, see Jay Tolson, *Pilgrim in the Ruins: A Life of Walker Percy* (New York: Simon and Schuster, 1992); Bertram Wyatt-Brown, *The House of Percy: Honor, Melancholy, and Imagination in a Southern Family* (New York and London: Oxford University Press, 1994); Patrick Samway, *Walker Percy: A Life* (New York: Farrar, Straus and Giroux, 1997); Paul Elie, *The Life You Save May Be Your Own: An American Pilgrimage* (New York: Farrar, Straus and Giroux, 2003); and *Conversations with Walker Percy*, eds. Lewis A. Lawson and Victor A. Kramer (Jackson: University Press of Mississippi, 1985).

THE MOVIEGOER

2.1–4   in gratitude to W.A.P.] William Alexander Percy (1885–1942), poet, lawyer, plantation overseer, and author of *Lanterns on the Levee* (1941); second cousin to Walker Percy and his brothers, and, after deaths of their parents, their adoptive father.

5.33–34   Lake Pontchartrain.] Saltwater estuary north of New Orleans.

6.24   Roosevelt Hotel.] Grand hotel in downtown New Orleans that opened in 1893.

6.34   Gentilly . . . suburb of New Orleans.] Located just south of Lake Pontchartrain.

6.37–38   old-style California bungalows or new-style Daytona cottages.] Affordable postwar housing construction.

6.39–7.1   the French Quarter] Also known as the Vieux Carré, low-lying historic district of New Orleans, with an intimate street plan and unique architecture that is a blend of French, Spanish, and Caribbean influences.

7.1   the Garden District.] Neighborhood in New Orleans distinguished by large freestanding homes set behind trees on broad streets, notably St. Charles Avenue.

7.3   Birmingham businessman . . . Bourbon Street] New Orleans is a destination for trade shows and conventions, bringing out-of-towners to Bourbon Street, location of many nightclubs by the 1950s.

7.4   homosexuals and patio connoisseurs on Royal Street.] The French Quarter, where Royal Street is located, has long had a vibrant gay community.

7.22   St Bernard Parish] Parish, or county, five miles southeast of New Orleans.

7.34   William Holden] American actor (1918–1981) in films such as *The Horse Soldiers* (1959), filmed in Mississippi and Louisiana.

8.8–10   John Wayne . . . in *Stagecoach*] John Wayne (1907–1979) plays daredevil outlaw the Ringo Kid in *Stagecoach* (1939), the first of many John Ford Westerns shot in Monument Valley.

8.10–11   the kitten . . . in *The Third Man*.] In the cat scene in Carol Reed's 1949 film noir, set in postwar Vienna, viewers realize for the first time that the racketeer Harry Lime, played by Orson Welles, is alive and well when his lover's cat runs up to a figure in a darkened alcove and licks his shoe.

8.19–23   a TV play . . . soul-searching.] The TV play starring American character actor Keenan Wynn (1916–1986)—known for his large, expressive features—is Percy's invention.

8.39   Ship Island] Barrier island off the coast of Mississippi.

9.25–26   Elysian Fields . . . Faubourg Marigny.] Elysian Fields Avenue, a broad avenue running north-south through New Orleans; the unofficial main street of the Faubourg Marigny, the district also known as the Marigny and the Seventh Ward.

9.36   the *Times-Picayune*] New Orleans daily newspaper, formed by the union of the *Picayune* with the *Times Democrat* in 1914.

9.38–39   remote neighborhood like Algiers or St Bernard—] Also known as the Fifteenth Ward, Algiers is across the river from the rest of New Orleans. See also note 7.22.

10.8   Alcoa] Acronymic name of the Aluminum Corporation of America, founded in Pittsburgh in 1888.

10.14–15   the queasy-quince taste of 1951 and the Orient.] Allusion to the Korean War (1950–1953), fought between North Korea and South Korea, with U.S. forces entering the conflict in 1950 in support of the latter.

10.16   a chindolea bush.] Percy's transliteration of 진달래 (Jin-dal-rae), the Korean rhododendron or rosebay, a shrub with bright pink flowers native to Northeast Asia.

10.18–19   the best times . . . the worst times . . . the best.] Cf. the opening line of Dickens's *A Tale of Two Cities* (1859).

11.9   Place d'Armes.] Hotel in the French Quarter comprising eighteenth-and nineteenth-century townhouses.

11.12   Chef Menteur] Bayou east of New Orleans.

11.21   Prince Val bangs] Pageboy haircut, like that of Prince Valiant, medieval hero of a comic strip created by Hal Foster in 1937 and adapted for the screen in 20th Century Fox's *Prince Valiant* (1951), starring Robert Wagner in the title role.

11.23   Amazons] Fierce warrior women of ancient Greek lore.

11.31–32 victim to the first little Mickey Rooney] Mickey Rooney, diminutive American actor (1920–2014) in vaudeville, film, and television who eventually married eight times.

12.29–30 the polls report . . . atheists and agnostics—] The Gallup polling company, in its surveys beginning in 1944, asked respondents, "Do you believe in God?"

13.24   Galatoire's] Restaurant in French Quarter specializing in French-Creole cuisine, located at 209 Bourbon Street since 1905.

14.16   Hattiesburg] Small city in eastern Mississippi.

15.8   a week before Mardi Gras] Carnival: In the week prior to Mardi Gras (French: Fat Tuesday) and the beginning of Lent, New Orleans celebrates with parades, dancing in the streets, and extravagant costumes.

15.12–13 Comus and Rex and Twelfth Night] Three of the oldest continuous Mardi Gras krewes in New Orleans. Krewes, or private social clubs, stage parades and balls during Carnival.

15.14–15 a group of Syrians . . . named Isis.] The krewe from Algiers is likely Percy's invention; a krewe from Jefferson Parish named Isis was formed in 1972, a decade after *The Moviegoer* was published.

16.10   Maison Blanche] French: White House. Large New Orleans department store on Canal Street that ceased operations in 1998.

16.14–15 a Charles-Boyer pout—] French-American actor Charles Boyer (1899–1958) personified Old World charm in dozens of films, including *Gas Light* (1944) and *The Buccaneers* (1958).

16.24   "Are you riding Neptune?"] Here, a krewe likely of the author's devising; a Krewe of Neptune was founded in 1981.

18.22–23 Feliciana Parish] Parish, or county, in Louisiana, founded in 1810 and divided into East and West parishes in 1824. See also Percy's prefatory note on page 4 in this volume).

18.33   dignified Adolph Menjou moustache] Adolphe Jean Menjou (1890–1963), a mustachioed American actor, portrayed sophisticated, worldly men in numerous silent films and talkies.

18.34–35 sulky as a Pullman porter's.] The Pullman Company was an American manufacturer and operator of railroad sleeping cars in the nineteenth and twentieth centuries. Until the 1960s, Pullman porters were exclusively Black and relied on tips from white clientele.

19.22 *The Life of the Buddha*] *The Life of the Buddha: Retold from Ancient Sources* (1955), an illustrated book by Anil de Silva-Vigier.

20.10–11 the Rosicrucians . . . *How to Harness Your Secret Powers*] The Rosicrucians are a secretive organization dedicated to alchemy, mysticism, and occult reputed to have been founded by Christian Rosenkreuz (most likely a fictional figure) in fifteenth-century Germany. The volume is Percy's own invention.

20.15 the *Picayune* cup] The *Times-Picayune* Loving Cup, awarded annually to a New Orleanian in recognition of public service.

20.25 the Schwarzwald.] Black Forest, in southwestern Germany.

20.28–29 the Rupert Brooke–Galahad sort of face] That of an ardent and idealistic young man, akin to Galahad of King Arthur's Round Table or Rupert Brooke, the author (1887–1915) of celebrated war poetry, whom W. B. Yeats called "the handsomest young man in England."

20.30 the Argonne] Forest in northeastern France, 135 miles east of Paris, through which American troops pushed in the final offensive of World War I, known as the Meuse-Argonne Offensive, which lasted from September 26, 1918, until the Armistice on November 11, 1918. American troops sustained more than 110,000 casualties.

20.31–32 Roberdeau Wheat . . . in 1862.] Chatham Roberdeau Wheat (1826–1862) was a Louisiana state legislator who fought in revolutions in Mexico, Cuba, and Italy before dying at the battle of Gaines Mill, June 27, 1862, a Civil War engagement won by the Confederate Army. Brigadier General John Bell Hood achieved the first breakthrough in the Union lines.

21.11–12 commissioned by the RCAF . . . the war.] Many American men sought commissions in the Royal Canadian Air Force prior to the U.S. entry into World War II, on December 8, 1941.

21.13 the wine dark sea.] Homeric epithet.

21.14 *A Shropshire Lad*] Book of poems (1896) by A. E. Housman, widely read by soldiers in the Great War.

21.19 Unilateral disarmament] The movement urging the nuclear powers to unilaterally renounce nuclear weapons was a topic of discussion in the late 1950s, following protest marches in England and elsewhere.

21.31 Biloxi] City in Mississippi, on the Gulf of Mexico.

22.39 Gypsy Rose.] Gypsy Rose Lee (1911–1970), burlesque entertainer whose life story was told in the memoir *Gypsy* (1957), the basis for the Broadway musical, with music by Jule Styne, lyrics by Stephen Sondheim, and a book by Arthur Laurents, that opened May 21, 1959, and closed March 25, 1961.

23.1 "Sodium pentobarbital.] Barbiturate used to treat seizures, insomnia, and other ailments.

24.20 the January selloff] Typically stock prices would rise in January after a sell-off in December, when stockholders reduced assets for tax purposes.

24.28–29 Jerry Dalrymple and Don Zimmerman and Billy Banker.] Football stars at Tulane University in the late twenties and early thirties.

24.30–32 King Arthur . . . the traitors.] Allusion to the Arthurian legends. In Malory's *Morte D'Arthur*, in the final battle between Mordred's followers and Arthur's loyalists, Arthur kills Mordred but is mortally wounded.

25.10 the City of Man . . . the City of God] Augustine of Hippo draws a sharp distinction between the two realms in *The City of God* (c. 1470).

25.29 the Natchez Pilgrimage] Annual tour of elegant houses in Natchez, Mississippi.

26.12–13 her Lorenzo posture] Akin to the pose in Michelangelo's sculpture of Lorenzo di Medici (1531), on Lorenzo's tomb in Florence.

26.24–25 Dryades Street."] Commercial Street in the Central City district of New Orleans.

26.30 "The barbarians at the inner gate] Allusion to the sack of Rome by the Goths in 410 C.E.

26.31 Don John of Austria?] An illegitimate son of Charles V, the Holy Roman Emperor, John (1547–1578) led the Holy Alliance fleet to victory over the Ottoman fleet at the battle of Lepanto.

26.35 Rosencrantz and Guildenstern."] Characters in Shakespeare's *Hamlet*, summoned to Elsinore to spy on their childhood friend, Prince Hamlet.

26.39–40 lock of hair . . . the MacArthur style] Douglas MacArthur (1880–1964), commander of U.S. forces in the Pacific during World War II and administrator of postwar Japan, wore his hair combed over.

29.1–2 Golden Fleece—] Student honor society at the University of North Carolina.

29.23 Samuel Hinds] American actor (1875–1948) cast in supporting roles, notably as Peter Bailey, father to George Bailey (James Stewart), in Frank Capra's *It's a Wonderful Life* (1946).

29.31 the SAEs, the Delta Psis, the Dekes, the KAs] Members of male campus fraternal organizations: Sigma Alpha Epsilon, Delta Psi Delta, Delta

Kappa Epsilon, Kappa Alpha. Percy was a Sigma Alpha Epsilon brother at the University of North Carolina, 1934–37.

30.17   ΔΨΔ—] Delta Psi Delta.

31.25   Tigre au Chenier.] A settlement on Vermilion Bay in Louisiana, destroyed by Hurricane Audrey in 1957.

31.27   boogalee] Cajun: slang for a person believed to have a mixture of Black and white ancestry.

32.31   Valdosta] Small city in southern Georgia, near Florida state line.

32.31–32   young Burl Ives . . . and guitar.] Burl Ives (1909–1995), American actor, musician, and radio personality, whose films include *Cat on a Hot Tin Roof* (1958), began his career during the Depression era as a traveling folksinger and guitarist.

33.34   Beale Street] Commercial strip in Memphis, Tennessee, known for clubs and bawdy nightlife.

36.19–20   when we Wagnerians . . . old Brahms—] In the late nineteenth century, the "War of the Romantics" set admirers of Franz Liszt and Richard Wagner against defenders of the Classical tradition such as Clara Schumann and Johannes Brahms.

36.28–29   Philharmonic upstairs . . . Gillette Cavalade in the basement.] *The Gillette Cavalcade of Sports* was a popular TV sports entertainment program on NBC that ran from 1946 to 1960. In many American households, the phonograph, or record player, was in the living room or parlor, and the television in the basement.

38.6   Western Auto] Now-defunct chain of auto-parts stores founded in Kansas City in 1909.

38.8–9   fishing camp on Bayou des Allemands] Bayou des Allemands is located on boundary of Lafourche and St. Charles Parishes in southeastern Louisiana; the town of Des Allemands is known as "the Catfish Capital of the Universe."

38.29   the Catos] Paragons of conservative thought: Marcus Portius Cato (234–149 B.C.E.), known as the Elder, was a Roman soldier, statesman, and historian; his great-grandson, Marcus Portius Cato "Uticensis" (95–46 B.C.E.), known as the Younger, was a Roman senator who sought to preserve the Republic against Julius Caesar.

38.36   Bayou Lafourche] One-hundred-mile-long bayou in southeastern Louisiana that stretches through Acadiana and flows into the Gulf of Mexico.

39.20   *Liebfraumilch*] German: Milk of Our Lady; a semisweet white German wine.

39.21   *Wilhelm Meister*] *Wilhelm Meister's Apprenticeship* (1795–96), a philo-sophical novel by Johann Wolfgang von Goethe (1749–1832). The German title is *Wilhelm Meisters Lehrjahre*.

39.22   your student prince] Allusion to *The Student Prince* (1924), an oper-etta by Sigmund Romberg and Dorothy Donnelly, set in Heidelberg, and adapted for the screen in 1954.

41.6–7   girl from Bennington] Bennington College in Vermont was founded as a liberal arts college for women in 1932 and did not become coeducational until 1969, eight years after the publication of *The Moviegoer*.

41.12   garçonnière] French: bachelor's pad.

41.23   Flat Rock] Town in North Carolina, known for the Biltmore estate.

41.27   Prytania] Prytania Street in New Orleans, location of the Prytania Theater, a movie theater in operation since 1914.

42.34–35   *Wanderjahr*] German: Year of travel; typically, a year spent abroad prior to or just after one's university education.

43.10–11   Euripides and Jean-Christophe?"] Euripides (480–406 B.C.E.), a classical dramatist of Athens whose works include *Medea*, *Electra*, and *Hip-polytus*. *Jean-Christophe* (1904–12), a French novel in ten volumes by Romain Rolland (1866–1944), recounting a life of a German Belgian musician.

44.33   Magazine Street] Busy commercial street in New Orleans, following the curve of the Mississippi River.

46.18–19   the Illinois Central] Rail line connecting Chicago to New Orleans.

47.37   the Tchoupitoulas docks.] Docks at the uptown end of Tchoupitoulas Street, bustling with river shipping commerce.

48.2   Negroes from Louisiana Avenue and Claiborne] Louisiana Avenue is the site of many Black-owned businesses and was for many years (1896–1983) the location of Flint-Goodridge Hospital, the first Black hospital in the South. Claiborne Avenue was the economic and cultural heart of New Orleans's Black neighborhoods until the construction of an elevated highway in the late 1960s.

48.8–9   Negroes dressed in dirty Ku Klux Klan robes] The Mardi Gras tradi-tion of the flambeaux—the Black men who carry flaming torches to light the Carnival parade routes.

48.34   *Panic in the Streets* with Richard Widmark] Gritty thriller (1950) directed by Elia Kazan. Widmark (1914–2008) had starred earlier in *Kiss of Death* (1947) in a far different role, as the sociopath Tommy Udo.

50.5   American Motors.] An American automotive company, 1954–88.

52.18–19   *Peyton Place*] Racy best-selling novel (1956) by American author Grace Metalious that was adapted for the screen the year following its publication in a film nominated for nine Academy Awards.

52.38   Birmingham Southern] Private liberal arts college in Alabama, founded in 1856.

53.2   Alcoa] See note 10.8.

53.5   Gregory Peckish sort of distance.] Peck (1916–2003) was a leading man in films of the forties and fifties, including *Spellbound* (1945), *The Gunfighter* (1950), and *The Man in the Gray Flannel Suit* (1956).

53.14   Rosenkavalier] *Der Rosenkavalier* (1911), a romantic-comic opera by Richard Strauss (1864–1949).

53.18   *Arabia Deserta*] *Travels in Arabia Deserta* (1888) by English writer Charles Montagu Dougherty.

53.37   *A Study of History*] Twelve-volume history of the rise and fall of civilizations (1934–61) by British historian Arnold Toynbee.

54.6–7   *The Expanding Universe*] Nonfiction work (1933) by English astronomer and physicist Arthur Eddington about "the Great Debate" in the early twentieth century concerning the scale of the universe.

54.12   *It Happened One Night*] Romantic comedy (1934) directed by Frank Capra, starring Clark Gable and Claudette Colbert.

54.29–30   the secretary in the Prell commercial.] Prell shampoo, introduced in 1947 by Procter & Gamble, ran many television commercials that targeted women.

56.8   Leo Carroll] English character actor (1886–1972) who appeared in many films, including Alfred Hitchcock's *Strangers on a Train* (1951) and *North by Northwest* (1959).

56.19–20   Massachusetts Investors Trust.] Early mutual fund, founded in 1924.

56.32   a Lockheed Connie] The Lockheed Constellation, a four-engine propeller airliner produced by the Lockheed Corporation, 1943–58.

56.39   Jane Powell] American actress, singer, and dancer (1929–2021) who starred in dozens of films beginning in the forties, including the musicals *Royal Wedding* (1951) and *Seven Brides for Seven Brothers* (1954).

57.33–38   José Ferrer . . . cheering up an old lady] In the Broadway production of Robert E. McEnroe's *The Silver Whistle*, Puerto Rican actor José Ferrer (1912–92) played Oliver Erwenter, a garrulous hobo who spreads happiness among the inmates of an old folks' home.

58.9–13   *Red River* . . . absurd scene] Climactic scene in 1948 Howard Hawks Western starring John Wayne and Montgomery Clift as a father-and-son tandem of Texas ranchers.

58.18   Joseph Cotten in *Holiday*] Joseph Cotten does not appear in George Cukor's 1938 romantic comedy *Holiday*. Cary Grant played the lead male role opposite Katharine Hepburn.

59.17   Rosebud] Last word spoken by protagonist Charles Kane on his deathbed in Orson Welles's *Citizen Kane* (1941), referring to a sled from Kane's childhood.

60.3–4   kindly old philosophers . . . portrayed by Thomas Mitchell] American character actor Thomas Mitchell portrayed a philosophical drunk in John Ford's *Stagecoach* (1939) and the likable, absent-minded Uncle Billy in Frank Capra's *It's a Wonderful Life* (1946).

60.14–17   Every moment . . . words of the Emperor Marcus Aurelius Antonius] *Meditations*, 2.5.

60.23   Currier and Ives] New York printmaking company (1835–1907) whose inexpensive lithographs hung in many American homes.

60.27–61.2   A play . . . with Dick Powell . . . political corruption.] American actor Dick Powell (1904–63) plays a newspaperman in the fantasy film *It Happened Tomorrow* (1944), based on a one-act play, but the play described here is Percy's invention.

61.9–10   *The Oxbow Incident*] Western (1943) based on Walter Van Tilburg Clark's novel of the same title, starring Henry Fonda.

61.13–14   *All Quiet on the Western Front*] Antiwar film (1930) based on Erich Maria Remarque's novel of the same title [German: *Im Westen nichts Neues*] about trench warfare in World War I.

61.26–31   A successful repetition. . . . peanuts in brittle.] Cf. the concept of *gentagelsen* (literally "taking again") articulated in *Repetition* (1843) by Danish philosopher Søren Kierkegaard (1813–1855).

61.32–34   German-language weekly . . . Nivea Creme] The popular moisturizer was first manufactured in Hamburg in 1911.

63.21   Tertullian, Archibald MacLeish, Alf Landon—] Quintus Septimius Florens Tertullianus (c. 160–c. 240 C.E.), early church father. Archibald MacLeish (1892–1982), American poet. Alf Landon (1887–1987), oilman, governor of Kansas, and 1936 Republican presidential candidate.

66.4–6   Edgar Kennedy . . . camping equipment.] American comedic film actor Edgar Kennedy (1890–1948), one of the original Keystone Cops, was known professionally as "Slow Burn" for his ability to portray mounting frustration.

66.26–27   the Junior Jets and the Lone Ranger pup tents] Children's toy gun and play tent, widely sold in the 1950s and '60s.

67.26–27   Tolstoy and St Exupery were right about war] *War and Peace* and *The Little Prince* dramatize the horrors of combat.

67.28   Rupert Brooke . . . full of expectancy."] English poet Rupert Brooke celebrated the glories of war and military service in poems such as "The Soldier"; he died at twenty-seven of sepsis while en route to the battle of Gallipoli. See also note 20.28–29.

68.15   theosophist] Adherent to the tenets of the Theosophical Society, founded by Helene Blavatsky and Henry Steel Olcott in London in 1875, one of which is a belief in human reincarnation.

68.36   Robinson Crusoe . . . the beach.] Pivotal moment in Daniel Defoe's *The Life and Strange Surprizing Adventures of Robinson Crusoe* (1719), in which the shipwrecked title character realizes he is not alone on the island.

69.4   MG] British sports car made by a company that grew out of Morris Garages, near Oxford.

70.14   a gold Hamilton."] American watchmaker whose products were featured prominently in films of the 1930s and afterward.

70.16–17   the works of Fabre] Jean-Henri Fabre (1823–1915), French naturalist and author of popular books on the lives of insects.

70.21   Browning] Robert Browning (1812–89), English poet.

71.37   snapshots of Ava Gardner . . . North Carolina.] Actress Ava Gardner (1922–1990) was discovered via photographs taken of her in her late teens.

72.38   Our name is Increase.] "Increase"—a name associated with the colonial Puritans, namely Increase Mather (1639–1723)—is a translation of the Hebrew name Joseph ("He will add").

73.7–11   old Gable . . . back pockets.] Before his film career Clark Gable (1901–1960) took various odd jobs, including factory work, lumberjacking, and a stint as a horse manager; on screen he played tough, stereotypically masculine characters in dozens of movies.

74.24–25   the king and queen of Iberia] Krewes annually elect or choose a king and queen for Carnival.

76.19   my Little Way] The Little Way, an outlook and spiritual practice popularized by St. Thérèse of Lisieux (1873–1897), involving the pursuit of holiness in mundane tasks and daily routine.

76.20   the happy shades in Elysian Fields.] "Dance of the Happy Shades" is the English title given to a ballet scene in Act Two of Christoph Willibald Gluck's opera *Orfeo ed Eurydice* (1762), in which spirits enjoying eternal blessedness after death dance in Elysium.

77.35 *The Prophet*] Book of mystical verse (1926) by Lebanese American poet Kahlil Gibran (1883–1931).

80.20–21 Studebaker-Packard.] Automaker created when Packard Motor Car acquired the Studebaker Corporation in 1954. It ceased operations in 1967.

80.37 Dana Andrew] American actor (1909–1992) whose credits include *The Best Years of Our Lives* (1946).

81.15–17 two children . . . an enchanted garden.] Allusion to Frances Hodgson Burnett's children's novel *A Secret Garden* (1910–11), adapted for the screen in a 1949 MGM production starring Margaret O'Brien and Dean Stockwell.

82.17–26 The marshal . . . fetch the padre] Likely *The Texan*, broadcast on CBS, 1958–59, which starred Rory Calhoun as a Civil War veteran serving as a marshal in Texas.

82.26–27 H. B. Warner] English actor (1876–1958) best known for the role of Mr. Gower, the pharmacist, in Frank Capra's *It's a Wonderful Life* (1946).

82.33 This I Believe] Radio program hosted by American broadcast journalist Edward R. Murrow (1908–1965), which aired on CBS, 1951–55.

82.34 compline] The last of the canonical hours of monastic prayer, said or chanted before monks retire to bed.

83.33 Mr Edward R. Murrow.] See note 82.33.

89.5–6 as enraptured . . . Eva Marie Saint.] Before playing a femme fatale in Alfred Hitchcock's *North by Northwest* (1959), Eva Marie Saint, in her film debut, starred opposite Marlon Brando in Elia Kazan's *On the Waterfront* (1954) as Edie Doyle, sister of murdered Joey Doyle.

92.25 Banquo's ghost.] In *Macbeth*, III.vi, the murdered Banquo returns as a ghost visible only to Macbeth.

97.1 inflicted on Rory Calhoun or Tony Curtis.] American actors Rory Calhoun (1922–1999) and Tony Curtis (1925–2010) appeared in Westerns in the 1950s.

97.15 the Chongchon River."] River in North Korea.

98.14 Rory] See note 97.1. Binx Bolling addresses the remainder of his narrative to Calhoun.

98.33–34 a 4-H excursion] Youth improvement organization—Head, Heart, Hands, and Health—founded in Ohio in 1902.

104.9 Howard Johnson's] Branch of a mid-century motel-and-restaurant chain. While the hotel chain continues, the restaurants have been shuttered.

106.18   Jackson's Valley campaign] Confederate Army offensive in the Shenandoah Valley in spring 1862, led by Major General Thomas J. "Stonewall" Jackson.

106.20   Rover boy eccentricity] The Rover Boys were protagonists of a series of boys' adventure novels (1899–1926) by American publisher and author Edward Stratemeyer, creator of the Hardy Boys and Nancy Drew series.

108.15   "*Fort Dobbs.*"] Western (1958) directed by Gordon Douglass, starring Clint Walker and Virginia Mayo.

110.19   *Dark Waters.*] Film noir (1944) set in the bayous of Louisiana, starring Thomas Mitchell and Merle Oberon.

115.8   I be John Brown] Idiom for "I'll be damned" or "I'll be hanged."

116.33   *The Greene Murder Case*] Mystery novel (1928) by American author S. S. Van Dine, adapted for the screen the year following its publication in an early talkie starring Dick Powell as amateur detective Philo Vance.

117.40   WWL?"] CBS television affiliate in New Orleans.

118.35   Horace Heidt and His Musical Knights."] Popular bandleader who performed on radio and television in the 1930s and '40s.

125.28   Akim] Akim Tamiroff (1899–1972), Armenian American actor whose films include *Dangerous to Know* (1938) and *Touch of Evil* (1958).

128.17–18   His hair . . . Nelson Eddy style] American actor and singer Nelson Eddy (1901–1967), who appeared in numerous musicals in the 1930s and '40s, wore his wavy hair longer on top, tapering gradually to his ears.

128.21–22   the old New Orleans *Item.*] Newspaper, 1871–1958.

131.3   Natasha Rostov.] Young Russian aristocrat in Tolstoy's *War and Peace*, portrayed by Audrey Hepburn in King Vidor's 1956 film adaptation.

136.36   Della Street] Secretary to fiction, radio, TV, and film detective Perry Mason.

137.36   *Winterreise*] German: Winter Journey, a songcycle (1824) by Franz Schubert.

137.38   Lotte Lehmann] German soprano (1888–1976).

138.3–4   *There Shall Be No Night*] Robert E. Sherwood's Pulitzer Prize–winning play ran on Broadway from April 29 to November 2, 1940.

138.5   the Carlyle] Luxury art deco hotel at 76th Street near Fifth Avenue in Manhattan.

138.32   the *Gita*] The *Bhagavad-Gita*, sacred Hindu text from the first century B.C.E.

143.25–27 Gary Merrill . . . pleasant self.] Gary Merrill (1915–1990) appeared in many films in the 1950s, including *All About Eve* (1950), in which he portrays sympathetic director Bill Sampson opposite Bette Davis's Margo Channing.

143.29 Galatoire's] See note 13.24.

144.36 Doukhobors] Sect of austere Christians that broke away from the Russian Orthodox Church in the eighteenth century.

149.20 Zion] Term for Jerusalem in the Hebrew Bible.

151.29–32 Tillie the Toiler . . . by Whipple.] *Tillie the Toiler*, a comic strip created in 1921 by Russell Westover (1886–1966), revolved around Tillie, a stylish young workingwoman, and her dealings with men, including her coworkers Mac and Mr. Whipple.

152.5 Rory] See notes 82.17–26, 97.1, and 98.14.

152.21–22 Scarlett enjoyed . . . Rhett's return] See chapter LVI in Margaret Mitchell's *Gone With the Wind* (1936), a novel foisted on Percy by "Uncle Will" Percy.

154.7 the Century of Progress] Title of the 1933–34 Chicago World's Fair, celebrating the city's centennial.

154.8 the World Series.] The Chicago Cubs played the Detroit Tigers in the 1935 World Series and hosted three games at Wrigley Field. Detroit won the series, 4–2.

154.24–25 Shiloh and the Wilderness and Vicksburg and Atlanta] Sites of Civil War battles in Tennessee, Virginia, Mississippi, and Georgia, respectively.

155.12–13 the pool where Tarzan-Johnnie-Weissmuller used to swim] The American freestyle swimmer Johnnie Weissmuller (1904–1984) trained at the Illinois Athletic Club on Michigan Avenue in Chicago; after winning five Olympic gold medals he went into show business, and played the title character in the Tarzan movies of the 1930s and 1940s.

155.19–20 tableau of Stone Age Man] Dioramas at Chicago's Field Museum of Natural History, removed in the late 1980s for their many historical inaccuracies.

158.5–6 Ozzie and Harriet] Ozzie and Harriet Nelson, a real-life married couple who starred in the television sitcom *The Adventures of Ozzie and Harriet*, which ran on ABC, 1952–66.

158.27 the DSC] The Distinguished Service Cross, awarded for extraordinary heroism in combat with an armed enemy force.

158.31 old Pete Longstreet] Nickname for Confederate lieutenant general James Longstreet (1821–1904).

158.36–37 Audie Murphy . . . a hero.] American actor and singer Audie

Murphy (1925–1971) was among the most highly decorated U.S. soldiers of World War II; he reprised his exploits in the memoir *To Hell and Back* (1949) and a 1955 film adaptation of the same name in which he portrayed himself.

159.19   Veronica Lake] American actress (1922–1973) known for femme fatale roles in the 1940s.

160.35–36   way down yonder in New Orleans?"] Allusion to "Way Down Yonder in New Orleans," a 1922 song featured in many recordings, among those by Al Jolson and the Andrews Sisters (1950), Freddie Cannon (1960), and Bing Crosby and Louis Armstrong (1960).

161.5   the Loop] Area of downtown Chicago encircled first by a cable-car line and then by elevated train tracks ("the El").

161.7–9   William Powell and George Brent and Patsy Kelly and Charley Chase] William Powell (1892–1994), actor who played Dashiell Hammett's detective Nick Charles in the 1934 film adaptation of *The Thin Man* and four sequels, and also starred in films such as *The Great Ziegfeld* (1936) and *My Man Godfrey* (1936). George Brent (1904–1979), Irish American actor who appeared in numerous films in the 1930s and '40s, including *Charlie Chan Carries On* (1931), the Rin-Tin-Tin serial *The Lightning Warrior* (1931), and *The Spiral Staircase* (1946). Patsy Kelly (1910–1981), American comedic actress who appeared in many shorts of the 1930s. Charley Chase (1893–1940), American actor who starred in shorts in the 1930s and '40s, and also directed and produced the shorts including those for The Three Stooges.

161.10–14   *The Young Philadelphians*. . . . his ideals.] The 1959 melodrama revolves around a group of friends and their overlapping romances, and stars Paul Newman (1925–2008) as a calculating attorney and the film's narrator.

162.35   Vieux Carré.] French: Old Square; used here colloquially to refer to the French Quarter.

163.17–18   *The Charterhouse of Parma*] Novel (1839) by French writer Stendhal (1783–1842).

168.8   as erect . . . the Black Prince] Edward the Black Prince (1330–1376), prince of Wales, knight and duke of Cornwall, was renowned for his military prowess and chivalry during the Hundred Years' War.

170.18   Laodiceans] See Revelation 3:14–22.

172.4   "R-r-r-ramonez chiminée du haut en bas!"] Creole song based on street calls of chimney sweepers: Sweep the chimney from top to bottom.

172.7   the *Crito*] Socratic dialogue by Plato in which the imprisoned Socrates says he will forfeit his life before compromising himself ethically.

172.10   *ramoneur*] French: chimney sweep.

173.13   Chef Menteur] See note 11.12.

174.38 "The Lord of Misrule] Rex, King of Carnival, traditionally chosen from among the elite businessmen of New Orleans. The Lord of Misrule shares his power with an annually anointed queen.

175.15–16 Old confederate Marlon Brando—] Brando (1924–2004) starred as Stanley Kowalski in *A Streetcar Named Desire* (1951), set in the Faubourg Marigny neighborhood of New Orleans.

175.24 Petrouchka] Ballet (1911) by Russian composer Igor Stravinsky (1882–1971).

175.30 Pat O'Brien's."] Bar and restaurant on St. Peter Street in the French Quarter, established 1933.

177.37–38 Archie Moore mustache] American boxer Archie Moore (1913–1998), world light heavyweight champion from December 1952 to May 1962, had a pencil-thin mustache.

180.2 my thirtieth year to heaven, as the poet called it.] Allusion to "Poem in October" (1945) by Welsh poet Dylan Thomas (1914–1953), which begins: "It was my thirtieth year to heaven."

180.28–30 the great Danish philosopher . . . the edifying.] Allusion to Søren Kierkegaard's *Edifying Discourses* (also translated as *Upbuilding Discourses*).

183.1 "When Our Lord . . . the last day] See John 6:35–51.

THE LAST GENTLEMAN

186.1 FOR BUNT] Mary Bernice "Bunt" Townsend Percy (1921–2012), Percy's wife. The couple married on November 7, 1946, at First Baptist Church in New Orleans.

187.1–2 *If a man . . . Either/Or*] From "The Rotation Method," in volume 1 of Soren Kierkegaard's *Either/Or* (1843).

187.3–11 . . . *We know now . . . The End of the Modern World*] Italian German theologian Romano Guardini (1885–1968) was a Catholic priest; *Das Ende der Neuzeit* (1950) appeared in an English translation as *The End of the Modern World* (1956).

189.7 the Great Meadow] Two of Central Park's largest grassy expanses are the Great Lawn and the Sheep Meadow.

190.24 Stuka] The "Stuka" (from *Sturzkampfflugzeug*), a German dive-bomber designed to give close support to ground troops, was used in the Spanish Civil War and World War II.

191.16–17 sad yellow 1901 concrete] 1901 is the section of the New York building code that sets the standards for concrete.

191.31–32   *Meet me . . . in St. Louis*] Allusion to the MGM movie musical *Meet Me in St. Louis* (1944), starring Judy Garland.

192.14–21   *Some say . . . thee resort.*] From Shakespeare's sonnet XCVI, lines 1–4.

193.5–6   the Y.M.C.A. . . . his room] The West Side YMCA, at 67th Street and Central Park West, made rooms available to men at a low rate; Percy lived at the Y when he arrived in New York to attend Columbia University's College of Physicians and Surgeons.

193.8   the Val-Pak] Wardrobe bag.

195.2–3   like an immigrant's son in Passaic] Town in New Jersey, west of Manhattan, with a sizable Eastern European immigrant population.

196.28–30   A German physician once remarked . . . *Lücken* or gaps.] Sigmund Freud is the "German" (Austrian) physician. See especially his *Interpretation of Dreams* (1899).

199.2   Schiller's *Die Räuber*] *The Robbers* (1781), the first dramatic work by Friedrich Schiller (1759–1805).

200.16   the Hit Parade] *Your Hit Parade*, an American musical variety show that ran on radio, 1935–53, and on television, 1950–59.

200.39–201.2   Shenandoah Valley . . . Stonewall Jackson.] During his campaign in the Shenandoah Valley, May 8–June 9, 1862, Confederate lieutenant general Thomas (Stonewall) Jackson (1824–1863) defeated three different Union commands in five battles and succeeded in keeping nearly 60,000 Union troops from advancing on Richmond.

203.1   the Carlyle] See note 138.5.

204.19–20   shadowy knoll . . . Mad Anthony Wayne.] During the Revolutionary War, "Mad" Anthony Wayne's Continentals captured the steep Hudson River promontory Stony Point, fortified by the British, on July 16, 1779.

205.24   hurricane Donna.] Hurricane that caused extensive damage from the Lesser Antilles to New England in September 1960.

205.25   Auchincloss] Prominent northeastern family of Scottish origin.

207.30–32   Mr. Magoo . . . the abyss.] The misadventures of cartoon character Mr. Magoo, created in 1949 by United Productions of America (UPA), are the result of his extreme nearsightedness.

208.27–29   let one stand . . . a Velázquez . . . dry museum.] Diego Velázquez (1599–1660) was a Spanish court painter; a number of his works are on display in the Metropolitan Museum of Art.

209.24–25   They knelt . . . Count Orgaz.] Allusion to *The Burial of the Count of Orgaz* (1586), a painting by El Greco.

220.18   Jodrell Bank] Radio astronomy laboratory, established in Cheshire, England, in 1945.

221.24–27   *From you . . . with him.*] From Shakespeare's sonnet XCVIII, lines 1–4.

222.3   Nedick's] A fast-food restaurant chain founded in New York in 1913, with many outlets around the city. The chain closed in 1981.

231.16   "Tractatus Log—"] *Tractatus Logico-Philosophicus* (1921) by Austrian philosopher Ludwig Wittgenstein (1889–1951). It concerns the limits of science and the relationship between logic and reality.

232.31   Monteagle]   Town in southern Tennessee.

232.32   Mentone] Town in northeastern Alabama, on Lookout Mountain.

236.13   Tavern-on-the-Green.] Restaurant in Central Park.

240.14   the "Bavarian Illuminati,"] Originally, a secret society of freethinkers founded in 1776 and thought by many at the time to have infiltrated Masonic organizations throughout Europe.

240.18–19   story of Judah P. Benjamin and John Slidell] Benjamin (1811–1884), the Confederate secretary of state, worked with Confederate foreign diplomat John Slidell (1793–1871) in unsuccessful efforts to gain official recognition of the Confederacy by France. On November 8, 1861, Slidell was one of two Confederate diplomats en route to Britain and France who were removed from the British mail packet *Trent* by the U.S. Navy after the vessel was intercepted, nearly setting off an Anglo-American war.

244.30   country matters.] *Hamlet*, III.ii.116.

245.10   middleweight at Princeton] See the first sentence in Ernest Hemingway's *The Sun Also Rises* (1926).

248.9   George Gipp . . . Notre Dame stadium.] Allusion to the climactic scene in *Knute Rockne, All American* (1940), a film dramatization of the career of the legendary University of Notre Dame football coach, with Ronald Reagan playing halfback George Gipp, who died of pneumonia shortly after a triumphant senior season.

248.26   sideways Lippo Lippi look] Fra Filippo Lippi (c. 1406–1469), also known as Lippo Lippi, was a Florentine artist. His "Coronation of the Virgin" incorporates a portrait of himself, as a kneeling monk, looking sideways at the viewer.

248.33   Merita cake] Brand of breads and cakes once common in the southeastern United States.

261.4–5 New Lots Avenue . . . Far Rockaway.] Last stops on two New York City subway lines, one in Brooklyn and the other in Queens, both near the shore of the Long Island Sound.

265.2 John von Neumann's *Theory of Games*—'"] *Theory of Games and Economic Behavior* (1944) by mathematician John van Neumann and economist Oskar Morgenstern.

265.11–12 the lance corporal in *Der Zauberberg.*] Hans Castorp, the protagonist of Thomas Mann's *The Magic Mountain* (1924), who volunteers for military service at the novel's conclusion.

265.36 "Ulysses."] Allusion to roaming protagonist of Homer's *Odyssey.*

268.26–29 quotation from Montaigne . . . the dozens.] Montaigne, "Apology for Raimond Sebond," *Essays* (1603).

269.6 the Philco] A phonograph that played 78 RPM records.

269.24 The Great Horn Theme] From the fourth movement of Brahms's Symphony No. 1 (1876).

270.17 BMT subway.] Brooklyn–Manhattan Transit Corporation lines; here, the Fifth Avenue–59th Street station.

272.19 Huichol Indians.] Indigenous people of Mexico.

273.22 Cuernavaca] City in Mexico, forty miles south of Mexico City.

275.21–23 sniper's den . . . the battle] On the second day of fighting at the Civil War battle of Gettysburg, July 1–3, 1863, Little Round Top was successfully defended by Union troops against a Confederate assault. Photographer Mathew Brady (c. 1823–1896) arrived at Gettysburg two weeks after fighting ended.

276.10 the old Northern Pacific yin-yang symbol] Seen on trains of the Northern Pacific Railroad, operating from Minnesota to Washington state.

278.6–8 as guttural . . . an Alabama voice as Tallulah Bankhead.] American actress Tallulah Bankhead (1902–1968) was born in Huntsville, Alabama.

279.14–15 the siege of Richmond and later of Petersburg.] Series of Civil War battles fought around Petersburg, Virginia, from June 9, 1864, to March 25, 1865.

279.22 the Crater."] On July 30, 1864, Union engineers exploded a mine beneath Confederate defenses at Petersburg, creating a crater into which Union soldiers rushed, with catastrophic consequences.

282.2–3 crippled and overcame it . . . like Glenn Cunningham] As a child, American middle-distance runner Glenn Cunningham (1909–1988) suffered serious burns to his legs in a schoolhouse fire.

282.12   Huntley–Brinkley] *The Huntley–Brinkley Report*, a news program named for its hosts, aired for fourteen years on NBC beginning in 1956.

282.37   Zuñi] Pueblo peoples from the Zuni River valley.

282.40   Ahaiyute myths.] Zuni tales featuring supernatural twins who figure as helpers to the Pueblo peoples.

288.22–23   Lucky Lindy's . . . in 1928.] American pilot Charles Lindbergh (1902–1974), nicknamed "Lucky Lindy," made his historic solo flight across the Atlantic, May 20–21, 1927. An eleven-year-old Percy shook hands with Lindbergh when Lindbergh visited Birmingham in 1927.

290.27   Fruehauf trailer.] Truck trailer manufactured by Fruehauf Trailer Corporation, 1918–89.

297.36   Rooney Lee . . . sojourn in the North] W.H.F. "Rooney" Lee (1837–1891), a son of Robert E. Lee and a major general in the Confederate Army, attended Harvard University prior to the Civil War.

299.16–17   reeling . . . Seven Days.] During the Seven Days' Battles outside Richmond (June 25, 1862–July 1, 1862), in which Rooney Lee participated, Confederate forces succeeded in driving the Army of the Potomac away from the eastern approaches to the city and forced it to retreat into a defensive position along the James River; however, the tactical Confederate victory was costly, with nearly 3,500 killed and 15,758 wounded.

300.29   Fiesole to Levittown,"] Fiesole is an ancient hilltop town outside of Florence, Italy. Levittown, Pennsylvania, outside Philadelphia, is the second of the prefabricated suburban developments of that name, built for returning World War II veterans.

301.24–25   *Les Caves du Vatican.*] *The Vatican Cellars* (1914), novel by French writer André Gide (1869–1951).

301.29–30   like Descartes among the Burghers of Amsterdam] French philosopher René Descartes (1596–1650) left his native France to settle in the Netherlands, where he composed his major works.

302.4   a cup of Duz.] Duz was a popular powdered soap—"Duz does Everything!"—produced by Procter and Gamble, 1929–80.

302.33   a regular La Pasionaria of the suburbs.] Isidora Dolores Ibárruri Gómez (1895–1989), known as *la Pasionaria* ("the Passionflower"), was a Communist and a Spanish Republican politician of the Spanish Civil War (1936–39), during which she delivered a series of fiery speeches.

309.21   an Esso map] While the Esso name remains common outside the United States, it was replaced in the States by the Exxon brand in 1972 after the company bought Humble Oil. Gas stations once offered free maps.

310.3–4   a battlefield. . . . Malvern Hill] The Union Army commanded by
Major General George B. McClellan (1826–1885) repulsed repeated Confeder-
ate attacks at Malvern Hill, Virginia, on July 1, 1862. The battle of Malvern
Hill was the last of the Seven Days' Battles.

311.14   Dynaflow transmission.] Automatic transmission built by General
Motors for its Buick cars, 1947–63.

312.36–37   doleful woods of Spotsylvania . . . plexiglass of Sheboygan.] The
Wilderness, a dense second-growth forest of scrub oak, pine, and underbrush in Spotsylvania County, Virginia, was the scene of two major Civil War
battles: the battle of Chancellorsville, May 1–4, 1863, in which Lee succeeded
in driving the Union Army back across the Rappahannock River, and the
battle of the Wilderness, in which Lee attacked the Union Army as it moved
south through the woods, May 5–6, 1864, but failed to prevent Grant from
continuing his southward advance toward Spotsylvania Court House. The
suggestion is that the camper was built in Sheboygan, Wisconsin.

317.34   Ulysses] See note 265.36.

318.4   Sir Tristram] Hero in a number of chivalric romances based on Celtic
legend, including Gottfried von Strassburg's *Tristan* (c. 1211–15), composed
in Middle High German, and Sir Thomas Malory's *Le Morte d'Arthur* (1485).

325.33   General Oglethorpe.] James Edward Oglethorpe (1696–1785), British
soldier, member of Parliament, and founder of the colony of Georgia.

327.4   ATO waltz at Mercer?"] Song for the chapter of the Alpha Theta
Omega sorority at Mercer University in Macon, Georgia.

327.34   Henry Grady] American journalist, orator, and civic worker (1850–
1889) who, after the conclusion of the Civil War, popularized the idea of a
"New South" based on industrial development.

329.35   *The Murder of Roger Ackroyd*] A mystery novel (1926) by British
writer Agatha Christie.

330.19–20   Mary Roberts Rinehart] Prolific American mystery writer
(1876–1958).

330.33   Bicycle cards] American brand of playing cards sold since 1895.

332.22   Hallicrafter] Brand of radios manufactured in Chicago, 1932–75.

336.1   Libman] Emmanuel Libman (1872–1946), bacteriologist and pathologist associated with Mount Sinai Hospital and Columbia University in New
York City.

339.7   Dizzy Dean] Hall of Fame baseball pitcher (1910–1974) for the St.
Louis Cardinals, 1932–37, and the Chicago Cubs, 1938–41.

340.10   Bobby Jones] American amateur golfer (1902–1971) who dominated the sport in the 1920s. During Percy's childhood, the Percy family met Jones in Birmingham, Alabama.

341.8–9   Roman structure . . . in honor of Juno] The temple of Jupiter, with Corinthian order, dedicated in 75 C.E.

346.27–28   swanky bars . . . Richard Barthelmess and William Powell] Barthelmess (1895–1963) and Powell (1892–1984), American movie actors, were close friends; with actor Ronald Colman, they were known as the "Three Musketeers."

353.13   Choate man.] A graduate of the Choate School for boys, in Wallingford, Connecticut. John F. Kennedy was a graduate of Choate. In 1974 Choate merged with the all-girls Rosemary Hall to form Choate Rosemary Hall.

356.35   D.A.R.] Daughters of the American Revolution, a conservative service organization founded in 1890 for women who are purportedly lineal descendants of persons who aided the cause of American independence.

359.39   Klonsul of the Klan] Attorney for the Ku Klux Klan.

360.13–14   Sister Johnette Mary Vianney."] Val has taken the name of St. John Vianney (1786–1859), French priest known as the Curé d'Ars and revered for his restoring the faithful after the persecution of the Church during the Reign of Terror.

364.7–8   dispatched like Polonius behind the arras] See *Hamlet*, III.iv.1–38.

364.14–17   "See the poem . . . all the rest?"] See Lee Hunt's "Abou Ben Adhem" (1834), which concludes, "And lo! Ben Adhem's name led all the rest."

364.26–27   sentimental Jean Hersholt . . . Judge Lee Cobb] Danish American actor Jean Hersholt (1886–1956) starred in *Heidi* (1938) opposite Shirley Temple as Heidi's hermit grandfather. American actor Lee Cobb (1911–1976) portrayed Judge Garth in the 1960s NBC television series *The Virginian*.

371.27–28   Freeman's *R.E. Lee*] Pulitzer Prize–winning biography of Robert E. Lee by Douglas Southall Freeman, published in four volumes in 1934.

372.25   Frank Gifford] American football player, actor, and sports broadcaster (1930–2015).

375.12   General Kirby Smith's surrender at Shreveport.] Confederate general Edmund Kirby Smith (1824–1893), who commanded Confederate forces west of the Mississippi, surrendered on June 2, 1865, almost two months after Robert E. Lee's surrender at Appomattox Court House on April 9, 1865.

375.22–23   a meeting of the Rothschilds . . . in 1857] To address a transatlantic banking crisis.

378.12 DeMolay] International fraternal organization for young men, founded in Kansas City, Missouri, in 1919.

380.20–21 in Ferrara . . . Lucrezia's husbands . . . been murdered.] Alfonso of Aragon, second husband of Lucrezia Borgia (1480–1590), was murdered in 1500, perhaps by Cesare Borgia, Lucrezia's brother. After Alfonso's death, Borgia married Alfonso d'Este, Duke of Ferrara, her third husband.

380.22–23 Lucrezia Bori . . . St. Bartholomew's Massacre.] Lucrezia Bori (1887–1960) was a Spanish soprano who performed at the Met. While serving as regent for her second son, Catherine de Medici (1519–1589) helped to plan the massacre of Huguenots in Paris on St. Bartholomew's Day, August 24, 1572, an attack that resulted in civil war in France.

384.27 Bobby Jones?] See note 340.10.

389.34 Rock City barns] From 1936 to 1969, sign painter Clark Byers painted "See Rock City" on more than 900 barns in the Southeast and Midwest. The popular tourist attraction is located on Lookout Mountain in Georgia.

390.24 L & N Railroad.] The Louisville & Nashville Railroad, 1850–1982.

392.22 a Russian writer . . . Goncharov] Ivan Goncharov (1812–1891), Russian author whose novels include *Oblomov* (1859) and *The Precipice* (1869).

396.28 *poilu*] French infantryman.

398.3–4 Ben Bernie and Ruth Etting and the Chase & Sanborn hour.] Ben Bernie (1891–1943), a bandleader and radio personality, and Ruth Etting (1896–1978), a singer, were familiar guests on the Chase and Sanborn Hour, a series of American comedy and variety radio shows sponsored by Chase & Sanborn Coffee, 1929–48.

398.21–22 Helen Wills . . . 'Little Miss Poker Face.'] Wills (1905–1998), an American tennis player who won thirty-one Grand Slam titles during her career, was nicknamed "Little Miss Poker Face" by the press for her phlegmatic presence on the court.

399.30–31 Rheims cathedral] Notre Dame de Reims, or Reims Cathedral, a High Gothic cathedral in the French city of the same name.

401.9 the *Commercial Appeal*] Memphis daily newspaper.

401.37 Garibaldi] Giuseppe Garibaldi (1807–1882), Italian revolutionary.

404.16 Mary Nestor] Tom Swift's girlfriend in the Tom Swift series, children's adventure novels created by Edward Stratemeyer (1863–1930) and continued by his fiction syndicate.

405.6 Rooney Lee.] See notes 297.36 and 299.16–17.

407.11 a Deke from Vanderbilt] Member of Delta Kappa Epsilon (DKE) at Vanderbilt University in Nashville, Tennessee.

411.26   *The Art of Loving*] Popular book (1956) by Erich Fromm (1900–1980), German psychoanalyst who settled in the U.S. in 1934.

416.9   Esso map] See note 309.21.

417.18–19   Whitehead's displacement of the Real] In *Process and Reality* (1929), English philosopher Alfred North Whitehead (1861–1947) proposed that what is commonly understood as "reality" is better understood as a concatenation of various processes continually interacting with one another.

421.32   G. E. Gold Medallion homes.] Beginning in 1957, as part of a nation-wide campaign to promote the benefits of electric power, General Electric and other electric companies conferred "Medallion" status on all-electric new homes.

427.5   *zwischen die Beinen*.] German: between the legs.

432.8   Kahlil Gibran] Lebanese-born American author (1883–1931) whose works include the best-selling book *The Prophet* (1923), a sequence of lyrical parables.

433.14   Pareto] Vilfredo Pareto (1848–1923), Italian economist and sociologist who laid the foundations for modern welfare economics.

433.15–16   John Dewey] American philosopher and education reformer (1859–1952).

434.13–15   the five proofs of God's existence . . . difference between a sub-stance and an accident.] In the writings of St. Thomas Aquinas (1225–1274), Dominican friar and Catholic philosopher.

434.37   like Adam on the First Day.] See Genesis 2:19.

436.38–437.1   Hudson Supersix] Automobile manufactured by the Hudson Motor Company, 1916–1951.

437.10   I.C.] Illinois Central Railroad.

437.15   admired Pericles more than Abraham] Pericles (c. 495–429 B.C.E.), an Athenian statesmen and military strategist. Abraham, the first of the Hebrew patriarchs, revered by Judaism, Christianity, and Islam.

439.35   Scandalous Thing] Reference to "the scandal of the Incarnation," as characterized by St. Irenaeus of Lyon, a second-century Christian theologian.

441.11   WWL] See note 117.40.

441.29–33   *for the world . . . for pain*—] From the final stanza of "Dover Beach" (1867) by English poet and critic Matthew Arnold (1822–1888).

443.26   Cary Middlecoff] American professional golfer (1921–1998) who competed on the PGA Tour, 1945–67.

444.8   Nicklaus and Palmer.] American professional golfers Jack Nicklaus (b. 1940) and Arnold Palmer (1929–2016).

452.9   Pelleas] Knight of Arthurian legend.

455.39–456.3   Theard Street . . . Milliken Bend] The names of streets in Covington, Louisiana, the town where Percy lived from the 1950s to his death in 1990, and where he wrote *The Last Gentleman*.

457.11   "Strike It Rich"] A game show on CBS television that featured financially needy contestants, 1951–58.

457.12   *Race and Reason*] Book (1961) by Carleton Putnam that defends racial segregation.

457.14   Bill Cullen.] American television personality (1920–1990) who was the original host of *The Price Is Right*, 1956–65.

459.21   the Great Horn Theme] See note 269.24.

461.28   Plattsburg issue] Prior to the U.S. entry into World War I, a series of summer military training camps for young American civilians was based in Plattsburg, New York.

461.29   Kaiser bill helmets] Kaiser Wilhelm II, the last German emperor, who abdicated in November 1918 at the end of World War I, was nicknamed "Kaiser Bill" in the English-speaking press; in drawings and caricatures he was often depicted wearing a spiked helmet.

463.32   Admiral Foote's] Andrew Hull Foote (1806–1863), naval officer who helped secure Union forces to capture Forts Henry and Donelson.

464.22   Heligoland] Island off North Sea coast of Germany.

464.23–24   when the bridge at Vicksburg was built] Construction was completed in 1930.

466.17   De Soto] Automobile marque manufactured by the Chrysler Corporation, 1928–61.

467.17   Goofy] Cartoon character—an anthropomorphic dog—created by the Walt Disney Corporation.

468.6   old round-eyed Zenith] Round-screen televisions manufactured by Zenith in the 1940s and '50s.

471.5   *pari passu*] Latin: without partiality.

471.21   Pandora's Box] In Greek mythology, Pandora, prompted by curiosity, opened a box or container entrusted to her husband, releasing all the ills of the world.

471.30–33   post-Christian . . . post-memory of Cx] In the 1960s, theologians

Gabriel Vahanian, Thomas Altizer, William Hamilton, and others proposed that Europe had become post-Christian; "Cx" is shorthand for "Christ."

472.14–16   Captain Kangaroo . . . and Mr. Greenjeans] Captain Kangaroo and Mister Greenjeans were the main characters in *Captain Kangaroo*, a children's television show that aired on CBS for nearly three decades beginning in 1955.

474.35   J.A.M.A.] *Journal of the American Medical Association.*

475.5–7   the Southwest which attracted Doc Holliday and Robert Oppenheimer] Holliday (1851–1887), a notorious gambler and gunfighter, participated in the gunfight at the O.K. Corral on October 26, 1881, in Tombstone, Arizona Territory; Oppenheimer (1904–1967), an American theoretical physicist, led the Los Alamos Laboratory in New Mexico where the atomic bomb was developed beginning in 1943.

475.21   10,000 devils . . . St. Anthony] In the legend of St. Anthony, monk and Desert Father in Egypt in the third and early fourth centuries, Anthony is tormented by devils.

475.33   Gretel-lost-in-the-woods] In *Grimm's Fairy Tales*, Hansel and Gretel, brother and sister, get lost in the woods and wind up in the clutches of a witch who lives in a house of gingerbread, cake, and candy.

476.14   Senator Oscar W. Underwood] Alabama politician (1862–1929) who ran for president in 1912 and 1924.

477.33   Humble station] Humble gas stations were rebranded as Exxon stations beginning in 1972. Humble Oil and Refining Co. existed as an independent company until September 1959.

479.14   La Fonda] Historic adobe hotel in downtown Sante Fe, New Mexico.

479.27   *Ich warte.*] German: I'm waiting.

480.11   Rancho la Merced] Wildlife preserve in Costa Rica.

482.14   Catherine wheel] Also known as a pinwheel, a type of firework.

482.32–37   the Battle of Valverde . . . to California] The Civil War battle of Valverde was fought along the Rio Grande, in New Mexico Territory, on February 20–21, 1862. It was a costly victory for Confederate general Henry Sibley, who had originally intended to march his troops westward from New Mexico to California.

483.13   *sub specie aeternitatis*] Latin: under the aspect of eternity.

487.2–3   O.K. Corral and Boot Hill] Boot Hill Cemetery in Tombstone, Arizona, is the burial place of outlaws Billy Clanton, Frank McLaury, and Tom McLaury, killed in the gunfight at the O.K. Corral on October 26, 1881.

487.34   Queen Bess.] Elizabeth I (1533–1603), queen of England and Ireland.

489.32 Walter Reed.] U.S. Army physician (1851–1902) who proved that yellow fever was transmitted by mosquitos.

490.27 Lucky Lindy] See note 288.22–23.

492.3 Ben Gunn] Marooned sailor in Robert Louis Stevenson's *Treasure Island* (1883).

495.8–9 Powder Puff Derby] An annual transcontinental air race for female pilots, 1944–77.

495.9 Lockheed P-38] Twin-engine fighter and fighter-bomber used by the U.S. Army Air Force during World War II.

498.5–9 Wittgenstein? . . . announced the dictum . . . keep silent.] In his *Tractatus Logico-Philosophicus* (1921).

499.36–37 a K.C. pamphlet] Publication issued by the Knights of Columbus, a Catholic fraternal organization.

499.39 Rotarian."] Member of Rotary International, a fraternal organization of service clubs for businessmen and professionals founded in 1905.

LOVE IN THE RUINS

528.1 *FOR SHELBY FOOTE*] American novelist and historian (1916–2005) who was a close friend of Percy's since their boyhood in Greenville, Mississippi.

532.13 Howard Johnson motel] See note 104.9.

532.28–29 Principalities and powers . . . high places.] See Ephesians 6:12: "For we wrestle not against flesh and blood, but against principalities, against powers, against the rulers of the darkness of this world, against wickedness in high places."

533.34–533.38 I believe . . . the world.] Cf. the Nicene Creed.

534.5–7 A man, wrote John . . . a liar.] 1 John 2:4.

535.28–29 Homer's first words . . . the anger of Achilles,"] In the *Iliad*.

535.29–31 Freud's last words . . . on their account"?] From the last sentence of the final lecture in Freud's series on psychoanalytic theory. See *New Introductory Lectures on Psycho-Analysis* (1933).

536.20 A & P supermarket.] American grocery chain, 1859–2015.

536.25–27 *Is it the truth? . . . better friendships?*] First three tenets of the Four-Way Test, a guide to ethical behavior promoted by Rotary International, a service organization founded in Chicago in 1905.

538.2–3 Physician, heal thyself. . . .] Luke 4:23.

538.13   The prophet Hosea . . . bad home life] In the deuterocanonical (apoc-
ryphal) Book of Hosea, the titular author's broken marriage and family life
symbolizes the broken covenant between God and the tribes of Israel.

538.25   island of Cozumel] In the Caribbean, off the coast of Mexico.

538.37   Bantus] In a letter to Percy, Thomas Merton makes reference to *La
philosophie bantoe* (1961) by Fr. Placidus Temples.

539.12–14   the Valley Forge Academy . . . Negroes out.] Military and
Christian academies, as private institutions, were not bound by the Supreme
Court's 1955 order to desegregate public schools with "all deliberate speed."

540.2   like King David before the Ark.] See 2 Samuel 6: David, king of Israel,
brings the ark of the covenant to Jerusalem, and dances before it.

540.5–6   *Wonderful World of Color*] Walt Disney television series that aired
on NBC, 1961–69.

540.9–10   "Finch 'han dal vino" from *Don Giovanni*] Aria for baritone from
Act I of Mozart's opera (1787).

540.10–11   "Holy God We Praise Thy Name,"] Traditional Catholic hymn.

540.28–29   the Dvořák concerto] Dvořák's Cello Concerto in B minor
(1895).

541.31   the Little Sisters of the Poor.] Catholic order of religious women
founded in France in 1839 to care for the needy elderly.

543.16–18   Here everyone . . . liberal and conservative.] See Galatians 3:28:
"There is neither Jew nor Greek, neither bond nor free . . . for ye all are one
in Christ Jesus."

544.11   Rhodesia] Rhodesia (now Zimbabwe) was a British colonial state in
southern Africa. Named for English imperialist Cecil Rhodes, the country
declared itself independent in 1965, with a minority white government and
significant repression of the Black population. Civil war ensued, and the
minority government was eventually overthrown in 1979.

544.14   the Knothead Party] Cf. the Know-Nothings, a nativist party in
nineteenth-century America.

544.18   CCCP] Russian abbreviation for the Union of Soviet Socialist
Republics (USSR).

545.1   The center did not hold.] See the first stanza of W. B. Yeats's "The
Second Coming" (1920). "The Center Did Not Hold" was one of the titles
Percy considered for *Love in the Ruins.*

545.12–13   *The Sound of Music, Flubber,* and *Ice Capades of 1981*] *The Sound of
Music* (1965), directed by Robert Wise and starring Julie Andrews as Maria
von Trapp, is an adaptation of Rogers and Hammerstein's stage musical. *The*

Absent Minded Professor (1961) and its sequel, *Son of Flubber* (1963), star Fred MacMurray as a college professor who creates an antigravity substance called "flubber." *Ice Capades of 1981* is a film of Percy's invention.

545.24–26 Harold Robbins . . . Jacqueline Susann . . . Gore Vidal] Robbins (1916–1997), a popular American novelist who dominated the best-seller lists in the 1950s, '60s, and '70s. Susann (1918–1974), an American actress and the author of numerous best-selling novels, including *Valley of the Dolls* (1966). Vidal (1925–2012), an American novelist and essayist, frequently at odds with famous contemporaries William F. Buckley Jr. and Norman Mailer.

545.35 Birchers] Members of the John Birch Society, an extreme right-wing political organization founded in Indiana in 1958 by candy manufacturer Robert Welch (1899–1985) and named after John Birch (1918–1945), an American intelligence officer killed by the Chinese Communists at the end of World War II.

545.36 the ACLU.] American Civil Liberties Union, advocacy group associated with liberal causes.

546.1 war in Ecuador] Percy's invention, suggesting parallels with the U.S. war in Vietnam, still ongoing in 1971 when *Love in the Ruins* was published.

548.8–11 Anglo-Saxon Catholics . . . Elizabeth got after them] After the Reformation, Elizabeth I used violence, compulsion, and other means to force Catholic "recusants" to attend Anglican services.

548.11–12 in Maryland . . . kicked them out.] Maryland, originally a colony named for Queen Maria Henrietta, Catholic spouse of Charles I, was settled by substantial numbers of Catholics in flight from religious persecution in England. In the decades following the passage of the Maryland Toleration Act in 1649, Protestants seized power and passed repressive, anti-Catholic measures.

548.12 Sir Thomas More] Lord High Chancellor of England under Henry VIII, statesman, and author (1478–1535) executed for refusing to recognize Henry as head of the Church of England and the annulment of his marriage to Catherine of Aragon. More was canonized by Pope Pius XI in 1935.

548.35–36 Beauregard next to . . . Presbyterian Stonewall Jackson] Confederate general Pierre Gustave Toutant-Beauregard (1818–1893) was a Catholic Creole.

548.37–38 third-degree Knight of Columbus] The Catholic fraternal organization, founded in Connecticut in 1882, has four degrees of membership, the highest of which is Knighthood.

549.26 the Catholic Einsteins, Salks, Oppenheimers?] Albert Einstein, Jonas Salk, and Robert J. Oppenheimer, scientists celebrated in postwar America, were Jewish.

550.21–22   Barbara Walters . . . *Today* show.] Broadcast journalist Barbara Walters (1929–2022) appeared on NBC's *Today* show in various roles, 1962–76.

550.29   Toynbee . . . speaks of the Return] In *The Growth of Civilizations* (1934), the third volume of *A Study of History*, by British historian Arnold J. Toynbee (1889–1975).

551.24–25   Oak Ridge or Los Alamos] Oak Ridge, Tennessee, and Los Alamos, New Mexico, were the two sites of the Manhattan Project, the joint effort of the U.S., Canada, and Great Britain to produce an atomic bomb, powered by stores of radioactive uranium and plutonium.

551.33–35   John Locke who said . . . the two?] In *An Essay Concerning Human Understanding* (1689), Locke defines knowledge as the "perception of the connection and agreement, or disagreement and repugnancy, of any of our ideas."

552.33   Brodmann Area 32] German neurologist Korbinian Brodmann (1868–1918) mapped the cerebral cortex, identifying fifty-two numbered regions.

553.3   *J.A.M.A.*] See note 474.35.

554.15–16   Edward Jenner's . . . the great pox.] Jenner (1749–1823), an English physician, developed the world's first vaccine, for treatment against smallpox.

556.9–10   Lion, Kiwanian, 33rd-degree Mason] Men's fraternal service organizations.

560.10   "angelism,"] The belief, often disparaged by Christian theologians, that humans are akin to angels, purely spiritual beings, and therefore not prone to sin.

567.16   Battle above the Clouds] Civil War battle, also known as the battle of Lookout Mountain, fought in heavy mist and rain on November 24, 1863, when Union troops under Major General Joseph Hooker (1814–1879) drove Confederate forces from much of Lookout Mountain outside of Chattanooga, Tennessee.

569.23–24   GM's famous Charley Kettering] Charles Franklin Kettering (1876–1958) was the head of research at General Motors, 1920–47. He developed GM's air-cooled engine.

569.39   Billy Graham] William Franklin Graham (1918–2018), the leading Protestant revivalist in postwar America.

570.22   Fletcher Christian . . . Pitcairn] Christian led the mutiny on the HMS *Bounty* in 1789, afterward settling with some of the mutineers and a dozen Tahitian women on Pitcairn Island in the southern Pacific Ocean.

570.33–34   Stedmann's *History of World War I*.] The book and author are Percy's own invention.

571.18   Jeb Stuart] Confederate lieutenant general J.E.B. Stuart (1833–1864), Robert E. Lee's cavalry commander.

571.40   Gene Sarazen] American professional golfer (1902–1999), one of only a handful of golfers to win all major championships.

572.1–2   Phoebus Apollo or Sir Lancelot] In Greek mythology, Apollo is the god of light. In the Arthurian legends, Sir Lancelot is one of the knights of the Round Table, bearing great love for Queen Guinevere.

572.6–7   Dick Taylor . . . the Red River campaign.] During the Red River Campaign in the Trans-Mississippi theater, Confederate major general Richard Taylor (1826–1879), a son of President Zachary Taylor, defended the Red River Valley against superior Union forces under the command of Major General Nathaniel Prentiss, defeating him at the battle of Mansfield, April 8, 1864, and the battle of Pleasant Hill, April 9, 1864.

572.23   Erle Stanley Gardner's . . . *The Case of the Velvet Claws*] Mystery novel (1933) featuring detective Perry Mason.

572.31   Pocahontas] Powhatan Indian woman (1596–1617) who intervened to spare the captive Jamestown leader, John Smith, and subsequently converted to Christianity, marrying colonist John Rolfe.

573.39   Holyoke vowels.] Mount Holyoke is a private liberal arts women's college in South Hadley, Massachusetts.

579.22–23   Ecuador and Bosnia-Herzegovina] The Ecuadorians fought a civil war, 1913–16; ethnic and religious divisions among the people of Bosnia-Herzegovina, a province of the Austro-Hungarian Empire, sparked a conflict that became World War I. See also note 546.1.

583.18   Tang] Powdered "space-age" drink that became popular after NASA chose it for the Gemini project in 1962.

583.21   the First Air Cav] The 1st Cavalry Division of the U.S. Army, whose actions figured prominently in the U.S. war in Vietnam.

583.27–29   Rikki-Tikki-Tavi . . . the bricks.] "Rikki-Tikki-Tavi" is a story in Rudyard Kipling's *The Jungle Book* (1894).

584.5   Brownie model.] Simple cardboard box camera that was produced by Eastman Kodak beginning in 1900.

585.21–23   *Siddhartha / Atlas Shrugged / ESP and the New Spirituality*] *Siddhartha* (1922), German Swiss writer Hermann Hesse's novel set in the time of the Buddha, first translated into English in 1951. *Atlas Shrugged* (1957), a novel by American writer and intellectual Ayn Rand. The third book is Percy's invention, its title combining the trending interest in ESP (extra-sensory perception) and the search for a "new spirituality" among many Catholics and mainline Protestants during the 1960s and '70s.

586.26   long-thighed Mercury] In art, Mercury, the Greek messenger god, is often depicted with long legs and wearing a short tunic.

587.8   To the lake isle of Innisfree."] See William Butler Yeats's poem "The Lake Isle of Innisfree" (1888), about the yearning to escape modern society and live a simple rural life.

587.34–35   Build thee more stately mansions, O my soul."] From the final stanza of "The Chambered Nautilus" (1858) by Oliver Wendell Holmes.

588.27–28   Hindoo reverence for life] The principle of *ahimsa* (Sanskrit: avoidance of harm) is found in the *Upanishads* and the *Vedas*, the major Hindu scriptures.

590.19–22   Ramakrishna . . . a bitch."] Ramakrishna Paramahamsa (1836–1886) was a renowned Hindu ascetic (or *fakir*) and mystic; his disciple-once-removed Swami Prabhavananda (1893–1976), based in Hollywood, attracted the writers Aldous Huxley and Christopher Isherwood (the latter was gay).

592.17   a Danish sling] Mid-century modern chair.

592.40   two-eyed Picasso profile.] In Picasso's Cubist portraits, such as *Seated Dora Maar* (1937), the figure's eyes appear to be on the same side of the face.

593.26   Choctaw cannab] Traditionally, some Choctaw rituals have involved the use of cannabis.

593.28–29   Verdun . . . Fort Douaumont?] During World War I, three months after the Germans began their offensive at Verdun, on February 21, 1916, they seized Fort Douaumont, a key French position. French troops temporarily regained control of part of the fort, in late May, but suffered heavy losses from German artillery and were forced to abandon their position. A French counteroffensive finally recaptured the fort on October 24, 1916.

594.6–7   *Don Giovanni* . . . Milton Cross.] Cross (1897–1975), radio announcer and commentator, hosted weekly broadcasts of the Metropolitan Opera, 1931–75; Mozart's *Don Giovanni* (1787) was, and is, a staple of the company's repertory.

595.11   Tara] The plantation at the center of Margaret Mitchell's novel *Gone With the Wind* (1936), the basis for the 1939 film starring Vivien Leigh and Clark Gable.

595.12   Guarnerius cello] The Guarneri family were makers of violins and other stringed instruments in northern Italy in the seventeenth and eighteenth centuries, their instruments prized by modern players.

595.21   the Liberty Lobby.] Political advocacy organization, now defunct, founded in Washington, D.C., in 1958, which produced a daily radio show promoting white nationalism and "America First," anti-Semitic conspiracy theories.

597.15   *Wienerblut*] *Wiener Blut* (1873), a waltz by the Austrian composer Johann Strauss II (1825–1899).

597.16   a Jules Verne gondola] Verne's novel *Five Men in a Balloon* (1863) concerns the protagonists' travels over Africa in a gondola suspended beneath a hot-air balloon.

598.34   N.I.M.H.] The National Institutes for Mental Health, the federal agency devoted to study and treatment of mental disorders.

599.1–2   *Wine, Women, and Song.*] A Strauss waltz (1869).

599.32   Victor Herbert] An Irish-born American composer of operettas and light music (1859–1925).

601.38   *Hills of Home*] Perhaps a reference to "The Holy Hills of Heaven Call Me" (1968), a gospel hit written by Dottie Rambo and recorded by her trio, The Rambos.

610.6   Perry Como's Christmas show] Beginning in 1948, American singer Perry Como (1912–2001) hosted television Christmas specials, which featured seasonal songs known from his recordings.

610.9–10   the Dvořák concerto] See note 540.28–29.

610.17   the *Don Quixote* theme] From *Don Quixote* (1897) by Richard Strauss.

614.30–31   his Santa hood . . . like a Carmelite's] Friars of the Carmelite order, founded in present-day Israel in the thirteenth century, wear hooded brown cloaks.

623.12–13   the Blue-Gray game] Annual all-star college football game, played in Alabama in late December, between players who attended schools in the North and players who attended schools in the South, 1939–2003.

623.37–38   like Saint Thomas Aquinas . . . connected up.] Aquinas's philosophy, set out in the *Summa Theologica* (1265–74), is rooted in the conviction that there is a divine order to the world and its phenomena.

624.7   Pascal wrote as if . . . for life] In his *Pensées* (1669–70), French philosopher Blaise Pascal (1623–1662) writes: "Picture a number of men in chains, all condemned to death, some of whose throats are cut each day in plain view of the others, while those who remain see their own fate reflected on the faces of their fellow inmates and, sorrowfully and without hope, await their turn. This is the condition of humankind."

626.1–2   Toulouse-Lautrec . . . rise much.] French impressionist painter Henri Toulouse-Lautrec (1864–1901) was about five feet tall; he possessed an adult-sized torso, but his legs were stunted because of a childhood accident.

626.13–14   the young Jesus confounding his elders.] See Luke 2:39–52.

626.39   Walpurgis night] Eve of the feast of Saint Walpurga, believed in German folklore to be the night of a witches' sabbath.

628.2   the annual Donnybrook."] Here, an occasion for drinking and disputation, evoking the fair held in Dublin, from the thirteenth century to the 1850s.

628.4–5   Manolete taking on Belmonte."] Manuel Laureano Rodríguez Sánchez (1917–1947), the Spanish bullfighter known as "Manolete," is often called the successor to Juan Belmonte (1892–1962).

634.23   Skinner box] Common name for a chamber used by behavioral scientists to observe animals' responses to stimuli as forms of conditioning; it was created by the American behavioral psychologist B. F. Skinner (1904–1990) while he was a graduate student.

635.23   Mazo de la Roche."] Canadian novelist (1879–1961) known for the sixteen-volume Jalna series, a family saga widely read in the middle of the century.

635.33   Scheherazade."] Symphonic suite (1888) by Nikolai Rimsky-Korsakov (1844–1908), based on the tales of the Arabian Nights.

637.6   Whiteoaks of Jalna] Eighth novel in Mazo de la Roche's Jalna series.

638.5–6   the que to the filio] Filioque ("and from the son") is a Latin term added to the Nicene Creed by the Third Council of Toledo in 589. It is the ongoing source of division between the Roman Catholic and Eastern Orthodox churches since the Schism of 1054.

639.16   Pat O'Brien] American actor (1899–1983) who played Irish-American characters in more than a hundred films.

639.25–26   Freud's first patient, Anna O.] Freud wrote about "Anna O.," not his patient but rather a patient of his friend Josef Breuer, who treated her from December 1880 to June 1882 for hysteria.

641.8   Zwei Herzen] German: Two Hearts, folk song popularized through a 1932 film of that title.

641.25   EEG's] Electroencephalograms, used to observe and measure brain activity.

642.1–3   She never . . . damask cheek.] Twelfth Night, II.iv.110–12.

642.18–19   Her cheek . . . the green.] From "Oh saw ye the lass," a Scottish ballad.

645.4   Che gelida manina.] Italian: What a frozen little hand, from the first act of Puccini's opera La Bohème (1895).

645.24   Dry Tortugas again? Chichén Itzá? Tombstone?"] Dry Tortugas, a national park in southern Florida. Chichén Itzá, a complex of Mayan ruins in Yucatán, Mexico. Tombstone, a territorial park in Yukon, Canada.

646.25 *"Mach schnell!"*] German: Hurry up!

647.26–28 *Is it the truth? . . . better friendships?*] See note 536.25–27.

648.11 Merida] Capital of the Mexican state of Yucatán.

648.24 Pompey!"] Roman town buried by eruption of Mount Vesuvius in 79 C.E.

649.3–4 Rod McKuen] American poet and singer-songwriter (1933–2015) who was popular in the 1960s and early '70s.

649.30–34 "The lion . . . his sleep."] Cf. Edward Fitzgerald's translation of Omar Khayyam's poem "They say the Lion and the Lizard keep."

649.36 Miss Clairol] Models featured in the television and print campaigns for Clairol hair-dye products.

651.5–6 *The Laughing Cavalier*] Portrait (1624) by the Dutch master Franz Hals.

651.14 "Far from the maddening crowd."] See line 73 in Thomas Gray's "Elegy Written in a Country Church Yard" (1751).

652.12 *Stanyan Street*] *Stanyan Street and Other Sorrows* (1966), a collection of poems and lyrics by Rod McKuen.

653.4 *Tantum Ergo*] Last two stanzas of the *Pangue Lingua*, a Latin hymn setting of a prayer attributed to St. Thomas Aquinas, often sung at the Benediction during the pre–Vatican II Latin Mass. The text begins: "Therefore, so greatly the Sacrament / Let us venerate with heads bowed . . ."

653.4–5 "Deh vieni alla finestra" from *Don Giovanni*] Aria for solo baritone from Act II of Mozart's opera.

653.6 *Gentle Ben*] CBS television series about the friendship between a boy and a bear, 1967–69, developed from the 1965 children's novel of the same title by American author Walter Morey.

664.34–35 Kingfish Huey P. Long . . . a king] Huey P. Long, nicknamed "the Kingfish," was governor of Louisiana from 1928 to 1932 and then a Democratic senator from the state until his assassination in 1935. A demagogue, he struck a populist note in a 1934 radio address, calling for the undoing of an American society in which "more is owned by twelve men than it is by 120 million people."

666.38 the ox-lot] Unique to the design of Covington (Percy's residence from the 1950s to his death in 1990), ox-lots are open spaces on each block for farmers and merchants to bring carts of goods for sale.

667.19–20 the *Ford Times*] Monthly magazine published by the Ford Motor Company, 1908–17 and 1943–93.

667.21   the S A E *Record*] Journal of the Sigma Alpha Epsilon fraternity.

670.23–26   *Glory be . . . chestnut falls*] From "Pied Beauty" (1918) by English poet and Jesuit priest Gerard Manley Hopkins (1844–1889).

673.34–36   Robert the Bruce . . . it succeeded."] Legend says that while on the run from Edward I of England, Robert the Bruce (1274–1329), King of Scots, took refuge in a coastal cave; inspired by the determination of the spider, he vowed to carry on his fight against the English, eventually crushing them and their allies in 1314 at Bannockburn.

677.5   Rudolfo and Mimi.] Lovers in Puccini's opera *La Bohème* (1895).

677.31–32   the German ace . . . the Immelmann turn?] German World War I ace Max Immelmann (1890–1916) is associated with an aerobatic turn whereby a pilot climbs above another plane after attacking it for a renewed attack from above and behind.

678.6.   Southern Bell] Regional phone company serving Alabama, Kentucky, Louisiana, Mississippi, and Tennessee until 1968.

679.14   N.I.M.H.] See note 598.34.

681.17   Holy Name man] Member of the Society of the Holy Name, a Catholic confraternity that traces its origins to the fifteenth century.

685.4–5   Property Rights Sunday] Holiday of Percy's invention, a conflation of segregationist practices rooted in business owners' "property rights" and the "right to property" affirmed by Pope Leo XIII in his encyclical *Rerum Novarum* (1891).

685.7   Saint Pius XII Church] Pope Pius XII was the head of the Roman Catholic Church from 1939 till his death in 1958; his successor, Pope John XXIII, convened the reformist Second Ecumenical Council of the Vatican, 1962–65, which introduced changes in the liturgy, alterations in the Church's relations with other churches and other religions, and other *aggiornamenti* (modernizations).

685.11   the Kaydettes] A precision drill team affiliated with the Army ROTC (Reserve Officers Training Corps).

686.30   "Ginger Rogers and Red Skelton were Cancers."] Film actress Ginger Rogers (1911–1995) and comic Red Skelton (1913–1997), who both began their careers in vaudeville, were born in July, under the astrological sign of Cancer.

688.13–14   Henry Miller . . . Jacksonville, Florida.] In his travel memoir *The Air-Conditioned Nightmare* (1945), American novelist Henry Miller (1891–1980) spends time in the park in Jacksonville, which he characterizes as the worst of American public spaces, frequented by "the respectable middle class: *clean clots of phlegm.*"

688.31   the Infant Jesus of Prague."] Here, a church named after the Infant Jesus of Prague, a sixteenth-century wooden statue, the locus for Catholic popular devotion.

688.40   a Catholic gnostic.] A Catholic interested in the occult. The allusion is to the Gnostic writings that flourished in the second century C.E., often described as radically dualistic and world-denying, which promoted salvation through esoteric knowledge and mystical spirituality.

690.21–22   Ricardo Montalban] Suave Mexican American film and television actor (1920–2009).

691.29–30   "Do you . . . what Scarlett . . . in *The Good Earth*?"] In Margaret Mitchell's *Gone With the Wind* (1936), Scarlett O'Hara takes to heart the advice given to her by her father: "'Land is the only thing in the world that amounts to anything . . . for 'tis the only thing in this world that lasts, and don't be forgetting it! 'Tis the only thing worth working for, worth fighting for—worth dying for.'" In Pearl S. Buck's *The Good Earth* (1931), a dying Wang Lung admonishes his sons not to sell the family property: "'It is the end of a family—when they begin to sell the land. . . . Out of the land we came and into it we must go—and if you hold your land you can live—no one can rob you of land—.'"

692.21–23   The present "Pope" . . . Pius XIII.] See note 685.7.

692.33–36   the words . . . *locum refrigerii* . . ."] The Second Ecumenical Council of the Vatican replaced the Mass in Latin with Mass in current local languages. A prayer in the Mass entreats for the faithful departed *locum refrigerii, lucis et pacis* (a place of refreshment, light, and peace).

692.37–693.1   the Gospel from Matthew . . . his tomb.] See Matthew 27:57–60.

693.1–2   the resurrection of Lazurus . . . well off.] See John 11. The interment of Lazarus's body in a tomb sealed by a stone is evidence that he was a person of means.

694.36   *The Lawrence Welk Show*—] American television musical variety show hosted by bandleader Lawrence Welk, which aired on ABC, 1955–71.

698.16   a Confederate Bible] The Confederate Bible Society printed and distributed editions of the New Testament during the U.S. Civil War.

698.26–29   Two freejacks . . . Battle of New Orleans.] Andrew Jackson defeated the British in the battle of New Orleans, January 8, 1815, the last skirmish in the War of 1812, with a patchwork of army regulars, free and enslaved Black people, frontiersmen, and Choctaw tribesmen. While bondsmen may have been promised freedom in return for their services, Jackson did not free them nor would he have had the power to do so.

698.36   Saint Aloysius Gonzaga] Italian Jesuit (1568–1591) who died at age twenty-three caring for plague victims.

699.19–24   At six o'clock . . . by artillery.] See note 593.28–29.

699.26–30   Grant lost . . . and Armstrong.] Grant's frontal assault on fortified Confederate positions at Cold Harbor, Virginia, on June 3, 1864, resulted in 7,000 casualties for the Union, compared to less than 1,500 for the Confederate Army.

700.34–36   Descartes . . . own house.] In *The Concept of Mind* (1949), British philosopher Gilbert Ryle famously characterized Cartesian dualism as "the ghost in the machine."

703.10   *Christianity Without God.*] Reference to the "death of God" movement that gained currency in the 1960s. The book is Percy's invention.

705.37   the bullring at Pamplona.] The Plaza de Toros de Pamplona, in Spain.

706.12   *estocada*] Spanish: the thrust of the sword by the matador into the bull in the final stage of a bullfight, designed to kill the bull.

715.5   *Eins zwei drei,*"] German: One two three.

715.24–25   my face . . . Saint James's epistle.] See James 1:23–24: "For if any be a hearer of the word, and not a doer, he is like unto a man beholding his natural face in a glass: For he beholdeth himself, and goeth his way, and straightway forgetteth what manner of man he was."

721.21   Physician, heal thyself."] See note 538.2–3.

723.27–28   Charlottesville . . . Saint Anthony's Hall.] The Upsilon Chapter of the Fraternity of Delta Psi, at the University of Virginia.

724.36   Dr. Spiro T. Agnew] Agnew (1918–1996), the running mate of Richard Nixon in 1968, was the thirty-ninth vice president of the United States (1969–73). He resigned his office on October 10, 1973 (two years after the publication of *Love in the Ruins*), following an investigation for financial improprieties committed while governor of Maryland in 1967–68.

724.38–40   Hermann Hesse . . . B. F. Skinner . . . Justice William O. Douglas] Hesse (1877–1962), Nobel Prize–winning German Austrian writer who explored spiritual and mystical themes in novels such as *Siddhartha* and *Steppenwolf.* Skinner, see note 634.23. Douglas (1898–1980), jurist who served on the U.S. Supreme Court from 1939 to 1975, supporting progressive and libertarian opinions.

725.35   Captain Queeg] Paranoid, unstable skipper of the USS Caine in Herman Wouk's novel *The Caine Mutiny* (1951), the basis for a 1954 film starring Humphrey Bogart as Queeg.

726.23–24   Gallic shrug . . . from Thibodeaux] Thibodeaux, a city in Louisiana, is home to many Cajuns, many of whom trace their ancestry to French settlers of the region.

728.2–3   Art Linkletter III] American television game-show host Arthur Gordon Linkletter (1912–2010) had a son named Arthur Jack Linkletter (1937–2007), also a television host; Percy invents a third-generation game-show host.

734.9   the Ocala frieze."] Percy's invention.

734.16   Narvaez expedition."] Spanish journey of exploration and colonization led by Panfilo de Narváez, beginning in 1527. Of the approximately six hundred soldiers, sailors, and colonists who began the expedition, only four survived to return to Spain.

734.18   the Franciscan files at Salamanca."] Salamanca, Spain, is the site of a renowned friary of the Franciscan order.

736.25   the Jews in Miami] Miami and other cities on Florida's eastern coast were popular postwar destinations for American Jews, many of whom made second homes there.

737.36–37   Brahms. . . . a summer night.] Among the works of German composer Johannes Brahms (1833–1897) is "Romantic Music for a Summer Night," Clarinet Trio in A minor, op. 114 (1891).

738.21–22   Cumberland Plateau.] West of the southern Appalachian Mountains.

739.19   *liebchen*] German: sweetheart.

741.27   monstrance] A circular vessel for the display of the Eucharist in Roman Catholic churches, typically with beams or springs of gold extending outward from the center.

744.27   St. Vitus's dance in the Middle Ages] Poorly understood social phenomenon in medieval Europe in which large groups of dancers worked themselves into a frenzy, often dropping from exhaustion.

745.21–26   A fair woman . . . Juvenal . . . didn't quite say that."] In *Satire* II, Juvenal blames Rome's moral decline on the feminization of its male citizens.

753.6   *Wine, Women and Song*] Waltz, op. 333 (1869), by Johann Strauss II (1825–1899).

753.24   *Wien Wien, du du allein*] *Wien, Wien, nur du allein* (Vienna, Vienna, You Alone), song by Austrian composer Rudolf Sieczynski (1879–1952).

755.5   *Louisiana Lou*] Song (1894) by English composer Leslie Stuart (1863–1928).

756.2   Mantovani music—] Annuncio Paolo Mantovani (1905–1980) was an Italian conductor and composer of light music, known for his cascading string arrangements.

756.6–7   *There's a Small Hotel with a Wishing Well.*] Song by Richard Rodgers, with lyrics by Lorenz Hart, featured in the musical *On Your Toes* (1936) and the film version of *Pal Joey* (1957), sung by Frank Sinatra.

758.32   the tiny ropes that bound Gulliver.] In Swift's *Gulliver's Travels* (1726), Gulliver washes ashore on the island of Lilliput, populated by tiny people, who tie him down while he sleeps.

760.40   "The Death of a Salesman."] Allusion to Arthur Miller's play *Death of a Salesman* (1949).

761.12   Knott's Berry Farm,"] Sweet wine made in Orange County, California.

761.17–18   Seven Flags over Texas.] Amusement park in Arlington, Texas.

761.23   Jerome Kern.] American theater and film composer (1885–1945).

761.30   Draw-Me arms and legs.] Well-proportioned arms and legs, like those of an instruction-by-mail art course of the period.

761.37   seven souls of Shiva.] Attributes of Shiva, one of the principal Hindu deities, the creator, preserver, and destroyer of the universe.

762.4–6   the Introductory Prom . . . a hat.] Single-sex Catholic schools would sponsor dances together, and students were paired in this way.

762.10   *Gunsmoke*] Western television drama broadcast on CBS, 1955–75.

762.15   "If"] Poem (1910) by Rudyard Kipling (1865–1936), once a fixture of American elementary and high school education.

772.28–29   *The world . . . our powers*] From William Wordsworth's sonnet "The World Is Too Much With Us" (1807), lines 1–2.

773.35–40   Origen . . . own member."] Most scholars believe Origen of Alexandria (c. 185–c. 253 C.E.), an early Christian scholar, rejected the notion of transmigration of souls. It is unclear whether Origen literally castrated himself.

775.20–21   *I Love Lucy*] American television sitcom starring Lucille Ball and Desi Arnaz, which aired on CBS, 1951–57.

779.35   David O. Selnick's] American film producer and studio executive (1903–1965) who produced *Gone With the Wind*.

780.27   "Là ci darem" from *Don Giovanni.*] "Là ci darem la mano" (Italian: There we will give each other our hands), a duet from Act I of Mozart's opera.

781.21   Datsun] Automotive brand, 1958–86, owned by Nissan.

783.10–12 "I've never seen . . . from Montgomery.] The National Guard in Montgomery, Alabama, were called in by President Lyndon B. Johnson in 1965 to protect participants in a civil rights march led by Rev. Dr. Martin Luther King Jr. from segregationist protestors; some members of the Guard went on to serve in the Vietnam War.

783.32 Farhad Grotto motorcycle] Vehicle decorated for parades, bearing an emblem of the nonprofit Farhad Grotto and a special license plate.

793.30–31 Saint Thomas Aquinas . . . Q.21, Obj. 4, Part I, *Sum. Theol.*] Aquinas, in the *Summa Theologica* (1265–74), addresses killing in self-defense in Question 64, article 7. Question 21 deals with the justice and mercy of God.

793.34 Zane Grey] Popular and prolific novelist (1872–1939) specializing in Westerns, including *Riders of the Purple Sage* (1912).

794.6–7 Coeur de Lion . . . Saladin] Lion-heart, sobriquet of King Richard I (1157–1199). In the Third Crusade (1189–92), Richard I of England failed to retake Jerusalem from the Egyptian sultan Salah ad-Din (Saladin). On September 2, 1192, they negotiated a three-year truce that left Jerusalem under Moslem rule, but allowed Christian pilgrims to visit the Holy Places.

794.8–9 Sir Walter Scott] Scottish novelist (1771–1832) whose works include *Ivanhoe* (1819) and *The Talisman* (1825), the latter concerning the relationship between Richard Lion-heart and Saladin.

798.3–4 the Fifth Symphony, the *Principia Mathematica*, the Uranus guidance system.] The Symphony No. 5 in C minor, op. 67 (1808), by Ludwig van Beethoven. *Principia Mathematica*, a three-volume work on mathematics (1910–13) by English mathematician-philosophers Alfred North Whitehead and Bertrand Russell. Guidance and control systems for the Apollo program were developed in the 1960s (the "Uranus guidance system" is Percy's invention).

798.31–33 "You've had Liberia . . . Haiti even longer."] Liberia, established in 1847, was the second Black republic; Haiti, which won independence from France in 1804, was the first.

799.4 George Washington Carver."] Black American agricultural scientist and inventor (1864–1943).

802.29 Sten gun] Submachine gun first used by British and Commonwealth forces in World War II.

804.11 Kodacolor murals] Color prints made from a brand of color film stock produced by Kodak. The Kodacolor name has not been used since the 1990s.

808.28 *The Drummer Boy*] Christmas carol written by American composer Katherine Kennicott Davis in 1941 and popularized by Harry Simeone's 1958 recording.

809.14   A & P] See note 536.20.

809.27   *Round yon virgin mother and child . . .*] Line from "Silent Night," Christmas carol composed, in German, by Joseph Mohr in 1816.

810.10   Duke Ellington] American pianist, composer, and bandleader (1899–1974).

811.7   *We three kings of orient are . . .*] First line of "We Three Kings," a Christmas carol composed in 1857 by John Henry Hopkins Jr., an American clergyman.

811.29–30   *The first Noel / The angels did sing . . .*] First line of "The First Noel," a traditional English Christmas carol, first published in 1823.

812.32   Duke Wayne] Nickname for American actor John Wayne (1907–79), star of many Western films.

815.18–19   as grave . . . as a CBS commentator.] Walter Cronkite (1916–2009), longtime host of the *CBS Evening News*, was praised for his calm gravitas during crises, as was his predecessor, Edward R. Murrow (1908–1965).

815.22   as somberly as Arnold Toynbee taking the long view.] British historian Arnold J. Toynbee's twelve-volume *A Study of History* (1934–61) analyzes the rise and fall of human civilizations.

819.31   *The Ice Capades of 1981.*] See note 545.12–13.

826.16   *"Zwei Herzen!*] See note 641.8.

831.31–33   *Everybody's talking . . . echoes of my mind.*] From the song "Everybody's Talkin'" (1966) by American singer-songwriter Fred Neil, popularized through a 1969 recording by Harry Nilsson and featured in the film *Midnight Cowboy* that same year.

832.11   *A partridge in a pear tree . . .*] Refrain of "The Twelve Days of Christmas," an English Christmas carol made popular by Bing Crosby and the Andrews Sisters.

832.23   a Dvořák Slavonic dance] One in a series of sixteen orchestral pieces by Dvořák published in two sets (1878 and 1886), op. 46 and op. 72.

833.21   Tarheel alma mater] School song of the University of North Carolina, Percy's alma mater.

834.10   H.G. Wells] Prolific English writer (1866–1946) best remembered for his science fiction novels, including *The Time Machine* (1895) and *The Island of Dr. Moreau* (1896).

835.38   Baylor, T.C.U., S.M.U.] Baylor University, in Waco, Texas, founded by Baptists; Texan Christian University, in Fort Worth, Texas, founded by members of the Disciples of Christ; Southern Methodist University, in Dallas, Texas, founded by Methodists.

836.16   LBJ Memorial auditorium] Lyndon Baines Johnson (1908–1973), the thirty-sixth president of the United States, under John F. Kennedy, was still alive when *Love in the Ruins* was published.

836.18–20   Van Cliburn . . . in Moscow] Harvey Lavan "Van" Cliburn (1934–2013), raised in Texas, gained fame by winning the Tchaikovsky Piano Competition in Moscow in 1958, during a tense period of the Cold War.

840.13–14   *Silent night, / Holy night.*] Opening of "Silent Night." See note 809.27.

840.19–20   Helen Gurley Brown] American author and longtime editor-in-chief of *Cosmopolitan* (1922–2012).

842.25–28   *There was a girl . . . October hill.*] From "Love's Been Good to Me," a song by Rod McKuen, known through a 1969 recording by Frank Sinatra.

849.13–14   Dr. Carl Weiss . . . Huey Long?] Weiss, a physician, assassinated U.S. senator Huey P. Long inside the Louisiana state capitol on September 8, 1935. See also note 664.34–35.

851.21–22   objective correlative,"] Literary-critical term introduced by T.S. Eliot, referring, in the poet's words, to "a set of objects, a situation, a chain of events which shall be the formula of that particular emotion." See Eliot's essay "Hamlet and His Problems," published in *The Sacred Wood* (1920).

853.4   "Transubstantiation . . . Roman popes,"] Catholic doctrine holding that in the act of consecration during the Mass, the bread and wine used sacramentally are "transubstantiated" into the body and blood of Christ.

862.14   a CO_2 Transylvania fog.] Artificial fog used as a special effect in horror films, for example *Dracula* (1931).

864.13   Invincible Ignorance."] In Catholic theology, a term describing the blameless condition of those without knowledge of the Christian message.

865.9   Lourdes] Village in France, site of miraculous apparitions of the Blessed Virgin Mary to the peasant girl Bernadette Soubirous in 1858.

865.10–11   the London Psychical Society] The Society for Psychical Research, founded in London in 1882, which gives attention to psychic and paranormal phenomena.

866.36–37   the Christ at Sacre Coeur in New Orleans.] Statue of Christ, with outstretched arms, above main doors of the Academy of the Sacred Heart, an all-girls Catholic prep school founded in 1867.

866.39   *Beautiful beautiful Copenhagen.*] From "Wonderful Copenhagen," a song written by Frank Loesser and released by Danny Kaye with Gordon Jenkins and His Chorus and Orchestra, 1952.

872.40–873.1   Robinson Crusoe] Title characters in Daniel Defoe's *The Life and Strange Surprizing Adventures of Robinson Crusoe* (1719), about the exploits of an Englishman who spends twenty-eight years as a castaway on a tropical island.

874.34–35   burned $100 bills like Oklahoma Indians of old.] The Osage Nation became wealthy after discovery of oil on tribal lands in Oklahoma at the end of the nineteenth century.

875.3–4   the U. of M.] The University of Michigan.

875.25   Lockheed] The Lockheed Corporation, an American aerospace company, 1926–95. Lockheed merged with the Martin Marietta Corporation in 1995.

875.25–26   Colonial Dames] The Colonial Dames of America, dedicated to historical preservation, with a chapter based in Atlanta.

876.11   Rudolph Friml.] Czech-born American composer of light instrumental and operatic music (1879–1972).

877.38   The *Anvil Chorus*] Chorus from Act II of *Il Trovatore* (1853) by Giuseppe Verdi (1813–1901).

878.14–15   "Waltz of the Flowers" from *Nutcracker*.] Orchestral piece from Act II of Tchaikovsky's ballet (1892).

878.23   *Barcarole*] Venetian boat song from Act III of the opera *The Tales of Hoffmann* by German-born French composer Jacques Offenbach (1819–1880).

881.36–37   the late Harry Belafonte.] The American actor, singer, and activist (1927–2023) was alive at the time of the publication of *Love in the Ruins*.

882.20   Holy Name man] See note 681.17.

884.13–14   *He's got . . . in his hands.*] From "He's Got the Whole World in His Hands," an African American spiritual made popular through several postwar recordings.

887.21–22   John XXIV . . . public penance] Pope John XXIV is a fictional invention, evoking John XXIII, who called the Second Vatican Council in 1962, after which the sacrament of penance went into abeyance in the United States and elsewhere. See also note 685.7.

887.28–29   Saint Aloysius Gonzaga] See note 698.35–36.

888.33–34   The new Hanseatic League of Black City-States—] Invented commercial alliance that alludes to the loosely aligned confederation of city-states in medieval Europe. *Hanse* in Middle Low German means a merchant guild.

889.7–8   Kennedy, Evers, Goldberg, Stevenson, L.Q.C. Lamar.] John F. Kennedy (1917–1963), thirty-fifth president of the United States, 1961–63. Medgar Evers (1925–1963), the field secretary of the Mississippi NAACP, 1954–63.

Arthur Goldberg (1908–1990), secretary of labor under Kennedy, 1961–62, and an associate justice of the U.S. Supreme Court, 1962–65. Adlai Stevenson II (1900–1965), Democratic nominee for president of the United States in 1952 and 1956, and U.S. ambassador to the United Nations under Kennedy, 1961–65. Lucius Quintus Cincinnatus Lamar (1825–1893), Democratic congressman from Mississippi, 1857–60 and 1873–77; U.S. senator, 1877–85; secretary of the interior, 1885–88; and an associate justice of the U.S. Supreme Court. Lamar is featured in John F. Kennedy's Pulitzer Prize–winning book *Profiles in Courage* (1956).

889.28–29   the *Salve Regina*] The traditional Catholic hymn "Hail, Holy Queen," sung in devotion to Mary.

889.29–30   Walter Huston doing a jig . . . the Sierra Madre.] In the film *The Treasure of the Sierra Madre* (1948), directed by the actor's son, John Huston.

890.13   To bed we go for a long winter's nap] See "A Visit from St. Nicholas" (1823), better known as "The Night Before Christmas," by American poet Clement Clarke Moore (1779–1863).

890.14   as the ivy twineth] See "The Ivy Green" (1836), a poem by Charles Dickens.

RELATED WRITINGS

893.1–2   *Accepting* . . . The Moviegoer] Percy's acceptance speech for the National Book Award for *The Moviegoer* was delivered on March 13, 1962, at the Astor Hotel in New York City.

893.12–13   Jean Stafford . . . Herbert Gold . . . Lewis Gannett] Stafford (1915–1979), American novelist and short story writer whose works include the novels *The Mountain Lion* (1947) and *The Catherine Wheel* (1952) as well as *A Mother in History* (1966), a journalistic portrait of Marguerite Oswald. Gold (b. 1924), American novelist and short story writer whose novels include *The Man Who Was Not With It* (1956), *Salt* (1963), and *Fathers* (1966). Gannett (1891–1966), editor and book reviewer, long associated with the *New York Herald Tribune*.

893.17–18   Elizabeth Otis] Literary agent and cofounder of the literary agency McIntosh and Otis (1900–1981). McIntosh and Otis represented Percy for the entirety of his career.

893.18   Stanley Kauffmann] American editor, film critic, and founder of *The New Republic* (1916–2013). At Alfred A. Knopf, Kauffmann acquired and edited *The Moviegoer* but was dismissed from the firm prior to the novel's publication.

895.1–3   "*Special Message*" . . . The Moviegoer.] The author's prefatory note appears in the Franklin Library's limited edition of *The Moviegoer* (1980).

895.19–24   I had written two novels . . . a hillock.] "The Charterhouse" and "The Gramercy Winner," respectively. Percy submitted both novels to publishers in the mid-1950s. A bound typescript draft of "The Gramercy Winner" is held in the Wilson Library at the University of North Carolina at Chapel Hill. "The Charterhouse" does not survive.

895.24   Hans Castorp] Protagonist of Thomas Mann's *The Magic Mountain* (1924).

897.1   *Concerning* Love in the Ruins] These prepared remarks were addressed to the Publishers' Publicity Association of the National Book Awards in New York City on March 4, 1971.

899.10   when people talk about the greening of America] The phrase was popularized by Charles R. Reich in *The Greening of America* (1970), a celebration of a new countercultural consciousness that, in Reich's words, had "emerged out of the wasteland of the Corporate State, like flowers pushing up through a concrete pavement."

This book is set in 10 point ITC Galliard, a face designed
for digital composition by Matthew Carter and based
on the sixteenth-century face Granjon. The paper is acid-free
lightweight opaque that will not turn yellow or brittle with age.
The binding is sewn, which allows the book to open easily and lie flat.
The binding board is covered in Brillianta, a woven rayon cloth
made by Van Heek–Scholco Textielfabrieken, Holland.
Composition by Publishers' Design and Production Services, Inc.
Printing by Sheridan, Grand Rapids, MI.
Binding by Dekker Bookbinding, Wyoming, MI.
Designed by Bruce Campbell.

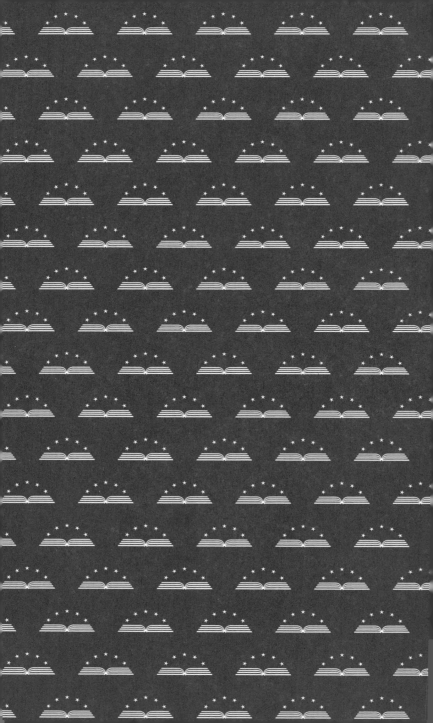